JAMIE MACGILLIVRAY

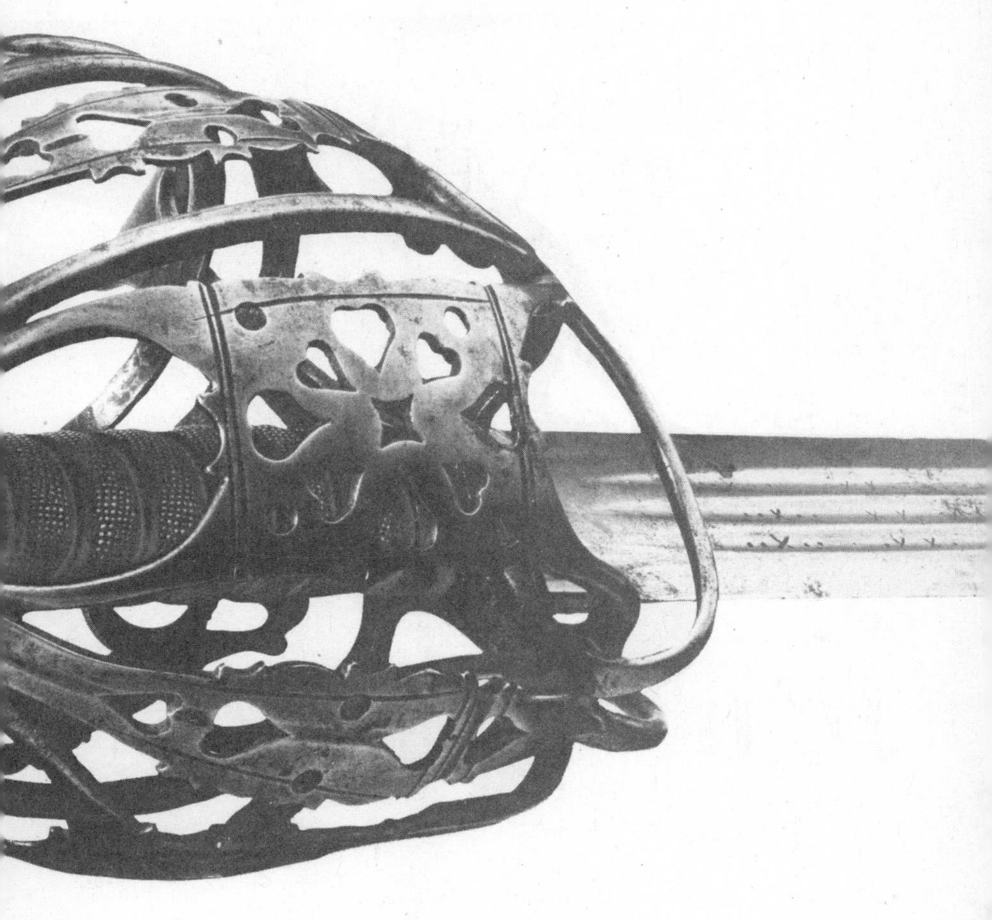

ALSO BY JOHN SAYLES

Pride of the Bimbos

Union Dues

The Anarchists' Convention

Thinking in Pictures: The Making of the Movie Matewan

Los Gusanos

Dillinger in Hollywood

A Moment in the Sun

Yellow Earth

JAMIE MACGILLIVRAY

the renegade's journey

JOHN SAYLES

MELVILLE HOUSE
BROOKLYN • LONDON

JAMIE MACGILLIVRAY

First published in 2022 by Melville House

First Melville House Printing: November 2022

Melville House Publishing
46 John Street
Brooklyn, NY 11201
and
Melville House UK
Suite 2000
16/18 Woodford Road
London E7 0HA

mhpbooks.com
@melvillehouse

ISBN: 978-1-61219-988-7
ISBN: 978-1-61219-989-4 (eBook)

Library of Congress Control Number 2022947921

Designed by Emily Considine

Printed in the United States of America

2nd Printing

A catalog record for this book is available from the Library of Congress

For Maggie

BO

O

CULLODEN MOOR

THE MARE SLIPS, CLIMBING THE RAIN-SLICK HILLside, white puffs huffing from her nostrils in the frigid evening air. Jamie MacGillivray, new-bought plaid draped over his head, leans forward in the cracked saddle, cooing to the beast in Erse. There are no trees. He knew this, of course, remembered it, but the bleak nakedness of the hills is still a shock after so much time away. Sudden scooting of dappled feathers to his left, but the mare is too weary to startle. Easier to snag a grouse in one's bare hands than to find the Laird Lovat if he wishes it not. At what the gentry call Castle Dounie, the resident Fraser secretary condescended to inform Jamie that the Auld Fox was not yet so vexed with age as to return straight to his clan seat after a narrow escape, and that even if he was there, the quest was pointless. But Jamie is a go-between by profession now, and the job requires patience. The more accomodating Fraser, who attends the Prince, cautioned Jamie of Lovat's calculated evasiveness, his eel-like ability to change direction, even shape, but stressed that he is the key to success in the impending carnage—then whispered the name of the great chieftan's most likely hideaway.

Jamie, cold and sodden, is unsurprised that no Highlander he's asked since has been willing to cede him the exact location, or even admit that such a place as Gortuleg exists. His only guess is that it lies somewhere here on the northern shore of Loch Mhòr, possibly over the next hill—

Jamie presses his knees tight to the mare's steaming flank. They gain the crest as the rain hardens to something like sleet, then pause to survey the other side, and there it lies, just below, chimney smoke blown sideways from a middling, whitewashed cottage left deceptively unguarded. Turf smoke, by the smell of it—the Auld Fox must save his kindling for honored guests.

A few bodies move about the cottage, none looking up the hill as Jamie allows the surly mare to rest. They have surely kenned his coming for an hour at the least—even with the young and vital away in arms, Frasers are not to be caught unawares—*Je suis prest* their motto. Jamie has seen Lovat only once, he and Dougal as boys fishing in the Moy Burn when the procession came through on a hunt to the north, the laird with a parade of his henchmen. The *óstair* first, leading the great man's stallion with a trio of young bodyguards trotting alongside, keeking the hills for danger, and then the sword bearer and the baggage man and the standard bearer, wavering as his flapping banner caught the wind and pulled him backward, and the piper, striding with his nose in the air, his own gillie shuffling behind with the bulky instrument draped upon him like a many-armed sea creature, and then the portly Auld Fox himself, legs outsplayed, riding the shoulders of his ruddy-cheeked *casflue* across the frigid water. *Je suis prest*, announced the banner, letters on the belt that circled the buck's head, *I am ready*, but they knew before they read it, Jamie and his brother standing with mouths gapped wide and poles forgotten in their hands. It was in the man's face, everything they'd ever heard of him, as he spread his wide, jack-o'-lantern grin and nodded to one of the half-dozen *luchd tighe* trotting to the rear with hands on their swords, and that ready young man flipped a tarnished shilling that Dougal snatched before it hit the water. Laird Lovat with the grin of a wolf, eager for whatever life might place before him.

Jamie prods the mare, and they start down the hill.

TWEEDIE WATCHES FROM THE DOOR AS THE STRANGER hands Rhory Bain the reins to his mount and steps forward. It is a tall mare, none of your shaggy little Galloways for this lad, who announces himself in Erse with a foreign lilt to it and waits in mud-caked boots and wet woolen breeches. Tweedie can hop it when he desires, but now drags his ruined leg emphatically across the cold plank floor to advertise the intrusion. It always hurts worse in the cold. Though at times the Laird will curse Tweedie's slowness and his clumsiness and the leaden scrape of his gait, and joke that if this crippled oaf is truly his blood the Frasers are doomed for certain, the Auld Fox is a great man, and they all, from the royal cousins to the lowest wandering thrasherman, strut prideful in the world to claim him as their chief.

The great man is on his chamber pot when Tweedie announces the visit.

"A MacGillivray, is it?" says the Laird, the meaning of his smile yet to be revealed. "Lead him in. And ale for the two of us."

Tweedie moves a mite quicker to cross the excuse for a hall and calls the stranger in, telling him to wait by the door. He pours twopenny from the bucket into a pair of tankards on the small table, then stirs the fire and hitches out past the visitor to the yard, only a thin, cold rain to contend with now.

Rhory Bain is watching the stranger's mare eat hay.

A MacGillivray, Tweedie informs the hostler, speaking Erse. One I've never seen before.

Another young man gone a-kingmaking, snarls Rhory Bain, not one to waste a soft word on a two-legged creature.

He wore no cockade.

He reeks of it. What else would stir a man out in this weather?

Tweedie moves to peer back inside. The men are standing at the table, drinking ale. He strains to listen.

They're talking Saxon.

Rhory Bain scowls. No good will come of it, he says, same as the Last One.

They are both old enough to remember the Last One, the '15, Tweedie still whole then and mustered to march back and forth across the country with never the occasion to fight.

The Laird knows what's right, he says.

He does indeed. That one—Rhory jerks his shaggy white head toward the doorway—will leave on the same horse he arrived on.

The Auld Fox stands by the fireplace, eyes gleaming red. "Spare yer tongue," he says, the burr of the Highlands a conscious filigree to his English. He's at home here, not preening for the peers in London, wig left snug in its powdered box. "Ma mind is fixed."

Jamie stands back from the flickering light, his bonnet wet under his arm, *épée de coeur* buckled at his hip, feeling the cold of the room at his back. "Ye've a son with the Prince," he says.

"And twa mair in the scrape with the Royal Fusiliers, standing by King George. Them that's left tae me are needed fer the plough."

The notorious master of intrigues, thinks Jamie, careful to gird both his flanks years ahead of Prince Charlie's impetuous fling at the throne.

"The French are coming with arms and men," he ventures—

"The French!" smiles the Auld Fox. "The French have been coming fer thretty years noo, and I've yet tae keek a mon of 'em in the flesh."

"I've ainly just been with the Prince—"

"I smelt it when ye strode in." The Auld Fox had been as canny in the '15, promising both parties the support of his clansmen but never quite joining either, conniving to hold on to nearly all his ill-gotten estates after the Defeat.

"T'will gae hard with ye when we've won," says Jamie, a statement rather than a threat.

"I've ma son with yer lot tae plead fer me."

"If he survives the fighting."

The Auld Fox shifts his head, eyes shadowed now. "Enough shall be lost," he says quietly, "withoot I add tae the sorra." He steps toward Jamie, looking him over from boots to crown. Snorts. "Yer father was as fu' of the Cause in his ain day—he'd hear nae counsel. If he'd listened, ye'd no be ferrying coals fer the MacIntosh."

The Auld Fox is as wide as he is tall, powerful, excesses of table expanding his girth while those of the court and the bedchamber still frolic in his wicked eyes, his constant smirk. Jamie notices that the heavy chairs set at the table have rings below the arms, rings to fit the poles with which, after a night of toasting one king or another, the neighboring laird and the three-bottle men and perhaps the Auld Fox himself, mumbling and cock-eyed, are carted off to sleep.

"There is Honor tae be considered." Jamie hears his echo in the stone cottage. No claymores cross over the mantelpiece here, no coat of arms like the secretary Robert Fraser stood before at Castle Dounie. This is the lair of a chief in exile, something better than a croft or a cave, but only meant as shelter till the outcome of the great struggle is known.

The Auld Fox smiles again, eyes crinkling into slits. "Aye, the French are great uns fer Honor."

And then the lame house gillie, breath wisping ghostly in the cold as he enters, informs them that there is a messenger from Inverness.

THE MEN SIT ON THEIR FOLDED PLAIDS ON THE COLD ground, hungry, awaiting word from the flock of Irishmen and rebel lairds who surround the willowy boy they wish to place on the throne. Since the stormy shambles of a battle at Falkirk Muir, they've done little but retreat, the Hessians in the game against them now under King George's porcine third son, Cumberland, who is in no hurry, it seems, to bring them to bay. "There's little enow iv Scotland left," the MacGillivray Chief muttered only this morning, "fer us tae run tae."

Dougal walks among his landsmen to be seen. They have been too long without a fight. Without a charge, a slaughter, a victory or defeat, the rest of it is only misery. It will be a hard winter, and each morning roll finds a handful missing, gone to mind their beasts and bairns. Clan Chattan had been given the center front at Falkirk, right beside young Fraser's troop, a greeting shot in the howling storm and then throwing down firelocks to charge, waving claymores and screaming their cry, the lobsterbacks firing one uneven volley with wet powder before they took to their heels. Lashed with sleet, cutting men down from behind no more perilous than houghing cattle, striking at their legs and leaving them in the mire to be finished with the thrust of a dirk. His men were raw at it, lunatic-eyed and near hysteria as they lingered to strip the dead, allowing the living, breathing red enemy to disappear into the wall of freezing rain.

"Where are we aff tae?"

It is the little printer from Inverness, scrawny and shivering, half whispering in English at Dougal's side, as if there are secrets to be shared.

"It hasnae been decidit."

The man had run broadsides for the Cause from his shop at night, colorful jeremiads to be read in passion and burned immediately, until he was denounced to the Lord President and forced into hiding. He'd lived as a wraith among his MacBean people till the Rising and now struggles to keep step with the regiment, dwarfed by the rusty claymore his father's father's father carried to fight Cromwell.

"But where'd'ye think?"

They have this conversation several times a day. "Are the King's cannon rainin' shot on our heids?" asks Dougal.

The man actually looks to the sky.

"They are no."

"Are his sojers formed in line to pierce us with bullets or spit us on their bayonets?"

The man frowns. "They are no."

"Then be glad fer it, and wait instruction."

The one they call Crawford's Fergal is cleaning his firelock. He was with the Highland men who fought for the Crown in Belgium but was mustered out on their return from the Continent as more trouble than his worth. Dougal has seen the man's naked back, welts upon welts from the King's Discipline, and knows him for a drunkard and a troublemaker and a magnificent hellion in battle.

If the other men had your vigilance, says Dougal in Erse, stepping past him, we'd be a force to contend with.

If the other men had whisky, mutters the veteran, I'd trade this for half a gill of it.

Neddy Coos is standing before Dougal now, one of his renters from home, wide and placid. Neddy can charm milk from an udder that hasn't yielded for days, is a master at bonding orphaned calves to barren cows. His eyes are a watery blue, and he speaks slowly and after much deliberation.

"Winter is upon us," he says.

Neddy is a good tenant, paying his tack in clabber and crowdie, never a complaint.

"The hay will be gan."

Dougal waits. Neddy carries a Lochaber axe into battle and has the shoulders to render it fearsome.

"The roof wants mending."

Like many of his kind, Neddy considers it impolite to begin a conversation with a question, first building a solid edifice of undeniable observation to house it.

"How much langer," he asks, finally letting it peek out, "will we be at war?"

Dougal lays a hand on Neddy's massive arm, speaking softly.

"No lang, I fear," he answers. "No lang at all."

The Chief allowed each man to keep whatever weapons he was

able to find on Falkirk Muir, but in the weeks since, the poorest have sold or traded their firelocks to those who know how to use them. They are a mongrel regiment, not only the usual jumble of MacIntoshes, MacPhersons, MacBeans, MacPhails, MacGillivrays, Farquarsons, Davidsons, Ritchies, and Smiths that form the confederation, but blooded gentry, tacksmen, tenants, tradesmen, and strolling laborers mixed together, few who've ever marched in order or raised a blade in anger. Half, perhaps, were seduced by the glory of it, Lady MacIntosh rosy-cheeked and bonny on her mount bringing the blood up in a man, riding among the clachans while her husband honored his legally sworn service to the Hanover King. "This is our Destiny," she told them. "Clan," she said, "God," she said, "King," she said, "Scotland," she said, and tears ran from old men's eyes. "Ma husband is bonded to the English, so MacGillivray of Dunmaglas shall lead you!" Barefoot cottars shouldered their pitchforks and scythes, kissed their women farewell, and followed her to the next smattering of huts, chuffed to belong to Lady Anne's Regiment.

The rest were shamed or threatened.

Dougal had a hand in that—only a wee step from tacksman to recruiting officer. No thatch was torched, no cattle taken, only a strong word and the ancient weight of the clan.

"If ye dinnae come oot, and we win, there will be nae life fer ye here," he explained. "And if we lose, yer still ainly Hieland filth tae the English. So ye've nowt but ane course tae take—"

Only the poorest, the harvest hands and gleaners, starvation in their bones, were without obligation. The tack for the land that tenants worked and squatted on was mostly paid in kind—oats or barley, beef and mutton and fowl, perhaps a week's labor when required—but belonging, being part of a great family that reaches back through the mists of memory . . . that, you pay in blood.

"Tis the Duke of Cumberland's birthday," says the Chief, in English, stepping over when the conference around the Prince breaks up.

"May the wee kraut-eater ne'er see another," says Dougal.

"Their troops rest at Nairn, and they'll be gi'en brandy tae celebrate."

The Chief is looking pensively at his underfed, exhausted men. "We'll march through the night, Murray with the right, Perth with the left, the Prince himsel' ahind us with the second line, and we'll a' fall upon them at dawn."

Dougal feels ill. The Prince's army—Highlanders and Irish and Scots in the French service and English deserters and the flighty, headstrong MacDonalds—is hard enough to herd together in daylight.

"And who is to guide us on this midnight crusade?"

"You are, Dougal," says the Chief, MacGillivray of Dunmaglas.

THE OLD MAN COOKS BANNOCK ON A TURF SPADE. THE shed, at the far edge of Fraser land, squats in the lee of a dozen horse-high stacks of drying turf on a rise just above the bog itself. His feet are wrapped in burlap rags, his fingers stained a reddish brown. Jamie saw the wisp of smoke in the last light, spoke as if he was on important business for the Auld Fox, and was invited to shelter for the night. The mare has been hobbled—nothing to tie it to on the great soggy mat of the moor—and Jamie is sitting on his grounded saddle in the dull glow of the peat fire. When his thoughts wander back to France, he thinks of being dry. Dry and warm.

The old man does not seem unintelligent, his Erse lively when he chooses to speak, and Jamie wonders what transgression might have caused his banishment this far from the heart of the clan to be the lonely minister of turf.

The old man flips the cake deftly, browned side up now. Jamie hasn't eaten oat bannock since he was a boy, hunting with Dougal and their father. You needed real coals, his father said, from a wood fire, though the old man seems to be doing well enough with what he has at hand.

Have there been many people by? asks Jamie, more to break the silence than for want of an answer. Sooner wrest a bloody chop from the teeth of a starving dog than coax a Highlander to reveal himself.

No one comes by, says the old man, eyes never leaving the cake. The spade is a blackened iron ell with a wooden handle.

People come to win their turf, and they go home.

Jamie hopes the Prince's army will be in Inverness tomorrow, though he is without good news to bear. None of the lairds holding men back have agreed to release them, and those stragglers he has seen on the roads have been deserting rather than hurrying to join the fight. The French have in fact landed some weapons and money, but no more troops, and he is only glad that he is not back in St. Germaine en Laye to hear them explain why. It is a beautiful language, French, for mendacity.

Still, there are so many moving about the country, says Jamie to the old man. Soldiers.

It's what soldiers do, says the old man.

There are more turf spades leaning against the one high wall of the shed and some other items, just at the edge of the firelight, laid out on an old scrap of sacking. Jamie moves to kneel on the damp floor beside them—a blackened, broken sword, a pair of bone-handled rondel daggers, some pottery—

They come up in the bog, says the old man.

—and a kind of blackish, leathery sack with stumplike appendages that Jamie gives a tentative poke with his finger.

And that was a man, says the turf minder.

Jamie sniffs but smells only bog.

Old?

Dead for a good while. He might have been one of the Painted People.

When it was nothing but savages here.

Something like a smile plays about the old man's lips, or perhaps it is only a trick of the firelight.

A man with matters to look after, no doubt, he says. Important things—vital things, but meaning nothing to us now.

It looks like a leather sack, says Jamie. He cannot imagine that the bannock will be edible. He wonders how he will sleep on the earthen floor with the wind moaning over the treeless moor. For the first time since the French boat left him ashore, he is losing hope.

Some come up in the bog, says the old man, shifting the flattish cake onto a slab of wood.

Most prefer to remain below it.

"THERE IS A 'WAYS A MOON," HIS FATHER USED TO SAY. "Whether it reveals itsel to licht our wee or no is another matter."

Dougal has always had the gift of direction, a sense of how the land is arranged, of what should lie ahead. He keeps south of the Inverness road, the river to their left now, able to move over the raw heath and scattered stubble of grain fields quickly enough. But except for the half dozen in the vanguard, Lord Murray's men seem unable to remain in contact. For every hour of traveling there is an hour of waiting for them to catch up and be reassembled, leaving a chorus of barking clachan dogs in their wake. Some are foraging, of course, rushing after startled chickens in the dark, and some are too exhausted or reluctant to do more than trudge mindlessly, staring at the back of the man before them, lost or not. Entire regiments wander astray. Dougal feels the darkness thinning, slipping away, as he makes out the distant tower of Cawdor Castle against the sky. Any royal-ass-licking Campbells knocking about within it will be the old and the infirm, the fighting men no doubt asleep in Nairn after celebrating the Duke of Cumberland's twenty-fifth year.

Dougal signals for the handful of men behind him to wait again, planning to steer the troop north from here when they arrive. First there will be a twitching of panicked hares, then the creaking and clanking of the multitude, or at least those who have not wandered too far astray. They are the right wing, meant to recross the Nairn behind the English while Perth's men confront them head on. There are meant to be runners keeping the two forces informed of the other's position and timing, but not one has arrived from either Perth on the left nor from the Prince back with the reserve.

Crawford's Fergal squats next to the rock Dougal sits upon. He wears grenadier's boots tugged off a corpse at Falkirk.

We'd go out on a night darker than this one, he says, his Erse a gargling hiss in the dark, lift a few dozen cattle from the Camerons, and be warm in our beds before cock's crow.

Dougal listens deep into the night, but no one is coming yet.

Cows are easier to lead than men, he says. They lack imagination.

Fergal smiles. I saw the royal lad himself at Tournai, you know. Cumberland. Stuffed in his uniform like a Christmas sausage and waving his hat about to rouse the troops. Sent us howling into the French center without a qualm.

It's a wondrous talent, says Dougal, sending men off to die.

Oh, he's steady enough himself when the shot is flying near. A King's son has the Almighty on his shoulder.

The MacGillivrays are Episcopal by tradition more than practice, Dougal's father always maintaining that if God could make the earth in less than seven days He had no need for a pack of pew-polishers and mess-Johns to help Him sort it out.

And when one king's son, says Dougal, meets another in battle?

The men never tire of comparing their slender, berry-lipped Prince with King George's corpulent third son, born only a year apart and seemingly fated to meet on the field of battle. Though few of the men are Catholic, the most fervent for the Cause treat their glimpses of the Prince as the touch of a holy relic, the tangible, polished bone of an ancient and miraculous saint. Others, with more worldly designs, think him now only the harried fox who centers the hunt.

Ah, when prince fights prince, says the scarred veteran, God is in his glory.

It is a long time, by the feel of it, the frigid heath silent without a breeze, before three hares bound past, changing direction with each leap, and then the sound of men on the move gathers shape behind them.

It is Lord Murray and his aide, the Lowlander the French have christened the Chevalier de Johnstone who claims to know Dougal's brother Jamie from the exile court, and one of the much-resented Irish advisors, O'Sullivan. Dougal stands and takes his bonnet off.

"Where are we now?" asks Lord Murray, clearly unhappy with the progress of his troop.

Dougal points in three directions. "Cawdor Castle," he says. "River. Nairn."

"But how far?"

Dougal, suddenly dizzy on his feet, tries not to yawn. "Nearly a league yet tae Culraick."

The officers look to the sky. They have run out of black night, and Dougal can clearly see Crawford's Fergal, who understands but never speaks English, glaring at them. No telling if Perth's men or the Prince's reserves are still on the march, and without the advantage of surprise—

There is a dampness in the air that will be rain in an hour. Morning rain.

"What does your Lord suggest?" asks de Johnstone.

Some think Murray a traitor because he tarried so long in joining the fight, because he argued so strongly for retreat from the enemy's territory, but he was stalwart in the '15 and has formed the Prince's rabble into something like an army.

"It will be an hour or more only to gather them all," he sighs to O'Sullivan. "At least we'll have the light for our return."

And it is a somber gray light by which they shuffle back on the Inverness road, raining lightly now, the men four abreast in their regiments, more lost warriors joining from either side. There is little talk. Dougal keeps after them, dragging the ones he finds sitting on the wayside to their feet. "Just a wink of sleep," they say, "and Ah'll be with ye. They're no chasin' us yet, are they?"

Neddy stands at the bend facing the stumbling troop, waiting for Dougal with his look of perpetual befuddlement. Dougal knows the question before he reaches the man.

"What was a' that fer?" asks Neddy Coos.

THE MARE IS WELL-JADED BY SUNRISE. SHE IS AN ILL-TEMPERED hunter he purchased from a trader in Glenfinnan, recalcitrant even on the well-traveled tracks during the early hours, huffing and faltering now over broken ground. Jamie notes the ragged group to the west, tottering under bundles of their belongings with the anxious air of people in flight. The mare, wet to the bone and studded with thorns, wearily carries him along the crest of the hill. There is smoke in the sky ahead, then the scattered bothies and byres of the clachan come into view. A whistle, echoing, and he knows he has been spotted.

He starts down the hill and sees a boy running out the back of a hut and off in the opposite direction. Somebody to warn, perhaps, or merely told to save himself.

Jamie stays mounted as the hunter drinks from the muddy burn that wanders crookedly between the dwellings, reins gripped tight. He calls, speaking in Erse, to the pair of blanket-shrouded women watching the drizzle from the shelter of a shed roof.

Where have the men gone?

With the cattle, answers the elder of the two.

I saw none on my journey here.

They're on the other side of Monadh Cruan, the woman answers, and pulls her friend inside.

There is not a thing, he realizes, to give away which party he serves, no white cockade in his bonnet, not a hint of uniform or rank in his dress. Only a man they believe they've never seen before, to be avoided.

A rheumy-eyed cow stands across the burn, staring at him dumbly, and a girl in her late teens steps out from the largest of the bothies with a wooden bucket half filled with oatmeal, which she sets beside the animal. She addresses Jamie in English without looking at him.

"They're ainly feart of ye."

"I'll do them nae harm."

She draws a knife with a broken handle and knicks at the cow's ear, holding it out then to drip blood into the pail of meal. She is a comely girl, unmarked by the pox, her eyes an unsettling light gray, almost clear, when she looks up to examine him. She notes his boots, his breeks. For soirées in Paris he'd wear the phillabeg kilt, French ladies invariably rendered giddy at the sight of a man's untrousered legs, but it is a garment ill designed for riding a horse.

"And how are ye called?" he asks.

"Jenny," she says. Only that.

When Jamie was a boy his father knew everyone they came across, knew who their closest kinsmen were, knew perhaps a meandering tale about what someone of their line did long ago. "This land was a' ours, then," he'd say. "And, Lord willing, so it shall be again."

"I was born near here," says Jamie, looking around at the sodden, puddled patch of ground, the roundstone-and-mud huts under tilting heaps of thatch.

"I ken ye—yer brother is tacksman fer the MacIntosh."

There is neither fear nor deceit in her steady gaze. He wishes his father were alive, to tell him her story.

"I'm no here fer the rent—"

"Yer after the fightin', then."

"There's been a battle?"

The girl lightly pinches the cow's ear where it has been cut, waiting for a scab to form.

"Ah've been telt of a great flockin' of sojers on the government road, marchin' tae Inverness."

"Redcoats?"

The girl's eyes are like fresh water held in glass.

"Nae," she says, cautiously. "Hielanders."

JAMIE OVERTAKES THEM AT THE BRIDGE OVER THE NESS. Young Simon, Master of Lovat, is mounted on the far side of the road, watching his four score of Frasers maunder toward the rumble of cannon, not far distant. He calls before Jamie has brought the mare to a halt.

"*Ave, nuntius, morituri te salutant.*"

They have met twice before, two students of the law employed as pawns in a game of kings. Jamie nods ahead as there is another grumbling volley.

"They've begun?"

Young Lovat resembles his father the Auld Fox, chin, nose, lips, but there is no sport in his eyes, a reluctant player. He listens to a volley. "Ainly the musicians tuning up," he says. "Three-pounders, still firing iron shot. Perhaps we've time tae make the dance."

"I've been tae see yer father."

A cloud passes over Simon's face. "Did he lift the mask?"

Jamie suspects that the young Master of Lovat, at this moment, requires no diplomacy. The cannon are very near.

"He is keen in his support of whiche'er party wins the contest, and has been frae the beginning."

"Wise of him."

Jamie turns toward the sound of the artillery. "Do ye ken where they've set their lines?"

"Ma runner says it's Drummossie Muir. Mair than half of ma regiment are a'ready there, standing atween yer lot and the Appin Stuarts."

It is well known among the troops that young Simon wants no part of the fighting, that he tarried in recruiting his Frasers, that but for his father's scheming ambition he would be safe in Rotterdam blowing the dust from ancient law texts.

"On the field of battle, then," says Jamie, urging the reluctant mare toward the thunder.

"Or on the hangman's platform!" calls the Master of Lovat.

THE YOUNG PRETENDER'S MEN ARE ASSEMBLED UPON the sodden moor, awaiting slaughter.

Dougal MacGillivray, sleepless and bone-weary, stands in the front line, sword and targe in hand as the enemy's cannon drop roundshot upon them, rarely a man struck with the ground too wet to send the balls skipping. Smoke drifts across from the enemy's guns and back from their own small pieces firing in front, sulfur stinging the nose and eyes, and the crofter's son beside him who joined after Falkirk and has not yet been blooded pisses a sharp-smelling, steaming puddle at his own feet.

"Pick yerself a redcoat in their first line," Dougal tells the boy without turning his head. "That's yer mon. Bear him in sight, and dinnae mind the rest."

It will be impossible, he knows, to pick out any single redcoat through the powder smoke of their first volley when it comes, but the boy has been given a musket and possibly even been instructed how to use it—perhaps he'll get a shot off before he's killed.

They have been standing far too long in the wind and sleet, a few meager leagues from where Dougal was born, waiting, outnumbered and outgunned by Cumberland's army lined in their ranks far across the rough meadow. He is with Lady MacIntosh's champions, honored with the very center of the line again, ready to leg it over too much wet ground to close with the bustling cannoneers, the rows of stolid infantry in red coats and slouched hats, the sergeants with their halberds, the nervously shifting horsemen.

A roof over my head and a few hours rest, thinks Dougal. Somebody—the Prince and his Irishmen, or Lord Murray, perhaps—has decided they will stand here, well armed and poorly fed, all of Clan Chattan able to lift a weapon ready to sell their lives dearly as the pipes moan up and down the regiments like a great suffering beast.

Only don't force a man to contemplate.

"There's sae mony of them," says the crofter's son, shivering as he scans the distant wall of redcoats.

"We've beaten twice our number in the past," Dougal tells him. "When we gae," Dougal tells him, "cry oot with a' yer might, as if yer a daemon frae hell that's come tae destroy them."

"Will they run?"

No, he thinks, not today. Not in daylight with the best of the ground and too much of it between them.

"Turn yer heid around, laddie, and keek what's ahind ye."

The boy turns, taking in the massed warriors, Perth's and Glenbucket's men in the second line, Strathallen's horsemen—

"Would ye haud yer ground afore that?"

The boy shows his pitted teeth in a grin, then flinches as a cannonball lands just before them with a huge wet smack, spraying water and mud and suddenly men all around are running forward, shouting, Dougal hearing no order but following the mass of them, struggling over the uneven pasture, his belted pistol digging into his hip, splashing in places and slipping in others, perhaps a hundred men in front of him with plaids flapping wetly and the battle cry and the pipes and they have crossed half the ground before the first scouring of canister is unleashed, Dougal dodging one man lying sprawled on his face and leaping over the torn body of another, screaming now as if when he is filled with the sound no shot can pierce him and a second cannonade with the jagged metal hissing past him and still-burning wadding afloat in the air as the crofter's son just ahead loses his legs and there are gaps between the running men to see through now, the front line of redcoats with their muskets held ready, the cannoneers before them sponging, priming, ramming the canister down the bore and stepping away as Dougal dives forward, spreading his arms to slide on tufts of slick grass before the final blast tears through the men still standing, and he is up and upon them, thrusting under the spongeman's outheld staff to kill him and the first musket volley crackling out, smoke rolling all down the English line as the clansmen still alive behind him dash past and over the redcoats, parrying bayonets, slashing, clubbing, bodies underfoot with Dougal caught up among them in a great deadly screaming wave finally broken upon the bristling wall of second-line bayonets, Dougal hacking with his blade as he feels the press of the clansmen piling up behind him, forward movement halted now, scrummed between two armies and losing his feet for a moment, carried, staring at a hand's length into the furious eyes of a cursing redcoat for an instant, his sword caught in another man's ribs and twisted from his grasp, something hard smashing him on the temple and when the blaze of light subsides, pulling the charged and primed pistol free to jam it against the nearest patch of red and yank the trigger, smell of burning wool the last clear sensation before a smothering weight overtakes him, driving him down upon a tangle of gutted Highlanders—

JAMIE STRIKES THE INVERNESS ROAD EAST OF THE TOWN at a trot, the sleet a little thicker now. The thunder of the cannon is well past, but there is still the crackle of musket fire carried by the wind. He turns the mare toward the sound, and the first beings he encounters are a pair of men in gory tartans, one supporting the other as they attempt to run through the rutted mud.

"It's lost!" cries the one who is not bleeding. "Lost!"

"And Clan Chattan?"

"Struck doon! A' of them kilt!"

Jamie kicks the mare's flanks but she is unsure of her footing and balks, skittering from side to side on the wet road, kicking up a spray of mud. The next man is French and on horseback, his white uniform coat spattered with red.

"*C'est un folie!*" he cries. "*Il y avait trop de terre pour traverser!*"

"*Et le Prince?*" Jamie shouts back at him. "*Il est échappé?*"

"*Qui peut savoir? C'est un debacle!*"

Then there is a scrambling torrent of men on foot, wounded and not, many without weapons, Jamie forced to ride well to the side of the road to avoid trampling them. Men weeping and cursing, men with bewilderment and disbelief in their eyes, men looking panic-stricken over their shoulders, a broken army in desperate flight. Then the road is empty again, and he forces the mare to a gallop, slowing only at the sight of a trio of Irish Picquets, the man in the middle staggering with his hands over his face, blood streaming through his fingers.

"Turn back!" cries the man on the left, waving his arms. "They're killin' all they can lay their hands upon!"

Riders appear in the distance behind them, a squadron of the King's dragoons moving in loose formation.

"Lord save us," mutters the Irishman, pulling an envelope from his breast and beginning to stride back toward the approaching horsemen, holding it high over his head. "French papers!" he cries out. "We've papers from the King of France!"

Jamie, with a tender letter from Ambrosine Reynaud in his pocket but no official commission, turns his mount and kicks his heels into her flanks, heading south off the road.

He had a fleet turkoman back in St. Germaine that would have understood the difference between sport and survival, but this animal is determined to show him its displeasure. It slips and founders as he drives forward, beginning to climb, the hooves of his pursuers' mounts splashing behind. The mare quits before the summit, head down, wheezing, and Jamie dismounts and steps away, drawing his sword, turning to see—

There are six of them, shifting into a half circle around him, closing. One man on each flank dismounts, draws his rifle, aiming it at Jamie. The man in the center, a captain, walks his mount forward. Jamie's short French sword, chosen more because its scabbard does not drag on the ground than for his skill in handling it, feels paltry in his grip. He thinks for a moment of the ball or the blade, of the singular lack of glory to be won on this forlorn mound of gorse, and thrusts the point deep into the soaked ground. The captain closes with him, draws his own saber, and presses the tip of it to Jamie's neck.

"Now here's a lad with a bit of *sense*."

MEN HAVE BEEN PASSING FOR DAYS, IN LARGE GROUPS and small, heading toward the government road and Inverness. Though it is not far, even without a cart or shoes to cover your feet, Jenny has only been there once, her father claiming that the city market is no place for an unmarried girl to be seen. That one time, shortly after they moved back east from Sheildaig, was in the summer, and they went to the dock where the Ness meets the Moray Firth leading out to the northern sea, and there were ships of all sizes and gulls in the air and the great old castle across the river and people, so many people, some of them who spoke languages that were neither Erse nor Scots nor English, and she even saw a tall man whose skin was so deep brown it was almost black. Mr. Higgenbotham had two paintings hung on the wall at his house in the west, one of a ship with many sails at sea that he said was a frigate and another of a flooded city where the streets are water and you travel from building to building—for in the painting there are only tall stone buildings and nothing like a crofter's hut—in narrow boats that are moved by pushing very long poles on the bottom. They must all be fishermen, she thinks, and wonders if in the painting it is high tide or low. Jenny has never been on board a great ship but twice has crossed the Ness on ferry rafts and once in a boat pulled by oars.

Men are allowed to go more places. The men who have been passing, some of them, brag about how close to London they've marched and list the names of towns and cities they've been through, advancing and retreating, as if now they own them. Jenny recognized the names of many but has no painting or picture to help her imagine what they look like. Of course these men are moving about in order to fight and kill, which must take much of the pleasure out of travel. She wonders if wars have ever come to the flooded city in the painting.

Maybe they fight from boats.

Jenny moves the rusted iron pot under the spot in the roof that is dripping the most. Water that comes through the thatch has a strong taste, but the cow will drink it. There is mending to deal with, something she dislikes, always happier to be outside though there's nothing new there to see or do. Sometimes if her father is away she will take the trail with the fewest nettles to the government road and wait for the coaches. There are four in a day, two coming and two heading back down south. You can't really see inside the box, but she pictures the people riding, wearing clothes like in the drawings in Mr. Higgenbotham's books, books he said he wished Jenny could read out loud to him because his eyes were now so poor. But it was only black markings to her, till you found another of the drawings and could build your own story around it.

There is a country called France, across the channel from London, a channel being like a firth but much wider.

There is a country called Italy, where the flooded city lies.

There is a country called Africa, where the brown people come from, and you might be stricken by a deadly sickness.

There is London, where Mr. Higgenbotham lived before he took to the ships, that he says is the greatest city in the world, greater even than Edinburgh, where Jenny has never been either.

If one of these men who have been passing were to look at Jenny and say, "Come with me," she would follow without question, as long as they were not heading only to a battle.

Jenny wonders if the men will be passing again soon, moving in the other direction. There has been talk in the clachan of victories and defeats, though both seem meaningless here. The same hovels, the same muck, the same handful of oats and miserable fowl skittering about the yard. She wonders where her father has gone, never a man for greetings or farewells.

The thatch above drips for hours even after the rain has ceased, making a kind of song in the pot and on the floor that is something like company when her father is away. Jenny takes up a pair of his old trews, worn through at the knees and in the seat, that she has mended twice before. There is nothing in this hut or on their little patch of earth that she has not done before and will not be tasked to do again and again. She threads the needle, ponders where to begin.

There is a country called America, covered with trees, where naked men run about carrying axes made of stone—

DOUGAL CRAWLS ON HIS BELLY. HE HAS BEEN BAYONETED twice in his right side and once in the back of the opposite thigh, his forehead gashed and sticky. He is able to push with one foot, pull with one arm. He thought of lying still among the other bodies as if dead till somber light bled from the sky, but then came the redcoats, methodical, under orders and doing a thorough job of it, driving their spoons into the living and the dead.

It was young Charles Fraser of Lovat's regiment, struggling to rise upon a knee, who afforded him the moment's distraction to slither away. Fraser calling out his name, his office, then a shout and a quick flocking of English officers in wig and braid, a muttered debate—Dougal had rolled into the gulley before the muffled pistol shot signaled their verdict.

I will bleed to death first, he thinks, pushing with a foot, pulling with an arm, a bone-deep cold beginning to overwhelm the agony of his wounds, *and never feel the blade go in.* He'd had no fear in the battle, if it could be named one. But now, empty-handed and face half submerged in a puddle, the idea of being skewered on an infantryman's steel terrifies him.

Pushing with a foot, pulling with an arm, torquing his mortified body as if to punish himself, Dougal crawls through the gully, the sleet in abeyance now, the bodies he encounters only mounds of cold flesh and sodden wool he struggles to move over or around. *I will bleed to death slowly,* he thinks. *Like falling asleep.*

The gulley is shallower now, the wet earth rising, and he sees ahead with his one eye not clotted shut with blood that there is a hut ahead at the edge of the moor, a pair of wounded MacPhersons stumbling to it and ducking inside. There are other people, barefoot beggarmen and local poor folk who've come to watch the slaughter and gather the spoils should their champions be victorious—they are staring at something above and behind Dougal, and then they begin to run in every direction, panicked, and a few rush into the hut and Dougal hears the splashing of many feet in the gulley behind him and buries his face in the muck of the berm, willing himself not to twitch or shiver.

The soldiers, perhaps a dozen of them, run past, a few planting their boots squarely in his back to climb the berm, knocking the breath from him, and there is shouting and rifle fire. Dougal lies still, breathing shallowly and willing the blood to drain from his body, sensing that he is becoming one with the clammy earth beneath him, sinking into it, until the screaming begins.

He only has to tilt his head slightly to see. Somewhere they've found dry hay and have piled it to fire the hut, thatch roof in flames already with a thick, black smoke boiling out from it, redcoats standing and kneeling with muskets leveled, a captain beside them tapping with his sword to elect which two are to dispatch the next burning soul to bolt from the opening. Dougal closes his good eye, lays his head to the side and prays he will die before they find him.

THE MEN NOT TOO BADLY WOUNDED STAND SHOULDER to shoulder in the wagon bed, steadying each other at the jolts, attempting not to tread on those moaning at their feet. Dragoons ride on either side of them, clothes and faces spattered with mud, joking with each other. Jamie stares out the rear, the moment seeming unreal as he listens to the clansmen mutter in Erse. The ground was ill-chosen, they say, the King's men given too much time to prepare, too much distance to shoot them down in. One says he saw Prince Charlie leave the field, unhurt. The wagon is rolling back toward the moor.

"I've been done fer," whines a tow-haired boy who lies curled upon himself, holding his stomach, again and again. "I've been done fer."

The banners of the King's regiments are planted all about the killing ground, hanging wet and limp as redcoats stroll in twos and threes across the grass, pausing at this or that heap of what was a man, thrusting their bayonets into it, moving on. Now and then a musket shot. There are women, Cumberland's camp followers, hopping like corbies among the dead, tugging at boots, hauling back on lengths of plaid till the obscenely white, naked bodies roll free of them. The dragoon captain is sweeping his arm about, explaining the battle to his troopers.

"As stupid as young bullocks," he is saying, "hurling themselves on our steel."

The tow-haired boy begins to choke.

They are carried a ways down the road to Nairn, till they come upon a battle-weary company of the King's infantry taking their ease on a berm. Their sergeant rouses them to their feet as the wagon is stopped, then waves his sword at the prisoners.

"Out with ye, then! 'Op it!"

The clansmen who are able climb down, Jamie attempting to stay within the crowd, waiting for his quality to be recognized when it will do him the most good. They are told to leave the badly wounded in the wagon and prodded toward the small rise on the north side of the road. The men balk, uneasy, and the sergeant, who looks as if he hasn't slept in days, yanks Jamie by the arm from their midst.

"Ye understand me?"

"Ah do." This can be managed, thinks Jamie, there is always something one can say—

"Tell 'em we're marching over the hill."

"What's there?"

"The rest of yer clansmen," says the sergeant. "Go on now, tell 'em—"

Jamie repeats the sergeant's words in Erse, and the men grudgingly move up the slope, infantrymen to their backs and a dragoon riding along on each side of the group. Jamie helps a large, bearded Stuart man whose right leg is ruined.

There is nobody waiting on the other side of the hill.

There is nobody waiting, but the men walk forward and Jamie feels that the redcoats have stopped and he hears the sergeant tell them to form their line and then there is a long ditch before them—

It is two quick steps before he throws himself in, the volley cracking before he hits the pile of bodies already lying there, then screams of other men as the redcoats rush forward to finish those only wounded. Somebody leaps over the ditch and there are more shots and he realizes he's been hit in the back of the leg while he was jumping and a dead man is thrown on top of him. Jamie closes his eyes and tries to breathe without moving his chest, but then he is stepped on, soldiers walking on top of the bodies, arranging them in the ditch, and he opens an eye to find a redcoat staring down at him, the butt of his musket poised to strike.

"Sorry, mate," he says before he smashes it down.

THEY STAY WELL BACK FROM HAWLEY'S MEN, CONSIDERing themselves soldiers and not executioners, making neat piles of swords and pistols taken from the dead, Cruikshank slipping the occasional dirk or smaller memento into his kit bag.

"A good deal of these was lifted from our dead at Prestonpans," says Kirby when they reach the first of the muskets thrown down in the charge. "A firearm 'as no bloody conscience."

"Nor a dragoon," says Cruikshank, pausing to allow one of Hawley's up ahead dispatch a whimpering Highlander.

"Orders is orders."

"But ye don't 'ave ter relish the worst of 'em."

"If their charge 'ad come any deeper, we'd feel different."

"Might. But ye know 'ow they go on about the 'eat of battle?

Well, me own 'eat cools off dead quick these days. When blades are flashin' and the lead is flyin', sure, ye want a bit of houtrage, ye want ter tear their bloody 'earts out then. But when the smoke clears—"

Scattered gunshots on the moor as Hawley's men obey the Duke's order.

"Lookit this one," says Kirby.

A boy of maybe fourteen, lying on top of a musket, very little left of his legs. Kirby rolls him over, checks the musket.

"It asn't been fired."

"Yer irregulars is fine fer abuscados and 'orse stealin—" says Cruikshank. "Ye remember them Oirish women in the 'ills above Limerick?"

"Bleedin' Amazons, 'ack ye ter death with a turf slane—"

"—but fer a nose-ter-nose affair like we just 'ad, yer professional sojer will prevail every time. It's the discipline does it, keepin' a cool 'ead whilst the blade-wavin' hellions are about ter overrun ye."

"Discipline as is beat inter yer 'ide."

"Tis a poor sojer learns nuffing from a stout whipping. I've earned a few stripes on me back over the years—"

"And 'ad the luck to duck a good number more ye deserved."

"True enough," muses Cruikshank. "But take this young'un 'ere. 'Is military career lasted all of—what would ye put it at, Kirby?"

Kirby looks back to the line of rebels killed by cannon while still in formation.

"A 'undred yards, per'aps."

"*Out, out, brief candle.* One minute yer pullin' spuds outer the ground—"

"I believe it's *oats* they've got up 'ere, Reg."

"Right ye are. One minute pickin' bugs out from the barley, and the next engaged in deadly combat, without an hour of drill, a notion of tactics, nor the opportunity ter discharge yer weapon in the direction of a target ter get the 'ang of it."

Kirby finds a spot on the ground unoccupied by a dead Jacobite and fires the musket into it. "Amateurs. The type as would leave a weapon primed an waitin' ter do mischief," he says.

"My point exactly. Don't bovver searchin' 'im fer coins, Bert, 'ee'll need any 'ee's got in the next world."

Kirby turns to survey the swath of corpses they've already examined. He sees movement by the hut that was fired, smoldering now. He points the musket with one hand—"Something stirring there."

They stroll back around the disarmed bodies toward the hut, a thin sleet dropping again, blowing into their faces.

"Nasty climate, this," says Kirby.

"I'd 'ave let the Pretender *'ave* it."

"And throw Carlisle inter the bargain?"

"All I'm sayin' is, they're a diffrint *race*. They don't think like you an' me, Bert. Take this poor bugger—"

Kirby bends to pull away the dirk strapped to a crawling man's calf, examines it. "Nice bit of work 'ere on the 'andle. The way they've carved the bone—"

"You or me, if we was poked through with 'oles on a battlefield, we'd likely lie still and wait fer further developments. But this worthy young gent—" he pushes the man over onto his back with his bootheel. It is hard to tell what is mud and what is gore. The man squints up at them through the sleet, breathing with great effort.

"Orders is ter leave none alive on the field," says Kirby, slipping the dirk into Cruikshank's near-full kit bag.

"But this one 'as the aspect of a chief, 'ee does. Lookit the way 'ee's dressed. 'Ee might 'ave vital information ter pass on ter them as draws up our campaigns—"

"Them that sits back under a roof somewheres, by a nice 'ot fire—"

"Get a dram into 'is gullet and 'ee'll probably give out with the Pretender's current location, though it might be all in Oirish—"

"Easier, though, ter just knock 'is brains out—"

"Easier, yes, but what of the larger canvas, Bert? We're only private sojers, I'll grant ye, but a bit of hinitiative—"

"Can get ye twenty on the back tied to a post."

"True enough, true enough, but—"

"Do ane or the other," interrupts Dougal, the wounded man on the ground. "But do it quick and get me oot of this fecking rain."

IT IS COLD, AND WHEN JAMIE BREATHES THERE IS MORE earth than air to it. Something hard digs into his ribs and he cries out, earth filling his mouth, and then someone is cursing in Erse. Jamie chokes and attempts to rise up, earth in his eyes, and when he blinks to see there is a crofter above him with a spade raised over his shoulder, ready to strike.

"*Òir!*" croaks Jamie, the word spewing from his mouth before a thought can form itself.

Gold! I know where gold is buried.

The crofter lowers his spade, scowling, suspicious. It is almost dark, and he has begun to fill his cart with clothing stripped off the dead in the ditch. It is difficult for Jamie to speak, one side of his face too swollen to move, but he tells the man that he has buried a fortune of French gold meant for the rebels not far from here, that he'll lead him to it when the English are not so thick in the land. But now he needs shelter.

The crofter has brought sacks of turnips to cover whatever he's plundered. Jamie crawls into the cart and the man lays them on top before he wrestles himself into the yoke and begins to plod toward home. The man is pondering, Jamie imagines, the probability of a reward for delivering him to the English against the possibility that the story of French gold is true. "We are withoot land nor title," his father would often comment upon passing a man behind a plow, "but we have no sunk tae *that*."

Each bump of the wooden cartwheels is a dagger behind Jamie's eyes, and he is buried again, straining to fill his lungs, then holding his breath each time the cart stops rolling. His father died this way, in bed, wheezing, his life narrowed to a struggle for air. Jamie can tell that his head is swollen, throbbing, and he feels as if he is going to vomit. *This will pass*, he wills himself to think, *and we will prevail.*

BRIGADE MAJOR WOLFE, NOT YET TWENTY, IS AN UNeasy rider. No fear of tumbling from the mount, which his groom says answers to the name of Derrick, but chagrin at the ungainly picture he makes upon it. *Aide de camp* to Lieutenant General Hawley, he is an infantry officer in a dragoon regiment, and at the end of each day in the saddle, painfully aware of it.

"Find my people," Hawley shouted to him before thundering away himself, "and have them muster at the bridge."

Hawley's people, principally the 1st Royal Dragoons, have galloped in several directions, chasing the remnants of the Pretender's shattered army, scything them down with cutlass strokes, then turning back to finish them with a pistol shot. Derrick, if that is indeed his name, is not distracted by the carnage, carefully stepping around and over bodies and parts of bodies, ears twitching with interest. Wolfe himself has seen worse, in the center of the first line in the chaos of Dettingen, a boy ensign willing himself not to tremble as iron shot tore the limbs from men around him, more worried about his younger brother than himself. He met, if that is the word for it, Cumberland then, the Duke himself only twenty-two on that day and as unconcerned by the shot and shell as if it had been a light rain. Or that was the impression he gave when Wolfe delivered him the message, and impression is what counts with the men, who must believe it is worth their lives to lift a fallen standard from the bloodied earth. He is tall and slender, Wolfe, too slender, and too young, he knows, to be properly intimidating as an officer, but today he is damned if he is going to appear be a poor horseman.

There is no life in the bodies he rides over. Many have been shot in the back of the head. This is a donkey's mission, given not as punishment but for lack of better employment to set him to. Dragoons have a way of always coming back together without plan or urging.

The men of the 1st Royal do not love or respect Lieutenant General Hawley. They fear him, fear his rough tongue and his rages and his orders to flog or to hang. Held in reserve today until the rebels broke and ran, they will not hesitate to execute his order, they will match his brutality with their own. The aide position is meant partly to serve as Major Wolfe's training, and what he has learned from Hawley is that for mounted troops, dash may be as important as discretion. But it was the portly young Duke of Cumberland in charge of tactics today—

"It would take four of you to equal the Duke," said Lieutenant Colonel Fosdick on first sight of Wolfe, then explained while his companions laughed that they'd just been discussing who best to shelter behind during a barrage of canister. The dragoon officers, if anything, cut an even more colorful figure than those of the grenadiers, their sexual exploits alone, though often difficult to believe, certainly more varied in location and detail. Wolfe will take a dram now and then, but avoids the card playing, billiards, and indiscriminate wagering in the barracks. Fosdick himself lost a considerable sum after the debacle at Falkirk to one of General Cope's officers, who had bet him Hawley would have no greater success in his first engagement with the rebels than Cope had at Prestonpans. Wolfe writes his mother whenever possible, has given up his practice of the flute, and has failed to take up either cursing or the use of snuff. Tolerated if not warmed to by the officers of equal rank, he is perhaps treated with a modicum of tact due to the black armband he wears for poor brother Ned, gone with the consumption less than a year ago.

The dead are fewer and farther between now, and he has yet to find his first dragoon. There is a euphoria, for those who survive it unscathed, that comes in the aftermath of battle. Of *course* one is not among the corpses, nothing could be clearer. After Dettingen he felt almost giddy, despite being made head of a detail meant to consolidate their casualties, and he remembers the vividness of the colors of flags and uniforms, the smell, almost a taste, of musket smoke wafting across the river. It is an illusion, he knows, the grim probabilities weighted against even the most intrepid of soldiers. Certainly if his seasickness had not overwhelmed him on his first campaign in uniform, if he had reached Jamaica under his father's command, he would have been one of the majority who perished. And if Barrell's Foot, when he was still with them, had been called up for the slaughter at Fontenoy—

It does not bear thinking about. Men who fight heroically one day may falter and quail on the next, and he believes overthinking to be the culprit. Life, at least military life, is constant assault, and one must face it unflinchingly.

He sees Captain Hargreaves ahead with a squadron of Barrell's men, roaming among the dead and collecting weapons. Wolfe pulls in the reins, slows to parallel Hargreaves. Only months ago the man had been his superior officer, a good twenty years his senior, but possessed neither wealth nor a father in high command.

"How goes it, Captain?"

"Tolerably well, sir, now that the hurly-burly has died down."

"You took the brunt of it."

"That we did."

It was difficult to watch from the flank, his former regiment nearly overwhelmed by the point of the rebel charge, redcoats falling under hacking swords and axes while Hawley chuckled with glee and anticipation beside him. The position was an honor, Barrell's Foot having stalwartly covered the retreat at Falkirk, but honor has its pitfalls—

"Have you reckoned your casualties?"

Hargreaves nods. He looks drawn and exhausted.

"Over a third," he says. "Lord Kerr had his head cleaved in two, Lieutenant Colonel Rich lost his hands—"

"You fought valiantly."

Hargreaves seems unfazed by the compliment. "We'd our own people's bayonets at our backs, nowhere to go—each man deals with what is before him."

Providence again. Wolfe is adequate with a sword, but frail compared to the private soldiers on the line, and no match for a blood-maddened Highlander. The most difficult task he's faced in this campaign has been explaining to Mrs. Gordon that yes, General Hawley will be billeting in her house, and no, she may not take any of her goods and possessions with her when she vacates it immediately. That her silver and china is now in Hawley's crates waiting shipment home is an uncomfortable thought, but facing her with the firmness and civility he believes required of an officer and a gentleman—

"Have you seen any of our dragoons?" he asks the captain.

"They kicked a good deal of mud in our faces," he says, pointing to the west. "Today is sport for the cavalry."

IN THE BYRE, JENNY WATCHES BY THE NERVOUS FLAME on a pine root as the man sleeps, if that's what it is, one eye twitching open from time to time, rolling wildly, the other swollen shut, his breath rapid puffs in the cold. She helped her father carry him in and lay him behind the cow, covering most of him with the last of the barley straw. Her father would not meet her eye, face set in a scowl, back stiff, inviting no question.

"There's been a great killin' on the Drummoissie Muir," shouted Bobby Strathallen, puckled with fear on his run to the wild north mountains, "and mair tae coom!"

She had hoped that returning here from the west would be safe at the least. In Sheildaig the runrig share they rented had been a mite better ground for planting, and a short, meandering donner brought you to the glorious sea, but the kirk there lay upon your every doings with a suffocating weight. It was unclear who started the rumor—so many eyes following you, so many tongues eager for someone to denounce—and as Jenny was young and bonny and working for the Englishman, Mr. Higgenbotham, she was called out as a harlot. Though no man or boy was ever named as her partner in debauchery, she was yanked by the hair and dressed in sackcloth and marooned upon the Sinner's Bench every Sabbath, her mother covering her own face with her *earasaid* through both services and her father daring any man to meet his glaring eye, then thrashing her when they were back home. Mr. Higgenbotham was bent with age, a retired navy man who kindly praised her artless cooking and taught her phrases in the English tongue, never laying a finger on her, but old women felt obligated to put their knobby hands on her belly and squeeze her breasts until they burned in hope of green milk that would prove her guilt. There was nothing to confess. Condemned by the Session despite her denials, her mother shamed, finally, into the grave, her father loaded the cart in the middle of a moonless night and took her, without the reverend's Testicat or the tacksman's leave, clear across the Highlands to this spouty, rock-strewn patch of misery. He had some people in the area, but the blood had run very thin, and it was a rare day that he did not mutter, in her presence, "I swore the sun would ne'er catch me here again."

It is past talking now, the two of them penned under the same moldering thatch, father hating daughter for the calumnies raised against her, daughter hating father for believing them. They are spoken to kindly enough in this clachan, but there is an edge to it, a slyness and a judgment. Whenever Jenny passes Mrs. Cumming and her friends, conspiring under their shawls as they grind oats to meal on the quern that it takes two of them to lift and hide from the tacksman's visits, there is a mocking sort of laughter. And the eyes of the men and older boys linger overlong when she is not at her father's side, as if they own a piece of her.

The wounded stranger wakes with a gasp.

His unbloodied eye casts about frantically before lighting on her face. A spark of recognition—

The man? he says, in Erse.

"My father."

"He's here?"

"He went oot," she says, pleased to use her Saxon.

"Went where?"

"Oot tae think. He dis that."

She has a pannikin of milk for him, but with his face still so swollen it is hard for him to drink, and some of it skitters down his front despite her holding his head. The cow is lying on its side, nearly motionless, the man pressed against its back for warmth.

"Is it dying?" he asks.

"Feed is scarce through the winter," she tells him. "Some days we need tae pull it tae its feet with ropes."

He looks like a different man than the one on the tall horse in the morning, bloodied now, his fine clothes a fright and hair matted and tangled with straw. He tries to sit up and she helps him and is suddenly shamed as he peers beyond the meager light of the pine root. The ceiling thatch is black with soot, only a low shelf separating the cow's byre from the space that she and her father eat in, sleep in, avoid each other's gaze in—

"Is he a guid mon?"

"Ma father?"

It is a strange and sudden question, but something about the stranger makes her feel as if she's known him all her life.

"Is he honest?"

She has never thought to apply the word to anyone.

"We're puir," she says.

The man searches her eyes for a long moment. She remembers thinking him bonny, in the morning, in his breeks and boots astride the flighty mare. He reaches inside his shirt, digging for something, then pulls out a gold ring, the band wide as the nail on her little finger.

"Ye take this," he says. "Twas ma mother's."

It is well polished, and glints pure in the flickering light.

"Ye dinnae need tae pay."

He presses the ring into Jenny's hand.

"Talk tae yer father."

She knows what he is afraid of. The ring feels heavy as she closes her hand on it. She's never touched gold before.

"What's yer name?"

"Jamie MacGillivray, of Dunmaglas," he says. "And you, I recollect, are Jenny."

She nods to him, and makes her way to the other side of the hut, snuffing out the flame.

THERE IS NO FEAST WITHOUT A SLAUGHTER.

The phrase has stuck in Lord Lovat's head all day as the women scurry about preparing the food and drink. There is no manner to ken the outcome of any battle, of course, but it would beggar providence to wait for confirmation. Yesterday's messenger, after the young MacGillivray had been dismissed, spoke of the plan for surprise attack, of the Prince regaining his boldness after weeks of retreat. So much of it, Lovat knows, is will and persistence, unlikely to develop in a lad who believes he owns a mandate from God—

Thomas, his host, steps in from the hillside, out of breath.

"Riders," he says. "From the east."

"Uniforms?"

"Mostly covered from sight. As if they're in flight."

No manner to ken.

"I'll stand," says the Auld Fox. "For whatever it be."

It takes both Tweedie and the hostler, Rhory Bain, to right him out of the chair and prop him with his staff in hand. Like an old house with rotting timbers, he thinks, ready to collapse. He hears the women wailing in Erse outside and knows it is the worst.

The food is quickly distributed, the Irish barely dismounting to eat before they hurry on, leaving Young Charles and his odd lot of nervous retainers behind.

"*Mon Prince*," says Lovat, lowering himself slightly with the help of the staff and indicating his humble hideaway, "A' that ye keek here is *à votre service*."

"A pleasure to meet you," the Prince replies, offering his hand. "*Mais je regret les circonstances*."

They sit then, the Prince attentive and mannerly despite his distracted air, his aspect that of a man expecting to be forced to bolt at any moment.

"*C'est seulement une bataille, pas la guerre entière*," Lovat reassures him.

"Of course," says the Prince. "But we did not retreat *en masse*. I'm afraid the army is broken—though some are making for Ruthven—"

"The chieftans will find their way tae their ain strongholds, and await the call tae reassemble. If ye'll ainly gae upon the heather fer a spell, up high where the redcoats dinnae dare set their feet, they'll rally round ye again."

"I should have waited for the French—"

"Nae time fer regrets. Think, if ye will, of Robert the Bruce. Defeated in eleven battles, he won Scotland in the twelth."

The Prince is looking past him.

"There will be French ships on the coast," he says, "waiting for me."

The Auld Fox has never thought the boy capable of regaining the Three Kingdoms. But Scotland, Scotland could be won back and defended, land and titles restored, a legitimate King in place for whenever the southerners wearied of their kraut-eating George. With will and persistence—

Young Charlie sighs. "I was misinformed," he says. "My advisors—"

By the third glass of wine the retainers are in a panic, in and out of the door urging the Prince not to tarry. With an effort he knows will cost him later, Lovat rises on his own power.

"*Je vous en supplie, mon Prince,*" he says, "*il faut que cherchez un lieu hors de danger, plus loin des Anglais.*"

It is dark outside, and cold, but he knows the Prince is not safe here and wishes to run. They embrace, and the women stand in a line to curtsy as he steps out to his horse.

If that wisp of a boy is the best we can do, thinks Lord Lovat as he watches the party hobble away, perhaps we deserve what is coming.

Tweedie is by his side, ready to support him if he totters.

"Make all ready," he tells the gillie. "We leave tonight."

He'll have to be carried, he knows, like a butchered steer you've not had time to quarter. The wine has angered his gout, his knees are aching—

"*Càite?*"

"To the mountains," answers Lord Lovat, putting his hand on the Tweedie's shoulder. "And then to the west."

THE IDEA, OF COURSE, WAS TO WIN BACK THAT WHICH had been lost. Exactly what that was, and when the losing of it had begun, was never totally clear to Jamie and his brother Dougal, only that it was worth dying for. "Lang syne we were great in the land," their father would say after a wee dram, "afore treachery and ill fortune stole it awee." He was a steady drinker, their father, never off his feet with it or even sluggard of tongue, but his days began with ale, built to claret, and ended with malty *uisce beatha* stilled in Black Isle by his smuggler cousins. He would snarl at the disgrace of Union, the vanity of Lowland political men and the perfidy of all Campbells, then call them forward—Dougal on the right and Jamie to the left—clutch their boyish shoulders in his massive hands, and bid them swear they would right it all. He was the mountain they dwelt beneath, their mother taken with the King's Evil, a gaunt, hollow-eyed woman who hacked into a fold of cloth to stifle the noise, and spoke, when she had breath to speak, the Erse of the western islands. Jamie has the memory of himself in her arms, pressing his wee hand on her chest and feeling the rale as she breathed, the purring thing that would kill her before he was five.

It is the clan's slogan—*Touch Not the Cat.*

And as Dougal would sooner roll naked in burdock than open a book, it was Jamie chosen to be the wit of the family's restoration. "Ye need the canny uns to keep holt o' that which the sword has won," their father would say. "Mair has been lost wi' the scratch iv a quill than tae the stroke iv a claymuir." It was afternoons with Reverend Ainsley for English, Latin, and the beginnings of the French tongue, and then, not a hair on Jamie's chin, on to Edinburgh. Their father, tacksman for Rennie MacIntosh, fair bled his tenants for the money to keep him there, a knowledge that gave Jamie more than a twinge of guilt on his drinking rounds with the lads.

It is torture for Jamie to turn his body, slowly working his more frozen parts against the bulk of the cow. He will have fleas by daybreak, but that will matter little if the girl's father chooses to sell him. The English will be on the country like a plague for some time to come, but as days pass their thirst for blood will wane, and it might be possible to venture out at night. He realizes he is hungry.

There are Campbells on sections of what his father claimed was MacGillivray land, and if the Prince and his followers had prevailed—

that was the dream. Restoration of a birthright he has never felt fully entitled to, a rise in status within Clan Chattan, the instant respect of men who know only his name. Touch Not the Cat. Jamie has never pictured himself borne across running water in a chaise supported by his gillies. And he has never pictured himself trembling and bloody in the muck of a byre, husband to a bony mass of beef and waiting to be skewered by redcoats, yet here he lies.

They are not dreams so much as a slackening of consciousness, cause drifting away from effect till it is one red place or another to be avoided, concentrations of pain that bring him back toward the surface for a moment only to slide back under, the events of the day fluttering anxiously beneath it all and once or twice the calm relief of gray eyes, eyes nearly clear, like pure water in a glass.

The smoke wakes him before the screaming makes sense to his brain. Men's voices shouting, the girl's voice screaming, the smoke and the smell of burning thatch, and there is no way he can unwedge himself from behind the pissing cow till it struggles to its wobbly legs and there are redcoats in the byre to drive it out and drag him along by one leg, leaving him stretched beside the weeping crofter, blood running out Jamie's nose and mouth already as they kick him. The girl, Jenny, screaming, screaming.

THERE ARE FOUR OF THEM, THE CORNERS OF THEIR mouths still blackened with gunpowder from yesterday's volleys, and each, breath thick with ale, takes a turn driving her into the dirt. Only the first one tears her, and the last stands, when he is finished, and holds the barrel of his musket to her forehead for the longest time, watching her body heave with sobs, before spitting on her and striding away. She lies still, hoping that the cold ground will numb her completely, until embers from the burning thatch float down and begin to blister her skin. She manages to stand, shakily, bleeding down her leg, and finds that her father and the man they were hiding have been taken away, the rest of the huts in the clachan still ablaze or pushed over, the people nowhere to be seen. The cow is still there, drooling with its head low, staring at the burning byre with rheumy eyes. Jenny makes it to the well and hauls up the bucket, needing to wash herself, but they've thrown filth down into that too and she vomits bile on the stone curbing. The gold ring, which she swallowed when she first heard the dogs barking, does not come up.

DOUGAL LIES STUCK TO THE TOLHOUSE FLOOR IN INverness, without the energy or will to shift himself. He can't tell if it is his own blood or another man's that has crusted and bound him to the stone. Men cry and moan and gibber prayers all around him, a writhing carpet of misery, calling for water, water, water and God's mercy. He can't tell if his own voice is among them, rolling to and away from himself like something caught in a swirling tide. Now and then there is light, someone with a lantern, shapes appearing on the ceiling where it was only black before, and he can tell from the glisten of the unblinking eyes that the man beside him is dead. Released. Dougal welcomes the cold of night at first, but then begins to shake with it, angering his wounds. His father held that pain was not a punishment, only a reminder that you were still alive, but he saw his father staring hollow-eyed from bed and longing for death. Lantern light again, and then a redcoat kicking him hard in the side and Dougal becomes unstuck, feeling new heat and wet beneath him. The man kicks again, perhaps to see if he's alive, or perhaps just because he can.

If I am to live, Dougal thinks as the pain rackets through his body, give me the chance to kill one more of these sons of whores—

BY DAYBREAK THERE IS BARELY ANYTHING LEFT THAT will burn and Jenny has not slept. She squats by the embers of the pyre she has fed all through the night, stirring it now and again with a charred stick for whatever flush of heat remains. She hears them in the mist before they take shape, orders shouted, some laughing, some cursing. There is nothing left standing in the clachan big enough to hide in or behind. Jenny lies on her side, curled in a ball, by the big stones of the grain shed they pulled down.

Only two step out of the mist. They wander apart, poking at the ruin with their boots, till one has gone out of sight and the other has meandered toward Jenny. He was one of them, she can see, one of the four, red hair and a lump on the bridge of his nose like it had been broken. He walks by and Jenny holds her breath and closes her eyes and when she opens them again the red soldier is standing by the cow, which is grazing in the patch of kale the Fergusons grow by their hut. The soldier watches it for a moment, then opens the flap on his cartridge case and pulls out a twist of paper. He tears the end off the paper with his teeth, pours a little powder onto the pan of his musket.

The quern stone that Jenny hoists onto her shoulder nearly pulls her off her feet. It is only a few quick steps to the man, who is ramming the wadded paper down the barrel of his musket when she reaches him. He senses her, turning slightly to be hit over the eye and falling awkwardly and she has to kneel on his back to smash his head again with the stone, driving it into the dirt. The cow only shifts slightly, attacking a new tangle of kale.

Jenny heaves the bloody stone and the dead man's musket, surprisingly heavy, down the well, watching for the other soldier. Her front is stained with blood. She climbs the hill that rises above the ruined clachan, mud squishing between her toes in the bare patches, a feeling she has always loved.

It is a long, cold walk north across the great moor and up to the shielings. There will be no one there at this time of year, cold and dank, but where there's nothing to loot you'll draw no lobsterbacks.

The few she crosses with now, a half dozen or less in each southbound group, barely give her a keek.

I must be a fright, she thinks, as they're well known for molesting the livestock if nothing human is at hand. She walks till neither of her bare feet has any sense left in them, following the rut of the cow path, passing a handful of grim crofter's wives and their gaunt children bearing bundles of whatever they've saved, reaching the foot of the Buachaille in the late day. She meanders then with the burn along its base, iced over near the banks, till she comes to the spring and the clootie tree that stands above it.

Wee Tess McNair, bold beyond her years, led her here last summer while they were hunting wayward lambs. Jenny tears a strip of muddy cloth from the hem of her shift, ties it to a low-swinging branch to join the dozens of others hung there, all the while cursing the man she's murdered to the fires of Hell and wishing a plague upon the ones she hasn't, a sickness to rot their innards and make blood run from their pizzles.

She sits then, already shivering, in the lee of the clootie tree, the wee spring muttering among the rocks and the tinkly things people have left in the branches next to the rags making their noise and sparkling in the last horizontal rays from the west. She wonders if falling asleep and slowly freezing feel like the same thing. There is a sharp pain in her stomach. Hunger, maybe, or the ring she was given by the handsome MacGillivray man unhappy in its present seat. Jenny lays back on the rise above the spring, tries to move her frozen toes, lets her eyelids slide. If there is a tale about sleeping under a clootie tree she has not heard it, but it is doubtless an unwise and unholy act. If the Devil should come, she thinks, beginning to drift, perhaps He'll bring a blanket.

THE KING'S MERCY

IT IS ALREADY GROWING DARK WHEN THEY ARE SENT from the house to tear the weirs apart. Most of the day has been taken up with looting the absent Laird's stores of liquor and food under the eagle eye of Brigadier Mordaunt's aides, Cruikshank's kit bag left a day's march behind in Inverness. Hundreds and hundreds of bottles of wine and spirits, wagonloads of grain, a library stuffed into crates with no time to peruse the titles—it has been chilly work with little rest. That Lovat deigns to call the great pile of stone a "castle" gives rise to a certain amount of humor, but all are impressed by the bounty they find in his cellars and outbuildings.

"All these riches fer one owd man," muses Private Kirby as they stroll toward the swift-flowing Beuly.

"The way it goes up 'ere, Bert, is the common people—crofters and shepherds and whatnot—give whatever they fish or 'unt or farm ter the chieftain, an 'ee's in charge of dolin' it out as the need arises."

"Why don't everybody just keep what they 'arvest fer themselves?"

Private Cruikshank whistles. "Dangerous talk, Bert. Don't let the Brigadier 'ear ye on about that."

"I've just got to say, hit's been very meager pickings up ter this point. Crofters absent, cupboards empty, livestock starved ter the bone. And as fer the crofter's wives—"

"Never you mind them—"

"Not a one of those doxies we found 'iding as looked worth a tumble."

"And since when 'as Bert Kirby become so partickilar? I've seen ye so blind drunk in a public 'ouse ye'd 'ave screwed yer own mother, and 'er three long years in the grave."

"It's the tales that lead a man ter 'esitate."

"Tales, is it?"

"Of the 'ighlanders. The men"—here Kirby lowers his voice, as if there is someone to hear—"they violate their *ewes*."

Cruikshank considers this. "Then we've done a great deed fer the sheep of England. To think what those maraudin bandits might've done in Suffolk—"

"Ye don't believe me—"

"Of course I do. Ye've put me off mutton fer life."

Sergeant Morse is upon them then, a plaster on his cheek, one of the few in the 20th Foot so much as grazed by a ball. They had been at the rear of the second line, moved forward to check the deepest penetration of the rebels.

"And what, may I inquire, might that be?"

He is pointing at the oddly shaped lump in one of Bert's pockets. Looting, it has been declared, will be punishable by—

"Hit could be vital evvydence, Sergeant," says the private, quickly pulling out a ceramic coffee mug and offering it to Morse. On it is a rendering of the Pretender, looking particularly curly-wigged and rosy-cheeked, with *Rex Nostrorum* scribed on a garland above his head.

"Ye pass this around to the squadron, they'll reckonize the very nib we're supposed ter be 'unting for when they sees 'im. I expect that's Oirish writ over 'is 'ead."

"I trust ye arrested the owner of this," says the sergeant, stuffing the mug in his own coat pocket.

"They wasn't in," says Kirby, "so we left a note."

The sergeant scowls and points to the river. "Into the drink with yez, then—on the double!"

When they reach the river, a detail is lugging two large creels full of flopping fish up the bank.

"We cleaned it out fer you, lads," calls the corporal with the dipping net balanced on his shoulder. "Enjoy yer swim."

Private Kirby steps in halfway up to his boot tops to tie rope around the most likely supports, but even with both of them pulling the first of the weirs won't budge.

"We want the artillery 'ere," says Cruikshank. "A twelve pounder might do the job."

"It's a task fer the marines," says Kirby, sitting to pull his boots off, "but they're all off on a sea cruise."

"We're going in?"

"The sergeant seemed ter 'ave 'is 'eart set on it."

The water is icy cold, and powerful even with the weir blocking most of its force. Cruikshank and Kirby carefully sidestep to the center of the contraption, holding on to the mossy saplings that make it up, then begin to yank and pull.

"We need an axe."

"Not standard issue, Reg. Insight and initiative, that's wot's wanted 'ere."

"Ye've been heavesdroppin' by the captain's billet again."

"Never too late ter add ter yer store of knowledge. Though an axe would come in very 'andy right now."

They are wet up to their armpits, the weir, saplings woven together with leather thongs, starting to unravel. Downstream a pair of soldiers heave stone querns from a wooden cart as far into the water as they can, making a contest of it.

"Did they really think this Lovat would wait around 'ere ter be snagged and brought ter trial?"

"If 'ee'adn't 'eard the outcome of the battle—"

"Then 'ee would've 'eard this mob coming five miles down the pike."

"Didn't 'ave time ter clear 'is goods out of the castle—"

"No. But I'll wager 'ee's buried some gowd and silver not too far from it."

"Pick and shovel, Reg. You shovel and I'll pick—pick where to dig—"

The center of the weir gives way then, Private Kirby holding on to the remnants but Private Cruikshank swept downstream by the sudden surge of water.

"Can't leave you two alone fer a minute," growls Sergeant Morse from the bank, with Lovat's castle now fully ablaze in the distance behind him. "Are ye done playin' about?"

Cruikshank manages to stagger to his feet on an outcropping of stones, a grin on his face and a writhing, three-foot-long salmon in his arms.

"'Ere's another that won't feed the rebels, sergeant," he calls. "There's no 'iding from the King's Justice."

IT MAKES A BEAUTIFUL LIGHT, CASTLE DOUNIE AND THE peat stacks around it, burning far below. The English must have been predisposed for its destruction to be there so quickly, no doubt organizing all they've plundered for shipment, enjoying his provisions as they warm themselves by the great fire. So much for one man, the common redcoats must be thinking, not understanding what Lovat is to the Frasers—their bank, their storehouse, their salvation from hard winters or failed crops.

The life that went into restoring that stone building, garnering that wealth. The desperate acts, the exile, imprisonment, the years of plotting and persuasion—no royal darling he, born secure of a title—he had to claw his way to the head of the clan, stealing away the ninth Lord's widow when her daughter wouldn't marry him, forcing himself on her, demanding his blood right, if it was a right at all—

"Enough," says the Auld Fox, turning his head away from the fire below, and the men lift him in the litter, struggling to climb even higher.

There are so many islands in the west, he thinks, that the English cannot search, must less occupy, all of them. Perfect for a respite, before designing his resurrection—

JAMIE HAS A LAST GLIMPSE OF THE TOWN BEFORE THEY shove him backward into the hold. The ruins of Fort George on the hill, the bridge spanning the Ness with its seven arches and beneath it a small tribe of women, coverings hiked to their hips, bending over their washing on the rocks, the water stinging cold but never freezing solid with so much sulfur in it, as a pair of fishing smacks head out for herring and smoke rises from the chimneys of the houses and the open fires of the venders at the Market Cross, straight white columns of smoke against a frigid, pearl-gray sky. A painting, he thinks, *Inverness in Winter,* sentimental and familiar but for the random daubs of scarlet—mounted hussars patrolling the bridge, artillerymen in their mitred hats mustered along the pier, a smear of infantry on the Castle Hill. Perhaps the last view of his nation—

Boots and coat stripped away, undershirt stuck to his flesh with blood, and still less than steady from the blows to his head, Jamie lands on top of a badly wounded man in the uniform of the *Garde Écossaise,* who cries out in anguish.

"Damnation!"

"I'm sorry," Jamie replies, rising to his knees and matching the lieutenant's English. "I was pushed."

"That doesn't make it hurt any less." The lieutenant is clutching his bloodied thigh in both hands, face flushed with perspiration. "Where are they taking us?"

"I believe that's meant tae remain a mystery till our arrival. Though I've heard 'the end of a guid, stiff rope' mentioned several times."

The lieutenant casts an eye about them as orders are barked and hawsers shift on the collier deck above. A motley collection, clansmen and townspeople, men of some rank and middling tacksmen and humblies who'd been too far back in the charge to have earned a scratch, crammed phiz-to-fanny in the grimy black of the hold, some clutching to the beams as they stand unsteadily, others trying to claim a spot on the floor.

"Either they've no sense of station or they're deliberately ignoring it," snarls the lieutenant. He still has on his silver-nailed riding boots, no doubt from the shop on Rue des Fossés where Jamie bought his own. "Tossed together like table scraps for the Master's hounds."

"We'll be sorted soon enow," says Jamie, nausea rising as the coal scow gets underway. "I've nae doot of that."

IT IS LATE MORNING BEFORE JENNY, BEGINNING TO shake with a fever, climbs to the first of the shieling huts with a fair-sized maukin she found dozing beneath the clootie tree upon waking and dispatched with a rock slung over her shoulder. She's barely inside, searching for the flint and bundle of sticks that are often left for travelers, when she hears the nicker of horses. She sits on the cold dirt floor with her back to the stones by the entryway, listening. Hooves on the turf, maybe three animals, stepping near, halting. A man's voice—

"We've spied ye from above. Ye might as well step out."

There are crags just above where a horse can't follow, but she can't outrun horses to reach them. Jenny stands, steps out into the light, still holding the hare by its hind legs.

Three mounted dragoons, with two bearded, bedraggled Highland men standing before them, the ropes around their necks tied to the riders' saddle horns. The oldest of the English speaks down to her.

"A piping stew fer the Pretender, is it?"

"I dinnae ken what yer after."

"Save it, luv, we know yer all related up here, cousins begetting cousins till yer all born bloody halfwits." His eyes drop to her dress, the soldier's blood dried upon it.

"Aiding and abetting," he says, "that's treason, and we'll have his whereabouts from ye in a nick. Will ye come along with us, or do we need the rope?"

Jenny feels nothing but the ache behind her eyes and the weariness in her bones, not sure if she slept through the dark hours or only dreamed of sleep. Her stomach rolls, bubbling. She holds the rabbit out before them, arm trembling with the weight of it.

"If I'm tae hang fer it, maun I no eat it first?"

THEY ARE DRIVEN, TWO AND THREE ABREAST IN THEIR rags, from the dockside at Leith to the Royal Mile. Perhaps seven score still with the use of their legs, the badly wounded and those in death's antechamber still being lowered on pallets over the side of the slop-bucket of a collier. Jamie MacGillivray, alert with his unswollen eye, sees the townspeople stare or turn away, the surgeons and skinners, butchers and hammermen, the cordwainers, weavers, fullers, and bonnetmakers, here and there a University student, perhaps one of the many who had rousingly formed the Volunteer Guard to protect the city from the Stuart rabble, then merrily piled their hodgepodge of weapons in the castle's courtyard when the Edinburgh Town Council voted to capitulate to the rebels without an angry shot. The Prince's men left the redcoats snug in the castle itself unchallenged but pressed a throng of citizens to witness his coronation in its very shadow.

"Don't linger, children, you'll miss your supper!"

It is the short one, prodding them from the north side of the High Street as they pass the Holyrood Palace—pillars, cupola, marble chimneys, yet another grand abbey despoiled by Cromwell's hordes and given over to the English. The wee bit of a green-eyed Hebridian at Jamie's heel has already dubbed them the Toad and the Hare, the soldier to the north squat, implacable, his lipless mouth sagging down at the sides toward the jawline, while their tormentor on the south side of the shambling coffle is tall, startle-eyed and vigilant, his head twitching this way and that to mark them, as if any or all of his prisoners are on the verge of desperate flight.

Faces turning toward them, caddies pulling up short from their errands to gawk, windows opening in the tottering residences—five, six, seven stories up—and the inhabitants leaning out to witness their misfortune. Jamie, who'd barely seen a tree more than twice his height in the Highlands, was cowed by them when he first came to University, keeping to the middle of the unpaved wynds and closes that rarely felt the sun, certain that stone could not be piled so high without tumbling. Harsh calls and recriminations from above now, and a pail of something yellowish spilled on the flat, tight-packed paving stones, the smoothest course for a wheel in all the Union, that only smacks hard and spatters the gaiters of the Hare as he skips away from it.

"Ye'd think it were London and nae the heart of Midlothian," grumbles the wee west islander.

At Inverness, in their parade through the Cross and to the docks, a pair of red-coated drummers punctuated their exile and the townspeople looked away, women pulling their *earasaids* over their faces in shame or sympathy, the men, those not overemployed in licking the invaders' boots, staring above or straight through them.

"Quiet there," calls the Hare in his reedy voice, "and steady on."

They continue eastward on the ridge of the High Street, what Jamie always thought of as the spine of the Dragon, with the Holyrood at its tail and the castle crag its erect head. They pass the Trone Church first, the way still five coaches wide here, and Jamie is struck again by the sheer mass of humanity packed into the Mile, nothing even in Paris or Amsterdam to compare to it, hundred-pound-a-year men hip and elbow with tinklers and poor mechanics, lords of session breathing the same foul air as the coarsest haddock monger. A squadron of soot-faced boys jeer at them from the steps, almost perpendicular, that rise between two buildings, and runners carrying ladies in sedans and vendors hustling handcarts swerve to either side of the procession, too hurried to spare more than a glance of annoyance.

"There's no sae mony beings in a' the Hielands," mutters the Hebridean, whose name is Lachlan.

Crowded and noisy and rank, Jamie a boy of fifteen on his arrival, Edinburgh seems now a friend who has turned away, grown strange. It was never a Jacobite stronghold, but there was a sense of revelry and tolerance beneath the stony Presbyterian eye, an appreciation of its distance from English King and Parliament. He wishes he'd had that day of the coronation in September with the Prince's army, returned to his beloved haunts a conqueror, wishes that he'd felt, if only for a moment, as if the city truly belonged to him—

Now the Luckenbooths, the long rectangle of shops and stalls swarming with patrons, and Allan Ramsey's bookshop, where those in his trust could partake of forbidden texts, and the spike on the Dragon's back, St. Giles, its cupola shaped like the Imperial Crown, the Cathedral now stone-quartered into High Kirk, Auld Kirk, Tolbooth Kirk, and Haddo's Hole.

And here, at its northwest corner, the Tolbooth itself.

How many times has he lingered in its shadow, has he wondered at the state of the wretches within, while never crossing the portal? For he stopped there during the Riot, waiting for the mob to drag the terrified Captain out, too cowardly to add his hand to the slaughter and too excited not to witness it.

It is a glum, steep-roofed edifice, nearly as tall as the Cathedral, suddenly narrowing the breadth of the High Street like a boulder thrown in a narrow burn. A pair of round turrets of five stories hug close to its southern wall, and since Jamie's time a low, squarish addition has been built on the western end, topped by a platform open to public view, a wooden gallows ready upon it.

The massive door, a foot or more thick, that the Riot mob had to fire before breaking through is now easily opened by a smirking gaoler with a ring of enormous keys in hand.

"Mair of the King's guests, I reckon," he smiles, stepping aside to allow them entrance.

They step in and are shunted to the east turret, the Hare in the lead, vaulting up the turnpike stairs with only his heels left in sight as he follows the curve, Toad roughly guiding them one by one to follow, a yank on the arm and a shove in the back and a "Get on with it, noo. Step lively."

They reach the second floor, where the Hare turns the first thirty in the group, Jamie well in the van, into a bare, stinking room with chopped bits of sodden straw on the floor and an iron door, a room already occupied by a solitary, shifty-eyed lad of perhaps fifteen, gobsmacked by the sudden influx.

"Holy saints in Heaven," the boy exclaims as he is pressed against the turret wall, the room soon more crowded, if possible, than the hold of the collier sailing down. "Wha've yez a' done tae be in here?"

"We've failed tae restore the rightful King of Scotland," answers wee Lachlan. "And yersel'?"

Voices rise below in the turnpike, and then a massive Highlander, wrists manacled and dragging a chain, staggers in with one gaoler riding his back and the turnkey waling at his ribs with a truncheon. The other prisoners make way as well as they can, the less nimble catching a blow or trodden upon, and when the Hare moves to aid his fellows the huge man spins him around and envelops him with the chain, the Hare able to raise an arm just in time to protect his neck from cracking. They struggle—bellowing clansman, Hare, turnkey, terrified jockey, and now the Toad, kicking at whatever legs he can reach to bring the whole thing down in the southwest corner of the iron room. There is a snap of bone, a scream from the Hare, a bucket of urine kicked over, and finally the great man subdued, the gaolers beating on him long after he is prone and unconscious.

"Clean daft, that un," wee Lachlan mutters to Jamie. "A MacGregor, and withoot the wit tae conceal the fact."

The Hare is led out, holding his broken wrist close to his chest, with the Toad turning for a parting word at the door.

"Any mair trouble frae this quarter," he says, bloody club held over his head, "and ye'll pay in kind."

The iron door makes a very large and hollow sound when it is hauled closed behind him.

Curses and mutterings from the entombed. There is only one barred window cut in the outside wall, higher than a tall man can reach, allowing but a meager light. Jamie wends his way through and over bodies to reach the MacGregor, who lies face down, his bloodied head already beginning to swell. With the help of another, Jamie drags the man clear of the puddle of spilled urine, propping him in a sitting position, back against the wall. The huge head droops down, blood drooling from the side of the man's mouth, but he appears to yet have breath in him.

Sitting beside him is the angry lieutenant, who seems to have accommodated himself to rough company. He watches as Jamie once again unsticks the cloth of his trews from the wound behind his leg, wincing from the sting of it.

"Still bleeding?"

"Aye."

"Ball still in you?"

"There's a wound in the rear and another nearby it—I believe it passed through the flesh."

"Fortunate."

"Mair fortunate if it had missed me completely."

The lieutenant nods toward his own wounded thigh. "They seem content that I retain my own souvenir."

"Ye can feel it?"

"If I shift the leg there is a grinding sensation."

"I had an uncle," Jamie tells him, "who carried a ball in his nether parts his entire life, with little effect."

"Received while relocating cattle by moonlight, no doubt."

Jamie allows the remark to pass.

"Aeneas Cameron," the lieutenant announces, "fourth Earl of Lochiel."

Jamie nods. "MacGillivray of Dunmaglas. Son of Ian Mor."

This pedigree apparently acceptable, Cameron nods back and indicates the room.

"What do you imagine their plans for us are?"

Jamie considers this. "Weel, after the '15 there was a rush of executions afore the Indemnity. Men of position forfeited their titles and property. Of course Mar, who set the torch tae the rebellion, made his way tae Paris—"

"I met him there when I was first in the French service." Cameron looks to be ten years Jamie's senior, a strongly built, fair-haired man. "But I expect there's to be a harsher reckoning this time—"

"Perhaps. I witnessed dozens, and them a'ready surrendered, who were butchered after Culloden."

"And they've become great with this business of transportation."

"The King's Mercy."

"Sweltering with Africans in some patch of cane—"

"They'll gae hardest with those closest to hame. The ones who rose in Manchester—"

"Have no doubt earned the halter through their actions."

Jamie sits by Cameron, a spell of dizziness coming over him. "If we survive this hole," he muses, "there will be worse tae coom."

THEY HAND HER A BLANKET BEFORE SHE BOARDS THE hulk. A thin scrap of cloth, to be sure, and crawling with nippers, but she wraps herself in it nonetheless. There are no more than a score of women among those held below, kept in a separate compartment and provided with an oil lamp hung from the beam overhead. It smells of tar and human excrement. The women already confined seem to be criminals all—petty thieves and strumpets, a young girl who slashed a rival's face with a boning knife, an older, witchy-looking woman wrapped in a black shawl who sings mournfully in Erse. Jenny, feverish now and running with the flux, follows her nose to the cramped space under the ladder from the deck and lowers herself onto the waste pot. She feels it all the way down and out, hard and sharp, and fishes in the warm scum beneath her till she catches it in her fingers. She cleans it as well as she can on the hem of her shift, lodges it snugly beneath the hemp of her belt, steps out feeling drained.

"Yer feelin' puir?" inquires the girl charged with the cutting, forced to duck her head beneath the low timbers.

"No sae bad," says Jenny, trying to catch her breath in the close chamber. "But me fortune's runnin' oot me arse."

THE BELLS OF ST. GILES STRIKE SIX OF THE EVENING, AND the keepers enter with four wooden kids of grayish meal to feed all in the room, the Hare waiting by the iron door with an ashplant under his healthy wing and his broken one in a sling. The prisoners wait until they have gone before turning to the food, famished but resolved not to grant their enemy the satisfaction of watching them fight each other over slops.

"It's eight men tae each," Jamie announces in both English and Erse when the iron door has been barred. "And fetch some tae those as can't shift fer themsels." The men follow his instruction, determined to proceed with some dignity, if only for the moment. Wee Lachlan, cradling his share of the meal in the hem of his shirt, sits beside Jamie to eat.

"Yer a MacGillivray."

"Of Dunmaglas. What of it?"

Lachlan intones the verse with a defiant air—

Oot stepped the great MacGillivray
Steadfast tae meet his doom
With ane wee bairn at mother's knee
And another in the womb—

Jamie eyes his oatmeal, still feeling queasy.

"They jailed yer father and took his lands."

"Our lands."

"A tragic injustice, some might say. Son of a chieftan, reduced tae a gillie's task fer the MacIntosh."

"Ye've a long tongue, friend."

Lachlan smiles. "I'm a *seanachaidh*, as the Irish would have it—I live by the word."

"Clan?"

"MacLeods iv Raasay. *Luceo Non Uro."*

"I shine, but dinnae burn."

"Ye were in the midst of the slaughter?"

Jamie forces a mouthful down. "I was unable tae reach the field."

"A wise decision." The Hebridean's eyes reveal more mischief than malice.

"Ma brother was with Lady Anne's regiment," Jamie tells him, "in the vanguard of the—"

"Ah, but I keeked it a' frae a height—and a wee distance."

"Also a wise decision."

Lachlan smiles. "A baird requires an overview of the situation, sae as no tae miss any detail."

"Or absorb any lead."

Again the wee *seanachaidh* grins and rises to strike a pose. Orating now to the entire incarcerated company, one arm raised, the opposite hand pressed to his heart—

Wet morn upon Drummossie Muir
Twa armies poised tae strike—
Hanover's rows of musketry
'Gainst claymuir, dirk, and pike.
Though mighty dae their cannon roar,
Dread missiles wheen and whir,
Withoot an order tae advance
Our champions canna stir.

The men leave off eating, watching Lachlan, who repeats each verse in Erse after laying it out in English, each with its own music—

Our fighting lads, altho' possessed
With naked steel and targe
And keen tae fight, they also need
A leader tae shout "Charge!"

A murmur from the men who survived the day, a spark of anger in their eyes. Lachlan continues, raising his tone—

But noo Clan Chattan's valiant men
Can check their pulse nae mair
And speed intae the jaws of Death
As bagpipes thrill the air!

He has them now, Lachlan, for he has the gift, able to rouse men's spirits, to lead them into battles past, real or imagined. His voice grows wistful, tears forming in his eyes—

Tae wide, tae wide, Drummossie Muir
Tae wide tae reach yer foe
The flower of the Hielands fall
Their fervent bluid doth flow
MacLachlans, Grants and Menzies fall
The sons of Nairn and Perth
Their bodies pierced by shot and shell
Tae stain the sodden earth
Tae wide the span of killing groond
Tae mony volleys crack
Tae mony brave young lads charge forth
Tae mony ne'er come back.

Jamie feels a twinge of regret. He was on his way. If he had arrived on time he'd have been at the front, beside his brother Dougal—

Bold MacIntosh, far in the van
His courage doth define
Impaled, alas, on closing with
The English second line
In swift retreat the spared noo fly
Baith Infantry and Horse
The wounded left fer Cumberland
Tae kill withoot remorse

More grumbling, a curse or two. Wee Lachlan thrusts his chest out, frowning, making a fist with his raised hand—

Sae lang, sae lang, we've borne our shame
Beneath the English heel
Sae lang we've suffered perfidy
Sae lang been forced tae kneel
And noo ma tongue doth rue tae speak
A tale tae strain belief
Fair Charlie, God's ain chosen Prince
Is hunted like a thief!

A silence when he is finished. Lachlan sits again by Jamie, and then there are low mutterings, a few men venturing that it was an accurate account of the fiasco.

"If we'd had as many muskets as they," announces the fourth Earl of Lochiel. "If the Prince had been more decisive—"

"If the French had landed as they promised," adds another man, a Farquarson.

"The French have their ain game tae play," says Jamie. "They're content tae maintain the Stuarts as a threat rather than a reality."

"Too many of our ain have been bought—"

"Or are afeart—"

"Or profit frae the Union," adds Jamie. "Each mon has his reasons."

"But tae oppose the will of God," muses the Farquarson, a long-faced Presbyterian, "is tae place reason aboon faith."

Jamie exchanges a look with Cameron. They've avoided speaking of France, too many traps to fall into, factions within factions, but both have been too near the workings of the exiled court to believe any Divine Will is involved.

"The English are craven blackguards, in thrall tae a Dutchman," says Lachlan. "And they've thrashed us soundly once again."

The warders return then, two of them bearing a near-dead prisoner on a pallet, dumping him roughly onto the straw next to the massive Highlander, who has regained consciousness only once, to vomit. While the Hare collects the empty kids, the Toad and another guard, tugging and pulling and making a good deal of sport of it, shackle the dying man, glassy-eyed and breathing with great difficulty, face to face with the prone MacGregor.

"That man's dying," says Cameron. "He's likely diseased."

"And so?"

"Chaining him tae—"

"Each will warm the other."

"It's inhuman."

The Toad stands over Cameron, speaking in a pleasant tone. "We could slip ye betwixt them, if ye'd like."

The Highlander groans and rolls onto his back, the dying man pulled on top of him.

"No? Then I suggest ye keep yer pie-hole shut and yer nose oot of affairs that dinnae concern ye. I bid yez a guid night, gentlemen."

This time when the iron door is shut they are left in darkness, the sun gone down behind the castle on the hill. Snatches of conversation, men shifting for a better position to sleep in, if sleep is possible, somebody weeping—

Jamie feels insects crawling on his body.

"*Vous êtes militaire, ou seulement conspirateur?*"

Cameron's voice, close to him.

"*Courrier, mais prêt pour le combat,*" Jamie answers softly.

He has made the crossing only twice before, carrying sealed messages in each direction, a journey always preceded by interrogations and swearings upon holy texts. But it is all up now, so little left to conceal.

I began at the Scots College in Paris, says Jamie, still in French.

Studying for the priesthood?

No, we're Church of Scotland. I read law here in Edinburgh, a bit of history in France.

His father's idea, from the first, was that Jamie would make secure with legal wiles what Dougal won back by force of arms. "Any one iv yer Latin-spouting bastarts in a robe," his father would snarl, "is the equal tae a platoon of fusiliers."

"But soon I was sent to Saint-Germaine-en-Laye—" says Jamie, switching to English.

"Where the Prince no longer dwelt—"

"The chateau was full of those loyal tae him—English fer the maist part—under the protection of the Duc de Noailles."

"I fought under Noailles at Dettingen and in Alsace-Lorraine," says Cameron. "I was brought over when The Lochiel was deposed after the '19."

"Yer mair French than Scots then. When ye come tae trial—"

"They'll argue that my treason has been of long duration. If they want our heads, they'll *have* them."

Quiet! calls somebody in Erse, and they leave off talking.

THERE HAD BEEN A SURPRISE AT HOW WELL HE SPOKE French, better than the majority of the English, Irish and few Scots residents at the Chateau St. Germaine-en-Laye.

"Ye've an ear fer it, laddie," Monsieur MacTavish, his tutor in Edinburgh, had always said, a compact man with a nearly impenetrable Shetland brogue when he spoke in English that Jamie assumed carried into his French. But in his first weeks abroad he was regularly complimented on his pronunciation and gradually adopted an educated but relatively unpretentious Parisian accent.

It was Phineas Guthrie who brought Jamie over by way of Rotterdam, gilding the occasion, as always, with a good deal more hugger-mugger than was necessary. Guthrie was the son of a friend of his father's who had offered his ships in service to the losing faction of the '15 and fled with his family to the protection of the Stuart court at St. Germaine, there to subsist on a modest pension from King James, who in turn was a dependent of Louis XIV. The younger Guthrie, only ten years Jamie's senior, had adopted a more active mode of survival than his attainted parent, volunteering for the French service under Adrien Maurice, Duc de Noailles, initially as secretary and *aide de camp*, but eventually he was wounded in action and made lame during the seemingly interminable War of the Polish Succession. At the time of Jamie's arrival, Guthrie was serving as a liaison between the Stuart retainers and Irish left in St. Germaine and the Duc, who was the appointed caretaker of the chateau, though most often away shooing Austrians from the Alsace-Lorraine. Guthrie, a good-humored fellow with a pronounced limp and a constant smile, accepted bribes from the exiles to influence his patron in this or that matter pertaining to the accommodations and allowed himself a substantial commission on all upkeep and workmen's payments associated with the chateau, in addition to his own military pension.

"*En service de la cause, tout est admissible*," he would say with a wink when discovered in one of these acts of larceny. He spoke French like a native and Scots as his father must have, sprinkling his conversation with tidbits of Italian he'd picked up in his jaunts to Rome, where the King, Prince Regent, and important courtiers had dwelled since the debacle of the 15, leaving their lesser dependents and a few thousand Irish fighting men behind in France.

"We never doubt the existence of the sun," one English dowager, wife of an abandoned equerry, put it, "but we do not enjoy its *warmth*."

"We've nane o' the Royal Bluid in residence," Guthrie warned Jamie upon his first visit to the chateau, "but a' iv their pretensions."

The French royal family had lived in the chateau for a century and a half, till Louis XIV moved permanently to the newly built Versailles only a few leagues to the south. He generously ceded the old chateau to King James upon his exile from Britain, the Stuarts and their ever-growing retinue eventually filling the chambers, hallways and staircases and spilling out into more modest habitation within the town. On his first viewing, the main façade of the structure seemed to Jamie the length of all of Edinburgh High Street, a four-story, flat-topped behemoth built of rectangular blocks of stone with a honeycomb of arched windows and a full complement of towers, turrets, parapets, and *gargouilles*. All this was set among rows of transplanted chestnut trees, gardens mostly returned to Nature and a vast set of terraces from which could be seen the winding Seine below and the rising ground of Montmartre to the east.

Entering between a pair of stone houses that at one time sheltered the defenders of the royal family in exile, Guthrie led Jamie across a small bridge and then beneath a pair of carved, heralding angels to pass through the vaulted *salle-des-gardes* into the irregularly shaped courtyard, the interior a series of arched galleries with balconies outside each apartment window, the narrowest of the sides taken up by three enormous panels of stained glass.

There was damp clothing hung on several of the balconies. Small children, shouting in both French and English, chased around the yard after a bundle of rags tied into a ball.

"*Résidence des Rois anciens*," Guthrie announced with his customary smirk, his voice echoing slightly off the galleries. "And beating heart of the Parallel Kingdom."

The inside of the structure was grand enough—vaulted red brick ceilings, tile floors in some of the larger chambers—but it was dank and cold and crowded with what seemed like hundreds of residents, most of whom appeared in the doorways of their apartments to gaze suspiciously at Jamie as Guthrie led him a tour.

"Of course, there's nae room fer ye here—I'll find something suitable in the village—but I want ye tae understand what ye've landed in. The King was bairn in these rooms, as was our young Prince Charlie, and though the shadow of neither has fallen upon these stanes fer twenty years, the spirit remains."

"The folk are loyal."

Guthrie laughed. "At some point ye'll be taken tae Beauvais tae keek the piece of the True Cross they keep there. Nowt but a wee sliver of wood, but ye'll see unco women and mony a grown mon fair swoon in the presence of it." He indicated the vaulted chamber around them. "We've mair than a sliver here."

The point of Jamie's sojourn was to serve as Guthrie's courier to the Duc de Noailles and other worthies among the French military and clergy, helping to convince them, as a very recent arrival, that the Highlands, to the man, were on tenterhooks to rise in support of any invasion meant to restore the Stuarts, and that many more in the north counties of England would immediately follow suit.

"I'm nae certain that's true," Jamie told him. "The clans I ken best, nae doot, but there's others—"

"If it's a flude yer after," Guthrie reassured him, laying an arm over his shoulder, "somebody needs tae kick the sluice gates open."

Jamie loved the travel. Supplied with a *passé-tout* by Guthrie, who smuggled French silk into England as a sideline and possessed an intimidating number of official stamps and seals, Jamie was able to move across the countryside with relative ease, to be invited into camps of war and Jesuit cloisters, to observe the customs and characteristics of the upper and lower echelons of French society.

The poverty in the hinterlands was no great shock, the *villes du pays* no meaner than the clachans he was raised among, but that in Paris was of a magnitude and desperation he had never witnessed. It seemed like one out of three persons was indigent or earning less than their daily bread, and many of those employed were no more than gillies sleeping in an attic or basement space, cruelly or indifferently used by their employers. When in the city Jamie regularly ate from the vendors on the street, unless his assignation was set for a café or tavern. He had a friend, Hugh Lowry, at the Scots

College on Rue du Cardinal Lemoine, and even attended some lectures there as a cover for his message-bearing activities. Sealed letters were sewn into the lining of his coat by Guthrie's mistress, a youngish French widow who acknowledged Jamie in phrases of three words or less, and there were passwords, often quotations in Latin from the ancient Romans, to prove his *bona fides* upon first interaction. He was never tempted to open either the missives dispatched by Guthrie or those sent in return by his correspondents and co-conspirators, less for fear of being caught than for his trust that the contents were somehow in aid of the eventual restoration of his family's property. It was, he admitted, a singularly self-serving motive to be in the game.

"When we've triumphed," Guthrie would tease him, "and ye're settin' back on yer rightful domains, ye'd dae well tae build yersel a wee *palace*. A laird's nae a laird that hasnae a great pile of stane tae amble aboot in."

They never met in the chateau—too many roving eyes and wagging tongues—but in the grottos built beneath the garden terraces.

"A pair of Italian *fratelli,*" Guthrie explained as they explored the Grotto of Hercules and those of Perseus, Andromeda and Orpheus, "clever in the art of *jeux d'eau,* were brought here tae devise the fountains that aince spouted, day and night, in the gardens. And the water frae the greatest of these was drained aff in pipes that ran below tae power various *automata*—there was a dragon that rose frae a pond, a water organ, gods that descended frae aboon by counterweights—"

"A' gan ferever, noo, I expect—"

"If ye've wars tae fight, Versailles tae build, fellow Kings and their dependents tae support, ye'll maun cut doon on the *choses d'amusement.* Twas a wonder in its time, though."

Jamie began to regard himself as a clandestine Mercury serving a cadre of outcast gods, all in all a somewhat romantic figure. Lady

Jane Porter thought so as well, she the very young wife of the increasingly befuddled Viscount of Arbuthnot, a title conferred upon him by King James as a consolation for both his loyalty, having been attainted of his position back in England, and for the indignity of being left behind when more useful retainers were transported to Rome. Born of a chambermaid in the chateau and still dwelling there, the Lady made up in imagination and intrigue what she lacked in the means to travel, her husband's allotted portion of the King's bounty being rather meager.

"Tell me about Orléans," she might say, or "Describe the ships at Le Havre."

Jamie was cautious at first, wondering by what device she knew he had been to these places, but then comforted himself with the thought that it was simple curiosity rather than espionage that piqued her interest. His frequent reports to her led to further intimacy, with the viscount off hunting each day, seemingly unaware or unconcerned that deer and wolves had been unprotected since the Royal relocation and were in decidedly short supply. Lady Jane was the sweetest part of the adventure, her marital status only another aspect of his feeling of being immune from the rules of conduct, somehow chosen, in this Parallel Kingdom, to trespass at will.

Her own chambers being under the vigilant eye of the chateau exiles, Jane sought pretexts to venture into the village, where Jamie was able to entertain her in the cleverly converted stable that Guthrie had procured for him. She was an energetic, even aggressive, lover, charmed by the rustic simplicity of his lodging.

"It's a prison, you know," she said of the chateau. "We might as well all be locked up in the Bastille."

"The villagers envy ye."

"The villagers hate us. *Les mauvais Anglais,* they call us—"

"They assume that the roof over yer heid disnae leak—"

"Small comfort—"

"And that yer courtyard is the scene of lavish banquets and frivolities, a' provided by their ain profligate King."

"We dine no better than they—"

"Ye dwell in a *pal*ace. There's few in this country whae can make that claim."

The lady's only shortcoming in his eyes was her fondness for Italians. Most annoying among these was Facchetti, a papal envoy of some sort with whom he had several times exchanged envelopes at the Scots College, where the diminutive Italian was a central figure in the expulsion of Jansenists. More than once Jamie found the viscountess strolling in the chateau courtyard with this dark, rapier-thin eminence, who treated him with polite condescension.

"*Il giovane senza pantaloni*," he would say in greeting, though Jamie had rarely affected a kilt since he left home for Edinburgh. "The bird who flies from the hand of Signor Guthrie."

"And how fares the pontiff?" Jamie would reply, stepping close to look down on the little dago. The current Bishop of Rome, Clement XII, was a man in his mid eighties, blind and bedridden, who had reinstated the popular public numbers lottery, thus insuring the financial health of the Vatican.

"*Molto bene, grazie.* As does your own monarch."

Facchetti was not shy to advertise his personal contact with King James and the Prince Regent, exaggerated or not, and dressed himself in the embroidered silk of an adventurer.

"Vittorio tells me that something is afoot," Jane would invariably report. "Military stratagems are debated, troops made ready to sail—"

"As they hae been every year since Ah was conceived," Jamie demurred. "If rumors was siller, we'd a' be rich."

Guthrie knew about Jane, of course, but only counseled Jamie to observe the French custom.

"There's a *comme il faut* tae it, lad. E'en if a' the world kens what yer up tae, an effort at discretion is expected."

Jamie's relations with the villagers were pleasant enough, as he paid for all services when engaged and with the local currency Guthrie parsimoniously supplied as the occasion merited. Accustomed to being hard-pressed in his college days, Jamie never complained of this obvious method of control. He was not in France to save wages.

A rainy afternoon with Jane in his stable room, which did leak, led to her insistence that their next assignment be at the chateau, leading to crisis. They were naked together in her alarmingly creaky bed when the door to the chamber was flung open. Rolling off and onto his knees, Jamie expected to see the viscount with a brace of quail in hand, but in fact it was Facchetti, cursing the lady in decidedly unpapal Italian. Rising to protest with only a small pillow to cover his shame, Jamie was struck in the face and challenged to a duel.

Guthrie, disconcertingly amused by the situation, filled him in on the protocol involved.

"As the insulted party, yer allowed the choice of weapons, and responsible fer their supply. Are ye expert with a pistol?"

"I've no had much cause fer it."

"Swords, then. I'll serve as yer second, and bring a pair tae the field of honor."

The venue, chosen by Facchetti, turned out to be the Doric gallery that adorned the third terrace of the chateau, in front of the Grotto of Neptune. Seconded by another Italian, a dance master named Luppo, Jamie's rival arrived dressed for the occasion in tight breeches and white silk shirt, strutting back and forth with an indignation that perhaps masked his anxiety. And when Guthrie unwrapped two of the largest claymores Jamie had ever seen, Facchetti lost what little composure he had left.

"*Non e possibile!*" he cried. "These are the weapons of a peasant!"

"Ye challenge a Hielander, peasant or laird," said Guthrie, making no great effort to conceal his delight, "yer maun tae wield a claymuir."

Jamie, a head taller than the Italian and not so finely built, stood by his employer with a blank countenance.

"I refuse to sully my hand with this," said Facchetti as Guthrie held out one of the swords, nearly as long as the Italian himself.

"Then yer afferin' an apology?"

Facchetti and the dance master put their heads together for a rapid-fire conference in their native tongue. The papal envoy then spoke to Guthrie, not deigning to meet Jamie's now haughty stare.

"I am due in Rome on important business. I will consider this matter before my return."

In consideration to the feelings of the aged viscount, who remained blissfully unaware of his wife's predicament, the duel had not been advertised. There were no witnesses to the Italian retreat but Jamie and his second.

"Ah'm no sure Ah could *lift* that thing," he said when they were out of sight. "Where'd ye find them?"

"On the wall of a chateau in Chartres. If there'd been a Lochaber axe or twa available—"

"Do ye believe it's finished noo?"

Guthrie considered this. "He maught dirk ye in the back some mirky nicht," he decided, "but yer duelin' days is over."

And shortly after, in the summer of '45, the Prince Regent's precipitous venture to Scotland caught Guthrie by surprise.

"God himsel' must have whispered in his ear," he told Jamie as he provided him the little gold he had to send and instructions as to which Highland notables were to be won over to the Cause. "Or mebbe it was the fecking Irish. But gan he is, and we're hurled intae the waters, sink or swim. There's a hoy rigged tae slip oot of Calais the moment ye've reached it." Guthrie slapped his gammy leg. "I'm with ye in spirit, if not in the flesh. Perhaps we'll raise a cup at yer Dunmaglas."

Viscountess Jane's goodbye was more pathetic. Overcome with tears, she begged Jamie to take her with him.

"It's *my* future at stake," she cried. "Why should I not be able to fight for it?"

Jamie sailed, in the dark, with a handful of coastal smugglers who assumed he spoke no French. The captain advised the crew not to rob him.

All who pay to be ferried over, he told them, will pay twice that when they're forced to return.

THEY ARE ALLOWED EIGHT CIRCUITS ABOUT THE DECK, the few sailors left on board giving way to the gruff, iron-haired marine left in charge of them, the seamen climbing the naked spars to observe the promenade and offer their comments. They are anchored near the mouth of the river, within a stone's throw of four of the other transports that sailed down from Inverness in convoy with the *HMS Winchelsea.* There are more men than women held on board, Jenny hearing them above during their one daily turn up top, though half of these, it is rumored, have already been taken off, dead or alive. As she walks, Jenny looks to the fort on the nearer shore, low walls in the form of a star, those facing the water well supplied with cannon, four bastions, and several huge stone blockhouses within.

"Fort Tilbury," says the girl who slashed her rival. Her name is Morag, from Bucksburn near Aberdeen, and would be a beauty if not for what the pox has done to her own face. "They've hunnerts of our lads kept in the powder hoose. Yer dusted wigs in Lunnon dinnae choose to be blain tae bits, so it's Tilbury where a' the explosives are docked."

"We're by Lunnon?"

Morag nods toward the gray water. "That's the Thames, lass. Where've ye been keepin' yersel'?"

"In a reeky hole belae the decks."

Morag smiles. For her own reasons she has singled Jenny out as a friend, though Morag is a town girl and a papist. She points to the far shore.

"That's Gravesend, there, and then the ships"—she points to each—"the *Jane of Alloway*, the *Pamela*, the *Thane of Fife* that coom doon with us, and the great tarry wreck with nae sails tae raise ner mast tae hang them on is the *Liberty and Property*, nowt but a floatin' pesthoose, meant tae sicken and starve our lads tae death afore their trials."

"And will we have a trial?"

Morag looks to see where the marine has gotten to. "Mebbe. Mebbe ainly a sentencing."

"And hoo d'ye ken a' this?"

Morag nods toward a grinning sailor, sitting on a yard halfway up the foremast.

"That un has a way through the hatch," she says, "and he'll slip ye cheese and biscuit fer a shag."

"Och. And well-informed tae boot."

Morag walks backward, looking Jenny over.

"Yer lookin' a mite peaky, lass. If yer tae survive this ye'll want muir than ox cheek and pease."

There is a shout, and they turn to see the Long Ferry easing past at no more than a stone's throw, with the spectators, as many women as men, lined up on the port side holding scented handkerchiefs over their noses. The pilot and their surly marine exchange a wave, no doubt some commerce involved between them to assure there are unfortunates on deck to gawk at before the ferry lands the gawkers for the Tilbury portion of their tour. Morag spits toward them, the offering falling short into the river.

"Snoolin' eedjits."

Jenny presses the hidden ring against her belly, as she does countless times in a day, reassuring herself that it is still there. There will be a moment, she is certain, when it will save her life.

"And what ship are we on?" she asks.

Morag gives her a disapproving look.

"I ken tis written on the hull somewhere," says Jenny, "but I come aboard in the night—"

"The *Jane of Leith*, twenty women and near eighty men held prisoner, or that's what we began with. Jem"—Morag points to the sailor grinning down at them from the spar—"the tarry-breeks as nicks rations fer me, says that e'er morn they fetch corpuses frae the men's hold aff in a jolly boat."

"A plague?"

Morag shrugs. "The water they gie us is drawn frae this river, as it carries a' the cess iv Lunnon oot to sea. And ye've smelt the slop they feed us."

Jenny turns to see, and the grinning sailor, Jem, has swiveled around the mast to follow their progress.

"I can make an introduction if ye'd like."

Jenny presses on the ring again. "No fer noo. If Ah'm tae market ma quim, Ah'll want mair than biscuit and cheese."

AT FIRST WHEN HE WAKES JAMIE CAN'T REMEMBER where he is.

Foul stench, black dark, men breathing heavily, a few snoring. Bits of chopped straw stuck to his face. And then the bells of St. Giles without, striking ten.

Ten was the hour, in Edinburgh, of waste hurled from high windows, the hour for dock-wallopers, porters, draymen, students and other drunkards to set off on their rounds of the city's plethora of gin shops and taverns. Jamie, Davie Falconer and poor Colum Munro fresh out of one of the coffeehouses that surrounded the college or from Ramsey's theater before the presbyter had it closed, released from study and free to roam, explored the havens of the night, both within and outside of the old wall. Colum the most avid tippler of the three, a wealthy merchant's son from Fife intent upon strong whisky and the bedevilment of various doctors of Divinity, Jamie there for Law and History, the first with Cromarty and the latter with the venerable Pitcairn. Davie was in for medicine, having been raised as one of the indigent boys in Heriot's Hospital and still living there as a proctor for the younger ones. Jamie and Colum shared one of the widow Dalhousie's rooms on the Cowgate, there being no residences at the college. No robes were worn, each professor was paid directly for lecture or lesson, and all instruction was complete by four in the afternoon. Students were an integral element of city life, distinguished by their dress, their high spirits, and the public conveyance of books.

A Highlander, a lowlands wastrel, and a Catholic foundling, they were united by a shared sense of the risible and a fervent Jacobitism.

"Tae the King," they would toast, reaching their glasses of port over a panniken of water to symbolize the sea between them and their exiled ruler, or perhaps "Doon with the Rump!" or "Long live PC!" if fairly certain they were not able to be heard in the din of a crowded drinking parlor. Davie's zeal began in religion and widened to more rational anti-Unionist principles, Colum's seethed with an inherited hatred of all Campbells and their allies, and Jamie, not yet twenty years of age, was the shining hope for restoration of his family's name and estate. But even in the presence of the Crown's enforcers it seemed a game, and they the very rakehells of the Royal Mile. Drink brought out Colum's fiery stripe of rebellion to an alarming degree, Davie remained rational, almost detachedly philosophic throughout, while Jamie, especially under the influence of wine, drifted into a pleasant sentiment of distance from it all, unburdened of his family mission, indifferent, almost, to which noble head the bloody crown should rest upon. In private and sober they debated political alliances, military strategy, the trustworthiness of the French and the Spaniards, the likelihood of this or that noble to risk all for the Cause, the willingness of the common man to bear arms. Whether browsing in the stalls of the Luckenbooths or visiting the legal texts kept beneath the old Parliament building, the Tolbooth was the physical axis of their perambulations, looming over them as a grim but apt appendage to St. Giles. *Attend not to the dour instruction given within the kirk,* it seemed to announce, *and this be your fate.*

The Tolbooth's residents during Jamie's student days had been simple debtors and scofflaws for the most part, some even ordering out for beer and victuals with what monies remained to them or were put at their disposal by supporters. The rarer hard cases—cutpurses, sneak thieves, the occasional bigamist or murderer, if not wealthy or highly connected, were kept in the iron room, but their sojourns within the prison were of shorter duration. There was no shortage of bloody history to the place, of course, heads once impaled on the sharpest points of the ironwork, but those times seemed long past. Jamie even had the beginnings of a romance with a barmaid named Una, a few years his senior, whose father was let out through the forbidding oaken door of the Tolbooth every morning to ply his trade as a bootmaker, then welcomed back each evening as if it were no more than an oversized boardinghouse.

The death sentence for Wilson, a notorious smuggler whose gang had made a shambles of robbing the Pittenweem excise collector of two hundred pounds, was given spice by his valorous sacrifice to help his partner Hall escape during their *vale vitae* sermon in St. Giles kirk. Thus his hanging, scheduled a few days later in the middle of April, drew far more than the usual morbid crew of witnesses. Ditties were composed, broadsides arguing the particulars of the case sold on the streets, a constant vigil of idlers camped in the narrow passage beside the Tolbooth, reenacting the particulars of the bold escape and hoping for a glimpse of their hero. As the ceremony was to take place on a Saturday, there were no academic matters to attend to.

"Whomever misses this," Colum Munro announced to his comrades, "would slumber through the Apocalypse."

They joined the sullen procession on the High Street, red-coated members of the Canongate regiment lining the way, apparently called out by the magistrates in reaction to the rumor that a further escape would be attempted. Wilson stood resolutely if not defiantly in the cart in his burial suit, wrists and elbows tied together before him to discourage any last-moment theatrics, giving him the aspect of a man about to pray. A flighty mare, ears all atwitch, pulled the cart, a psalm-muttering clergyman walking on either side and guards from the Tolbooth both preceeding and following. Jamie had watched such a parade twice before, but never followed one to its mournful conclusion. The crowd seemed tense but quiet, only a random shout of sympathy for the prisoner heard over the steady tattoo of the drummer boy who strode before the cart, cries of "Down the Union!" ignored by the stoic regimentals. The cart rattled hard on the more uneven pavement as they turned down steep and crooked Bow Street, Wilson shifting his feet to attempt to keep his balance. Jamie was struck by the diverse nature of the condemned man's ever-growing retinue, not only the likely idlers, petty criminals and night workers, but a good number of small-scale merchants, some very well known to him, perhaps believers that even a highwayman's response to the Excise was a blow for liberty.

"Tis like Beltane's Day in Ayrshire," grinned Colum, his spirits somewhat lighter than the occasion suggested. "We'll have bonfires and a caber toss by the end of it."

As the way opened up onto the Grassmarket, Jamie was struck by the extreme height of the black gallows tree, two thick uprights topped with a flattish crossbeam erected only that morning, with

Castle Rock and the Royal Palace looming above it. A company of the much detested City Guard awaited the crowd, drawn up around the scaffolding in their blue uniforms, with their Captain, Jock Porteous, strutting officiously about the periphery.

"If it's a riot they're feart of," Davie observed, "they've done a' that's needed tae provoke one."

They were well to the rear of the throng as the executioner, a solid, gray-haired man, supervised the placement of the cart beneath the tree.

"We'd profit frae a higher vantage fer the crowning act," said Colum, on his toes to see over the taller men surrounding him. "Follae me."

They made their way around the edges of the crowd as the charges and sentence were called out by a court official reading from a roll of documents, coming to the south row of the tipsy buildings that defined the long rectangle of the Grassmarket, Jamie musing that the condemned man's most vivid final impression might be of the rich, insistent aroma of hay and horse manure, a reminder of the enclosure's most frequent employment. A flock of dusky jackdaws, disturbed from their trove of insects and nesting material, rose and fell, rose and fell, searching for a patch of ground not occupied by the jostling spectators.

A bit laddie sat at the entrance to one of the taller edifices, probing his nose with a dirty finger.

"Do ye bide here?" Colum asked him.

"It's ma hame."

"And yer nae intrigued by the spectacle?" Colum asked him.

The boy yawned. "There's a lang spell of jabbering tae come first. When the drums start fer earnest, I'll nick up tae our rooms and keek it through the windae."

"Might we join ye?"

The boy removed his finger from his nose and looked them over. "Twelvepence the view," he said, "An that's fer each of yeez."

The rooms were no more squalid than those offered by the widow Dalhousie, and the fourth-story window offered a vertiginous outlook almost straight down over the condemned's left shoulder as he stood at the rear of the cart. One of the clergymen was finishing his oration, addressing the spectators with only a rare lift of his head up to Wilson, while the executioner fiddled with his halter, drawing the brass ring up and down to adjust the opening of the noose.

"I seed a lag that keeched his breeks, once," remarked the boy, squeezed between Jamie and Colum. "And most a' of them wets their front when they're stretched."

"An involuntary reflex," Davie added, always eager to pass on an arcane facet of human anatomy. "The sphincter, which functions something like a knot being drawn tight, suddenly relaxes—"

"When it's a' over the hangman'll sell the halter," the boy told them. "And at times the mon's claes as well. The mair desperate the brigand, the mair siller they'll fetch."

Jamie was suddenly struck with his own height above the ground, imagining a rushing four-story drop before the snap of the hemp, the head surely ripped from the body—

The executioner stepped up on the cart with Wilson then, placing a white nightcap on his head.

"As if he's being readied fer sleep."

"Tae spare his dear uns the sight of the waeful faces he'll pull." The boy cricked his neck to one side, bugging his eyes and sticking his tongue out.

"Ye've witnessed a good deal of this?" asked Jamie, his stomach climbing to his throat.

The boy shrugged. "Most days it's ainly cuddies and coos, but five have been topped ere we've dwelt in the Market."

The executioner slipped the noose over Wilson's neck, tightened and adjusted it, then helped him step up onto a wooden crate.

"If the drop is nae high enow," explained the wee laddie, "he'll kick till the sun falls ahind the Castle. I've kent family folk tae glaum ontae a mon's knees and pull doon tae speed the end."

The executioner reached up to gently tug the nightcap over Wilson's face, then climbed out of the cart. The drummer boy, now joined by two of his fellows, busied his sticks in an anticipatory roll.

Jamie somehow missed whatever blow or signal the executioner gave to the flighty horse, but it suddenly bolted forward, the crowd exclaiming as one, and the cart was no longer beneath the hanging man.

Wilson did not kick for long. The executioner stepped beneath to still the body's swaying, then hugged it close, lifting slightly so one of tallest of the City Guards could climb onto another crate and saw through the rope above the brass ring. People began to make rude noises, closing in around the Guards who ringed the gallows tree, epithets sullying the air. The wee lad was indignant.

"Clarty bastarts! He's meant tae swing fer an hour!"

"It seems a mercy to remove him thus—"

"Where's the respeckit? If a cutpurse or a cattle thief is gien an hour, is Wilson no worthy of the same?" The boy struck his fists on the windowsill. "They're feart of the people, is a'."

A hail of stones, transported to Grassmarket that morning for the very purpose, began to sail through the air, the executioner stumbling toward the waiting cart with Wilson's body over his shoulder, shouts erupting between Porteous and the crowd, and suddenly a shot fired, black smoke blooming around the pistol held forward in the hand of the snarling captain and a scream and then a rapid, murderous volley from the City Guards nearest him, the crowd surging back in terror with three of their number left prone on the ground, Jamie and the others leaning out to see the executioner hurriedly wheel the rattling cart with Wilson's body up the steep incline of the Bow, Porteous and most of the Guard peeling after him in some disarray, then an order barked out and half the Guards whirling to fire another ragged volley at the pursuing spectators.

Jamie later supposed that a number of the guardsmen, pricked by conscience, had aimed high, several of their balls chipping the brick around the window and one striking Colum in the throat. It was in a daze that he carried his friend by the ankles, backing down the stairs with Davie, bizarrely calm, supporting Colum under the shoulders and directing Jamie's movements out into the Grassmarket and weaving through the furious rag ends of the mob, jackdaws fluttering about in confusion. They were halfway to the house of Dr. Kerr when Jamie was seized from behind by a sergeant of the regulars, another pair of soldiers taking up Colum's writhing body with Davie and hurrying away.

"Yer a witness, and we'll have yer story weel it's fresh," said the sergeant, an iron grip on Jamie's shoulder. "Ye'll gae with me."

Passed through the ranks then, Jamie was standing in front of the Thistle and Plow recounting his version of the event to a red-faced major with an English accent he could barely comprehend when it was shouted that the most choleric of the horde from below had beseiged the Guard House, wherein Porteous had blithely, as at the end of any day's business, retired. Jamie was dragged along with the major and two dozen hardy troopers to extract the Captain, lacking only his hat, from that smaller redoubt and march him the several hundred yards to the more secure confines of the Tolbooth. Eventually mollified by the major's announcement that Porteous would be tried for murder, the mob dispersed, Jamie able to drift away unnoticed with a phalanx of laborers from the cooperage in Leith.

When Jamie reached Dr. Kerr's house, Davie was sitting on the front steps, head in his hands.

"He's gan," Davie told him, red-eyed, hands shaking. "He'd lost tae much bluid."

More troops arrived to augment the regulars in the weeks that followed, strolling unarmed about the city as a reminder, firm though not overtly hostile, of the Crown's distaste for opposition. It fell to Jamie to take the ferry to Inverkeithing to explain to Colum's parents how their son had been slain, Mr. Munro's political sympathies unguarded in his reaction.

"Tis the bluidy, reeking Union that's kilt him," he hissed as his wife wept into a handkerchief. "And t'will bury a thousand mair ere it's settled!"

Jamie was called as well to recount his story at the trial of Porteous, listening with growing anxiety as he waited to each witness contradicting the previous. With none claiming to have heard Porteous read the Riot Act first, the hub of contention was whether the Captain had ordered his guardsmen to fire or if they had only reacted in panic due to his insufficient mastery of the situation. When Jamie was finally in the witness dock and had given what detail of the event he could remember, the barrister for the Captain's defense began by approaching to examine him as if he were a pile of excrement suddenly sprouting legs and a mouth to speak with.

"You are from Inverness?" opened the barrister.

"Dunmaglas."

"In the *Highlands*." He spoke it as if a malady.

"And proud tae be so." As whenever pressed, Jamie's blood came up of a sudden. *Touch Not the Cat.*

"And you are a student here—"

"Of the law."

A smattering of laughter here, earning a glare from the magistrate.

"And how is your father employed?"

"Ma father is deid."

"He was a gentleman?"

"He was."

"And what do you have yearly from your lands?"

Jamie answered before the prosecutor could raise his objection.

"Our lands," he said, raising his voice, "were forfeit in wake of the '15—"

"Objection!"

"I wish only to establish the provenance of the foregoing testimony," said the barrister, already with back turned to Jamie and strolling away. "I'll have nothing more from this lad."

Jamie returned to a seat at the rear of the gallery, feeling soiled.

But influenced, no doubt, by the multitude of interested parties screaming for vengeance in the High Street outside the chamber of justice, a verdict of guilty was found and the officer condemned to suffer the same punishment as Wilson, the execution scheduled for the beginning of September.

"If the Crown allows Porteous tae swing," Davie commented on the verdict, "I'll eat ma bonnet."

"*It must be obvious to all right-thinking citizens,*" read an opinion in the *Edinburgh Evening Courant*, "*that the punishment ordained for Captain Porteous, if carried to its conclusion, bodes ill for the maintenance of order in the whole of Northern England. If our duly appointed City Guard be at the mercy of a seditious and criminally inclined rabble, what hope enforcement of the King's laws and levies?*"

"Should they dare tae spring the murthering bastart," promised Selkirk, the butcher, bloody cleaver in hand, "we'll maun hang him oursels!"

But then came a packet from Dougal, the letter inside apologizing for the meager stipend within, cottars paying so often in mutton rather than silver, and Jamie, facing examinations and sobered by the death of Colum, returned to his studies. It was on a rare hiatus from his Civil Law texts, sitting with Davie in the Rod and Anvil, that he learned of the reversal.

"Sodding Walpole's pushed his snout in!" cried the Cowgate smithy, bursting into the low-ceilinged tavern. "The hanging's aff!"

Queries and protestations then, the story emerging that at the fervent intercession of the Prime Minister and the absence of the King, Queen Caroline had granted Porteous a reprieve.

"A reprieve is not clemency—"

"Tis ainly the caution afore the cauld fact. We're tae be bodgered by degrees."

"The folk winnae stand fer it."

"There's another regiment of lobsterbacks been shipped tae make sure we do. As if the lot setting on their hunkers by the Canongate is no enow."

There was a change in the pitch of the city over the next few days, tinklers still shouting their wares, carts and carriages rattling in the streets, but at the corners there were groups of men in sullen conversation, casting dark looks to any who would come near, there were shops that closed early, and a constant vigil, complete with runners poised to spread the alarm if need be, outside the Tolbooth.

"The six already dead are no sufficient," Davie lamented. "They'll have a massacre."

It was planned for the day prior to the arrival of the reinforcements. Planned, because the core of the mob moved too directly, were too efficient in their actions for it to be a spontaneous outburst. Jamie and Davie were in Imbrie's tavern, a much smaller contingent of revelers at the tables than the average Friday evening, when they heard the shouting from without.

"A' them as wish tae seek vengeance fer innocent bluid," went the cry, "join us noo!"

The men in the van of the marching throng carried torches made from pine boughs, others with weapons they had taken by force of numbers from the undermanned City Guard barracks. Jamie and Davie were immediately braced by a trio of hearties with faces masked with cloth like highwaymen.

"It's nae hope fer yez tae go runnin' tae the sojers at Canongate! We've taen a' the ports tae the city and destroyed ilka drum that could give warning!"

"Our dearest friend was killed by the Guard," answered Davie, cool as ever. "We've nae motive tae oppose ye."

"On with us, then!"

Once joined with the mob Jamie ceased to be aware of his own legs moving, swept along with the mood and motion of it, the torches floating down the High Street to the looming prison. Tools had been proffered, voluntarily or no, at an ironmonger's along the way, and so hammers of various lengths and sizes were available to assault the imposing, vaulted Tolbooth door, men taking turns laying into it but producing nothing but splinters. A fire was then carefully set with several barrels of pitch, boys standing by with water buckets to control the blaze and masked men haranguing the crowd to keep their spirits inflamed. The charred wood finally gave way to a rush with a sturdy ladder used as a battering ram, and a dozen men clambered up the turnpike to the upper apartments.

Jamie had seen Jock Porteous out of uniform once, strolling on the Bruntsfield Links just below the southern wall in a foursome that included Rattray the surgeon. The Captain had been a barrel-chested cock stalking a wee stitched leather ball with a lethal-looking hickory club. The man now carried out of the Tolbooth was in his bedclothes, his hair stuck out in every direction like the stubs of scythed barley, his eyes glistening white in the torchlight. A dozen fellow prisoners followed him out of the entrance, quickly losing themselves in the crowd, as a pair of men linked arms to carry their captive in the King's Cushion across the Lawnmarket to the West Bow, and then down to the Grassmarket. No gallows tree had been erected, so the condemned man was awkwardly noosed and hung from a dyer's pole. Pushed to the fore of the executioners, Jamie saw it all, the Captain twisting and kicking till it was observed he had gotten a hand between the hemp and his neck, and so was flailed at with the flat of an axe, then pulled down, stripped of his nightgown and shirt and hauled up again, his tormented body going slack, eyeballs distended, head swollen to a darker hue than his naked torso, only a moment before the bells of St. Giles tolled for midnight.

An eerie quiet then, one of the masked men announcing that the body would be no further mutilated, but carried with all due ceremony to the Greyfriar's yard and left for burial. The rioters dispersed, torches bobbing away in all directions, and Jamie and Davie walked without speaking all the way to the field that bordered the old palace at the foot of King Arthur's Seat. Custom had it that debtors had found sanctuary there when there were still trees to hide behind.

"Justice," said Davie finally, "is nae mair bonny than perfidy."

"I saw a murderer broken on the wheel in Paris," mused Jamie. They sat on the wall, brooding on the night's activity, hearts beating almost normally again. "Leastways, I keeked the first two blows of the hammer."

"We had the Maiden here in Edinburgh," said Davie. "A machine tae separate heids frae bodies. Simple gravity, like the hangman's drop, but ever sae muir reliable. The Earl of Morton was it's greatest advocate—and one of the first tae lose his heid beneath it."

"Ye have a point?"

Davie pondered before answering. "Ye start a fire in the bracken," he said finally, "and there's nae telling what it may consume."

Jamie, lying now in the lightless iron room, wonders if Porteous was held here or in a more comfortable but less secure apartment, imagines him hearing the shouted imprecations of the approaching mob, the smashing of hammers on the door, wonders if he could smell the burning tar before the trampling of his persecutors' feet up the turnpike to his hiding place—

If it's to be the halter for Jamie, he hopes it will not be left in the hands of amateurs.

Suddenly the void is filled, a voice roaring in Erse about devils. Then a chorus of epithets, in several languages, from the other awakened prisoners. There is a thumping and a clanking of metal that accompanies the roaring voice, as if some great beast is struggling to be loosed upon them. Then the echo of the iron door unlocked, and a quartet of angry keepers, one leading with a torch and the rest with truncheons in hand, rush into the room, swatting at whichever unfortunate inmate dares to raise his head.

It is the enormous Highlander, Fergal, returned to consciousness in the absolute dark to discover he is intertwined by shackles, belly to belly and face to face with a corpse that has begun to putrify. The gaolers' first response is an attempt to beat the man senseless again, but he somehow manages to contort himself and the corpse into such a position that he is able the fend their blows with feet and knees, shouting and cursing them all the while. Jamie rises, careful to remain well shy of the truncheons' reach, and offers to talk to the man if they'll promise to free him from the corpse.

"Whate'er ye like, damn ye, just so's he'll shut his gob."

"Stand awee, then."

The keepers back off, and Jamie squats and tries to catch the panicked Highlander's eye, cooing to him in Erse, repeating himself several times.

Quiet yourself, he tells the man, and they'll take the other away.

The Highlander does not so much comply as wear himself out, voice growing hoarse and losing its power, his great muscles beginning to quiver, till he lies on his side, chest heaving, twisting his neck so that his bearded cheek is separated from the mouth of the deceased, whose purple lips have pulled back now to reveal yellowed teeth.

The smith from the Cowgate stables is roused from his bed, bringing his tools, and is set to the task of disentangling the living from the dead, the Highlander casting a wary eye upon him, very like a wild Galloway being shod for the first time.

"The deadun's a' swollen aboot the shackles," the smith declares, brow asweat from his efforts. "Twill gae smoother tae cut flesh than iron."

This is agreed on and a hacksaw is produced, some of the prisoners and all of the keepers looking away as first a hand, and then a foot are severed from the body. Finally, the smith steps away.

"It's yers tae take away. I've tetched it enow."

Two of the keepers pull the body away cautiously, peeling back the Highlander's massive arms, cramped in an embrace, while another gathers up the severed parts. The fourth holds the torch near to be certain none of the smith's instruments remain in the iron room. As they leave, Jamie catches a last torch-lit glimpse of the huge man, able to support his back up against the wall now, eyes gleaming madly, muttering to himself.

He's still with me, the man is saying. He's crawled inside.

JENNY IS TRAINING HERSELF NOT TO THINK OF WHAT will come. The moment is all—the ship rocking gently or enough to make you lose the bit of scran they've allowed you, the damp from the ballast beneath them, the constant stench, the daily promenade above, faces ever more haggard in the open light. The tide will ebb and flow without her aid, the Law will bide its time before disposing of her. If there is no tomorrow there is no wishing, and therefore no disappointment. There are moments when Jenny becomes aware of herself, a sudden I am here and alive, and knows her eyes have been open for hours, knows it is pointless to wonder what day it is in the other people's world, or how many of her fellow prisoners have passed since she last took stock of herself. In the hold of the ship it matters not when the sun rises or sets, if it still does so. The cow is likely dead, and perhaps her father as well and there is nobody on the *Jane of Leith* who knows just how she came to be here. On her circuits above, Jenny watches the gulls, free to come and go, their flocks ever-changing in shape and number and each bird a rival to the other. She cannot imagine that they think beyond the moment, beyond the discovery of whether that gob floating on the next wave is worth fighting over or not. On rainy days, which are many, the deckwalking women lift their faces to the sky and open their mouths, though the lot of them together barely swallow a gill. On clear days when the tide is low she can see that the supports of the Tilbury dock are crusted with wee creatures, so fixed in place that they must glean their nourishment from the water of the Thames. What can it profit them, if they think at all, to fret each day if the tide will rise again, or that a dockie might arrive tasked to scrape them from their hold on life? Airy thoughts, thoughts of matters over which Jenny has no dominion, and can therefore neither harm nor help her. The *Jane of Leith* rocks fore and aft now. Morag lies asleep, or perhaps only with her eyes closed and in the same state of timelessness, in Jenny's lap. No one stirs on the deck above, and she can hear a squawking of gulls shifting from one side of the river to the other. At some moment to come there will be shouted orders to eat this or do that.

Or perhaps not.

IN THE DREAM, NONE OF IT KILLS HIM. THOUGH HE BIDS them not to, they pull the cap over his eyes, and from then on there is only a strained light, like what makes its way through uncolored church glass on a dismal morning. Strong hands push and pull at him till he is in place, the hemp chafes against the skin of his neck and is then drawn snug. There are voices, but none of the sounds have meaning. The cart beneath him shifts to and fro—he is afraid of tumbling but his hands are bound behind him, helpless to aid his balance. And then a crack and the floor jerking out from under him and a precipitous drop, feeling, hearing his neck snap with a loud pop and a flash of white but not over, not killed yet but swinging, and a cheer from those attending and now strong arms around his legs pulling down on his body, the pain like nothing he has ever experienced and constant now, even when he is suddenly lifted and laid back on the ground by many hands, new pain then as the knife punches in just below where the rope has cut through the skin of his neck, sawing now, opening him from breastbone to navel—

Asweat in the ascent from his hanging, Jamie imagines, almost conscious now, other ends. Skewered on the dragoon's sword on the muddy hill, lying with a ball through his skull in the trench, bodies below, bodies thrown upon him, the smell of wet earth as it chokes off the air above. And then the slow inventory of his living body, bones sharp against the scraps of hay on the floor, the noises of the men sleeping, perhaps dreaming, around him, the weary effort to remember where, precisely, in the world he is lying—

CAMERON IS TAKEN OUT FIRST, NO WORD OF THE PURpose, and then a lowlander with a gangrenous foot. It is just afternoon, by the bells, when they come for Jamie, Toad on his one arm and Hare on the other, guided brusquely down a corridor to a room with good light that has been set up as a kind of hospital. Jamie realizes at once that his wound is to be examined, and then that the physician attending is his companion of college days, Davie Falconer.

"Strip yer trews aff, if yer able," says Davie, without meeting his eye.

One of the Tolhouse screws, in the pay of the gaol's owner and not the Crown, stands guard by the door, but there is no uniform for spies. Jamie is able to peel his trousers down below the bullet hole, the scabbed flesh only bleeding a little now. Davie cleans the wound, front and rear, with a liquid that throws off a stinging aroma.

"In and oot," says Davie, "possibly to dae mischief to the mon ahind ye."

"It entered frae the rear," Jamie corrects him, "and came oot the front of me."

"In retreat, then."

"I was standing afore a ditch filled with the dead." Davie flicks his eyes to Jamie's at this. "Twas puir aim rather than mercy that spared me."

Davie palpates the flesh at the entry and exit points as if judging the freshness of a sole.

"The human body is a miracle sometimes," he announces. "What it can withstand."

"As is the human spirit."

Davie leans back to look frankly at his friend.

"I've seen yer cell mate. Cameron—"

"Fourth Earl of Lochiel."

"Which he would truly be," says Davie, "were he no the natural son of a natural son."

"Ah."

"His uncle Arch was ahead of me in the medical school. Arch seems tae've joined his brother in the recent unpleasantness."

The Tolhouse screw's face betrays no sign of comprehension, but here in Edinburgh it is unlikely he has no English.

"Arch Cameron was sent tae Loch nan Uamh," says Jamie, "tae convince Prince Charlie twas no the moment fer an uprising."

"Then he failed in his mission."

"There's nae arguing with the Divine Right of Kings."

It is a topic they argued many a night, switching sides at times to explore all the subtleties, with only poor Colum accepting the doctrine *ex facae*. Davie points to a pile of coarse but unstained clothing.

"See if anything there fits ye."

"Frae yer closet?"

"Tis drawn frae the workhoose."

"I'll want better fer my trial," says Jamie, sizing a pair of britches to replace his own bloodied tatters. "As an afficer in the French service—"

"If yer born in the Kingdom, that maun no serve ye." Davie has not so much put on weight as grown more stolid, a set to his features that speaks of experience and resignation. "The Crown is set tae issue their edicts as tae what will be tolerated."

Jamie nods. "And Cameron? He'll live?"

"Live tae be tried. I removed the ball, though it discomposed him greatly. Lead creates toxins—"

"And why the sudden concern?" Jamie leans closer to Davie, lowering his voice. "Why've ye been allooed tae treat us?"

"No allooed, instructed."

Always the most cautious of them, Davie, orphan himself, challenged to navigate the world alone.

"Why, then?"

Davie turns to his instruments as Jamie pulls on a gray workhouse shirt, muttering so the Tolhouse guard may not hear.

"They've decreed that nane will be tried in Scotland," he says. "So yer aff tae London by the tail of the week."

TOLBOOTH TAE LEITH,
We were marched twa abreast
Ne're again tae roam proud and free
The Dutchess of Fife, *with puir captives impressed*
Set sail and put oot tae sea—

Lachlan is one of the few short enough to stand in the low, stifling compartment, sweating freely in the July heat. The men, demoralized and seasick, have demanded a verse, and he does not hesitate, mind racing only a few lines ahead of his tongue—

Chained and condemned, in steerage confined
The ship was nae sooner unmuired
When a tempest swept down, having made up its mind
Tae drown every mon that's aboord

The heavens stained black, ship swamped in the blow
Her crew fast-despairing did weep
Twas certain it seemed, that a', friend and foe
Were fated tae rest in the Deep

There had been more cursing than weeping above deck, but it was a storm such as none Jamie had encountered, the ship lurching fore and aft, starboard and larboard, cold saltwater slapping down upon them through the grate, the sounds of great sails torn loose and flapping, at least one cannon-crack as the boom split—

But then a' at once, the wind and the wave
As quick as they'd rose settled down
And thus we were spared frae a watery grave
For our necks a' belang tae the Crown—

A bitter laugh from the men. Jamie sits huddled, struggling for breath in the sultry, almost liquid air, rocking with the steady surge of the ship. It feels like they are running before the wind now, sliding down the coast with ease, drawing nearer to what comes next—

Sky blue and seas calm, we continued tae sail
When ainly a day oot of port
Begrimed and bedraggled, louse-ridden and pale
The Englishmen made us their sport
The vengeful Jack Tars their captain implored
Determined tae give us a dip
Young Cyrus McNabb was tied by a cord
And dragged neath the keel of the ship
Our task was tae hoist the lad oot of the swell
We feart he were sentenced tae death

Though we pulled with our hearts it was simple tae tell
McNabb would nae mair draw a breath—

They were arranged in a straight line with the rope at their feet, a marine with a musket at each end and the captain, a man called Grissom, supervising from the poop deck. McNabb was pushed off the bowsprit, a splash, and then they had to wait an agonizing moment, hoping their comrade was sinking deep—

"Now!" cried Grissom, his eyes feverish, and they snatched up the rope and began to pull it through the blocks, hand over hand, their feet slipping on the wet deck, the weight of McNabb and all the water he plowed before him unbelievably stubborn, the barefoot sailors cheering or jeering them on, then a lightening as he came out of the water, two sailors stretching to pull him over the rail and the captain walking aft to peruse the result. McNabb lay on his side with his hair swept over his face and water drooling out of his open mouth, clothing shredded and beginning to blossom red, lifeless in a puddle.

If his wrists had not been bound together, thought Jamie, he might have had a chance.

"Just as I thought," said Grissom. "Not a hopping flea left on him."

The sailors who'd gaffed him in looked away, but the captain strolled down the line of prisoners, many bent over and gasping for air, till he met with Jamie's steady glare.

"Name?"

"MacGillivray." Holding the glare, wishing hellfire upon the captain—

Nae satisfied yet, twas Jamie they chose
As next tae be tossed in the drink
"I'm no such a weighty carcass tae tow,"
He said, and then dove with a wink—

He tried to meet each of his comrades' eyes as he was led away, making light of it to calm his heart. He and Dougal had competed as boys, holding their breath under the cold river, poking the other's ribs to make him break, and he knew the trick of it was calm. To relax as if the water was your true element, to look around, explore the bottom. He made sure to turn himself before he was perched on the bowsprit with wrists bound and the towline fastened round his ankles, for a last shouted jest and a look at the boys in the stern.

Then the sailor's kick, and falling, trying to arch his body to cut the water, willing himself to sink before the line jerked his legs and he began to be hauled belly-up through the water, careful to push bubbles slowly out through his nose and bring his rope-bound hands up to cover his face—

He scraped the hull three times, jolting his knees upward to torque off from it, razor-sharp barnacles slicing to the bone, arching his back and feeling his lungs vise shut, tight as angry fists, his chest ready to implode, and then jerked up feet first and hung dripping like a flounder on a hook—

Sae frantic we heaved, hands clutched tae the line
Sich effort has rarely been seen
His very first words, when pulled oot frae the brine
"God save us, I'm finally clean!"

More laughter from the men, Lachlan making a little bow before he sits.

It was only a brief moment, shivering and gasping on the deck, even a few of the sailors grinning for him, then the captain's angry command and all thrown back into the filth of the hold. The hatch was barely closed upon them when they heard McNabb's body splash overboard, no ceremony wasted.

Jamie's ankles are still throbbing from where the cords cut in, his soaked clothes stuck tight to his body, saltwater acid in his bloody stripes. Drowning was never on his list of imagined expirations, his taste running toward a quick bullet to the brain on a battlefield or a simple passing into sleep as a very old man.

"Tell me," he says to Lachlan huddled beside him, "did ye put yer back tae ma lifeline, or were ye composing the verse?"

Lachlan smiles, but before he can answer the hatch is opened, light glaring from above, and the boatswain calls down.

"Prepare yerselves, gentlemen." There is a tattoo of running feet upon the boards above, the screech of rope through the blocks, the mate's voice shouting instruction. "The whole town's come out to greet ye."

THEY DOCK AT BANKSIDE PIER, PRISONERS KEPT BELOW till all is made fast. Once on deck Jamie is more attentive to the sight of the London Bridge, just upriver, than the instruction of the marine sergeant or the crowd already hooting at them from shore. The Pont Neuf would be its equal if the Île de la Cité did not bisect it, and unlike the Parisian structure, this is topped by hundreds of buildings, some of them several stories high, the few gaps between them revealing a rather narrow carriageway. Vehicles of various sizes and shapes, as well as single horsemen and pedestrians, are currently massed in a state of waiting for the central drawbridge, located over the tallest of the many support arches, to be lowered after the passage of a tall-masted fishing smack.

"It appears they've a shortage of land doon here," Lachlan remarks, staring beside Jamie, "tae build a wee city aboon the water."

Just then a barrage of turds is loosed from one of the series of privies cantilevered over the near side of the bridge, splashing onto the water's surface and then floating with the tide.

Lachlan nods his head in appreciation. "On our island we've a wee bridge that shakes frae time tae time, but nane that can *shite*."

A wherry rowed by two husky men, with a trio of well-dressed passengers in the stern, shoots past the smack, aiming for one of the narrower arches, a tidal rip frothing through it at great speed. Jamie's fellow prisoners make quick wagers as to its fate, the foremost oarsman swiveling to look anxiously over his shoulder as they rush to the opening, trying to keep his bow pointed dead center. The two rowers ship oars as the current takes hold, passengers gripping the gunwales with one hand and their wigs with the other, then a cheer and a rattling of shackles as the wherry is flushed through with only one splintering thump of its hull against the side of the stone arch and spat out on the other side like a rotten pea.

The marines from the *Dutchess of Fife* unchain and line them up two abreast then, and they are marched down the gangway into the tumult on the pier. It seems all of Southwark has been informed of their coming—shops closed, apprentices given a holiday, the schools, if any of the jeering, stone-throwing urchins who dog their steps actually attend them, at recess. A local greengrocer has contributed enough overripe fruit for several volleys, and if Jamie is not mistaken, so engaged in dodging missiles himself, Cameron is struck on the face with a recently deceased cat. The crowd, braving the sun's midday blaze, strings along with them on both sides as they are prodded along down Watling Street, the boldest of the boys darting past the marines to poke or thwack prisoners with sticks, and a contingent of painted ladies, available for rent at other times, provide the crudest of the commentary.

"They ort to cut yez into mincemeat and feed yez to the dogs!" shouts one of the younger strumpets, over and over. "Fecking papist murtherers!"

That there might be less than a half-dozen Catholics in the entire miserable company does not belay the religious slander, and the fate of the Prince Regent, much speculated upon during the sojourn in the Tolbooth and the passage by sail, is revealed in other comments.

"When we catch yer bowsy Pretender," promises a burly fellow, by the stains on his apron a purveyor of meat, "we'll nail him to yon bridge by his prick and let him 'ang!"

"He's still in hiding, then," hisses Lachlan, pressed close against Jamie for shelter from the continuing fusillade.

"Or nipped aff tae France."

They pass onto the Borough High Street, where even more tormentors await. A woman with crazed eyes dodges in to push Jamie nearly off his feet.

"Ye'll burn in Hell, ye Jacobite scum!" she shrieks. "Ye'll drown in a lake of fire!"

They are halted in front of a cluster of three-story brick and wooden buildings, steep-roofed with dormers on the front face. The marine sergeant calls out names from a list, ordering those identified to step forward. Jamie, Lachlan, Aeneas Cameron and a score of other men are thus separated from the main body as the enveloping throng screams for their heads.

"You lot to remain here, the rest on to the King's Bench," announces the sergeant, leaving only two of the marines to shepherd them into the waiting residences. There is nothing to keep me from bolting for freedom, thinks Jamie as both the marines turn their backs to him. Nothing but the club-and rope-wielding population of Southwark.

They step into a turreted lodge at the front of the middle building, then are pushed into a side room, where a bland-looking, carefully dressed man stands on a wooden chair to survey them.

"If I might have your attention, please."

He is wearing an ill-fitting horsehair periwig and spectacles that make his light blue eyes look enormous, a faint smile on his lips as he addresses them.

"Here at Marshalsea," he begins, "we offer two very distinct options for our residents. We have a number of rooms available on the masters' side of the establishment, at twelve shillings a week if one is sharing, no more than three permitted to a room, and a pound for the privacy of a single habitation. There is a restaurant and a taproom on the ground floor, as well as access to the racket courts. Though our masters residents are normally allowed to leave the premises during the daylight hours, I'm afraid that option will not be available to you veterans of the recent *contretemps* in the north."

The man looks about the room expectantly. "Would any gentlemen here care to opt for the masters' side?"

There are undoubtedly many who would, Jamie thinks, but whatever currency they possess is hidden back in Scotland or has been appropriated by the invaders.

The man waits a moment, then sighs. "It would seem, then, that you'll be lodged on the common side, which I'm afraid offers very few amenities and very much less space. Mr. Micklejohn?"

A stooping, cadaverous-looking man in the doorway makes a small grunting noise.

"I leave them in your charge."

As it is revealed, there are only nine small rooms on the commons side, housing hundreds of prisoners, to which are added the Jacobite captives, crowded into a sweltering garret with a dozen incumbent prisoners. The most ferocious-looking of these, a fellow with a broken nose and one blind eye cast in a permanent leftward gaze, steps forward, in the paltry space available to step, to greet them.

"Time to cough up the garnish, mates," he growls. "Empty yer pockets."

One or two other inmates of criminal aspect stand uneasily behind their leader, but most of the men already in the room, some appearing to be in a very poor state, barely look up from their resting places on the barren floor.

"Unless you have both cannon and cavalry at your disposal, I would reconsider that demand." Cameron has regained much of his strength since Davie's ministrations, though he still walks stiffly and with a pensive air, as if listening for the pain.

"We've been gan over by yer army, yer navy, and yer marines," adds Lachlan. "We're dead skint, friend."

The one-eyed man shrugs. "More's the pity. They'll bring beer if ye've the scratch."

"And if ye dinnae ?" asks Jamie.

"If ye don't pay, ye don't eat, ye don't step outside in the yard, and if yer sick, it's ten shillins to be fetched to the infirmry, which is where coves that's mindful of their cellmates' comfort and 'ealth goes ter snuff it."

It is steamier in the slope-ceilinged garret than it was in the hold of the *Dutchess of Fife*, Jamie moving immediately to the small dormer window, which has only a few shards of glass left sticking out from the jambs and sill. He thrusts his head out, but there is no breeze. The one-eyed man appears beside him.

"We take turns wif that."

"I expect ye do."

"Nipper Wilde's me monicker. Resale merchant."

"Jamie MacGillivray." He indicates the window. "Is it possible tae communicate?"

"Wif the outside? Messages come and go, as do visitors, if ye can pay. I've got a woman on Blackfriars, brings me what she can. If she should get pinched as well, I'm done fer. I'm already deep in arrears ter Mr. Whipshaw."

"Whipshaw—?"

"The jasper as probably threw ye a sermon in the pound. Wears a duster on 'is nob, mild as milk—"

"That's him."

"Whipshaw pays the marshal fer the privilege of running this little sponge'ouse. He charges near a pound a week fer them in the commons, plus whatever extras they can pop fer, food, visitors, change of situation ter a bigger room—"

"We're being charged—"

"I don't know about you political gents, the Crown might lay summat on the table, but fer us," he nods to the men lying about on scattered tufts of straw, "which is mostly yer dodgers and defaulters, not independent tradesmen like me, he'll bleed ye every time ye roll over. I'm only waiting trial, see, and I awready owe the mewling whoreson a year's pickings."

He gives Jamie a squinting onceover. "Yer an eddycated cove."

"Moderately."

Nipper points down to the courtyard below them. A little weed-choked strip of dirt, then a wall just high enough to block a standing man's view, and beyond it a larger, grassy section of yard, on which three men are playing at skittles.

"That's where ye want ter be, then. Wif the *qual*ity."

AT FIRST JENNY HAD WELCOMED THE TASK AS A DIVERSION, something to occupy her mind through the stretches of waking time. But the ropes were old and full of tar or even paint, hard enough to untwist them to the piles, then into singles, and by the time she was pulling fibers apart her nails were broken and fingers bleeding.

"I've picked a ton of junk in me day," says Poll, the oldest woman in the hold, who had been a notorious cutpurse in her youth. She drops her length of rope in her lap to show her fingers, blackened down to the first joint "Enough to caulk a ship of the line."

"And that on yer thumb?" asks Morag, who scowls continuously as she works.

Old Poll waggles her right thumb, which has a T branded on it.

"The first time I was burnt fer thievin', I pled bennyfit of clergy and they 'ad me read from the Bible to prove I was quallyfied. In them days they'd brand yer thumb and let ye skip fer the first offense, but ye was marked inellygible fer the next."

"Ye can read?"

"Not a bleedin' word. But Squint, 'e was our schoolmaster, in a manner of speakin, 'e 'ad us all memorize the Fifty-first Psalm—that's like a poem in the Book—which is where they'd open it to fer the test. We called it the neck verse." Old Poll closes her eyes to remember. "*'Ave mercy upon me, oh God, according to thy loving kindness, according unto the multytude of thy tender mercies blot out my transgressions. Wash me thoroughly from mine iniquity, and cleanse me from my sin.*"

She opens her eyes, smiling toothlessly. "If ye practices iniquities it's a good un to know."

Jenny pushes the tangle of picked oakum between her ankles away, raises her arms over her head. "I've heared they can brand yer face."

"Not anymore, dear. But ye've nowt to worry, it's likely ye'll not even be tried."

"And why no?"

Old Poll glances at the other women who sit about them, tugging strands of rope apart.

"Of all of yez that's here fer aiding the Pretender and his mob, how many 'ave the English tongue?"

"Ainly masel' and ane other—"

"And ye've family with means?"

"We're a' puir."

"Witnesses to call? Clergy to swear to yer character?"

"Nane."

"Then they'll likely just ship yez to the islands, to stoop in the cane fields with niggers and Oirishmen."

"That's where I'm headed," says Morag, who was convicted and sentenced back in Inverness, "if I dunnae hang mysel' with this fecking rope afore."

"But they're supposed tae give ye a trial—" says Jenny.

"When it were ma go in the docket they heared a tale," says Morag, yanking viciously at her rope. "Nane of yer mumble-jumble in Latin and oot the door with the bitch, thank ye very much. The fecking hussy I done the wrang tae was there with a' her family and dinnae trust Scots law tae do its duty, so I blisthered their lugs with a description of her low behavior—"

"If ye anger the magistrate it will always go harder fer ye," Poll advises.

"Angry or no, they maun hear me oot! I've naething left on this airth but ma feelins, and I'll no surrender those with nary a peep."

"It's the islands, ye reckon?" asks Jenny. This is not good, something to think about, something maybe to be dreaded. "And what is it like there?"

"I've never been, love, and never will now," says Old Poll. "They only want them that's young and sprightly. Fer the *fields*, ye know—it's none of yer little snippin' and sewin' as ye'll find at the parish workhouse." She shakes her head. "An owd bag of bones like me isn't worth the passage to 'em. But you girls is *ripe*."

"IT'S A' LINKED UP TAE THE SUCCESSION," SAYS JAMIE.

They do the promenade twice a day, all the rebels not in chains or so muddled as big Fergal MacGregor, while Jamie serenades them with aspects of his university learning, intriguing if not often useful, and Nipper Wilde sits in the middle with the few other common criminals, suspicious of any activity not directly leading to profit or inebriation. Lachlan has asked Jamie to fill in the larger canvas of recent events—

"The Austrian Succession—it has the sound of a novel dance step—"

"It is, of a sort. A dance where the partners is apt tae shift positions afore the music ends, a dance that begins with the demise of the Holy Roman Emperor."

"An Italian gentleman—?"

"A royal Austrian of the Habsburg line—"

"Who lives in Rome?"

"Who lives in Vienna and is elected tae reign ower a muckle of states on the Continent that was at ane time under the imperial rule of Julius Caesar and that lot—"

"Which is where yer Romans step intae it—"

"Aye. Weel, this fella, Charles the Sixth, Mr. Habsburg, was also King of Bohemia, King of Hungary, King of Croatia, King of Serbia, as well as the Archduke of Austria—"

"Which calls, I assume, fer a plethora of royal appurtenances—"

"Thrones, castles, flags, armies—"

"Rods and scepters fer every occasion—"

"So wot *'appens* when this 'oly Roman cove kicks off?" prods Nipper Wilde, content to be entertained but always impatient with digression.

"Kicks aff," adds Jamie, "withoot leavin' a male heir."

Lachlan nods his head, beginning to see a pathway into the puzzle. "Highly inconsiderate, when ye think of a' them kingdoms tae be ruled ower—"

"Indeed. His contention, on his deathbed, and that of maist of his inner circle, was that his daughter, Maria Theresa, should inherit the lands and title."

"They let ye do that?" asks Nipper. "A woman—?"

"You English have had yer Elizabeth—"

"And a grand owd bird she was. So it's not a problem—"

"Unless certain other parties, principally the French and the Prussians—"

"Wot, exackly, is a *Prus*sian?"

"A sort of a Dutchman," answers Lachlan.

"Ah—"

"But with a stiffer spine."

"These other parties," Jamie continues, "declared that on account of the Salic Law, Maria Theresa is no eligible tae rule, and the crown should instead be gien tae the closest male relative—"

"Now 'oo are the *Sa*lics?"

"It's the Frankish people of lang syne, and their law was that *terra Salica* can ne'er be inherited by a woman."

"And these Frankish were—?"

"What the French was calt a thousand years ago."

"A thousand years?" Lachlan always walks directly behind Jamie, to better engage in the dialogue. "And why is somebody gan sae lang tae be consultit?"

"Because if yer oot tae snatch a kingdom, ye want a legal foundation—"

"A terrible shaky one, I'd say—"

"There's law that gets settled in court," says Jamie, the only one in the room who has studied at the bar, "and there's law that requires the deliberations of great armies in mortal strife. This situation belangs tae the latter."

"Yer sayin' there's a battle?"

"A *war.* The French and Prussians begin tae fight Maria Theresa's advocates, which at the beginning is maistly what ye'd call Austrians—"

"Confusion tae 'em a', I say. If it wisna tae be this Maria Theresa, who'd they want tae hand the crown tae?"

"Charles Albert of Bavaria, a gentleman married tae the recently deceased Holy Emperor's niece—"

"Yer royal blood's gettin' a mite *thin* by then, innit?" observes Nipper.

"If we're tracing royal bloodlines," Cameron interjects from where he sits by the wall, still nursing his leg, "I would propose that your German George's claim to an English throne is even thinner—"

Nipper points a warning finger. "'Old on, now, mate—no bloody *pol*itics allowed in 'ere—"

"And what aboot the Spanish?" asks Lachlan.

"England was a'ready at war with Spain—"

"'Ave been ever since the Dagos cut off poor Jenkins' ear—"

"Ye see, His Majesty George the Second," Jamie explains, "is no ainly King of England, he is also the Elector of Hanover."

"And Hanover is—?"

"Down past Croydon, innit?"

"E'en further. Yer George is Serene Highness of that Imperial Estate across the ocean, and therefore serves as ane of the Electors of the Holy Roman Emperor."

"An Emperor that needs tae be elecktit?"

"Aye, though fer three hunnert years it's a'ways been the next male in the Habsburg line twas handed the staff—"

"The people's choice, is it?"

"The difficulty being," Jamie explains, "that with such a raggle-taggle of an empire, dozens of peoples and tongues that they speak, alliances here and ancient feuds there, as mony enemies as ye've got borders, ye never ken when ye'll be dragged intae a dispute that leads tae a full-oot war."

"And thus the dance of the Secession—"

Jamie nods, lifting his knees high as he walks. Whipshaw charges dearly for the privilege of a stroll outside, but Jamie knows from Davie Falconer that inactivity allows the blood to settle in the wrong areas—

"Sae the French, as well as Frederic of Prussia and Charles of

Bavaria and a few other assorted dutchies and protectorates, are attacking Maria Theresa's troops in Austria, with some bit of success, when who comes over at the head of the Pragmatic Army tae join the party—"

"None of this sounds pragmatic tae me—"

"—but George the Second himsel'—"

"God save our King," interjects Nipper.

"—and afore ye can blink yer een, he's met the French under Marshal Noailles at Dettingen."

"I was there," says Cameron, somewhat bitterly.

"The English were there, the Dutch were there, the Austrians and the Hanoverians, and they prevailed over Mr. Cameron here and Marshal Noailles on that occasion, driving the French back toward the Rhine." Jamie turns to walk backward for a moment, looking at Lachlan. "Noo begin the complications."

"Och—and afore twas so simple—"

"Them that's in support of Maria Theresa believe the Russians are gang to join them, but then the plot tae remove Tzarina Elisabeth is exposed—"

"I'm shocked. And tae replace her with another Hopsbug?"

"Nae, with Ivan the Sixth, who was nowt but a wee bye—"

"Hopin' he'd be properly grateful once he'd grown tae the task—"

"But the plot is *foiled*, and because the English are suspeckit of being a part of it, the Russians fall oot of the alliance—and the Swedes come in."

"I'm tickled tae ken it. It must've been a torture fer the puir Swedes, the pipers a' screelin', and them no invited tae dance—"

"But then the Austrians finally make peace with the Sardinians—"

"Ah've ne'er heard of the animal—"

"And it's at this moment the French decide tae invade England."

Lachlan claps his hands, bringing a jailer to look in through the grated window. "I was feart they'd ne'er get aroond tae it."

"They prepared an invasion force tae sail from Dunkirk, tae be headed, at least in spirit, by the Prince Regent, Young Charles—"

"Yer Pretender," says Nipper Wilde.

"Our hope and joy, with the hooly mission of placing his father James back on the throne, whilst forcing the English tae withdraw their troops frae the continent in order tae fight us in the north."

"A bold strategy—"

"A brilliant secret plan, of which Ah heard countless versions," says Jamie. "Until a great storm rose up, wreckin' and scatterin' the entire fleet—"

"The Protestant Wind," says Nipper Wilde. "There was sellybrations 'eld over that, like it were the King's birfday."

"Sae instead, the French marched intae Flanders—"

"Which is . . . mair Dutchmen?"

"Of a sort. The French met with little resistance at first, while Frederic and his Prussians were taking over Bohemia."

"I won't even ax where that might be," says Lachlan. "And then?"

"And then King Louis of France is stricken with the smallpox and the French become distracted—"

"They're difficult enow when ye've got their full attention—"

"*But*—he recovers—"

"And there is rejoicing in the streets of Paris—"

"While Charles of Bavaria, who if ye remember, has been named Holy Roman Emperor by his allies—"

"But has yet tae lower his fanny ontae the royal chair—"

"—*dies,* and a new election becomes necessary."

"Dinnae they just give it tae his son?"

"No e'en considered. The French and the Prussians have their hands full, as they lay siege tae the city of Tournay, and who comes tae the rescue this time but the bluidy Duke of Cumberland, barely o'er twenty he is, commanding the Pragmatic Army at the Battle of Fontenoy, where our friend Cameron here also served with distinction."

"It was a slaughterhouse," says Cameron, his eyes closed.

"Leading tae an English retreat, and their sad recognition that they maun need mair troops tae prevail—"

"They tried ter press me inter the Foot, they did," says Nipper. "But the magistrate 'ad prior claim."

"And it is at this moment that our Charles Edward Stuart, the Prince Regent, decides tae land in the north of Scotland of his ain volition and with ainly a handful of sojers, expectin' a' the great Hieland clans tae gae oot fer him."

"Did ye e'er keek him in the flesh?" asks Lachlan.

"Briefly, and through a windae. He was ainly a pale stick of a lad, dressed in plaids, but still it made ma heart race."

"As we speak," asks Nipper, eager for clarification, "exactly 'oo is the bleedin' 'Oly Roman Emperor? Or Empress?"

"This remains tae be decided," says Jamie. "Cumberland and his murderers will be shipped back tae the Continent tae continue the argument."

"Then our stand, at best," says Lachlan, "was ainly a diversion?"

"Tae the French and the other belligerants, yes. But tae you and me—"

Lachlan shakes his head, troubled. "On Raasay, when we speak of 'the world'—*an saoghal*—tis rare that we signify owt that's not found betwixt North Ulst and Aberdeen. A' this that yer tellin' me—"

Jamie looks him deep in the eye. "If ye'd kent the hale of it, *seanachaidh*, dae ye think yer clansmen would still have come oot fer Charlie?"

Lachlan walks for a long moment while pondering this. "Tis our duty bairn on the islands tae obey our lairds and no ax questions," he says. "Tis well kent there, fer instance, that MacLeod of Skye was kept oot of the rebellion coz the Laird President caught him sellin' his ain people tae the plantations."

Cameron opens his eyes, shocked. "Selling MacLeods?"

"Them as was ahind in the rent. A laird has the right—"

"A laird has a responsi*bil*ity—"

"Perhaps he had his ain debts tae pay."

"That would do for a *mer*chant," says Cameron with some disgust. "We see half of Galway climbing over each other to enter the tobacco trade. But for a clan chieftain, a man of honor and tradition—"

Lachlan holds his hands up as if to defend himself. "A' Ah'm sayin' is twas well kent, but naebody cared tae speak of it abroad. Ah made a lovely verse aboot the first of the ships tae sail, but twould've meant the forfeit of ma heid tae sing it."

They make a full circuit around the cell before anyone speaks again.

"Face it, gents," muses Nipper Wilde. "Yer Monarchs and Emperors are the tides of the ocean, and the likes of us are nowt but grains of *sand*."

Micklejohn enters the room then, followed by a pair who by their rags are likely fellow prisoners, one of them with a tangle of chain looped over his shoulders.

"Pendergast and Nance," whispers Nipper Wilde, turning casually to watch them. "Whipshaw points and they're the boys as make it 'appen."

Micklejohn stands over Aeneas Cameron, still wearing the boots, britches, and waistcoat of a French officer. "This one," he says.

The two convicts are upon him, clapping rusty shackles to his wrists and ankles. Cameron does not resist, in fact holds out his hands for their convenience, staring haughtily up at the gaunt turnkey.

"Might I ask as to the motive for this encumberment?"

"It has been ordered," answers Micklejohn.

"Ah."

"However, easement of irons is only ten pounds. Per week."

"Ye're ainly squeezing him fer the money then," calls Jamie from the window. Nipper quickly eases from his side as Micklejohn crosses the room, men on the floor scooting away to make a path.

"We have punishment more fearsome than irons, here," he says.

Jamie holds his tongue. Micklejohn cocks his head to study him from crown to toe, as if measuring him for a suit of clothing.

"To the strongroom with him," he says, and briskly exits, stepping over the ones who can't shift quickly enough.

Pendergast and Nance advance then, smiling in anticipation, one full set of teeth between the two of them.

"Don't fight 'em, mate," advises Nipper. "They'll 'ave at ye with a bull pizzle."

"Such torture," spake MacGillivray.
Doth truly vex ma soul—

Lachlan calls out as Jamie is escorted from the garret—

Affronted by this bold display
They chucked him in the hole.

IF NOT FOR THE BROGUES DAVIE SUPPLIED HIM, JAMIE would not have survived the night. The rats crept in before the last of the light squeezed through the tiny chink above the door, and he feigned sleep, resting on his shoulder with shoe in hand, till the boldest ventured near enough to stun with a blow and then finish with several more. The other two fled then, squealing, somehow able to contort their bodies and escape out a gap in a rotten plank no wider than three of Jamie's fingers. He jammed the dead rodent into the space, put on the brogue, and stamped it in more securely, then spent the night either pacing—three short steps, turn, three short steps, turn—or not quite sleeping on the floor with his back against the wall and the brogue with the bloody heel at the ready.

There is no movement of the air within the cramped strongroom, and that thick enough with the reek of sewage to saw into rounds. The heat does not dissipate with the night—Jamie soaking through his clothes and attempting to breathe slowly, evenly, to dispel the panic that he'll suffocate. There are noises in the dark, scuttery things, and it feels a century between each tolling from St. George the Martyr, but eventually the oppressive details of the tiny chamber rematerialize, as well as sounds of human activity from the Borough High Street. He stares at the spot in the far corner for a long while, uncertain, then crosses to look. The vermin's corpse is gone.

It is still early, he believes, when the door is unlatched with much clanking and creaking and opened to reveal Whipshaw, bewigged and bedecked for a special occasion.

"Come along, if you're able," he says pleasantly. "We've got to bid farewell to some of your cohort."

A long open brewery wagon is waiting in front of the Marshalsea, several benches bolted to the floor within it, and the other Jacobite prisoners, less one, bolted to them. A long chain passes through the leg fetters of each on a bench to discourage individual enterprise. Jamie is secured at the rear of the wagon, seated next to Lachlan.

"Ye're a' reet?"

"I am that. And Cameron?"

"Still fast tae the wall in the garret. Has he nae friend or relation tae buy the irons aff him?"

"Them as would favor him is likely dead, captured, or on the shank in the crags with redcoats at their heels." Jamie looks around, bleary eyed, as the pair of Suffolk Sorrels are whipped into motion and swing the wagon onto the High Street. "Are we tae be run past the rabble again?"

Lachlan shakes his head. "They've a' gan ahead," he says, and indeed the street seems uncommonly inactive. "They're topping the Manchesters today."

Jamie had ridden through Carlisle shortly after the Prince and his army began their long retreat to the north, leaving his English followers, the Manchester Regiment, to garrison that city. He brought sealed orders for Colonel Townley, whom he had met once in Chartres.

"We're to be the chops you toss out of the hamper when you're trailed by a wolf," the colonel said on that day after glumly reading the orders. "I've less than three hundred at my disposal and Hamilton has even fewer in the Castle—barely a snack for the Crown's army."

Townley's men were already of a sullen humor, lounging about the town, ill-equipped for battle and feeling abandoned. They were barbers and linen drapers and stewards and tallow chandlers, many of them Catholic, with Townley, who had distinguished himself fighting for the French under the Duke of Berwick in the Rhine Valley, the only true military man among them. The Prince had offered him command of this assemblage of Stuart supporters who had come forward in Manchester while the Prince was still on the march toward London, and he accepted it with equanimity, if not enthusiasm.

"While the Prince's army were still in Scotland, the rebellion were only rumor, I minded my tongue with all and sundry," a rueful former publican with a rusted sword on his hip told Jamie. "But when it marched down to me very doorstep—what's an honest man to do?"

They are nearing Lambeth when they overtake a trio of horse-drawn sledges, really only rectangles of wattle fence, upon which the condemned men, two pairs and a trio gyved together for exhibit, are dragged from the New Gaol to Kennington Common. A few hundred Londoners, mocking but abstaining from open assault, follow along. Jamie recognizes only Townley, wearing a suit of black velvet that appears newly made. There are seven of them to be dragged on the traitor's course, all in the bloom of young manhood, all attempting to look straight ahead and not at their persecutors.

A cheer is raised as their procession enters the Commons, several hundred more spectators out for the festivity, with a company of guards creating a symmetrical hollow around the platform itself. The wagons bearing Jamie and those others whose day has not yet come are positioned close for viewing, while the condemned are dragged about the periphery of the Commons on their hurdles so all might have a closer look. A burly man dressed in white busies himself at firing a pile of faggots set close to a block formed from the stump of a tree with an oversized axe leaning beside it. Seven coffins are lined up in a row beyond this, and several nervous officials confer with each other behind their raised hands.

"The heidsman hasna a mask over his face," remarks Lachlan.

"Tis warm enough withoot ye stick yer heid in a sack," says Jamie. "He's an agent of the Crown, as well, and proud tae play his role in its preservation."

The next hour is taken up with various acts of devotion, those of the condemned who choose to speak more keen to pledge their souls to their Creator than to extol the righteousness of their fugitive Prince. Jamie's attention wanders—he sees a pair of young men holding strangely shaped shinty bats, as if their game has been interrupted by the solemn ceremony, no patch of ground sizeable enough to beat a rug left unpopulated at the moment. Vendors make their way through the crowd selling foodstuffs and toys depicting hanged men made of sticks and yarn. Finally the eight are led up upon the platform, each haltered with a noose, and linen caps pulled over their faces, one by one.

There is a tilt mechanism fitted to the long plank they stand upon—this is operated by a lever, which the executioner swiftly employs to send them on the first leg of their journey.

There is no real drop to it.

The hemp has been knotted so as to strangle rather than break the necks of its victims, who writhe and kick to the amusement of many and the horror of some in the morbid assembly. Townley is cut down first, clearly still alive, and carried to be laid on his back over the block. Whipshaw has appeared beside them, looking on with mild amusement, and Jamie and Lachlan take this as their cue to appear unimpressed.

"Bairn in Manchester is a greater treason than bairn in Argyll," says Jamie offhandedly. "Tis ainly a warning tae us frae the Crown."

"And the folk seem mair diverted than terrified."

"The tradition, of course," observes Whipshaw, "is for the traitor to view his own bowels torn out and tossed upon the fire."

A collective gasp now as the headsman takes up his axe and brings it down once, twice, three times without the desired effect, then quickly draws a knife and slits Townley's throat.

"A mon of some compassion, Ah see," says Jamie.

The headsman decapitates Townley with a large cleaver, the man's head bouncing once as it hits the ground.

Jamie could close his eyes. He has seen cattle and sheep slaughtered, has flayed rabbits and grouse himself, but those were only animals, the white bone and red flesh beneath their skin somehow different from what he's imagined to be the state of a man. He tries to watch through the eyes of Davie Falconer—what isn't anatomy is only meat, thinks Jamie, meat and blood and sinew and bone—

"God save King George!" cries the blood-spattered executioner, grasping Townley's severed head by the hair and raising it for the eyes of that worthy's subjects.

One of the Marshalsea prisoners, a tailor from Fife, faints and is held upright on the bench by the men chained beside him.

There is a cry of reaction from the throng with each new act of evisceration or dismemberment, bowels and heart pulled out of the open cavity of the body and thrown into the fire, much flailing with the axe to separate legs and arms from the torso. Smoke bearing the stench of burning organs wafts over them as the headsman carefully arranges the various pieces of Townley in the first coffin.

"I trust you gentlemen are suitably impressed," says Whipshaw as the headsman employs his various tools. "That head will be fixed to a spike on Temple-Bar, where it shall remain to instruct the public."

"And do they want the sheep's heid upon their table," says Jamie, eyes running with tears from the acrid smoke, "when they sit doon tae mutton?"

MOST DON'T EVEN LOOK UP. ASSUMING THE LADDERS are only there for repairs or in too great a hurry to wonder, they pass through the Bar, many with their robes flying around them, from Westminster to London, from London to Westminster, ignoring little Noddy on the ground with the basket and Alf up tying himself a secure purchase on the curved apex of the wall. He is used to being ignored by barristers, near invisible as he fixes whatever needs fixing in the Temple Inn, muttering his "Excuse me, Sir," and "Just a moment, please, gentlemen," working as quietly as the task will allow. Little Noddy is no trouble in this regard, his sister's boy simple and nearly mute, but able to pass a tool or hold the other end. Alf tolerates the work, but relishes the vocabulary. Surrounded by lawyers conversing, arguing their points, crowing over their triumphs every day, and bringing a bundle of new words, some even in Latin, to try out on Minerva every night.

Intemperate.

Perspicacity.

Emolument.

Altitude—

"Altitude" is the one that comes to mind at present.

"Nothing on the *roof,* is there?" he was careful to ask before accepting the janitor's position. The mere thought of heights is enough to make his palms sweat, and when he surrendered to Minerva's desire to move in from Dagenham it was with the understanding that a dwelling on the ground floor would be rented. It would have been simpler here, of course, to step through the window of the neighboring banking house onto the bridge level, but the manager there objected on political grounds. So two ladders it is—

"'Ow's the view up there?" shouts some wag in passing, and Alf does not answer, keeping his eyes firmly on the stone of the cap, on the iron spikes out in the middle of it, the highest point over the street far below.

This was certainly not presented as one of his duties when the employment was offered, but of course there was no foreseeing the necessity. As it was, he declined the mission till informed he would be fulfilling the King's personal desire, and that refusal would place his loyalties in question.

"Think of it as an honor," said his supervisor at the Inns, Mr. Chiswick.

Alf would prefer to navigate the curve of the roof on his rear, but he can hear that people are watching now and he doesn't care to add to the spectacle. Then there are the spikes to consider, nearly a dozen of them evenly spaced, with a human skull crookedly topping the one in the very middle. He has been instructed to use this as his centerpiece.

"For the symmetry," said Mr. Chiswick.

Alf crouches, anchored rope in hand, and shuffles ever so slowly up toward the center of the roof, carefully placing one foot, then the next, aware of a good-sized crowd gathering below but too terrified to look for them.

"Ye gonter stand on yer 'ead?" calls another man, and there is laughter. Alf has never been able to watch acrobats as they begin to climb, the very idea of a tightrope walker enough to suck the wind from his lungs.

Alf reaches the spike with the skull and sits to straddle it, facing London and Fleet Street, the Strand at his back. The skull appears to have been there a long while, missing several teeth and bronzed with exposure. He lifts the coil at the end of his safety rope from around his neck and drops it, not caring what passer-through might be hit. He looks to the building that rises up to the right—a women is staring straight at him from her fourth-story window, her expression somewhere between concern and curiosity. How people can live so high, even if they keep their curtains drawn—

Alf feels the tug on the rope from Noddy. He hopes the boy has tied the basket in proper balance, so that nothing will spill out. You can't assume Noddy will understand the point of any task, though from time to time he will surprise you. Just last week, Mr. Winkle, one of the older barristers who frequents the Temple Inn, mistook him for a page and sent him out for newspapers. Noddy returned with a half dozen, exactly as ordered, and blithely offered Winkle only half the change he was due. Alf pulls up the basket, surprisingly heavy, hand over hand.

He realizes, with it resting in his lap, that Mr. Chiswick has given him no instruction as to which direction the gentlemen should *face*. The skull is no indicator—rattling loosely, it could have been blown in circles any number of times over the years, and is currently regarding the tall building on the left with cocked head and empty eye sockets. Is this exhibition meant to reassure the citizens of London that the Crown is ever vigilant, or to awe the denizens of Westminster as they dare to enter the realm of the Law? Or both, since there remains the option of pointing one toward Fleet Street and the other toward the Strand?

Perhaps, Alf thinks, gingerly peeling the first one out of its sack, it is meant as an inducement to caution for the legal gentlemen who populate the Temple liberties—neglect your preparation, misplace your witnesses, argue insipidly before the bench, and your clients shall end up here.

London it will be.

He hears a wagon creak to a stop, hears a collective gasp, hears the first cries of "Traitor! Traitor!" as the head comes free. It has been well-bled and feels cold to the touch, like a pig's nob you might lug home from the butcher. No telling if this is Townley or Fletcher, even if he had ever seen the gentlemen in the flesh, and they are meant to have equal dominion over the Bar. He had imagined lifting it by the hair, like the Greek fellow with the serpent-tressed lady in the illustration. But there is not enough to get a grip on, so he holds the thing with his fingers on the forehead and thumbs under the cheekbones, leaning to fit the opening of the neck over the spike to his left, then wrestling it down till well-fixed, nose pointed straight down Fleet Street. He gets up into his crouching position again, lays his hand on top of the crown of the head and puts his weight to it. Mr. Chiswick was adamant on this point, that the spike be driven well into the brainpan, so that when the flesh begins to fall away—

"Ye should be ashamed of yerself!" shouts a woman from below, followed by other angry voices, several arguments breaking out. There must be several dozen stopped to watch now, by the sound of them, groupings on either side of the gateway. Alf has personally passed though the pedestrian arches every day for several years without looking up, and was surprised today to notice the statues in the niches, two on each side, that are now below his feet. Three long-dead kings and a queen, no doubt, and the skull on the very zenith a total wonder. If the point is to confront His Majesty's subjects, loyal or not, with the consequences of rebellion, a more down-to-earth location might be more effective—suspended over the main entrance to the Royal Theater in Covent Garden, for instance, for all the drama enthusiasts and greengrocers to ponder.

The second is easier now that he has a feel for it. Alf wonders if all the spikes have ever been occupied at once, and where any surplus heads were dispatched to. The woman is at it again—

"Hit's a bloody sacrilege, hit is! These belong with their corpuses, buried in the ground!"

More debate from below. The second head ends up pointing toward the woman in the window, who finally does pull her curtains closed, no longer pleased with her view, and Alf has to twist it right, the sound nearly bringing his supper up.

He is a bit dizzy sidling back off the curved roof, trying to focus on his feet and nothing beyond them. He backs down the first ladder to some applause and some jeers, his turn completed, cue the dancing monkey, then hands that ladder and the rope down to Noddy. The second ladder is easy, keep your eyes on the rungs, and there is another small round of applause as he reaches *terra firma*, his heart palpably beginning to slow a bit. He sees that Noddy has placed his cap on the sidewalk and people have left coins in it, a gleeful smirk on the boy's face.

"'Oo's that then?" asks the drayman from the cart that has stopped in the middle of the street, blocking the outgoing vehicles behind him.

"Two of them as was topped at Kennington t'other day," says Alf. "Jacobite rebels."

"Well, that'll teach 'em, won't it? Mucking about with kings. Keep yer 'ead *low*, that's my motto."

Alf steps back and cranes his neck to survey his handiwork. From here, with the naked eye, you can just tell that they had been men, or the heads of men, though the bare skull exhibits a good deal more expression. Neither of the gentlemen had their eyes open when drawn from the sack, and Alf, wondering if vertigo might continue after death, did nothing to remedy that state.

He and Noddy each take a ladder and head back toward the Temple Inn. A dark-looking fellow, possibly a Turk or a Jew, has set up a small table on the walk, laying an array of shopworn mariner's spyglasses upon it.

"See the notorious rebel chieftans up close!" he cries. "Only an 'aepenny a gander!"

Ab uno disce omnes—Virgil
TO THE TRUE PATRIOT
March 20, 1747

DEAR SIR
Though not a subscriber to any of our august political parties, abjuring their constant and purposeless petty contentions and rivalries, I remain a steadfast advocate of the Protestant faith in the highest of its many variations, *id est* the Anglican church, and a resolute supporter of the Divinely appointed Ruler of our much-blessed Kingdom. It is these characteristics (dare I say attributes?) that have occasioned much upset, not to mention sleepless nights, *in re* the present legal proceedings obliged by the ramifications of the late and deeply lamentable rebellion. When the outcome of that desperate contest was still uncertain, my thoughts sometimes led me to meditate upon what we were likely to expect should success attend the prospective ravagers of our country and usurpers of our rights. Nay, I had even gone so far as to suppose them actual victors, and such horrors I would wish on no man, whatever his race or nation.

Happily, such gloomy considerations have been vanquished through the valiant efforts of our soldiery,

> and the tasks of securing the hard-won peace and meting out just punishment to the malefactors responsible for the conflict are upon us. At first, I admit, I was highly critical of the ongoing trials, not only for their expense and waste of our legislators' valuable time and effort, but that the process seemed to *honor* those dishonorables with consideration they had not earned. To the gallows, I thought then, swiftly and without mercy, seeking rough justice and a return to pleasanter concerns. Fortunately I have since realized that these tribunals are held not for the benefit of the intriguers and turncoats before the Bench, but for ourselves, that the light of our jurisprudence, our Rule of Law, shines out like a beacon in a dark and savage world. Having no doubt regarding the eventual verdict that shall be reached, my misgivings now center on the *utility* of the sentence that must be rendered—

The Pamphleteer works by oil lamp, his children asleep in the next room. They are respectful of his work, playing quietly nearby in the daylight hours, understanding that he earns their bread through his scribblings, but they are so precious to him, such a joy, and so shipwrecked at the death of their dear mother that he cannot help but put aside quill and ink to engage them in some favored pastime. He is a colossus in their eyes, of course, though much maligned by others, unjust though they be. Yes, if you are one of Walpole's benighted admirers, the Pamphleteer appears to be an unequivocal and long-nosed Whig poltroon. Yes, he has been effectively banned from the stage by legal edict, being in fact one of the chief irritants inspiring the Theatrical Licensing Act that has put a muzzle on every playwright of a satirical bent. And yes, he is marrying his deceased wife's maid, who is presently with child. But he is still and all a patriot, and though too old at forty and too sickly by nature to shoulder a musket, he is willing and able to render his service with the pen—

> Public execution has been with us since the Romans established their province of Britannia, ever intended as not only just deserts for the troublemaker but as a caution to any tempted to follow in the path of outlawry and depredation. Neatly effective in the first case but, I venture, absolutely futile in the second. Have murders ceased? Thievery, blasphemy, unholy intercourse, all of these hanging offenses and duly endorsed, but they are as rife today, if not more prevalent, than in those Roman times. Of course there is the theatrical and rabble-rousing aspect of the ceremony, *ad captandum vulgas*, but beyond the low entertainment and opportunity for tinkers to vend their wares to a sizable, court-approved assembly, the execution itself, be it ever so grisly, makes only an ephemeral impression on the *hoi polloi*. I therefore offer a polite suggestion—

The Pamphleteer, like others of his breed, suffers a constant dearth of funds. *The Female Husband*, sixpence worth of scandal from the pen of Anonymous, sold well enough to stock the larder for a season, but with two offspring and a third on the way he must devise a larger piece—a novel, say—that excites the imagination of the reading public. Till then, this weekly diatribe. He suffers a minor pang that *The Patriot* owes its existence to the subsidy of certain of his friends in the Ministries, secretly buying out most of the copies and having them sent about the country to enlighten the masses, but even at three pennies a number his share amounts to little, and since the good gentlemen never instruct him as to what he should write—

Might we not improve upon the admonitory quality of the punishment and extend the agony of the justly condemned by placing them on display in the meanest of circumstances? The number of suicides reported from our various debt-houses and bridewells suggests that close confinement and loss of familiar company in themselves are a crushing burden on the spirit, but add to this the specter of broad and constant ridicule, and I believe we have a rung of Hell unimagined by the immortal Dante. What if the offenders of lower estate—Jacobite officers, renegade priests, minor chieftans—were kept as exhibits alongside the common beasts of commerce in an enclosure to be constructed at the Smithfield market? The likelihood that the Highlanders might infect the livestock with pests of the scrofulous ilk would be far outweighed by the public's opportunity to view and revile these ruffians whilst they select a likely calf for butchery. The expense would be small, the prisoners' sustenance that fit for swine and kine and no more, and the pedantic benefits immeasurable.

As for those Lords who allied themselves with the accursed House of Stuart in the recent debacle, the Lovats, Kilmarnocks, Balmerinos, *et alia*, their elevated rank should be recognized by their addition to His Majesty's menagerie at the Tower. Rare specimens, they, chained for perusal among the curiosities of five continents, perhaps neighbors to their fellow predators the wolves and the jackals. I am convinced that these worthies would soon be pleading for the axeman's block—

It would profit the Pamphleteer to become more famous, the

name of Fielding forever elevated above those of the crapulent denizens of Grub Street, but there is both craft and shelter in a *nom de plume*. The shammed letter to the editor is a wondrous sword, double-edged, enabling one to both lampoon the supposed author of the missive and also allow him or her *droit de farceur* over whatever target has been chosen. Thinkers during the Inquisition were adept at their "dialogues"—inventing a fictive advocate to propound, often with excellent reasoning, some heretical concept (and so much good sense was labeled heresy in that epoch), then brilliantly refuting it in their own name. No matter his friendship with Pitt and Lyttelton, the line between fame and notoriety (or even prosecution) is a fine one.

> As those entrusted with the care of exotic beasts will avow, the more ferocious the *genus* and the more recent the apprehension, the likelier the captive will be to soon lose appetite, grow lethargic, and quickly descend into indifference and death. To prevent this subversion of our design, I advise that the wretches be kept in their native dress, fed whisky and oatmeal once a month, and, when notably unresponsive, subjected to the ministrations of a Highland piper (one only, please) retained to stir them to greater activity. That the plaid and the pipe, as well as the Irish tongue, have been wisely now prohibited in our Kingdom will render this display all the more poignant and indelibly instruct the public, especially the young, that nothing in our world becomes extinct but for ample cause and the Lord's will.
>
> *Castigat ridendo mores*—
>
> Your respectful servant,
> Percival Whallop

Lovat, once the Auld Fox is finally run to earth, will forfeit his wigholder, of course, but perhaps the next time—and there will no doubt be one soon enough—the wanton bloodlust of Parliament and public will be somewhat diminished, with those with some memory of the Pamphleteer's forays into satire wary not to become the object of their earlier derision.

The Pamphleteer puts Percival Whallop to bed, then tiptoes to peek in on his other creations. Sleeping peacefully. As recounted in the letter, he actually experienced a number of daydreams, morbid reveries, really, at the time that the Pretender had crossed the border and those generals and their troops not contesting the French in other corners of the globe seemed to be stumbling over each other rather than stopping him. Plaid-wearing hillskippers in the streets, himself dragged from his children, royal statuary pulled down and replaced by enormous papist crosses—he did not exaggerate these nightmares too awfully much in *The Patriot*. But the public demands novelty—another few heads to roll, a shipload or two of malcontents off to the Americas, and it will all soon be but a memory, and thus not worth his bookseller's ink.

A novel, then, something epic, but in prose, and comical on the surface—

NOSEWORTHY, THE SOLICITOR, IS LESS THAN SANGUINE about Jamie's prospects.

"Colonel Townley, yesterday's unfortunate recipient of the King's pleasure, fought for some years for the French crown, and indeed held a commission in their army," he states. "All of which, rather than affording him any immunity to prosecution, was held much in his disfavor."

They sit in the taproom on the masters' side of Marshalsea, a concern operated by a former prisoner there. Completely unfettered, to

Jamie the moment is thrillingly redolent of actual freedom, despite Pendergast and Nance sitting over ale at a nearby table.

"But I ne'er led a troop on English soil," he protests.

"But you did serve as a courier, and importuned more than one recalcitrant chieftain to join the fray on the Pretender's behalf."

"Aye, but nane committed tae arms—"

"If incompetence were a defense, your whole sorry lot would merit acquittal."

Noseworthy is a self-professed Whig and loyalist, procured for Jamie by his medical friend in Edinburgh, "who prudently wishes to remain *in clandestinus* given the current political tension in that fair city." He is a tall, hatchet-faced man of middle age who wears his own hair and smells of *eau de cologne.*

"You studied law, I believe?"

"Scots Law, aye—"

"I'm afraid you'll find very little precedent in your favor in the statutes covering treasonable behavior. Of course, the law is not hostage to statutes. Do you have any particular friends who are highly placed here in the south? No conduit to the Duke of Newcastle, for instance?"

"A' that I ken iv the gentleman," says Jamie, "is tae wish him ill."

Noseworthy sighs, rubs between his eyes. "When you were apprehended after the debacle at Culloden, did you attempt to fight to the death?"

"Nae."

A decision Jamie began to rue only when the third Manchester man cut down from the gallows, pronounced dead and not sentenced for beheading, regained full consciousness as he was being eviscerated.

"Then I don't see the point of any displays of defiance during the legal procedures that lay ahead. You will be taken before the Special

Commission for arraignment, at which time your indictment will be read and you will be requested to enter a plea. I would strongly advise that you admit to guilt and surrender yourself to the mercy of the Court."

"And if I dinnae recognize their authority tae—"

"Makes no difference in the outcome of the hearing, unless you are unwise enough to broadcast such a view. Your father was out in the '15, I believe?"

"He was—"

"Another black mark against you. There are witnesses who have already been deponed—a secretary of the Prince's, a certain Murray of Broughton—"

"What of Murray?"

"He has chosen to turn the King's evidence."

Murray was supposed to meet the French ships that put in at Borrodale, to transfer the gold they were to bring—nearly forty thousand pounds was promised—to finance the rebellion. Jamie wonders how much Noseworthy knows of his success—

"As has a gentlemen known as Captain Vere—"

"Vere is a fecking liar! He's kenned fer a scoundrel wherever he's set his foot."

"More's the pity for you. When it comes to perjury, give me a man without principle every time."

"And if Ah do plead guilty?"

Noseworthy sighs, answering carefully. "There will be . . . opportunity . . . to inform the Court of mitigating circumstances supporting an appeal for clemency before you are sentenced. I have letters extolling your character from two of your professors at Edinburgh, there is your youth to consider, the fact that you—as far as is known—took no life in the course of your activities—"

"Is there no a mon tae be *bought*, then?"

The solicitor is not discomfited by the suggestion.

"Your medical friend has supplied me with only enough to insure your comfort—your relative comfort—till the dispensation of your case is complete. Even the most basely corrupted justice of the peace would require more to alter his course—"

"So there's naething mair I can do."

"If you have faith in the power of prayer," says Noseworthy, gathering his papers and rising to go, "I advise you to petition our Savior's intervention."

WHIPSHAW IS IN THE GARRET ROOM WHEN JAMIE IS REturned there, supervising the replacement of the broken window.

"The cost of this will be dunned from your rations," he announces to all present.

Nipper Wilde snorts a laugh. "As if ye want cause to steal more of what the society folks send us."

Jamie sees that Cameron is still shackled to the wall, a new prisoner with a bloodied face sprawled on the floor beside him.

"What's yer fee fer easement of irons?" he calls out to Whipshaw.

"By the day or by the week?"

Jamie turns to look at the gaoler. "Fer the length of his residence here."

"There's no telling how long—"

"He'll die in chains or be hanged within the month," say Jamie. "Ye ken that well."

Whipshaw calculates for a moment. "It could be done for fifteen pounds."

The solicitor had paid ten to release Jamie from the strongroom, where he had been returned after the executions. He had cautioned prudence and patience, citing the surety of more desperate predicaments to come.

"Yer familiar with Noseworthy?"

Whipshaw smiles. "He is representative for some of our guests on the masters' side."

"He'll settle with ye, then. I want them aff afore the night falls."

The gaoler offers him an ironic bow. "Delighted," he says, and exits with the glazier.

"I thank you," says Cameron when they are gone. "I've no feeling in my hands nor feet."

The bloody man beside him raises his head, squints through swollen eyes. "He's a saft-hearted ane. Has been since he's a wee barra."

It is Jamie's brother.

"IT APPEARS," SAYS BROTHER DOUGAL AFTER HE HAS been embraced and helped to a more comfortable perch on fresh straw next to Jamie, "that ye've come intae a fortune. French gold, nae doot."

"It's me friend Davie, but nae fortune."

"I'd hoped ye'd been able tae jink around the red-coated gentry and nipped intae the heather. But here ye be."

"And yersel'?" asks Jamie. "Ye've been ill-used, frae the look of yer gob."

"They kept me in the Inverness Tolbooth fer a spell, a foot in Death's door, then it was shipboard with a regiment of fellow unfortunates—cabined, cribbed, and confined. Hoo's the scran in here?"

"Water gruel with a rumor of beef," offers Nipper, who has been listening. "Unless ye can pay, and then it's a guinea a week."

Dougal winces as he shifts on the straw. "Sich opulent lodgings, ye canna expect them tae feed us as well."

"The heat is murderous."

"Och, I'll be blythe tae bide here awheel. I dunna fare well on the sea—makes me cowk."

"And this?" Jamie indicates the blood dried on Dougal's swollen lip and chin.

"A trifle," says Dougal. "It seems I made mysel' obnoxious tae the dobbers that brang me here, and one of them fetched me a crunt on ma napper, then the baith of them drug me up the stairs by the feet. It's been mair of the same since we baucled the fight at Culloden."

"Ye were wounded?"

"It feels like the blades is still within me."

"I tried tae join ye, but—"

"Dinnae fash yersel' o'er that, lad. Ye were a'ways a canny one, and tis wrang tae waste such talent on a battlefield. Ye served us better as a go-between."

Jamie knows this is meant as a compliment of his diplomatic abilities and not to disparage his skill as a fighting man, which remains entirely unproven.

"We were sae close tae hame, at the end," he says.

"Did ye see it? Did ye see Dunmaglas?"

They roamed the whole of it as boys, flatlands and crags, fishing along the Findhorn, climbing Bein Dubcharaidh to find the nests of the golden eagles, hunting in the braes of Strathnaim for pheasant, grouse, hares, occasionally creeping around the old mansion house where their father was born. He would launch into his long stories, ale on his breath and a lost look in his eye, reciting the genealogy of centuries, who married who and begat a third, who feued what parcel of the land to another on what date, who, when pinched, was forced to wadset another portion to a neighbor whose spawn never left it, always ending with the disaster of the '15. Dozens of his tenants, bound to follow him into that adventure, were taken at Preston and transported to the West Indies to be sold as slaves—he would name every one, rank and file—and then of course the land itself forfeited.

"Every stane ye trod upon in yer wanderins," he would say, "is a MacGillivray stane, every drap of water that flows down the burns, every field and farra."

Their great-grandfather, called The Mountain because of his size, had signed the Clan Chattan bond in 1664, swearing that he and his charges would support the MacIntosh against their rival Evan Cameron. Their grandfather had been mortally wounded in a clan war at Lochaber, and their father, who could lift a stone-hewn quern over his head till the year of his death, after the '15 lived as a vagabond on the lands that had come to him by blood, renting poorer and poorer cottages from the MacIntosh who had bought them from the impecunious Earl who'd been granted them by the Crown after the Defeat and subsequent Acts of Attainder. Walking with him was a journey into struggles and scandals long past, a rest by a spring where he had courted their mother, a walk up Tomnashangan, Ant Hill, where a tenant's wife had been taken by the fairies and kept for a year to dance an endless reel with them. He took them to the upright slab of rock near Easter Gask, squatting to study the druidical markings, circles and spirals carved upon it, and point out the one discolored edge.

"MacGillivrays through the ages hae come here afore a battle," he told them, "tae sharpen their blades."

It had all been theirs, as boys—not the rents or the harvest, of course, but the joyous run of it, the feeling that the glens and the waters knew them, welcomed them, were bound to them by more than their mere presence.

"I rode through on the way to Culloden," Jamie tells his brother. "In the wet and the wind."

"I'd love tae set ma een on it once mair, in any weather."

"I've a solicitor," Jamie offers. "No that he advises I demand a trial, but—"

"We're fair knackered, Jamie, face the truth of it. But we've found each other noo, and that's a blessing I dinnae expect."

"NOT HAVING THE FEAR OF GOD IN THEIR HEARTS," DEclares the crown advocate, Sir John Strange, stooping a bit under an impressive but cumbersome new wig, "or having any regard for the duty of their allegiance, but being moved and seduced by the instigation of the devil, as false traitors and rebels against our said present sovereign lord the King, their supreme, true, natural, lawful, and undoubted sovereign lord—"

Noseworthy sits at the rear of the gallery in the Town Hall, which has been converted into a court for the proceedings. He has only two clients, brothers, among the two dozen standing at the bar, the Special Commission dispensing with individual arraignment in the interest of expediency. Various scribblers for the scandal sheets and polemic magazines sit near him, hoping for an outburst of contumely, if not an escape attempt, to report. A matter of morbid distraction is the constant hammering outside, though it is not a hangman's scaffold being erected but several theatrical booths for the coming Southwark Fair.

"—entirely withdrawing that cordial love, true and due obedience, fidelity, and allegiance which every subject of right ought to bear toward our said present sovereign lord the King—"

Strange is laying it on with a trowel, but such verbal obeisance is to be expected in times of regal anxiety, each man wishing to be overheard as more a Loyalist than the next—

"—also devising most wickedly and traitorously to change and subvert the rule and government of this King and to put and bring our said present sovereign lord the King to death and destruction—"

He'll need to ride the old boy a bit at lunch, perhaps suggest that more effort be taken in defining the legal issues than in polishing the King's buckles—

"—and to raise and exalt the person pre*tend*ed to be Prince of Wales to the crown and royal state, and to the imperial rule and government of this kingdom."

A rather long silence, Judge Heathcoate staring at the crown advocate from behind the bench, a hastily erected wooden placard bearing the Royal Arms hung on the wall behind him. Noseworthy notes that the Scottish unicorn, sinister supporter to the quartered shield, is yet restrained by a golden chain.

"We charge treason, Your Honor."

"Very well." Heathcoate, seated on what is normally the Lord Mayor's perch, supported by a statue of Justice on one side and of Wisdom on the other, tilts his enormous head to regard the prisoners. "You've heard the charge. Your name will be called and you will be required to enter a plea. Kindly attempt to do so audibly, and, if possible, in the English tongue."

He knows that perhaps a third of them have no English and have understood not a whit of Sir John's performance. Under the present circumstances that is considered their failing and not the Court's responsibility, and they are only here on account of their rank or an unfortunate drawing in the lottery.

Names are called and men make their pleas, many with a well-rehearsed "Guilty, Your Honor, and I beg the King's Mercy." The roll moves down the line, guilty, guilty, guilty, till his Highland brothers are reached.

"Guilty," states the older one, Dougal, rather more loudly than his comrades have done, "and fair proud of it!"

Murmurings and scribbling from the ink-stained wretches of the press. Noseworthy can imagine the diatribes, mostly anti-papist cant, that will be launched. The Scotch are a haughty, deluded, and self-destructive race, he muses, though perhaps more worth the effort of correction than the Irish.

"I demand a trial," says the younger, Jamie. "I wish tae look ma accusers in the eye."

Or perhaps not.

More murmurs and scribbling as Snodgrass, his barrister, looks back in a panic. It is an inconvenience, yes, but one must always prepare as if battle will be engaged, even though most cases are settled by cloakroom diplomacy. Noseworthy is accustomed to advising the better class of business cheats and men of property sued by other men of property, a group undoubtedly less principled than young MacGillivray but with a superior sense of what will serve in a court of law. A case of some interest except for its inevitable result, he thinks, and he is certain that Sir John will advise him as to how fervent a defense can be presented without damaging his own position.

Another important aspect of the trade never touched upon in the law colleges.

The prisoners, duly arraigned, are marched out past him on their way back to the dens of iniquity where they are kept. Whipshaw of the Marshalsea is not the most avaricious of the proprietors, only the most adept at turning a profit from every aspect of his concern—Titty Doll's, the restaurant lodged on the ground floor of the masters' side, even serves a creditable steak. Acton, Whipshaw's predecessor, had been tried for cruelty and manslaughter, and would certainly have been convicted had not his pet prisoners, hardened criminals who he employed to rule the sponging house in lieu of having to pay warders, chosen to testify in his behalf.

The Law is a lady, Noseworthy is fond of telling his acolytes, whose undergarments bear little scrutiny.

It is the older brother, Dougal, who catches his eye on leaving. Something of a stalwart within the rebel military, his chances for avoiding the gallows are practically nil, perhaps explaining his rather pathetic show of defiance.

"Do what ye can fer the lad," he says, almost apologetically. "He warrants a square go."

THEY ARE ALL ABUZZ AT THE WHITE HART WHEN THE Moralist steps in.

"If the Devil were an elderly man," Dora is muttering as she clears the remains of somebody's meal from the long table and rolls her eyes toward the upstairs apartment, "that's wot 'e'd look like."

An unusual number of men in uniform lounge about the entrance to the Inn, smoking and chatting with each other, the Moralist giving them a friendly nod and noting the face of a pox-ravaged corporal. Striking in a painting with the color to bring it out, but once it's been through the engraver's hands—

"To which of our political gentlemen are you referring?" he asks, a regular here and in no need of introduction.

"Hit's the Auld Fox," says Tom Puffin, who minds the Inn till the shopkeepers and scriveners return from the city after their working day. Tom points to the room above him. "Carried down from the 'Ighlands ter face the consequences."

"Lovat? Here?"

"We don't discriminate, sir. As well 'e's got an official escort."

There is a young lieutenant who needs a word or two, and then the Moralist is brought up. Lord Lovat sits for the ministrations of a barber, face and head covered with lather. When he sees the Moralist his wide mouth curls with delight, and he makes a great effort to stand for an embrace.

"Hogarth! Well met!"

The Moralist's arms fall far short of enveloping the Lord's bulk, and he steps away with lather on his cheek.

"My Lord. You look—"

"I look a fright. I've been bundled and trundled like a side of beef, hauled ontae ships with a sling like cargo, suspended betwixt plodding beasts in a kind of cradle—but for all that I still draw breath, which is the point of this brief sojourn—the Crown is terrified that I'll expire from age and ailment before they can do away with me."

"I have been following the news of your—your difficulties—"

"Lend me a hand, here—"

The Moralist and the barber help the old man back into his chair.

"They've got me treed, this time, I'm afraid. But I ran 'em across half the map."

Lovat was his favorite of the Scotch lords in London, generous, funny, a lover of gossip and pretty barmaids. An admirer of the Moralist's work as well, his comments about the *Progress* series very perceptive—nothing in the plethora of detail escaped him.

"You're too late to invite to dine with me," says the Auld Fox. "And I must confess I am much reduced as a host. They've taken all my silver—"

He has an amazing ear, Lovat, able to speak like an English gentleman when required, ready to drift into Scotch for a joke or to make a countryman more at ease, fluent in French, versed in Latin. This linguistic dexterity has no doubt been of service in his many intrigues.

"May I sit with you a while?"

"A pleasure, on my word. But keep your weapons sheathed until my tonsorial friend here has finished his business."

Lovat has always made much of the Moralist's satirical abilities: "a pen sharper than any dagger."

"I am sorry to see you in this situation," says the Moralist, watching the barber quickly shave the Lord's head. Always the best policy if one is to affect a wig, as almost everyone down to the butcher's boy is doing these days, as a precaution against the various crawling things that yearn to dwell in them.

"I suppose," the Moralist continues, cautiously, "now that it is over, and revealed to be a folly—"

"The great comic personages of the stage believe themselves exemplars, heroes—"

He brought his friend Garrick to meet the Auld Fox once, and the comedian walked away from it muttering about Falstaff and Richard Three, though the Lord was not a fulsome admirer of Shakespeare.

"I dinnae fash masel' tae be snoolin' aboot airin' ma woes tae the spectators," he complained of the many soliloquies found in that master's work, laying on the Scotch for effect. "Just dirk the mon or make awa' with yersel' and be doon with it."

"Yes," says the Moralist. "My own father decided to gamble our family's meager fortune on the establishment of a coffeehouse in St. John's Gate where only *Latin* was spoken."

Lord Lovat laughs with his prodigious belly, the barber holding his razor away to avoid cutting him.

"A novel idea—"

"And so he still maintained when I'd visit him in the Fleet."

"Ensnared in a sponge house?"

"For five years."

"There's a score of men as owes me money, but I'd never stoop to gaoling them. Leave them out where they may work the debt off, and until then—" he winks and holds his palm up, then closes his fist, "I own their souls."

The barber wipes the last of the lather away and Lovat calls for his gillie. "My coat and wig, Tweedie! And look sharp!"

A man well past his prime with a severe limp appears to dress and coif the chieftain. Though it is not cold in the Inn, the Auld Fox has several layers of clothes on, his stockings lumpy, his immense girth exaggerated. The coat, if rigged to a mast, could propel one to back to the Hebrides.

There is some adjusting of the wig before his Lord is satisfied, Tweedie apparently new to that particular task. Through the open window they can hear the soldiers and constables laughing.

"Quite a carnival, they'll make of it," says Lovat. "And I'm the dancing bear. Come ahead, then—draw your blade."

"A portrait?"

"I'd be honored."

The Moralist turns the sketchpad sideways to honor the bulk of the man, begins to draw with a piece of charcoal. His good friend the Pamphleteer, scourge of papists and Jacobites, will not approve unless the portrayal is vicious, but that won't be necessary. No series of drawings, no *Clansman's Progress*, can surpass what is all there in this face—intelligence, humor, greed, wickedness, pride—wide as a pumpkin and still lusty for whatever is on offer. And the body—whatever horses hauled him from the north must be well jaded if not dead of the accomplishment.

"I could have just made a conjecture," says Lovat, leaning forward avidly as he speaks. "Bet my fortune, my life, on one king or another like any brainless chub at a cockfight. But no, that won't get you through the world. Does a captain peek at the sky, set his sails, and leave them thus throughout the storm? You have to ride the beast, ever sensitive to the wind, or it's bound to turn and drown you."

"You believed the Pretender could triumph?"

"If he'd had the sense to wait for French boots on Scots soil, if he'd been content to stay in the north and forget the Three Thrones, if I'd been able enough to join the campaign instead of learning of it in retrospect through visits and correspondence—"

The Auld Fox ticks off each one of these ifs with a fat finger to his thumb, a gesture the Moralist quickly captures, the hands as alive as the countenance—

"Forbes sending me daily warning from Inverness, with his gillie MacLeod pitching in from Skye, while the Prince kept insisting thousands were waiting for my commitment, the young hotbloods in the hills restless to fight on one side or the other, my dear Simon caught between as well—"

The old man shakes his head. "If I'd sent my Frasers to the Crown, what would I have now? A traitor's name on the lips of my dearest friends and a cursed legacy for my son. Simon, twelfth Lord Lovat, a pennyboy to the Whigamores of London."

He suddenly looks heavy, Lovat, his body a burden rather than the reward for his indulgent life. The Moralist can add the filigree later, long practice allowing him to see a detail on paper before he has drawn it.

"I am nearly finished," he says, shading detail into the stockings.

"As am I," smiles Lord Lovat, leaning back in a chair that barely supports him. "Castle Dounie looted, burnt to the ground, my lands and titles forfeited, my son held in Edinburgh Castle with no hint of his fate—" he gestures toward the Moralist's sketch. "This may be all that's left of me."

"MAY IT PLEASE YOUR LORDSHIP, AND YOU, GENTLEMEN of the Jury, I am of counsel on the side of the prosecution against the prisoner at the bar, who stands indicted for levying war against the King, in his realm, which is declared to be high treason by the express words of the Statute of the 25th—"

One must always keep in mind that the jury, whatever their various backgrounds, knows nothing. Well versed in rumor, perhaps, even having some acquaintance with the particulars at hand, they must nevertheless be considered lost children to be guided along a somewhat circuitous path to an inevitable destination. Judge Heathcoate has heard this opening from him many times now, so Strange directs his peroration completely to the twelve wise men—

"And on this occasion," he tells them, "the matter be submitted to the consideration of you, Gentlemen of the Jury, will be plain and easy, for you will not be involved in difficulties that attend the unraveling of dark and intricate plots, carried on by fictitious names, cant words and cyphers, the result of private and midnight transactions, nor in attending what the law calls interpretive or constructive levyings of war, which may be matters of doubt and difficulty, but we are only called upon to deliver a plain, simple question of *fact*—"

Though he has numerus witnesses to call upon, none can claim to have seen the young man fire a shot or strike a blow, and anticipating some claim to foreign commission as a defense, he strikes at its underpinnings—

"That *fact* being whether the prisoner at the bar is one of those who joined in the late rebellion or not. It is with infinite gratitude and pleasure I call it the late rebellion, since I think that by the blessing of God, his Majesty's paternal care of his people, and the prudent, cautious, and intrepid behavior of his Royal Highness the Duke of Cumberland, we have all reasonable foundation to think this wicked rebellion is at an end."

A murmur of approval from the gallery, and Sir John can see the third juror from the right, front row, a Smithfield cattle broker, mouth, "Hear, hear." One attempts to foster the sense that prosecution and jury have an important job to do together, that they are, depending on which judge is presiding, perhaps the only fourteen rational men in the courtroom—

"In order to bring the prisoner at the bar to justice, he is charged, first, to have assembled with a great multitude of traitors and rebels, armed and arrayed in warlike and hostile manner, with colors displayed, drums beating, pipes playing—"

The Scotch pipes have proven to be something of a bugbear for London juries, the thought of their screeching provoking images of savagery and violence, perhaps even eliciting thoughts of the three days of incoherent panic at the news of the Pretender's almost bloodless conquest of Manchester on his southward march. First the menacing drone, then the banshee wail, and finally a hirsute, tartan-clad behemoth with his claymore at your neck. Strange will at some point remind them that the instruments have been banned by Royal Decree—

"Second—to have actually armed, arrayed, and disposed himself in such manner—"

He has the deposition from the officer who disarmed and apprehended MacGillivray, and Captain Vere will swear to have seen a pistol in the lad's possession. Vere has done a great deal of swearing in the last several weeks, and fortunately this jury has not been privy to any of it. No Garrick he, the captain has a manner that does not inspire confidence in his veracity, a shallowness to his affect. When stating his name and address one feels he has a dozen possibilities to choose from—

"And finally—to have been an instrument in both the preparation and the levy of this cruel and public war against our King in his realm."

The myrmidons who Sir John sends throughout the city have not the perspicacity to understand the messages they deliver, even if they should condescend to open and read them, but apparently this young rebel has been to university and will be hard-pressed to argue he was a courier innocent of the plot that was unfolding about him. And should his familiarity with the law seduce him into a desire to direct his own defense—well, it is always fascinating to watch a man eviscerate himself.

Geoff Noseworthy's man, Snodgrass, rises, his voice more of an oboe than Sir John's throaty bassoon.

"Your Lordship, Gentlemen of the Jury, I must express my heartfelt concurrence with the sentiments of the Crown's representative concerning the end of hostilities. We are indeed fortunate to live under the protection of such a wise and forceful ruler."

He is the most intelligent of Noseworthy's barristers, the most logical, chosen no doubt in view of Heathcoate's antipathy toward emotional outburst and calls to sentiment—

"However, we must remember that although *inter arma enim silent legis,* the conflict is now happily at an end, and we can once again apply the more humane and just characteristic of the law to the unfortunates who were drawn into the Pretender's cause."

Victims, all of them, pressed, dragged even, into service by their bellicose chieftains, duped, extorted, merely out searching the glen for lost lambs when of a sudden the entire rebel army appeared and swept them into battle—

"The young man at the bar, compelled into folly by Highland fable and imprudent elders, ventured abroad, attending the Scots College in Paris, where, under the influence of *Jes*uits—"

A worthy thrust, the average English juryman believing these clerics nothing less than the devil's most adept subordinates, able to bewitch the dull and unwary. But the boy is not even a Catholic—

"—he was drawn deeper into conspiracy, flattered and slyly remunerated till he became emissary to those dark forces who so recently held our kingdom in peril."

A father in the '15, a brother gory with the blood of valiant royal troopers—this is no corrupted innocent but a traitor born. And it has already been established, in the last month's parade of *pro forma* convictions, that a commission in the army of a foreign state does not entitle the holder, being an Englishman (which as of the Act of Union includes the Scotch) to be treated as a prisoner of war. The French Gambit has heretofore only served actual Frenchmen, many of whom have already been exchanged, leading, no doubt, to some just-redeemed infantryman captured on the Rhine raising a tankard of ale to their idiocy in a Cheapside public house at this very moment—

"These parties, Frenchmen, papist Italians, and yes, disgraced and exiled Scotsmen with aspirations to perfidious usurpation, so filled his head with treacherous fantasy that his rational understanding of what is countenanced under our law, not to mention what is moral and *right*, was gradually eroded, and though the beneficiary of some education, he began to *think* like a foreigner."

Ignorancia juris non excusat, as you very well know, muses Sir John, wondering if this is the best Noseworthy has to offer—

"But fortunately for us all, as our esteemed prosecutor has pointed out, the rebellion came to nothing, ill designed and badly executed, and my client's part in it was never played—he was apprehended a league shy of the battlefield at Culloden and in any case would not have arrived until after its glorious conclusion. Gentlemen of the Jury, we judge men by their actions in this country, not by what lies in their hearts."

Sir John has to smile. *Cogitationis peonam nemo patitur*—he's not positing innocence but incompetence. A novel stratagem, which will make for a livelier afternoon than expected—he'll have to thank Noseworthy for the diversion when they meet at the Serjeant's Arms. It won't serve, of course—there is ample evidence of MacGillivray's energetic efforts to become involved in the fray, and if needed he can call on Fraser, who he was hoping to reserve for the trial of Lord Lovat, to recount the particulars of the lad's entreaties to the Auld Fox to take a more active role in the rebellion. It will want some instruction to the jury as to the legal niceties, though he imagines most of them firmly *do* believe in persecuting men for what lies in their hearts.

As Snodgrass sits, Sir John happens to catch the eye of young MacGillivray, and it is the most remarkable thing. Not malice, not the dull glower of incomprehension, but a frank and personal gaze, as if they might be persons to share a conversation or a meal. The lad is a fanatic—no other explanation for a man of any intelligence becoming entangled with the Stuarts and their forlorn Cause—but the look seems so honest, so calm, so unembarrassed by his paucity of defense. "But for the fortunes of war," it seems to declare, "you and I would be standing with our positions reversed."

The Law is a game fashioned by philosopher-kings, muses Sir John, and determined at the point of a sword.

THEY ARE MUSTERED IN THE YARD FACING THE KING'S Bench, joining the Jacobite prisoners from there as well as nearly fifty more brought over from the New Gaol, prodded into rows and their names taken. Lachlan is behind the MacGregor, whose Christian name is Fergal, and thus finds it difficult to see what their captors are up to in the front. Fergal seems to have remained a bit cracked since his ordeal shackled to the corpse—something in his eye, the way he mutters constantly to himself.

The MacGillivray brothers and Aeneas Cameron have been left behind, "not being Gentlemen or Men of Estates, but above Common men" and therefore destined for the more particular attentions of the Crown, with Jamie fairly treading on the tiger's tail by demanding his day in court. This ceremony, however, is in the charge of a glowering hulk of a lieutenant, nose in the air as if detecting a foul odor.

"As your name is called," he announces, "you will step forward and draw one slip of paper from a hat containing many. If you receive a paper with a black ball scribed upon it, you will be separated from your fellows and appointed for trial. If you receive a blank paper, you will be allowed to petition for the King's Mercy without trial and suffer transportation from this realm."

In their many idle hours this possibility has been much commented on, with horrible stories of slaver's whips on steamy tropical plantations or mutilation and death at the hands of red Indians circulated by men who "have heard," though none has ever been there nor met a transport, with return to the Kingdom proscribed by death. Lachlan, born on an island, hopes that whatever new situation he might be brought to will be near the sea.

"I might add," continues the lieutenant, "that we have arranged the papers so that roughly one out of every twenty of you shall be held to trial. You are in the hands of Providence."

A sergeant begins to calls out names, prisoners stepping forward to reach into the capacious, fur-trimmed bonnet that Whipshaw from the Marshalsea has volunteered, each pulling out a scrap of paper, glancing at it quickly, then handing it to a clerk standing behind a barrelhead that has been set up for his listkeeping. Lachlan bends around big Fergal to see as the fourth man called is pulled aside by the sergeant after surrendering his paper.

"Ferguson, Alexander," the clerk intones, scratching pen to ledger. "Blackballed."

Pell-mell ye rushed tae battle as their volleys rent the air
A ball was meant tae kill ye, but it missed ye by a hair
Sae sure the Laird had spared ye
Ye left that bluidy stage
With nae idea that fatal ball awaits ye on a page

There is shelter in verse, distance, the phrases dulling the sound of flesh hacked by steel, the cries of men, the sudden, deadly shriek of wayward artillery. To sit and observe from a height, even if your mortal body is left helpless amid the carnage—

Ye've gien yer a' fer Scotland, survived the final stand
Sich reckless acts of valor should be knane throughoot the land
But one man oot of twenty
Will dangle by the neck
Condemned noo by a drap of ink nae bigger than a speck

"MacLeod, Lachlan," reads the sergeant from his list.

Lachlan steps forward. There are three men in the condemned line already, and he tries to calculate his chances, closing his eyes to reach into Whipshaw's beaver hat. He opens them to see the verdict—

The paper is blank, blank as a clear summer sky over Raasay.

A sky that bodes fair weather, that exudes a healing light
Nae black mark clouds the future, nor defiles the virgin white
Like westward flocks wind-driven, betimes we'll blindly soar
Till Time and Fate deposit us
On what benighted shore?

WHEN JAMIE IS BROUGHT BACK UP TO THE GARRET AT Marshalsea, Dougal is waiting for him, having been sentenced that morning with Cameron and three others who had pled guilty.

"What did he say to you?" Jamie asks.

Dougal frowns down at his brother and puts on his best English accent. "Let the several prisoners above-named return to the gaol from whence they came—and from there they must be drawn to the place of execution—and when they come there they must be severally hanged by the neck, but not till they be dead, for they must be cut down alive—then their bowels must be taken out and burnt before their faces—then their heads must be severed from their bodies, and their bodies severally divided into four quarters—and these must be at the King's disposal."

Jamie looks to find Cameron, sitting in a corner with his head in his hands.

"King's disposal, is it?" continues Dougal. "I wonder what the gowkie German bastart will do with them? Ma quarters, I mean. Dangle them o'er the bed he crawls intae tae kip at night? Feed them tae the hounds—?"

"He read me the same act."

Dougal grins. "And here I'd thought they'd ask ye intae their Parlyment. Convicted, ye say?"

Jamie shrugs. "Twas worth the bother I caused them. And if ma eyes could spit fire that fecking Vere would be a cinder."

"There's still hope," says Lachlan, sidling closer to them from the group of men not lotted for trial. "Yer not hung till yer toes leave the ground."

Dougal looks to Jamie, raising his eyebrows. "And what patch of thistle did this wee brownie hop oot from?"

"He's a *seanachaidh*."

"Och." Dougal lays a hand on Lachlan's head, looks him hard in the eye. "When ye sing ma epitaph, baird, tis 'Noble Dougal, of Dunmaglas'—and be mindful iv what ye rhyme it with."

"The King has been known tae allow fer pardons," says Lachlan.

"The King," Dougal declares, "may kiss ma royal Scottish fanny flaps."

JENNY HAS ALWAYS WANTED TO SEE LONDON. OLD MR. Higgenbotham painted such pictures in her head, and now, moving slowly through the gut of the city, she holds onto the bars of the cage and looks till her eyes hurt. The other women are more cowed by the spectators who stare in and point, the jeering boys who run alongside, but as they are believed to be only common criminals, there are no attacks.

Bound by wrists two and two they were passed down into the lighter and rowed up the great river, much jabber in Erse about the consequences if the boat should tip, and even that short ride was a marvel, passing the White Tower where great Lords are kept before their heads are taken, the Customs House with a dozen vessels waiting inspection, the Bridge supporting a small city on its back ahead of them, and finally turning in to the market at Billingsgate, a great reek of fish with gulls wheeling overhead and a collier being shoveled out by laborers so black with the dust that the skin around their eyes, washed, perhaps, by tears, bore the only evidence that they were white men. At the market they were roughly transferred into a pair of wheeled iron cages drawn by spavined horses whose rib bones protruded like the bars of a cell, and began to clatter in from the great river.

Smoke then, great dark billows of it issuing from where she cannot locate, clearing some then and they are surrounded—chair-men, mostly young, strapping fellows, rush fore and aft of the covered sedans they carry on poles, Jenny with no clue as to what manner of gentlefolk lounge inside, mere pedestrians wisely ceding these athletes and their cargo passage. There is greater noise made by the activities of more people than she ever imagined existed in the world—the iron tires of dray wagons and carriages shuddering on uneven granite setts or cobblestones, horsemen passing to look down into the cage from their seats, men and women bent behind pushcarts, higglers shouting their wares or blowing horns to announce them, and here a small crowd around a ballad singer on a corner, his voice sweet, the air fetching, but moving quickly past after only a snatch of it.

"That's ma life," she says to Flora, who was a sempstress in Perth and speaks English well. "Half a verse and it's say farewell."

It is a wonder to her that so many of the men wear wigs, not just gentlemen and officers but tradesmen, even some of the porters have bag wigs affixed to their heads as they fly by bearing their loads, the queues bobbing after them.

A young woman steps near, throwing a pail of ashes into the channel, but even though it's clear she is only a maidservant she's wearing a silk gown. Gentlemen in narrow-shouldered smartcoats pass, tipping their hats to the ladies, and an older woman in a dress with enough material to stock a midsized draper's shop ploughs along the walk with head held high and a pair of fussily clothed footmen in her wake, bearing an array of parcels.

"Fart-catchers tae trail after yez," says Jenny. "Can ye imagine that?"

"What must the lads've been drinking," muses Flora, who has been flogged twice on the ship for relieving herself in the ballast and holds herself like an oft-kicked dog, awed by the scene, "tae believe they could prevail ower a' of this?"

"Tis ainly city folk."

"But there's *le*gions of them."

Their gaol wagon has to halt at the cross to let a mob of sheep pass through, their wool grayish with dust.

"And that's us," says Jenny. "Lambs tae the slaughter."

"D'ye believe sae?"

Jenny keeps her hold on the bars and her eyes on the street. "What I ken is that we've nae mair power in the matter than these puir hoggies do."

The last of the animals driven through, they turn onto a lovely street, large houses set back from a kerb lined with giant elms, bigger trees than she's ever seen, set in a neat row on either side.

"Can ye picture having a place in sich a hoose?" says Flora. "Polishing their plate, tending the fire that's in every room, a clean apron each day—"

A gilded coach-and-six careens past them, the liveried driver half standing to reach the lead horses with his long whip, a footman in shining boots and a red coat clinging to the rear, the queue of his beribboned bag wig flying behind him and a look of pure pleasure on his countenance.

"That's the position ah'll take," says Jenny.

"But it's ainly fer men."

"If we're dreamin' that's of nae import. Fancy the *speed* of it."

The trees are smaller on each succeeding block, and then there are none. The dwellings now, wooden structures on the verge of toppling this way or that, crowd the unpaved street and there are human wrecks about them, also on the verge of toppling, one of them noisily easing his sluices against a wall. There are scrawny children here, many with shaved and scabbed heads, and women, painted so luridly it is hard to determine their age, who stand or stroll holding up one side of their gowns, touting their availability. Two of these approach when the wagon stops again to accommodate workmen rolling a score of barrels into a public house.

"Bound fer the Old Bailey, is it?" asks the taller.

"They dinnae tell us nowt but get aff the ship and ontae the wagon," says Flora.

"And what've they nicked ye for?"

Flora speaks before Jenny can plant an elbow in her side. "They say I was an aid tae the rebellion," she says. "When it were ainly a kindness I'd show tae e'en a stranger."

The tall one backs away a step.

"Yer them popish whoors!" she snarls, her spit hitting one of the bars and sliding down it. "They'll sort ye out soon enough!"

The other girl, for Jenny can see now that she is very young, stays while her companion struts away, muttering curses.

"Do ye think they'll scrag ye?" she asks, Irish by her music.

"I doot it," says Jenny.

"But haven't they already murthered a pair of their own titled gents?"

"That's fer the betrayal. We're naething tae them—they'll dispose of us in whate'er way is least dear."

"Does a hangin' cost them money?"

"If it's done with any ceremony, I'd suppose sae. And with nae ceremony, where's the example of it fer a' tae see?"

The barrels cleared, the wagon jolts into motion again. The Irish girl gives them a small wave.

"Grand fortune to yez, then," she calls. "Mebbe ye'll be home soon."

Flora turns her back to the street. "I'll ne'er see hame again."

"I've nane tae miss," says Jenny. "There's no a clod of turf in Scotland tae welcome me back."

They roll past a pawn shop with numerous lovely things hung in the window—boots and watches and musical instruments and even a pair of embroidered bodice stays, a dark man who Jenny assumes is a Jew, though she's never seen such a creature, stepping outside to view their passing. Jenny wonders at the spectacle they must make, the clothes they were taken in turned to rags by now, all of them afflicted with the itch and mercifully not suffered to see their reflections in a glass for months. A flock of miserable harridans off to the knacker, she supposes, the shabbiest beasts in the menagerie.

They come alongside a squat rectangle of stone, narrow, barred windows high on the wall at each corner, the massive structure throwing a shadow over the street. A man holding forth at great volume to nobody in particular from his bantering booth set up on the walk before the prison leaves off and comes forward when he sees them. He is of middling age, wears his own hair, and is dressed in black with a thick black book stuck to his hand as if part of it. He claps his iron gaze on Jenny.

"Are you remanded to a cell, sister?"

"What is this place?"

"Newgate."

She has heard the women held for local offenses speak of it.

"We're tae be tried."

The man nods gravely but does not ask her crime. "You understand that it is not too late for you?"

"Tis later than that. We'll be judged fer who we are, no what we've doon."

"I'm speaking of your immortal soul. Trust me—nothing is destined. It is never too late to allow Christ into your heart."

This is a sentiment Jenny has never heard in the kirk. "What are ye, then?" she asks, wondering if the holy book in his hand could be the same that Reverend MacPherson waved in her face so many times. "Some manner of hedge preacher—"

"Only a Christian," says the man, walking alongside the cage as it rolls, "but there is a Method to my piety."

"And they suffer ye tae stand oot here, airing yer fancies?"

A wisp of a smile crosses his lips. "I've been gaoled, I've been dunned, I've been persecuted, but in time they've wearied of it."

"They're no sae weary tae deal with us. If we dinnae serve as fruit fer the gallows, they'll dispatch us across the sea."

The Christian nods again. "I've been to the Georgia Colony."

"Did it strike ye well?"

He ponders this a moment. "There is God even in the Wilderness," he says. "But I was not yet prepared to do His work there."

The evangelist veers away as they come to a building with several banners fluttering before it and a squadron of alibi men clustered at the door, these immediately flocking to surround the cages as the wagons are halted, spouting promises.

"Tell me yer offense, lovely lady," opens the one nearest Jenny, a man with a glistening moustache, "with the calendar date and time of day of the perpetration, and fer five guineas I'll swear ye was with me at the Scepter and Stallion the whole while."

"The sixteen of April of the previous year," Jenny tells him, "a wee stroll west frae Dalcrombie."

The alibi man snatches his hand from the bar as it it's been burnt. "Handmaidens to the Pretender!" he cries. "They'll sort ye out inside!"

The warders pull them from the cages then, two by two, perhaps a hundred passersby gathering to watch, and then they are marched into the courthouse.

There is only one other woman present inside, a beautifully dressed spectator watching from the balcony. The women from the *Jane of Leith* are arranged standing in a row with men in robes above and behind them, and after a few shouted instructions from a bailiff with a heavy staff in hand there is a long conversation, mostly in English, between the man with the most imposing wig and the highest seat and another man standing before him in a lesser wig who seems to be speaking on their behalf. The paper with writing on it that has followed Jenny throughout her captivities is produced again, and read from by the man in the heavier wig, repeating the story that she was taken while on the way to feed the fugitive Prince of Scotland, and though questioned by several officers—the paper does not mention her beating—refused to tell them where he was cowering. Then the man in the lesser wig, who they have also never seen before, utters a good number of sounds Jenny doesn't comprehend, and one of the Catholic girls informs her in a whisper that this is Latin, which is spoken by the clergy of her outlawed faith. The sense of it all, from what Jenny can deduce, is that they are an ignorant but wholly remorseful group of Scotch women who humbly beg for the King's Mercy.

She hears the word "guilty" from the mouth of the man in the highest seat, their judge, who then delivers them a lecture in language that might as well be Latin.

Taken back out and loaded, two by two, into the mobile cages, Jenny sees the evangelist being quick-stepped away from his bantering booth, a grim constable on each arm, his meager audience dispersing without complaint. There is more smoke in the air on their return to the Billingsgate dock, people burning refuse outdoors, and the streets chosen by their drivers provide a rougher passage. A group of the convicts behind Jenny debate in Erse for a spell, then ask her if she understands what has just been decided.

If we don't die before they can arrange a ship, she tells them, we're bound for the fever islands.

More deliberation among the women then, accounts related of blacks and whites sheltered together like beasts, of women strapped to plows and straining under the whip till they topple to the sun-baked earth and perish.

She has heard tales of the Georgia Colony and wonders if the evangelist was there as a prisoner or a free man. His holy book clearly offered no protection from English law.

And if she could, indeed, allow Christ into her heart, thinks Jenny, why ever would He wish to dwell there?

THERE IS A FINE BALANCE BETWEEN LOSING TRANSports or slaves to sickness during a voyage and losing your profit by overprovisioning them. With the Liverpool to Maryland Colony run averaging seven weeks and that to Barbados or Antigua often a full month more, the numbers must be thoroughly rendered before proceeding. Gildart has the Crown promised to compensate the firm at five pounds, one shilling per transport, and the last he heard from Rawlings in Maryland was that white men were bringing at least £15 worth of tobacco in trade, as opposed to £20 for negroes, the latter being less able to find safe haven should they escape. The firm has experimented with the conveyance of indentures, but as those are allowed to arrange their own terms with potential masters, waiting time in port is drawn out and the passage money surpassed by expenses. Whereas transports, indentured at embarkation to the captain, are sold by him at his will and a speedy exchange of cargoes assured.

There are risks involved, of course, though Gildart has been able to quantify many of these in his half century at the trade. A hold full of negroes may promise sure revenue on the page, but mortality, the threat of rebellion and the loss of captain and crew to disease while laying off of Calabar can easily be a venture's ruin. His worthy rivals—Tarleton, Cunliffe, Golightly—are only now learning this and have failed to diversify. The only true peril to a ship full of transports is that some muddleheaded colonial assembly will outlaw their importation during the voyage and they'll need to be carried on to a friendlier port until the Crown can impose its will again.

If only Maryland and Virginia could offer elephant's teeth as well as tobacco.

The *Johnson* sits ready in the harbor, as well as the *Venture*, and his namesake the *Gildart,* with half the decent sailors in the Kingdom lolling about town waiting for a berth. A certain number of these worthies has proven indispensible, but so many of the tasks on board can be managed by novices, eager young men who will sign on for a pittance and prove adequate even if Irish. Gildart has learned to discount his captains' fulsome objection to this economy, and the firm has not lost a ship, at least not due to mutiny or incompetence, in years.

He has written to Sir John Strange offering to provide, at a mere £5 per prisoner, an adequate number of irons with which to restrain the transports till their delivery, a precaution especially apt in the case of the recently vanquished Jacobites, who are after all men of violence with some history of concerted action. The Crown is notably parsimonious in such matters, however, and he has included the expense of two dozen sets of leg shackles into his calculations. Unlike the Africans, who are apt, if left unfettered, to hurl themselves into the sea, transports customarily respond to example and do not have to be restrained *en masse.*

That there are women included on the lists sent by the Commission is only a minor inconvenience—if the captains cannot spare a separate compartment, a barricado such as those constructed on the firm's slavers can be provided, a half day's work for the ship's carpenter. Women don't travel as well as men, of course, and tend to command a lower sum on arrival, but they also consume less throughout the voyage. Barring the interventions of buccaneers or unseasonable hurricanes, it looks on paper like a good business, though the amount of revenue will depend on the state of the servant market on arrival, vulnerable to the bold underpricing of certain rather desperate Bristol traders, and the typical depredations of the brigands at the Customs House upon return. Captain Holmes, fortunately, has no moral qualms about offloading half of the return cargo on the Isle of Man, to be later brought ashore more discretely, untaxed beyond a few pounds to the ever-amenable Manxmen.

It is not with small pride that Gildart can look from the window of his office and view the gently tossing forest of mainmasts in the Old Dock, itself somewhat the brainchild of his father-in-law, who began the firm. With the original Pool now sheltered from the Mersey's rambunctious tides by a river gate, a ship can be loaded or unloaded in a mere two days, a feat not to be replicated elsewhere in the Kingdom. Twice mayor of Liverpool and currently standing for the district in Parliament, Gildart has seen the city grow apace with the Crown's islands and colonies to the west. The bulk of the laboring population is made up of immigrants, as to be expected in a port, the firm's salt works hosting Irish, Dutch, Flemish, and outcasts from the Austrian empire. But it has been the triangular commerce that has made so many wealthy men—he spots the *Benin* just heading out, laden with brass, cloth, muskets, and powder to exchange for a Guinea cargo and then on to the Caribbean to trade that for cotton and sugar—a skyrocket of a business, despite its many drawbacks and vagaries. I scratch my pen to paper here in my nook, thinks Gildart, and Hottentot kings make war on each other, gaolbirds are whisked from London hovels to the wilds of Carolina, the looms of Manchester are kept humming, rural squires have sugar for their tea, dozens of ships and thousands of men surrender their destinies to ocean and wind. The walls of his office are covered in maps, many of them nautical charts, though he has never taken water passage farther than from one shore of the river to the other. Blobs of color with names affixed to them arranged on a blue background, increasingly conjectural the farther west you look, but he feels like he has been to many of those places, like he is presently there, through the agency of the firm, the far-flung outposts of the empire his chessboard.

Gildart dips his pen, begins a missive to his partner Smith, who is in London keeping track of the trials and travels of the Jacobite prisoners. The *Veteran* will hold one hundred and fifty transports without overcrowding, he writes, the *Johnson* and the *Gildart* each half that, captains and principal crew in place. The *Duke of Argyll* is also ready to sail, fitted belowdecks to receive two hundred and fifty negroes, and then on to the island of Antigua, God willing—

THE AULD FOX KNEELS, AS THEY HAVE ALLOWED, NOT bothering to strain his ears as the Crown's counsel tallies and elaborates upon his many acts of sedition.

"I do not hear," he informed them at the beginning of the trial, "I do not see—" though he can read by candlelight in his room at the Tower and eavesdrop well enough when the occasion merits it. Let them believe him a ruin, not worth the effort of execution.

"An offense of the blackest dye," says the counsel—this one is called Strange—"with intent to introduce popish bigotry and superstition instead of Protestant religion, and an arbitrary, tyrannical power instead of a free government."

There isn't a one of the hundred seventeen gathered peers struggling to stay awake during this peroration, he thinks, who would recognize a free government were they to pull it from their fundament. They are Hanover's puppies, allowed to yap and tussle amongst themselves but ever held on a short tether. Most men are terrified of true freedom, while a handful, those who have the stomach for it, wish to *rule.* The majority of these Lords owe their titles to nothing more than an accident of birth, while the Auld Fox, Lord Lovat, has had to wrest his from Fortune. A fourth cousin, remote from the Fraser line of succession, he felt the blood of a true Highland chieftain flowing through his veins and dedicated the first half of his life to obtaining that position. Outlawed, exiled, accused of rape and murder, he has prevailed, as he believes the founders of all the clans must have, through cunning and remorselessness.

The Crown counsel seems to be addressing him directly now—

"The weight of this accusation, the solemn manner of exhibiting and prosecuting it, and the awfulness of this supreme Judicature, the most illustrious in the world, are circumstances that may naturally strike your mind with anxious and alarming apprehensions—"

Actually, kneeling flanked by the Lieutenant of the Tower on his right and the Gentleman Gaoler—terrible axe in hand, but the cutting edge still turned away from him—to the left, he is flattered by their attention. He, Lovat, has filled the vast interior of the Westminster Hall with the flower of the nation, its Parliament abjuring the business of state to determine the fate of one of their number. Every day of the trial has begun with their prayers in the House of Lords, and then the solemn procession into the court—the Lord High Steward's Gentlemen Attendants, two by two, the Masters of Chancery, the four Judges, the peers' eldest sons and minors, the York and Windsor Heralds, the four Sergeants at Arms with their maces, the Yeoman Usher of the House, then the peers themselves, beginning with the youngest baron, two by two, till their area is filled with them, bewigged and robed in red with ermine trimmings, then four more Sergeants at Arms with maces, then the Sergeant at Arms attending the Great Seal and the Pursebearer, followed by the Garter King at Arms, Gentleman Usher of the Black Rod (carrying the white staff), and finally the Lord High Steward himself, Philip, Lord Harkwicke, his train borne by a pair of pages till he is deposited on the uppermost Woolsack, all duly admired by the hundreds who paid six guineas to watch from the balconies. The reverences made, the Sergeant at Arms calling his "Oyez, oyez," the peers rising to uncover as the Lord High Steward is handed his staff and purse—all this for a crag-hopping Highlander, Lord of a rabble of neep-eaters and cattle thieves.

"Such is the generous compassion of your Lords' noble hearts," proclaims Sir John Strange to the nodding peers, "that you will acquit with pleasure but condemn with reluctance."

Absolutely, thinks the Auld Fox. And hyenas make the finest nursemaids.

Robert Fraser, never worth a shilling, has verified the authorship of each of the letters brought forward, though the Auld Fox had often torn them artfully to remove his signature. He always counseled his friends in the Stuart association to write in general terms, but when arms and men must be directed, when one is corresponding with the person you believe will be your new King, this becomes impractical. That the disloyal secretary also "happened" to read missives left upon his desk does not surprise him, only that the man's memory of these during his testimony was so exact. The scoundrel must have been collecting information to shop, should the rebellion fail, from his first day of employment.

As for Murray of Broughton, the nonentity the Prince took on as his own secretary, Murray's bonny wife prancing about like the Jacobite Queen of the May with a brace of pistols on her hip—there is no word in the four languages Lovat is versed in to adequately describe the squalor of his character. A fellow guest at the Tower, he has gone so far beyond the confession necessary to avoid his own hanging as to suggest a sort of enthusiasm, a desire to play the great man before the assembled Lords, exaggerating his own factotum's role in the drama while blithely cooking the goose of men not yet indicted.

And Hugh Fraser, his most trusted aide who had barely survived the charge across Drummossie Moor, admitting in the box that were he not captured and threatened with the gallows he should not offer a word, carefully crafting his statements to condemn the father and perhaps acquit the son. Hugh, on the first word of the Prince's ill-timed and unexpected landing, had advised Lovat to send the boy to continue his studies in the Low Countries, and at first he had been tempted to do so. Young Simon was so inclined, with no passion for the Stuarts in his heart, but in his age and infirmity the Auld Fox needed an avatar, a pawn—no, a knight to move about the board to keep all in speculation as to his intentions. It troubles him still, his only true regret in the affair. The boy, not yet twenty, with tears of anger hurling the white cockade into the fire and lamenting that he had been made a tool and a fool by his own father, finally submitting to join the Prince with his tardily raised troops, and, blessedly, arriving at Culloden just after the curtain had come down.

The portrait of young Simon painted during the trial—reluctant warrior, grudgingly obedient to his scheming, ruthless Lord and father—is one that may well save his life. But to what end? No title, no estate, no line of inheritance continued—whatever the boy's fate, the Auld Fox has been undone in his posterity, his name only fit to grace the list of those nobles so rudely dispatched on Tower Hill.

One of the sergeants at arms whispers to the Lieutenant of the Tower, who places a hand on Lovat's shoulder. It seems his peers are ready to pass judgment—

"Time for my curtain call?"

"It is, my Lord."

"If you gentlemen would help me to my feet, then."

"Guilty, by my honor," does not take long to say. It is the reading of the titles, some of them multiple, no scrap of dubious nobility to be dismissed with, that accounts for his agonizing ordeal on foot before them, each Lord rising much too slowly to drive the next spike into his coffin, capped by the Lord High Steward himself, with hand on breast—

"My Lords, we find that Simon, Lord Lovat, is guilty of the high treason whereof he stands impeached, upon my honor."

He was carried often in the days of his vitality as a form of honor, a reminder to subalterns and tenants as to his position and authority, as the lavish dinners at Dounie were of his beneficence. But he needs carrying now, needs support, his trembling knees a locus of constant pain, his feet swollen, his balance uncertain—

The Lord High Steward receives the white staff from the Usher and breaks it in two, exciting a good deal of chatter in the balconies. The Gentleman Gaoler, who has been napping during much of the ceremony, turns the sharpened blade of the great axe toward the Auld Fox.

IN THE DREAM THE SCAFFOLD IS WOOD BENEATH HIS feet. Though he has bid them not to, they've pulled the cap over his eyes, and there is only a strained light, like what makes its way through uncolored church glass on a dismal morning. Strong hands push and prod him till he stands on what he senses is the trap. The hemp chafes against the skin of his neck and then is drawn snug. There are voices, but none of the sounds have meaning. And then a crack and the floor beneath his feet gives way and it is a sickening drop before the snap of his neck, a white flash and pain like he has never experienced, but his fall is still not broken, falling, falling, the cheer of the watchers fading above and falling, the cloth blown from his face and his eyes wide open but black, nothing but black and no wind against his skin but only the nauseous, endless falling into black nothing that he realizes will never end—

Asweat as the floor begins to press against him again, Jamie imagines, almost conscious now, lying wrapped in a shroud beneath the earth but not dead, cold to the bone and knowing this is for eternity. And then the inventory of his body, bones sharp against the scraps of hay on the floor, the noises of the men sleeping, perhaps dreaming, around him, the weary effort to remember where, precisely, in the world he is lying—

Ah, that's right. And this is The Day.

HE'S ALWAYS BEEN CHARGED TO PROTECT THE WEE FELLOW. "That un's canny, Dougal', their father would say. "But canny dinnae keep ye hale till ye've coom iv age." Jamie was always free with his opinions, even when they might earn him a clout on the nob, blithe in the knowledge that his fearsome older brother was at his back, whether present or not. It was a matter of blood—*Touch Not the Cat*, and no insult left unanswered. The idea was that when the lands were theirs again Dougal would be laird and Jamie his counselor, schooled in the intrigues of London and Paris and able to help navigate the shoals of both local and national politicking. The dream. It gave them a purpose in the world, a confidence and a bearing that they did not, apparently, merit. When Dougal would be hard with a tenant, demanding cash or something that could be sold for it, he soothed his ragged conscience with the thought that it was for the Resurrection, that all would benefit once the MacGillivray brothers were in their rightful position once more. A lovely delusion, he thinks, but one drifted away with the cannon smoke on Drummossie Moor.

There are no jests on this morning, not between the brothers or from the other prisoners, Scot or English. Why Jamie's date has been set so quickly and Dougal's left indeterminate remains a mystery. Pendergast and Nance enter and stand by the door, truncheons held solemnly behind their backs, waiting. No one speaks. The men on the floor or standing by the one window watch the condemned, somber, forcing themselves not even to scratch their pest-plagued hides, even Crawford's Fergal, who has clearly gone mad, ceasing his incessant muttering.

Dougal grasps Cameron's hand and gives him a thump on the shoulder, then embraces his brother. He was always a slender reed, Jamie, but the months of nothing but prison scran have reduced him to a wisp, and Dougal is careful not to squeeze the bones too tightly.

They step to the warders, seemingly calm, resigned, then Jamie turns and gives the wee *seanachaidh* a look.

"Well?" he says, forcing a grin. "Have ye gan dumb on us?"

The islander lifts his chin, puffs his chest out.

MacGillivray strides bravely—

—he proclaims—

As though there's nowt amiss
Where he's gang maun no be Scotland
But tis a better place than this.

JAMIE AND AENEAS CAMERON ARE NOT DEEMED WORthy of the sledges, conveyed to Kennington Common instead in a tradesman's cart pulled by a single hackney, into which, uninvited, an open-air celebrant of the Holy Word has placed himself.

"If you would only repent of your sins," he tells the condemned men, "the Savior will absolve you."

"I've nowt tae be absolved of," says Jamie, watching the paltry few who walk along with the cart in a holiday spirit. "It's them as passed judgment needs fergiving."

"Be thou not proud in thy iniquity."

"And there's nowt tae be proud of, we've made such a bollocks of it."

"No matter the hour, thy soul can be saved."

"Ma soul is nae worry, it's ma *heid* they're after."

The holy man turns to Cameron.

"Would you say a prayer with me?"

Aeneas has been broody for days, speaking rarely, and then only of his service to the long and illustrious line of Camerons, as if he stood to lose or gain anything but moral satisfaction and reflected glory from their fate. Jamie, cold poor but a MacGillivray by direct ascendancy, wonders how Dr. Arch Cameron or even the chieftain Lochiel might respond if confronted with this natural son of a second cousin.

"Leave it till we're on the gallows," says the purported fourth Earl, gently pushing the outthrust book of prayer away from his face.

There are a few hundred spectators gathered in the common, a visibly shabbier group, on the whole, than those who came to witness Colonel Townley and his comrades' departure. There is considerably less ceremony, this being a simple hanging and of rebels considered less egregious in their treachery, if only for having been born on Scottish rather than English soil.

"Almighty God, we remember before you today your faithful servant James MacGillivray," mutters the evangelist, who has apparently seen their names published, "and we pray that, as you open to him the gates of larger life, you will receive him into your joyful service—"

Jamie feels numb as he is helped out of the cart, his manacled hands of no use, numb in body, mind and spirit. He has had ample time to contemplate this moment, but it has always seemed a distant possibility, a storm at sea that might never strike the coast, and Dougal has kept him in such easy disposition that the fact, the very day, has crept up upon him.

"—that, with all who have faithfully served You in the past, he may share in the eternal victory of Jesus Christ our Lord; who lives and reigns with You—"

Dougal has offspring, including a son, to carry forward for him, he has been a warrior, a leader, he is a Highland gentleman of perhaps three hundred pounds a year and all the kale he can stomach. And I? At most a linguist and go-between, a gadfly of intrigues, the tacksman's lesser brother.

At the end of his brief trial, the jury had been charged by the court—"What goods and chattels, lands and tenements had the prisoner at the time of said High Treason?"

"None," replied the speaker for the jury.

If Dougal is hanged as well, which is their intent, who will bury them, and where? To be only a gust of wind, a zephyr, ruffling the gorse for an instant and then gone as if never having existed—

"—in the unity of the Holy Spirit, one God, for ever and ever. Amen."

They have pulled the white sack over his face and tightened the hemp around his neck before the announcement is made.

It is the Sheriff of London who addresses the spectators, prompting a multitude of curses. The cloth is removed, the halters loosed with some difficulty and pushed aside, swinging free of their promised burdens. Jamie finds that he has wet himself.

"I knew since last evening," the Sheriff tells them. "But the Crown wished to make an impression on you gentlemen. Nothing like true familiarity with the steps and the string to engender remorse."

"What is to become of us?" asks Cameron, looking bewildered.

"If you will but petition the Duke of Newcastle, your punishment will be commuted to transportation."

The holy man is beaming. "Tis not what I prayed for you," he says, "but may you go with God."

But the crowd, furious that the pageant of rough justice has been robbed from them, begin to evade the score of guardsmen and press around the platform. Jamie at first believes his legs are trembling, then realizes the frustrated spectators have a hold on the gallows supports and are attempting to pull it down. Visions of Captain Porteous spirited by torchlight through the streets of Edinburgh—

"We had better make haste," says the apprehensive Sheriff as a phalanx of the King's soldiers rush up to protect them, "before someone is harmed."

THE CHAPEL IS JUST A BRIEF HOBBLE FROM HIS ROOM IN the White Tower, all pillars and arches, the chamber where the Knights of Bath would congregate before a coronation. The Auld Fox kneels, making his peace with whatever God still dwells here. He has passed for Presbyterian, Anglican and Catholic in his time, but those are the institutions of man, beset with lethal politics, well below the notice or concern of any Being who can have created the world in six days. The Lord Lovat's God is a practical fellow, who understands that there is no feast without a slaughter, and will judge him accordingly.

There were visitors to the Tower yesterday, a party of diplomatic macaronis from Milan, but they had come to see the menagerie and not to goggle at the condemned nobleman. There is a fine pair of

Barbary lions, some camels and assorted deerlike creatures, and an enormous, flea-ridden bear from the Virginia Colony. He brought young Simon to see them as a wee laddie, but the boy, head filled with grisly tales of royal intrigue and retribution, kept looking up to the White Tower.

"Tis where they keep ye afore the axe falls," he remembers saying. "The anteroom tae Heaven or Hell."

He hears the echo of footsteps behind him. It is Cornwallis, the Lieutenant of the Tower.

"We'll have to get you ready, your Lordship."

"Has my wig been combed?"

"It has just been returned. Everything has been laid out."

Two of the warders, stepping in after Cornwallis, move to his sides to help haul him to his throbbing feet. It was particularly bad last night, and he barely slept.

"Are they come to the Hill yet?"

"The galleries are being erected, and the crowd is not yet substantial."

"No conjecture of rain?"

"Not a cloud in the sky."

The Auld Fox grins. "Then we shall have a festive time of it."

The warders help him move from the chapel toward his room.

"Your Lordship is in excellent spirits," Cornwallis observes, "given the occasion."

"I don't know why there should be a bustle about taking off an old gray head. Think of how many other citizens of the Three Kingdoms will meet their end on this day—some of them quite unexpectedly."

"But none shall equal your eminence."

Lord Lovat smiles again. "Leave off or you'll swell my head too large for its covering."

The King has honored his eminence by ordering a mere beheading, sparing the Auld Fox and his audience the sight of his venerable and most likely diseased viscera being torn from his middle and roasted in a fire. Several other rebels have already suffered this extensive punishment, and perhaps a climate of moderation is prevailing, the Crown and loyal subjects' thirst for revenge already quenched. He has been hoping to die in his sleep one of these nights and rob them of their satisfaction, but that end is now out of reach.

He'd been able to stay abed longer during the trial, what with Westminster Hall, too vast to light by flame, requiring the sun well risen before jury and judge are able to see each other, but today the ritual is scheduled for noon. The young man they've allowed him to assist with his wardrobe is adequate, though he misses speaking to his Toby in Erse. So much to miss, but none of it in this Tower.

Cornwallis brings the axeman in to meet him, a shambling, beetle-browed fellow who directs his gaze to the floor.

"This is John Thrift."

"Not a former banker, I trust?"

"I was a smithy, yer Lordship," says Thrift without raising his eyes. "But it didn't add up."

"Very little does, I'm afraid. You've performed this service before?"

"I have, sir, several times."

"Because if you fail to strike true, it will be very inconvenient."

"I'll do my best, your Lordship."

The executioner is dismissed then, offering the Auld Fox a little crouching bow as he goes.

"You're certain he's experienced?"

Cornwallis nods. "It's just that he's never dealt with a peer before."

"See that he has a dram. We can't have an axeman whose knees have gone to jelly."

By the time they are in the carriage Thrift looks better, sitting beside the Chaplain of the Tower, cheeks glowing, axe held between his knees with the edge turned toward Lord Lovat, who hands him a small purse with five guineas in it. "I'm not sure what is customary at these events," he says, "this being my first."

"Very handsome of you, sir."

They ride out through the Court Gate and join the procession and there is a merry throng lining the way, eyes sparkling and jaws slackened as they bend for a glance in through the windows, with none inclined to the abuse or launching of projectiles that characterized each morning's ride to Westminster during the trial.

I am no longer "an intestine enemy to His Sacred Majesty," but merely the midday entertainment.

He wonders if the American bear regards those faces that bob over its pale in the King's menagerie with equal disinterest. He wonders if a memorable utterance will be expected of him on the platform.

He did everything but wash the feet of each peer in his statement after the verdict was read, thanking them and the Crown counsel and the Lord High Steward a million of times for their forbearance with an old and infirm sinner, even praising Hanover as if the dimwitted sausage-eater had indeed been the sovereign he endeavored to serve, while in his heart thinking of the toast he raised so often with Lochiel and Traquair and Drummond—"Confusion to the white horse and all the generation of them." But that was when there was still hope of commutation, when there was still a forum to crusade for the life of his son.

What he most wanted to divest himself of was his disappointment with the Pretender—for that is what he proved himself to be—and how precariously near to dissolution their precious Union had been. The Prince was a well-looking young man when he appeared at Gortuleg the day after the Defeat, but the Auld Fox realized then that their Charlie was more dreamer than general and more Italian than Scotsman, regarding the Highlands as a primitive backwater rather than the fervent heart of his natural kingdom. And while still at the bar unburdening himself, he might have solicited their pity for any man attempting concerted action with the Highland clans, that vipers' nest of blood feuds, unfounded vanity, and equivocation.

Of which I, thinks the Auld Fox with a grin, am the *sans pareil.*

There is a great disturbance as he is helped from the carriage at the foot of Tower Hill, screams and rushing about, and at first he believes it to be an attack intended on his person.

"No cause for apprehension, your Lordship," says Cornwallis, signaling to the warders who will convey Lovat up the hill on a litter. "One of the galleries, hastily made, has collapsed and crushed a score of spectators."

The Auld Fox laughs. "Only a score?"

The platform waits above, framed by a crimson company of guardsmen, firelocks in hand, bayonets glistening in the sunlight, eyes held directly forward. He is being carried up. He remembers a day on a hunt to the north, crossing the Moy Burn on the shoulders of his *casflue*, preceded across the frigid water by his *óstair* leading temperamental Rob Roy, his stallion, a trio of young bodyguards trotting along to keek the hills for danger, and the sword bearer and the baggage man and the standard bearer wavering as his flapping banner caught the wind and the piper, striding with his nose in the air as his own gillie splashed behind with the bulky instrument draped upon him. *Je suis prest*, announced the banner, letters on the belt that circled the stag's head, *I am ready.* There were some wee lads fishing there, and he signaled one of his rear guard to flip them a shilling. A bright day, like this one, at the height of his powers, with everything seemingly before him—

There is a cheer as he stands, without assistance, upon the platform, waving the jabbering Chaplain away and turning to face the multitude. He gives it all of his lungs, observing that several of the nearest are his peers, who will understand and pass the words along to make his legend.

"*Dulce et decorum est pro patria mori!*" declares the Auld Fox.

Let them sort out which *patria* he is referring to.

He turns to see John Thrift waiting with the instrument of release held over his shoulder and a rather nervous person on the other side of the block holding a velvet sack to capture his cranium as it falls.

"Let the medical gentlemen observe," he says with a wink to the axeman, "an infallible cure for the gout."

He is helped to his knees. He lays his head in the groove.

Je suis prest.

BO
TW

AT SEA

NO CROWDS ATTEND THEIR LOADING INTO THE transport. The sight of prisoners, even those so notorious as adherents to the Jacobite cause, being shipped into exile while the odd Negro is hauled ashore is so common in Liverpool as to arouse only economic musings from the few dockside observers.

That will bring a pretty penny.

Jamie stands with the others on the slippery deck of the *Gildart,* stripped naked, unsteadied by the mild rocking of the frigate outside the breakwater that defines the Pool, waiting to be examined. There are over four score men about in similar undress who will augment the ship's cargo to the plantations, Jamie recognizing a few despite the effects on them of nearly two year's confinement on scraps and gruel. Alexander Stewart, the Prince's footman, given to him by the traitor Murray of Broughton, is aboard, as well as Lamond, the Duke of Perth's groom, undistinguished in their naked state from the various butchers, bakers, dyers, shoemakers, laborers—

Dougal is left in Southwark, waiting to be hanged as a "rebel of distinction."

"Bend and spread," orders the marine tasked with inspecting them for hidden weapons or tools. Jamie complies, blood rushing into his lowered head, fingers spanning his buttocks apart till the marine grunts, "Up," and moves on to the next prisoner. They have been lined up a dozen at a time for the process, the *Gildart*'s barefoot crew nimbly stepping around or swinging from ratlines over them as they ready the ship for sail, bronzed and active and seeming a species distinct from the toadstool-pale convicts.

"Dress yerself," orders another Marine strolling down the line in front of him. Jamie hurries on his breeks and shirt—all that is left to him—and stands waiting for the next instruction. He has sealed an indenture to serve Richard Gildart of Liverpool, or his assigns in the Colonies, for the term of his natural life. A half-dozen merchant ships take on supplies within the Pool, while the *Gildart* and its sister ship the *Johnson* lay anchored a short ways out into the harbor, the latter still receiving boatloads of shackled men, made fast to the thwarts for the trip out, then exchanging their land irons for seagoing ones once on deck. Gulls swoop above, mocking, and the afternoon sun of a late spring day sparkles on the water. It is the best Jamie has felt since well before Culloden.

"Count by six," orders a third Marine, pointing to Lachlan at the end of their line "starting here." They were hand-cuffed by twos for the transfer in an open boat pulled by a yawl with four oarsmen, but here on the *Gildart*, explained the captain, whose name is Holmes and will be considered their Master till they're sold to another on the far side, they will be kept in sixes. Lachlan, Aeneas Cameron, Jamie, the huge Fergal, and two Duncans from Dundee who were in Oglivy's regiment are told to sit on the deck to accept their notably rusty leg irons.

"The Hanoverian pleat," says Lachlan, watching as his are bolted tight around his ankles. "I'd float awee withoot them."

There is shouting to starboard after the yawl is propelled past their bow, Jamie standing to see over the side as the prisoner boat it is dragging fouls the cable from one of the *Johnson*'s bower anchors, tipping it sideways to spill its passengers into the sea. The crews of both ships rush to watch as well—more shouting, somebody on the yawl cutting the hawser free, the prisoner boat floating upside down, till only a single Marine guard, his musket lost, struggles back to the surface.

"I counted eight," says Cameron as lines are hurled from the deck of the *Johnson* to the paddling survivor. "Four pairs, bound to each other."

"That's eight will no be sold tae the buckskins."

"Oot of Mr. Gildart's pocket," says Lachlan, "and intae the drink."

"Hands," orders the marine, and they hold their hands out for their manacles.

THEY HAVE BEEN IN THE HOLD, WHICH REEKS OF TObacco, for several hours when they hear the mate bark an order to man the capstan, then the scrapings and clankings of various anchors weighed till the pitch and yaw of the hull around them evens out, the ship moving steadily in one direction.

"We're underwee."

"We're lost," says Cameron, tears in his eyes.

"Ye'd rather swing frae the halter?"

"Everything will be new," says Cameron. "Each man without loyalty, without history, tied neither to clan nor King, belonging to nothing—"

"We'll belang tae whoever lays ten pound on the barrelhead," says Jamie.

Lachlan grins. "Ye think ye'll bring sae much as that?"

"I've heared of blacks sold fer forty."

"Ah, but yer Africans is bred fer heat and hardship, and no sae stubborn as a Hielander."

They are confined between watertight bulkheads at each end of the compartment, newly installed by the ship's carpenter, with one hatch overhead through which a ladder can be lowered. Each chained set of six men has a bench to sit upon, leg shackles fastened to it. The floor is a metal grate under which bilge sloshes, fore and aft at the moment, with a pair of wooden grates above their heads admitting slanted bars of light that swing about with the action of the ship. They've been told that when it is time to sleep canvas and straw will be provided, and there are several tubs available for their waste, Jamie's coffle-mates already agreeing to attempt to relieve themselves as a group. Most have been held in worse places, though a few men have already puked from the tobacco stench and the ship's rolling.

"They've red Indians in the Colonies," says Lachlan. "Said to be wilder and e'en mair savage than MacGregors."

Fergal does not react. He hasn't spoken since they came aboard the *Gildart,* not even to mutter, but keeps a wary eye on his surroundings, like a great beast newly caged.

"Some are said tae be cannybuls—the red men, no the MacGregors—and they gad aboot wearin' the hides of wild beasties they've slaughtered, with painted faces and the thumbs of enemies they've kilt hangin' frae their necks as jewry. If ye should fall intae their bluidy hands ye'll mourn yer ain birth."

"I already mourn your birth," says Cameron, four shackled men between him and the *seanachaidh*, "and we're still within sight of Liverpool.

THEY'VE MADE AN ALLEY WITH STICKS, NOT TOTALLY straight on either side, and even have a boy paid tuppence to spot the pins. It is Dougal's third day out in the little courtyard, and the first in which the sun has broken through the haze of smoke from chimneys and street fires in Southwark.

"Drat!" cries Cousins after his first ball.

"The landlord don't care for you," grins Smythe.

"The landlord," Cousins complains as the boy hustles the ball back to him, "is the chief impediment to my leaving this establishment. Despite my assurances of imminent employment—"

"Not a patient lot, landlords—"

"Or ladies. Mrs. Goldsmith, I pled, if you'd only bear with me—"

"Goldsmith, is it?"

"Not a Jew. Though with her attitude—"

Dougal has watched the skittles players from the one cell window above, wondering what they could be talking about, their conversation never ceasing as pins are set up and bowled over.

"Odds that I can bowl a spare on this?"

Smythe regards the upstanding pins, with the landlord, set just behind the felled king pin, guarding the back of the diamond and a lone winger off to the side.

"You haven't a chance. They're scattered like a madwoman's shit."

"Then give me generous odds."

"One hundred to one."

"I accept."

Both men, he has learned, are hopeless gamblers who have squandered modest fortunes to end up here in Marshalsea, each with family willing to maintain them in the masters' side of the prison but not to buy their freedom. Wagering on every event short of the sunrise, on any day one might owe the other thousands of pounds in imaginary currency.

Cousins rolls, throwing a good deal of velocity into it, neatly taking out the landlord and the pins behind but leaving the winger untouched.

"Drat!"

"I don't believe you've felled that pin all afternoon."

"The boy must be screwing it down. You've bribed him—"

"No, but an excellent idea. Set them up, Dickie!"

Dougal continues his stroll around the courtyard as the boy resets the pins for Smythe's frame. His first day out, arranged through the generosity of Jamie's doctor friend, they tried to draw him into the game and were quickly disappointed in his lack both of interest and tangible funds.

"You Scotch have your own more primitive contests," Cousins had observed. "Hurling some sort of boulder through the air, if I'm not mistaken?"

Dougal let it pass, happy enough to test his legs out of the cell for an hour. The wounds still throb at night, but despite the sorry excuse for sustenance offered to the common side prisoners he has gained a good deal of his strength back. Whether he is now strong enough—

"Well done!" shouts Cousins as ninepins fly. "But our obstinate little sentry remains."

Smythe has knocked over all but the same winger. He is a round, florid-faced man, while Cousins is slender and pale. There is another, older gent, Shaftsbury, who spends his courtyard hour sitting on a spindly-legged wooden chair glumly contemplating the sky, a walking stick idle in his hand.

"Talk to me," says Smythe.

"Three to two."

"I'll accept that."

Smythe holds his second ball in both hands by his hip, staring for a long moment at the remaining pin as if visualizing its demise, then takes three quick steps to the line drawn in the dirt and unleashes—

"Cush!" cries Cousins as the ball nicks the gutter sticks and caroms back in to down the winger.

"The pitch isn't level! It rained last night—"

"Always the same sad story. Now, if you had called a cush shot and made it—"

"Which I seem to do, more often than not—"

Dougal sees that Giles, the keeper who daydreams in the doorway to the masters' side house, has left for his daily visit to the taproom. He quickens his pace, heading for Mr. Shaftsbury.

"Where do we stand?"

"The three to two, at a pound—"

"I only bet a shilling."

"You didn't say that."

"But we have agreed that unless stated, wagers are always in shillings—"

The old man looks up, startled, as Dougal lays a hand on his shoulder.

"Good afternoon, sir," says Dougal, bending to speak softly to the man. "If ye'd be sae kind, I'd like tae borra yer chair fer a moment."

There is a lag as Shaftsbury realizes he is being addressed in the English tongue. He leans heavily on the walking stick, manages to stand, and makes a little bow.

"My pleasure, sir."

Excellent manners, the English, when they're not invading your homeland.

Dougal takes the chair in hand and rushes it to the base of the lowest of the buildings that enclose the courtyard. He leans it against the red brick wall and is up on the back of the chair, able to reach the bars across the lowest of the second story windows. His arms shake a bit, but he is able to pull himself up, weaker but also lighter of body than he's been in years, the constant joke being that Whipshaw will starve them till they can pass between the bars. Now getting a toehold on the sill, digging into the seams in the brick face with his fingers, clawing up toward the next window—

"Five to two he doesn't make it to the roof," he hears Cousins say behind. "That's *pounds*."

"Give me three to one—"

"You just don't want to figure the maths—"

"Granted. Do we have a wager?"

It is a slate roof with a gentle slope, the first tile he lays a hand on cracking loose and tumbling to the ground.

"I mean *feet* on the roof."

"Granted. Dickie, bring Mr. Shaftsbury back his chair—there's a good lad—"

Dougal gets his chin over the edge of the slate, then both hands, palms flat and pressing down, then inches upward, digging the edges of the square-toed workman's shoes Davie Falconer has supplied him into the brick face below, glad there was no fog this morning and that all the surfaces are dry—

"If he'd brought a rope he'd be over by now."

"And where would he procure this rope?"

"Money opens every door—"

"The only rope our Scotch friend is going to encounter will be around his neck."

"Look at that—he's gaining, he's gaining—"

Dougal climbed the sheerest faces of Ben Nevis as a younger man, nearly vertical at times and a few times more than vertical, hugging knobs of rock with his bare knees, learning to think with the pads of his fingers, to consider with his toes, to test his weight on a shift of position without committing till he was certain—or nearly certain. Then standing on the top, triumphant and content to take the long, easy way down while watching columns of red-coated soldiers march into Fort William. The sweat on Dougal's palms serves as a kind of bond with the slate, giving him purchase, and he is able to shimmy a hip, then his entire leg over, gravity seeming to lessen its pull on his body.

"He's made it!"

"I said *feet*."

Dougal digs his knees in to move up to the peak of the roof, hugging it till he can feel his trembling muscles take shape again.

He's never been to the other side of this building, his one trip to court following a different route. Like our doomed army, he thinks, with no real plan once south of Carlisle—

"Do you think we'll be rewarded if we raise an alarm?"

"Do you mean released?"

"He's condemned to swing, isn't he? He must be important—"

"And how would that rest on your conscience?"

Dougal listens intently as there is a pause for consideration.

"A point well taken."

Legs still shaking, Dougal raises himself into a crouch, straddling the peak of the roof.

"Feet on the shingles! You are in my debt, sir."

Below on the far side is King Street, currently unoccupied, and the pile of waste Nipper Wilde said would be there, a bit of wood ash thrown on the top to confound the flies. Dougal sits and carefully slides down the slope on his rear, stopping at the edge. He sees only the top of one narrow windowsill for a footing before the drop. He can hear people shouting and wagons rattling on the Borough High Street around the corner and knows he won't remain unseen for long.

The objective is not to land on your head.

Dougal hangs a leg over the edge of the roof, reaching blindly to contact the sill. The trews the doctor provided fit him badly, too long with the cuffs rolled up and the rope around them for a belt beginning to slip. Two of the other condemned have ordered new clothes made to be hanged and buried in.

"If I'm tae die a pauper I'll look the part," he told them, knowing that if it were in Scotland before his own people he'd want to make a show.

There are three wee boys standing on King Street now, looking up at him.

Dougal wedges his foot between the sill and the brick, grips an overhanging slate tile that seems solidly fixed. He shifts his weight slowly, approaching the point of no return. There was only one moment on Ben Nevis when he was sure he would die, and then it passed, the little sideways jump he made, a shoulder's width at the most, landing him in a vertical crack for support. Keep your feet pointed down and knees bent, he thought even then, when there was no hope of survival should he fall—

He manages to catch a bit of the sill with his fingers as he slides past, willing himself into the brick but falling backward from his heels when he hits the refuse pile.

The wee boys watch solemnly as he struggles to his feet, nothing broken, but his tailbone feeling hammered.

The smallest of the boys points to the building he has just fallen off of.

"Me da's in there."

"And he thinks of ye every day, laddie," says Dougal, hurrying off toward the High Street. His trews are smeared with filth up to the knees, and he grabs an empty, broken barrel and throws it up on his shoulder, hoping to be taken for a working man on an errand.

It is the midday crowd they hear through the cell window, Dougal turning right to jostle among the message boys and the porters and the draymen and the loungers-about, a man with a job to do and no time to tarry.

The street bends and he sees in the reflection of a draper's window that someone is following him. A hollow-eyed fellow with reddish hair sticking out in every direction, shuffling along in shoes with no buckles and a greatcoat that has had its pockets torn off, keeping to the far side of the street and the same distance behind. Dougal considers turning to brain him with the barrel, but there are so many potential witnesses—window-gazers and shopkeepers, passing tradesmen, idlers, an old man selling chestnuts from a brazier—that the urge subsides. The follower is afflicted with a catarrh, snorting mucus loudly enough to be heard through the peddler's cries and horse hooves striking the stones, a kind of rhythmic prod at Dougal's back. He drops the barrel onto a pile of old crates being noisily broken up for kindling, quickens his pace, with the phlegmy snuffling increasing in frequency and rising in pitch. Dougal knows from his few visits to Edinburgh that a running man is always suspect—

"Now here's a handsome fella," calls a young woman, dressed in yellow silk, from a doorway. "And a bit iv a divvil, I'm thinkin'."

Dougal pauses to look at her. From the corner of his eye he sees the follower pass, then slow and wait ahead, pretending to eye one of the lamb carcasses hanging out over the sidewalk.

"Perhaps ye'd like ta pay me a visit later."

"I'd like it noo," says Dougal.

The young woman eyes his filth-smeared trews.

"But wouldn't yer master be expectin ye?"

"He can wait. Do ye have a place?"

The young woman, an Irish girl, attempts a smile. "Folla me, then," she says, "but stay a tad behind."

Dougal listens as she leads him back along the High Road and cuts left onto Nag's Head, but if the man is tailing him he has overcome his nasal difficulties.

The house is leaning forward as if to tumble into the street, and the stairs leading up to the second floor are an uneven jumble, a few of them missing. The room has only a window, a low cot and a cracked water basin on a stand. The girl turns when he shuts the door behind them.

"What's yer pleasure, sor?"

She has on more rouge than is necessary on so young a girl, and Dougal can make out freckles at the side of her nose.

"May I know yer name?"

"Tis Moira."

"Then Moira, I beg yer pardon, but I'm ainly with ye here tae keep me gob aff the street fer a spell."

"Yer in flight from one iv the sponge houses."

"Is it that plain?"

Moira waves a hand toward the little window—

"There's four of 'em within the sound iv St. George's bells. And I have to tell ye, the streets is full iv informers."

"Och—"

"Little finger-pointin' divvils that'll be after putting it in my Toby's ear that I'm up here with a fella as looks to be without a penny to his name."

"And he'll gae hard with ye?"

Moira shrugs. "He's a sanctuary man, Toby, that only steps out iv a Sunday to settle his accounts. Excaped from prison as you have."

"Would ye care tae sit, then?" says Dougal, indicating the bed. The plan was to get to the river, somehow get on a ship heading north—

"I'd love it. I'll be on me feet—when I'm not on me back—till the last lamp is doused." She sits and Dougal sits beside her. "Ye've got until two bells."

"I thank ye. If I had a coin tae spare—"

"Then ye'd not be runnin' from the keepers. Yer Scotch, is it?"

"I am—"

"One iv Prince Charlie's byes?"

"I was."

Moira nods. "I've a brother went off to France to folly them Stuarts. Anything to vex the Tommy Lobsters."

"And here we sit, in the bowels of the beastie."

"Do ye know what they've in mind fer ye?"

Dougal mimes a rope around his neck.

"There's some," says Moira, "would consider it an honor."

St. George's bell rings twice.

"Even if ye had paid me, that bell would be the end iv it," she tells him. "Toby is jealous iv me time."

They stand then, Dougal dipping his chafed hands in the water in the basin, and then he leaves Moira, happy to find nobody waiting for him on the hodgepodge of stairs.

The follower stands across Nag's Head, blowing his nose into a grayish handkerchief.

And Whipshaw is waiting for him, playfully swinging a set of manacles, with Giles and another of the warders along for support.

"A pleasant interlude with the lady, I trust?"

"I ainly just met her—"

"I am aware of that. I am aware of all that transpires in this neighborhood." They have begun to walk back toward the Marshalsea, the two keepers a step behind Dougal and Whipshaw. "A shilling proffered here and there, but also a great number of the residents have loved ones inside our penal edifices, requiring a favor now and again."

"Some hae managed tae escape, though—"

"Very few under my watch. And those were much more highly connected than you."

"Aye. Why should prison be any different frae the rest iv life?"

Whipshaw smiles. "This will mean some time in the Hole, I'm afraid."

Dougal wishes now he'd had the price of Moira, anxiety about the pox nothing to a man facing the halter. To feel her breath on his face—

"Unless, of course," adds Whipshaw, "we can arrive at a financial accommodation."

IT IS SOMETHING LIKE SENDING YOUR CHILDREN OUT into the world. You prepare them, of course, provide them with a store of example and instruction, see to their needs both physical and emotional, until they are able, you hope, to venture forth on their own. You have given them a proper course, and they must steer it. Gildart watches from the quay as the *Veteran* weighs anchor, a complicated process with so many ships crowded together, a minimum of sail raised and the rest at the ready. He loves to see, from this distance, the crew scurry about like monkeys, the mate's shouted orders drifting to him a heartbeat after they have been attended to. He has the *Johnson* and the *Gildart* already three days out, heading for the Colonies with a fleet of merchantmen, he has three vessels that should be, God willing, well on their way home, and now the *Veteran*, with John Ricky in charge, off to the Leewards. *Go forth and multiply*, he thinks proudly as the mainsail shoots up the mast and the crew's huzzah reaches the quay.

There are details, some rather vexing, to consider, of course. The blundering loss of eight transports and all its ramifications—too late to replace them or remove the proper percentage of victuals meant for their sustenance, a galling amount of paperwork to be filed with the Ministry, the shortfall in revenue compared to the cost of the voyage, always a matter of some rather speculative computation. Who is to say whether a skilled artisan—a weaver or watchmaker, for instance—will raise a higher sum than a laborer, young, well-made, and in reasonable health? His factotums pass on whatever news they glean when a ship sails into port from one of those far-flung islands—tales of crop failures, hurricanes, smoldering volcanoes and insurrections raised and crushed. Notwithstanding, however, that sugar, molasses, and now coffee continue to be unloaded on the docks, and the trade grows more and more lucrative, if one understands its vagaries, with every year. Many of the more cautious gentlemen in Liverpool have begun to spread their risk, investing a quarter or less of the outlay for several ventures, softening the blow should any one ship meet disaster, though diminishing the return when great success is won. Gildart, born into the trade, prides himself on his combination of boldness and acuity, his success in attracting the best of the port's seamen to man his ships, whether they be transports, slavers, or simple merchantmen. Ten percent profit on a voyage is nothing to sniff at, and when all runs as planned he can realize many times that.

Sometimes, in whimsy, he imagines what it must be like for those bound below—for man, no matter what his station, is a thinking animal. Man considers his past, ponders his fate. The transports have only themselves to blame for their situation, yes, but have now been torn asunder from the familiar regimen of gaol and gallows and sent off into a Great Unknown. What fears must incubate within their breasts, what misery, or, perhaps, what glimmer of hope?

The women, more than a dozen of them on the *Veteran* along with one hundred and fifty male transports, are always a worry. He holds a petition for mercy from one of them, a woman twice widowed during the recent rebellion, that he will hold on to till the ship is four days at sea—she is beyond pardon, and there is no sense in delaying the voyage for legal niceties. Ricky is an able master who will brook no debauchery aboard, and the women, most of them camp followers of the vanquished rebels, will be delivered with whatever virtue they still possess intact. Their destiny from that point on is difficult to foresee, depending of their age, health, domestic skills and feminine wiles. No doubt a well-looking Highland lass, given the dearth of white women there, might charm her way into some enviable position in Antigua or St. Kitts, for while the Frenchman or Spaniard have no qualms about creating mulattos and even, in extreme cases, giving them their names, the Englishman of stature is not so prone to decadence. What character may develop in even the white sons and daughters of these planters, raised in the tropics from birth and subject to indolence of climate and lassitude of social constraint, is beyond his ken. He has counseled his sons to limit their own travels to the tide tables and the chart room.

The *Veteran* is a speck of white on the horizon now, and till its return will remain an account unsettled in his ledger. A farewell shot from one of its paltry eight guns will have sunk to the bottom of the sea before the sound of its firing, should it be audible at all, reaches his ears. The entire island of Nevis or Barbados might have already sunk beneath the waves for all he knows, Jamaica might be in the hands of rioting maroons, the act across the water and knowledge of that act in the civilized world separated by geography and time. Common laborers he has transported to the Colonies might be kings in the wilderness by now—for certainly kings of Africa have left his ships to become common laborers.

The sea air is invigorating, but it is time to return to his figures, to his correspondence. The speck of white disappears where water meets sky.

THEY'VE GIVEN JENNY SHOES. NOT PROPER BROGANS, more like the *cuarans* the bog keepers wear, raw oxhide tied around the foot with a leather thong, hairy side out, that once wet seem to remain that way forever. Hers are wet now, the smallish boat they were carried out in taking water over the bow, but she'll keep them on till she thinks of a better place to hide the ring, held between her toes. They've a separate compartment, the fifteen of them, and much has been made of their freedom from chains. They know the lads are belowdecks as well, perhaps in the stern of the ship. Most of the women were taken together at Carlisle with the force abandoned there as the Prince and his Army retreated. Several seem to be sisters, and only a few have only Erse. They've been told they'll be given food a while into the day's voyage, when their stomachs have settled. Jenny has never been out of sight of land before. One of the older women, a MacFarlane from Perth, says that they'll be allowed on deck once a day, but so far that is only rumor. Morag says they'll be given to the sailors as part of their wages, but this has been discounted by the others. The sounds the ship's hull makes, creakings and groanings and occasionally a wooden snap, were frightening at first but now seem normal, the thumping of waves against the bow settling into a rhythm that changes pitch and direction every now and then. They are going somewhere.

Jenny wishes she'd seen more of Liverpool before they left.

> Ship's log *Gildart*, Wednesday May 10th, 1747. 5 days at sea. Watch commences moderate winds with heavy swell from west. Midday part moderate breezes and showers. Latter part fine breeze with passing showers. Lat 51' 28" Long 14' 49". Distance per log 68 miles.

Keach, shuffling on ruined legs, supervises the feeding. The hatch is opened, one of the ship's boys ducking his head down to be sure all are securely fettered and in their places, then the ladder is dropped and they begin to pass down trenchers of the day's swill. Smaller bowls that the sailors call "crews" are put before each of the groups of six, the men sharing whatever is dumped into them. Keach totters about making sure equal portions are dealt, then the boys are dismissed, while Barlow sits on a rung of the ladder with a belaying pin in hand, a thong attached to it wrapped about his wrist and arm to ensure it cannot easily be taken from him.

"Mair of this scran," mutters Lachlan, regarding the trough of thin gruel, "and we'll be up tae our oxters in liquid shite."

The other men begin to eat silently, as they have been instructed, avoiding the lame sailor's augerlike gaze. Keach allows them only a few swallows before addressing the perilous state of their immortal souls.

"Wot you lot don't realize is that our Supreme Father is not only a jealous and all-powerful God, but that 'ee is an *angry* God."

Keach's voice is amplified in the closed chamber like that of a reverend with a soundboard over his kirk pulpit, overpowering the thrashing of bow and waves.

"Ye're worldly men—steeped in sin an corrupshin from the day yez are born, and some've yez even *pa*pists, followers of a Satanic doctrine."

Jamie tries to choke down a small handful of the scurvy grass that is placed before them every day. Many of his fellow prisoners don't bother, hating the bitter taste or sure the English mean to poison them. But Jamie, knowing they are to be sold at the end of the journey, assumes that their Master will try to keep them at least as healthy as he would cattle or sheep being shipped for market.

"Ye've no idear 'ow offensive ye are ter 'is eye," says Keach, shuffling between the benches, his color rising.

"The God that 'olds you over the Pit iv 'ell as one 'olds a spider or other loavesome insect over a fire, 'oo abhors you, an' is dreadfully provoked."

Keach looks about at them, a disgusted grimace contorting his face. "You are unrepentant sinners 'oo will spend millions and millions of ages in suffering the agonies of 'Is mighty Vengeance, consumed in liquid fire but never knowing the peace of death, only to discover that at what you think must be the *end*, it 'as all been but a miniscule point in time to what remains!"

Big Fergal rocks a bit, as he always does when Keach holds forth. Jamie knows that Barlow, belaying pin or no, would be no match for the MacGregor.

"But now," Keach announces, his voice softening, "ye've got an extrawdinry opportunity, a day wherein Christ 'as flung the door of Mercy wide open, and stands in that door callin' and cryin' with a loud voice ter poor sinners, a day wherein many are flockin' ter 'Im, and pressin' theirselves inter the Kingdom of God!"

There are hellfire captains, Jamie has heard, who insist their crews abjure from cursing and the drinking of grog during their sojourn aboard. There are papist captains and Quaker captains and captains innocent of religious affiliation. What goes on abovedecks on the *Gildart* is still a matter of speculation for the transports, the captain, Holmes, speaking to them directly only once and the sailors colorful liars by nature. Keach may be proselytizing at his own whim, ruler of this captive kingdom.

Keach taps Cameron's foot with his own, suddenly back in the worldly realm.

"You six," he says. "On deck."

Climbing the ladder requires some care, moving one rung at a time with a great deal of repositioning of heavy chain. Once on top they wait for the next six chosen by Keach to step up, a dozen being Captain Holmes' limit for prisoners on deck at any one time. The ship's boys are sent back down to bring out the trenchers and waste buckets then, while Barlow herds the two coffles of transports to the afterdeck.

Jamie sees the fins, three of them, slicing the water's surface as the creatures swim parallel to each other, remaining the exact same distance behind the *Gildart* as if they are being towed.

"Devilfish," says Barlow, stepping to the taffrail to watch them. "Joined us after Belfast and 'aven't left off."

"Dae they no sleep?" asks Jamie.

Barlow winks. "Mysteries of the deep."

They are ordered to "dance," then, shuffling in place while raising their arms over their heads and bringing their knees as high as they can, the heavy irons chafing sores already open, to the beat of Barlow's belaying pin on the mainmast, another sailor indolently pointing a musket at them from on top of the longboat.

Keach and two of the boys reappear, carrying the body of MacCaffrey, who died in the night and has just been pried loose from his companions. They lay him on the deck, stuffing ballast stones in his shirt and breeks, then lift him up again. It is an awkward load, carried with quick, small steps to the very stern then unceremoniously heaved over. Jamie hears the splash, sees the fins—one, two, three—slide under the waves.

"One of the more fortunate," says Keach. "Not like you wretches. Where yer 'eaded, there's them that'll cook a man alive, bit by bit, and eat the cooked parts while the victim watches."

"Civvylized enow tae cook their food, is it?" says Lachlan, hopping slightly sideways on one foot and then the other. "That's a comfort tae ken."

"If ye was smart lads ye'd throw yerselfs ter them devilfish," says Keach. "Save yerselfs a life of mizzry."

"Where exactly is it we're to be delivered?" asks Cameron. There are several possibilities, and if the sailors know, they aren't telling.

"All ye really need ter understand," Keach tells them as the water in their wake boils with fury and a crimson rose begins to spread, "is that it is a Godless wasteland."

> Ship's log *Veteran*, May 13th, 1747. Pleasant weather. Sighted a brigantine standing to the east. Latitude 51' 08" north. Long 15' 04" west. Distance by log 169 miles.

Unfettered, they are set to picking oakum. "Merely as a diversion for the passage of time," stated the captain, though if any of them come short at the end of a day their deck privileges are curtailed. Jenny claws the tarry bits of rope apart with bloodied fingers, sitting on the edge of the shelflike platform they all sleep upon, listening to the others talk. Today it is the youngest of the three Lochaber sisters, nearly whispering in Erse as the bilge sloshes beneath them and the women pick away. The group held at Carlisle together, nine of them including the Lochaber Camerons, have become something of a family through their lengthy confinement together, tolerating Jenny but shunning to speak with Morag and the other two women transported for crimes other than support of the Cause. Those three keep their own sorority, laughing a good deal more than the others, while one of the Carlisle captives, Elizabeth, prefers to sit alone, her hands idle in her lap and as a punishment allowed on deck only once every few days. Jenny and the rest are brought up once a day, made to hop about and be leered at by the sailors.

She lost two men to it, explains Effie, the darkest of the sisters, no doubt with selkie blood in her veins.

The first was killed at Clifton, in the battle there. The Prince's army, though they'd won, had to move on quickly, leaving us that followed them behind. She was new a widow then, poor Liz, stumbling through snow that was over the knees at times and cold, cold like I've never felt it. We were taken by the Duke's men between Clifton and Carlisle, and made to walk, tied together by cords now, all the way through Appleby to the York Castle.

Jenny steals a glance at the woman, sitting peaceably, swaying gently with the motion of the ship, as if waiting for some finer conveyance to arrive and whisk her away.

There were a number of our men already prisoner there, some badly wounded, and among these was Edmund Clavering. He was a bold, difficult fellow, though very near a gentleman, and though the English keepers there despised him, they allowed our Liz to treat his wounds best as she was able, him slowly recovering his health till he could do what a man will do with a woman.

She looks near Jenny's age, Elizabeth, smallish and too young to be twice a widow. She is the only one of them wearing silk.

She was married in that gown, whispers Effie, noticing Jenny's gaze. There was a priest held in the castle, a real priest, Catholic, as was called Monox Hervey. Clavering was a Catholic as well, and prevailed upon the man to marry them—"To prevent sin," as he said. We were many of us there at the ceremony, having bribed the warders, but when the officer in command of the castle heard about it he was greatly distressed, all papist ritual being outside the law.

They were allowed together after?

Not once the marriage was made public. It reflected badly on the commander. Not long after there was a trial for most of the men held in the bailey, with Clavering one of those sentenced to die. It was winter by then, all of us freezing within those cold stones on the great hill by the river, and we watched the condemned taken away—nine of them—then saw as they were brought back from their hanging in town. Most were dragged in rough coffins on sledges, but Edmund and one other were returned in a hearse pulled by four black horses. As I said, he was nearly a gentleman.

Jenny stands and walks the few steps back and forth that are possible in the compartment. Morag has told her that the ship has been used as a slaver, but Jenny believes it would then smell worse, that it would be haunted in the dark. But the ship sounds at night are mostly comforting to her, like being in a giant cradle, and the men held below are too far away for the sound of their irons to be heard.

"What're them bitches mutterin' aboot?" asks Morag.

"Love, perhaps," says Jenny. "And hae our fortune is no in our ane hands."

"Or twixt our ane legs," says Morag, and the other criminal girls laugh.

"Of course," muses Jenny, "who'd ever want tae ken just what will happen next?"

Ship's log *Gildart*, May 15th, 1747. Early day blowing hard with all hands employed in ship's duty. Wind

> from NW but slackened. Carpenter drunk again, forced to give him correction with crew as witness. Lat 42' 30 ½" Longitude 15' 44" w (10 days out).

"It needs be at night," says Jamie. "Toward the end of first watch, when them that's still on deck is getting dozy."

It is their only entertainment, debating the best course of action to overpower the crew and take the ship, though much like the years of rebel talk that preceded Prince Charlie's abrupt appearance in the north, it is mere speculation.

"When the weather is tranquil," adds Cameron, "and few hands are required."

"Aye, with a steady breeze tae lull them asleep."

The ship's cat is suddenly in the compartment, gray and sturdy with bits of tar stuck to its fur, moving with a rolling gait like a sailor. They watch it pad about for a moment, ignoring them completely as if to flaunt its liberty. A rat has been spotted a few times, wriggling up from the bilge, but the two seem to be avoiding each other.

"It's just *there*," says Kemlo, a blacksmith from Aberdeen. "I've never keeked it comin' nor gang."

Lachlan attempts to make the Sign of the Cross, his manacles clinking together. "Wickit creaturs," he says.

Jamie continues with his assessment, keeping his voice low.

"I count ainly nineteen deckhands, if ye include the ship's byes," he says. "With the carpenter, bosun, surgeon, armorer, two mates, and Captain Holmes, that's twenty-six."

"Twenty-six capable of bearing arms," nods Cameron.

"The cannon cannae be tornt inward, and the small arms are a' kept in a locker by the captain's berth, but maist of the sailors will keep a dirk by them in their hammocks."

"Familiars of Satan," Lachlan persists. "Did ye ken that the he-cat has barbs on his pizzle? Once they've thrust themsel' intae the she-cat it cannae slip oot."

"Ye've made a study of this, have ye?"

"When the she-cat cries and screeches, is no passion, but *pain* she's feelin'."

"We'd need to spare one of the mates," says Cameron. "There's not a sailor among us, and someone must be trusted with the navigation."

"But where would we sail *to?*" asks one of the Duncans. "The English are a' over the coast where we're headed."

"Ye can tell it by their een," says Lachlan, staring at the cat. "The way they glows like fire at night—"

"Leave aff with that, will ye?"

"There is a wee bit of hard rock and green airth as sticks up frae the sea in the far west," Lachlan continues, raising his voice, "calt Pabbay Island. The wild, naked people that come afore us lived there lang ago, and then there was monks who dwelt in towers of stane they'd built, sending up their monkish prayers tae Heaven till the Norsemen landed and kilt them all."

"A warning as to the effectiveness of prayer," says Cameron.

"At the time I'm tellin', the only men upon the isle was a fearsome ootlaw named Kincaid and his three companions, each of 'em crooler and mair desprit than the next. As there was naething on Pabbay tae rob but fer the nests of the flocks of birds as raised their bairns there, it was ainly fit as shelter fer these bold men, a place tae hide and lick their wounds after a raid upon the other islands. They'd many an enemy at this time, Kincaid and his band, among them the sheriff and a' his bailiffs, as well as other banditti of the area who dinnae appreciate the compytition. The band were hard prest, watchin' frae a height each dee fer boats tae row up intae Bàgh Bàn, the harbor there, with a party of men set tae hunt them doon.

"The dee come when Kincaid had had his fill of this and says tae his mates, he says, 'What is wanted here is an al*li*ance, a pact, if ye will, with somebody that every mon of them that chase us is feert of.'

"'And who'd that be?' asks the boldest of his men. 'There's nary a mon in the west doesnae despise us and wish us deid.'

"'Fetch me three black cats,' says Kincaid, 'the blacker the better, and ye'll meet Him soon enow.'"

Touch Not the Cat, thinks Jamie, who was told this tale by his father's father.

"Noo, at this time twas written in the law books that cats was never tae be brung tae Pabbay, as they'd soon breed and overrun the isle, killin' aff the great flocks of seabirds as nestit there. But Kincaid's men was sore afeert of his distempers, and rowed aff tae Skye in search of the creaturs.

"Twas night when they returned, a night withoot a moon, carryin' three black cats held in a sack. Kincaid was waitin' fer them oot on Rosinish, a wee headland on the east of the isle that's conneckit tae it by ainly a narra bridge of rock, and he's set a great bonfire there, which they'd never done afore through fear of discovery. He'd cut a thin pole frae a sapling, Kincaid, and he holds it oot and he says, 'Tie me ane of them cats tae this here, sae as it may no struggle free.'

"His men pull oot the first of the black cats, which is scratching and bitin' at em, but they bind it tae the end of the pole, hangin' doon like a hare aboot tae be cooked, and Kincaid says, 'Keep yer swords in yer hands, lads, we might have company.' And with that he swings the cat over the bonfire and commences tae roast it slowly over the flames.

"Noo, ye can imagine the yowlin' and screechin' as follyed, the black cat writhin' as its hair is singed and its skin is blisthered aff, the tail catchin' fire and twistin' aboot, with Kincaid's men scairt clear tae their banes, sure that the racket and the light of the bonfire will draw the sheriff and his hanchmen. But what should emerge frae the dark around them but an *imp*—a wee, crookit fella with the face of a mole and scabs a' over his hide, walkin' on bare feet that has claws on them.

"'Leave aff with that,' he warns, 'or ye'll wake Him fer sure.'

"'Ye scurry back tae where ye dwell,' says Kincaid, bold as brass, 'ye oogly, skelpin' daemon, and ye tell Him we're waitin.'

"Well, the imp, he spits something yella and nasty oot that sizzles when it hits the ground, but aff he gaes, back intae the darkness. By this time the first cat is naethin' but char and gristle, sae Kincaid orders, 'Fetch me another cat!' and his men, near oot of their nobs with fear by noo, do as he says, binding the second scratchin', bitin' creatur tae the pole.

"This one sets up an even greater racket than the first, wailin' like a *ban sith*, the sound of it echoin' oot over the dark water as surrounds Rosinish, fillin' the moonless nicht with its terrible agony, the smell of its burnin' flesh enow tae turn yer stummick. Noo, that cat has barely a twitch of life left in it when oot frae the dark aboot them steps the *Shelly*coat, rattlin' as he walks, hair of brown seaweed, teeth gnarled and yella, the puir fella's hide crusted with shells and barnacles, webbing atween his toes like a duck, his voice like the screechin' of gulls.

"'Ye've woke Him noo, and he's clean vexed!' cried the Shellycoat. 'Leave aff with that or He says he'll take measures.'

"Kincaid only grins at this, crazed as a loon, and says, 'Tell him we're waitin'."

"Sae the Shellycoat rattles aff intae the dark, and Kincaid says 'Fetch me the last of them cats.'

"Noo this cat has heert the dyin' screams of his companions in the sack, and fights tooth and claw tae break loose frae their grip, but the ootlaws finally bind him tae the pole and Kincaid swings him over the flame.

"The final black cat screeches tae bring the Divvil—twistin' and writhin' on the pole as his flesh is burnt awee, Kincaid's men coverin' their lugs with their hands at the horror of the sound. And at last, when this final cat is ainly a wailing cinder on a stick, does another figure step oot frae the dark. Twas Auld Clootie-foot himsel', black and poxy, oogly as sin, and fit tae bite their heids aff.

"'Ye've woke me,' he says through teeth like brambles.

"'And fer a purpose,' says Kincaid, no sae cheeky noo, but able tae keek the Divvil in the een withoot tremblin'.

"Clootie-foot looks the lot of them over, sees what's left of the cat on the pole, and grins a terrible grin. 'What'll ye have, then?' he says.

"'We've enemies aboot the islands,' explains Kincaid, 'and I want ye tae join us agin them.'

"Clootie-foot considers this, smiling noo, which is a fearsome thing tae keek, stroking at his beard with his knobby fingers. 'Could be done,' he says, 'but it'll cost ye.'

"'What price?' asks Kincaid.

"'Four souls,' replies the Divvil.

"Then it's Kincaid's turn tae smile. 'Sae yer a powerful hand with a claymuir?'

"'Never a better ane,' says Clootie-foot.

"'Then join us against our enemies, and whenever ye care tae collect yer due, see if ye can best the four of us with the blade.'

"'I'd shake yer hand on that,' says the Divvil, 'but twould burn yer fingers awee.'

"And with that he fades back intae the black night.

"'What've ye done?' cries the boldest of his men.

"'Dinnae worry,' says Kincaid. 'I ken hoo tae deal with *that* gentleman.'

"And with that he commences tae throw seawater on the bonfire, quellin' the flames, till when they're nearly a' doused his men see Kincaid's claymuir, glowerin' among the embers.

"'It's been tempered noo,' he tells them, 'in the bluid of them black cats. It's become a weapon nae man nor creatur can vanquish.'

"And there follows a round of thievin' and plunder' as the isles had never knane afore, Kincaid and his lads makin' their raids in the light of dee, but whenever ootnumbered by their pursuers they'd turn and stand tae fight, Auld Clootie-foot appearin' at their side as agreed upon, the very Divvil with a sword, striking doon whomever dared tae challenge him and scarin' the others awee with only his fearsome appearance. Soon Kincaid and his band had ainly tae strike upon a door in whichever wee village they'd chosen and the inhabbytants would toss oot their treasures—better tae lose a portion of yer wealth than yer heid tae the Prince of Hell. Nae langer did the band need tae shelter on Pabbay Island—they strutted aboot like masters of the realm, takin' their fill of the drink and the women as was no well hidden or sent tae the mainland. Like kings they lived, and near fergot aboot the pact they'd made with Auld Clootie-foot.

"Comes the dee, they're a' the wee up tae Skye, carousing ootside a tavern in Portree Harbor, drunk as lairds, when the Divvil appears afore them, a claymuir in each hand.

"'Ye've had yer frolic in the sun,' He says, 'but noo it's time tae give up yer souls.'

"Kincaid and his lads draw their ane steel—'Come and take them, if ye dare,' he says, and they have at it.

"Weel, the other lads is nae match fer Clootie-foot and his twa swords, and there's clangin' and sparks flying and each gaes doon in his turn, cloven in twa frae chops tae nave, leavin' ainly Kincaid and his magic sword tae face the Divvil.

"'I've nae had sae much sport,' says Auld Clootie-foot, swingin' his claymuirs at a divvilish speed, 'since ma fall frae grace.'

"But Kincaid's sword is e'en faster than the twa of his opponent, merely a blur as it fends each killin' stroke awee, blue sparks flyin' and a' the town of Portree, such as it was then, watchin' frae their windaes and doorwees, mouths gappin' open in fear and wonder.

Auld Clootie-foot begins tae tire of this, his arms wearyin', and he says, 'I fergot tae remind ye, there's somebody else wants a portion of this fight,' and there by his side appears an enormous black cat, bigger and mair fearsome than e'en Fergal MacGregor here, standin' up on twa feet with his een blazin' with anger, and he croaks, 'Burn *me* in a fire, will ye?' and with ane swipe of his mighty paw he knocks the magic sword clear frae Kincaid's hand.

"Weel, Kincaid kens that he's done fer noo, and he kneels down afore Auld Clootie-foot, who wastes nae time in cleavin' the ootlaw's heid frae his shoulders, the heid rollin' tae a stop on the ground, his een fixit on the Divvil, his lips still able tae move. 'I'm yers, Master,' says the severed head of Rhory Kincaid, 'till the end of time.'"

It is quiet in the compartment for a moment then, and they realize the ship's cat is gone and no one has witnessed by what egress.

"Wickit creaturs,"says Lachlan, "that means naebody well."

> Ship's log *Veteran*, May 23rd, 1747. Took on water at Palma, Canary Is. Lat 29' 22" N. Long 18' 47' W—tomorrow to island of Ferro—15 days out.

Apex.

It is a beautiful word, a sturdy word, scribed on the paper with a towering "A." It is the word Captain Ricky keeps in his mind throughout the day as they continue their westing, himself at the very point, the very pinnacle of that A once there is water under the keel and wind in the sails. On shore and even just off the dock there are others above him, of course, Smith in London and Gildart in Liverpool, the Royal Navy, the Houses of Commons and Lords, all the way up to the King and His Divine Right.

There's an apex for you. One that looms above his every order, his every whim aboard the *Veteran* as he paces, without agitation at the moment, upon the quarterdeck. Every wretched tar with mutiny in his heart knows that even if captain and officers be vanquished, there is nowhere in the wide world he will find shelter from the Empire's justice. For though the base beneath the apex is much, much wider, the weight from above is crushing, is absolute.

Ricky can feel that every hand on deck, without giving him so much as a glance, is aware of his presence. *The Old Man's abroad.* There is respect in it, he the master of winds and currents, the savant of reefing, a veteran himself of a dozen voyages as captain and countless others when he was still ascending the ladder. But there must be an element of fear, as well—the horse that never feels the bit grows indolent, temperamental. No floggings have been needed yet, but he put Grimes on half rations, no grog for a week for pestering the female transports, and there is one of the landsmen, a sullen brute of a harvest hand already disenchanted with the sea, who will make a fine example. The crew have their pets, but this rustic is not one of them.

His officers and key men, the bar beneath the apex of the A, are solid enough, the mates having sailed with him before, the surgeon young but willing, the ship's carpenter never completely sober but adept at his trade, the armorer a Vulcan with the shackles and chains, though rather overzealous to employ weapons. Test-firing muskets whenever the male transports are brought up is a waste of powder. Ricky wishes he had more than two sailors who had actually fired a cannon in battle, but hauling transports rather than denser cargo leaves the *Veteran* a sprightly and maneuverable ship—quick action in the yards is always preferable to exchanging broadsides with a privateer.

Ricky strolls with his hands clasped behind his back, gazing at the horizon. Some, the landsmen especially, must believe him a man of leisure, and none can know just how much cogitation is required of his position. Just preparing for the voyage—the endless wrangle with the bandits who fit and provision the ship, delaying, delaying, their prices magically swelling as the window of favorable weather begins to close, butchers, bakers, stevedores, ship's chandlers, customs agents, all to be negotiated with, cajoled, flattered, threatened, while simultaneously enticing a crew to sign on. Good sailors, once back in port, do not bide their time to wait to rejoin a particular captain. They are flotsam, stirred by the currents of cheap rum and cheap women till their silver runs out and they wash aboard whatever likely vessel is about to sail, often delivered by a bailiff and with half their pay already advanced to landladies and publicans. Thinking of the future, in the orderly, cautious manner Ricky is required to do it, has no dominion with sailors.

Then at sea there is the course to chart, so many ways to skin the cat, so many variables of sea and sky to contend with, the abilities of the crew to gauge and, if possible, improve upon, the state of the ship itself to monitor. The *Veteran* is a smallish brig, no sheathing on its hull despite long forays in tropical waters, sound for its age but apt to yaw to the starboard when fully loaded. He has the transports, a potentially troublesome lot, to supervise. Rebels and traitors, all of them now inveterate jailbirds, and pledged to their common cause—at least with a Guinea cargo there is a mix of tribes, a gumbo of languages, even some blood feuds to keep the captives from cooperating in a plot. His current savages are all of the same blood, some able to understand what is spoken by the crew, and, being a species of white man, better able to formulate their mischief.

Give him a hold full of cutpurses and counterfeiters any day.

The man at the apex must also be a master of numbers. There are the degrees divined from the sextant, of course, the ability to steer the ship to flyspeck islands in the vastness of the ocean, but also the numbers of commerce. His status in the trade is tied inexorably to profit and loss. How much volume in trade goods can be given over to water and victuals for the crew and transports? How much westing given up to search for a man overboard? How many of the cannon to be fully functional and how many to serve only as show? When are the prices for sugar, rum, tobacco, likely to rise or fall? What is too dear for the risk involved, too likely to spoil on the homeward journey, what balance between filling the hold completely and setting sail at a propitious time of year? What customs fees, bribes, extortions to pay or evade? The competition from other ships, other nations, must be factored in, unknown political events imagined, the values of different currencies understood. How many pounds of tobacco is a man, a reasonably fit Scotsman, in this case, worth to a planter in Barbados? Before or immediately after an epidemic of the yellow fever?

The women have been brought up on deck. Less obstreperous than the usual whores and pickpockets, some alleged to possess skill at spinning and sewing and a few of them very well-looking. They are a distraction for the crew, of course, but thus far only Grimes has fallen off his spar. Ricky will auction them first, after a bit of rum punch with the planters, entertaining them with his version of the Jacobite rebellion and its vanquishing. Still very few white women in the islands, and these should be a welcome sight. There is some fine cloth aboard, and if he can calculate the value of the few yards needed to furnish new dresses against the potential increase in sale price—

> Ship's log *Gildart*, June 12th, 1747. 39 days at sea, paltry breezes. At 38' 31" north, lat by dead reckoning 30' 04" west, sighted derelict ship, no flag. Investigate—

The *Gildart* glides vaguely westward, sails only half full, the ocean's surface rolling almost imperceptibly beneath a cloudless sky. Captain Holmes stands at the bow with a glass to his eye as he speaks to the mate.

"Bring one up," he says. "And be sure he has a Christian tongue in his head."

Jamie steps up from the ladder, squinting, and stands, rubbing the now-exposed sores on his wrists where the manacles chafe. There is another ship to their lee, with three masts, one of them broken, from which hang the tatters of rigging and canvas. The crew of the *Gildart* stand at the gunwale, staring with obvious misgiving. Keach pokes Jamie from behind with a belaying pin.

"Cap'n wishes ter speak with ye."

The sailors eye him suspiciously as he is led forward, Holmes watching from above.

"Name?"

"MacGillivray."

"Right. You're to row over and board that—" he indicates the drifting frigate, "and have a look around. Touch as little as you can."

He is placed in the dinghy, swinging against the hull a few times with a soft thump before they lower it into the water. Jamie has not rowed three strokes before he is aware of the forms about him—devilfish, dozens of them, circling the derelict *Dahomey Queen* and now peeling off to investigate his tiny vessel. One bumps the hull of the dinghy and Jamie puts his back to the oars.

It takes him three tries with the line and boarding hook to catch fast on the gunwale, netting strung about the deck making a clean throw difficult. Halfway up the side he doubts he has the strength, but the thought of the sharks waiting below prompts a surge of resolve, and he is over the side, wrestling past the netting.

The stench is like a curtain that must be pushed through, Jamie pulling the tail of his threadbare shirt up over his nose as his bare feet meet the deck. It is eerily quiet—water lapping against the sides of the hull, wood and hemp creaking, the forlorn luff of a nearly limp sail.

A barricado nearly twice his height has been built at midships, extending from rail to rail and a few feet beyond, Jamie on the higher stern deck. Here it is black women, nearly naked, and a few white sailors—all dead. He sees that *DQ* has been branded on the bare buttocks of the women, that the sailors are not armed, though the swivel gun on top of the barricade is swung to aim down onto the other side. One dead man lies beside the wheel, his wrist lashed to it with a cord, waving with the rocking of the ship.

A man with shoes upon his feet, perhaps the mate, sits against the door of the captain's cabin, his face swollen and distorted as the others. Jamie pushes him out of the way with his foot, opens the door.

Blood and bits of brain matter have dried on the wall behind the captain's head, the discharged pistol still in his hand. A long procession of brown ants march up the lapel of his jacket to what is left of his face. Jamie takes the ship's log, only slightly spattered, with him as he leaves.

He can see the sunburnt faces on the *Gildart* following his progress as he crosses the afterdeck, ducking under loose ropes and hanging sailcloth, stepping over and around the twisted bodies of crew and cargo. There is a small door that leads through the barricado, a dead sailor with a musket lying beside him next to it. The door is not blocked, and Jamie passes through.

Only dead sailors on the other side. His count of white men, or those he assumes to be white men, given their clothing, ends at twenty-two. He squats by one, considers the dirk strapped to the man's thigh, then realizes he will surely be stripped and searched upon his return. The stench is thicker over the raised rectangle of grating on the foredeck, and he tries to hold his breath as he crawls upon it to look down. The sun is straight overhead and at first his own shadow obscures what lies below, until he turns sideward to allow the light in.

The hold is full of the bodies of African men, crowded one upon the next on a low platform, hands and feet swollen twice their natural size around their fetters. The men are bound in twos, hand to hand and foot to foot, and here and there he can see the *DQ* brand. These men are more emaciated then the negro women on deck, ribs nearly poking through their skin, though from their faces it appears they are not as long dead. Jamie calls down, and there is no answer. He hurries to the side to vomit through the netting, a swirl of sharks rushing to the spot where it splashes the surface.

Following his captain's instructions, Jamie crosses back to the other side of the barricade and locates an earthen jug of lamp oil in the armorer's shed, removes the flints from a pair of muskets, makes a pile of the driest canvas and rope he can find, topping it with a loose ball of oakum found in the carpenter's chest. He drenches it all in lamp oil, strikes the flints till the oakum is fired, and hurries back to where the boathook is fast.

The sharks are still cruising around the dinghy, which looks to be a great distance below. Jamie can hear flame crackling as he slides down the line, burning the palms of his hands, careful to yank the dinghy well under him before he falls aboard.

He is alongside the bow of the *Gildart,* easily able to keep pace with its progress, when Captain Holmes calls down.

"What did you see?"

It would be prudent, Jamie knows, if not strictly humane for the captain to abandon him here, and if there was more wind he might already have done so.

"I'll tell ye when I'm back on deck!" he calls.

Holmes confers with the mate and a line is thrown down to him. Jamie holding tight as he is pulled to a rope ladder, following Keach's instruction as to where to knot the line to the dinghy before starting up.

"So?" says Captain Holmes, backing up a step when Jamie steps too near.

"Slaver. I'd wager the crew and the cargo as was above, the women, died of some sickness they brought from the Slave Coast, and the men as was below then starved. Ah," he says pulling the logbook from his shirt, "and the captain sent a ball through his brain."

Holmes nods, and the mate takes the logbook from him.

"Quarantine," says the mate, and Keach is pushing him with the belaying pin again. Jamie sees black smoke rising above the *Dahomey Queen* as he is prodded toward the afterdeck.

"Was it bad?" hisses Keach as they pass the scowling crew.

"Terrible bad."

"May God 'ave mercy on their souls," mutters the sailor. "The wretches below, and the sinners as stole them away."

There is so little wind that even at twelve bells the crew on watch can still make out the blaze on the horizon, the slaver and all aboard burning long into the night. Jamie MacGillivray, alone below the waterline, sits in absolute darkness.

> Ship's log *Gildart*, June 21st, 1747. Afternoon heavy squall from the NE, continued dark squally weather, all hands employed in ship's duty. Distance per log 35 miles due to shifting winds. Long 38' 11" north, lat 35' 14" west.

He can hear Keach at the open hatch above. Jamie is quarantined indefinitely in the orlop deck with the spare anchors and cables, below the waterline. Twice a day the crippled sailor lowers food and water, remaining to talk while Jamie eats, the glow from his lantern the only light he is allowed. He worries he will go blind.

"We'd been on the Slave Coast fer a month," says Keach, "tryin' ter fill our cargo. But in some places there'd been no wars, in others the Dutch or the Spanish 'ad come just before us and bought all the people as was offered. So Cap'n Roberts says ter me and Georgie Baines, he says, 'Ye'll need ter go upriver ter trade before aw 'ere dies of the flux.'

Even without light Jamie has learned the position of the various obstacles laid on the deck, but now he uses the glow to navigate over and around them more quickly, feeling his pulse quicken. They've left the fetters off, and he feels light on his feet, too light, as if each day there is less of him.

"We 'eaded up the Cross River from New Town in Old Callybar in a log canoe, me and Georgie and three of the darkies as worked fer the local king on the coast, the big fat fella 'oo sat on the golden stool with a fly switch in his 'and. Two days at the paddles and we're ter the first station, which is only a little clearin' by the river surrounded by their spiny trees that's always got ants or spiders—somethin that'll bite ye—crawlin on 'em, and there's a few 'uts and this closure made with stakes and bramblebush where they keep the poor buggers as 'ave been captured in wars or kidnappins."

There has been meat in the food every few days, and some broken pieces of sea biscuit, and Jamie wonders if Keach is worried about losing his only trustworthy confessor on board the *Gildart*.

"There was only a dozen in the jail when we got there, and we bought 'em fer a fair price right off and then 'ad to wait. They give me and Georgie each a wench—twas the custom on the coast—mine was younger than I was at the time, though it's 'ard ter figure age with them, and black as I never seen before. The ones 'oo rowed us upriver was a reddish color, Aros, they called 'em, but my wench and the others 'eld fer sale was Igbos and from farther inter the wilderness. I called 'er Mary.

"It was rocky goin' betwixt the two of us at first—me thinkin' she'll cut my throat some night and the rest will 'ave me fer breakfast, Mary sure that when I tire of the pokin' I'll 'ave *'er* cooked and eat 'er—but we settled down. There was nothin' ter do fer weeks but swat flies, scratch yer bug bites, roll around in the 'ammock with yer wench and wait fer more captives ter be brought in. Mary got to trust me, or at least not ter shake nearly out of 'er skin when I'd come near, and maybe she thought there was a way I might save 'er from what come next. The Aros 'ad told 'er an' the others that the woods around was nothing but snakes and panthers waiting ter rip their 'ides, so it was no use runnin' off, they were too far from 'ome now. See, they tie their 'ands and put these collars around their necks, that are connectit to a long pole, maybe six or ten of the wretches tied together that way and marched fer days, then carried downriver in longboats. This is people as 'as never wandered far from their own little village before."

It is too deep in the hull to hear even the ship's bells, so Jamie has lost track of time, Keach's visits now his sun and his stars, though he has also lost count of the visits. He often doesn't know if he's awake or dreaming—

"When yer young, with wimmin, ye've very little sense—I was only sure she was no 'arbor strumpet bound to gi' me the pox and 'appy 'er teeth wasn't filed to points like some I'd seen. When there was noises from the beasts outside at night, enough to chill yer blood, she'd 'old closer to me, as if I could protect her. I'd never been with a woman as wasn't a strumpet, and never more than a single coupling with each, and—well, ye can't call it love, can ye, but it was *some*thin'.

"So protect 'er I did, in a way, at least fer a spell. When enough 'ad come in we set off down the river with three longboats full of 'em be'ind us, the captives all tied ter each other but for Mary and Anne, which is what Georgie Baines called 'is wench. I don't know what gone on between 'em, 'ee never spoke a word about it ter me, but we come ter a fast place in the river, water boilin' ower the rocks, and Anne throws 'erself off the boat and is lost in the current."

In many of the dreams, if they are dreams, Jamie sees the men lying below the grate on the *Dahomey Queen,* all in a jumble, hard to tell which limbs belonged to which body, many of their eyes open and filled with feeding insects. Jamie will strike his own face with his fists then, slam his bare feet on the orlop floor till he has a sense of his own body as separate from the darkness, and force himself to utter out loud the name of everyone, living and dead, who he is related to by blood.

He always starts with Dougal, who may be living or may be dead by now.

"Georgie was in a bad state, 'ad the sweats and the chills, and 'ardly looks inter the water after her. My Mary gives me a look from the boat a'ead and I shake my 'ead no—there's water dragons in that river, and sharks nearer to the coast, and by now I knew 'er greatest fear was that 'er body might be eaten."

A pause then.

"Are ye still there, MacGillivray?"

"Where else maut I be?" answers Jamie.

"You transports may be a devious lot, but ye don't go in fer pitchin' yerselves overboard. We always 'ad netting up on the slavers, like ye seen on that ghost ship, to keep 'em from going over as a body—there's ships as 'ave lost 'alf their cargo that way.

"When we got aboard the ship, Cap'n Roberts was fit to be tied. It 'ad been over a month, and four of our shipmates 'ad died from the foul air of that place. Georgie was little use fer anything in 'is state and I 'ad these bumps, fly bites, all over me legs that itched like the blazes. We got the cargo below as quick as we could, 'opin they'd be too cowed by white men swingin' the cat to note 'ow few was left of our crew now, and we raised anchor fer Jamaica.

"I'd made it clear that Mary was mine, which kept the other byes off of 'er, and she'd come to lie wif me wherever I found on deck ter sleep—with the cargo aboard there was no room fer our 'ammocks. There's no privacy on a slaver, and no modesty—Cap'n Roberts was lax in that regard, and ye'd see sailors, not on their watch, of course—couplin' with the wimmen out under the sun and the stars. The wimmen was never bound unless we caught 'em plotting, and were kept on our side of the barricado. T'isn't a fact, of course, but it felt at times like the darkies was used better than the crew—Roberts 'ad ordered the cat laid 'ard on us since we come ter the Bight of Biafra, ye'd be flogged fer lookin' cross-eyed at an officer, and ye can be sure the ill treatment was passed on ter the cargo by sailors with welts on their backs. Dragging their chains too loud, upendin' the waste tubs, refusin' ter eat their dabdab—we'd take it out of their 'ides.

"And before we'd lost sight of the coast, them bumps on me legs—it's the spawn of the flies under yer skin—they started ter poke their ugly 'eads out, little worms that I'd yank out when there was an inch of 'em to 'owd onter. The surgeon give me some salve, but both legs was infected, open sores gettin' bigger every day and we were a crew of skeletons manning that ship. Ye've never 'eard such misery, day and night, in all their gibberin' tongues, chained one atop the other in a floatin' lazar 'ouse, torn away from everything they've ever known and ready ter murder us all."

Other than Keach, Jamie has had only the one visit from the surgeon, lantern in hand, keeping his distance but not so far that the rummy fog of his breath didn't make Jamie nearly swoon. He judged the quarantined transport healthy enough at five paces and made a brisk retreat.

"Did they try?" asks Jamie. He is right under the hatch, can see a bit of Keach's knee in the lantern glow.

"Only once, when we were a day out of Bermuda. At eight bells we'd lift the grates—the stench that come out was like the Jaws of Death just opened—and bring 'em up ter feed and water and make 'em stir about. Two at a time, till all are up on deck and we set two of the fellows ter the drums, as would beat out a tattoo fer the others ter dance by—it's mostly 'oppin' up and down in their chains, but the surgeon said without it they'd all die or be useless by the time we made port. It's Georgie's duty that day ter be the one left on their side by the passage door, with the blunderbuss filled with scrap metal, the mate sittin' above 'im between the spikes on the top of the barricado ter mind that all was done proper.

"Well, Georgie is pretty well gone at this point, can't keep 'is weapon up and ready in 'is arms, and the black buggers see this and they make a rush and scrag 'im with a 'andspike they'd stolen. 'Ee never got off a shot. They tried ter force the passage door and 'ave at us, but I'm at one of the swivel guns that day—I could 'ardly stand with me legs oozin' pus and throbbin', so it was good to 'ave somethin' to lean on. That door starts ter be pried open, arms reachin' through, and the mate orders me ter fire inter the mass of 'em. It was a 'alf dozen went down, dead or wounded, and the blast brings the rest of the crew up with their muskets and before ye know it the savage wretches've all nicked back down inter the 'old.

"There was three dead and one bad wounded, so Cap'n Roberts, ee 'as two of the ones 'oo seem ter be talkers, that can savvy two or three different tongues among the cargo, and 'as them brung up ter watch while first 'e drops the corpses to the sharks that are always followin' us—a 'ole fleet of 'em, by now—and then 'ee 'as me and Jemmy Wren tie the wounded nigger like trawlin' bait and lower 'im, just ter the waist, inter the wake of the *Sovereign*. Well, the cries 'ee give out, and the look on the faces of them two talkers when we pulled what was left of the poor bugger out from the water—"

Keach is quiet for a long while. Jamie sits on a coil of hemp, studying the outline of his body parts in the dim light. He is still here.

"We'd started with thirty-two 'ands, officers included, and was down ter a dozen, and them only 'alf alive. Roberts was fine, 'ee spent 'alf this leg of the voyage drinking in 'is cabin, coming out only ter curse us for a mob of wharf scum and landsmen, so it was the mate, 'oos name was Imbrie, Mungo Imbrie, as got us ter Kingston.

"There was such a hunger fer new bodies for the plantations at that time, with the sugar work killin' eight out of ten within a year or two, that they 'ad the buying right on shipboard rather than on the dock. Undermanned so greatly, we 'adn't bothered ter do the usual over'aul on the cargo—shaving the men, blacking their 'air if there was any gray, rubbing their bodies with palm oil. It made no difference ter the scramble of planters and their agents as crawled over the deck. When she was claimed, right at the beginning, this fat fellow throwin' a cord over Mary's neck, she tried ter run ter me but he pulled 'er down and dragged 'er—

Keach is quiet for a moment. He starts up again, voice unsteady. "It was like the sorrows of Judgment Day all around, children torn from mothers, all of 'em convinced this is where they'd be eaten, and she give me a look, Mary, as 'er body was pulled away across the deck—I'll 'ave it wif me a'ways. I'd never made a promise, we didn't speak a word of each other's lingo, but—she *trusted* me. Can ye fancy that? As if an ignorant sailor 'as any power in the world."

Another silence. Ambrosine Reynaud had asked Jamie to go to the Catholic confession with her once, the papist priest behind a screen, chiding him in French for the sins he invented. He wonders now if that priest—he knows him only as a vague shape and an echoing voice—heard stories like this one.

"As for me," says Keach finally, "I was put off with 'alf pay. On yer slavers, the last leg—from the Indies 'ome—only needs the smallest crew, for there's no threat of rebellion from casks of sugar and molasses. The owners a'ways instruct their captains ter winnow the payroll if the miasmas in Africa 'asn't done it already. My legs was not so bad as ter warrant the scalpel and the saw, but my days climbin' in the yards was over for good. I spent years in bloody Jamaica as a wharf rat, beggin' on the docks, living off the charity of able-bodied sailors in their high rum spirits when they was between ships. Then I found the Lord, and Cap'n 'olmes found me and give me this job, ferrying lost souls from Penitence ter Perdition."

From the smell of the hold Jamie supposes they'll be sold to raise tobacco, but has no idea what that entails. His father forbade him and Dougal from planting, ploughing, or pulling of any kind, their station to live off the riches of the earth without stooping to touch it. He has never been whipped—

"They say," muses Keach, wistfully, above him, "that all sin and transgression will be fergiven ter them as discover righteousness."

Jamie raps the now empty bucket against the floor and Keach pulls it up on a line.

"But I'd leifer 'ave Mary's fergiveness than the Lord's."

> Ship's log *Veteran*, June 31st, 1747. 54 days at sea, Lat by observation 23' 08", Long 47' 42" west, distance 216 miles.

The fight is not so boisterous as to draw their keepers down from the deck. Morag bears some scratches on her face, the Perth woman a bloody nose. Jenny and the Irish girl are holding Morag fast while the Lochaber sisters tend to MacFarlane.

"I'll tear yer fecking innards oot!" Morag promises, not straining too hard to break free. "Say ma name once mair and I'll destroy ye!"

MacFarlane does not respond. She had been discussing "certain people" in a voice meant for all, and then turned to the topic of what was and what was not natural, and as Morag and the Irish girl have taken to sleeping in each other's arms, nothing more, offense was taken.

"She dinnae say yer name," Jenny coos to her friend. "Nor anybody's."

Morag begins to curse in Erse then, which MacFarlane does not understand, two of the Lochaber sisters covering their ears and the third giggling into her hands.

There is oakum strewn all over the planks beneath their feet, and Lizzie Robb on her knees gathering it up. The weather has been very bad the last two days, nobody allowed on deck, and they have been confined together for far too long. It is hot in their compartment now, June, and close to the Equator according to the second mate who oversees their feeding. He says that this Equator is a belt around the middle of the earth, which is round like a ball, and that it is always hot there.

They arrange themselves, Jenny now with the criminal women on one side of the compartment and those transported for treason on the other. People will find a reason, she knows, to dislike one another.

The Irish girl has been quiet during all of this, embarrassed rather than chuffed that women have been fighting over her honor. She is a lovely girl, pale with hair the color of barley late in the field, and was caught in Piccadilly as her brother, who was hanged in April, passed her a watch he had just stolen. Perhaps it was only jealousy, thinks Jenny, the wee girl's bosom a softer berth than she's known since the redcoats came to Torgormack.

Ship's log *Gildart*, July 4th, 1747. Lat 38' 12", long 55' 03", high seas, gale wind from west, all hands engaged.

The hull shouldn't be rising so high out of the water. Jamie can tell that much from down in the orlop, each sickening tilt and timber-shuddering slam in the dark sending him rolling over the cables, unable to find an anchor to hold on to. The sea is doing its best to smash the *Gildart* to pieces. He thinks to cry out, but of course they have forgotten him, and if not, he is their last concern.

There is water now, nearly up to his chest as he steadies himself on hands and knees, water where it is not supposed to be. The water runs away as the hull tilts, rising, then rushes back for the tremendous impact—

Keach, on deck, sees fear in his shipmates' eyes whenever the lightning reveals them, then it is back to wet and howling wind and whipping canvas and men's shouts and the ship's bow slamming down off the swells. He and two of the landsmen, both scared witless, work the pump, driving the bars of the capstan, slipping and rising, glad to have something solid to grab onto. Holmes himself is shouting the instructions to the men in the yards, all of the masts intact but the mate at the helm unable to keep the *Gildart* from yawing wildly as it goes over the crests, each precipitous slide down at a different angle. They have shipped a lot of water, the canvas of the transports' grating torn free long ago. Keach puts his back into it, futile as it seems, better to strain at any task than to sit and consider the likelihood of their sinking. There was some shouting from the hold at first, men despairing in their Erse tongue, or perhaps begging to be unchained, but it has gone silent below. They are panicked, no doubt, their waste sloshing around their knees with the rise and fall of the hull—

Then Keach recognizes the voice. It is the little one, the one who says rude things in Erse that make the others laugh when he comes to feed them, the one he's almost fogged a half dozen times but somehow forgiven. The one with the beautiful singing voice—

Why doth me darlin' Peggie grieve
Wha promised me tae marry?
She's kent I'm fated noo tae leave
The shores iv Inveraray—

—a voice surprisingly powerful in a small man, heard now cutting through the roaring wind and slapping rain and the hull-slam of the pitiless ocean—

A bounty placed upon me heid
Nae langer I maun tarry

A fugitive who's ne'er tae wed
Exiled frae Inveraray—

—a pulse of lightning, and Keach sees that the crew can hear the singer, their exertions suddenly less frantic, just sailors weathering a storm—

Nae mair we'll stroll aboot Loch Fyne
Nae mair her basket carry
Me Peggie's left tae weep and pine
Alone in Inveraray—

—the other transports joining in now, deeper voices—

Oh Peggie dear, I've gan awee
Who promised ye tae marry
A thousand leagues across the sea
Sae far frae Inveraray—

—another flash, and he sees that one of the landsmen is staring at him, troubled by the song.

"Not yet dead," says Keach, calm now, steadily muscling the capstan around, "and their souls already on the wind."

The hare neath fading heather lies
The eagle in its aerie
Ma heart in waeful yearning cries
Farewell tae Inveraray!

Ship's log *Veteran*, July 28th, 1747. Lat 13' 23" N Long 60' 16 W. Contested waters, Snow sighted—

He has fought this engagement a hundred times in his imagination. The sail, tiny at first, peeking over the larboard horizon, men leaping into the yards as he orders the topgallants readied, his eye pressed to the glass and the vessel taking shape, taking shape, but offering no flag, not even a false one, as it pursues—for he is certain now that it is a pursuit. It is identifiably a snow—sharp-beaked, trisail mast abaft the mainmast—riding too high in the mild swells to be carrying heavy cargo. The crew cheer, frightened and excited, as he orders them to lay on as much canvas as the *Veteran* can bear, all hands on and the transports left untended.

The last storm blew them past Barbados, or else they might be in the pocket of a trade convoy now, possibly even with one of His Majesty's gunships along. Decisions at sea are measured and logical for a prudent captain until there is weather or trouble, and then they must be made and implemented firmly and promptly, the number of options diminishing as the crisis develops. Mr. Bowles, the gunner, is getting his people not needed in the rigging into position, though the snow, gaining on them more slowly now, won't be abreast for several hours. They've performed rather badly in the drills Captain Ricky has ordered, only four thus far, as Mr. Gildart has often waxed apoplectic over waste of powder. They have five fully operable twelve pounders on the larboard, four on the starboard, and a pair of swivel guns meant for control of the transports that might be of use should it come to an attempt to board. For now, Ricky hopes for a change in the admirable sailing weather—fleecy clouds, a hearty blow out of the southwest—or that the snow is an English privateer only having a little sport with them.

In his imagined sea battles he has always twice as many guns and twice as many hands who know how to use them.

It is a strange afternoon for the captain, coolly strolling the quarterdeck to keep the men from panicking, double-checking to be sure everything above and belowdecks is prepared, having Jenkins charge his pistols and strap them around his waist. Ricky feels a sudden rush of affection for his crew, even for those landsmen who have been more obstacle than aid in the running of the ship. These cannot help but stand and gawk at the snow as it relentlessly grows larger, almost directly astern now, as if staring at a thing might cause it to go away.

In one of the daydreams he confounds the privateer by coming about and nearly ramming it bow to bow, smashing it to splinters with an expertly timed volley of twenty-four pounders. He has a cousin in the Royal Navy who saw action against the Spanish and speaks at great volume and length about the superiority of His Majesty's fighting ships. But the *Veteran* is only an undergunned transport, a floating Newgate with a crew unblooded in combat.

Hawkins, his mate, approaches.

"How long would you prefer to resist, Captain?"

It is not an impertinent question. *Some* fight must be put up, that is their duty, but there is a point where further sacrifice is pointless—

"If it shows the black flag, we'll loose the male transports and arm them—they'll understand which is the lesser of two evils, and we shall fight to the end."

"If it be French?"

He would prefer it to be French, some rules of engagement to rely on, the likelihood of exchange if he survives—

"We don't want to hand them a prize in top condition, do we Mr. Hawkins?"

"No, sir."

"Then if they render the *Veteran* unfit to sail, we'll consider capitulation."

He hears the transports shouting through their grate then, clamoring for food and water, and tells the mate to deal with them. Turning them out on deck and giving them arms is an act of desperation he prefers not to contemplate—though there are no sailors among the rebels they are the remnants of a somewhat organized military force and convicted traitors. And if the vessel is French, they are the enemy's natural allies.

There is time for the cook to feed the entire crew and for a round of grog, officers abstaining. Ricky only allows the rum up one keg at a time, with the armorer and the mate having the only keys to its access. For the last hour they seem to be suspended in time, wind steady, sky unchanging, only the pursuing snow edging closer, closer. He surveys his ship—it has weathered the voyage remarkably well, the rigging in good order, the deck shining scrubbed and almost white in the sun, the hull still free of the growths and wormholes that come with docking in tropic waters. A miraculous harmony of wood, rope, and canvas about to be pounded to splinters with iron shot—

We all know that one day we will die, muses Captain Ricky. It is an event on every horizon, but few can foresee just when that day will arrive. His father, also a sea captain in his day, is ailing, unlikely to survive till his son returns from the Leewards. Every day now, thinks Ricky, he must see that vessel gaining on him, closer, closer—

The sun is eight fingers above the horizon ahead of them, the white of the full sails astern brilliant against the sky and water. A cheer from the snow as the French flag is run up and Ricky feels a flush of relief run through him. There will be rules, protocols to obey. Talbot, the Boston man who claims to a have been a whaler, steps up to the edge of the quarterdeck, carrying an American long rifle with which he has entertained the crew by shooting sharks.

"If ye'd like me to, sir, I could put a ball in their captain when 'e's near enough ter make out."

The targeting of officers being contagious once the hands get a taste of it, Ricky demurs. "It would do us greater service," he says, "if you could dislodge whoever is at the helm."

The French snow swings wide as it catches up with them, men in the yards trimming a bit of sail to keep the ships parallel. There is a puff of smoke from their forwardmost gunport, then the deep thud of the cannon preceding the whistling of a shot across their bow.

The gunner has his head just above the hatch to the gun deck, like an expectant badger.

"Put one in their rigging, Mr. Bowles."

Bowles disappears and almost immediately there is the thump of their own best gun.

He can follow the arcing flight of the ball, can see, then hear the shuddering of the snow's foremast as it loses a yard arm and the sail buckles. A cheer from his men, quickly drowned by the roar of the first French volley—Ricky counts eleven guns firing from the single decker—and their own complement of sail is shredded.

"Mr. Hawkins!"

"At once, sir," calls the mate, his head bleeding as he untangles himself from a mess of fallen rigging. "Cut 'em away, men"

The best of the yard monkeys have been waiting with axes in hand and coils of line looped over their shoulders. They leap into the shambles above and begin to sever and disentangle.

"Return fire, Mr. Bowles!"

Their reply is not heartening, one gun misfiring, the other three balls passing through the top of the snow with sparse effect. Ricky sees his surgeon on deck, helping to carry an unconscious crewman below. Just below him Talbot fires the long rifle, and the French helmsman falls, the snow suddenly veering toward them before another man snatches the wheel and turns the snow parallel again, much closer now, for the second volley—

—which decapitates the bosun, smashes a hole through Captain Ricky's quarters, thoroughly destroys the longboat, and chops enough of the mainmast away that the greater part of it topples toward the bow till it is hung up at a diagonal by the other rigging.

The *Veteran* begins to yaw, bow turned toward the snow. Ricky can see the French captain now, the only man on board in a uniform, staring at him. He calls to Jasper, wrestling with the wheel.

"Does she steer?"

"She does not, Captain."

"Belay firing, Mr. Bowles—"

"Aye aye."

He holds his palm out to the French captain of *Le Diamant*, the name of the snow plain to read now, and gives it a thought. The gun crews are poised on both vessels, he knows, the matches smoldering at the end of their linstocks held just above the touchholes, waiting for the order to blow each other apart—

"*Soyez sage, mon Capitain,*" calls the Frenchman. "*Ça suffit, non?*"

Ricky appraises the disarray above, notes that there is a splinter of wood sticking out from his thigh, the trouser leg darkening with wet. This was in none of his imaginings. He looks to his mate.

"White flag, Mr. Hawkins."

BONDSMAN

THERE IS NO LAND IN SIGHT WHEN THEY ARE brought up, eight at a time, for the bathing. Jamie is pale and shaky, the rum-breathing ship's surgeon giving him a brisk once-over to be sure that whatever killed the people on the slaver has not invaded his body before allowing him to join the others.

As they are to be sold, it is the purser, whose name is Horner, who oversees the procedure, prisoners freed of their irons and told to strip naked, a crewman wielding a long boathook to flip these rags into a fetid pile that will be burned, then each man allowed a dip in seawater sloshing in a huge iron kettle Keach says is otherwise used to render whale blubber, before a final dousing with a bucket of tepid rainwater. The guards employ their muskets to poke them into a line, and one by one they sit, still naked, waiting to be shaved by the surgeon's boy.

All but Fergal.

"I put a razor ter that one he'll bite me finger off," says the boy, waving the big man away.

The skin on Fergal's ankles and wrists has broken and bled, scabbed over and broken again so many times it has formed into raised, purplish bands. He is an even more fearsome creature naked than clothed.

"We're nearly there, then," says Lachlan, hopefully.

"Where?" says Keach, toying with them as he swabs the deck around the giant kettle.

"Where'ere yer fecking taking us."

"That be a sensible conclusion."

"Slicking us up fer the slave market."

"If ye was black cargo yed've had better feed fer a week, and we'd be oiling yer hides, make ye shine. This is only ter rid yer of the crawlies—most of 'em, at least."

Each man in his turn, face scraped hairless, steps to a bundle of what the sailors call slops, square-cut trews and shirts of an unbleached cloth nearly as stiff as canvas, trying to find a reasonable fit for what their bodies have become in two years of confinement. There are no shoes.

"Shoes encourage walking," says the purser, checking off on a list of names as each man dresses. "Walking leads to running. Running leads to running away."

The new clothes feel pleasantly rough against Jamie's skin, stiff and ill-fitting as they are. He has not been up on deck for weeks, and the air and the space around him is intoxicating.

"If we gae back down," he says, "we'll be as filthy as afore."

Horner checks his name off on the list. "You'll sleep on the deck tonight, and once you're all up your quarters will be smoked."

Once dressed, they are shackled again, not too tightly, with the chains connecting them run through eyebolts in the deck. Mats are rolled out and they sit, crowded shoulder to shoulder at midship. Whatever is to come next, the anticipation of change is thrilling.

"Tis no hot enow fer the islands," says Alexander Stewart, who served as a footman to Murray of Broughton and was loaned to Prince Charlie for the campaign. Though neither young nor brawny, he has been treated like a dangerous criminal. "Sae it's like tae be Virginia Colony, and we'll be set oot in the tobacca."

"I'd like tae see the trees it grows upon," says Lachlan.

"It sprouts frae the ground, as kale does."

"Sae we'll spread the kelp, cut the leaves—"

"Alangside the blackies."

"The mair the better. I've heert they're mighty toilers."

"And what do they eat in the Colonies?" asks a weaver from Dundee.

"Hares and hinds," says Lachlan. "I keeked a pickter in a book once. A great giant of a buckskin steppin' oot frae the woods with a rifle o'er ane shoulder and a stag o'er the other."

"There maun be fish as well," says the weaver.

"Tis a country of burns and rivers, as Scotland is," Stewart tells him. "The maps a' show it tae be so."

It is a warm evening, the *Gildart* running before a light wind, sails billowing over their heads and the crew quick-stepping around them at the mate's orders. Jamie lays back on the deck to look up at the straining canvas.

"Gulls," he says.

The others look up. Beyond the sails, worn to a yellowish brown on the journey, there are suddenly white gulls soaring, gliding lazily across each other's paths, backed by an untroubled blue sky.

"We've not seen birds for a month," says Cameron. "We must be near to it."

"Do ye smell land?"

"Tis no what I smell," says Lachlan, looking around, nearly all of them washed and shaved and clothed anew, "tis what I *din*nae. The reek in that hold is like a full-growed Galloway bull setting on yer face. "

"There was crofters on the MacIntosh lands," muses Jamie, "puir, starvin' bastarts who never straightened their backs frae sun up tae sun doon, scrapin' at the airth tae feed their bairns—but they was free men, and proud of it."

"That was before Culloden," Cameron reminds him. "It isn't the *shack*les that make the slave."

They are quiet for a while, each man wondering where he will be taken, how he will be used. Jamie thinks of Dougal, likely buried on the lonely hill by the gallows, grave unmarked, neighbor to rebels, thieves and cutthroats.

Then a sailor, perched up near the soaring gulls, shouts that he sees land.

THEY ENTER THE GREAT BAY, OTHER SHIPS BLOOMING suddenly on both sides, the smaller ones crossing to the northern or southern shore, the larger headed out to sea. The sailors are grinning as they monkey into the rigging and prepare the *Gildart* for port, singing out as they echo the orders from Captain Holmes, and Jamie wishes he was one of them, riding the uppermost spar, surveying the new land as it takes shape on the horizon.

There is no ceremony when they drop anchor near the mouth of a wide, swift-flowing river. A smattering of low, rough-hewn log buildings crowd the shore, and beyond them a flat expanse of marsh and woods. Captain Holmes and the mate go ashore in the skiff while the crew reef the sails. Keach has been here before.

"North Potomac," he says. "Captain will deal with the customs, and when the tide shifts we'll move upriver."

"Tae where?"

"Buckwood Cove, I'd reckon. The planters will be gathered there."

There is another ship, a Guineaman with a barricado at its center, dozens of African men climbing dazedly onto the deck within it, hands still bound together, while a score of black women are clustered by the forecastle, all of them carefully watched by crewmen with muskets and pikes. They stare at the land off the larboard, then discover the prisoners of the *Gildart,* anchored only a hundred yards away.

"Will ye lookit them gawpin' at us, as if they've never keeked a white mon afore," says Lamond, who'd been a groom to the Duke of Perth.

"And us gawpin' at them," adds Lachlan. He bends to snatch up a length of the rusty chain that connects them, raising and shaking it. One of the black men on the *Monarch* does the same.

"They're in fer it, that lot," says Keach, watching with a strained look on his face.

"As are we."

The sailor shakes his head. "Ye'll be hard used, perhaps, but not as beasts. There's something in a black hide that summons up the devil in a white master."

Horner raps a belaying pin against the mainmast to draw their attention away from the Africans.

"We'll be at the auction soon," he calls to them, "and you'd be wise to comport yourselves well."

"Or we'll lock ye in chains," Lachlan whispers to Jamie. "Tis nae great threat."

The supercargo continues. "Once you are chosen, you will sign your indenture over from Captain Holmes to your new master. Maryland Colony requires only a seven year indenture—if you perform your tasks diligently and do not attempt to escape you will be discharged after that time, with your master required to furnish you with a rifle, a pick, a mattock, and a suit of clothes."

A good deal of muttering then as Horner's statement is translated to the men with no English.

"Ma sentence reads 'fer the term of yer natural life,'" says Alexander Stewart.

"And it means what it says," Horner answers. "Any man caught returning to the Three Kingdoms will be hanged upon discovery. But here—" he indicates the raw land around them—"here you will be freed from your bond after seven years, and expected to keep yourself."

Jamie's first thought is that they've already stolen his homeland and two years of his life. Seven more years is unthinkable.

"Have I made myself understood?"

Nobody responds to the purser, again talking among themselves. Alexander Stewart catches the eye of every man around him.

"Sign naething," he says.

The tide is beginning to roll in when Captain Holmes and the mate return, and the anchor is quickly weighed, a few sails run up the masts and they turn up the river, narrowing slightly before they turn to the larboard up a tributary on the right bank.

"The Wicomico River," says Keach to the prisoners. "Yer a lucky mob. Savannah or Charleston, ye'd be burnt ter cracklin' within a year. But this country is easy on a body."

Some of the trees along the banks are familiar to Jamie—he's seen pines like this on the western coast of France, though these rise up and up before there are any branches. There are even bigger trees growing straight out of the water, with triangular bases that narrow into a long, straight bole, also rising high before the branches and leaves begin. The Wicomico is mirror smooth, the tide propelling them more than the bit of canvas hung in the rigging, and they seem to drift deeper and deeper into a marshy forest that seems untouched since the day God made it. They float past screeching green birds with yellow necks and red faces flocked in some of the scrubbier trees.

"Parrots," Keach tells them, smiling now that they are clear of the slaver. "Up from the south."

It is early afternoon when there is a shout and a crude dock appears, reaching out into the water ahead, and the *Gildart* drags anchor to moor a stone's fling from the shore. A trio of rowboats pull out to greet them, each with a black man rowing and two well-dressed white men looking forward on the seats. Keach and three of the sailors have pulled up the mats and now arrange the convicts into a large semicircle, dragging chains and fastening them again through the deck bolts.

"That's yer masters comin'," says Keach, on his knees dealing with the irons. "Ye'll do well ter keep yer tongues in yer teeth and yer eyes on the future."

Captain Holmes greets the planters, solid men in buff and gray coats without lace or periwigs, and they retire to his cabin for a friendly drop. The Scotsmen are left standing under the sun of late July, sweat beginning to run down their foreheads, eyes blinking at the sting.

"Stay as you are," calls Horner, striding before them. "We'll be underway soon enough."

Jamie watches a seahawk flapping overhead, wings laboring as it carries a large fish.

"They shift it somehow," he says to Lachlan beside him, "afore they lift up, so the heid of the fishie is a'ways held forward."

"And can keek where it's gang tae."

"Which is down a hatchling's gullet. But first they get tae *fly.* A' we got is salt junk and seabiscuit and twa months in the bilgewater."

"They're no gang tae eat us, Jamie."

"Says you."

Horner does most of the talking when it begins, standing on an overturned wash bucket singing praises and giving directions to the planters as they approach and examine the shackled men. Chests and arms are thumped, mouths pried open and peered into, a sailor with a handspike shadowing each of the buyers to insure an uneventful perusal of the cargo.

"That's Thomas Laing ye've got there, twas a mine laborer in

Aberdeen, and if it's a strong back ye're seeking—I have an offer, eight pounds sterling, let's be serious, gentlemen, there we are, nine and six, but still it's pure theft for this lad—I see ten, ten, do we have a gentleman to top it? Ten and five, that's reasonable, ye'll not find the like of him elsewhere, in mint condition from the voyage and ready to lay his shoulder to whatever ye please—ten and five going once, twice—"

"They'll pay in tobacca," observes Keach, standing at a tall barrel behind Jamie, Lachlan, Aeneas Cameron, and big Fergal, who are chained together. "A few months from now, what goes ter acquire yer sorry hides will be thumbed up the Duke of Cumberland's beak and sneezed out in the Royal Palace."

"George Baillee, as was a bonnetmaker in Dundee, but I'm certain he will turn his hand to whatever ye've a need for. Feed him a bit of meal, let him find his land legs, and he'll serve ye well. A good, steady man, guaranteed not to turn rabbit on ye, and look at the head of hair on the man—healthy as a hound—"

The planters come near but Fergal's gaze, fierce and steady into their eyes, drives them away. As men are sold and unshackled they are led to Keach, who has been turning a long iron in a lit brazier.

"Right hand, on the barrelhead," he says to each, then applies the hot tip of the iron to a spot between the thumb and forefinger. Jamie smells burning flesh.

"Only a precaution ter flight," says Keach. "Be grateful it's not on yer cheek."

The branded man is then stepped forward to another barrel, where Captain Holmes spreads his indenture out to be signed over to the new owner.

"John Lucky there, that's a fisherman in his former life, and lucky's the man that buys him. Got all of his teeth and two strong arms, and no stranger to the water, which will serve ye well in this swamp-ridden neck of the woods. What do I hear for this fine specimen of a Scotsman? The bidding starts at nine pounds sterling, gentlemen, let's not be coy—"

The first to leave are a pair of buyers who seem to have a secret agreement with Captain Holmes and the purser, exchanging nods as certain of the prisoners are pulled out from the line. They each take seven men, who are lowered down into the waiting rowboats.

"A' of them Catholics," says Lachlan.

"Yer sure of that?"

"I've watched them pray together. And the captain as well. They maun be free men afore the sun sets."

"Mair power tae them if it's true."

"Tis the Roman Pope," Lachlan assures Jamie with a wink. "He casts a lang shadda."

Most of the men have been chosen, branded and legally bonded before a final rowboat arrives. On it are a man introduced as Colonel Thomas Lee, who is the local magistrate, along with two buckskins, men in leathern trews and homespun shirts, each carrying a rifle. Last aboard is a final planter, a tall, gaunt man with bloodshot eyes and stubble on his face, furious to have arrived after the best men have been spoken for. This one stations himself in front of Jamie's group as the Colonel joins Captain Holmes, who has been arguing with Alexander Stewart.

"This one won't sign," he says.

The Colonel, broad shouldered and graying at the temples, takes a slow walk around the prisoner, examining him from head to toe.

"Speak English?"

"Ah do."

"You understand that you've been sold."

"Ah dinnae accept it."

"Accept it or not, you've got only two choices here—go peaceably with your new owner, or remain bonded to Captain Holmes here. In which case he will send you back into the hold—which I can smell has just had the vinegar and fire treatment—and be returned to Liverpool, where you will be hanged upon arrival."

Stewart's face flushes red, his cuffed hands beginning to tremble.

"But as you'll no longer be valuable cargo, the captain is under no obligation to his employer to feed or care for you in any way. You won't make the voyage, my friend."

Stewart, without looking at either man, bends to lift the pen and awkwardly sign the indenture papers.

"That is Fergal MacGregor before you," calls Horner as he sees where the new planter is looking. "A Highlands crofter and cattle thief, worth three men or one mule if you'll hitch him to a plow. Don't be daunted by his fierce aspect, the Scotch can be broken to service by any—"

"I'm weel aweer of what a Scotsman might do," corrects the gaunt planter without lifting his fiery gaze from Fergal's. "I'll give ye forty pound in siller fer the lot of 'em."

He indicates the four men chained together. Horner looks to the captain, who sighs and nods.

"Sold, then! Sold to—may I inquire—?"

"Crozier," says the gaunt planter. "Jock Crozier of the Georgia Colony."

Jamie is branded first, holding his own wrist steady on the barrelhead with his left hand. There is a sharp pain, a tiny sizzling sound, and then a B-shaped welt rising up.

"There ye are, lad," says Keach. "It hurts less if ye offer it up."

When it is Fergal's turn he begins to fight, cursing in Erse and struggling with three of the burliest of the ship's crew. They have him down, a foot to the back of his neck, when Crozier kneels to look him in the eye and speak quietly, miming the actions with his hands.

"Ye'll have it markit," he says, "or I'll have it cut *aff*."

Fergal opens his hand and Keach applies the red-hot iron.

They are loaded into two boats, Cameron and Fergal crammed in with Colonel Lee and the buckskins, while Jamie and Lachlan, hands still bound, ride with Jock Crozier as his black man rows. The planter catches Jamie looking at the African, who has symmetrical markings scarred into each cheek.

"I call that'un Bonnie Prince Charlie," grins Crozier. "Ye'd do well no tae vex him."

THEY ARE GREETED AS CONQUERING HEROES.

The Scots have all been transferred to the French ship, as well as Captain Ricky, locked in the French captain's quarters while his crew remain out in the harbor on the *Veteran*, shackled in the same irons that held their rebel enemies for so long. Ferried in on longboats a dozen at a time, the rebels are embraced and kissed, on both cheeks, when they step onto the long, slippery wooden dock, a cheer rising up and a band playing a marching song, then formed into a double line with the women in the lead and promenaded toward the fort. The people here are dressed more brightly than Jenny has ever seen, the ones doing the hugging and kissing all white, while there are dozens, maybe hundreds of dark-skinned people, men and women, dancing and singing and making music with drums, an overwhelming rush of noise and color and Jenny can barely keep her feet, holding to Morag in order not to tumble.

"Tis solid ground," laughs Morag. "We've ainly fergot hoo tae walk upon it."

In the parade ground of the low fort that overlooks the harbor they are formed up again and again surrounded by people, many of these in uniform, and proclaimed at for a long while by a man in a silk coat and a powdered wig who might be the mayor or the governor, ending the speech with "*Vous êtes toutes liberées!*" which sets off more cheering and drum-thumping. One of the newly liberated men, who'd been a dominie outside of Inverness before he was swept into the service of the Prince, tells them all what this means and Jenny feels even more swoony. Beyond the low fort walls there is a looming greeness that goes up and up and up, the top of it swallowed by clouds.

The rags that Jenny and the other women wear are soaked with sweat and bilgewater, clinging to their bodies, and they are embarrassed before this foreign crowd as it presses upon them with more embraces and cheek kissing, well aware of what they look like. There is a heat she has never experienced before, a liquid heat, and the colors of the strange trees and plants about them as she and the other women are taken somewhere with a name she can't understand in a long, flat wagon are so intense that she feels like she is about to pass out. She is seated beside the driver, an older black man wearing a conical straw hat, who has a kindly smile on his face as he wields the reins, chatting constantly to the pair of oxen pulling in the traces. Free now, if the important man in the silk coat was telling the truth, she decides to be bold.

"Can ye tell me what is this place?"

He looks at her, still smiling. Jenny waves her hand to include all—the trees and the flowered bushes and the great mountain that rises in the distance to the left of them.

"What's it calt, this place?"

The driver makes a circle with his finger.

"*C'est une île dans la mer. C'est Martinique.*"

"Mairtaneek. And that there—" she points to the massive, cloud-shrouded peak. "The mountain—?"

The driver chuckles. "*C'est un volcan. Ça, c'est Pelée.*" He chuckles again, shaking his head. "*Un jè, Pelée va bruler tout'omme ici.*"

"What did he say?" calls Morag from behind.

"I think he said that we're on an island calt Mairtaneek," Jenny tells her, "and that we'll be safe here."

IT IS A FULL DAY'S SAIL IN THE SCHOONER TO COME OUT of the great bay again, both shores visible but miles away. Watched over by Colonel Lee and his buckskins, they are put to loading the craft—perhaps half the length of the *Gildart* and fitted with triangular sails rigged fore and aft—with supplies that Crozier assures them are not available where they are headed. Tools, barrels of grain, barrels of shot and powder, an iron plow, new sets of manacles and shackles. Once on board and ready to sail, they are fitted with ball and chain attached to their manacles, the chain short enough that they are compelled to carry the ball, more than a stone in weight, in order to stand up straight.

"If yer temptit tae swim fer land," Crozier advises them, "them iron baw's dinnae *float*."

They tack south at the mouth of the bay, hugging the coast. The captain of the schooner is a scrawny man with a tangled patch of beard who wears the rough clothes of a common seaman and spends most of his time at the tiller. The negro, Prince Charlie, is set to the meaner shipboard tasks, mopping the deck, hauling and stowing and tarring as directed by the small and surly crew, who, like their captain, rarely speak except to curse.

"What lies belae Maryland?" ask Lachlan, sitting with the heavy ball in his lap and watching the wooded coastline pass on the larboard.

"Virginia Colony," Cameron tells him. "Then the Carolinas, then Oglethorpe's debtors, and then you have the Spanish to deal with—"

"And red Indians in a' parts?"

"I've not been here. It's all stories."

The sun is sitting just above the strip of dark land when they are roused to their feet by a pair of the sailors poking with cutlasses, Crozier just behind them.

"Ye'll spend the night below," he informs them.

"And we'll sail this close tae land in the dark?" asks Jamie.

"Aye. There'll be a moon, and we need tae pass Hatteras at dawn."

"Tis a bad place, Hatteras?"

The planter shows them a sickly grin. "The Divvil's ain shoals and currents. If we need tae lessen our draft, ye'll be the first o'erboard."

There is little room in the hold, but they are able to recline on sacks of meal rather than hard benches, and there is no reek of human waste.

"He's nae Hielander, our master," says Lachlan when they are settled, the schooner rocking fore and aft over a light swell.

"I'm hearin' Glesga or thereaboots," says Jamie.

"And he most certainly is no gentleman," adds Cameron.

Prince Charlie is there with them, apparently not trusted on deck in the dark, but without a ball and chain for impediment. He squats on his haunches, seeming to listen to something far away.

"He looks a right cutthroat," says Lachlan.

"Wheesht! He's right there."

"What of it?"

Jamie leans forward till he catches the African's eye.

"Do ye understand what we're sayin'?"

The African only stares at him.

"Try him in Erse," suggests Lachlan.

Jamie sits back against the grain sacks. "He's come further than we, and been here langer. Did ye keek the stripes on his back?"

"They maun be frae his voyage."

"Or the work of our Master Crozier. The sooner we lose sight of that'un, the better fer a' of us."

The African yawns, then curls up to sleep.

"Weel, as soon as Ah'm free of this wee pebble," says Lachlan, shifting the iron ball to his left side, "Ah'm yer mon."

In the morning they are brought up on deck for the shoals.

There is a seemingly endless string of long, sand-and-scrub islands to the port, a brisk wind behind them and a confusion of swift water under the bow, a dozen shades of green with patches of white foam. Prince Charlie sits straddling the bowsprit with his knees, leaning forward to stare into the sea ahead and stretch one arm or the other out to signal the helmsman. The sailors stand ready to reef or haul, glancing over the bulwarks with grim faces. Jamie can see by the movement relative to shore that they are not going nearly as fast as the water running under the ship would indicate, the boilings of a tide race suddenly appearing and disappearing on all sides, and that they are on the very edge of control.

"We're pushed ahind by the wind," he says, "but the current is drivin' up frae the south."

"Ma father sailed through the Strait of Corryvreckan as a young mon," says Lachlan, crouching beneath the foremast with his iron ball held to his chest. "There's a whirlpool there as can swalla a ship and a' that's on her."

"By Raasay?"

"Betwixt the isles of Jura and Scarba."

"And this in a coracle, I suppose?"

"Nay, a proper sailing ship. He wrote a ballad—"

"A ballad that I do not wish to hear," says Cameron, who swivels his head between Prince Charlie waving his arms at the bow and the captain, standing beside the helmsman and looking as if the touch of a finger will shatter him to pieces. "Do ye think they will truly toss us over as ballast?"

"If a lowlander the stamp of Crozier pries forty pounds oot of his fist tae purchase something," says Jamie, watching the sandbar islands roll past, "he'll no part with it sae easy."

It is an exhausting day for the crew, all hands so engaged in small adjustments of canvas that they do not stop to eat or change watches, the four prisoners kneeling huddled together and trying to keep out of the way, while Crozier sits atop the captain's little aft cabin, smoking a pipe whenever he can get it lit in the wind, watching the struggle on deck as if it is a show staged for his amusement.

A pair of large herons, one seeming to follow the other, soars over the shoals just ahead of them for a spell, then swing back to the long string of islands. The shoals are nothing to them, thinks Jamie, nor would be the drowning of all aboard the schooner. And an hour's delay of his arrival at Culloden, he muses further, would have changed his life completely. A French invasion scuttled by a storm at sea, a bullet meant to cripple or kill him only passing through his flesh, the whim of a bewigged magistrate on the day before his hanging—it all seems more accident than design. And now his brother is dead, his country veined with red columns of enemy soldiers, his future that of exile in some forlorn corner of this vast wilderness—

And Cain went out from the Lord and dwelt in the land of Nod, thinks Jamie, *to the east of Eden.*

He feels himself a flyweight speck on the world's surface, his only substance the iron ball that lies between his knees.

He feels himself glowing.

"I'll no drown," he states to his companions.

Lachlan and Cameron look at him, the *seanachaidh* grinning. "Him that is bairn tae be hanged shall ne'r be drowned."

"If sech was ma fate, Ah'd have drowned on the passage tae Edinburgh, when they doused me in the sea. Water is no the manner of ma death, I'm sure."

"Yer meant fer a nobler end, is it?"

"I've nae idea of the partickilars, but it winnae come on this day."

"Then ye should inform the captain, and alloo him tae untwist his innards."

Twice, after a signal from Prince Charlie, the captain screams out orders, the helmsman jerking the wheel and the ship heeling as it veers, spray flying into the air and the sailors cursing, narrowly escaping some jagged obstacle just below them. But it all drifts away from Jamie, welcoming the spray that bursts over the bow to soak them, giving himself up to wind and wave, the vessel so long on the brink of disaster that fear dissolves into a pleasant numbness, the bonded men only realizing late in the day that they have not been fed or given water.

"Are we through it?" asks Lachlan when a pair of sailors, apparently following orders, come to stuff them back into the hold.

"Aye, and barely," answers one of them, a Boston man with a strip of beard that follows his jawline up to his ears. "I'd liefer spend an extra week at sea than run through them hull-rippers agin, but yer master is pressed to be home."

"Do ye ken where that lies?"

The Boston man shrugs. "Further south than I've been on this coast—I'm not certain it has a name."

There is no lantern in the hold at night, the only light coming from a slice of moon through the scuttle grating.

"Ah'm never tae spy Dùn Can again," says Lachlan from the murk.

"There's muckle mountains in this land, ah'm sure of it," comforts Jamie.

"But they're no *mine.* Tis no the thing itsel' that's sae grand, as is yer tie tae it."

"Well said, that."

"I'm wondrin'—once yer nowt but bones in the ground, is yer soul ferever tied tae that place ye've been planted?"

"Ah was tae the gallows, aboot tae join them as had been stretched afore," says Jamie. "But Ah dinnae have a visit frae nane of their spirits."

"Ye had yer eye on the hemp. They might've whisked yer breeks aff and ye'd no have kent it."

"Our souls will shift for themselves," says Cameron, the tiniest spot of moonlight catching his eye. "I'm more concerned with what this Crozier has planned for our bodies."

THEY ARE ALLOWED TO LINGER IN THE BATH, STEAM rising up from the warm springs as the dozen dark-skinned women who circle them giggle and point at their pale naked bodies. Jenny manages to hold her head under for a long while, hoping that the sulfur-smelling water might kill the crawlies in her hair. After, she is toweled dry by two of the dark women, a strange but pleasant sensation, and given a colorfully patterned shift made of some light cloth and a belt and things that have no tops to them but cling to your feet by thongs of hemp, and they are arranged before a delegation of who, by their dress, must be the important white people of the town.

It has the feel of a cattle auction, but polite, none of the French people drunk and near as many women there to observe and make their bids as men. When Jenny is quickly chosen by a well-looking man in a pretty blue military uniform, there is much laughter among them, the officer's face reddening a mite.

"Yer tae go wi' him and work in his hoose," says the rebel who understands their talk. "His name is Lieutenant St. Cyr, but ye should call him Monsieur, which means 'mister.'"

"Mesyuh Sanseer," Jenny tries, and the people laugh. "Am Ah his slave, then?"

"Nae," says the rebel, "ye'll be paid some sort of a wage. But we've scant option here. Mysel', I've signed fer their infantry."

"*Suivez-moi,*" says the Lieutenant after giving her a closer look, and Jenny follows him away, walking with some difficulty in the half-shoes.

PRINCE CHARLIE DRIVES THE WAGON, A PAIR OF RUNTY, scab-colored horses pulling along the sandy, narrow trace between stands of low palm trees and prickly underbrush. They are perhaps a mile in from where the schooner dropped them on a beach, though it is hard to tell with the view so monotonously strange and the draft animals so loathe to be hurried. The bondsmen, unshackled now and clueless as to where they are, sit wherever they can find purchase on the pile of supplies in the wagon bed, while Crozier, a charged pistol in his lap, rides beside the African.

Aeneas Cameron, incessantly waving at flies, leans forward to call to the master.

"Might I ask where we're being taken?"

The master does not turn to answer. "Ye'll be working on ma plantation," he says, "which is at the bottom of Lord Oglethorpe's Folly, the Georgia Colony." He taps a bit of snuff tobacco between his knuckles, snorts it in without sneezing. "He expects a white mon tae work in the fever swamp like the savages do, which is a bluidy joke. But we'll see the last of him soon enow."

He looks over to Prince Charlie, the African impassive, appearing not to listen.

"These dairkies is the future here, though ye'd cut me throat if ever ye had the chance, wouldn't ye, ma fine handsome cannybal?"

Prince Charlie watches the path through the scrub. Cameron shifts uncomfortably on the barrel he's claimed.

"I will not grub in the field with negroes," he announces. "I shall not submit to—"

Crozier turns quickly to face him, filling his hand with the pistol.

"Yer a Cameron, are ye?"

"Cameron of Lochiel, the fourth Earl of—"

Crozier swiftly lifts the pistol to rest the barrel against Cameron's forehead, cocking it.

"The world could do with mair tame neggers and fewer wild Camerons."

Jamie senses that the pitch of the insects' constant buzzing has changed around them, and there is a rotting smell from ahead.

"Are we near water?"

Crozier uncocks the pistol, turns back to look ahead.

"Such as they name it doon here," he grumbles. "Ye'd find mair fit tae drink in a peat hag."

THE RIVER, SUCH AS IT IS, SNAKES LAZILY BETWEEN more of the trees with the triangular bases, bony knobs of their root systems poking up from the pea-green water, with some kind of growth, like witches' hair, thinks Jamie, hanging down from the branches that arch over their heads. They are alternately rowing and poling a longboat made from a single, hollowed tree, with a skiff filled with the supplies tied behind. Prince Charlie stands in the prow, his bare toes hooked over the gunnels, guiding them around obstacles with a shaved length of sapling for a pole. He has covered his skin wherever bare with mud, which has dried a whitish gray, giving the tall, angular man a ghostly look.

They are plagued by small, buzzing, biting insects, which settle on their necks and faces as they work the oars, Fergal cursing in Erse at the rear of the longboat. Crozier, sitting just behind the African in the fore, has put flame to some foul-smelling grass in a tin can which he has set on the grain sack by his knees, the smoke from it rising about his face, then trailing behind too wispily to serve the bondsmen against the pests.

"If ye've a mind tae run," he calls back to them, "yer mair than welcome. After the snakes and scairpyins have had their turn, the red men will do wi' what's left iv ye."

They keep rowing.

With the current moving only sluggishly against them, they glide deeper and deeper into the strange, drowned forest, till they come to a party waiting on a cleared spot at the river's bank. Two miserable-looking black men, stripped to the waist, sit bound back to back on the ground, watched over by a man dressed in animal skins who carries a long rifle. Crozier has them pull the boat up on shore a ways downstream, then walks with Prince Charlie behind him to speak with the armed man.

"Is that a red Indian, then?" asks Lachlan.

"I dinnae believe so."

"But his face—"

"Has been under this sun fer some great while. And in a' the drawings of the red men, I've no keeked ane twas fully bearded."

"He looks a right savage."

"As will we, soon enow. As will we."

A bargain is struck between Crozier and the tangle-haired buckskin, money passing hands, and Prince Charlie arranges the bindings on the two black men so they are able to walk one beside the other. He speaks a few words to them, but they appear not to understand and are fastened on top of the goods in the skiff for the rest of the journey.

THE COLORED GIRL, WHO, TAPPING FINGERS TO CHEST, declares her name to be Amély, leads Jenny into the smallish stone building that houses the cookstove.

"*Ça c'est vot travaille ici,*" she says, lifting a skillet. "*Fé cuisine pou le maît.*"

"I'm nae use in a kitchen," says Jenny, shaking her head.

Amély shrugs. "*L'aut cuisinié, Mathilde, s'enfuit.*" She indicates running away with her fingers. "*Elle rivée récenment, comme vous, mais tou sauvage. Et je suis nettoyeuse.*"

She makes scrubbing gestures with her hands, then points to herself.

"But I dinnae ken what there is here tae eat, nor hoo tae prepare it."

The girl shrugs and giggles. She is slight and bonny, gleaming white teeth flashing with her ready smile and dimples in her tawny cheeks, her black, tightly curled hair wrapped in a bright yellow headscarf with one twisted corner sticking up straight, like a feather. Jenny is fascinated with the look of her and catches herself staring. Amély waves her to lean close.

"*Le maît*," she whispers, nodding her head toward the big house where the Lieutenant sits reading yellowed newspapers on the verandah, "*est un nom vec mains trés libe. Il touche beaucoup*," and here she pinches her own nipples, and grabs hold of her hind end, giggling. "*Gadé vous, M'amselle*."

"But hasna he bought me? Am Ah no a slave like yersel'?"

"*Esclave?*"

"Aye—"

Amély laughs loudly, points to herself again. "*Je suis esclave, comme presque tous les negs ici en Martinique. Mais vous*—" and here she puts her hand on Jenny's shoulder, looking her in the eye with some sympathy, "*vous n'êtes pas esclave ni libe, mais réfugiée, une orpheline du destin*."

"*Orphan*, Ah ken, and it's true enow, I'll reckon. If Ah've a father yet, and a hame, Ah'll ne'er lay een upon them again. But what Ah am no," she says, waving her hands at the stove, "is a *cook*."

Amély smiles, pointing to the scrawny, long-legged corpse of a hen with Wbeautifully bright plumage that lays on the knife-scarred table. "*C'est le dejeuner,*" she says, starting out of the kitchen. "*Bon chans*."

THE TREES ARE MOSTLY SCRUBBY PINES AND PALMS OF various heights and thicknesses. The bondsmen and the black Africans, trusted with axes while under guard by the rifle-toting overseer, Moncrief, and his companion Pike, a walleyed local white man, fell the trees and hack out the underbrush and drag it to a large pile that fills most of a sandy clearing on Crozier's land.

"Ye can't name it a plantation," Lachlan has observed, "when there's naething been *plan*tit."

Fergal, accepting his servitude for the moment, works with Prince Charlie to harness the one obstreperous mule to pull stumps, the African the only one of them capable of convincing the beast to strain forward, while the massive Highlander levers an iron bar from the other side, roots popping and earth flying as the twisted remnants are yanked free.

They have woven themselves hats of palm frond, their hands and bare feet blistered, then hardened by the work. There is no keeping the sting of sweat from their eyes, no protection from the swarms of biting insects. By midday it is not unusual for Jamie, Lachlan or Cameron to collapse and lie in the sand, stepped around by the Africans as they continue to toil, until Moncrief or Pike arrive with kicks and prods to revive them.

"It needs four of these great, strapping hillskippers," says Moncrief, another lowlander and somehow kin to Crozier, "tae equal the work of one puny negger."

Pike has a laugh that is more like a wheeze as he raps Jamie hard in the ribs with the butt of his rifle.

"Noo if it was cattle needed theivin', oh, they're clever uns at that." Moncrief circles Jamie, somewhat unsteadily. He and Pike often have rum on their breath, and Jamie has more than once seen Moncrief hiding a clay jug near the section to be cleared in the morning.

"Nip a few coos, get pie-eyed on the whisky, stab yer cousin with a dirk—that's a Hielander's dee fer ye."

He wanders over to where Fergal is digging around a stump with a pick.

"Lookit this un—big as an ox and simple as a wee bairn. Clean skite he is—tis the inbreeding does it."

"Yer fortunate he can't understand ye," says Cameron, passing with an armful of branches.

"Too bluidy feckless tae learn the King's English. Nekked, they were, yer Hielanders, until recent times. Painted their arses blue and run aboot the muirs beatin' ane another with clubs."

"Lowland scum," mutters Cameron.

The overseer moves to block his path.

"Laird of the manor, is it? I'd advise ye tae mind yer tongue with me, Mister High-and-Mighty. We had a laddie like you a wheel back—what was his name?"

"Buchanon," says Pike, spitting brown tobacco juice into the sand.

"Aye, Buchanon of Ballaghulan. Acted like the bluidy Duke of Atholl. Run aff intae the bush as soon as he spied the chance. The red men caught him—opened him up with a knife and tied ane end of his guts tae a tree. Then they beat him—have ye seen their tommyhawks? Forced him aroond and aroond till the guts was a' played oot. A great bluidy mess it was when we found him."

He claps Cameron on the shoulder, grins crookedly. "Nae, lads, ye'd better stick close tae Robbie Moncrief. Oot there"—he looks to the woods—"tis the Divvil's ane playground."

Jamie notices that whenever Moncrief leaves to relieve himself in the scrub he returns smelling more of rum, and then Pike does the same with the same result, the two then laughing over their shared indulgence in whatever patch of shade they find or create to supervise the work from. Master Crozier has informed them all that he is Kirk of Scotland to the core and regards his immediate neighbors—white, Spanish, and Indian—to be hellbound in their drunkenness.

The land does not yield willingly. Whatever Crozier's designs for planting, the soil is poor, sandy with orts of broken shell throughout, even well away from the ocean, and what prickly weed grows in it clings desperately to remain rooted. The days are heat and insects and hacking and hauling and at least one smoky, crackling trash fire to tend, and at times Jamie feels a pure hatred for the country, for its decadent vegetation and relentless sun, for its sudden, brief showers that do nothing to lessen their toil. But then a sudden curse or blow from Moncrief, an insulting jeremiad from the master, and he remembers who the real enemy is.

In time Jamie becomes aware that Prince Charlie, more than the other blacks on the so-called plantation, is subtly, constantly watching the overseers, measuring his effort throughout the day, working enough to avoid their punishment but slacking off whenever possible, carrying a lighter load, making one trip into three.

"Yer a canny fella," says Jamie, wrestling a huge, hacked-down palmetto through the scrub and coming upon Prince Charlie standing to stare at a trio of the strange birds that Pike calls pellycans, soaring wing-to-wing above them. "And yer the leader of yer mob, aren't ye?"

The black man's countenance reveals no comprehension, staring straight up.

"I've an idea we've the same thought in our heids," Jamie continues, "and it'd behoove us tae a' pull together."

Prince Charlie looks at him then, or perhaps through him, then grabs onto the tree and helps drag it to the burn pile.

Their food, other than a few berries found in passing, is provided by Crozier's cook, an ancient, tattooed Indian woman named Mercedes who speaks, when Jamie can get a word out of her, in Spanish. She tends a garden protected on all sides by thornbushes, feeding them beans and corn fritters and a kind of green squash that grows from a vine that climbs up dead trees, feeds them palm cabbage and strong-smelling guavas and the meat of gopher turtles and orange-tinted arrowroot biscuits made from a flour pounded out from what she calls *koonti.* In their few moments alone together Jamie tries his French on her and they make some sense, the old women telling him she is of a tribe that is nearly gone.

"*Mocama,*" she says, tapping her chest. "*Mocama,*" she repeats, pointing to the sea. "*Soy una de las últimas. Los padres catolicos me vendieron al maestro.*"

The others of her people, she makes him understand, have mostly died of fevers brought by the *españoles* or been killed in wars with them.

"*Despues de yo,*" she says, thumping herself on the chest again, "*nada.*"

The master is killing flies, his favorite pastime. He sits on the porch of his rough plank house in the little clearing, seemingly in a trance, waiting for one of the buzzing insects to land on a part of his body within reach of his long, calloused hands, which rest lightly on his knees. Jamie and Lachlan hear each lightning slap as they pile firewood at the far end of the porch, occasionally stealing a glance to see him examining the victim between his fingers before dropping it onto the pile of carcasses at his feet. The plank house is sealed tightly with dried clay, and the master could be free of flying pests if he sat inside, so it must be sport that keeps him out in the hottest part of the day.

If only he'd let them bite him, Lachlan mutters in Erse, they'd be dead soon enough.

Crozier dwells in the plank house, alone, and seems to have done something to poison the ground around it, for the jungle, which is what the crowded palm scrub on all sides amounts to, maintains a respectful distance. In other places it grows lasciviously, patches that Jamie and the others have cleared only days ago already crawling with tentative shoots and runners. Moncrief and Pike sleep in an unbalanced pile of sticks and saplings some distance away, hoping, perhaps, that the master cannot hear their drunken rumblings at night, and Mercedes in the same palm hut where she cooks their meals. Down a little slope from the overseers is what Mercedes calls a *chickee*, a platform with a palmetto roof above that has no walls, where the slaves and bondsmen lie on woven mats at night feeding the tiny, whining *mosquitos*—Spanish for the spawn of Hell. With no discussion of the matter, the blacks have settled on one side of this structure and the whites on the other.

"Godforsaken pestilence," Crozier announces suddenly. "Air unfit tae breathe. Garden of bluidy serpents."

"If it disnae suit ye," says Jamie softly, keeping his eyes on the growing pile of firewood, "yer free tae sail hame."

Crozier stares at Jamie and Lachlan for a long moment before he speaks. "I was telt of a crofter's paradise. I was telt of tobacca and barleycorn, of rivers tae water yer crop, of trees sae tall ye'd only tae trim the branches fer a mainmast."

"Further north, perhaps," says Jamie.

"I'll be buried here," says Crozier, eyes red, flies buzzing about his face. The master has not been drinking liquor, the master does not tipple, but there is a drunken melancholy to his words. "And ma only comfort is I'll see you sons of Hieland bitches buried first."

OLD YOLANDE WATCHES JENNY CUT THE VEGETABLES. Though the ancient negress, bought to teach her to cook after the first disastrous meal for the Lieutenant and his planter *amis*, speaks an even more extreme form of the French tongue than Amély, Jenny is able to communicate with her with substantial effort. Ensconced in the kitchen much of the day, her vocabulary here is mostly the types of *vivres*, and she revels in their variety and colors as well as the sounds of the words for them. The fruits alone—*l'orange amère, noix de coco, gouyave, pomélo, citron vert, papaye, maricuja*, the orange-fleshed *sapote mamey* and *mangues*, the surprising *tamarin*—all eaten straight off the tree or bush or used in their cooking. *Sucre* and *café* of course, things the lairds and town swells had back in Scotland but that Jenny has never tasted before, and some kind of meat—chicken or pork or even beef—for the *maître* several times a week and the drink they make from the *cacao* beans and all the lovely kinds of fish and *lambi*, which is an immense snail pulled out from the most beautiful pink and white shell, then pounded with a mallet till it is tender enough to cook. Jenny has sampled it all, liking even the simple *manioc* flour—what they have here instead of oatmeal—mixed with salt cod that the *noires* eat almost daily, her body rounding after her release from the starvation of the prison ships. And each day old Yolande teaches her, in words she does not fully understand and gestures that she does, new ways to combine and cook them that make her swoon to think of.

Today it is *courtbouillon.*

Jenny chops bright red *tomate*—a wonderful thing something between a vegetable and a fruit—and adds the cubes to the onions and garlic already heating in the stock made from fish heads, then begins to add the spices, following Yolande's admonitions of *plus, plus* or *ça suffit*—thinking of the months passed back home without even salt for their clabber and still amazed at the number and uses of the powders and potions the Creole woman has her sprinkle in, only slowly beginning to be able to taste their effect on what she prepares. The last added is a fine mince of fiery Bonda Man Jacques, a glistening red pepper grown on a bush just behind the Lieutenant's seaside house. Jenny has learned from painful experience to wash her hands thoroughly after using it, to lick her fingers as a test before touching her eyes or any other part of her body.

The ritual at meals is to deliver the latest creation to the table—Jenny clumsily holding the large trays in front of her rather than balancing them on her head as Amély demonstrated—then wait quietly for the *maître* to take his place, taste the offering, and render his judgment. St. Cyr is a discriminate eater, idling at table for hours even when dining alone, carefully nibbling at first, then either nudging the dish away with a sighed *C'est pas correcte* or digging in with a small but satisfied grunt.

Allowing the mix to simmer, Jenny cuts the scaled fish—*daurade* and *abadèche rouge*—into chunks and dusts them liberally with *sal*, *piment* and a few other colorful substances she can't remember the names of.

The Lieutenant's house sits on short pillars that lift it off the sandy ground, whitewashed, with large window openings that hold no glass but have wooden *louvres* that can be angled different ways depending on the wind, and a wide stairway up to a covered *gallerie* that runs all the way around, St. Cyr sitting out on it in a chair that is part wood and part woven, smoking and reading French newspapers that are six months old. He is an artillery officer attached to the *Compagnie Franche de la Marine*, in charge of the cannon and battlements of Fort Royal, but it is clear to Jenny that he is a man of some family wealth, strolling through this tropical colony as if he owns it. He watches her with a bemused smile on his lips, Jenny barefoot when inside, wearing one of the colorful *tabliers* Amély has provided, her hair washed every day now and tied back with a ribbon, but only once has she been forced to utter the *Ne me touche pas* the colored women have taught her.

It is bound to happen.

Jenny sees no way to avoid it, the Lieutenant a confident, well-looking man, a *maître béké* accustomed to having his will served, and the papist church here, though everywhere present, seems willing to ignore relations between men and women that would have your ear pinned to the kirk door back in Scotland. If she can only have him know her a wee bit, to at least learn to look her in the eye, before surrender—

She has seen Morag a few times at the *marché*, buying *vivres* for the family she is in service to. "Most of them that was Catholics," the girl told her of their fellow captives, "has taken passage tae France. But ma mistress here is easily pleased, and the auld man's tae decrepit tae fox me intae a corner, sae I expect I'll stick it oot fer a wee bit, find me a sojer. The scran is dead nasty, thoo—these people eat *snails*."

Jenny declined to tell her that she hopes never to leave.

The Lieutenant's house is situated so that there is always an ocean breeze wafting through it to keep the biting insects at bay, with the sound of the waves lulling her to sleep each night in her little cell of a room at the back, and on the many holidays and saints days of important white men there is music made by the black people that makes her long to dance.

As for the *esclaves noires* she has had to deal with, her main surprise is that they are so rarely sullen. The women at the market laugh together, chattering in their rhythmic *patois*, and even the bare-chested laborers on the docks will venture a work song or a smile under the angry gaze of a white, *baton*-wielding *surveillant*. There is an undertone to it all, though, and Jenny, in the limbo of her free-but-*dépendante* status, is allowed to see and hear things other whites are not. Mockery, sometimes—Guillaume, the hostler, is expert at mimicking the Lieutenant's nose-in-the-air gait—and sometimes there is open hostility, *les sales békés* cursed to their backs more than once in her presence.

Jenny eases the fish chunks into the broth and old Yolande frowns at the bubbling surface of the pot. The woman is *neg-guinée*, born long ago in Africa and stolen away to this island, her face rutted like a plowed field. There is no telling how old she is, though she has all her teeth still, which she brushes clean once a day with the fibers of a broken section of sugar cane. There is a brand, a raised scar on the black skin on the back of her right hand, and the lobes of her ears hang down, separated from the rest of the flesh and stretched at some time in the past. She gives the *courtbouillon* a sniff.

"*Pas mal*," she says, and pats Jenny on the cheek.

DAYS PASS IN A DREAM STATE, ONE DIFFICULT TO DISTINguish from the other, seemingly endless stretches of brute labor broken by moments of much-begrudged rest, the sun unrelenting, the superheated air a challenge to breathe. There is little novelty to interrupt the fugue, and no explanation of the tasks they are set to—lift this, move that, dig, chop, haul—even the overseers dare not examine the master's instructions in search of purpose. They seem to be clearing land, but with no fences, no marked boundaries, it is sometimes hard to find yesterday's work site in the jumble of sawgrass hammock and marsh. There are eight of them—the bondsmen, the two slaves picked up on the river, Prince Charlie, and an older African called Juba who was waiting by Crozier's plank house when they arrived. Each day, with each task, a pace of work is established, the laborers with no idea of what will be demanded next and therefore saving themselves, the overseers striking when they see idle limbs or just become bored watching other men toil. They are only allowed to rest during meals, announced at the whim of their guards, with the slaves and bondsmen often too exhausted to speak, struggling to summon the energy to chew and swallow. Crozier appears rarely, staring at some thicket or muckhole to formulate a plan he does not share. A belief grows among the men that their labors are pointless, designed only to numb their minds and break their bodies.

Jamie, a spade over his shoulder, makes his way around the cypress knees, ankle deep in muck. He is burning with a fever, sweat pouring from him as it did all through the night. The colors of the trees around him become more intense, almost painful to look at, and then fade. He was dizzy when he first stood up this morning, and he lurches through the tangle of swamp, his bare feet making sucking noises as he jerks them up from the marl. There is an easier path to the clearing, drier ground, but their overseers insist they take the shorter route through the swamp, Pike prodding them into it with his rifle and Moncrief waiting, smirking, at the other side.

When he catches an ankle and falls it is face forward, the spade flying clear, jamming an elbow on a cypress trunk and taking in a mouthful of scummy green water. Jamie curses in Erse, reaches to haul himself up—

"Dwunt move!"

Prince Charlie's voice, behind him.

It is a beautiful thing, really, buff-colored with darker brown crossbands down all of its length, coiled tightly upon itself on the hip of a tree within half an armspan of Jamie's raised hand, its triangular head arched back and mouth gapped open to display the fangs and pearly white insides.

Jamie holds his breath, holds his hand as steady as he can. He hears munching footsteps, then the blade of the spade eases past his head and the African's shadow covers him. There is a quick, twisting flick and he hears the snake hit a tree somewhere off to the left with a wet smack.

Prince Charlie bends to hand Jamie the spade, then moves ahead.

"I thank ye," calls Jamie.

The African keeps walking.

MONCRIEF IS ALREADY SMELLING OF RUM WHEN JAMIE stumbles out into the clearing. The overseer notes the swamp scum still wet on his clothes, laughs.

"Had yerself a wee bath, is it?" he says. "Well this is no spa fer gentlemen—get busy with that spade."

They have discovered a patch of loamy earth that goes down several feet and have been filling huge baskets with it to spread upon the clearing surface.

"Yer no lookin' weel, Jamie," says Lachlan, digging beside him, the little islander up to his navel in the pit they've made.

"Ah'm burnin' up."

"Tis nae climate fer a Scotsman, nor fer any but a red Indian."

"Ye don't keek them diggin' holes under the hot sun."

"Ye barely keek them a'tall. Which is just as weel."

There have been a few men with stripes tattooed on their faces and wearing beautiful shirts with horizontal bands of color come to trade with Crozier, men he calls *Muskogee*, and Jamie has witnessed one long negotiation where they seemed to be trying to purchase Prince Charlie.

"They observe us, I'll venture." Jamie stabs the spade down into the black earth till enough has come loose, then tosses it up into the basket. "Amused by us, as the folk of quality who visit Bedlam are entertained by the lunatics."

"Ah, but those are meant tae leave a donation. We pervide our spectacle *gratis*."

They are allowed to take the midday meal at the same time, the transports and the slaves, but sit apart on driftwood benches to eat it. Careful to avoid the beached seaweed that is always hopping with tiny fleas, today they eat lumps of corn fritter with a kind of squash stew Mercedes provides, lifting it with spoonlike shells out of bowls made from gourds. Pike and Moncrief, lounging on an overturned rowboat with a gaping hole in its bottom, have roasted an opposum, a huge, long-snouted rodent with evil-looking pointy teeth, and are passing the forbidden jug back and forth.

"He's crackit, ye ken, the master," says Moncrief, loud enough for all to hear. "Gan round the bend. But he's still canny as a fox, and nae mon tae diddle with."

"What is meant to be planted here?" asks Cameron, who always sits on the sand with his bad leg extended rather than perching on the driftwood.

"No that it's any of yer concern, but as the master explained it tae me, there's a wee wormie that eats nowt but the leaves of a certain tree, and that tree is what will be set in the ground here—as soon as the seeds fer it arrive."

"Silk?"

"Tis the plan. They weave themselves a wee tent, these wormies, and frae that is made the cloth."

"He means to raise silkworms from the mulberry."

"As I stated—the mon's crackit in the heid."

THE BONDSMEN LIE ON THEIR WOVEN MATS BENEATH palmetto thatch, Fergal muttering Erse in his sleep, Jamie, knackered by the long day's labor, still drenched with sweat, waving his bloodied, calloused hands to keep a small cloud of mosquitos from settling on him. The Africans remain sitting around the little cook fire, faces devilish, lit by flame in the black night, speaking little as they practice some handiwork. Lachlan begins to coo a verse—

Doon at luck and Godforsaken
Heat nae mon can lang enduir
Cursed each dee tae once mair waken
Stranded on this wretched shuir—

He makes the effort, Lachlan, to keep up with the others, to dig as much, lift as much, haul as much, but he is wee and frail and receives the brunt of the overseers' abuse, slapped and kicked from dawn to dusk, at times denied food in punishment for poor performance—

Here they toil in desperation
Dissolute, bereft of zeal
Robbed of valor, base in station
Pinioned 'neath the tyrant's heel—

There is nothing cocksure or heroic left in the *seanachaidh*'s ballads, snarling them out as he wrestles roots from the withholding earth, old clan victories forgotten in the pall of the endless, scorching days of labor—

When will these four slip their irons
Captors' bloodhounds tae evade
Fleeing tae far aff environs
Dwelling free and unafraid?

The wee islander goes quiet then, the high, rhythmic chirping of frogs and the crackling of the Africans' fire filling the silence. Jamie rises, hops down from the platform and approaches the slaves. Scratching at the latest accretion of insect bites on his arms and neck, he sits beside Prince Charlie, who stares moodily into the fire.

"They dinnae bite ye?"

The black man indicates the smoke with a nod, then holds his nose.

"Ah. Listen, Prince Charlie—"

"*Yaw*," says the African, tapping his chest with his hand.

"Yer actual name is Yaw?"

He nods.

"I'm Jamie."

"Ken dat."

"Tell me then, Yaw, hoo lang have ye been here with master Crozier?"

Yaw frowns.

"Dae ye ken what a year is?"

Yaw nods, hold up three fingers.

"Laird preserve us—and he hasn't kilt ye yet. And Juba as well?"

"Juba 'eer when Yaw come."

The two men picked up by the river are carefully slitting open the stems of sago palm leaves with shells they have sharpened into blades while old Juba digs out the whitish pith, saving it in a small leather sack.

"Is that tae eat, then?"

Yaw shakes his head. "Dat fa masta, mekkim die." He hold his hands around his neck as if to choke himself.

Jamie smiles. "A capital idea, that." He takes up a stick yet untouched by the flame.

"A' reet, then, Yaw—ye've been aboot much mair than any of us, up and doon the river"—he smooths a place in the sand between them. "Show me where we are."

IT BEGINS WHEN THE LIEUTENANT OVERHEARS JENNY speaking in *kréyol* with Amély and is appalled.

"*Tu dois parler un français correct, comme une maîtresse blanche!*" he protests, and when Jenny replies that she is the mistress of nobody and that it is difficult for her to tell the difference between "proper French" and what the blacks speak among themselves, he resolves to teach her. At some point each day after his return from the fort there is a lesson, something like what she experienced with old Mr. Higgenbotham, but with a more intimate feel to it.

St. Cyr begins with the words for the parts of her body, softly touching each as he names it, and has her repeat.

"*La tête,*" he begins the first lesson, gently cradling Jenny's head in his fingers as she stands before him on the *gallerie* in front of the house. "*Repetez, s'il vous plait.*"

"*La tête.*"

"*Les sourcils,*" he says, tracing her eyebrows with the tips of his fingers. "*Repetez.*"

"*Les sourcils.*"

"*Et les yeux, pour voire votre maître,*" tapping under each of her eyes, his own looking into her.

"*Les yeux.*"

The words are more flowing than in *kréyol*, with a softer music. St. Cyr brushes her cheek with the side of his finger.

"*Et c'est la joue ici.*"

"*La joue.*"

He lifts her hair from the nape of her neck, giving her a swift and pleasant little chill. "*Les cheveux—trés belles—*"

"*Les cheveux.*"

He runs the tips of his fingers slowly, softly around her mouth. Twice.

"*Et la bouche—tellement tendre, tellement douce—*"

"*La bouche—*"

He holds her chin up to him, smiles. "*Ça suffit pour aujourd-hui. Tu es une bonne elève.*"

He leaves her standing there, feeling a bit weak-kneed, a bit resentful, but her skin alive where he touched. Nobody has ever handled her so gently—

AMÉLY IS VERY PLEASED. "*QUÈ BON CHANS, CHÈ, Q'TU LE plait,*" she exclaims when Jenny informs her of the lesson, of the touching. Soon, she says, Jenny will not have to cook, she will have plenty of pretty dresses, possibly of silk, and even real shoes, more than one pair. She has been worried about the Lieutenant, alone here, *tellement loin de l'épouse—*

"He has a *wife*?"

"*Bien sûr, en France.*"

Jenny thinks of the voyage from London. France is on the other side of the world.

"And here—*ici—le lieutenant a-t-il d'autres femmes?*"

Amély shrugs, makes a dismissive noise. "*Seulment les negresses.*"

There are slaves of all shades on the island, but Jenny has not been sure if they might arrive that way on the boats or be the result of—

"*Et avec toi?*"

"*Moi*?" laughs Amély, slapping a hand to her chest. "*C'est impossible!*"

"*Tu es trés belle, jeune—*"

"*Mais c'est mon frè!*"

Jenny is shocked. "Yer brother? *Comment*—?"

"*Nous avons le même pè,*" Amély explains, explains that the Lieutenant's father was a planter here who sired many children of color, each of whom was rewarded with a job in the household rather than the fields. That the old man—the *vié béké*—died while St. Cyr was in Paris receiving his education, and that upon returning as an artillery officer the Lieutenant sold most of the plantation land and dedicated himself to cannons and cockfighting.

"'*Vec les cousins, pas de problème, mais les frès et les soeurs—ça c'est un péché grave.*"

Despite the papist priests, thinks Jenny, there are so many fewer things considered sins here than at home, and those still recognized seem easily erased in their confessions. Amély grows serious.

"*Fó qu'et prudente,*" she warns, warns that Jenny must not let the *maître* take her lightly, that if properly played, a white consort can earn certain rights and may even be brought out into society. She explains how at the *quadrilles blancs* many of the officers bring women to dance with who are not their wives, how even when wives are present on the island, *châteaux d'amour* maintained expressly for side women are common, smaller houses complete with servants and gardens.

Jenny is studying the housekeeper's face, and yes, there is a resemblance, Amély's skin the shade of coffee with milk stirred in, but her nose and eyes shaped much like those of the *maître.*

"*T'es viege?*"

When Mr. Higgenbotham taught Jenny the English word for *virgin* she was so rattled she couldn't repeat it at first. She has never spoken to anyone, not even Morag, about the soldiers on the day after the great battle, and has pressed her hand to her belly every morning since, grateful that it has not swelled.

"*Pas—pas exactement.*"

Amély looks into her eyes then, accepts this as an answer.

"*Alors—c'est mieux fé semblant que t'es innocente, c'est pas dificile.*"

"D'ye think he'll believe it? *Il me croyez?*"

Amély flashes her beautiful smile, presses her palm to her chest.

I have been a virgin so many times, she says. "*C'est comme un miracle.*"

JAMIE AND YAW ARE ON A SHALLOW, SLOW-MOVING river, smelling of decay, having rowed Crozier several miles to trade. The master, mute and glaring, sits in the rear facing them the whole way, loaded pistol in his lap, the foul smoker can set before him. Lachlan and Fergal are towed behind in the little skiff with a roll of animal skins and a cloth sack nearly full of sea turtle shells. Jamie is unable to identify landmarks—one stretch of moss-laden trees near identical to the last, nothing blazed or painted. He reckons that they are traveling inland, due west from the sea—sun at their backs the entire morning—which agrees with the crude map Yaw has drawn for him. The wider part of the river, to the south of Crozier's cropless plantation, is more likely a channel between the shore and a series of long coastal islands, leading down to the realm of the Spanish. He sees several snakes in the water, oozing along the surface, and they flush the same heron a number of times, the huge, unlikely bird flapping ahead around a bend and settling, only to be dislodged again when they catch up to it. Jamie's shoulders ache, but he prefers rowing to digging, and the overhang from the trees breaks the force of the sun.

He recognizes the cleared spot by the river when they come to it, Crozier directing them to pull up on the bank. Crozier steps to solid ground, waves the pistol at them.

"Ye'll toss them oars up here," he says, "and stay in the boats till yer needed."

They doze in the beached dugout, serenaded by parrots, till the buckskin from before appears, his leather jerkin filthier, sporting a necklace made from the claws of some large animal. He's brought supplies as near as he can by sledge, and they are to portage the goods the rest of the way. The buckskin, whose name is Shiflett, leads the way, the party crossing two streams, the water of the second waist-high and more swift-moving than the river.

"Does he use ye hard?" asks Shiflett once Crozier has lagged behind out of earshot.

"Hard enow," Jamie answers. "Can ye say what's north of here?"

The buckskin grins, showing brown-pitted teeth. "Mostly yer Muskogee, and then yer Cherokee, which is both as apt to trade as to lift hair. And then mebbe the Shawanese, they'll wander down this way—they be vagabonds, near as I can tell."

"Dangerous?"

"Mercenary. Tis known there's a bounty fer runaways, and all is on the lookout to collect it. If yer lucky, *I'll* find ye before the savages do."

"Ye'll hunt us?"

Again the terrible grin. "Some feckless darky takes it on the shank, Shiflett's the man they call fer."

They are on the way back with the first load when Fergal shies at the shallower stream, dropping the barrels from off his shoulders and crying out in Erse.

"*An diabhal, an diabhal!*"

It is one of the water dragons, crouched on the far side of the stream, huge maw opened and hissing at them.

Lachlan steps to the water's edge, sets his burden down. "Will ye look at the creatur—a monster swum up frae hell!"

They hear Crozier shouting from back in the woods to keep the damned goods moving.

"It could swalla ye hale with that mouth—"

The master is beside them. "Don't fash yersel', lad. We'll take care of Mr. Reptile afore he can make aff with ye. Shiflett—"

The buckskin loads his rifle, a longer barrel on it than Jamie has ever seen, and kneels to aim at the alligator. The ball hits one of the hard scales on its back, chipping it away, and the fearsome beast melts down into the stream, Jamie watching its snout and eyes, held just above the surface, as it swims downstream.

Fergal seems not to have noticed, sitting on the forest floor well back from the water, muttering to himself and still trembling.

Crozier turns to Jamie. "Tell yer witless friend tae carry his load across."

The huge MacGregor shouts at the master, hands gripping the earth at his sides.

"He says ye can kill him if ye'd like, but he's no crossing that stream with the divvil floatin' in it."

"We'll leave him, then. See hoo that sets with the daft booby."

They are halfway back to the boats when they hear Fergal crashing through the brush behind them. He even has the barrels tucked under his arms.

The last thing to go into the towboat is an enormous, wedge-headed turtle that Shiflett holds up by the stick it has clamped its jaws on, legs slowly paddling the air.

"Ain't he a beauty? Near took my foot off."

The reptile is stuffed head first into a burlap sack and tossed to Fergal, who quickly pins it beneath his feet.

"I fear we're meant tae eat that creatur," says Jamie to Lachlan as they set off down the river. "Or perhaps tae ride it."

MONCRIEF DOES THE FLOGGING. THE AFRICANS ARE given the task of surprising Fergal to bind his arms and legs, managing to adequately hogtie him but unable to drag him to the tree that Crozier indicates, so the overseer has to keep pace with the massive Highlander as he wriggles and rolls across the yard in front of the master's plank house, the shirt flogged from his back and dragging in bloody tatters.

Crozier watches from the porch, calling out fifty blows of the knotted rope, purposely losing count twice as his laborers, black and white, are required at musket-point to stand in witness.

By the end Fergal has ceased his movement, lying still on his face for the final dozen lashes.

The master turns and enters his house. Jamie and Lachlan go to Fergal, Lachlan kneeling to comfort the man with soft words as Jamie struggles to pull his bindings loose. When they manage to sit him up he is fully conscious, and though his face is drained of color the look in his eyes is the most cogent they've seen since he was shackled to a corpse back in the Tolbooth. He croaks a whisper to them.

"What did he say?" asks Aeneas Cameron.

"He says he'll kill every bluidy mon of them."

"*LES BRAS*," SAYS LIEUTENANT ST. CYR, RUNNING HIS hand slowly down Jenny's arm. It is evening and they are in the *maître*'s study, an oil lamp worried by dozens of moths hanging overhead.

"*Les bras*," Jenny repeats. He has begun by touching again each part of her from the last lesson, holding her eyes with his own, and she has practiced saying them in the French style.

"*Les épaules*," he says, holding her shoulders and stepping slightly closer to her.

"*Les épaules*."

"*Le cou.*" Bending his head to place his lips on the back of her neck now. Jenny shifts away slightly and touches her throat.

"*Ici?*"

He faces her again, a slight smile on his lips. "*Non, c'est la gorge.*" He slides his hands down around her waist—

"*La taille.*"

"*La taille.*"

Then to her hips—

"*Les hanches.*"

"Ye barely ken ma name."

"*Comment?*"

"*Vous ne savez pas mon nom.*"

"*Tu es Jeannie, mon 'tite captive.*"

He has called her his little captive before, but never addressed her as *tu*.

"*J'etait captive des mauvais anglais, pas de vous, M'sieur. Ici je suis seulement cuisinière.*"

She is not paid wages as a cook, of course, only sheltered and fed in exchange, and in her ignorance of the island often feels less "free" than the bonded servants around her.

"*Je m'excuse, mademoiselle,*" says the Lieutenant with a bow meant to be ironic.

She loves to speak this language, so many new things and manners here that she often wonders if there are even words for them in the English tongue—certainly not in Erse. Speaking it makes her feel like a different Jenny, unrelated to the grimy clachan lass condemned in the English courts and styed in their floating bridewells, a Jenny able to make a choice or two in the world—

The Lieutenant begins to slide his hands up toward her breasts till Jenny blocks them with her own.

"*C'est assez pour aujourd'hui, M'sieur. Si il y a trop de mots, je ne peut pas rappeler tous.*" It is true, more than seven or eight new words a day are wasted on her.

St. Cyr steps away, smiling. "*Tu es coquette.*"

"Ah'm nowt but a puir crofter's daughter—*fille d'un paysan*—but ah'm nae strumpet."

The Lieutenant makes a face at the word. "*Qu'est-ce c'est?*"

"*Swè pas bouzen.*"

"*En français correct*—"

"Ye ken what ah'm sayin," Jenny tells him, smiling, easing herself out of his hands and backing toward the door. "*Autre leçon demain, j'espère?*"

IN THE MORNING THEY BEGIN TO PLANT MULBERRY trees. Crozier hovers with the sack of seeds carried down from Savannah, doling each out to the men working on their knees as if it is a golden nugget.

"Make them holes deeper, damn ye, and no sae bluidy close tae the next un. I've telt ye, five paces betwixt trees, five paces betwixt rows!"

It is a task Lachlan finds himself well suited for.

"Mary, the wife of our Chief MacLeod on Raasay, owns a silken gown or twa. A lovely sheen tae the cloth."

"And very dear," says Jamie, tamping a seed down with his measuring stick.

"As ye'd expect. Some puir twat has tae pull a' them wee wormie houses apart, twist them intae threads—"

"The Chinese invented it."

"Did they, noo?"

"Silk and explosives."

"Clever bastarts. All Ah ken aboot Chinamen is that there's a great muckle number of them. D'ye think these will grow intae trees?"

"Someone thinks so. The buckskin telt me that if yer gi'en land in the Georgia Colony, yer expectit tae plant them."

They hear Crozier cursing the Africans at the other end of the clearing.

"He hopes tae win a fortune."

Jamie shrugs his shoulders. "Them orange fruits as grow here is tae bitter tae eat, his maize and indigo died, and even if ye could raise a crop in this sand, who's near enow tae purchase? Sae the puir fool dreams of silk."

They are done sowing by the afternoon, and spend the rest of the day carrying water from the river, half a league away, with Aeneas drizzling it on each new mound using a gourd drilled full of holes.

"Twice a dee," Crozier announces to Cameron, "withoot fail, yer tae do the same. The neggers will hale the water."

Cameron's gait is uneven, unable to bend the one leg, but he rarely falls behind and is too proud to complain.

"Is it possible to give them too much?"

"If they dinnae sprout, laddie, ah'll have yer hide fer it."

When dark comes they feast on a stew the Africans make of the snapping turtle. They share the same fire at night now, Jamie distinguishing more than one tongue spoken among the blacks. Fergal sits rocking quietly, the new shirt of coarse linen provided him crumpled in his lap, with a poultice of mashed leaves Juba prepared laid on the raw, bloody welts crossing old scars on his back.

Inspired, perhaps, by the meal, Lachlan stands, dramatically lit by the flame, and begins to declaim one of his older verses, his voice rising above the music of frogs and insects—

Black flowers grow on the brae
nurtured by the bluid of Campbells.
Fearless strode MacColl's legion
against the sallow sons iv Argyll—

The Africans watch, fascinated, their bodies swaying sideways with the cadence of the verse—

With venomous blades they hacked
the paws of treacherous foe
And strew the bare-rocked heights
With feast fer hawks encircling—

Juba is grinding handfuls of dried toadstools into a powder, then adding it to his sack with the sago palm pith—

Mony a warrior left sword and bow
Tae swim the cold water iv Nevis
Mony a warrior, though lauded in song
Runs yet frae our mighty onslaught—

Fergal listens, understanding words that have never graced his tongue, with tears in his eyes—

Remember this day, betrayers of Scotland!
The bluid iv great kings flows hot in our veins!

Lachlan, moved by his own eloquence, looks out past the sparks of the fire for a moment when he is done, then shrugs apologetically as he sits.

"I've no yet been able tae make it sing in Erse."

One of the younger African men, the one Yaw calls Cudjo, stands then, excited. He begins to recite an equally impassioned tale, stamping his foot and thumping his chest at various moments, the other black men repeating short phrases as a chorus. It is almost a song, and he seems to grow larger as he tells it.

Jamie can faintly see the overseers' shack on the little hill above them, can smell the iodine odor of sea wrack rotting on the beach, can look up at the stars, none in their proper place here, and is filled with an incredible sense of loss.

I belong here now, he thinks, not even with those two in their hovel or snug in the master's plank house. Here by this fire, in this benighted swampland, MacGillivray of Dunmaglas bound to dwell till body and spirit are broken, lower than a harvest hand and lackey to a madman.

Firelight glistens in the African's eyes, sweat shining on his bare chest, the sounds from his lips full of fury and longing. Even Cameron is rapt, leaning forward as if aching to comprehend. The man pleads his story till he grows hoarse and can say no more.

"I dinnae ken a word ye spake, laddie," Lachlan says to Cudjo when he is finished and seated again. "But yer a warrior and a poet."

THERE IS A BEAUTY TO THE MATHEMATICS OF DEATH. ST. Cyr understands the numbers on paper, of course, but even in the tumult of battle, air thick with smoke and bitter to inhale, he can glance at a battery piece and know it has reached that point where further elevation will rob distance, can spot an enemy guidon and tell how many metres away it lies, know that the twelve pounder, with a slight adjustment for wind—

Little Zézé, who trains his fighting birds, steps forward with a jet black *coq* in hand, cooing to it in his *patois*, a steady stream of instruction and encouragement.

"*Lequel est-il?*" asks St. Cyr.

"*Ça, c'est Gaspar l'Assassin.*"

"*Alors, il est trés audacieux?*"

"*Le plus vicieux de tous les coqs, M'sieu.*"

It does look like a killer, entire body trembling slightly with tension, jerking its head this way and that, searching for something worthy of attack.

"*Allez, allez—*"

Though the other *jouers* here would be loathe to admit it, there is no mathematics to cockfighting, all their strategies serving only to make them feel clever when winning and somehow betrayed when their bird is killed. You must have a good handler, of course, who keeps the birds well fed and sufficiently angry, the gaffs must be sharpened and strapped on correctly, but once the *combattants* are let loose in the pit with each other it is simply a blur of beaks and claws and feathers, two forces bred only to attack until victory or death.

Le Monnier, whose all-white rooster Bec-Fort is to go into the pit with Gaspar, catches his eye and flashes ten digits. Le Monnier has one of the largest plantations to the north—cane, cacao, coffee, all for export—and is a genial if obsessive gambler to whom St. Cyr already owes hundreds of *livres*. Not to be cowed by the wealthy planter, he answers with twelve digits and Le Monnier cedes him a smile and a slight bow.

The betting around the pit is spirited, both the birds triumphant on earlier evenings, with the *maîtres* discussing with their black handlers the merits of the opponents as if there is more complexity to the match than a roll of dice. There must be moments, St. Cyr thinks, when field generals abandon all thought of position and firepower and surrender to the urge to charge, just charge, straight into and over the enemy's cannon and have done with the academic chess match of battle. A gentleman must have that kind of resignation, that *sang-froid,* even to consider stepping up to a gaming table or cockpit, and the rule of combat nobody wishes to admit is that whatever the qualities of their armed forces, long wars end when one side runs out of money.

Zézé and Le Monnier's handlers hold the birds, the black and the white, with their faces an inch from each other, flaccid combs filling tight with rage, as the *arbitre* announces that the time for wagering has ended.

Whatever his skill as a *bombardier*—and St. Cyr believes he has no match in all the *Îles de Vent*—there is no mathematics, no magic formula to the *politique des militaires*. Despite the well-reasoned critiques of de Gribeauval and the success of the Prussians with a more scientific approach to the art, artillery officers are still more likely to rise due to family connections or personal favoritism rather than merit, and in many cases a basic competency is lacking. It is a game with too many variables (not to mention that news of war or treaty with the English arrives here six months after its declaration), a game that St. Cyr will never learn to relish. His father was a successful planter, teaching his son the proper way to handle both slaves and free men, but never followed his own advice, entangling himself with the comelier *bonnes* in his charge till St. Cyr is unable to travel a league on the island without stumbling over one of his *bâtarde mulatte* half brothers or sisters, each with a hand out and expecting special consideration. Not that he has been any wiser—this affair with Jeannie, being remarkable because of her color, will no doubt be advertised abroad. Wives learn things, even if they are back in Giverny, and wives have fathers—this one a *Marichal de l'Armee*.

Perhaps, he thinks, as the *coqs* are placed with their claws on the dirt of the pit but not released, the *arbitre* bending to place his hand between them, perhaps I should have been a *corsaire*. Government commission in hand, strutting around Fort Royal and Saint Pierre dressed according to their whims, saluting nobody, carousing on the gold their prizes have won them, each their own *maître* and regarded as heroes by the creole population. There are several of them here tonight, shoulder to shoulder with gentlemen officers and planters, a bit drunk, their accents insufferable, but—St. Cyr has to admit—excellent cannoneers, performing every task not only better than his boys do but on the violently pitching deck of a ship at sea.

The *arbitre* cries out *commencez!* and the birds are let loose, flapping at each other, rising straight up in a flurry of beak and claw as the *jouers* cheer for their champions—

—and it is over in less than a minute, Gaspar splayed flat on the dirt with blood pulsing from his neck, tiny golden eye staring up at the thatch of the roof, while Bec-Fort, certain to also die from his wounds, is cosseted in the arms of Le Monnier's handler. St. Cyr gives the planter an offhand salute—the amount will be added to his debt. Zézé lifts the limp black body, tears in his eyes. Perhaps old Yolande can teach his petite captive how to stew her tasty *ragoût de perdant*.

Loser chicken.

WITH THE *MAÎTRE* OUT MATCHING HIS BIRDS, AMÉLY takes Jenny to listen to a *conteur*. They are among the first to join the rough circle marked with torches, sitting on a bench made of bamboo stalks, Amély greeting each new arrival, mostly field slaves wearing the conical *chapeau bakoua* on their heads and strips of colored cloth tied around their arms and legs or women who sell things from baskets, usually perched on their heads, on the streets. These *belles* are much admired and courted by the men, women of many shades in the low-cut, embroidered *chemises*, in a skirt kept long in back but tucked up high in front to allow them free movement, a colorful silk *foulard* draped over their shoulders and the bright yellow turban fixed front and sides with silver brooches. None of them, busy with their flirting, rapid flow of talk, pay Jenny much attention. She is given a drink in a half coconut shell, rum and sugar cane juice and some spice, that makes her feel lovely inside.

I might be Amély's puppy, she thinks, with everyone assured that I don't bite.

The storyteller, when he comes, is a skinny, older man with skin like an overripe banana and one dead eye, the iris a milky blue. He sizes up his two dozen listeners with his good eye, head jerking sideways like a chicken as he leans on a knobby wooden staff. The people, both men and women, continue their drinking and gossiping with each other as if he's not there, speaking so quickly in *kréyol* that Jenny can only catch a word or two.

"*Kric!*" shouts the conteur suddenly.

"*Krac!*" the blacks shout back, coming to attention.

The storyteller begins slowly, using his hands to emphasize or indicate, mimicking the leaves of trees or the movement of water or the quick snatch of claws, soon dropping the staff and moving about, his voice changing as he inhabits different characters in the narrative, making animal noises or sounds of human emotion, eliciting laughter and gasps and head shaking from his audience, some of the women covering their eyes or ears at certain moments. Eventually a young man, eyes closed and rocking slightly, begins to beat a *tambor* softly, weaving the beat around the words of the *conteur*, and the people take more of a part in the stories, calling out observations or warnings or repeating phrases the old man has just uttered. From the gasps and nervous laughter Jenny guesses that he is telling of the dangerous night spirits now, and she thinks of the *Cailleach Bhéara,* the hammer-wielding hag of the wild places who formed the great craggy mountains and brings the killing winter, who herds the wild deer and uses the whirlpool at Corryvreckan for a washtub, her exploits whispered by ancient country people when free from the shadow of the kirk—

"*Kric!?*" the storyteller calls out, pleading for affirmation—

"*Krac!*" call his listeners, and the story goes on, shifting tone and theme, the old man a dozen characters, male and female, human and spirit, the sweet rum flowing freely in the crowd and for an instant, only that, Jenny forgets that she is not one of them, not a chattel slave bound for life at the mercy of any white man with a sense of his own importance and a rod in his hand, transported in this moment to a magical zone.

Though early morning, it is still dark when they start home. Day and night are always nearly equal here, like two men with arms locked in a struggle neither can win. There is no lingering dawn or dusk—and at day's end the sun spreads, suddenly brilliant, along the horizon of the western sea and then is gone, like a candle blown out with one puff. They walk hand in hand, Amély pensive, perhaps a bit frightened. Jenny speaks softly.

"The last story—*le dernier histoire—de quelle trait?*"

"*De not' pays.*"

"Yer hame? Mairtinique?"

"*Non—not' pays à travé de la mer. Afrique.*"

"Ah—"

"*J'ai peur que jamais le vé—*"

"That ye'll never see it? But ye've never *been* there—"

"*Mais quand mó les neg, ils revié a la tè d'Afrique.*"

"If that's true, then yer sure tae go there when yer dead—"

Amély swipes a hand across her cheek. "*Vec cette couleur?*"

"And why not—whatever yer color? *Ça ne import pas.*"

Amély looks at her as if she is a child. "*Demi blanche, demi noire—qui sait que fé le bon Dieu?*"

Jenny doubts that her own soul, should she posses such a thing, will return to Scotland upon her death. And the English judge made it very clear that if she returns while still breathing she'll be hanged and hurled into the paupers' pit.

They enter a thick section of wood that St. Cyr has warned her against.

"*C'est dangereux ici? Avec les serpents?*"

"*Pas maintenant, chè,*" Amély reassures her, tilting her cheek on her folded hands to indicate a sleeping snake. "*Les fé-de-lance et les aut serpents dódó pour les nuits.*"

And then proceeds to inform Jenny of all the more frightsome demons and *djables* they might encounter—

JAMIE AND CAMERON ARE THE FIRST TO WAKE UNDER the *chickee* roof, cold, last night's coals fallen to ash. Jamie speaks softly, thinking aloud.

"We've been branded as bondsmen."

"Aye, and that's for life."

"So if we run—"

"We're any man's prize."

"Unless we have some form of release—a document—"

"Ye mean to get hold of paper and quill?"

"Ah mean tae strike an agreement with Crozier."

Cameron snorts. "Tis not an agreeable man."

"Aye, but no an ignorant ane, either. Ah'll present an appeal tae Reason. Lowlanders chuff themsels fer their canny nature—"

"He's not a man anymore, he's a *ma*ster. What is reasonable to you or me—"

"It's worth an effort."

There is a long silence before Cameron speaks again.

"If we dodge his gillies and go on the shank," he says finally, "I'll be nothing but an anchor. If there's another way, you're welcome to try it."

MONCRIEF RESTS HIS LONG RIFLE LAZILY ON HIS SHOULDER as he leads Jamie down a path through a section of scrub that is new to him.

"What'ere it is ye've got on yer mind, laddie, Ah'd advise ye tae save yer wind. He dinnae care a whit fer me, and Ah'm a *free* mon. You, he'd trade fer a sack of wheat flour—"

"You ainly *think* yer free."

The overseer scowls. "Ah could march oot frae this plantation t'dee, and the master couldnae raise a finger tae stop me."

"Sae yer content here?"

"Ah've got plans."

"And roosters has wings," says Jamie, "that'll no carry them as far as their crow can be heert."

They step into a small clearing to find Crozier on his knees, laying wildflowers by a carved tupelo cross. Jamie stands close enough to read the words cut into the bar—

LORNA ROSE CROZIER – LOVING WIFE

"What's this?" asks the master, rising red-eyed to face them.

"He wishes tae speak with ye, sir."

"Does he, then?"

"Ah come with a proposition—"

The men laugh.

"The others, the bondsmen—axed me tae bring it tae ye—"

"Weel?"

"My countrymen and mysel' will agree tae work tae the best of our abilities withoot resistance fer a period of three years—"

"The cheek—"

"With the understanding that we will be released frae yer bond at the end of that period. Otherwise—"

"Insolent—"

"—*other*wise, our efforts will be as can be expected frae slaves—grudging, neglectful—"

Crozier steps forward to strike Jamie hard across the face. Moncrief jams the barrel of his rifle to his neck. The master leans close, his breath hot, his eyes blazing—

"On this plantation Jock Crozier is *king!* Ye've been bound tae me by law—and ye'll do what yer telt or Ah'll feed yer ballocks tae the blackamuirs!"

The planter spits on ground.

"Get him oot of ma sight."

AENEAS IS BENT OVER NEXT TO MERCEDES, HELPING her smoke strips of mullet over fire on a rack made of green sapling branches, when Jamie arrives, flushed and angry. His fever comes and goes now, more sweat and head pain than actual rise in his temperature, the bark tea the old Timacuan woman brews for him easing the relapses. He sits at the edge of the *chickee* platform, brooding, till Cameron approaches.

"And so?"

"We'll start tae hoard our food. Anything that winnae spoil."

IT IS AN EVENING WHEN ALL THE HOUSE SLAVES HAVE been sent away on errands that the final anatomy lesson occurs. The Lieutenant, very pleased with the *volant frit et calalou* old Yolande helped her concoct, has taken more than his usual glass of *ti-punch* after dining. He calls Jenny into his *chambre à coucher* to help him off with his boots, a task usually reserved for his *valet*, Étienne.

"*Les orteils*," he says once his feet are bared, pointing to his own naked toes and then to Jenny's.

"*Les orteils*."

He is seated on a plush stool, Jenny standing before him, readying herself for what she knows will happen next. She's had a feeling all day, what Amély calls a *frisson*, and after midday meal was finished quickly bathed herself in the servants' tub behind the stable.

"*Le cheville*," taking hold of her ankle—

"*Le cheville*—"

St. Cyr slowly slides both of his hands up over the calf of her leg—

"*Et la jambe*—"

Jenny feels her breath catch as he continues upward—

"*Repetez, s'il vous plait*—"

He is in his uniform still, a beautiful white with golden braid and buttons, showing blue where the cuffs and tail are turned back. There is not a speck of red upon him—

"*La jambe.*"

He stands then and takes hold of her breasts, squeezing them tenderly—

"*Les seines avec les 'tit tetons. Et autre fois la bouche*—"

He kisses her on the mouth then, breath sweet with rum punch. Jenny feels new in his arms.

"*Il y a autres partes plus intimes, mais il faut que deshabiller pour les voir.*"

Jenny knows the parts of her he is talking about, is ready to have them named.

"I'll want shoes," she declares, looking him in the eye. "*Chaussseurs du dame.* At least twa pair of em."

Afterward, when he is asleep and she is sitting up in his boatlike frame bed wondering if she should stay till morning or return to her little cell in the rear of the house, she knows no shame. Having endured so many sabbaths on the sinners' bench, guilty of nothing but arousing jealousy, she feels she has earned this wicked pleasure. St. Cyr is her *maître* and she his possession and that will not change, but his talk of shoes and dresses and even a tutor for her French leads her to believe she might be a possession that is decorated and displayed.

"*La chatte,*" she whispers. She wonders if it is the real word, or only like when rude clachan boys tell you to show them your fud. On the whole it was so much nicer than what she's seen from animals doing it, and she didn't think more than once about the redcoats. Jenny looks at her bare toes, wiggles them. She's only worn shoes to kirk and they always hurt her feet, but it is a matter of pride.

A matter of pride.

MONCRIEF INFORMS THE MEN THAT THE MASTER HAS ordered the head-high pile of cuttings, palm fronds brown and crispy now, to be moved branch by branch to a distant spot instead of burned where it is in the far corner of the mulberry orchard.

"Does he think the smoke will harm his precious trees?" asks Cameron.

"The master dinnae need tae explain," Moncrief tells them. "He gives an order, yer tae stir yer sorry carcasses intae motion."

It is a brutally hot day, and Juba, always the most silent, the most stoic of the Africans, begins to speak in a high, tight voice, eyeing the pile as he circles it. The others hesitate to begin, till Moncrief lays the hot metal barrel of his rifle on Juba's bare shoulder, burning it, and Pike jabs Lachlan, always his favorite target, in the ribs with the butt of his.

"Get tae yer work, damn ye, or I'll lay the cat on yer hides!"

It is shortly after this that Juba cries out, jerking his arm away from the pile with a diamondback snake clamped onto his bicep, the overseers skittering away as he sends it flying.

Juba gives the puncture wounds in his arm a glance, then crosses to sit on the ground with his back against a sweet gum tree. When Yaw approaches him with an axe, offering to sever the arm and possibly save his life, he is waved away, Juba's yellow eyes growing distant as the arm quickly swells to twice its thickness. Moncrief sends Pike running to fetch the master.

"Tis a bluidy serpent's nest ye've put us to," Lachlan accuses. "We'll no be shiftin it aboot."

Juba begins to spasm then, writhing on the ground until he is dead.

"Do ye ken how much that negger cost me?" snarls Crozier when he arrives to look down on the corpse.

"I dinnae ken where every bluidy snake on yer plantation is layin'," replies Moncrief, offended. "It might've been any of them was bitten."

"Have them bury this one and then move them branches."

"They winnae gae near it noo."

"Then wait till the wind shifts," says the master, walking away, "and have it burnt."

They dig the hole in the soft dirt beneath the trees at the edge of the beach, Cudjo looking out across the water and chanting something that sounds like a prayer. Only a few feet down the hole begins to fill with water, so they lay Juba's body, hands folded across his chest and feet facing the ocean, in a bed of moss and cover him with dirt and then pile driftwood logs above it.

As they head away, the overseers keeping their distance behind, Jamie sees that Yaw has taken the leather sack from around Juba's neck and hung it around his own. The African catches his eye.

"Tomorrow," he says.

AT NIGHT, AROUND THEIR SMALL FIRE, THE AFRICANS sing softly in their different tongues while the white bondsmen ready their few possessions. Mercedes has brought them a gourd full of guava wine she has made and left Jamie with a small bundle of the fever tree bark.

"*Para el viaje*," she says, somehow knowing what they plan.

There is just enough wine, passing it around, to set their minds wandering, Lachlan musing as he wraps smoked meat into a palm leaf—

Their ebon comrade slain
Neath foreign soil noo lying
Nae mair they'll feel the lash
Nae mair their base complying
Free men they'll stand again
Or perish in the trying—

"I'll have his pistol," says Cameron.

Jamie looks to the fourth Earl of Lochiel, gloomy in his rags, staring into the fire.

"And after I've employed it to send Jock Crozier to hell, I'll have it with me in case—" he looks to Jamie. "You won't leave me without a pistol and a ball, will you?"

"We won't leave you."

"I'll do my best to keep along—but if I falter—"

"We'll have need of ye, as well as that pistol, should we encounter savages of the wrong stripe."

Cameron nods, resigned if not heartened. The Africans sing until Yaw tells them to sleep, tells them to rest for their journey.

YAW LISTENS TO THE RHYTHM OF THE AXES BITING INTO the wood. There are bootprints in the dirt that lead him to the tree with the notch where Moncrief caches his jug. Yaw quickly uncorks it, empties half his sack of the powder into the rum, shakes the jug, corks it and places it back in the notch. He scuffs dirt, uses leaves and scraps of bark to disguise his own tracks on the way back to the new clearing.

Jamie and Lachlan drag a huge cedar log through the scrub. Three men could lift it and make better time, but Moncrief only follows lazily, rifle held by the barrel over his shoulder. They grunt and gasp in Erse between bouts of ploughing the dirt with the tree bole.

There are red men to the south of here known to take in Africans as free men, says Jamie. And to the north there are Scotsmen, Highlanders—

How far north?

"Give yer tongues a rest and put yer backs tae the work!" shouts Moncrief behind them. "Lazy buggers—yer no fit fer sharkbait."

They apply themselves to the log, rolling it when the path is wide enough, able only to manage a trio of mighty heaves before needing another rest. They pass Moncrief's tree, and the overseer snatches his jug up, finger through the hole in the handle, and brings it along. When they reach the new clearing, Yaw, who is chopping at one side of a substantial tree while Cudjo whacks at the other, gives Jamie a small nod.

You'll make a verse of what's coming, Jamie tells Lachlan.

They drag the cypress log to the spot Moncrief selects, then are set to gathering up the branches the others have trimmed, destined for the master's woodpile. Fergal is not allowed an axe, he and Cameron wielding a two-handed saw to cut planks from what the Africans have downed. It is slow going, the wood still too green with sap and the teeth of the saw too dull not to stick.

"Feckless at common labor," observes Moncrief, sitting now on the cypress log with Pike, passing the jug back and forth, their rifles on their laps. "The ane's a halfwit and t'other fancies himsel' a gent. Whate'er the master paid fer these boobies, it were too dear."

Pike laughs, rum coming up through his nose, and suffers a mild choking fit.

THEIR MIDDAY MEAL IS ALWAYS TAKEN ON THE BEACH, the bondsmen and slaves out on the sand under the sun "where ye can be watchit" and the overseers just back in the shade of the scrub palms. Today Pike is curled on the sand, complaining of his stomach, while Moncrief, sweating profusely, stands on suddenly wobbly legs. Both have been dosing themelves with rum, convinced of its healing powers.

"Another wee nip'll do ye wonders," says Moncrief, offering the jug. "In any case, ye'll need to get up and mind these lags, fer Ah've tae aff and lighten ma load."

The men on the sand eat their smoked fish and corn dodgers silently, not meeting each other's eye.

Moncrief gets Pike sitting up, rifle in hand.

"My guts're twistin," Pike complains.

"Weel, ye'll have tae bear it fer a moment—Ah'll be back in a wink."

They wait for Moncrief to disappear into the scrub, then Yaw stands, pulling something from the waist of his trousers, and steps toward Pike, holding it out to show.

"What the devil have ye got there, ye heathen bastard?"

It is a small figure of a man, carved in tupelo wood, complete with a swatch of human hair atop its head.

Pike frowns at the figure, unsettled, and then Yaw throws the sand held in his other hand into the overseer's eyes and is upon him, rifle wrested away and the man's mouth stopped with the wooden fetish. Jamie is immediately on his feet with the others, grabbing a chunk of driftwood for a club, trotting into the trees.

He finds Moncrief squatting with his back to the beach, rifle laid on the ground before him, the knife he wears on his hip stuck in the dirt. He is slowly duck-walking forward from the slick of liquid shit he has produced, a tangle of flies already upon it. Jamie swings the driftwood with both hands—

The overseer is easier to drag than a cypress log. When Jamie reaches the beach with him the others have Pike rolled on his belly in the sand, hands bound behind his back with the cord they have been saving, the wooden figure tied fast in his open mouth. Cameron has Pike's rifle in hand and the Africans are debating something, exclaiming in all of their languages. Moncrief comes conscious again in the shade provided by Fergal, an axe gripped in the Highlander's meaty hands.

"Oh, God, please," mutters the overseer, "hae mercy on me!"

Yaw stuffs a wild orange into Moncrief's mouth, wraps a band of rag around his head and knots it taught. The overseer is rolled onto his belly next to Pike, hands bound behind his back. Cudjo yanks the man's boots off—one of the other Africans has already pulled Pike's on, stomping in the sand to test them for size—and then Yaw takes the knife offered by Jamie, kneels and swiftly severs the tendon above the right heel on each man, a spray of blood and muffled screams.

"Crozier now," says Aeneas Cameron, and they leave the two lying halfway between the water's edge and the high tide line.

The mulberry orchard is on the way to Crozier's plank house. The saplings grow amazingly fast, hip high already, and the roots sunk deep enough that it is easiest for the Africans to slash away with their axes to destroy them all. There is no hurry, really, but Cameron is impatient.

"He'll slip from our hands," he keeps saying as the planting, months of their toil, is laid waste.

CROZIER'S HORSES AND WAGON ARE GONE FROM THE shed. The master is not in his rough plank castle.

"Damn the luck!" cries Cameron as the others strip the cabin of anything useful for their flight, Yaw finding a large pouch filled with tobacco, Lachlan stuffing tree moss into a pair of Crozier's shoes till they fit snug on his feet. Jamie, having never passed through the door before this, stands before a painting of a beautiful young woman, hung on the wall.

"The late Missus Crozier, Ah take it," says Lachlan.

The Africans have gathered around behind them to stare at her.

"He brought her tae this land and it kilt her," says Jamie.

"We go now," says Yaw from the doorway.

As they hurry toward the river, Jamie can recognize most of Crozier's clothing on his fellow fugitives.

"Perhaps he's gan aff tae fetch the wee silk spinners," muses Lachlan, trying to keep up in the oversize shoes. "Or tae buy a mon tae replace puir Juba. I'd love tae keek his mug when he returns."

They have found no currency, but Cameron leaves with Crozier's pistol and a handful of lead balls. Mercedes, drunk on her own wine, watches mutely from the cook hut as they pass.

THE *COTILLION* IS HELD AT THE PLANTATION HOUSE OF one of the Lieutenant's cousins, the smell of burnt sugar overwhelming the fruitier scents that envelop the various *dames du bal.* Despite the dress of a breathtaking blue, the bodice mashing her breasts upward till they are in danger of spilling out, despite the petticoats and the satin shoes, light as a whisper on her feet, Jenny cannot contrive to move like the other women. She has none of Amély's talent for mimickry, the housekeeper herself now in an orange and red *douilette* fit for her new role, peeking through a side door with the other ladies' maids, their laughter plain to hear whenever the small orchestra, all black men in fine white livery, cease playing.

"*Sois belle et muette*," the Lieutenant has instructed her, holding a cautionary finger over his lips, declaring that her youth and the novelty of her situation will be found charming, but not her atrocious *kréyol*-polluted French or lack of *savoir faire*.

So Jenny smiles as pleasantly as she can, making little attempts at curtsies as she is introduced to the other women, attempting to be beautiful and mute, feigning a total lack of comprehension when they voice their evaluations while looking her in the eye.

Only a kitchen servant, they say, but white women are in such short supply.

It is widely known that the Scots never wear undergarments, they say, neither the men nor the women.

She may be his *chouchou favori* at the moment, they say, but he'll soon drift back to his negresses, like all the other weak and aimless men on the island.

Jenny remains blank as they gossip, learning that in this ballroom full of finely dressed *grands blancs* there are those who were born in France and those who were not, and among the latter there are those who have *been* to France and those who have not, and that this seems to matter a great deal. The women are kind enough to Jenny, who never having been to France nor ever wishing to go there, is no threat to any of them.

In the first part of the evening the men and women remain separate from each other, a deeper pitch and a veil of smoke on the male side of the room, with much speculation about what the English might be up to and the fickle market for cane, while in the female half there is gossip not only local but directly, if tardily, from the corridors of Versailles. The latest presumptions of Madame de Pompadour and the tragedy of the poor Spanish *dauphine*, dead within days of delivering her first royal child (a girl, *Hélas!*), compete with the story of Ghislaine Léandre, standing brazenly by the punch bowl in her baize chiffon, and her affair with an affluent smuggler from Saint-Pierre who is rumored to be a *quarteron*.

Halfway through the evening Jenny realizes that she is not wearing the dress but carrying it around to be admired, and that very little of the *accoutrement* and behavior around her is without calculation. Though the participants are neither as drunken nor as likely to cross swords with each other as those at a highland *cailidh*, this is a battleground, each hairstyle, beauty patch, fleck of gilt or turn of phrase a *sortie*, with coveted social territory to be won or lost.

It is the dancing that saves the night for her, Jenny always nimble when there is a piper to be heard and no kirk elders within earshot. The steps are not difficult to learn, whether *minuet*, *gavotte*, or even the more complicated ring dances, Jenny moving with the music and following the gentlemen's guidance, and the Lieutenant is pleased by how many of the officers and planters wish to lead her onto the floor. She wonders at the musicians, if these black men have other duties in the daytime or if their skill with an instrument has saved them from the cane. If so she vows to be like them, a performer with a perpetual smile, and in the carriage returning through the burnt sugar night the Lieutenant holds her hand and compliments Jenny on her comportment.

"*Tu fais une trés belle figure*," he says, petting her. "*Trés belle*."

Later, Amély, eyes ablaze with excitement and still in her new gown, slips in to sit at the edge of Jenny's bed.

"*Ça va, ma chè?*" she says, telling Jenny how good this could be for both of them, that the Lieutenant seems enchanted with her, that once the hook is set a wise fisherman knows how to coax even the most recalcitrant *poisson* into the boat. Tells her that if she is careful, if she can learn to read the man correctly, she will be settled for life.

"*Comme une vrai maîtresse blanche*."

While Jenny sits on the edge of the bed in blue silk, staring past her lady's maid to the mirror fixed on the wall, searching for the clachan girl who crushed a man's skull with a stone quern.

IT IS WITH A GIDDY ENERGY THAT JAMIE DODGES through the scrub, his first moments of true liberty since Drummossie Moor. He tries to keep the Africans ahead of him in sight without leaving Cameron, carrying a rifle now and lurching from tree to tree in his effort to keep up. Nobody is chasing them, of course, not yet, but moving as rapidly as possible away from Crozier's ruined plantation seems vital. It feels like they are moving to the west, though the sun is directly overhead and it is hard to be sure, and it is nearly an hour of rapid flight before Yaw stops them at the edge of a great, foul-smelling swamp.

Yaw waits for Cameron to stumble through the cane to join them, then taps himself on the chest and points into the swamp, to the south. "We go dis wee," he says, then turns and points to the north. "White foke go dat wee."

"And where be the red people?" asks Lachlan, down on one knee and breathing heavily.

Yaw makes a large circle with his arm. "All place."

He says something in one of the African tongues and Cudjo hands a pistol and a small sack of powder to Lachlan, then the three of them disappear into the moss-covered swamp trees.

Cameron turns to look north. "We'll proceed, then," he says, "till it's too dark to see."

JAMIE WAKES THE NEXT MORNING, STIFF AND COLD ON a bed of pine boughs, and has a panicked moment trying to remember where he might be. There is a ground mist so thick he can barely make out the bodies of the men sleeping immediately beside him. Aeneas Cameron rouses, lifts himself on his elbows and peers into the white.

"Which way did we come?"

Jamie has no answer to this. "When the sun appears," he says, unsure that such an event will come to pass, "we'll keep it on our right."

A loud snort and crackling nearby wakes Lachlan, who fumbles with the pistol that was resting on his chest and sits up, blurting in Erse.

"*Dé o shealbh?*"

Jamie hushes him, listening, as Cameron charges his rifle.

A huge, shaggy beast appears from behind them, snorting, walking ponderously past, then another and another, the mist beginning to thin and reveal that they are among a herd of the massive animals, Fergal awake now, looking stunned. The bison ignore them, snuffling at the ground but not pausing to graze, their breath snorted out in clouds in the cold morning air.

Cameron takes aim at the humpbacked monster nearest him, but Jamie pushes the barrel of his rifle down, taps his ear.

"We dinnae ken who's oot there."

"The divvil's ain playground," mutters Lachlan as the creatures, like a herd of strolling mountains, fade into the mist.

They wait, gnawing on jerked meat, till a bit of sun fights through the pine canopy to them, then head what they hope is north again, traveling steadily with Jamie in the lead. There are different flying insects here, smaller, and different birds that they hear but do not see. The sun is overhead before they totter out onto the bank of a river running directly across their path, with Cameron sinking exhaustedly to the ground to lean his back against a tree, the other men falling to their knees around him.

"We're already bloody lost."

"We are no. We gae north tae a great river—"

"This one?"

"Nae—"

"We've already crossed two—"

"A river sae wide ye've got tae swim tae get acrost, then continue north—"

"What you *think* is north—"

"Weel, we cannae gae *back*, can we?"

Cameron's bad leg, which he is kneading with his fingers, jumps suddenly, and there is the shaft of a feathered arrow sticking in it, and then shrieking red men swinging war clubs are upon them, most of them surrounding Fergal to bait him like a bear, thrashing and retreating, thrashing and retreating, while Jamie scrambles to his feet and is immediately thumped on the back of his head, driving him to the ground, where he sees a tall Indian with bones hung clacking around his neck step up to Cameron, snatching the half-primed rifle from his hands and cracking him in the forehead with the butt of it.

THE CAPTIVE'S NARRATIVE

THE FOUR SCOTS ARE TIED ONE BEHIND THE OTHER by the painted warriors, leather cords digging into their necks, and goaded into a brisk trot, each hugging a heavy bundle of hides to their chests. It is an hour, dodging branches and moving at a rapid trot, before Jamie can be certain that there are only nine, though it seemed like dozens during the attack.

"I can't do it!" cries Cameron behind him, the shaft of the arrow still protruding from his thigh.

"Ye must—if ye falter they'll murder ye!"

"I *can't!*"

"We'll stop soon, I promise ye. Even these divvils cannae run forever!"

Jamie's assurance is met by a jab to his side with a war club, and the party hustles forward.

None of what they run through is familiar to Jamie, just identical pines on all sides, and he notes that the red men are constantly looking about alertly, as if they are the trespassers here. The ground is soft needles, gentle on their feet, but the pace is relentless. A very young warrior, not much more than a boy, leads the way, while the man with the clacking bone necklace takes up the rear, constantly prodding Cameron to move faster. Their captors' faces are smeared with black and red paint, and the hair on their heads has been shaved off save for a clump at the top of their foreheads, and that interwoven with small feathers and bits of colored yarn. They lope along with fire-blacked clubs and small hatchets in hand, the man with the bone necklace in possession of both the rifle and pistol taken from Crozier's.

Empty the mind and move, thinks Jamie. They haven't murdered me yet—

The sun is down behind the trees when they reach a small clearing and the leader, Bone, calls a halt, the prisoners relieved of their bundles, goaded to sit with backs against an enormous tree trunk, arms forced back and then bound to it and each other. The red men squat to confer.

"Do they mean tae kill us?" asks Lachlan.

"Not while we carry their goods, I'm guessing," says Jamie. "They seem in a hurry tae leave this coontry."

"I can't feel my foot." Cameron is deathly pale, breathing shallowly, the blood around where the arrow sticks from his thigh dried black now.

"Try tae move yer toes."

Cameron gingerly touches the wooden shaft with the tips of his fingers. "The arrowhead is grinding inside—I can feel it with every step."

"Twill wiggle itsel' oot," lies Jamie. "Ye've got tae show them yer no afeart."

Bone separates from the others then and bends to look at them one by one, evaluating, as if judging cattle. He pokes Fergal in the chest, leans in to examine the brand on the hands of Jamie and Lachlan, then twists the arrow shaft stuck in Cameron's leg. Aeneas glares back at him, sweat streaming down his face, but allows himself no moan of protest. The Indian pulls an iron hatchet from his belt and with an abrupt motion and a terrible sound drives it squarely into Cameron's forehead. Jamie, sprayed with blood, has to close his eyes and turn his head away as Bone draws a knife and begins to saw at the front edge of Cameron's hair, the tiny speck of life fading from the Highland gentleman's eyes.

Leaving their friend stripped naked on the forest floor, the captives are soon moving again, whipped by branches in the spreading darkness, Bone having wrapped his necklace in cloth and tucked it away to muffle its noise and the other red men as wary as before. Jamie sees the space immediately in front of him and nothing more. Lachlan has no verse for the occasion. When it is too dark to see anything they are tied to another tree.

On the second day they are given strips of their own dried mullet to eat.

On the third day they hide, along with their captors, in the bushes beside a river as a party of differently dressed red men pass by in canoes, the dip of their many paddles without sound.

On the fourth day they reach a village.

HE SAYS HE WANTS TO SHOW JENNY HIS WORK, BUT REally *she* is the display. As St. Cyr escorts her around the fortifications and batteries that guard the bay, his men—and there are fifty of them directly under his command—enjoy a thorough review of her qualities. The *maître* has chosen her clothes carefully, sorting through the recent purchases and then having Amély lay out what he thinks appropriate. He prefers Jenny in blue, stating that crimson is too *gauche* and that white-skinned people should never wear yellow. Even the parasol he has chosen to shade her from the harsh sun out on the parapets is blue, the material so light that several times Jenny forgets that she is holding it.

"*La tête haute, marcher avec petit pas*—" he mutters as they move along, correcting her posture and gait. She has learned to lock her hips in place, the Lieutenant assuring her that only *les negresses et les putaines* let them sway from side to side.

It is impressive, really, as they inspect the multitude of cannons he is responsible for, how much St. Cyr knows about firing shot and shell. He explains the principle of an explosion contained in a rigid tube, how the energy of the gas created must find a way out and thus propels the missile, explains the equation of thrust, elevation and distance, the rainbow arc of a mortar, the devastating horizontal blast of cannister shot, explains how the future of his profession, despite the recalcitrance of *les generals anciens* back in Paris, lies in lighter pieces with shorter barrels, the prolonged seige no longer the *méthode juste* for battle.

"*La mobilité, c'est tout,*" he insists, complaining of the need to use civilians—barefoot slaves, here on Martinique—instead of trained soldiers for the transport of cannon in the field, and then enthuses about the innovations Prince Liechtenstein is pursuing in Austria—moving the axles of the gun carriages forward, replacing the old unreliable quoins and chocks with an elevation screw for better accuracy, laying by a supply of prepared cartridge ammuniton rather than relying on men under fire to wield a powder shovel and judge their loads in the smoky havoc of battle.

He has his team on the *batterie du sur* demonstrate by firing their piece. One man standing at the left of the cannon hefts an iron ball of *douze livres* as another man standing on the right rams a cloth bag of black powder and then a small wad of hay down the barrel with a very long pole that has something like a lambskin mop on the other end. The ball is rolled down into the barrel, then pushed with the pole to set it, and then the *capitaine* orders a fourth, burlier man to shift the piece slightly to the right, then tilt it up a mite, using small wooden wedges to achieve the desired angle. A fifth man, who has had his thumb over the touch hole, now fills it with more powder from a small sack and at the *capitaine*'s order yet another man, who has been holding a forked stick with a lit slow-match stuck in it, puts it to the touch hole and there is a great explosion, the heavy piece hopping backward and frightening Jenny.

"*Avec la pratique*," crows St. Cyr, not even watching as the ball smacks into the water far out in the bay, "*on peut tirer trois fois pour une minute*."

Jenny nods, hoping to look amazed. She wonders how many times a minute the cannon on English warships can fire, how many each warship can point to the shore, how many ships they might send—

The Lieutenant has his men bring Jenny examples of the many projectiles—cast iron balls of different sizes and weights, each with a *fleur-de-lis* of appropriate proportion molded onto its surface, has one of them open a cannister to reveal the many metal balls of different sizes that will burst from it upon firing, and smiles, delighted, as she shakily lifts a twenty-four-pound ball over her head.

On their way home the Lieutenant explains that though his trade is in fact "*la combinaison de la physique et les mathématiques*," he considers it more art than science, and boasts that he is the conductor of a great, deadly orchestra that must rehearse but has rare occasion to play. His words, though he sits right beside her in the carriage, sound hollow and distant, and she realizes she neglected to put her fingers in her ears when the cannon was fired. St. Cyr is noticeably hard of hearing, a hazard of his profession, and she has witnessed him watching people's lips as they speak. Amély makes very bold with this, often venting her opinions out loud behind the master's back, understanding at just what volume she begins to run a risk.

"*Tu es impressionée?*" he asks her. It is not really a question.

"*Il faut que pèser lourdement, cet responsibilité*," she says, and she truly cannot imagine having the lives of fifty men, and a dozen more if you include his *esclaves de maison*, under your command. Now that Amély has been assigned as her *bonne* it is vexing to order her about, and Jenny has to check herself from clearing the plates from the table once a meal is finished.

"*Mais le noblesse oblige*," shrugs the Lieutenant, and calls to Maigrichon to put his whip to the horses.

CHARTIER WALKS A SLOW, UNIMPRESSED CIRCLE around the three that Bone and his raiding party have brought in. If there is an advantage to being *métis*, it is that one can play the unimpressed Frenchman or the unpredictable savage to fit the occasion. He scowls, noting the bond marks on the captives' hands, the terror on the face of the smallest, the look of animal rage on that of the largest, the watchfulness, possibly cunning, of the third. White people are always more trouble than they're worth.

Three months in the southern colonies, he says disdainfully, and this is all you bring me?

The hides, though adequate in number, have been hastily prepared and won't fetch much from an experienced trader. When they all left the Coosa together, Bone bragged how he and his young men would linger to raise havoc among their enemies, but here is Bone with only three scalps hanging from his belt.

The woods were full of Choctaw, says Bone.

And what am I supposed to do with these white men?

Your father, the great Louis, will buy them. As he does the scalps.

There has been no official declaration, nothing from Montreal, yet Bone and many of the other *Chaouanons* believe this to be true. Chartier suspects that other traders, whether French or English, must be doling out rum and rumors to disrupt the market.

Scalps don't have to be fed, he says to Bone.

Then don't feed them.

The one who might be cunning is following their conversation in Shawnee as if trying to understand it. They are in a temporary village—a half-dozen mud-and-wattle huts, a main *cabane* with a thatched roof, a mix of Muskogee, Mingos and his own *Chaouanons* paused by the river fork on their way north or west, most of them refugees from the whites or the encroachment of other tribes. Bone has the sour look he was born with on his face, and his young men are circled around, angry at the lack of celebration greeting their arrival. Bone wants to be a war chief, and this southern adventure, if more successful, could have affirmed his status.

And these skins, says Chartier, shaking his head, the haughty trader now. Such poor quality—

The woods were full of Choctaw—

They haven't been cured properly.

You can still sell them—

Chartier sighs. He is a chief of the Pekowi Turtle Clan, leader of those driven from Pennsylvania by the English, his name respected even in places he's never been—but soon Bone will be an important warrior and there is no sense in making enemies.

Let's have some brandy, he says, and see what we can work out.

The cunning-looking one, bound hand and foot on the ground with his companions, speaks up—

"*Excusez moi, Monsieur.*"

The accent is not that of an *habitant* or *voyageur.*

"*Nous ne sommes pas anglais—nous sommes écossais. Écossais et grands enemies de le Roi Georges. Je suis grand ami de le Compte Villiers de Fontenot, fiancé à sa fille—*"

"What're ye saying?" asks the little one.

Chartier gives the Paris-tongued captive a rude nudge with his foot, acting the red savage now, and addresses him in gutteral French.

"*Vous vous trompez—je ne suis pas gentilhomme blanc, je suis un chef des Chauouons. À présent, vous êtes prisonniers—rien de plus.*"

Prisoners and nothing else, he says, with no more rights than any other item of trade, explaining that any further protestations will surely result in their throats being cut.

Bone stands fingering the fetish he wears around his neck, comprehending just enough of the French to add a snort of agreement. Chartier turns to address the young warriors.

So, my brothers, let's see about that brandy . . .

IN THE MORNING THEY ARE UNBOUND FROM EACH other and taken in separate canoes, Fergal with the mixed-blood trader and two men Jamie recognizes as Muskogee, Lachlan with three of the men who captured them, and Jamie in a buffalo-hide canoe with Bone, two of his warriors, and most of the hides, all of the captives forced to help row.

Jamie's back and knees, still sore from the forced march north, are screaming in pain as he kneels and tries to match the strokes of the Indians, only Bone not with an oar in hand, scowling at him from the prow of the boat. The rivers are deeper here, flowing more swiftly, and they struggle against the current. His arms are feeling too leaden to continue when he hears Lachlan, in the boat behind, singing out in rhythm—

The French are a peculiar race
Malod'rous and uncouth
They'll tell ye lies straight tae yer face
And swear that it's the truth—

There is nothing that cannot be borne, Jamie assures himself, and death is only a release. His arms, in fact, will move even when numb with weariness.

The French engage in pointless wars—

Lachlan continues, sounding almost cheerful—

Frae cradle tae the tomb
They never bathe or change their drawers
And hide it with perfume—

DURING A WEEK OF UNSEASONABLE GALES LIEUTENANT St. Cyr is ordered to Saint Pierre to take stock of the armaments there, and the *maître* decides to bring Jenny along. High and violent seas on the west coast preclude an ocean voyage, and it is decided to follow the *Trace des Jesuits* over the various *mornes* on the way to the *pitons* of Carbet, then hug the base of massive Pelée to the coast and Saint Pierre—a more picturesque but much slower route.

Such an absence prompts the Lieutenant to meet with his *économe*, Octave Renaud, a man he neither likes nor trusts, but an adept hand at managing *gens de couleur.* At this meeting Renaud, the middle son of a neighboring landowner, is reminded again that this is only a household and not a sugar plantation, requiring a light hand on the rod and a sense of the long game. Better a spell of laxity in the *maître*'s absence than a staff of moody *noirs*, a people known to hurl themselves from the tops of coconut palms or into the teeth of cane crushers, to drown, hang, or sicken themselves to the point of death by eating dirt if rendered morose through overly harsh treatment. The *économe*, Jenny has observed, is far gentler with their little coterie of livestock than with Guillaume the hostler or Zézé who keeps the chickens or Étienne, the Lieutenant's valet, or Micheline the new cook, or the coachman Maigrichon, or even her sweet Amély. There are no vast fields of crops to be planted or to harvest, of course, only a garden to be protected from vermin, a small orchard out back to be pruned and tended, the eggs to be collected and the cow to be milked, all tasks the Lieutenant has now forbidden Jenny to take part in.

"*Il faut être strict mais juste*," the Lieutenant counsels Renaud, specifying that his *gens* be fed on salt cod only every other day, that they be warned away from excessive *tafia* drinking and all-night *bamboula* dancing, and that if Micheline gets with child it had better come out darker skinned than she is. Amély has labeled Renaud *le crabe* because he is always pinching her, and keeps a pair of scissors in her belt to ward him off.

"*Absolument, M'sieu*," nods the manager, who as a civilian chooses to ignore St. Cyr's uniform. "*Comme toujours*."

They begin on the backs of their riding mares, Sofie and Cleothilde, with oilskin capes folded behind their saddles to deal with the daily *déluge* of twenty to thirty minutes that relieves neither the heat nor humidity, with Guillaume leading the way bareback on a very short mule, his feet nearly brushing the ground. Despite high winds it is the usual brilliant day on the coast, and Jenny is struck again by the myriad shades of green on the island, green that will fade to brown only if a plant is cut with a *machette de canne* or killed by heat and drought. She loves the new sensation of being on a horse's back, always agog as a girl when some gentleman would ride by the clachan, and she has a brief thought of the doomed young MacGillivray who passed through before the battle and then was dragged away by redcoats. Jenny wears the ring he gave her hung between her breasts on a thin silver chain that was a present from St. Cyr, telling her *maître* the ring was passed down from her grandmother, that her people were once more than poor muckskippers and had been brought low by generations of English perfidy.

It is one of her few lies.

On the way up the muddy path from the outskirts of Fort Royal the Lieutenant tests her memory and pronunciation.

"*Dis-moi tous les oiseaux que tu connais*," he begins.

It was the first thing she asked to know the names of, so many beautiful birds in colors that never brightened the Highlands.

"*Le canard routoutou*," she begins, one of her favorites, a red-bodied duck with a black mask and a powder-blue beak. "*Et le colibri fal rouge*," a multi-colored hummingbird she sees in the garden, "*et le perroquet Amazone*," a burly green parrot with orange on its wings, "*et le gri-gri*," a falcon she has seen drop out of the heavens and leave only a fluttering of loose white feathers where there had been a gull, "*et, bien sûr, le martin-pecheur*," a red, white, and blue kingfisher that looks like it should be somebody's flag.

"*Et les autres rapteurs?*"

"*Il y a l'aiglon, le busard, le malfini—*"

On the windy slope of the Buachaille one day when she was a girl, Jenny saw an eagle try to take a week old lamb, hoisting it an inch from the ground and straining its enormous wings to lift, carrying it laterally away from the flock and up and down three times before giving up and flapping away.

"*Et le plus bel?*"

There are so many lovely ones, but she doesn't have to think. "*Pour moi, c'est l'euplecte franciscain*."

This is a bird with a startling orange body and a black head and wings. St. Cyr sighs and shakes his head.

"*Tu as le même gout que mes gens negres*."

It is something he says often, wondering if her taste has been coarsened by her contact with his slaves or if it was always so vulgar. He does not seem to mind, though he forbids her to wear head scarves like Micheline and Amély.

The rain hits them on the way up the first of the *mornes*, the sound of it splatting on the broad leaves of the tamarinds like a battery of snare drums, and then stops abruptly, sunlight sneaking here and there through the thick overhead canopy of thirty-meter tree ferns and buttressed ceibas, steam rising from the ground, and Jenny watches the flowers of the lianas opening, intense reds and yellows and purples, and again there is birdsong and the screeching of parrots. Every few kilometers there is another shrine, usually the papists' Virgin, set on a shelf fastened to a tree bole or in a niche carved into one of the many outcroppings of black lava rock. Guillaume removes his straw hat each time one is passed.

"*C'est Notre Dame de la Déliverance,*" St. Cyr tells her. "*La sainte patronne de Martinique.*"

The path narrows so they have to ride one behind the other, this part of the Trace through thick woods an almost solid mass of trees that seem to wrap around each other or grow from each other's sides, with lianas and creeper vines, some as thick as a dockworker's arm, yoking the upper reaches together like ship's rigging fouled by a storm. It is all struggle, she thinks, each tree clawing up the back of its neighbor for a blessed touch of sunshine.

The jungle closes in even more, forcing Jenny to lean one way or the other to avoid hanging branches and vines, Guillaume on his mule seeming to be swallowed up in the green tangle though he stays barely ten yards ahead of her.

"*Ne touches pas les arbres,*" St. Cyr warns her from behind. "*Ils avaient des épines trés agouts.*"

She heeds his advice, some of the trees indeed covered with a solid fuzz of tiny spines or bristling with larger ones, others oozing caustic saps of bilious color. Jenny attempts to breathe shallowly in the close, damp hollow beneath the jungle canopy, Amély having warned her of the *miasme* that *békés* are especially susceptible to, though the Lieutenant maintains that it is the *noirs* who are most affected, with half of the slaves who ever died on his boyhood plantation afflicted with rotting lungs.

"*C'est bon, cet pays,*" Amély often says of the island, "*mais la beauté est toujou dangereux.*"

As if privy to her thoughts, St. Cyr repeats his lecture concerning the deadly *fer de lance*, describing the flat head, the yellow underside, its extreme irritability and ability to spray venom from its fangs, its habits of hiding in the underbrush or hanging from tree branches, finally naming the people he's known who have been bitten by it and the effects of its poison, the flesh of limbs rotting off the bone when the victim does not die within the first day. Jenny has already been so frightened by the stories Amély has told her that she no longer ventures into the garden without wearing her new riding boots—which the Lieutenant assures her will be of no service should the *serpent* be a full-grown and aggressive female.

All this lovely heat, beautiful sounds and colors, delicious things to eat and drink, this paradise of luxuriant growth, thinks Jenny—of *course* there's a poison snake.

The river is well above its usual depth, and St. Cyr insists it will float a *canot*. Two waiting *bateliers*, their bare skin blacker than any Jenny has seen on the island, have been hired to row and navigate the twisting course. She is warned to keep her hands in her lap and make no sudden movements, as the hollowed *gommier* longboat is narrow and less than steady. It sits low in the water, a beautiful gliding motion as the black men alternately paddle or pole them along, tree branches sliding overhead, now and then a turtle or two sunning on a beached log sliding under the surface as they come near. The current slows and then nearly stops, the water full of thick reeds and a floating carpet of vegetation, and the *bateliers* hop out to move the boat along, immersed to their armpits, one pulling, one pushing. Jenny asks if they are free men.

"*Mais non*," the Lieutenant answers. "*Ils sont esclaves. Ils doivent partager leur paie avec le maître.*"

When Jenny asks how much of this pay their master will keep, he only shrugs. "*C'est son affaire.*"

The men are in the water for most of the rest of the river passage, and when they ease back into the *canot* Jenny can see bright green leeches clinging to their bare chests and legs, thin streams of watery blood running down from them, which they ignore as they begin to paddle again. When finally she is helped out of the boat to resume the journey on fresh horses, St. Cyr jingles coins in a leather purse, then drops five *sols* into each outstreched hand and frowns when Jenny thanks them, calling them *Messieurs.*

"*Ma petite sauvage,*" he calls her when they are mounted and riding again, "*tellement innocente de notre coutumes.*"

Not so much innocent of their customs, thinks Jenny, as made uneasy by them.

The men who now accompany them around the base of mist-shrouded Pelée are as silent as the boatmen, the wall of the mountain rising so steeply here it seems like a giant wave set to crash down upon them. St. Cyr does not acknowledge the guides. Would you say hello to a strange horse? he will chide if she mentions it, though he did in fact greet his new mount with a few calming phrases. The man who leads looks back only when holding aside a branch that might strike them, and the man behind dozes now and then on his mule's back.

On your belly shall ye crawl, Jenny thinks, a phrase from one of the kirk sermons back home—*and dust ye shall eat for all of your days.*

She is not a slave and she is not a wife, and when they have come down the final steep *morne* to the outskirts of Saint Pierre the man from the rear kneels on all fours so she can step on his back to ease her way to the ground. This is no gillie serving the head of his clan, it is the true snake in the garden, she thinks, so many more blacks than whites on the island, their obeisance taken for granted just as it is assumed that Pelée will never explode. Once she understood just what a volcano was, Jenny began to ask Martinicans what they thought would happen if it erupted.

It's been dead for years, the whites would assure her, shrugging to dismiss the question even on days when smoke could be seen wisping straight up from several of the fissures on its side. "*Un volcan mort mais trés beau.*"

"*C'est pas en not' mains,*" the slaves and free blacks would shrug, often actually holding their hands out, palms up, as if to indicate how helpless they were to change anything on the island, then looking toward the mist-shrouded peak of Pelée with a sigh. "*C'est l'volonté du bon Dieu.*"

THE CAPTIVES HELP TO ROW THE CANOES UP RIVERS that cut through deep forest, help to carry the heavy boats, rolls of skins and barrels of trade goods still in them, down narrow wooded pathways that lead to yet another river, paddling at the bottom of rocky gorges and steering through sections of rapids and short falls, more chesnut and other broad-leafed trees than pines now, sleeping entombed beneath the beached, overturned boats at night.

Jamie is truly lost now, places without names, or not even places but only miles of flat wooded country veined with cold rivers, no mountains or castles to navigate by, and at night the stars always in the wrong place. In the Highlands he knew each fold of the land and who it belonged to, and even in a dense fog a two minute walk would reveal his location.

They are paddling hard up the widest of the rivers for half a day before they come to a large village and are ordered to turn for the bank.

The village is laid out on both sides of the flowing water, patches of cultivated field interspersed with smaller, circular sapling and bark dwellings and a few squarish log cabins and one great long-house with an arched roof and low openings at either end. He has seen clachans as seemingly disorganized, but never on this scale, well over a hundred people out of their lodgings on this side of the river and dozens more watching now from the far bank. Children, the smaller ones naked, shout gleefully as they rush forward to gape at the visitors and their prisoners, dashing in to poke the Scots with a finger and daring their friends to do the same. Dozens of older natives soon join these, staring and pointing and laughing. Jamie notes that nothing is thrown at them, the sole improvement upon their reception in the London streets, though Bone is suddenly prodding at them again with his war club as if to assert his ownership.

"Are we in Carolina?" asks Lachlan.

"Ah've no bluidy idea."

Loaded again with the hides and barrels, they follow Chartier to the longhouse, where a short, solid man of perhaps thirty years stands waiting, a leather pouch with a long-stemmed pipe sticking out from it hung round his neck.

"*Shingas! Ça fait trop longtemps que je n'ai pas vu mon frère,*" says Chartier.

The man replies in his own language, reaching to touch the half-breed trader on the arm, then repeating the greeting with Bone. He is dressed no finer than the other men who crowd around, wearing only a worn calico shirt and a deerskin cloth that is folded and belted to cover his genitals and buttocks somewhat and a pair of the little half-shoes the Shawanese warriors travel in, but Jamie has the feeling he is their principal man.

He waves his hand and says something, and several of the local men take hold of Jamie and Lachlan and Fergal, leading them away to a large wooden pole that has been driven upright into the ground, where they are made to sit with their backs to it then lashed tightly with leather thongs and left to be surrounded by a throng of children and young people. Teen girls with shining black hair falling over their shoulders giggle and poke them with sticks, while adolescent boys get up close in their faces to shout what must be insults, drawing laughter from their comrades. Jamie tries to focus his eyes beyond them.

"Filthy wee bastarts," mutters Lachlan.

"Dinnae alloo them tae vex ye," Jamie tells him. "They'll tire of it and leave us if we dinnae give them a show."

Fergal curses in Erse as a boy smacks him in the head with a hurled clod of mud.

A well-looking young woman, perhaps not as dark as the others, pauses in passing with a pair of younger girl companions to assess them. She wears a doeskin gown undistinguished from that of the other women in the camp, but Jamie notes that her eyes are light brown instead of pure black, that her hair is not so straight, and her bearing exaggerated and self-conscious, as if playing a role. She snatches a long stick from one of the boys and prods at Jamie's tadger with it, to the great merriment of all.

"*Attention à ne rien casser,*" says Jamie. Only the young woman reacts, lashing at his face with the stick before throwing it at him and stalking away.

"There's a princess who'll no save yer neck frae the axe," says Lachlan. "Whae'd ye say to her?"

"That I'd prefer tae keep ma bollocks intact, if she dinnae mind."

"Ye've a silver tongue with the lasses."

SHINGAS WATCHES CHARTIER SHAKE THE TURTLE SHELL, hands cupped over the openings, the peach pits rattling inside. The trader pulls one hand away and dumps the pits onto the stiff hide that lies between them—four painted sides up, three down. They each have a tin cup of Chartier's rum, the trader drinking freely, while Bone, who trusts nobody, is keeping track of how many times the cups have been filled. Cloud Woman moves about around them, letting her presence be felt, muttering just quietly enough that Shingas can't make out her words.

Four is the number to beat, Chartier tells them. Shawnee sounds enough like Lenape that Shingas can understand it, but when the details of the trade are to be made final he will switch to his own tongue. The *mengwe* up north call his people stutterers, but only because the *mengwe* are vain and ignorant and have no ear for language.

I bet you one musket, says Shingas, picking up the turtle shell and scooping the pits into it.

We have enough muskets, mutters his wife, laying bowls of hominy and venison next to each of the men.

Shingas shakes the pits in the shell, seeming to ignore her.

In fact, I bet you *two* muskets—

LACHLAN AND FERGAL, EXHAUSTED FROM THE MORNING'S exertions, doze against the pole, while Jamie tries to make sense of the scene around him. Most of the people have gone back to their fields or little conical huts, while the children are off to his left rolling a hoop on the ground while shooting arrows at it. A man who might be white, though in the garb of an Indian, steps close and squats to look Jamie in the eye, a slightly embarrassed smile on his face.

"*Anglais?*"

"*Éscossais.*"

"*Encore mieux.*" The man flexes his biceps. "Strong workaire—" He glances at Fergal, who is snoring, then touches the raw cut on Jamie's cheek where the young woman's stick hit him.

"*Vous êtes guerriers?*"

Jamie, feeling distinctly less than warrior-like, nods. "When it's needed."

The man, his own face raw where he has plucked out the beginning of a beard, cocks his head at the branded B on the back of Jamie's hand.

"And at times you are *esclave.*" He points at Lachlan. "And thees one?"

"*Il est un barde.*"

The man laughs.

Jamie lifts his chin to indicate the camp around them. "Where are we?"

"*Mais, dans le village,*" the man shrugs, then taps himself on the chest. "*Je suis LaCroix.*"

"But what land is this?"

LaCroix considers for a moment before he answers.

"The French, they call us the Wolf—*les Loups*—but we are Lenape. *C'est le village de Shingas.*"

"That's a place or a mon?"

LaCroix points to the hut that Chartier, Bone, and the man in charge entered. "*Cette homme, là.*"

"He's yer king?"

"We do not 'ave a king. But if Shingas lead, *nous suivons.*" He smiles and gives the thongs binding Jamie's hands a poke. "If you think to escape—*il y a gens de peaux rouge en toutes côtés.*" He makes a circle with his arm, as if to include both sides of the river and the woods beyond.

"And what will they do with us now?"

LaCroix looks again to the hut of the leader. "*Cela dépend de la chance. Ils jouent*—they play—and you, *mon ami*, you are the prize."

JUST BEFORE THE MORNING SUN APPEARS, MIST ON THE river hiding the dwellings on its far side, Lachlan stands, softly singing a lament in Erse, a few curious women coming out of their huts to listen, till Bone shoves him into the long canoe with the other Shawnee men.

Fergal, seemingly resigned to whatever his fate may be, helps Chartier and his Muskogee travelers load their boat with bundles of skins bartered for in the camp and what's left of their trade goods in chests and barrels, then climbs into the center and takes up the oars.

Jamie stands with the women on the bank, hands still bound, watching as the Shawnee push out into the current and begin to paddle with it back to the south, while the trader and his Muskogee companions chop at the water with greater effort, heading north.

Just as he is about to disappear into the mist, Lachlan looks back to fix his mournful gaze on Jamie, then resumes his song, the only human sound in the gray morning—

My soul like ship unmanned
Pulled far from hearth and kin
Drifting, drifting
On a sea withoot a shore—

Those on the bank listen until he can be heard no more, and then Cloud Woman strikes Jamie on the shoulder with a stick and grunts something at him. He turns to follow her back to the village.

THE LAND DESCENDS PRECIPITOUSLY FROM MORNE Rouge to the sea, with Saint Pierre clinging at the very edge of the water. It is not so much bigger than Fort Royal, but crowded with four times as many people and countless stone houses painted yellow or peach and almost no streets that are not crooked and steeply pitched. These are nevertheless full of carts and carriages, full of black and mulatto women with their hair twisted up in colorful plaid handkerchiefs and wooden trays piled with items for sale balanced upon their heads, full of soldiers in light blue uniforms marching here and there, and, in the shady hours of the late afternoon, *grands dames blanches* strolling in outfits that Jenny suspects must be imported from France.

Her days are aimless. St. Cyr is at the seawall supervising the repair of the massive cannons of the d'Esnotz battery, their range much greater than anything an English warship can carry on board, and usually dines in the officers' mess. Jenny quickly tires of sitting in the small *cabane a louer* he has found and begins to wander the city, if it can be called such, tailed by the sullen Hyppolite, her *garde du corps* who is normally employed polishing the boots of artillery officers. Without the *maître* to chasten her, Jenny smiles and says hello to the *vendeuses* as she passes them on the Grand Rue, some struck mute in surprise but most smiling back and responding—

"*Bonjou, chè. Comment ou yé?*"

"*'Tout douce,*" Jenny replies, "*Et ou?*"

Almost all of the women will then look back, having to turn their whole bodies so as not to topple the burdens on their heads, trying to place her status. Some must assume she is a *sang melé*—one hundred twenty-seven drops of white blood to a single drop of the African, dressed a bit above her station. The combinations, as St. Cyr has explained them and Amély elaborated for her, are impossible to keep track of, *mûlatresses* and *chabines* and *quarteronnés* and *métisses* and *mameloucs*—Jenny suspects that beyond one generation nobody really knows the true mix.

Yet understands that they have come to care, obsessively.

The *vendeuses* call out their wares as they gracefully stride down the main avenue, mangoes, papayas, the creamy pear with the skin of a green lizard they call an *avocat,* tasty cooked *pan-mi* and *akras* wrapped in banana leaves, one woman with a heap of huge, ebony-hued river crayfish, true monsters with black-bead eyes and wavering feelers, writhing on her head tray. Other women sell live crabs from the barrels they are kept in, fed on little balls of manioc to fatten them and sweeten their meat. There are women selling cloth and embroidered *mouchoirs* and toys made of bamboo and bracelets and beads—Jenny buys a necklace from one of these, the beads of varying sizes and made of a beautiful dark hardwood instead of the hollow metal ones on the *colliers-choux* the street vendors wear, and when the Lieutenant sees her with it around her neck he laughs and informs her it is a *rosaire* that the Catholic women use to keep track of their prayers.

On most days she walks as far as the Rivière Roxelane, where the contingent of *blanchisseuses* scrub linen in the cold mountain water, then gather it into a shape perfect for smacking down on the boulders, the collective sound like a distant cannonade. The women are in the water all day, maintaining a constant, songlike conversation shouted over the roar of the swift current. Several white-painted bridges cross the Roxelane, and Jenny likes to linger at the rail of the *Pont-bois* and look down on the women wrestling the wet linen about, standing beside porters and errand boys who have found excuses to come by and flirt from a height while the passing *vendeuses* and housemaids pause to yell greetings and gossip to their friends. At the midday meal Jenny finds them sitting on the rocks with their feet still in the water as they eat, the river flashing white with linen draped out to bleach and dry in the sun.

Across the bridge is the high ground and the fort, palm trees towering over the thick stone walls, and the *marché du fort* in the open space of the Savane. Huge tamarinds surround the market, with one side of the ground dedicated to fruits and vegetables, the other to meat and fish, while next to the fountain at the center entire rowboats are carried in, filled to the gunwales with shark, tuna, swordfish, and the shiny, winged *volants*. Jenny asks the names of the foods she doesn't recognize, buys a sample, and if they don't need to be cooked, eats them right at the stall to the amusement of the locals.

It is not enough to fill the day.

Even with the sea breeze, the air is so steamy here that Jenny finds herself sleeping while the sun is up for the first time in her life, having to change her sweat-sodden clothes at least once before the ringing of the second carillon. There is a *hamac* slung between two palms in front of their red-roofed cottage, and Jenny is flipped to the ground twice before she learns the balance of it. After a week the sea calms enough so that Amély, left with a travel billet by St. Cyr, is able to take the boat to join her, the *bonne* sleeping on a pallet on the floor beside Jenny's bed, ready to make herself scarce if the *maître* chooses to visit.

Saint Pierre might as well be Paris to Amély.

"*Tant de gens pou voi,*" she exclaims on the first day, walking almost beside Jenny on the Grand Rue, "*tant à faire!*"

And within days Amély has a new *douxdoux,* a dockworker named Abélarde, tall and well-made and very dark, with a full head of hair like black lamb's wool. Abélarde is *kreyòl* like Amély, but born in a mountain town on the other side of the island.

"*N'est pas n'om sophistiqué,*" she says of her conquest, "*mais peut-êt qu'un jou il sera libe.*"

One day he might be free. Abélarde, though owned by a local shipwright, is able to "find" things on the dock that he can convert to cash, hoping to some day buy his way out of bondage. Jenny thinks of herself in the hold of the *Jane of Leith,* afraid to even imagine of such a thing.

Their days have a routine, with the sun rising late behind the bulk of Pelée, lighting the ocean far beyond the harbor before its luminence rolls back into the town. A lovely barefoot girl brings St. Cyr his wake-up coffee and *corossol,* a fruit with a spiny exterior and creamy white insides smelling of pineapple, with Jenny not required to make an appearance. She rises shortly after the *vendeuses* begin to call on the street outside, and by the time the church carillon has rung for the first time she has washed herself, using the lovely *l'eau de gouave* that flows down from the volcano, running free in the streets or channeled by bamboo pipes. In Fort Royal the *maître* cautioned her not to drink water unless made safe with a healthy dash of rum or from a *dobanne* of captured rain, but here everyone drinks the sweet run-off from Pelée.

She then has her own breakfast, usually a tart from the *boulanger,* who comes to the door wearing his white *chapeau de chef,* while Amély deals with the insects. Every house in Saint Pierre seems to be infested with giant spiders, hairy creatures too big for even the largest of their resident lizards to confront, as well as the pale, slinky *mille pattes* that make your flesh crawl just to look at. She escorts the spiders out the door with a broom, scolding them gently, and uses the heel of one of St. Cyr's boots to smash the centipedes into mush. Jenny has learned to examine her shoes, now that she wears them every day, before putting them on, tiny scorpions and biting bugs likely to lodge within them overnight.

Jenny generally takes her midday meal on the street, though she is one of the few white women to do so, and she and Amély stroll the market together, her *bonne* somehow already well-informed as to the backgrounds and peccadillos of the people, both vendors and buyers, they see there.

This one stabbed her uncle, she might say, never pointing but the culprit being obvious, or that one was her master's mistress, *comme tu,* but has gotten too old and been pitched onto the street. And that one, she often says, gently leading Jenny away by the arm, is a *pratiquante* of the dark arts, and meets with *zombis* in the cemetery.

Night begins well before the third carillon, and when St. Cyr dines with his fellows Jenny and Amély sit outside for a spell, no lantern hung in respect to the flying insects it must draw, and listen to the tree frogs trilling and the rasp of the *cabri-des-bois* crickets and the soft, disembodied voices of the last passersby. Jenny has never been so idle, her one responsibility to *être joli,* and as pleasant as she finds this island, sometimes it seems like a punishment.

"*Je suis absolutment inutile,*" she sighs, holding out her empty, softening hands.

The white woman's disease, says Amély, sympathizing.

Jenny has no idea what the normal French custom is, but St. Cyr has never invited her to stay the night in his bed. In Fort Royal he would most often visit her little *chambre de servante,* perhaps enjoying the sense of forbidden alliance, but even here, with so many fewer rooms, he maintains the separation. It is just as well, as he comes in very late, smelling of tobacco and rum and grumbling over his losses at the card table, and it is only a small wait for Jenny to know if she should prepare herself for a bout of lovemaking or go back to sleep. Some nights he will take out his violin and begin to play, not especially well, the same song over and over, as if trying to learn it. She is not welcome to join him unless summoned, and his lessons here, usually held in the dead of night, all have a military character.

"*Le général command le colonel.*"

"*Le général command le colonel.*"

"*Le colonel est plus haut que le capitaine. Repetez—*"

"*Le colonel est plus haut que le capitaine.*"

"*Et le lieutenant mange la merde du capitaine.*"

There is a *capitaine* above him, a *petit bourgeois* from Châlons-sur-Marne, but a captain nonetheless, French-born and overly proud of the fact, who has become St. Cyr's tormentor here in the capital, treating him like a lackey and a fool. The other lieutenants St. Cyr plays *Trois Jeux* with commiserate as they take his money, telling him that Heureux treats all his subordinates like shit, that ridicule is what fuels society back in *la Patrie* and that he is lucky to be here where languid climate and moral laxity soften all things, even army life.

"Ye've nae need tae stay in, if ye loathe it," Jenny tells him when he sits at the edge of her bed venting his frustration. "*Vous êtes un homme aisé.*"

And then he confesses to her that his means are not what they once were, his presence at the card games almost a duty for any officer who wishes to be respected, but his luck at them nonexistant. He wonders if some wizened *quimbosier*, perhaps a resentful slave from his days as a plantation owner, has cursed him.

Jenny is flattered by his openess, sitting up to take his hand, but the moment comes when St. Cyr shakes his head, muttering "*Ça ne va pas*," and goes back to collapse in his own bed. He can barely look at her in the morning, embarrassed.

"*Le maître sufre beaucoup*," Amély observes when he is gone. "*Les békés riches ne faisent pas bon esclaves*."

If this is so it is a slavery the *maître* has chosen, and from what she's seen he treats the *bombardiers* below his rank as he does his *gens de couleur* in the Fort Royal house, with a mixture of amusement and condescension.

These are very simple men, he has explained to her. Poor, ignorant, but eager to learn. A firm hand, he says, and consistency is what they want, a stern but predictable father. The deference of army protocol, the saluting, the drumming and display of flags, all seem to her a mask for something very savage, a way for men to organize themselves to kill others without killing each other.

They look splendid in the uniforms.

On a day when Capitain Heureux is known to be in the north, St. Cyr brings her to the d'Esnotz battery. There are eleven of the incredibly long, heavy guns, perched on the stone wall built at the edge of the sea, pointing out into the vast ocean. He indicates the horizon.

"*Les anglais viendrant de là-bas*," he announces, "*avec touts leurs navires*."

Jenny tries to imagine it, the sea that is now only dotted with the sails of a few coast-hugging transports suddenly blooming with English warships spouting smoke and fire, their missiles whistling overhead and smashing the flimsy structures in the town behind them. She touches the ring beneath her blouse.

"And if they triumph, I'll be theirs once mair," she muses. "*Autre fois une prisonierre*."

St. Cyr laughs. He has beautiful teeth, shining white in his tanned face. He waves toward the row of massive cannon.

All this is for your protection, *ma 'tite sauvage*, he tells her. "*Nous nous battons pour ta liberté*."

And though she is certain none of the fortifications are in fact dedicated to her particular freedom, Jenny is comforted to witness the volley St. Cyr orders fired in her honor, the simultaneous explosions shaking the ground under her feet, the sound an enormous, physical thing, the smoke from their barrels taking a long time to dissipate and smelling like an exotic pepper.

Let the English fleet come, she thinks, and be blown to splinters.

AMONG THE WOLVES

IN THE TIME WHEN THE FROGS BEGIN TO SING, JAMIE jabs the pointed stick into the ground, again and again. The tasks are not so different than what he was forced to perform for Crozier, but the tools are inferior. Around him Lenape women chop at the earth with short wooden hoes, chatting, while a few of them kneel pushing seeds into the ground where it has been thoroughly turned and weeded, a few little girls assisting them. The children here, Jamie has observed, are allowed to run about like wild Indians, though when required to help with something useful they are eager to comply, even to volunteer.

He misses the iron rod supplied by Crozier for breaking soil, but tries to match the rhythm of the Lenape women. Now and then Cloud Woman, who seems to be his owner, will hit him with a clod of dirt to catch his attention, then indicate some new patch of the field he is to stab at. Like the others, he tries to stay turned toward the river, watching for arrivals.

The Lenape men do not work in the field unless there are trees to be felled. He sees them strolling between huts to visit, or squatting around blankets laid on the ground to gamble, or walking down the bank of the river to fish in the shallows, slender spears in hand. Most of the men beyond their teens have at least one design or image tattooed onto their skin, some with many, even on their faces. Some have their noses or lower lips pierced with silver bangles hanging down, and many have separated the flesh of the lobes from the rest of their ears, weights hung from these to gradually stretch them until there is room to wrap them with shiny brass wire and dangle feathers from them. The lobes of a few of the older men touch their shoulders, jingling with ornaments as they walk. They are bare-legged in this warm weather, wearing a rectangle of cloth or buckskin held fast by a cord around their waists that hangs down front and rear to conceal their private parts. Above this there is most often a colorful linen shirt, buttons removed to leave the chest bare, that has obviously been gotten in trade with white men. These are worn every day and apparently never washed until so ragged as to fall off the wearer. The adult men often have a blanket thrown over one shoulder, giving them the aspect of somewhat gaudy Roman senators, and there is invariably a furry pouch made from an entire small animal, like the Highland sporrans fashioned with otter hide, hanging on their breast, the long clay pipes they use for their tobacco sticking from the top.

These men look through Jamie if he crosses their pathway, and he is as careful as the camp dogs to avoid being kicked. Every time he hears a shout from the river bank he stops to look over, hoping for the canoe full of white traders who will barter for his freedom. The village must have contact with such men, as no iron is forged here, no powder or shot produced, no stroud milled, no rifles repaired, and yet the people have all these things. In his first week Jamie often caught the smell of coffee brewing from the hut of Shingas and Cloud Woman, then the supply must have run out.

Someone will come.

Soon, he hopes.

Until then Jamie stabs the dibble into the ground, again and again, working hard enough to not be murdered as useless, but not so well that these savages hesitate to part with him.

He watches and he listens.

When the women around him laugh, which they do often, what has been said? He learned his French and Latin with tutors, with written symbols to compare the words to, but here there are still only sounds, becoming more familiar as he hears them again and again—

The sound for wake up!

The sound for sit on the ground—

The sounds for stay here—

The sound for dig it up—

He has always had a talent for language, though, an ability to almost see the sounds as solid things, each with a distinctive shape, which when fitted together become something with meaning. The language, the sounds, become his obsession, being the barriers—no—the doorways leading to his escape, to his salvation. He grasps at them as a drowning man to a log afloat—

The sound for eat—

The sound for drink—

The sound for white man.

In the time when apple trees blossom, Jamie, barefoot, bearded and in rags, kneels in the riverside field pulling weeds among the ankle-high shoots. He begins to tug at an especially stubborn one when Cloud Woman thumps him in the back with her hoe, shouting angrily and pointing to a nearby plant that has begun to sprout tiny bean pods.

The sound for stupid.

The plant looks nearly identical to the one in Jamie's hands, and he realizes she is scolding him not to destroy it. He notes her use of the negative, *màtach*, which in some form appears in almost everything the woman says to him, and searches for a different weed to pull.

The language is breathier than Erse, nothing in it to make you swallow your tongue, and not as predictable as Latin, with each of its squadrons of declensions marching in order from the body of the verb like disciplined centurions. Attempting to appear uninterested, a dullard, even, Jamie begins to organize the sounds he hears spoken around him into something like words, their meanings beginning to be perceptible, like the details of a shore emerging from the fog. Lenape seems to use fewer distinct words, with similar sounds twisted in various ways to express states or actions of the same person or object. LaCroix, whose status in the village is clearly not that of the full-blooded men, tends to avoid him, but has condescended to supply the names of some the people closest to Jamie. The headman is *Shingas*, which means a boggy place, while his wife, Jamie's most consistent tormentor, is *Kùmhókw*, Cloud Woman, and many of the other names describe places or animals or attributes of the person so titled.

LaCroix himself is known by his neighbors as *Kahtalenape*, Wants-to-Be-One-of-Us, an apellation he does not relish.

The word for deer.

The word for bear.

The word for wolf.

The word for turtle.

The word for squirrel.

The word for rabbit.

The words for killing.

IN THE TIME WHEN THE SHAD RETURN, JAMIE SMASHES kernels of maize with a thick wooden pestle on a quern made from a tree stump. When they are rendered into a meal fine enough that Cloud Women won't beat him, he scoops it out into a flat basket with a kind of screen over it, dumping the particles that do not pass through back into the quern for further pounding and grinding. There is a cry, and dogs barking, then men and women rushing past to where the ones he knows as Digs Deep, Killbuck, and Red Warrior emerge from the woods behind the village, between them carrying the carcasses of two deer they have slain. Jamie watches for a moment, then notices that the other person who has not run to greet the hunters is Ange, the rude young woman who prodded his genitals the day he arrived, still grinding her own maize in front of the rather shabby *wikëwam* she lives in alone. She is watching Jamie, as she often does, as she pounds the grain. LaCroix says that she is his sister, and that she is possessed by a *manëtuwàk*, an uneasy spirit that attracts men and makes women curse her under their breath.

Game seems to be plentiful at this time of year, often cooked and eaten immediately when it is brought into camp, no matter what the time of day. The animals are skinned, of course, women providing this service, the hides later worked and stretched to dry for use or trade, with tails, paws, hoofs and sometimes even heads kept aside to make ornaments or tools with. No meat is wasted, with unwanted organs tossed to the camp dogs, and entire animals are consumed at one sitting. Jamie has witnessed no salt or other seasoning thrown into a pot, and the scraps he is thrown are torn fresh from the carcass and not unlike the scran on a prison ship. They will mix the meal he is grinding into a porridge, or make a sort of bannock cake with it, and do something similar with roasted acorns.

The young woman, Ange, says something he does not understand. She dresses as the other women do, a simple skirt wrapped around her hips that reaches only to her knees and sandals made from braided cornhusks, but her neck, ears, throat, and arms are adorned with more bands, bracelets, and bangles than any three of her sisters combined. She repeats the phrase.

Jamie looks about. There is nobody she could be speaking to but him.

"*C'est pas pour nous*," she says, switching into French.

It isn't for us.

He understands that none of the game brought into the village is for him, but no one has included themselves in that exclusion before.

"*C'est tristement vrai, Mademoiselle.*"

She scowls at him then, as if he may have insulted her, and goes back to her grinding.

WRITING OF ANY SORT MAKES THE RED MEN UNEASY. Unfamiliar symbols, a code the white people use to trick them, threatening enough on a scroll of parchment, but here, graven on metal and about to be buried beneath the ground, like a secret curse—

Maintenu par les armes says the lead plate the party of French soldiers have carried, with great effort, to this spot. Their claim to the land, in their minds mandated by their one and only God, to be "maintained by arms." But Chartier knows that the land is vast and their arms, from what he has witnessed, inadequate to the task.

They are half a league south of Sonnontio, the largest of the Shawnee villages. There were no whites there four years ago when the Pennsylvanias wanted to arrest Chartier and he came for shelter. There was no stockade from which to shoot rifles and make holes in the French flag, no English *commerçants* to hide inside it and poison the hearts of his people. But Croghan and his *métis* partner Montour have been in that stockade recently, he knows, spreading lies and handing out gifts and perhaps making claims of ownership for their father George. And now, though Chevalier Céleron has been ordered to honor the peace made across the Great Water at a place named Utrecht, one does not travel into a strange country with two hundred soldiers and two dozen armed *guerriers à la peau rouge* as a gesture of good will.

When a male wolf urinates on a stump it isn't because his bladder is full.

Chartier watches the faces of the warriors as the shovel bites into the earth, squatting on their haunches in a group to the side of the uniformed white men standing in formation. The Ottawa will be no problem, these are not their hunting grounds being claimed, and some are still hoping for scalps and plunder on this journey. The Mingo, of course, have come partly to spy for the *confédération iroquoise.* It is his own Shawnee, their principal village less than a day's journey up the great river and then the Scioto, and English traders living among them, who have the most to fear.

The young *corporel* does not dig deep. The point seems to be to establish precedence for the French crown, the *droit de première découverte.* But do they truly believe that the old men wearing other men's hair while they dicker over a treaty across the Great Water will bother to send someone to this obscure bend in a wilderness river to search for a lead tablet engraved with words in French?

White people and their strange rituals—

The Chevalier Céleron de Blainville, who is a good leader in a fight but no statesman, has used the royal "We" in the inscription.

Nous, Céleron, commandant d'un detachement envoie par Monsieur le Marquis de la Galissoniere le commandant général de la Nouvelle France pour retablir la tranqilité dans quelques villages sauvages—

A noble claim, but Chartier is certain that none of the villages they've passed through have become more tranquil since their visit. The English traders who have crept in to the area will be anxious, as they should be, the Miami will be on the alert for another massacre, and his Shawnee, forced to move so many times and with no trust in whites and their promises, are spoiling for a fight.

The plate is laid in the shallow hole and buried as the drummer boy rattles the air with his sticks, the Chevalier Céleron holding his hand over his heart, the *drapeau français* fluttering listlessly overhead on a pole, and both regular troops and *canadiens* standing absolutely motionless, muskets shouldered, eyes staring forward at nothing.

They become wooden, as his people say.

What do the scratches mean? asks Bone, who has stepped up silently beside him.

Bone who has run his fingertips over the markings on the plate, scowling, uneasy in the presence of dark medicine—

It says that the French are the loyal friends of the red man, Chartier tells him. And that they are here to protect us from the English, who wish to take our land.

It is almost true. The French do want to be rid of English traders who offer superior goods for lower recompense, and have no plans to bring white settlers to the valley of the Belle Rivière. But they are not merely visitors—

—prés de la Ohio, autrement connu comme la Belle Rivière, et de tous des terres de deux côtes jusqu'au source des dittes rivières—

—but here to "renew" their claim to the great river, the Ohio, and all its tributaries and all the land that borders it. Chartier has been paid well to bring his people back to the fire of their great friend Louis, to help them recognize the English for the liars and thieves that they are. For whether they have planted lead plates or not, both the Pennsylvania and the Virginia colonies also claim the Ohio, as does their father, King George.

If the French are our friends, says Bone, why do they bury magic stones in our ground?

The stones are for the English to read.

But they are buried—

We will leave another piece of metal, Chartier explains, telling all white men where to find our warning.

Bone searches his face.

Chartier shrugs. You know that white men are like children, he says. Their actions do not always make sense.

But Bone trusts nobody, especially if they have white blood like Pierre Chartier.

Céleron begins his little pronouncement now, the same speech he made at the bend in the Alligewinenk where they buried the first plate. He does not mention *les droits du Roi* or possession, aware that many of the warriors present understand some French. The Chevalier does not much care for traders, English or French, considering them, as a breed, less than honorable, and has treated the chief men of the various tribes they have encountered like potential allies and not as inferiors. If he had been born over the Great Water instead of in *la Nouvelle France*, Céleron would be a general by now.

Our orders are not to rob or kill the English traders, he has told Chartier many a time, but this may be encouraged among those we leave behind.

Let the moon grow full two times after our leaving, Chartier has told the *Indigènes* in the villages they have passed through, and then treat the English as you wish.

Bone watches intently as a tin plaque with the royal coat of arms and directions to find the lead plate is nailed to a chestnut. Bone and his little *cadre* of followers will not wait even two days before returning, Chartier knows, to dig up the plate with the graven symbols on it, and will either melt it in a fire to make lead balls to kill their enemies with or hand it over to an English trader and demand reward. Bone desires that the two great white tribes make war on each other, which will happen soon enough, but expecting them to kill each other down to the last man is perhaps too much to ask of the Creator of All Things.

But there will be profit in such a war, Chartier knows—gifts to be received, scalps to be taken, songs of boldness and courage to be sung in one's honor. Bone is already teaching the little *écossais* he captured and kept, a man too puny to carry a load and worthless in a fight but with an ear for every sound, to speak the Shawnee tongue—

I am the captive of the terrible Bone, he has been taught to cry out, walking ahead of the warrior as they enter a new village. *Keep your distance lest you be scorched by his wrath!*

Maintenu par les armes, says the lead plate in the ground. Chartier has been to both Montreál and Québec in the north and has seen the armies the French keep there, sufficient perhaps to oppose the fighting men of the Pennsylvanias or Virginias, but if the great English father George sends more of his redcoats across the Great Water, French armies alone will have no chance to hold this land. And thus the Miamis must be threatened, and the Ottawa and the Wyandots and the Mingos and the Lenape and his Shawnee won over, the Iroquois kept neutral, so that English traders and English settlers can never be sure that they will not be robbed, that they will not be killed by red men.

"*—au nomme de notre Roi bien-aimé, Louis Quinze*," finishes Céleron, and a dozen of his fusiliers fire a volley into the air, the shots echoing off the valley walls. The Ohio, *la Belle Rivière*, can be seen through the trees, flowing as it always has, lead plates or no, summer light glistening on its surface, a flotilla of ducks gabbling at the far bank. *Les canards de Louis Quinze*, thinks Chartier with a smile. He sees Bone separate himself from the troop, sees him turning his back and lifting his breechclout.

Pissing on a tree.

IN THE TIME OF THE GREEN CORN, JAMIE HOES WEEDS in the chest-high maize with several women. The hoe is too short and he has to bend over to work, has to avoid chopping the vines of the squash and tomatoes, now that he recognizes them, that grow between the rows. There is a shout and the women rush to one side of the field, Jamie daring to follow them.

Cloud Woman has a *shixikwe,* a thick, mottled snake with a cluster of rattling lumps on its tail, pinned to the ground with a long forked stick. The other women, fascinated but not stepping too near, are full of advice as to what should be done, then go silent when Ange arrives and squats by the head of the serpent.

Ange has a glistening chunk of meat in her hand, what looks to Jamie like the liver of a small, just-killed animal. She takes a firm grip behind the serpent's head, then carefully impales the liver on the creature's bared fangs, stroking what on a person would be the throat with one of her thumbs. She finally pulls the liver away and stands, placing it in a colorfully decorated pouch she wears around her neck. She gives Jamie a wicked smile and rubs shoulders with him as she slinks away.

"*Nuchihëwès,*" says Cloud Woman.

"Witch," mutters Jamie.

Then Cloud Woman thanks the rattlesnake for his warning and flips him into the edge of the woods.

The word for I see.

The word for I hear.

The word for I smell.

The word for I know.

IN THE TIME OF THE HONEY BEE, JAMIE LABORS OVER A raw deer hide laid upon wrist-thick logs using a bone scraper to remove the flesh from the inner side. Beside him kneels a very dark-skinned woman, also a captive, though dressed in the Lenape style, who is mashing the deer's brains to make a paste the skin will be steeped in to soften the leather. Behind them Cloud Woman and her friend, possibly her sister, Spits Far, are chatting as they flay a just-killed buck, one tugging hide while the other cuts.

Jamie's knees, bare and bloody through the holes in what is left of his trews, mutters under his breath as he scrapes.

"Treat me like a bluidy woman."

The African beside him snorts.

"Woman got respeck here," she says. "Woman got a *name*. You hear them call you somethin'?"

Jamie has had no occasion to talk to her and is startled to hear her speak English.

"No—"

"Won't give a dog a name, neither. Might got to *eat* the dog."

"And I take it ye've earned a title fer yersel'?"

The woman keeps mashing, a trio of skinny curs loitering nearby, tails wagging.

"White foke as used to own me call me Silvy. These here, what they call me mean 'Buffalo Hair,' on account mine not *straight* like theirs is. My mam had a Affican name fo me, but I don't know if it mean somethin' or not."

"What was it?"

Buffalo Hair gives him a sidelong glance, frowning. "I don't say it out loud. That way it stay *mine*."

She continues to study him as he works the hide.

"Jes so's you know, you could do wuss than these Delawares. They mostly real peaceable—but they *watch*in', don't miss a thing. And you run away, they take that fo a *in*sult."

The word for content.

The word for sad.

The word for heart.

The word for angry.

IN THE TIME WHEN THE SQUIRRELS HIDE ACORNS, JAMIE huddles on the ground just outside the *wikëwam* that Shingas and Cloud Woman dwell in, stars looking cold in the sky above, wondering if he'll be allowed inside somewhere when the first frost arrives. Already leaves on many of the trees on both sides of the river are turning colors, and he has only a worn, dirty blanket to cover himself with. Cloud Woman appears with an iron pot in hand, pitching out the dregs of dinner, camp dogs immediately crowding to lap at it. She starts inside, as she always does, then as an afterthought—or is it meant to be a statement? lays the pot down next to Jamie. He keeps his head turned from it till she is inside, then quickly begins to dig out the crust of burnt hominy in the bottom with his fingers, kicking away a dog with his bare foot.

He hears a laugh, looks across to see Ange, entertaining yet another of her young men. Sometimes they enter her hut, sometimes not. She looks past her suitor to Jamie, smiling, and he turns so his back is to her before bolting down his dinner.

JAMIE KNEELS AT THE RIVER'S EDGE SCRUBBING OUT pots with sand and the tops of rushes, then filling them from a swift-whirling eddy to take back to his mistress. Lenape boys swim nearby, splashing each other, the water bone-chillingly cold. They now tend to ignore him, which is a relief, Jamie never sure if he as a captive is allowed to fight back when chldren are involved. The boys are thin but well formed and always in motion, and make him think of himself and Dougal in their free-ranging days. A pair of strange Indians glide past him in a small canoe, waving to men lounging outside in the village. There are over two hundred people on Jamie's side of the river, many seeming to be related to each other in ways he has not yet determined, and there are at least two other tribes beside the Shawnee who come to visit and to trade.

He lifts the water-heavy pots, starts up the bank to the village.

The word for stranger.

The word for water

The word for sky.

The word for captive.

IN THE TIME OF THE FALLING LEAVES, JAMIE GATHERS kindling at the edge of the woods, picking it up from the ground or breaking it from trees with the small hatchet he is trusted with. The hatchet is iron, obviously a trade item as he has seen evidence neither of mining nor smelting here, and he realizes the adolescent boy also gathering a few yards away is meant to watch him. It is the farthest he's been from the hut of Shingas and Cloud Woman since he was purchased, the smoke escaping through the small holes in the roofs of the *wikwahëma* dissipating in the sky behind him.

The only *shëwanahkòk*—the only white men he has heard spoken of—have been French traders like Chartier, traders who make long journeys down several rivers to reach the village. His world here is spacious compared to the English dungeons and prison ship holds, but having so little idea of where it lies and what surrounds it unsettles Jamie, as if he is not truly living but only floating at the edges of life.

And no one here has yet given him a name.

Jamie steps into the hut of Shingas and Cloud Woman with a load of firewood on his back, the tumpline that supports it pulled taut across his chest. The headman, smoking a long pipe by the fire, as usual does not stir or raise his eyes to look at him, Jamie apparently too low a creature to merit his notice. It is Cloud Woman who plays Prospero to his wretched Caliban, ordering him, correcting him, at times beating him, and only lately guarding her words when in his presence, as if aware of his growing understanding.

Jamie kneels and piles the kindling by the empty baskets. The interior of the dwelling is very spare, a pallet that he assumes is their bed, with fur robes and trade blankets rolled on it during the day, a long-barreled rifle leaning against the wall, a bow and some gourds and other vegetables hung from above, the two iron pots and a few crude cooking tools resting by the fire. A very poor kingdom, if this is all the ruler has collected. Though men come in here to sit and smoke with Shingas for hours, Jamie has yet to see him issue a decree or plan a miitary campaign. Perhaps this village, *Kittanning*, they call it, is for those of the tribe who have retired from competitive life, a backwater of reduced ambitions.

Jamie exits without ceremony, the stolid chief still smoking, staring into the flames.

THAT ONE BEARS WATCHING, THINKS SHINGAS. CRAFTY and patient, like the crow, qualities he thought he sensed in the man when he chose him among the three offered. Reports are received each day of white men on the move, white men taking their iron axes to trees, making clearings, building structures too large to be only trading posts. The French and the King George men have settled a peace, it is reported, in their lands across the Great Water, but here they watch each other like scavenger wolves that hunger for the same carcass.

Shingas taps the ash from his pipe, fills it with a small plug of tobacco, and lights it.

That one does not fight back, does not run, but he is not broken. His mind remains whole, and he hides his intentions well. This is a skill desirable in a talker, who must turn your words into the other party's language honestly but without revealing what is in your heart, especially when dealing with men as treacherous as the French or the King George men or the Haudenosaunee. Tanaghrisson, who the Seneca have sent to live among them and to spy and to sign white man's papers in their name, understands Lenape and Shawnee well enough, speaks the King George tongue very well, but is ignorant of French and sworn to make war on those who speak it. Wants-to-Be-One-of-Us understands much of each but cannot be trusted, with a French father and a mother who was of a stinkard people, a tribe so weak their survivors were forced to beg protection from the Lenape. Such a man has no character.

That one bears watching. If he survives the winter he should be tested. He speaks so little, and that mostly to himself, like the moaning of an old dog when it rises upon its legs. Shingas hopes the man does not prove clumsy of tongue.

BACK IN FORT ROYAL, THERE IS EVEN LESS TO DO. EVEN St. Cyr, who never seems to exert himself or perspire, seems bored, only the odd cannon-shot of greeting as a merchantman sails into port to keep him occupied. Jenny has brought the *hamac* down from Saint Pierre and spends much of her day in it. None of the *dames blanches* in town, not even the few other white concubines, has invited her to tea, and Morag has followed her new soldier to duty on Guadaloupe. Amély misses her Abélarde, praying nightly for his safety and faithfulness in front of her little shrine, a small plaster Virgin on a wall bracket, a candle kept lit beside her night and day. She also keeps a clipping of his hair in a small leather sack, holding it to her heart now and then and muttering words in what Jenny thinks might be African. Amély refuses to explain.

"*Si je t'explique, le fétiche péd la puissance.*"

The old mountain people were the same back home, willing to cast a spell but never to reveal their methods, hinting that such knowledge was tantamount to becoming the devil's gillie. If Jenny knew such magic she would apply it to St. Cyr, who delights in telling strangers the story of her deliverance to Martinique, but never asks after her mood or opinion.

There are much worse men that she could have become attached to.

One of these is Charbonnel, the Lieutenant's childhood friend who bought his old plantation. They visit him there, across the bay in Les Trois-Îlets, the oldest of the house slaves making a great fuss over *mon ti' Alphonse* when St. Cyr arrives. Charbonnel, though like the *maître* only in his late thirties, has the ruddy face and mishapen nose of a three-bottle man.

"*Sans tache?*" he asks as he looks her over from head to toe, searching for a sign of African blood.

"*Elle est éscossaise, un île que n'avait pas les negres.*"

St. Cyr was disbelieving of this when she first reported it, but she assured him she had never even seen a Frenchman, much less someone stolen from Africa, before the *Diamante* brought her to this island.

"*Quelle chance pour eux,*" says Charbonnel, and goes on to bemoan his own misfortune at being the master of over one hundred *esclaves noires*, whose indolence and perversity have driven him to drink. Three have just run off into the hills, while another pair, just to spite him, have killed themselves by eating dirt. And the rest of his *atelier*, many of them recent imports yet unbroken to the routines of work and discipline, are far behind in the vital harvest.

St. Cyr smiles tolerantly, agreeing that it is a dog's life and he is very content to have given it up. Jenny wanders through the house, a mansion of grand proportion with lushly upholstered furniture imported from France that is not faring well in the tropical climate. Amély is with her, related on her mother's side to some of the house servants and having been born in one of the thatched cabins that line the edge of the cane fields.

I know everyone here, she tells Jenny. "*Les vivants et les morts.*"

And perhaps more of the dead than the living. When Jenny is given her own room, Amély will not enter it.

"*C'est la chamb ou ma mé nous a laissé,*" she says, crossing herself as the Catholics do, and explaining that her mother, never happy in her relationship with St. Cyr's father, chose this room to sit in and shoot herself with his pistol. If Jenny hears a cock crow at night, she says, she can rise to watch the blood stain on the wall reappear.

Charbonnel's wife prefers to live in Saint Pierre, so Jenny is alone at table with him and St. Cyr, the men beginning with port and moving on to unadorned rum as the dinner progresses, reminding each other of youthful adventures that sound much too energetic for her languid *maître*. She is, thankfully, mostly left out of the conversation and allowed to retire early, Amély leading her by candlelight through the many unused rooms to her own. The night is even livelier here than in Saint Pierre, frogs and insects and birds shrilly voicing their opinions, and once Jenny does hear a cock crow but can find no stain on the walls.

In the morning Amély takes her to watch the field cook, Edwige, and her girls prepare *manioc*—peeling and grating lengths of the thick root, boiling it in fresh water, cautious not to inhale the toxic vapor given off, then pressing the water out and drying the meal to grind it to powder, this last operation with the aid of a mill operated by a hand crank. The workers in the *atelier* are given this, mixed with a little water, to eat with their strips of salt cod every day, while in the house it is used to make a sweet pudding, full of little gelatinous balls like fish eggs. Preparing enough *farine de manioc* for the work crew is a matter of several days' meticulous labor, important to leach out all the poison before feeding it to anybody.

Later in the day St. Cyr and Charbonnel take Jenny with them to watch the *récolte* in the lower fields. It is something like what she has imagined war to be. A long line of *coupeurs,* all men, advance on the cane, blades flashing in the sun, followed closely by the female *amarreuses*—barefoot women hustling across the sharp stubble to bundle, bind and stack the severed cane stalks. This is the job she'd be slaving at, thinks Jenny, had the *Veteran* completed its voyage to the English islands. Behind the cutters and gatherers come a trio of drummers, beating a tattoo on their *tambores*, and their overseer, a huge black man with a rawhide whip in one hand and a pistol in his belt. The cane has been scorched by a controlled fire to burn off sharp leaves and bring the sugar sap up in the stalks, and wisps of black fluff dance in the air as the line hacks its way forward. Jenny asks if there are snakes in the field.

"*Bien sûr*," Charbonnel assures her, explaining that they are driven back before the cutters until the last few rows become crowded with them, a true vipers' nest. One loses a good negro now and then, he admits, but the serpents also serve to keep the rat population under control.

While they are observing, two of the three runaways are dragged in by a party of *chasseurs*, men who make their living tracking slaves overcome by delusions of freedom. They are in rags, cut and bleeding from the misfortunes of their flight, both trembling with fear as Charbonnel has them bound to the side of a wagon and calls over his *commandeur*. At the first crack of the giant negro's whip, limbering it for service, Jenny asks to be excused.

"*C'est necessaire*," Charbonnel insists, blaming the runaways' flight on the influence of free blacks from town and the persistent rumors of wild *marrons*, who alledgedly manage to survive off the bounty of Nature up in the high *mornes*.

And *par ailleurs*, the law forbids more than twenty-nine lashes for any single offense—

"*Elle possède un coeur tendre*," St. Cyr explains, taking her arm to lead her back to the mansion. "*Comme tous les femmes de qualité*."

Not so much a tender heart, thinks Jenny, as no stomach for torture.

He escorts her past the noisy, smoke-emitting mill, more dozens of black men feeding cane into the rolling press while women pile the *bagasse* extruded on the other side for fuel and fodder, he shows her the great boiling vats, the fires beneath them stoked constantly by men stripped to loincloths, sweat pouring off their dark skin, shows her the curing house and the molds in which the crystals are held to whiten, the shop where hogshead barrels are fashioned to ship the refined sugar to distant ports, a half-dozen barefoot men sitting in the sawdust wielding chisels and mallets.

"A' of these people," muses Jenny, "and ainly yer friend tae be the king iv em."

"*C'est une mode de vie*," shrugs St. Cyr, who understands her English but refuses to speak it. "*Tous comprends leur place*."

"And if they ferget their place," she mutters, "there's somebody close by with a whip or a musket tae remind them."

That night it is not St. Cyr but Charbonnel, very drunk, who enters her room without a candle, mumbling something to the effect that consorts are meant to be shared, and despite the number of items in the room—a stout pole to work the window louvers, a heavy porceline chamber pot—she could employ to beat his brains from his skull, Jenny attempts to remain good-humored in her refusals, eventually managing to escort the planter from the room.

In the morning Amély tells her that Charbonnel next went searching for her, prompting her to spend the night hiding in the *cas-de-vent*, a low stone structure used for shelter during hurricanes.

THEY PASS THE CANE FIELDS AGAIN ON THEIR WAY BACK to Fort Royal, St. Cyr moodily nursing a rum headache in the rear of the carriage next to Jenny while Amély sits up front with Maigrichon. A small army of dark-skinned people in grimy white *vêtements de travail* are laying seige to another section of yellow-green cane. Jenny has toiled barefoot in fields, has wrested turnips and potatoes from stony turf, but cannot imagine the misery of this inferno of heat and long knives, choking dust in the air, buzzards circling constantly overhead to swoop down on the rats and toads exposed by the cutters.

Boats stacked with young black men stolen from Africa are unloaded at the port every month, Amély tells her as they roll past one crew so exhausted they lay in the dirt by the side of the road like dead men, a paste of sweat and dust on their skin. But the number of *esclaves noires* in the cane never increases.

White people eat sugar cane, Amély grimly observes, "*et la canne à sucre mange les negre*."

IN THE TIME WHEN THE FIREFLIES PLAY AT NIGHT, JAMIE wakes huddled with two of the camp dogs, all three of them scratching at fleas. Disgusted, he sends the curs yelping away and pulls his ragged shirt off, uncovering a multitude of red welts on his chest and arms. He rises and heads toward the river.

At the bank he tears off the remnants of his trews, then immerses himself in an eddy where the current is not strong, the cold taking his breath away at first. He crouches there until his itching skin feels numb, then climbs onto a flat rock with water rushing around each side of it, watching the early risers leaving their huts on the far side of the river and allowing the morning breeze to dry him. There is laughter behind, and he turns to see a trio of small boys running away with the remains of his clothes.

Jamie walks, fully naked, back through the village. The men who are up do their best to ignore him, while a few of the women giggle and point. Cloud Woman stands outside the *wikëwam* shaking blankets when he arrives.

"A good morning to ye, Madame," he says, taking a hoe left leaning against the wall and heading for the fields. Ange sits outside of her hut, examining the blade of the knife given as a gift from one of her young men. She watches without comment as Jamie passes by.

He chops at the weeds in a fury. To his surprise he does not hate Cloud Woman—she toils nearly as hard as he does, though at her own pace and volition. The renters back home must have felt worse than this, he thinks, when he or Dougal, having done nothing to wrest a crop from the infertile soil, darkened their doorways demanding the tack.

Something is hurled to the ground at his feet.

Cloud Women walks away without a word.

Jamie kneels to examine the clothes—the woolen vest of a white man, a piece of cord and a long strip of buckskin a little over a foot in width, and a pair of leggings. It requires several attempts to arrange the breechclout evenly. He is still barefoot, and the garments feel heavy and strange, but he takes their delivery as a sign. He has risen above the dogs.

Jamie attacks the weeds with less passion now, moving toward a stand of maize that now sways even with his eyes. He finds a fallen ear, checks that no one else is in sight, then quickly rips the husk off and devours the parts not too compromised by worms. The final harvest must be coming soon.

Women and girls join him then, the women never without a task to lay their hands to, preparing meat and hides, weaving and mending, gathering berries or mushrooms, sewing together clothing from animal skins or traders' stroud, tending the various fields and gardens. A few are recent mothers, carrying their babies strapped to a wooden board that they prop or hang somewhere shaded near their work, the infant snugly cocooned with dry moss to absorb their excretions and seemingly content enough to watch from there. They are released from this portable bondage when they are ready to walk and are soon trailing after the slightly older mob of children. One of the little girls, who is called Pretty Weasel, has begun to include him when she brings gourds of cool water to the working women, sometimes shyly petting his beard with the palm of her hand. From her he has learned the words *mpi*, *xkànakhàkw*, and *sànkweyok*, for water, gourd, and weasel, and repeats them to himself, as he works, with the hundreds of other words and phrases he has picked up, trying to put a name to everyone and everything he lays his eyes on during the day. The outer life of the village makes sense to him now, the women responsible for the immediacy of food and clothing, the men, between trips away for trade or hunting, lounging about to smoke and gamble and joke with their comrades. The inner life, the dances and other rituals he's witnessed from a distance and the ceremonies held within the confines of the longhouse, remain a mystery.

On this day the women, with no signal for him to follow, leave the field early. Jamie works until the sun is low, understanding now what is plant and what is weed. When he returns to the dwellings there is nobody walking about, but a deep and insistant drumming heard from within the longhouse. He finds LaCroix sitting outside the hut he shares with Buffalo Hair, the negress fashioning a doll from corn shucks.

"*Asseyez-vous, mon ami,*" offers LaCroix, and Jamie sits wearily beside them. There is chanting, many voices raised together, along with the drumming now.

"*Le cérémonie de maïs,*" explains LaCroix. "For twelve night they sing like this."

"And ye cannae join them?"

LaCroix indicates Buffalo Hair. "This woman, she is a prize of war, *comme vous*, and I am the son of a Frenchman and a *pouant*—" he points across to Ange, sitting unhappily in front of her own *wikëwam*, "*et ma soeur aussi.*"

"A stinkard?"

"*Ma mère*, she is born *dans un tribu* who does not have the right or the respect of other tribe."

"MacGregors, then—"

"Magregaire—?"

"A cursed people. Ootlaws—"

"Our people were defeat by the Haudenosaunee—almost all of them is kill. *Les survivants*, they go to other tribes, beg to live with them." He crosses two fingers together. "But they are not the blood."

Jamie turns to Buffalo Hair. "And ye're a captive as well—"

"Shingas, 'e take her on a raid *contre les Sherokee.* Then I buy 'er from 'eem."

"She belangs tae ye?"

LaCroix makes a shrugging gesture. "*Nous avons un accord*—"

"Thas right—" says Buffalo Hair, adding cornsilk to the doll to make hair. "The agreement is he don't ack like a master, and I don't cut his throat whilst he sleepin'."

LaCroix looks amused.

They listen to the rhythmic chanting for a while, a reddish glow of firelight spilling from the small opening nearest them.

"Does it vex ye tae be left oot?"

Again LaCroix shrugs. "*C'est la vie. Mais Ange*,"—and here he nods toward Ange, who is chanting softly along with the ones inside and rocking gently to the beat of the drum, tears rolling down her cheeks—"my sister she is *désespérée* to be Lenape."

THERE IS A RUN OF SOME SORT OF FISH IN THE RIVER, and the whole of Kittanning is enlisted in their harvest. Jamie is directed to join the women, chanting and smacking the surface of the hip-deep water as they march forward in a line toward several of the sturdier men holding the deep end of a woven net that spans across half the river, struggling to fight the current.

Jamie feels something wiggle up under his breechclout from behind, making him jump.

It is not a panicked fish but Ange, who grins wickedly and moves away.

When the net is so heavy with perch caught by their gills that it cannot be held, all walk it in and drag the squirming mass ashore, the quick hands of young boys and girls untangling the prizes and ferrying them to higher ground. This is done five times, until Shingas, staring into the water, declares that the catch will no longer be worth the effort.

In the afternoon Jamie sits with Buffalo Hair, beheading and gutting the fish and tossing the innards to the waiting dogs, then splitting the bodies open to be salted and dried on racks. Ange has moved close to them, busily reducing firewood to kindling with a hatchet.

"She like you," says Buffalo Hair.

Jamie considers Ange, sinewy and quick eyed, always with an air of hunger. “She likes a’ the young men.”

“Alla them give her things. But she *like* you.”

This is news to Jamie. “I am flattered.”

“You damn well ought to be.”

THEY BEGIN TO HARVEST THE LAST OF THE MAIZE, EVEN some of the men from both sides of the river helping to carry heavy baskets full of the ears to the spot where it is either husked or tied together for hanging and drying. There is a festive mood to the activity, like the reaping of the oat fields when Jamie was a boy, and on the afternoon of the final day of the picking the whole village gathers in a large fallow field that has been tromped flat, a tall pole erected at either end of it, perhaps two hundred yards apart. Jamie notices, as he stands at the edge of the activity wondering what this gathering will become, that several of the younger men and women are holding long sticks bent into a loop at the end, and that loop fitted with a small basket of leather strips. Shingas appears before him with one of these, thrusting it into his hands and giving him rapid and fervent instructions, the words coming so fast that all he can distinguish is *mpapi*—play.

“Shingas, ’e has wager much upon this contest,” says LaCroix, coming up behind him, “and ’ees *équipe manque les jouers*.”

“I dinnae ken the game nor the rules—”

“*Trés facile*—you are with the clan of the Wolf. You ’ave to knock down the Turtle.”

Those without sticks in their hands are stepping away, while Shingas continues to push Jamie toward the young players.

“But I dinnae ken which clan they belong tae!”

LaCroix smiles and shrugs. “*Tant pis pour toi*.”

A hard round ball is thrown in the air and the game begins amid cheering and whoops from the spectators. At first it seems only to be mayhem, a great deal of flailing with sticks and tripping and blows with the elbow, the ball traded from the little basket on one person's stick to another several times but never leaving the center of the field. Then one player breaks away with it, half the participants chasing him and the other half trying to escort him toward one of the poles.

"Shinty, is it?" mutters Jamie, and then is thwacked on the back with a stick, driving him to his knees.

"*Bouge de là!*" calls Ange, grinning as she trots away.

As he gets back to his feet Jamie notes the spectators who are pointing at him, much amused.

"Laugh, ye ignorant bastarts!" he says and then there is a warning shout and he looks up to see the ball flying at him, reflexively bringing his stick up to protect his face, the sphere landing solidly in the net, as everybody on the field suddenly rushes toward him, weapons in hand.

"*Qui est un loup?!*" he cries, sidestepping to dodge the first attacker. "Who's a bluidy Wolf?!"

Receiving no reply, Jamie manages to duck and feint away from a few, then turns to sprint for the near post in the hope of reaching it before he can be hacked to death. One young man, well ahead of him, turns to block his path, but Jamie flips the ball in the air, catching it in the webbing on the other side of him, eliciting whoops from the watchers. But several players catch up to run alongside of him, flailing with their sticks to thrash him in the ribs, the legs, across the face, and there is Shingas standing before the goal post, a pistol leveled at him and waving his other hand, shouting for him to run the other way. Jamie whirls and flings the ball well over the heads of his pursuers, where it comes to ground and rolls to the feet of Killbuck, lagging behind all to catch his breath. He scoops it up and runs uncontested for the opposite goal post, the crowd of players reversing direction in pursuit. Jamie sinks to his knees, out of breath, smarting in a dozen places. Shingas runs past him, whooping happily, firing his pistol into the air.

And then Ange is there, grinning, offering her hand. He takes it cautiously and she helps him to his feet.

"*Bien joué*," she says, then slaps him on the buttocks and runs after the others. Jamie watches, gently fingering the bridge of his nose to see if it has been broken.

In the evening Jamie limps through the village, scraped and bruised, wondering if all those out celebrating are members of the Wolf Clan. Killbuck passes unsteadily, thumping him on the back and saying something about *linàm*, luck, and then Buffalo Hair, looking worried, waves him over to her *wikëwam*.

"You best stay out of sight fo a spell."

"Our clan won."

"Gonna be some traders' rum passed round tonight. The mens gets testy, commence to playin' with their knives." She looks over to Ange's lonely hut. "Gonna be busy in there, too."

But Ange stands in the doorway, beckoning to him.

"You seen what she done with that snake," calls Buffalo Hair when he starts away.

Ange waves for him to enter, then points to a bearskin robe spread by the fire. He sits. There are far more things in here than inside the hut of Shingas and Cloud Woman, most of them trinkets, a few of them practical. Ange has a warm poultice, something wet and wrapped in leaves, in her hand, and kneels by Jamie to apply it to the swelling around his right eye.

He doesn't know what to say in any language.

She studies his face for a moment, then brings her own close and kisses him.

"*Je suis Ange*," she says then. "*Tous les jeunes hommes m'apportant des cadeaux*."

Jamie holds his empty palms up. "I've naething tae give ye."

She smiles. "*Je penserai à quelque chose.*" And kisses him again.

Parts of him hurt and parts of him feel wonderful as they make love, just as one half of him is hot and the other cold lying next to the fire, and not since his trysts with Lady Jane Porter has he been given so much instruction. Ange smells of woodsmoke and of the bear grease the women use to make their hair shine and speaks in Lenape more than in French, but it is the first he has been touched without malice for several years and extremely welcome.

Later, Jamie is adding sticks to the fire when Sees the Light, one of Ange's frequent visitors, stumbles in, drunken, surprised to see him there. Sees the Light begins to complain, spitting his words, but Ange sits up and crossly tells him to leave. He glares at Jamie, grumbles something with *mwekane*, their word for dog, in it, then leaves, falling to his knees when he ducks through the entrance and crawling away.

Ange shakes her head.

The young ones, she says, have no manners.

"*J'AI BESOIN DE TON AIDE.*"

He has been moody, St. Cyr, for over a month, irritable, silent at meals, coming home later and later. Jenny has only dared once to ask what the trouble might be, prompting a glacial "*Cette une affaire des hommes.*"

She is to travel back to Saint Pierre, this time by boat, to deliver a letter to a certain Dutchman, van der Wal, a noted clothier in the city, and he will give her something in return. She will spend the rest of her day purchasing items of no great expense and sail back on the morrow. Amély is to accompany her for appearance's sake, but not to be informed of the actual mission, as slaves are incapable of keeping a secret from others of their station, and soon the entire island would be buzzing with the news. The Lieutenant does not reveal either the purpose or any further detail of this transaction.

But Jenny assumes it is money trouble.

It is good sport playing the *grand dame* aboard the ship, dressed in her finest, strolling the deck with parasol always in hand, Amély following a half step behind. The voyage is smooth, a pod of dolphins cavorting alongside for miles and the crew members touching their hats when they pass her. There is no one picking oakum in the hold, of course, but when offered a peek belowdecks by the captain she politely defers. Some of the sailors are mulattos, possibly even free men, and Amély enjoys flirting with these.

The *auberge* St. Cyr has chosen for them is clean enough, and they retire early. She has been pretending that the trip is only a whim on her part, that she is bored in Fort Royal and the Lieutenant has acceded to her pleas for diversion.

Amély is not fooled.

Whatever you have been sent to do, she says, "*Je suis à ton service.*"

Jenny thanks her, then shrugs her shoulders apologetically, wishing she could share the adventure. "*Cette une affaire des blancs.*"

Once outside van der Wal's establishment, only a few winding blocks from the inn, Jenny suggests that Amély might want to see if she can locate her Abélarde, who she has been mooning over since their return to Fort Royal.

"*À vot souhait, Mam'selle,*" says her *bonne* with a grin and a curtsy, and then hurries away. She still calls Jenny *cher* at home when the Lieutenant is not present, but loves to play the ladies' maid in public, enjoying the demonstrations of *politesse* as much as the improvement in wardrobe.

Jenny has not been in this shop before. Dresses and other items of women's clothing are displayed on one side of the principal aisle, bolts of cloth, some of very fine material, stacked on a roller system on the other. A wisp of a young man in very tight breeches, a measuring cord draped over one arm, gives her a slight bow.

"*Puis-je vous aidez, Madame?*"

"*Je cherche Monsieur van der Wal.*"

"*Un instant, s'il vous plaît, il est de retour.*"

The young man steps through a door into the rear of the shop. Jenny has the letter, which she has not even considered opening, clutched in her hand, and experiences a little *frisson* of nerves. Whatever her *maître* is up to is obviously illegal, and as someone who has suffered at the whimsy of the law—

The young man steps out, indicates the open door beside him.

"*Il vous invite à le rejoindre, Madame.*"

The rear is a forest of hanging cloth and uncovered metal dress forms. Van der Wal, florid of face and with hair so blond it seems white, does not rise from the chair he sits in behind a desk covered with papers.

He looks her over boldly before he speaks in English.

"You haf something to gif me, *mijn schat?*"

"Ye ken what I'm here fer, then—"

"You are St. Cyr's doxy, *ja?*"

Not knowing how much trouble her *maître* is in, Jenny cannot pretend to be insulted. The Dutchman holds out his hand.

"Gif."

She hands him the letter, which he opens and reads with a bemused look on his face.

"You know what this is saying?"

"I have an idea. Yer tae give me something—"

"Perhaps."

"Not perhaps. I've come a' this way."

Van der Wal points to a small cot in the corner of the room.

"You sit there, and maybe we do a business."

Jenny sees nothing handy to smash the man with. "Tis no part of the agreement."

The Dutchman smiles, handing the letter back to her. "But it is. There in the third sentence—"

Jenny recognizes St. Cyr's hand, but has no idea where sentences might begin or end. She experiences another *frisson*, this one of anger—the Lieutenant is too jealous a man to have written what is being suggested, and this Dutchman is counting on her ignorance. She lays the letter back down on the desk, bends to bring her face very close to his.

"Whatever the twa of ye is up tae, he's the mon who's got muckle fellas with guns in their hands at his beck and call. Ye'd dae well tae keep that in mind."

Van der Wal laughs then, his jowls shaking. "You are staying at the Bijou de Port, *ja?* I haf it sent there."

"I leave tomorra—"

He waves her away. "No worries. Go."

Jenny spends the afternoon wandering among her favorite shops on the Grand Rue, buying only a few *mouchoirs* for Amély. Her *bonne* is waiting in the room when she returns to the inn, along with a sizable leather-covered chest sitting on the floor beside her bed.

"*C'était ici quand je suis rivé*," Amély explains, waving at it, and Jenny doesn't ask her to leave. The chest is filled only with scraps of cloth, but it takes the both of them to drag it to a corner away from the bed. Jenny arranges the handkerchiefs she bought neatly on top of the scraps, then straps the chest closed. Amély sits on it then, grinning wickedly.

"*Un 'tit cadeaux pour le maître*?"

"*Quoi d'autre?*" says Jenny, wanting to hug her. "*Et as-tu trouvé ton Abélarde?*"

The grin grows wider. A short visit, says Amély, but a sweet one.

Jenny hires the porter from the *auberge* to haul the chest to the ship, the captain ordering it safely stowed in his cabin. There are no dolphins to escort the return voyage, the sea much rougher, and Jenny spends her time within the cabin comforting Amély, stricken with *mal de mer.*

St. Cyr invites her to his room for the opening of the chest.

Beneath the mass of cloth is a false bottom, and that is filled with coins—copper, brass, silver, a few of gold. Jenny helps the Lieutenant sort them into piles on his bed, he muttering all the while as he keeps a tally.

"*Aucune pròbleme avec le Hollandais*?" he asks when he is satisfied in full.

Jenny has a twinge of doubt, wondering at exactly what the letter may have stated, but shakes her head.

"*Seulement un commerce*," she shrugs.

St. Cyr confesses then that his gambling has nearly ruined them, and that with payment of his debts no longer able to be honorably postponed, he has been forced to delve into the *marché noir* for salvation. A privateer of his aquaintance is in touch with the captain of an English merchantman with a hold full of prohibited goods, which the Dutchman was eager to receive and sell to discreet customers. The privateer's men handled the clandestine docking, the unloading, and land transport of the cargo, with St. Cyr responsible only for transferring a few soldiers from their observation posts on the coast. But van der Wal has been slow in paying, claiming that he first had to sell the merchandise, obliging the stern letter from the Lieutenant—

"*Et cela suffira?*" asks Jenny, indicating the treasure spread out on the bed.

The privateer has already been paid, he assures her, and this will just answer his obligations. As for the future—

"*Mais vous avez votre salaire*—"

St. Cyr laughs, telling her that the salary of a Lieutenant of *bombardiers* is far from equal to the expenses of the household.

"Perhaps ye sud no hae selt yer plantation."

He takes her hand then, sitting with the piles of coins toppling behind them, and tells her how when he was still only a boy *la variole*—the smallpox—had swept the island, killing hundreds in the cities and larger towns, and how his father, determined to insure the continuance of the St. Cyr name, sent him away to a tutor in a mountain village. On his return a year later, the *variole* having exhausted itself, his mother and sisters lay in their graves. His one great desire from that time on was to have nothing to do with his father's plantation. The land has collected its ransom from him, he declares, and he owes it not a moment of his care or consideration.

"But ye'll no a'ways be ainly a lieutenant," says Jenny, offering some comfort. "There's promotion tae be had."

The *maître* smiles sadly, understanding.

"*Cela dépend*," he tells her, "*en nos amis les anglais*."

Then asks her to stay the night in his bed.

WHEN JAMIE COMES OUT FROM ANGE'S HUT THERE ARE already people hurrying toward the river. Emerging from several canoes are a white man in his early thirties, surrounded by Haudenosaunee carrying bundles. One of these lags behind and draws the largest group of excited onlookers as he pulls a shying horse off a raft that has had one corner pulled up on shore.

Killbuck appears to block Jamie's way, telling him that Shingas wants him in the longhouse.

He has only been in the huge, windowless structure once, laying in a stock of firewood under Cloud Woman's supervision. The room features a low wooden platform running the length of one side, all draped with reed mats and furs, with a large firepit at each end and ample space on the pounded earth floor for dancing and celebration. When he is able to push through the crowd around the south entrance, past the post bearing the ubiquitous carved countenance of a man, the *mesingw*, Living Solid Face, and duck inside, Jamie finds that Shingas is already sitting at the far end, flanked by a few of the other important village men—Red Warrior, Killbuck, Shingas's brother Tamaqua, which means Beaver—with LaCroix standing behind the wise men, visibly upset to see Jamie approaching.

The white man sits facing them on a bear robe, beside him a light-skinned man who wears typical trader's clothes but has a stripe of red paint across his forehead and earlobes extended and wound with brass wire and feathers. The other Haudenosaunee—Oneida, by Jamie's guess—have unrolled woolen Hudson Bay Company blankets, white with stripes of indigo, yellow, red and green, and are laying out the gifts that have been brought upon them—a trio of long rifles, powder, metal pots, and axes and knives, a small chest full of glass beads, and, most notably, a gleaming officer's saber.

When these are settled and the Haudenosaunee men seated, it is Tamaqua, Beaver, who begins to speak in Lenape, never taking his eyes off the white man, who he addressed as *xinkòlëpay*—their word for a buck deer. Jamie is surprised at how much he understands, the orator speaking slowly and formally while the Buck and his mixed-blood companion listen with polite and undivided attention. A fire is lit behind them, a shaft of sun slanting in through the smokehole above, and there are torches stuck in the ground on either side of Shingas, flame light playing on his face as he stares at his guests without expression.

When Beaver is finished there is a moment of silence, as if allowing the words time to be considered, like food digested after a meal, and then without prompting LaCroix repeats the entire greeting in French, even to the point of using the French word

Iroquois for Haudenosaunee. The guests look not at him but into the eyes of Shingas and the other men of the Lenape council, and when LaCroix is finished there is another long silence.

A very long silence.

Until the white man turns to look at Jamie, standing awkwardly to one side of the gathering.

"I believe it'd be your turn now, lad."

Jamie has been following the words closely, hoping to improve his Lenape, and is able to the address the white man, who turns his attention back to the council.

"He says it's been a long journey that brings ye tae us. He—he brushes the dust frae yer feet—he wipes the weariness frae yer eyes that ye might see the truth, and he—"

"And he lifts the hivvy burthen from me shoulders."

An Irishman.

"Aye," says Jamie. "He does that."

"Ye can skep the rest iv the formalities and tell them I come here with gifts from his good friend George—"

"George?"

Smiling pleasantly, the Irishman does not take his eyes from Shingas or raise his voice. "*King* George, ye feckin' eejit. And mind ye be polite in the sayin' iv it."

Jamie stumbles after the first couple words in Lenape.

"*En français*," says LaCroix.

"*Ils vient ici avec des cadeaux de votre bon ami Georges*—"

LaCroix translates this to Lenape, and Jamie realizes he is in for a very long day.

Expressions of respect and good will are exhanged, only Beaver and the Irishman, whose name is Croghan, and occasionally his mixed-blood partner, Montour, speaking as the others listen without moving a muscle. Food is brought in then, only LaCroix and Jamie left standing and not invited to eat, and as Cloud Woman and a few of the more attractive young girls clear the bowls and remains, the Buck praises the hospitality of his hosts and the warmth of their lodge. There is an underlying tension, however, always present during the visits of the Haudenosaunee. One man in particular, a Seneca called Tanaghrisson and called by LaCroix "*le demi-roi*," has made several visits strolling about the village with a superior air and leaving Shingas in a black mood.

"*Ils pensent qu'ils sont les maîtres de tous*," LaCroix has warned him, that it was the Haudenosaunee who destroyed his own people and who had defeated the Lenape in a great war in the past, thus claiming dominion over them. They are like a great storm from the north, always rumbling, threatening to sweep down and wreak havoc—

The Irishman rises and lays the saber in front of Shingas, then sits back in his place.

"I offer this long knife to me great friend Shingas, that he might wield it agin his enemies."

Jamie repeats this in French, and LaCroix into Lenape.

"And now, me lad," says the Buck, raising his voice a bit higher but keeping his eye on the council members, "ye can do yerself a favor. Ye do a proper job convincin' the wee fella to go our way, and I'll see what I can do about buying ye back from these savages."

Jamie manages to keep his face a blank.

"And what dae ye want fer me tae say?"

"Tell him first that when the Dellyware return from their winter hunt, their good friend George will be eager to buy all the skins they've taken."

Jamie and LaCroix translate this.

"And as he very well knows, our goods is both chaper and iv better quality than them iv certain ither parties, and that his good friend George is prepared to be much more genrous than in the past."

They translate, LaCroix allowing his upset to color his voice as he realizes where the talk is heading. It is Shingas who speaks now, his voice mild, as if they are chatting, and LaCroix responds for him—

"*Et que voudrai t'il notre grand ami Georges en échange?*"

"And what would our great friend George expect in return?"

"In return, is it?" says the Irishman, putting on his most benevolent expression. "Why, only the peltries as yer men bring us to trade. Of course—and I'm spakin' of a very unlikely possibility now—if there was to again be some sort of—of *dif*ficulty between George and this other party—"

"*Louis*," Jamie interjects, giving it the French pronunciation.

"That's the fella. Well—as they say, the enemy iv my friend is *my* enemy."

Shingas and Croghan, the Irishman, keep their eyes locked as the translation proceeds. At the end of it Shingas speaks again, then LaCroix looks to Jamie.

"*Il veut savoir ce que vous pensez de cet homme.*"

Meaning the Irishman.

Jamie believes, from watching their faces, that the mixed-blood Montour, and possibly even Croghan, understand French.

He speaks slowly in Lenape, struggling to make some of the sounds.

I know very little of this man, he tells Shingas, but he speaks for the English, and the English are snakes.

He sees Montour's jaw tighten as he says the word *xkukàk*, snakes.

"What are ye sayin'?" asks Croghan, still not looking at him.

"I told him that everything he has heert about the great King George is true."

Shingas speaks again, and LaCroix translates into French and then nods to Jamie.

"He says ye've traveled far and spoken well," Jamie tells the visitors. "He says ye're welcome in his village and nae harm shall come tae ye here. Killbuck will show ye to yer shelter fer the night."

AS THE PARTY FOLLOWS KILLBUCK OUT FROM THE LONG-house, Croghan mutters to Andrew Montour.

"Did the little shite say what I think?"

The Oneida considers before answering.

"He does not love the English."

Shingas and elders remain silent for a long while. Jamie waits to be dismissed, but then Shingas speaks directly to him in Lenape.

There is bad blood still between his people, the English, and our friend Louis.

Jamie agrees that this is true.

The headman nods solemnly, thinking.

Those who trade for our friend Louis will come soon, offering more gifts.

Jamie tells him that this is not a bad thing.

Shingas holds his eyes, Jamie realizing that everyone else in the room is watching him.

A woman may accept gifts from many young men, Shingas tells him, but a day comes when she must choose which one to lie with.

AS JAMIE LEAVES THE LONGHOUSE, CLOUD WOMAN meets his eyes, but has no instruction for him, as if he is no longer her servant.

But Ange has Jamie recount every detail that night, her eyes sparkling with the reflection of their little fire as they lie together. It is a great thing to be invited into the longhouse, she says, a place she has never viewed, and a greater one to be trusted to pass the words of important men to each other. She uses the word *mengwe*, men without penises, for the Haudenosaunee, and tells him that Croghan is not only a great and wealthy trader, but also an appointed spokesman for the council fire of Pennsylvania. She vows to help Jamie improve his skill with Lenape, so that at the next council her brother will not be needed. And then she makes eager love to him, Jamie used to her smell by now and Ange never complaining about his.

He sleeps very little, naming, in his mind, every object in the village in the Indian tongue, even waking Ange up once to ask the word for war club.

"*Pakàskinkwehikànēm*," she says, groggily.

He has to pronounce it several times, with her help, before it is his.

"*Et pourquoi penses-tu à la guerre?*" she asks.

He tells her of his capture, of Aeneas Cameron brained and scalped by the Shawnee.

But it was good luck for you, she tells him in Lenape. For it has brought you among the First People.

SHINGAS DOES NOT SLEEP WELL EITHER, SMOKING BY the fire in his *wikëwam* well into the night. There is much to consider, his people in a spot in the river where the current does not run clearly in one direction or the other, but seems to swirl on all sides, threatening to pull a swimmer or even an entire canoe under the water. Though the French and the King George people claim to be at peace, it is obvious that their traders are hoping to steal the hearts of the various tribes of red people from the other, using bribery and lies and sometimes even killings, as young Langlade has done in attacking the Twightwee at Pickawillanee in the far west country. During the last white man's war there had been some, especially the Haudenosaunee, who grew fat by threatening one side that they would defect to the other if not given gifts of powder and shot and special consideration in trading. This was easy for those close to the French or English strong houses and armies, but a dangerous game out here far from white men but situated between their forces.

Two of the thirteen great fires of the King George men, Pennsylvania and Virginia, have brought Shingas and others to their capitals to make them promises, promises that also contain threats, while the French, though not so numerous, join with their friends the Shawnee and Wyandot to harass English traders and those who deal with them.

There are some, like his Shawnee brother Bone, who say it is good when the white nations fight, that even if they do not manage to kill each other off completely, it weakens them and slows the movement of their mongrel people into Indian lands. But great wars, he knows, are like the firing of a wood on a windy day—they can change direction in a moment.

CROGHAN AND HIS PARTY LEAVE IN THE MORNING WITH no ceremony, paddling their canoes to the north.

Jamie is summoned to go to Shingas, the headman stroking the muzzle of his new horse that is tied to a post by the longhouse.

This is a fine gift our friend George has sent me.

Jamie looks the animal over. He has never seen a Lenape on a horse here in Kittanning, though he believes their word *nehënaonkès* is used to name the beast.

It needs to be fed and groomed, he says.

Shingas hands him the reins. You will do these things.

Jamie nods, wondering if this is a test. There are pathways through the woods leading away from the village that might be wide enough to ride on, but he has no idea how far they go or where they lead to.

I will, he says.

Shingas looks into the great liquid eye of the horse.

Gifts from white men, he says, have a way of becoming burdens.

THEY HEAR ST. CYR CALLING FOR AMÉLY, HEAR SOMEthing crash to the floor. Amély lights a lamp for each of them, and they find him in the room his father used to conduct business in, now full of trunks and unneeded furniture.

"*Je cherche l'épée de mon père!*" he announces loudly. The *maître* does not say why he needs his father's sword, but staggering in at this hour, reeking of liquor and shouting, it is of no avail to question him. Jenny sees a light blaze on in the carriage house where Guillaume sleeps, more comfortably now that the horses have been sold to satisfy gambling debts. Amély quickly finds the épée, unsheathed but unbent, in one of the trunks, and St. Cyr proceeds to pace the room swishing it about, the women stepping quickly to stay out of his path.

"*J'en ai besoin,*" he says, over and over. "*J'en ai besoin!*"

"*Et pourquoi?*" Jenny finally ventures.

It spills out of him then, with considerable venom, LeGrasse a braggart and a knave, and, worse than that, of equal rank to Lieutenant St. Cyr and therefore not to be denied satisfaction when he demanded it in response to the *maître* accusing him of clumsily palming the ace of clubs, a fact none of the junior officers at the table dared to comment upon.

The result is that they must duel.

"*Duel? Quand?*"

"*Quand je suis prêt, bien sûr!*" he says as if it is obvious. "*Nous ne sommes pas des montagnards écossaises!*" then goes on to explain that he, as an officer of the artillery, cannot be expected to be as proficient a swordsman as LeGrasse, who trained for the infantry before his transfer to the marines, and therefore adequate time must be given for him to prepare.

Jenny does not ask if his opponent is forbidden to also practice during this period, becoming even more skilled, or to wonder out loud what became of St. Cyr's resolution to do his drinking at home and refrain from gambling altogether.

A tutor is engaged the next day, a handsome *insigne*, roughly Jenny's age, named Paillard, who is reputed to be a terror with the *épée*. Each day, instead of indulging in the afternoon mess with his peers, St. Cyr retires behind the house to cross swords, *épée* tips carefully buttoned, with this prodigy of the blade. Jenny is invited to watch his progress, sitting in the shade beside a small table on which Amély places cooling drinks for the *épéistes*. At some point Paillard sits beside her to observe his pupil's form as he battles an imaginary opponent—the *attaque au fer*, the *glissé*, the *balestras* and *ripostes*, the rapid *flèche*, the deceptive *coupé*—all the while making verbal love to her.

It is not unflattering.

Paillard says that she is the most exquisite woman he has yet seen on this island. He compliments not only her beauty but her obvious intelligence, her freedom from the affectations that plague most of the other *dames blanches* here, he even tells her there is a charming lilt to her pronunciation of his language, a *soupçon* of celtic mystery to it, that inflames his passion and makes him wish to suggest that which, given his rank and station, he dare not. But as much as Jenny would like to be or even somewhat resemble the creature he describes, he says all these things in French, which she loves to speak and loves to hear and does not trust a word of. Something in the music of it, perhaps, like song with more flourish than melody, something in the way he coos to her while rarely taking his eye off his superior officer, parrying *pointe a pointe* with an invisible LeGrasse. Jenny tells him, pleasantly, that his misgivings are valid, and that he'll be wise to make no more suggestions.

She chooses not to bother the Lieutenant with this, more concerned about the duel, which has still no fixed date, and her *protecteur*'s chances of surviving it. Her first thoughts upon contemplating that St. Cyr might, if the character and swordfighting prowess of his opponent are not exaggerated, be killed, are to wonder what will become of her, an unmarried foreign refugee on this island of masters and slaves. She has seen a few women in Saint Pierre who

Amély assured her are prostitutes, and knows of a few more who manage and possibly own inns or shops. And then, if young Paillard is good for his word, she could become his mistress, with a considerably reduced *style de vie.*

She has seen a few dirk fights in the clachan, brief and nasty, and is no judge of swordwork, but the Lieutenant shows no promise of ever becoming as catlike of foot and deft of wrist as his tutor, in fact appearing not to have improved at all after several weeks of training.

"*Qu'est-ce qui se passarait si*—" she begins one night in his sturdy boat of a bed after they have made love, finding it difficult to find the right words in any language, "*si*—if ye don't win yer duel?"

"*C'est possible, oui,*" he acknowledges.

"*Mais si tu es tué*—"

St. Cyr reassures her that in most cases the seconds intercede when first blood is drawn.

"*Mais si ce sang vient de ton coeur*—"

Flattered by her concern, he again reassures her that the heart is an organ not easily penetrated, and begins to explain the various defensive gambits by which he will avoid such an outcome.

"*Mais si l'insigne ne tu donne son meilleur instruction*—"

It is a mistake.

St. Cyr asks why in the world Paillard would *not* be giving him his best advice, for what could he possibly have to gain, and when Jenny has no answer, he knows all.

"*Qu'est'ce q'il t'a dit?*"

He is never crude, Paillard, only comparing her to beautiful things and proposing what he'd do if circumstances were different—

Jenny shakes her head. "*Rien*—"

"*Dits moi. C'est mon droit de savoir.*"

"*Seulement les bêtises*—in French the words sound daft tae me."

Try as he might, Jenny does not reveal to St. Cyr details of any of the silly things the boy has said, pretending that perhaps her comprehesion has failed her and that she is mistaken about his interest. St. Cyr does not ask her what, if anything, she has said to him in response or if she is attracted to him, ending her attempts to explain his suspicions away by placing two fingers over her lips.

"*Tais-toi, mon amour. Cette une affaire des hommes.*"

Two weeks pass without incident, with the Lieutenant, *épée* in hand, giving his young instructor a very formal *salut* before they engage, and though he does seem to be concentrating more intensely on the lessons, especially when they are *engagé*, Jenny sees no rancor in his movement. Paillard sits by her as usual, stepping up his campaign of blandishment somewhat though never quite proposing a specific time or place for an assignation, till Jenny wonders if this might only be practice for him, something to maintain his form until a real contest presents itself.

She does not see the button on St. Cyr's *épée*, loosened somehow, fly off the point, and apparently neither does Paillard, not in time to disengage before the Lieutenant drives the sword several inches into the flesh just beneath his collarbone with a *doublé* he has never exhibited before.

St. Cyr extracts his sword carefully and has his skewered ensign sit by the small table, then sends Amély running to the barracks to summon the surgeon. Paillard presses his thumb hard against the puncture wound, but blood begins to soak his shirt around it. Jenny, on her feet and unprepared for this moment, is asked by her *maître* to look in the grass for the missing button, as if to prevent his épée from doing any further mischief.

"*Quel accident,*" croons St. Cyr with great sincerity. "*Avoir une lame nue juste au moment que j'ai eu de la chance.*"

Not luck at all, Paillard, who is beginning to breathe with some difficulty, assures him, his *compétance* has grown admirably. Perhaps Lieutenant LeGrasse should be informed that the field of honor can be prepared—

WAKENED BY A SENSE OF THINGS MOVING WITHOUT HIM, Jamie steps from Ange's hut to see several groups of men already out in the light before sunrise, three distinct groups of them gearing up to leave. Killbuck, bow in hand and a bulging duffel slung over his shoulder, passes with Red Warrior and LaCroix.

"*Où allez vous?*"

LaCroix explains, in Lenape, that it is time for the men who are able to go on a long hunt.

And what should I do? asks Jamie.

LaCroix winks, something Jamie has never seen a full-blooded Lenape do. Keep the women happy, he says.

As LaCroix and his companions join a group of others heading on foot toward the distant tree line, Jamie sees that Cloud Woman is out, helping Shingas to prepare. There are things a Lenape woman does not touch, and others that she is welcome to. Shingas, though acknowleged as the leader of the village, has no spoken title that Jamie is aware of and seems not to receive any form of tribute, in fact always being the last to help himself at any communal feast.

"Winter comin'."

Buffalo Hair is beside him, holding a robe of raccoon skins stitched together around herself. He joins her in walking toward the river.

"Ever year the French wants more skins for what they give us. English, too. An ever year you got to go farther away to fine any deer."

Villagers step around them, hurrying to see their hunters off.

"Our men goin' up into where the *mengwe* hunts, or down round the Catawbas, Cherokees and Muskogees—whilst they comin' up here lookin for the same thing. Make for a lot more contention."

"So why not stop trading with them?"

The black woman raises her eyebrows at him. "You know how to make a axe outta stone? Make a pot from the mud, or gunpowder, or where you find the flint you use to set it off?"

"No—"

"An neither does most of these people, not anymore. You gonna get a rifle to hunt with, axe, knife, iron pot, wool blanket—you best have you somethin' the white fokes *want*."

"And there's the rum—"

"Rum take a bit of the *sting* away, but it run you into debt quicker than the gamblin' do. Most of these men sit down to barter, they already owes the trader for the powder and shot they used to get the skins."

The river is full of canoes now, full of hunters pulling away from the bank, some heading upstream, some down. The women and children and old men left behind watch as the canoes glide away.

THEY ARE BUILDING A BIGGER FIRE IN ANGE'S *WIKËWAM* for the nights now, cold creeping in along the ground from the outside like spilled water till it begins to fill you up. Ange always pushes him toward the fire, warming his other side under the fur robe. He can feel by her breathing that she is not asleep.

Have you traveled far from here? he asks.

They have agreed, without stating it, to speak mostly in Lenape, Jamie having to rehearse the phrases quickly in his head before speaking.

Ange wriggles from beneath the fur, then crawls away from him. Her shape blurs as she moves away from the fire.

If you walk three or four days and nobody kills you, she says without turning to look at him, there are towns of white men.

Those must be upstream.

Yes. And to the east.

In the flicker from the fire Jamie sees the bow hung near the dooway, wonders which of her lovers among the young men presented that to her.

The men have left me here—

They're afraid if they take you on the hunt you'll frighten the game away.

A three day walk, he thinks, if one prepares and has an idea of where one is going—

LaCroix has said that captives who try to run away, thus insulting the First People, are brought back and tortured in various horrible ways before they are thrown into a great fire. Unless they are caught first by the *mengwe*, who will cook and eat them.

Ange reappears, holding something, then laying them on his chest.

A pair of new moccasins, beautifully crafted, porcupine quills dyed red and blue used for the stitching around the toe.

"*Pour moi?*"

Who else?

Jamie sits up to look at them, moved. He has seen other village women fashioning these for their men, knows something of the work involved—

You made these?

Ange comes back under the fur, brushing his hip and turning her body so he can't see her face.

So that when you run away from me, she says, your feet won't be injured.

EACH DAY IS COLDER THAN THE NEXT, THE BROADLEAF trees bare now and the forest floor soft with disintegrating piles of what has fallen. There is no more weeding or harvesting to do, most of the women and many of the children searching the nearby woods for the last of the chestnuts, most of the yellow-green burrs open enough by now to reveal the glossy brown fruits within, and now that the closest deer have all been hunted out for trade hides, squirrels are the main competitor for their collection. Jamie has ventured farther than he ever has before, discovering a good yield under a tree that doesn't seem to have been visited before, when the screams begin.

He breaks out of the woods, empty handed, to see perhaps a dozen Indians he does not recognize hurrying acoss his path carrying bundles of cured deer hides and dragging three children and a teenage girl from the village along with them. Three of the party in the rear spot Jamie and begin to run for him, war clubs in hand. He sprints for the huts, smoke beginning to issue from the top and sides of several of them, racing the invaders. An arrow slices through the air, passing his hip, and he hears a cry from one of the pursuers immediately behind him. Ange stands outside her *wikëwam*, bow dangling from her wrist as she pushes the head of her next arrow into the little sack she stores her poison in, then notches it and draws as Jamie runs past her to the headman's house, too quickly to register why Cloud Woman is wailing and tearing at her own hair.

The saber from Croghan hangs from a cord on the back wall. By the time Jamie is out again there are other villagers massing, many with hoes or axes in hand, and he yanks the reins from the pole and is on the wild-eyed horse's back, slapping at its rump with the flat of the sword to goad it between two burning huts.

The animal has been ridden before.

Ange is already running after the retreating men, one with an arrow in his thigh held between his two comrades, when Jamie rides by her, not understanding the phrase that she screams. He gallops across the stubble of maize left on the field, bending forward to hug the horse's neck as one of the retreating men turns to fire his musket, then up raising the saber crying *Ionnsaigh!* before he slashes down completely through the man's wrist and across his neck, continuing the gallop toward the men trailing with the captives, only a few hundred yards from the edge of the woods and again the attack cry in Erse as he dashes into the center of them, men and captives scattering, Jamie managing to slow and turn the horse just before they crash into the trees and galloping back, saber held out low to scythe down another running warrior, seeing that the three older captives are loose and running back toward the village, while the last, Pretty Weasel, is still held by the hair by a painted raider. Jamie wheels and heads toward this man, who pushes the girl away and plants himself solidly, gripping a lance ready to impale Jamie or his mount. Jamie squeezes the horse with his knees and feels it respond, quickening its stride, heading straight for the warrior and then veering off at the last moment, dropping the saber and leaning to sweep the girl up with his arm and lay her across the horse's withers.

Trotting back to the village he passes several of the women hacking with hoes and hatchets at the two men he downed, passes the other freed captives in the arms of family and friends. He eases Pretty Weasel down as the woman he recognizes as her mother rushes forward, making an exultant yipping sound. The raiders have all disappeared into the woods with a treasure in deer hides, several bark huts are burning to the ground, but Jamie feels an incredible sense of joy, like his heart is growing, filling up his chest, and he is about to cry out in triumph when he realizes what he is riding over is the brains of Digs Deep, the older brother of Cloud Woman, his head smashed open like a rotten squash.

Jamie dismounts, steps toward Ange, who stares furiously at the tree line, as if her wrath could follow the raiders and kill them.

I hit three, she says. The poison will make them swell until their skin rips open and they will die in pain.

Buffalo Hair approaches, a bloody knife in hand. "Cherokees. Must be getting desprit, comin' up so far from the south."

Ange is staring at Jamie.

I thought you were running away, she says.

Jamie ties the horse back to the post next to Shingas's hut, pats its lathered flank.

A fine animal, he says.

THE DETAILS COME TO HIM AT NIGHT. THEY COME IN fragments and not in the order in which they occurred—the feeling in his hand as the saber chopped through bone, splitting the first Cherokee's shoulder from his neck, the thrill close to nausea, the horse beneath his legs, responding—with a horse like that at Culloden, he might have escaped. There was no thought while it was happening, except the first one as he stepped from the trees—*they're stealing our people.* And now, with her sleeping warm beside him, he realizes if Ange had not been there with her bow he would be dead, scalped, and a quiver of dread jolts through him. There is no safety in this world.

Jamie recalls a day stalking deer with Dougal when he was a boy, much too far onto Fraser land to claim ignorance, and Dougal bringing a buck down with their father's ancient doglock musket, recalls the mix of fear and exhilaration he felt the moment he left clan territory, the tug of sinew against the blade when his brother had him finish the wounded animal. It is all he knows of trespass, all he knows of killing, and for the men of the village it is their life. No wonder the ceremony, the dancing and chanting and purification, the burning of tobacco to please the Great Spirit and solicit its blessing. No wonder Ange collecting poison, no wonder the murder of Aeneas Cameron—killing a man who could not keep pace in enemy territory was no more to Bone than abandoning a leaky canoe.

The fire makes unpredictable, shifting patterns of light and shadow on the ceiling of the *wikëwam*. The recovered saber lies on the floor by Jamie, within easy reach of his hand.

THE DUEL IS POSTPONED INDEFINITELY. MAJOR DE LIANcourt chooses to acknowledge the talk of the *querelle* between his lieutenants, and not only calls them together to forbid their crossing swords, but transfers LeGrasse to Saint Pierre on permanent duty. And LeGrasse, perhaps considering the news that Lieutenant St. Cyr has administered a wound *presque fatal* to his reknowned fencing instructor, makes no great effort to pursue honor outside of official sanction, as any true *homme de valeur* back in France would be expected to.

St. Cyr is philsophical regarding the matter. "*Mes mains sont attachées*," he is often heard to sigh, pressing his wrists together as if they are bound by a cord.

More disturbingly, his superior officer seems to blame him for the *contretemps*, stating that as an older and more experienced man he should know better than to fall into debt, that gambling is the vice of the vain and indolent, and that if they were home instead of in this remote and decadent outpost, sterner measures would have been applied.

St. Cyr does not remind the Major that this *is* his home.

"*Ils gardent les nez en l'air*," he grumbles to Jenny, a charge she has heard a score of *créoles* level against their friends and neighbors born in France. And goes on to complain that he is humiliated in front of his men, that he is used as a lackey, and that if he was not mired in the present *marais économique* he would resign his commission, place his uniforms, everyday and ceremonial, into storage, travel to Saint Pierre to dispatch that *crapule* LeGrasse and then retire to the life of a gentleman.

These rantings are so frequent and so passionate that Jenny decides it is not yet time to share with him the news that Amély has confirmed, through physical observation and a ritual involving a hen's egg in a glass of *anisette*, that she is with child. Her suspicions began with a sudden nausea at the smell of coffee brewing, then a feeling that her clothes were too tight, then the constant urge to pish. Jenny's acceptance of her condition varies from moment to moment, swinging from certainty that it is a curse that will lead to her abandonment and ruin to a kind of wonder that an ignorant, cast off hillskipper living in sin such as herself might be capable of giving life. In her less emotional moments she realizes that she, and this new being, if it survives, will thrive or suffer at the whim of Lieutenant St. Cyr. Amély assures her that if the Lieutenant already had any white *enfants bâtards* on the island she would know—so perhaps he will welcome an heir, legitimate or no. Or, in his straitened circumstances, the expense of keeping a mistress might already be questionable, without adding a child to the burden.

Though Amély's advice is to leave the matter *en les mains de bon Dieu*, Jenny wakes one day determined to marshal her courage and inform St. Cyr on his return from the fort. She rehearses various approaches, some meant to draw out his attitude before the revelation, others much more simple and direct. He arrives much earlier than expected, a somewhat stunned look on his face.

"*Y-a-t'il un problème?*" she asks, seeing his distress.

"*C'est seulment un catastrophe!*" he snorts bitterly, as if she already knows the problem and is making light of it.

Jenny does not instantly panic. A Scots crofter explaining the failure of his crop will admit to "a wee reversal iv fortune," but the Frenchmen she has met here suffer nothing that is short of disaster.

"*Quel genre de catastrophe?*"

St. Cyr looks her in the eye, face drained of color, voice trembling. I'm being transferred, he tells her. "*Ils m'envoient au Canada.*"

THERE ARE ONLY MEN AT THE CEREMONY, IF IT CAN BE named such. Jamie stands before a dozen of the men in the longhouse as Shingas presents him with the saber.

You will have this Long Knife.

"I thank ye," says Jamie. "*Wanìshi.*"

And it will be your name as well. *Kitshikàn*.

The men around Jamie repeat the name approvingly.

"*Kitshikàn.*"

As he is led from the longhouse to the *wikëwam* of Fox Dreaming, he spies Buffalo Hair and LaCroix standing before their hut, the negress smiling and the half Frenchman looking morose.

"*Kitshikàn,*" says Buffalo Hair, somehow having already heard.

"They canna eat me noo," says Jamie.

FOX DREAMING IS ONE OF THE ELDERS, HIS BODY AND face so covered with tattoos it is impossible to judge his age. Jamie's shirt is taken from him and he is told to lie on a bear robe on the ground in front of the hut. The old man sits beside him, laying out on a cloth an array of steel and bone needles of varied thickness, as well as a small bowl with a black paste in it. He begins to carefully draw a figure on Jamie's left breast, dipping his forefinger into the paste between lines. LaCroix arrives and kneels at his head, flashing a steel trader's razor before his eyes.

"When I was *petit garçon*, they pull the 'air each one at a time. But this make it go more fast."

He begins to shave Jamie's tangle of a beard, not gently. Between strokes Jamie is able to look down to see the design taking shape on his chest.

"*C'est la tortue,*" LaCroix explains. "Cloud Woman she wish you to take the place of 'Ee Who Digs Deep. *C'est un grand honneur.*"

"Ah'll be her brother?"

"You must attempt to be as good a man. And Cloud Woman, she is of *l'clan des Tortues*, and so you will carry this image," he says, touching his own unmarked left breast over the heart. "*Proche du coeur.*"

Fox Dreaming begins to insert the needles then, deep enough to draw blood, and occasionally work paste into the new wounds with his thumb. It hurts less than what LaCroix is doing to his face.

"Sae ah'm tae be a Turtle."

"*Il y a seulement trois clans*—the Turtle, the Turkey, the Wolf. Shingas, 'ee is Wolf. When there is *un mariage* it must not be of a man and women of the same clan."

Jamie steals another look. The smear the old man is pricking and rubbing at is roughly the shape of a turtle.

"And what is Ange?"

LaCroix has wrapped one of the hairs at the back of Jamie's head around a small bone with grooves cut into it, like a screw. He yanks the hair out swiftly.

"We 'ave no clan."

Young men wander over to watch for a few minutes, sometimes grunting in approbation. Jamie understands that there is a test to this, that no matter the pain he must not react. He has seen the men, who go nowhere without one of the palm-sized looking glasses they receive in trade, spending long hours plucking their own hair, whether on scalp, face or body, one by one, using either a small clam shell or metal pincers. Jamie hopes that the operation becomes easier and hurts less than it does at present.

When Fox Dreaming is done with his design he rinses off the paste to examine the pattern of welts rising around the needle punctures he's made, nodding with satisfaction. He says something Jamie does not understand.

"'E ask if you 'ave *un guide spirituel.*"

"Guide—?"

"Before, in your other life—"

Jamie thinks. His father was a fearsome enough man, nearly a laird before the forfeiture, that he was able to keep the kirk at arm's distance without consequence. France, of course, was rampant with crosses, being both papist and Latinate, but when Jamie thinks of a symbol it is on the flag his people carried at Culloden—

"The MacGillivrays are of Clan Chattan," he says. "The clan of the cat."

"*Kwèn'shùwënay*," says LaCroix to the old man, giving him the name for a cougar.

Fox Dreaming nods and begins to draw on Jamie's right breast with the black paste.

Jamie knows stories of the Painted Men, those who the Roman legions encountered when they ventured north of the Clyde, said to be fierce warriors who ran naked, though tattooed from head to foot, into battle.

He hopes that Fox Dreaming will be satisfied with only a pair of drawings.

LaCroix, working quickly, has denuded Jamie's head except for a small lock just above the center of his forehead, which he now separates into three strands woven together, decorating these with bits of feather and colored yarn and pausing now and again to show Jamie the results with his small looking glass.

"*Trés beau*," he says. "*Comme un vrai guerrier Lenape*."

IN HER HUT THAT NIGHT ANGE MAKES A KIND OF OINTment, mixing ingredients from her collection of little animals' bladder sacs with bear grease and smoothing it over the proud skin on his chest. She gently traces the outline of the turtle.

Whatever woman you take as a wife, she muses, she will be a Lenape too.

I suppose she will, says Jamie.

It won't matter what her father was.

Jamie lifts her chin with his hand till she reluctantly meets his eyes.

"Ye want that mair than anything, don't ye?"

ANGE WAITS, THE NEXT DAY, FOR THE HOUR WHEN THE most people will be in the village to make her fire. She lays down a base of her driest kindling, tops it with a large reed basket, then fills it with every gift she has ever received from one of her young admirers, one by one, entering and exiting her *wikëwam* each time. No one stops to look, but Jamie has observed that though staring is considered impolite here, the Lenape miss nothing. When the basket is full, her bow laid across the top of it, she drizzles pitch over it all and sets a torch to it. She stands by Jamie as they watch the fire. Cloud Woman steps out from her hut, looks at the fire, then goes back inside. LaCroix has told him he is not to work with the women anymore, which would be an insult to Digs Deep, but he has not yet been invited to join the men in any of their activities. All he knows of his status is that he is allowed to stay with Ange at night and is no longer watched if he wanders near the woods.

The smoke drifts toward them, his newly naked scalp alive to the breeze. The swelling has already begun to diminish around the designs on his chest, a turtle and the head of a cat, bluish black. Standing beside him Ange is chanting something, low and constant, looking as if she will burst with pride. He mutters to himself.

"May God fergive ye, Jamie MacGillivray."

IN THE TIME WHEN THE SNOW FALLS AND COVERS THE ground, Jamie is allowed to join the bear hunters. He is given neither bow nor rifle, but instructed to carry a duffel filled with sticks and dried moss, bulky without having much weight. It is Killbuck and his brother Throws Away and Beaver and Jamie, all with their moccasins filled with moss against the cold and with webbed, oblong hoops tied onto them that allow them to walk on top of the snow without sinking through. Moving with them requires a particular gait that takes Jamie some time to master, the other men breaking trail ahead of him never quite getting out of sight. Once he has found the proper balance and stride, Jamie realizes they have been holding back for his sake, and by the afternoon, now able to match their pace, he is damp with sweat under the hooded elkskin robe, something like a Franciscan habit, that Ange has made for him.

Nothing, of course, is familiar to him, and he is very aware that if their tracks were snowed over he would be lost without his companions. They stop occasionally, Killbuck studying small animal tracks in the snow, but move steadily to what Jamie believes to be the northwest. The men do not speak. They take turns walking in the fore, only Jamie, who does not know where they are or where they are going, absolved of this responsibility, the leader choosing their path through thick stands of trees, choosing whether to go over or around the deadfall, leaving his tracks for the others to step into. Killbuck, the tallest of them, adjusts his stride so that none have to stretch to follow. The men do not speak even when the shadows grow long and they halt in a gully somewhat sheltered from the wind to make camp, do not speak until after they have cut saplings to make a shelter low to the ground and pine branches to start a small fire and eaten the parched corn and leathery strips of venison they have brought and smoked a pipe of tobacco.

Then Killbuck, who is a fellow Turtle and somehow related to Cloud Woman and therefore to Jamie, addresses him in the patient, formal manner that is used when something needs to be understood.

Brother, he says, looking Jamie in the eye across the flames of the fire, as you have only lived with white people, and therefore must be taken by the hand, there are things you must be told that to another man would be obvious. We go at the sun's rising to a country that is not our own. The people there have not our tongue, have not our ways. Their hunters may also venture into our lands, looking for deer, looking for elk, looking for bear, but this does not mean that we share. In the time before the white men came these animals were many and we did not travel far to find them. But now we need the white man's guns, his things made of metal, his woven blankets, and to have them we trade the animal skins. Deer are killed, elk are killed, and their flesh is left for the wolves. So we must trespass in the country of other people and soon we are at war.

Brother—in this country we go to we must be like the owl that makes no sound in flight, we must be like the great cat that hunts but is never seen. We will use our bows and not our rifles in this country, so as not to make a sound, and if we do meet with other men there, we must hope that they are happy and well fed, like the bear whose belly is so filled with fish that he does not stir to fight.

Jamie waits, the fire crackling softly, but Killbuck has no more to say.

I thank you, Brother, for your guidance in these matters, he responds. On this journey I am like the pup whose eyes have newly opened. As we go on, if there are things you must tell me, by word or by sign, I will be grateful.

The men return to their smoking then, and one by one they roll themselves into their blanket to sleep.

In the morning they scatter the saplings of the lean-to and bury the ashes from their fire. The pace of travel is the same, though they seem to pause slightly to look and listen every twenty rods or so. Everything they carry is fastened tightly so it does not rattle or squeak, the Lenape men even wearing a band around their heads to keep their extended earlobes from flapping. The webbed hoops make only the softest thud against the snow, and the leader is careful to avoid spots where fallen branches or protruding rocks might betray their passing.

It is most of the day winding through the trees, never stopping to eat, the men scooping clean snow up in their mittens and melting it in their mouths to drink, eyes on the ground and on the bark of the trees. Jamie's shadow is as long as he is tall when Beaver discovers an old elm with claw marks about the base, pointing to a hollow in it above the first thick branches, maybe thirty feet up.

Killbuck signs to Jamie that he is to pull out sticks and moss from his duffel, the men quickly making a kind of ball from it, as big as

Killbuck's chest, that can be suspended on a longer stick. Beaver stuffs a bit of the dried moss into this, then kneels over it with his musket, sparks lighting it as the flint hits the steel mizzen. The smoldering ball on a stick is handed to Jamie, and Killbuck points up to the hollow.

Jamie speaks in a near whisper.

Once I have done this, Brother, where am I to go?

The men smile.

Move to the far side of the tree, Killbuck tells him, so the bear does not kill you and you are out of the path of our arrows.

Jamie has not climbed a tree in many years. But the bark of the elm is old and rough enough to provide toeholds, and hugging with his knees and digging his fingers into the indentations left by bear claws with his one free hand Jamie slowly struggles his way up the tree, the tangled ball beginning to smoke, till he is within reach of the hollow. It takes several attempts to wedge the ball into the opening, Jamie hoping the creature is in as deep a sleep as Beaver has described to him. Once this is secure he descends as quickly as he can, corkscrewing to the far side of the bole and reaching the ground to find all three of the hunters with bows drawn, pointed up at the hollow, waiting. Their arms hold tension on the bowstring without trembling.

The bear that emerges from the smoke and begins to scrabble down the tree is twice the size that Jamie imagined could fit through the opening, fat and black with claws as long as Jamie's fingers. Beaver puts the first arrow in him, just below the shoulder, and then Killbuck and then Throws Away, the hunters backing up on their snowshoes as Jamie plunges knee deep in snow to the next tree, the bear reaching the ground and loping straight at the men as they calmly notch arrows and fire again, the final arrow driving through the standing bear's neck and sticking out the back and it does not roar but makes an angry huffing sound, steam snorting from its nostrils in the cold air and the shaft of one of the arrows snapping as it drops to all fours and contnues to charge, Beaver fending it off for a moment by jabbing with the sharp end of his bow in his hand but slapped away and the bear stands a final time, makes a coughing sound, and falls forward dead.

Beaver kneels in the snow before the animal and lifts its massive, shaggy head in his heads, looking into the rapidly clouding, open eyes.

Brother, you have acted bravely, for which we thank you. You have done honor to the Spirit of Bear, and we hope to gain strength and courage from your flesh.

They move quickly then, Throws Away gutting the animal, steam blowing out from its innards, and cutting the liver away to hand slices of the raw meat to Killbuck and Beaver as they flay the bear, Jamie helping to tug the hide away from the carcass. Once this is free and laid out, chunks of meat and fat that Killbuck hews loose with his axe are placed in the center of it, then it is rolled and tied off at the paws into a kind of long satchel that Jamie and Throws Away each take an end of. This was a thinking creature only moments ago, thinks Jamie, and now it is in pieces, snow stained red relating the tale of its final moments.

They avoid their own tracks on their route back to Lenape territory, wary that an enemy may be waiting in ambush by these. Before long it grows dark, and they camp without a fire. It is a night colder than any that Jamie has ever experienced, and after using sinew to hang the sections of meat from a high branch, Jamie and Throws Away are rolled into the hide, furry side inward.

Even there, in absolute dark, Jamie is not sure if he is falling asleep or freezing to death. He dreams, at some point, of being a wasp in a hive that is filling with smoke.

In the middle of the next day the men begin to speak again, now and then, no longer anxious about being on strangers' ground.

It is an excellent bear, Beaver announces, an old warrior of a bear, but only one bite for each mouth we have to feed.

He looks around, then reaches up to touch a low branch on the chesnut he stands beside.

We shall search for tracks, he says. And when the sun touches upon this spot we shall return to declare what we have found.

They head in three separate directions then, leaving Jamie with the meat and an improvised cudgel to discourage any wolves who might be following, though Beaver claims that the cold air stops their noses.

Jamie is glad for the rest. He listens to the forest around him, no insect buzz or birdsong, only a deep stillness. He walks in circles around the bulk of the rolled hide, working his fingers inside of his fur mittens. He eats some of the liver that remains, thawing a small piece inside his mouth before chewing and swallowing. He tries to remember details of where they have been and how they have come, but it is still only trees and snow in his mind.

The sun has crept around the trees blocking it and is about to touch on the bough that Beaver chose when Jamie hears, or rather feels the first approaching footfall. Something like a rhythm, the rhythm of a man walking with a peculiar, labored gait. The hunters arrive within moments of each other, with Throws Away, the last, holding up two fingers and pointing in the direction he came from.

They work quickly to haul the entire bear hide and contents well above the ground, and Jamie joins the hunters in hurrying back over Throws Away's tracks.

They stop when they come to a pair of deer tracks, parallel in the snow. The trees are thinner here, but very close together, Jamie judging that there is no straight shot that could fly for more than forty yards before hitting wood.

Stay here, Beaver tells Jamie, and if they come, try to catch the bigger doe.

They leave him again, the three fanning out from each other. It is even colder now, a small breeze moving over the snow, but it is not long before Jamie hears a gunshot and then movement, rapid movement, off to his left, and then a whoop that sounds like Killbuck. The movement seems to drift across in front of him, then to the right, with more whoops, the last from very near and then there is a doe running back at him down the trail it left earlier, struggling in the deep snow, veering away when it sees him and he is chasing, making long loping strides in the snowshoes and falling more than once but the doe is falling too, lurching, sometimes up to her belly in the deep snow, bucking forward and digging with her hind legs and then she just stops, exhausted beyond movement, sinking into the snow, sides heaving as Jamie struggles to catch up with her. Empty handed, he falls sitting into the snow beside her, her eyes bulging with panic but not focusing on him, and then Killbuck catches up, wheezing slightly with the effort, and kills her with a blow of his tomahawk.

They gut the doe and the smaller deer Beaver has shot but do not dress them further, cutting new sinew to poke behind and through the tendons by the hooves, Killbuck throwing one over his shoulder and Beaver the other, while Jamie and Throws Away stagger along with the bundle of bear.

They are able to make a fire that night, and roast deer liver in caul fat from the bear, and the hunters smoke their pipes. Throws Away tells a story that Jamie cannot tell if it is true or fable, about a hunter able to make the sounds of a she-bear in heat, and Killbuck laughs and remarks that that is a very dangerous skill to practice unless one is brave and well armed. Jamie struggles to keep his eyes open, and in the morning wakes to find himself once again wrapped in the bearskin.

Killbuck has them stop in the woods when they can see the smoke of the village above the treetops. Using the axe and his knife he takes the top of the bear's head off, scraping out the brains and fastening it on top of Jamie's head, the upper jaw protruding over his eyes. Jamie hopes this is an honor, and they are surrounded by the people as they step out toward the huts, with much whooping back and forth. It is a heavy load on his neck and a sticky liquid runs off his bare scalp and down the sides of his face, but Ange's eyes are filled with pride as they pass her, and little boys who used to pelt him with mud run in circles around him, chanting Long Knife, Long Knife! as he bows his legs and tries to walk like a bear.

Next time, perhaps, they'll let him bring a weapon.

THE DECK IS FILLED WITH SOLDIERS TRYING TO STAY OUT of the way of the crewmen rushing up and down the yards to wrestle with the wet, whipping sails, everyone drenched from the rain and the hard sheets of seawater crashing over the gunwales. The storm is in its third day, driving them back down the American coast, the captain, Boisson, attempting to keep his ship heading into the scouring, shifting wind. Jenny and Amély are in his cabin, the only place on board without water sloshing underfoot, and have rarely stirred from its confines since they passed between the Spanish islands. They are the only women on board, allowed as a perquisite for Lieutenant St. Cyr, the ranking land officer on board, and as such are regarded both as treasured cargo and something of a liability. There is nothing for them to do, not even to play at *cartes* each evening like the Lieutenant and Captain Boisson, who have drained one keg of brandy and most of the second dedicated to the voyage. Torn from her warm and beautiful Martinique, Amély has retreated into a near wordless funk, while Jenny, though relieved not to be abandoned, has heard nothing encouraging about their destination, both soldiers and sailors referring to it as *la glacière*—the Icebox.

And she has still not informed the *maître* of her condition.

It doesn't feel right. Though she has never been pregnant before, she knows that it doesn't feel right, her insides changing but no sense of life there.

"*Qu'est-ce que tu penses?*" she will say, taking Amély's hand and pressing it to her slightly swollen belly, but her *bonne*, always in a mood, will only shrug and declare that she is no *sage-femme*, has never borne a child herself, and besides, white women have a different type of organ than *les negresses*.

The air inside reeks of bananas, as Boisson is a *connoisseur* of the fruit and has festooned every available surface with bunches of them, unsure when or if he will be ordered back to the islands by the navy and having been assured that they are not available *au Canada*. Jenny is not sure if it is their odor or the pitching of the vessel that is responsible for her constant nausea. The sleeping arrangement is better than anything belowdecks but does not provide enough privacy for intimacy, though St. Cyr has favorably noted her slight change of shape.

"*Tu ne ressembles plus à une réfugiée*," he says, smiling and putting his hands around her waist. He credits the French cuisine, superior, even aboard this battered transport, to anything consumed by the Scots or the English.

She plead with him not to bring Amély along, knowing the dislocation would break the young woman's spirit, but he explained in a very direct manner that there was only a narrow line between a *paramour* and a *putaine*, and that the presence of a ladies' maid would make the distinction clear. As for his wife, he has written to her of his transfer but is certain she is not apt to give up her comfortable life in Grenoble for an adventure in the frontiers of *la Nouvelle-France*.

They sit on a small bench together, Jenny holding to the sides of it to avoid being pitched to the floor and listening to the shrieking wind and the cries of *le seconde* to the sailors beyond the cabin walls, Amély fingering the beautiful wooden crucifix Jenny passed on to her and muttering prayers. The lantern hung from the ceiling swings crazily, light and shadow swirling around them as the *Moineau* smashes through the waves.

"*Peut être*," says Jenny, "perhaps" being the way she begins most conversations with her friend since they left Port-au-Prince, "*Peut-être le nord ce sera trés beau.*"

Jenny has seen snow, of course, and thought it beautiful when she was not too miserable from the cold.

Amély keeps muttering.

"*C'est bon de voir autres pays.*"

She despaired, as a girl, that she would never be able to leave the Highlands, but a trip to Edinburgh had been the height of her aspiration. And more recently, she had wondered what Dominica and Guadaloupe were like—

"*Si n'est pas l'Afrique*," says Amély, not looking up from her beads, "*je m'en fous.*"

Jenny feels a sudden warmth beneath her and looks down. Blood stains her dress and is beginning to puddle at her feet.

"*Je saigne*—" she says before she hits the floor—

THE VILLAGE IS COVERED IN SNOW. SNOW DRIFTS HIGH against the riverside of the huts, a brief thaw and a quick freeze forming a crust on top of it that makes it pointless to hunt, each footfall a snapping alert to the game. Thick chunks of ice are jumbled on both banks, crowding each other and heaving upward, only a narrow stream of water uncovered in the middle of the river. Smoke rises from the holes at either end of the longhouse.

Jamie stands before the council fire, the warriors and old men sitting closest to him, women and children on the benches that run down the long sides waiting, listening.

My father's name was Duncan MacGillivray, he begins.

The name in English will be only a sound to them, as theirs were to him when he was first brought here, so he adds the Erse sobriquet—

—who was also called *sliabh*, the Mountain, after his own father. He was chief of one of the greatest of the clans of the Highland people—

For this he uses *luwàneyunki*, the people who live in the north—

—and when they fought side by side with the MacIntoshes and the MacBeans and the Shaws and the MacPhersons and the other people of the area they formed Clan Chattan—the Clan of the Cat.

They use *pushis* for a house cat, and though there are none in the village, they remember them from those owned by the white people who were their neighbors and who then drove them out of what is now the Pennsylvania Colony—

But a great enemy lived to the south, who claimed dominion over land they had never set foot upon. My father and the other Highland people fought against this enemy in a great war.

Mahtakenk is simply war, and he does not know if they have the concept of rebellion—

They were defeated—by stupidity and cowardice and the treachery of those who spoke their own tongue but fought for the enemy.

The men are nodding, some of them commenting that this is true. Jamie has learned from Shingas and Beaver that well beyond the oldest living man's memory the Lenape warred with the great confederation of *mengwe* to the north and were defeated, and that since then they have been considered as women, forbidden to make war or forge alliances without permission, a kind of Iroquois vice-regent always assigned to monitor their actions, and that most of their land in the Pennsylvania Colony has been sold to the English, often without even a consultation, by their conquerors.

My father was captured, and the lands he—

There is the word *nehëlatànk*, which means "owner," but he has never heard it used with the concept of land—

—the lands he had hunted and fished upon, the lands where he and his father and his father's father and all of the grandfathers going back to the beginning of stories lived, were taken away by the enemy—

Again the men nod and mutter in sympathy. Shingas does not watch him but stares into the council fire, deep in thought—

—so my brother and I grew up by the fire of another clan. We were neither wealthy nor poor, neither chief nor crofter, outcasts in our own country. There was a peace of thirty years—a bitter, rankling peace in which the enemy came into our land and taxed our possessions and insulted our women, and we were made to walk in the world with empty hands, with no weapon to hunt with or defend ourselves.

Our greatest hope—our only hope—lay across the Great Water. For there lived the son of the highest chief of the Highland people, and it was whispered that when he grew to manhood he would return to lead us into battle against the enemy once more, and that our lands would be restored and the ways of our people followed again and all would be as it was before the coming of the enemy. So when young Prince Charlie landed, it was remembered where arms, many that had been used in the '15, were cached or buried—

Ange is here, sitting among the other women, her first time inside the longhouse with permission, proud that her man has been asked to relate his story. The wives of the most successful and fiercest warriors are deferred to by the unmarried women or those who have allied themselves with insubtantial men, and these sit far from the light of the council fire. None of these levels of distinction are spoken of, but all are understood, as the camp dogs will know when a hunter is about to return to the villlage long before he is seen or heard.

And when I came of age, says Jamie, I went to live in the country ruled by our friend Louis—

LaCroix sits near the youngest of the men, the untried warriors. He has not been on a raid with the Lenape, has not killed an enemy in defense of the village as Jamie has, he is not marked on his body with pride of clan or kill—

—our great friend Louis who claimed to be a brother to the Highland people, who claimed that when the great battle came he would send men and weapons and gold to help us. One day the son of the highest chief of our people returned, and word of this spread as men rode about the land bearing a fiery cross, which is a signal that all are to take their arms from where they have hidden them and join in the march to battle.

The small children have been placed close to the fire at the other end of the longhouse, the flames and the heat from the bodies of all the people filling the room to make a warm place in a frozen world, some of the men now dropping the Hudson Bay Company blankets from their shoulders, Jamie's breath no longer visible when he speaks—

First there were hundreds and then there were thousands, thousands marching behind the son of our highest chief, and we defeated our enemy in battle and pushed his warriors back into their own land, and then we followed and defeated them close to their own fires. But there was stupidity among our leaders and there was cowardice, and there were those who spoke our tongue yet chose to fight for the enemy. By the time I returned from across the Great Water, bearing little but words that were as air from our friend Louis, our warriors had retreated. Out of the land of our enemy, retreating north till their backs were against the water.

He is learning to find a way to make what is general into a picture that is simple and common. When friends are angry at each other a tree has fallen across the path between them. Foreign territory is either beyond the mountain or across the Great Water.

The Shawnee are the ones from the south, or the people who move from here to there. Those who hesitate to speak have their throats closed with dust—

The son of our greatest chief was a brave man, I believe, he tells them, a man who made our hearts beat more rapidly in our chests, but he was not—he was not a great war chief.

He sees the look of concern on the faces of the warriors seated near him. They are living the story, and have been hoping for a satisfying end to it—

We faced the enemy in a final great battle at a place called Culloden.

He hears Killbuck repeat the word softly—Cuh-lo-den.

The ground was wet and difficult to cross, and there was too much of it—

He struggles to express this—

—by the time a fast-running man could cross, his enemy could load and fire his rifle many times. But the son of our highest chief told us to attack, and the Highland men—the Highland men will do many things, and some of them are bad, it is true, but they will not shrink from a fight!

Tears are running down Jamie's cheeks now. He has not thought of this for a long time, has not spoken of it since his captive countrymen were rowed away down the great river—

The enemy shot us down with their muskets and cannon, as one cuts the tall weeds with a long knife. The traitors, the Campbells, were there on our right, behind a stone wall, but we ran forward—

He does not know if they have a word for "charge," perhaps it is not one of their tactics when in battle—

—the MacGillivrays, the MacIntoshes, the MacBeans, the Shaws, the MacPhersons, the Camerons, the Stewarts, the MacLeods, the MacDonalds, MacGregors—all the fine flower of the Highlands, the fiercest of our clans—lost.

He sees Fox Dreaming wipe a tear away, the old man staring into the council fire and rocking slightly, side to side—

Our people, our ways—lost.

Jamie feels a bit dizzy. He sits.

Silence. The fire crackles. The Lenape ponder their fate.

B

TИ

OVERTURE

EN *ACADIE*, THE SEA HATES THE LAND, SMASHING it with a fury or skulking off the coast with low, chopping waves, a constant, sullen gray. The tides here are like the moods of a drunkard, receding far out into the *Baie de Fundy* to strand countless shallops and small sailing boats, or up high, menacing the edge of the fields. It is in between now, the *bateaux de pêche* dragged onto the rocks and surrounded by women who appraise each creature as it is pulled from the nets. Amély tugs her mittens off to squeeze the bodies of the *morue*. The fishermen always claim their catch is fresh from the sea, but they are famous liars and Amély's nose is running constantly here, useless to smell with. She chooses the firmest and the *pêcheur* wraps it in dried seaweed before she places it in her bag.

"*Tu ne mangeras jamais mieux*," says the fisherman, in the *français atroce* that all the people here speak, quacking it through their noses like ducks. Amély pays him with some of the paper money the government makes from playing cards and heads back, looking across the flat marsh to what is left of the village of Beaubassin. A few crooked chimneys still standing, the stone parts of the church, all blackened by fire. She knows the English are *une malédiction* in this land, their own small fort smugly overlooking the ruins, but to burn your own homes in order to spite them—

It was the work of the crazy priest, Abbé le Loutre. Scheming, in their own language, with the *peaux rouges* he has converted, exhorting the poor white people here like a canefield *surveillant* to dig and carry, dig and carry, building dykes as if one could keep out the angry sea—passing in the new village, he stares with his burning eyes at Amély as if her skin is the punishment of *le bon Dieu*. She is enough of an oddity to the white people, who stare and whisper, but his savage Mi'kmaqs are bolder, poking and stroking, even offering the skins of wild animals in trade for her. St. Cyr claims that most of the red men by now are Catholics, and needed here to keep les *mauvais anglais* from taking even more land, but they scare Amély, and each time she encounters one she clasps at the holy beads that Jenny gave her.

It is a long, bumpy trek from the sea across the frozen marsh to the new village, Beauséjour, laid out in front of the French fort with the same name, the wind mercifully at her back. Amély wears a hooded cape and as many layers of heavy clothing as she can fit beneath it, a walk in the raw air tiring even with little to carry. At least there is only a dusting of snow on the ground, as she has not yet learned to move with the strange *raquettes* tied to her feet, making tracks like some monster. She was excited the first time she saw it fall, pretty and dancing in the air the way her *maîtresse* had described to her, but it kept falling and falling, covering everything, then was swept by the cutting wind into drifts that sealed the door of their house, Amély and the Lieutenant having to crawl out a window and shovel a tunnel through it.

Though fresh, *morue* for dinner again will be a disappointment. Amély has only tasted salt cod back on her island, a yellowish shoe leather you need to soak for days to be able to swallow down, the cheap feed thrown to the cane cutters. Pulled from the sea here, you can boil it or bake it or even fry it, but without any real spices—

There are men on the roof of the new church. Mad Abbé le

Loutre is having the bell he saved from the Beaubassin *église* hung here, the bell he claims was blessed by the bishop in faraway Québec, the place the Lieutenant was hoping to be stationed. *Acadien* men are nailing shingles on the roof while le Loutre watches from below, surrounded by some of his Mi'kmaq acolytes, the women wearing their strange red hats that come to a high, sharp point like a steeple. The Indians all turn to stare at her. Amély touches her holy beads and hurries by.

The small house they have been given is made of white-painted boards and has a steep-pitched roof. The *maître* spends several nights a week in the officers' quarters at the fort, for appearances, he claims, though both she and Jenny know it is when he is so full of brandy that even the short walk to town in the freezing night seems too much bother. He is billeted here with his handful of *bombardiers* to improve the fort's defenses, but in this season the ground is like stone and digging is nearly impossible.

The English are just as cold as we, the Lieutenant assures them, and not so craven as to mount a surprise attack in such murderous weather. With the treaty signed at a place named Aix-de-la-Chapelle, the only allowable warfare left to English and French here is a building contest, the sawing and hammering from Fort Lawrence audible at Fort Beauséjour when the tide is low and the waves far from the rocks. Local vendors and workmen, *acadiens* whose families have been here for over a hundred years, are engaged by both detachments and happily spy on the progress of each. But an attack, should the peace not hold, will not come by land, says the *maître*, not with the bay in sight and English navy guns far superior in their reach than anything available at Fort Lawrence. This was the constant threat in Martinique, enemy warships only a few islands away, but that always seemed as unlikely as Pelée erupting and pouring molten rock down upon Saint Pierre.

Here, though, caught between the violent sea and the brooding *peaux rouges*—

Jenny sits by the fire, where she spends most of her day, shivering. The ceiling is low, the house more like a *cabane d'esclaves* than anything Amély has lived in with the *maître*, and smoke sulks just beneath the rafters. At least Jenny is not coughing. She has been weakened from the *fausse couche* on the ship, and may still be mourning the loss of the child, though this miserable climate alone is enough to break one's spirit. Amély puts her bag down and immediately adds a few more logs to the fire.

"*Je suis désolée*," Jenny sighs. She apologizes to Amély at least once a day.

"*Et pourquoi?*"

For being weak, says the *maîtresse*. I could have insisted that St. Cyr leave you behind—

So he could sell me?

"Och, he'd nivver sell ye," says Jenny, breaking into English as she does when excited or miserable. "Yer like family."

"*Peut-être*." Amély squeezes the leather bellows, and flames appear to lick at the dry wood. White people always love their dogs and their horses and their slaves, she muses. But when they need money—

Jenny's eyes are liquid, on the verge of tears.

What would I do without you?

You'd do well enough.

The wind is up again, howling mournfully outside. There is so much land here compared to her island—why don't people just start walking south till they reach where it's warm? The *maître* has explained that in Québec and Montreál there are men who own *gens noires*, usually calling them servants rather than slaves, and that in the colonies to the south there are plantations like the one he owned on Martinique, some with dozens of *esclaves de terrain* picking tobacco or indigo. The weather would have to be far worse than this for her to wish she was there.

Amély peels the seaweed wrapping away from the *morue,* guts it, then rubs its flesh with salt and dried sumac berry, a red powder the *peaux rouges* mix with their smoking tobacco to give a bit of tang to it. She wets the seaweed, rewraps the fish, then makes a pocket of embers in the fireplace with the iron rod and lays the whole package into it.

Who did you meet today? asks Jenny. She never takes long walks like she did in Martinique, never ventures out to look at the *maître*'s cannons and be shown off to his men.

I don't meet anybody. I do errands and I buy things.

Buy from what people?

The fisherman. The woman who sells dried apples. I bought a small barrel of flour from the miller himself, a man named Desjardins. His children are Indians.

They look like Indians?

Not the way they dress, but in the face, their hair.

So he has an Indian wife.

She must be dead.

How do you know?

Amély stirs dried corn in a skillet with hot butter and begins to crumble into it some of the biscuit the *maître* brings from the fort, hard as bark but not as tasty.

Because he doesn't look at me the way a married man does, she says.

What way is that?

He looks, but he doesn't look guilty.

Jenny laughs. It is so good to see her smile. She is all I have here, thinks Amély. My master's mistress.

It is nearly dark outside now. This has been the hardest to adjust to, so little daylight, such long nights, as if dark and light are at war and dark is winning. The *maître* claims the season will change, that there will come a time of more day than night, but Amély will believe this when she sees it.

"*Ça vous manque terriblement?*" asks Jenny. "Martinique?"

She does miss her home, terribly, but as her *maman* used to say, life is not given to us—it must be taken. And the first thing that must be dealt with here is to survive this endless winter.

I miss home, she says, but I would miss you so much more.

It is not totally true but what needs to be heard. Jenny stands from the fireside to embrace her then, weeping.

"*Je suis vraiment désolé*—"

"*Calm-toi, ma petite,*" coos Amély, patting her *maîtresse* on the back.

The *meunier*, Desjardins, a man as short and sturdy as his stone-walled mill on the bank of the narrow, frozen river that separates the French from the English here, has six children in all, and his Indian wife was taken by the *tubercule*. He says he keeps back some flour every winter, "for those who grow desperate." He looked her in the eye and asked her about her home, about her reason for being here, listening intently as she told her story. His children obviously adore him.

Six children who have never seen a mango.

THE RIVER, WHICH THE PEOPLE CALL THE ALLEGHENY, is too frozen for a canoe but not so solid it can be walked upon.

I would ride my horse, says Shingas as they make their way along the shore, showshoes tied to their backs in case of a blizzard, but that might ruin its legs.

Though he likes to sit regally on the horse's back when an important guest is about to arrive, Shingas is no rider. Killbuck, who has the biggest feet, takes the lead, breaking trail when necessary. Jamie follows him, and then Shingas and his brother, Beaver. It is bitter cold, their breath puffing out in clouds of white frost in front of their faces, the giant sycamore trees bare, the earth glazed with a sharp crust of snow, and there is not another creature to be seen.

If He Who Created All Things had been in a sour mood when He made our world, says Beaver, this would be our only season.

It is the time when men prefer to sit in the warmth of their *wikëwams*, smoking and telling stories and eating the things they have dried and stored away earlier in the year. But Shingas returned to the village to say that an officer of the Virginias, white men who live to the south and speak English, has summoned the chiefs of the tribes who dwell by the Ohio to a parlay, and that Jamie must come to help judge his words. Jamie has never been this far from the village, even the few times he has gone hunting with Killbuck. The winter moccasins and leggings Ange made for him fit well, but his face and fingers ache with the cold, which is like nothing he has ever experienced. They walk steadily on the west side of the river, not stopping to eat but occasionally chewing on dried meat and corn as they go. They are a small party, vulnerable to attack, but Shingas has assured him that their enemies to the south, the Catawba, never bother to come raiding in winter.

And the Haudenosaunee, he says with a trace of bitterness, will be expecting us in Logstown.

There were no villages in this whole river valley, he has explained, for many years, tribes only coming to hunt with the permisson of the Onondaga Council. But as the Pennsylvanias and other whites have increased in number and power, the real people, first the Shawnee and then the Lenape, have chosen to move farther west, as have some of the *mengwe*, Haudenosaunee people who the whites call Mingos.

We have managed to live here in peace together, says Shingas, for as long as I have been alive.

They reach a camping place just before dark, a clearing on a rise that overlooks a large island in the middle of the near-frozen river, dozens of snow-covered stumps giving it the appearance of an old and disorderly graveyard. They take shelter in the remains of a trader's cabin, its roof half collapsed and half filled with snow, collecting wood to make a fire in the open part, ignoring the plugged chimney.

The town that once was here, Shingas tells Jamie, was built by Chartier, the man I won you from. When he lived here with his Shawnee people and some English traders it was a town nearly as big as our Kittanning, with dwellings on both sides of the river. But then he fought with the English traders because they fed his people rum in order to cheat them and he angered the Pennsylvanias, and the Shawnee had to move further west. The last I heard of him, he was with the French who came to nail metal on trees and bury lead plates with lies scratched upon them, claiming that all this land belongs to their king Louis.

Such a good place for a town, says Jamie. But nobody has come back.

Some Shawnee have come back from the west and from the south, says Shingas, but not to this place. They believe a bad spirit dwells here.

Do you believe it?

I am not Shawnee, says Shingas, smiling.

Killbuck cooks some corn and venison in the pot he has carried and the men eat quickly and then light their pipes. The smoke from the fire rises straight into the hole of black sky above them and Jamie can sense the cold all around, a hostile, amorphous spirit waiting to creep into their bodies if the flames should die.

Long before I was born, says Shingas, firelight dancing on his face, the people your Ange comes from, the Cats, lived here. But then the white men arrived to the east, and said they would trade many fine things, rifles and powder and iron pots and looking glasses and other things the real people had never seen before, all for the skin of the beaver. The people were content for a while, pleased by these new things, but soon there was a great tree fallen across their path.

He Who Created All Things had put only so many beavers into the world.

At first the tribes killed only the beavers that lived near them, trading their skins to the white men, but soon the dams were all broken, the ponds empty, and they had to search on their neighbor's land for more. This led to angry words, and then to theft and murder, and then to a great killing—not of beavers but of men.

And as the Haudenosaunee had united the council fires of the Mohawk, Onondaga, Oneida, Cayuga and Seneca as one and were thus so many, they were able to defeat the people who lived in this land, the Cats, as well as the Shawnee and the Lenape who lived farther to the east.

So few of the Erie—the Cats—were left alive that they became stinkards, begging other tribes to take them in as orphans, and for many years this land was empty of men, and belonged only to the wolves.

Since this great killing, since the defeat of the Lenape, long before I was born, says Shingas, bitterly, the Haudenosaunee have made us as women. Their Great Council appoints emissaries who come to throw their shadows upon us, *mengwe* who have the power to grant or deny us permission to lift the tomahawk against our enemies, or to sell land, or to move from one area to another. More than once they have sold the ground beneath our feet to the English.

And when we meet for parlay, says Shingas, they will pretend to own even our words.

Jamie has been told much of this by Ange and LaCroix. The details, once each of the royal colonies and the tribes within them are added, are no less complex than the Austrian Succession.

It's the Union, he says, when they took away our Parliament. The English claimed my country with a treaty, as if two nations were making a friendly agreement, but it was nothing but bloodshed and bribery.

You speak English, says Beaver, trying to understand, but they are not your people—

We have our own language.

Let us hear it, says Killbuck.

> *"Ò gur mòr mo chùis mhulaid—"*

—says Jamie, recalling one of Lachlan's short verses, the rhythm of it on his tongue bringing tears to his eyes—

> *"'S mi ri caoineadh na guin atà 'm thìr"*

The men contemplate this for a moment before speaking.

There is something bad in your throat, says Shingas, that you wish to cough up.

Beaver smothers the fire, spreading the embers out, then spreads earth from the covered part of the cabin floor over them. They lay on their blankets on top of this while Killbuck makes another small fire nearby, Jamie feeling the heat come up from the ground beneath him. It is absolutely still outside, not the rustling of an animal or a whisper of wind, and they might be the only people left alive in the world.

Killbuck, who is a big man, snores throughout the night.

They leave Chartier's Old Town at first light and continue along the river. It is slower going now, huge chunks of ice that have done battle with each other as they are pressed toward the riverbank lying in an exhausted jumble that make it impassable, and many stretches where they cannot find even a deer path through the trees. Jamie constantly flexes his fingers and toes, unable to feel them. Not a word is spoken. When they come to a hollow giant of a sycamore with a dozen black crows sitting on its branches, Shingas stops the party to watch them.

The crows, silent and unmoving, watch the men.

The men stare at the crows.

They are the wisest of the birds, whispers Beaver. And the most treacherous.

If they are so wise, asks Jamie, why have they not fled to the south with the other birds?

These are perhaps the souls of warriors who have been slain, says Beaver, and not received a proper burial.

The crows are alive, light from the white winter sky reflected in the little black beads of their eyes, but so still they might be in a painting.

Or perhaps, muses Shingas, they're waiting for more men to be slain, so that they may pick at their innards.

The group moves on then, and when Jamie looks back the crows have turned to watch them leave.

The river widens a bit, open water to be seen flowing in the middle, and in the late afternoon they reach Shannopin's Town, a village that has been more recently abandoned. There is another trader's cabin here, this one with its roof intact, and signs inside—fresh ashes in the fireplace, a small wooden cask that contained rum—that white men have just left.

Queen Alliquippa of the *mengwe* was the last to have her people in this town, says Shingas. But she is very old now, and much afraid of the French, so has moved farther south to live beside the waters of the Youghiogheny.

The French are her enemy? asks Jamie.

French brandy is her enemy, Shingas answers. The Queen cannot control her young men when they are full of it.

As the chimney in this cabin has not been filled with snow and animals' nests, they are able to make a proper fire. Once they have eaten and settled with their pipes, Shingas begins to speak, in the casual manner that always signifies that one is meant to draw a lesson or warning from his words.

We watch the turtle, he says.

And though it seems to do nothing, seems rarely even to move, over time we have learned its ways, have learned when we may find it sunning on the rocks or when it will be buried in the mud at the banks of the river.

And the deer, he says, though it moves so swiftly that we catch only glimpses of it, we have hunted for so many years that we also know its ways, we can read the sign that it leaves, we know when the bucks will be knocking their heads together and when the does will be carrying fawns in their bellies and when their coats will fade from red to tan.

But men, says Shingas, we may watch forever and never know what they will do.

Because men have words.

He allows this statement to drift, like smoke above a campsite, before speaking again.

Words are like the colors and shapes on the back of a snake, he says. They may be very bold, very beautiful, and serve to warn the weaker creatures away. Or they may blend in with what is around them, and serve to hide the snake in a tree or on the forest floor, so it can attack and kill.

Words, says Shingas, are like the white man's liquor that fills us with a wonderful heat and a laughing forgetfulness, that causes us to do foolish things.

Where we are going we will hear many words—they are like a fog that from a distance seems a solid thing, but when you step inside proves to be nothing but air.

He looks to Jamie. I will let you know when to tell me what they say, and I will let you know when to speak for me.

But you must listen with your own ears.

EARLY IN THE MORNING THEY PASS THE FORKS WHERE the three great rivers meet, pausing there to feel the power of the place, and then follow the widest of the rivers, the Ohio, to the north. The footing is better here and they travel rapidly, able to see the smoke from Logstown in the sky by the middle of the day.

There are at least thirty cabins, built above the old village one winter by the French, with Mingo, Shawnee, Lenape and even people from some of the western tribes living in and around them. It is so busy with people moving about, even on this freezing day, that at first little note is made of their arrival.

Shingas points to a sturdy cabin that sits above the others.

That is one of the trading posts of George Croghan, says Shingas, the dog who barks for the Pennsylvanias.

Shingas scowls at a memory.

It was in that house that I was crowned as a king.

Our uncle, whose name was Sassoonan, had been called this thing by the Pennsylvanias for years. The white man cannot believe that our people follow no one man, that they are free to listen to their own heart speak, to remain at peace even when all others have taken up the tomahawk.

And so because we have no king, they must invent one.

This was our uncle, Sassoonan, a good man, who held the council bag in which our people keep their belts of wampum and other special things. But he was also a weak man.

He was taken to Philadelphia, their great town, where he was flattered and given white men's clothes and white men's rum and instructed by them and by our Haudenosaunee keeper to put his name on pieces of paper. Each time he did this the real people discovered they would have to move farther west, into the land where there were only wolves.

Beaver has turned his back to stare at the river as his uncle is being spoken of. He is a bit older than Shingas, taller, and speaks just as much when there is a council. The people in Kittanning call Shingas the war chief, even though there is not presently a war.

Finally Sassoonan was so lost in the rum, says Shingas, that he fought with our cousin Shackatalin, who would have been the next great man of the Lenape, and stabbed him to death.

He was so ashamed of this deed that he refused to eat, and as he was then well into his years above the earth, he soon died.

A trio of men, one carrying a drum, are coming down the hill toward them.

There was a council here in Logstown, says Shingas, with many of the important Pennsylvanias, who said we must choose a new king for them to deal with. Our eldest brother Pisquetomen would have been the choice of our people, but he had already had sharp words with the Pennsylvanias about them taking our land, and so was feared by them.

My brother Beaver, who is a wise and cautious man, would have been the next choice of the people, but the people were not here to speak for themselves.

Instead there was Tanaghrisson, the *mengwe* who lives here to watch over us for the Haudenosaunee, who loves to strut and crow in front of the white people, who call him the Half King in mockery. Because I was the youngest, and because he thought he could make me his dog, and because I was not here to protest, Tanaghrisson told the Pennsylvanias that I was their man.

Shingas holds his arms out, looking to Jamie and speaking in English.

"And so you see him—the King of the Delawares."

Then they are invited to eat and drummed into Logstown.

THE CABINS ARE WELL BUILT, MANY WITH STONE CHIMneys and windows that can be shuttered in the winter months, and it is in the largest of these that they meet. There is no furniture as such, only some thick logs set against the walls to serve as benches, with furs laid over to make them more comfortable, and a rusted, long-barreled rifle hung over the fireplace mantel. They are fed a stew of meat and corn and turnips that has been cooked in bear fat, the wise men of the tribes wrapped in blankets and eating from wooden troughs, facing the young Virginia major and his party, who sit on furs spread on the floor with their backs to the fire, eating from metal plates.

Jamie sits at the right shoulder of Shingas, waiting to be told what to do.

Jamie's fingers burn and tingle, his face still raw from the days of travel in cutting wind. He uses a trader's razor to scrape his face clean each morning, rather than plucking the hairs out one at a time like the other Lenape do, and has kept his head shaved but for the topknot. A few from the white man's party have stared at him, but only one, an Irishman named Davidson, has spoken to him, in somewhat accented French. Jamie walked away from him without response.

He wonders if Virginians think of themselves as English, or if they are more like the Irish or the Scots. Killbuck told him of a Highlander, John Fraser, a gunsmith and trader forced to leave his cabin at Venango by the French, who has moved now down to Turtle Creek on the Monongahela, and it set him wondering. If he wanted to leave the Lenape, to live as a white man again, would this Fraser help? Jamie looks to his hand, where the branded T has become part of the shell of a turtle. Perhaps he could attach himself to this Virginia major, this Washington, could change his name, become a new person—

But it would be disloyal.

Old chief Paxinosa is here, as well as his grown sons and many other Shawnee, many of whom live here in Logstown. Of the Mingo, the most important are Guyasuta, known as an expert guide, then the viceroys, Scaraoudy and Tanaghrisson, the one who the English call the Half King.

Those two are the men the Haudenosaunee have sent to watch over us, says Shingas as they eat. We may speak, but they are the ones who must be listened to.

The Virginia major, the only one of the whites in a uniform, is tall, having to bend low when entering the cabin, with reddish hair and a pox-scarred face and so young he might not yet need a razor. He seems supremely confident though, calmly studying the red men over his long nose.

This is a new buck, says Jamie softly in Lenape, whose antlers are still soft and green. Why have all these great men come to meet him?

He is no buck, Shingas tells him, but the first bird who precedes the flock.

When the last of the food is cleared away, Tanaghrisson, the Half King, a man in his fifties with a tattooed face who wears a tricorn hat trimmed with lace and engraved medals of silver and gold around his neck, stands to begin the formalities, speaking English well and emphatically.

"Brothers!" he says. "We welcome all of you. We brush the snow, which has collected on your long journey, from your weary feet."

Guyasuta echoes the Half King's words in the Seneca dialect of Haudenosaunee, while one of the sons of Paxinosa translates for the Shawnee, and Jamie repeats in Lenape.

"Brothers!" says the Half King. "We clear your ears with soft cotton, that you might understand well what is spoken here.

"Brothers!" he says. "May your hearts be warmed at our fire, that they might be open to our friendship."

Gifts are exchanged then, only a few because this is not a trading expedition or a treaty to be made. Washington is given a ceremonial pipe, and he in turn presents the Half King with a belt of wampum, purple and white, of perhaps two hundred grains. Another pipe is passed around for all to smoke, needing to be refilled with tobacco several times. Jamie watches the white men trying unsuccessfully to hide their impatience, all but the buckskin named Gist who sits by the Virginia major. These two are both land stealers, Shingas has told him, men who come into Indian territory bearing sticks and chains and a magic metal needle that shows them where the sun will rise and set, who draw pictures in their notebooks so that other whites will know which places are worth taking.

Washington stands finally, or rather stoops, his head by the rafters, to speak.

"Brothers—" he says, "your people have come to us complaining that the French have been building a line of forts, coming down the rivers from the north, bringing their soldiers and their cannon into land they claim but do not own."

The major knows enough to allow time between his statements for translation.

"Your good friend, King George, shares your anger at this intrusion," Washington continues. "And I have been sent with a letter from his loyal servant, Governor Dinwiddie of the Virginia Colony, to tell the French that they must leave."

Jamie wonders if the tall major is truly so confident. There are hundreds of French soldiers already at Fort LeBoeuf to the north, and Virginia is very far away—

"I have come here to speak with you wise men, that you may

add your voices, and the voices of your warriors, to our instruction, and that you may go with us to warn these intruders that they must leave."

And then he is done.

It is not what an Indian would consider a proper speech. Shingas looks to Jamie.

He wishes to threaten the French, he tells Shingas, using our tomahawk.

The Half King rises then, facing the wise men on the floor, speaking in English so the Virginias may understand him.

"I have been to their Fort LeBoeuf," he sneers, "and seen the men and the weapons the French have brought there to steal our land with. I told their chief, Captain Marin, that we have not asked him to come here, that this river he has built his fort upon belongs to me and my warriors, who fought to win it!"

There is no ho! of agreement from the wise men on the floor, which seems to annoy the Half King.

"This Marin then said that my warriors and I were like people who had lost their minds, that the river and all the land around it, the land upon which the Mingo and the Lenape and the Shawnee now dwell, belongs to Louis, the King of France."

Muttering in many tongues over this. Shingas does not touch his shoulder, so Jamie does not bother to translate.

"'I despise all the stupid things that you say,' the French Captain told me, 'and I will continue on my way, building new forts, and if there are any bold enough to hinder my path, I shall *crush* them.'"

The wise men consider this indignity solemnly. Jamie steals a glance at Shingas, still no expression on his face.

"I then took the belt of wampum he had given me," says the Half King, miming with his hands, "and I *threw* it at his feet! 'If you do not leave at once,' I told him, 'I will strike with my Rod all over this land, let it hurt who it will!'"

The Seneca is flushed with anger now, his blanket fallen to the floor.

"I now ask you wise men, you chiefs, to bring me all the belts that the French have given to you over the years, that I might return them to Captain Marin with our promise that if he does not leave the river we will destroy him and make spoil of his property!"

The Half King turns to look at Shingas.

"Shingas," he says, challenging, "will you bring me the many belts the French have given to your people?"

Shingas speaks directly to the Half King in Lenape, not rising from the floor.

Most of our belts of friendship, as you know, were traded by my uncle Sassoonan to the white man for liquor. Shingas nods at the belt given by Major Washington, which is draped over the Half King's shoulder. Perhaps that is one of them. The few left are in Venango, with Custaloga, who is the chief man there. This young Virginia man may ask for them himself as he passes through.

The Half King, scowling, replies in Lenape, which he speaks as well as he does English.

This is not an answer.

The white men look back and forth between the two, sensing the tension, while the other Indians in the room turn their heads away.

I will send a messenger ahead to Custaloga, asking for the belts, says Shingas lazily. Let us hope that they, too, have not been traded for rum and poured down some Indian's gullet.

The Half King does not avert his gaze.

May I remind the great Shingas, he says with mockery in his tone, that it was I who named him chief man of the Lenape, choosing him over his own brothers.

I do not forget, says Shingas. The white people, the Pennsylvanias, wished the Lenape to have a king to make their business with. So you had them write my name in their book.

A long silence, the Half King glaring until he turns to old Paxinosa, speaking in his tongue.

Your people, the Shawnee, have also accepted many gifts from the French. The day after I left Fort LeBoeuf, you and others met with their Captain Marin, and he gave you—

All of our belts are held by my nephew Bone, says the old man. And Bone has left to raid our enemies in the south.

The Half King is furious, but tries not to display it in front of the white men. He speaks softly, in a mix of Lenape and Shawnee, tongues that are cousins to each other.

Do not forget, he says, that we Haudenosaunee have put a dress on you people, and that as women you must obey our counsel in important matters.

We never forget this, says Shingas, seeming very calm. If we look to the sky, our brother Tanaghrisson floats there as a cloud. If we gaze into the river, he swims beneath us as a fish. If we step upon the earth, he is beneath our feet, like a snake.

The two men stare at each other. Jamie is glad that the drinking always comes after the trading has been done or the negotiations finished, and that his chief has always left by then.

But may a woman ask a question? asks Shingas.

The Half King scowls, his arms folded in front of his chest.

That is why we have come here.

Shingas turns to Jamie. Ask the tall man what words are in his paper.

Jamie stands to face the Virginia major. "Shingas, chief mon of the Lenape, would like ye tae read the letter tae us."

Washington's eyes harden, looking him over as if seeing him for the first time. "It is a sealed letter from Governor Dinwiddie," he says. "I know not the specifics of it."

"Ah," says Jamie. "Then yer ainly a messenger."

Washington glares for an instant at Jamie, then flicks his gaze to

Shingas. "I can say, though, that it will behoove you people to make up your minds whether you're with us or not, and rather *promptly*. Great forces are involved here, great kingdoms, and one cannot remain neutral in the woods."

Shingas looks to Jamie, puzzled. There are few words for abstract ideas in Lenape, though the concepts themselves exist.

He warns us, says Jamie, that we must stand on one side of the tree or the other.

Shingas smiles. Then ask him what our good friends in Virginia intend to do to help us keep the French away.

"Shingas, chief mon of the Lenape, wishes tae know what aid yer king George and the people of Virginia plan tae offer us, that we might chase the French frae our land."

Washington takes a moment to confer in whispers with the buckskin, Christopher Gist, and the big Dutchman at his other side.

"We intend to build a strong house," Washington answers. "Not a fort with many soldiers, like the French have built, but a place where the Lenape and the Shawnee and the Mingo can trade for the things they need, including guns and powder, to oppose the intruders in their own fashion. I have studied the land during my journey and believe the ideal location for this is on the point at the forks of the three great rivers."

It takes a moment for this to be translated, for it to be repeated and understood. Scaraoudy, who has watched the Half King's performance without emotion, stands to face the white men. He too speaks English very clearly—

"Brothers—you have bid us to take care of our own lands, to turn our backs toward the French," he says. "And this we shall do. But we ask you not to build this strong house. During these troublesome times, we desire to keep our country clear of white settlements."

Once translated there is a scattered ho! from the wise men on the floor.

Washington offers Scaraoudy a slight bow. “Understood. I shall deliver your sentiments to Governor Dinwiddie upon my return.”

“Who of you will come with us,” asks the Half King, looking over the wise men who sit before him, “so that the French will take this warning to heart?”

Though I wish the young messenger good fortune, says Shingas, my wife, Cloud Woman, is very ill, and I must return to her side.

Cloud Woman, who Jamie last saw carrying a load of firewood on her back, the snow up to her knees.

I am very old, says Paxinosa, and not fit for a long journey in this cold season. But I will encourage some of my warriors to go along with you.

“They’re not coming,” Jamie can hear Gist muttering to the Virginia major. “They’re afraid of the French.”

There is very little more to the parlay, Paxinosa asking for intercession in freeing some Shawnee warriors held by the colony of South Carolina, and then the Half King, clearly vexed, declaring that he hopes that all present will hold fast to the Chain of Friendship.

SHINGAS AND HIS PARTY HAVE BEEN GIVEN THEIR OWN cabin to spend the night in, logs already blazing in the fireplace. There is mostly cedar in the fire, crackling and shooting sparks, and they listen to it for a long while, smoking, before anyone speaks.

Have their grown men all died, says Beaver finally, for them to send this boy?

He is hungry to be great in the world, says Killbuck. And carries himself as if it is already so.

He travels with a message from his governor, says Shingas, staring moodily into the flames, but he has his own designs. As does our brother Tanaghrisson.

A soft ho! of agreement from the other Lenape men.

When the Half King spoke of his visit to the French, Shingas continues, he spoke only for the Mingo who follow him in this valley, not for the Great Council of Onondaga.

How do you know this? asks Jamie.

The more frightened the dog, the louder the bark. He threatened the French at their fort with only his dozen of Mingos behind him, hoping they would believe it was the thousands of the Haudenosaunee.

The Half King is ambitious, says Jamie. But also his mind is bitter toward the French—

Shingas turns to look at Jamie.

As yours is toward the English. Perhaps they have murdered someone close to his heart.

Killbuck throws another log on the fire, the men brushing from their blankets the crackling fireflies that spit out from it.

Will you ask Custaloga to give him the belts? asks Jamie.

The Half King does not expect me to, says Shingas. That was only his show for the Virginias, and to remind us that we have been made women. Just as Scaraoudy's protest about the strong house at the forks was a show.

You think so?

The *mengwe* have no doubt met privately before with the whites, as they will do again, perhaps later this night. It is then that the true agreements will be made.

I don't believe that the governor's letter was sealed, says Beaver.

Nor do I, says Shingas. And if it is a only a warning to the French, why would the major not let us hear the words of it?

Jamie understands that there is no shelter, even if he sought it, for him in the Virginia Colony. He felt himself already judged and convicted in the gaze of the tall young man, whose bearing heralded him as an enthusiastic servant of the Crown.

Major Washington carries a message from his governor, says Jamie. And his governor is appointed by King George.

This is so.

Do you suppose, in the letter, King George says, "You Frenchmen must quit this land, because it belongs to my friends, the red men, the Lenape and the Shawnee"?

The men smoke their pipes, trying to imagine this.

No, Jamie tells them. King George says, "You Frenchmen must quit this land because it is *mine*."

JENNY WISHES THE ROAD WOULD GO ON FOREVER. ST. Cyr is in one of his joyful moods, rarer and rarer, with only two glasses of brandy in him, and there is a new, late season snow on the ground, pure white and not so deep that the horse has to struggle pulling the *traîneau*. She is wearing only one layer of clothes, a first since she arrived in this country, and the sky is without a cloud. The Lieutenant assures her that he has traveled in this direction before and that it is absolutely safe.

"*Le prêtre sauvage est occupé*," he says. Abbé le Loutre will be saying Mass all morning, too busy to be out hatching plots against the English with his red men. The *acadiens* are not so tolerant of officers and their mistresses as are the *blancs* of Martinique, and St. Cyr is not a man to push Jenny under their noses on their holy day. So Sundays without kirk are a bright interlude in her dreary weeks.

It was Amély who finally pulled her out of the house, insisting that she could not understand the *acadiens*, nor they her, and needed an interpreter along on her errands. Laying her *patois* on so thickly that nobody but a Saint Pierre street vendor could understand her, she dragged Jenny to the butcher, the baker, the woman who sold dried fruit and nuts, the other women who did laundry for the soldiers, and finally to the millhouse and René Desjardins.

He is a quiet and plainspoken man, polite in a country way, and kept referring to her as *votre amie* to Amély in a manner no shopkeeper in Martinique would dare. His son Modeste, well made and handsome the way the Indian boys are before they shave their heads and tattoo their faces, was there mending jute sacks and watching the exchange intently.

"*Qu'est-ce que tu penses?*" asked Amély the minute they had left, a small sack of cornmeal in hand.

I think he's a very nice man.

But do you think he likes me?

Why wouldn't he?

I mean *likes* me.

It had not even occurred to Jenny, and suddenly she was very ashamed. Even attached to the Lieutenant, Jenny was an exile, a refugee in Martinique, while Amély had been born there, had friends, people related to her by blood. Here, she might as well be an animal in a zoo, an animal with fur not thick enough—

The horse shies. There is a monster in the road.

Blowing puffs of steam from its huge nostrils, rough haired and tall as a man on a donkey, staring at them. Jenny has seen only the head of one of these creatures, stuffed and hanging on the wall of the officers' mess at Fort Beauséjour, enormous flat bones branching from each side of its skull.

"*Mais ou sont les bois?*" she whispers.

The antlers drop off in the winter, St. Cyr tells her. And you needn't whisper—the moose knows we're here and will do what it will.

The huge beast lowers its head, staring at them as if unsure of what they might be. St. Cyr pulls his pistol from under his coat, pulls the hammer back—

Hold on tight, he says.

Their horse, Christophe, decides the matter, whinnying in terror and skittering off the road, pulling them in a wide arc around the moose, its long head swiveling to follow their progress. St. Cyr muscles the reins to get them back on track once it is out of sight behind them.

"*Une bête très dangereuse*," he says when they are on their way again. And ugly, like everything in this country.

I don't think it's so ugly here, says Jenny, "*mais il y a de trop*." Too big, too cold, too far from anything I recognise. The *acadiens*, she says, must have been poor as Highlanders to come here of their own will.

The road bends to cut through forest, tall, snow-laden pines giving way to bare oak and maple trees, so many and so thick around it is no wonder that half the ships leaving for France are filled with timber. The day has grown warmer than when they left, clumps of melting snow falling to the ground around them with a soft plop, the runners of the sleigh making a high shussing sound, a woodpecker rattling somewhere off to the left.

It is exhilarating to be out of the house, to feel like spring will actually come. Jenny had been more resigned than excited about the baby, but when she lost it a kind of heaviness descended on her, as if she was living under water. Voices seemed distant, air difficult to breath, even Amély's attempts to be cheerful annoying. And then a blizzard on their second day ashore, as if sent purposely to bury her mournful soul. But with each lengthening day her spirits have risen, Amély offering no protest when Jenny announced that she would not only serve as *traductrice* for their shopping expeditions but chop all their kindling from now on, suddenly eager to climb from beneath the heavy blankets at sunrise. St. Cyr has told her that many animals here sleep throughout the winter—bears, skunks, raccoons, squirrels—huddling up in holes inside of trees and living off their fat. She wonders if they feel the same elation when they wake.

We could have ended up in much worse places, he says.

"*Bien sûr*."

There are officers every day sent to build and maintain forts, he says, that are more like tiny trading posts with a few cannon, and no *petit ville de gens blancs* nearby for company. A line of little forts that stretches all the way down to the wilds of the Ohio Valley.

She thinks of the redcoats who may still be barracked near her clachan in the Highlands, lonely, surrounded by people who despise them—

I even know a lieutenant who was sent to Cayenne, in *la Guyane français*, says St. Cyr. But he was suspected of being a Jew, who had insulted his commandant—

And suddenly they are among savages.

"*N'aie pas peur*," says the Lieutenant, climbing out of the sleigh and raising his hand to greet one of the *indigènes* stepping toward him. Jenny feels her heart racing, looks around. They are Mi'kmaq people, "our Indians," as St. Cyr calls them, men and women wearing blankets and fur robes and cooking something in a huge brass kettle on a fire, none paying special attention to her.

"*Bienvenus*," smiles the man who has come forward, the tattoos on his cheeks crinkling.

You're missing Mass, says the Lieutenant, who must know him.

"*Et vous aussi*," answers the *indien*, who wears both a necklace of bear claws and a silver gorget with the image of Louis Quatorze stamped on it around his neck. "*Avec ta femme*."

St. Cyr introduces Jenny to Chief Bâtard, and the Mi'kmaq nods his head, still smiling. They are like children, St. Cyr has told her, and not always to be trusted, especially when they are drunk.

She hopes they are not making liquor.

Jenny has seen a few in town, there to trade, has seen the ones who camp just outside the walls of Fort Beauséjour, and has watched them paddle their big fishing canoes out into the bay. Unless their faces and bodies are painted, St. Cyr has told her, they are not likely to be up to mischief.

"*Le sirop est presque fini,*" says the man, gesturing toward the kettle, and then leads them around from tree to tree to display the process—the tapped trees still bleeding sap into receptacles fashioned from birchbark, women filtering the collect through a square of cheesecloth before adding it to the boiling brew, making sure that the mixture remains at a certain level. Finally the chief—for that is how St. Cyr addresses him—dips a ladle deep into the bubbling liquid, showing no fear of burning his hand, then dribbles a bit of it onto a patch of clean snow.

"*Prêt pour la dame,*" he says, and St. Cyr scoops up the golden snow to offer it to Jenny. It is so sweet and aromatic she has to close her eyes.

The chief says they will continue to boil the syrup down, then stir it with a paddle till it becomes sugar, which they will store for themselves after selling some to both forts.

"*Vous vendez le sucre à l'anglais?*" St. Cyr asks him, raising his eyebrows.

"*Bien sûr,*" says the chief. "*Nous sommes tous en paix.*"

Peace. Jenny has heard talk of raids, cabins of English settlers farther inland burned, men and women murdered with hatchets. The English soldiers must be too lazy or too frightened to venture out and make their own sugar.

St. Cyr steps aside with the chief for a moment then, speaking quietly and more seriously. Jenny does not want to know the details. For every Abbé le Loutre, says the Lieutenant, there is an English trader inciting his own savages, the Iroquois, to murder French-speaking settlers. A very strange peace—

They seem so normal, so *hu*man working by the smoking kettles, talking among themselves, the children making balls of the snow and throwing them at each other, careful to avoid hitting an adult. It reminds her of a cattle auction or sheep-shearing at home, only there would be fiddlers, and whisky, and some brawling later in the day. The chief laughs, teeth flashing white in his swarthy face. She didn't know the men could laugh—

"*Reviens bientôt!*" calls the chief, waving, as they start away in the sleigh, a small packet of finished sugar in Jenny's hand.

They are gliding smoothly on the way back, nearly out of the woods, when St. Cyr begins to muse upon the oddities of their new home.

Deer the size of camels, he says, *loups de mer*, seals with the eyes of beautiful women, and loyal friends such as chief Étienne Bâtard who make sugar from maple trees and collect other men's hair as a *passe-temps*.

"*Vraiment?*"

Jenny has heard the rumors about Bâtard and his exploits under the direction of Abbé le Loutre, heard the jokes about keeping your hat tightly on your head, has even met one man, an old *acadien*, who has a shiny oval patch of scar just above his forehead, scalped alive when he was a young man.

St. Cyr assures her that he has seen at least twenty of the hairy discs, though that may not be the entire collection, hanging in their host's lodge.

"*Un assassin trés charmant.*"

THEY WATCH THE BUILDING AT THE FORKS FROM THE trees on the south side of the Ohio.

They arrived in time, Jamie and Killbuck and LaCroix, to meet the English party, forty men in all, more laborers than soldiers. There in time to hear Captain Trent say that the strong house they will put up is meant to help their good friends the Indians of the Ohio country defend themselves against persons pretending to be subjects of his most Christian Majesty the King of France. There to hear the Half King, speaking more to the few dozen curious Shawnee and Lenape who had gathered than to the whites, say that this fort will belong to both the English and the Indians, and that they should make war on any who come to oppose its building.

There to see the Half King proudly lay down the first log.

Trent and the Half King then asked the Shawnee and Lenape to go hunt meat to feed the men who would build, but most just drifted away. Jamie volunteered that he and Killbuck and LaCroix would look for game, but instead only walked out of sight and then crossed the river to come back and watch, serving as eyes for Shingas.

"All of these traders now wear the uniform," said LaCroix at the time. "Trent, the captain, is partner to George Croghan, and is marry to 'ees sister. The young ensign, Ward, has work for Croghan and is 'ees 'alf-brother. Fraser, *le deuxieme*, is a man 'oo fix rifle, and has a cabin for the trading near to this place."

"They think there will be a war," said Jamie.

"They think, *peut être*, that after thees war they will *own* the land they build upon."

At first there is very little to see. Two weeks are spent clearing the point so that all three of the rivers may be seen clearly from the raised ground they will build on. The wood is like iron in the extreme cold, and the axemen first set fires around the tree to be cut down, waiting till the bark has turned black and started to peel away before attacking from both sides. Squaring the logs is nearly as difficult, and the days are still very short. There is a lot of shouting, mostly from Trent, and one morning it looks like the men refuse to work until some promise is made to them. Nobody brings food, and the provisions brought on their raft are too meager to keep them strong. Jamie is ordered to watch from dawn till dusk, while LaCroix and Killbuck search in the woods for something to shoot. He resents it at first, then realizes that they don't believe he will run away, only that he is a poor hunter.

They eat a lot of squirrels, and at night travel down to Queen Alliquippa's new town, where Killbuck has a sister, and sleep in a warm *wickëwam*.

A fort—or a very small facsimile of a fort—slowly begins to take shape. Jamie finds he has to change position often, moving carefully from the shelter of one great pine to another, in order not to freeze, and often envies the men across the river who have heavy logs to carry and saw, who have bonfires of cut branches burning all around them.

Those fires burn all night. And he knows they are seen by every Indian who travels through the forks, the water still full of ice but flowing freely now, and that word of the building has likely spread, at least among the red people, from Canada to the Carolinas.

The strong house is almost finished, only the front gate yet to be hung, when Killbuck and LaCroix return with a raccoon they have smoked out of hibernation and news from afar.

"We meet with this young man Silver'eels 'oo is a runner, a *messager* for the *mengwe*," says LaCroix, excited. "'Ee says that the *français*, they are come down the river in many *bateaux*, many *canots*, with hundred and hundred of soldier and bringing the big cannon as well. 'Ee also say that the *jeune homme de Virginie*, this Washington, 'ee also come, from the east, with not so many soldier and not so many cannon."

Killbuck is happy as well.

With good fortune they will meet here, he says, and we'll be able to watch the white men kill each other.

That evening they bring the raccoon to Queen Alliquippa's town, sharing it with Killbuck's sister and her family. They speak only of hunting.

Many years ago, when I was little more than a boy who had grown tall, Killbuck begins, we lived much closer to where the sun comes out of the earth, near to the city of the Pennsylvanias. There was a great sickness in our village, many of the people dying from this, and one of them was my father. As my mother had only sisters, there was no grown man to provide for us, and so it was left to me to bring meat to the fire.

He was very tall already, says Killbuck's sister, who is called the Swan, as she puts chocolate in the pot to boil for them. But he had seen only fourteen winters—truly a boy—

This was the Year of Too Much Rain, Killbuck continues, when the fields of corn and squash were flooded and the chesnuts that fell in the woods rotted on the ground and the animals could find little to eat. Because of the sickness and because of the rain very little was put away for winter, which came that year as if trying to bury us, with many great blizzards and snow so heavy it broke the branches of the trees. It was hard to move from one place to another without the snowshoes on your feet, and this is a very tiring way to walk, even for a tall boy like I was. But my mother and brothers and sisters needed to eat, and so I went out to look for food.

As I have said, there was little to eat for the animals in the forest, and the ones who lived closest to our village had all been killed, so I walked over the snow until I came to this western country, where there were few people but we were allowed by the Haudenosaunee to hunt. My father's rifle had been broken, and without something to trade with the white people it could not be fixed or replaced, so I had only a bow and some arrows to hunt with, and some meal made from acorns in a small bag.

On my first day in this country I heard only the echo of my own footsteps—not a bird, not a squirrel, nothing. I found no tracks in the snow, I saw no claw marks on the side of a tree where a bear or raccoon had climbed. For this kind of hunting one has to stop and listen, stop and listen—I would hold my breath even, but I could not even hear the great rivers nearby, as they had frozen solid and were under drifts of snow.

The second day, in the afternoon, I began to feel like I was being watched. And when I'd stop to listen, sometimes I would hear one more step. But not an echo, it was not the sound a snowshoe makes. After a few hours of this I finally saw him—a gray wolf, long and thin, who was following me. When our eyes met he froze still, staring at me, one of his paws held in the air.

"Brother," I said to him, "you are welcome to be my shadow. And if you promise not to scare the game away I will share whatever I kill with you."

For the rest of that day he followed me—I could feel him more than I could see him—and at night when I looked out from my fire I could see the yellow reflection of his eyes.

On the third day my meal was all gone and I was starting to weaken. Again I felt something watching me, and by stopping and listening, stopping and listening, finally I saw the wolf. But it was a different one, bigger, with black fur and his back slightly hunched behind his neck, as is often seen.

"Brother," I said to the black wolf when we met our eyes, "you are welcome to be my shadow. I know that we are both hungry, and if you promise not to scare the game away I will share whatever I kill with you."

And for the rest of that day I could sense the black wolf following me, and once crossed the track of the gray wolf, which had two toes missing from one of its front paws, but I found no game.

That night as I looked out from my fire I saw no eyes. But later I was awakened by the sound of snarling and fighting. The two wolves had found each other. At first I grew afraid that they would join in hunting me, but then realized they were not of the same pack, not of a pack at all but *xuha tëme*—the ones who hunt alone.

On the fourth day I was very weak—when I stood still to listen, the trees would not stop swimming around me, and it was a great effort to lift each leg with a snowshoe on the end of it, as if they were tied to the earth. Again I could sense something watching me now and then, but had no idea which of the wolves it might be.

And then I saw a buck. I saw him through the trees, on the other side of a ravine, too far away to shoot with an arrow. It was a buck in his prime, of the ones who father all the new deer, holding his head up to sniff the air. I was downwind from him but knew I was too weak to move close enough for a shot before he saw me.

Killbuck leaves the animal poised on the other side of the ravine while he thumbs tobacco into his pipe, lights it, and takes a few thoughtful puffs.

And then it began to run, he says. It began to run toward me, and I saw that the gray wolf was above it, loping down the side of the ravine, chasing it in my direction. I readied my bow then, drawing it, holding, waiting, waiting until it struggled up the close side of the ravine and appeared again to me, and I put the arrow just under its throat and into its heart.

All men used to be expert with a bow, says the Swan, bringing cups of hot chocolate, sweetened with maple sugar, a drink the white traders have taught them to desire. But the young ones now think of a bow as only as a toy.

The buck was dead before I could reach him over the snow, Killbuck continues. But as I drew my skinning knife there was a snarl, and I turned to see the wolf, the black wolf, very close, showing me all of his sharp teeth and making small steps forward with his head low to the ground. Though I had spoken to him before, he wanted all the meat, and as I had only the skinning knife in hand and was very weak, I could not argue. I backed away from him slowly, my eyes never leaving his, kept stepping back and back, which as you know is a very difficult thing to do when wearing snowshoes, backed away until he turned to the carcass of the buck and I could pick my bow up from where I had stuck it upright in the snow.

He must have been very hungry, because a wolf—which is the symbol of my clan—will usually have better sense. I waited for this greedy wolf to start ripping at the buck's belly, then put an arrow through his throat, closing it so he could swallow no more.

He took a long time to die. I had nothing else to do and leaned upon my bow to rest, the trees still swimming a little. While the greedy wolf was still writhing in the snow, making it red, the other one, the gray wolf, came forward out of the trees and sat on his haunches to watch. He was on the other side of the dead buck from me, but I could see there were fresh red scars on his muzzle from the fight. I called to him.

"Brother," I said, "if you will just have patience, we will have something to eat and neither of us will suffer a bite."

Soon the black wolf ceased to move, and I came forward with my skinning knife and my pack with the hatchet in it, while the gray wolf sat where he was, politely, watching me.

The black wolf had already opened the buck's middle, so I cut away its heart, which I tossed to the gray wolf, and its liver, which I ate myself. It is a wonderful thing what meat will do when you are hungry, and knowing that there is more to come is even better. The trees around me stopped their swimming, and my legs were no longer tied to the earth.

With my hatchet I cut away one of the legs—one of the rear legs, which have more to eat on them—and dragged it toward the gray wolf. The wolf waited until I was very close before it stood up, trembling a little, and that is when I dropped the leg and went back to deal with the rest of the buck.

I skinned the buck and hacked it into pieces that would be easier to carry home, leaving aside the head with its sharp horns sticking up. I then skinned the black wolf and rolled its pelt to be carried as well, hoping to trade it to a white man who could repair rifles. Without his skin the black wolf looked very small, and I hoped that whoever later wore its hide as a coat would not become as greedy.

That night by the fire I could not only see the shine of the gray wolf's yellow eyes, but I could hear its teeth, breaking the hollow bone of the buck's leg.

He was still there when the sun came up out of the earth, sitting, watching me, with snow stained red and some scraps of bone beside him.

"Brother," I called to him when I was packed like a trader's horse with meat and skins, "I thank you for your help, and for your company." And I left him a large piece of the meat that lies between the shoulder blades, which is always good. As he was a polite wolf and also proud, he waited till I was out of sight to step forward and eat it.

The Swan makes a happy sound in her throat, liking to hear the story again.

The men sit smoking, listening to the fire and drawing their conclusions.

All wolves are not alike, says LaCroix finally.

Ho! says Killbuck, agreeing.

And one must always go forth with at least two arrows.

IN THE MORNING THEY WATCH AS THE FRENCH FLOtilla—for it is that impressive—passes the men building on the point, swinging around and up the Allegheny to camp at abandoned Shannopin's Town. Jamie counts at least sixty *bateaux* and over three hundred canoes, filled with French *troupes de la marine*, Canadian militia, and Indians, at least five hundred men in all. They fly the white flag with the golden *fleur-de-lis* and carry eighteen cannon, uncovered so that the shivering English workers and their tiny military escort, rifles, hammers, and saws in hand, can get a good look at them.

They'll give them a day to think about it, says Killbuck, and then tomorrow something will happen.

And if Washington and his men arrive?

Then it will be more interesting.

They leave Jamie to watch and go off hunting. An officer accompanied by two drummers and a northern Indian comes from the French to the young ensign, Ward, who has been left in charge. They stand in front of the strong house, its gate just hung, as a summons is read and explained, the Half King appearing at Ward's side to make angry gestures. Ward is then paddled down the Monongahela, looking worried, perhaps going to bring his senior officer Fraser back to deal with the situation. A few hours later he is paddled back, without Fraser at his side. After a heated exchange with the Half King, he has himself rowed to the French camp.

It is almost dark when Killbuck and LaCroix return, having killed a deer, an old doe with her tongue hanging out of the side of her mouth.

An offering for tomorrow, says Killbuck.

The many campfires of the French are within sight of the few campfires of the English, and the new arrivals sing for much of the night.

There is morning mist over the rivers when they step out into the great clearing the English have made on the point, Jamie and LaCroix coming first with their hands spread wide, showing they have no weapons, and Killbuck following with the doe draped over his massive shoulders.

We had to go back to Kittanning, he says innocently when the Half King steps out from the strong house to glare at them. But we thought we would come down to see how the strong house is coming along.

The Half King does not respond, looking instead behind them, where another emissary from the French is approaching. The man, whose uniform used to be white, disappears into the strong house for a moment, then steps out with young Ward and another Virginia soldier, heading for the canoe awaiting them at the riverbank.

We'll cut this up and cook it, says Killbuck, strolling with the doe over to one of the bonfires that has been kept burning. I'm sure the men inside are hungry.

Killbuck is quick with his knife, and Jamie and LaCroix help him roast pieces of the doe over the flames. The smell soon brings men out from the strong house, and they tear at the venison while it is still smoking, having had nothing but salt meat and biscuit for weeks. Jamie and LaCroix and Killbuck squat nearby, quietly watching them.

Jamie finds a huge axeman with a huge black beard staring at him.

"What are ye, then?" the man asks.

Jamie answers in Lenape, saying that he is a warrior of the Turtle Clan.

"Don't give me any of that," snarls the axeman. "I can see yer not a red man."

Jamie answers again, this time in Erse, saying that he is a MacGillivray, of Clan Chattan.

The axeman frowns and nudges the man eating beside him.

"Do that sound like French?"

The Half King steps out from the new-made building then, followed by three Mingos, walking to the edge of the trees that haven't been cleared and sitting on their folded blankets to wait.

"Red devils," says the axemen. "Now they'll want our hair."

The food has all been eaten up by the time Ensign Ward returns, the workmen and Virginia soldiers crowding around him before going back into the strong house to gather their things. Jamie and LaCroix and Killbuck move back to their own canoe to watch, ready for a quick retreat if necessary. Perhaps only a hundred of the newcomers, French regulars in well-worn uniforms, come for the exchange ceremony, bringing along their own drummers.

They stand in two ranks, leaving a gap between them, drums roll, and Ward leads his ragged party out from the little strong house, which they had called Fort Prince George, saluting the French captain and stepping through his troop to the *bateaux* they have been offered to travel home in. The workmen hold axes and shovels on their shoulders like they are muskets. When they are all loaded and have pushed out into the current, the Half King begins to shout, in vehement French, to the victors.

"*Ce fort est à moi!*" he yells. "*Et je vous verrai brûlé dedans!*"

And then fades into the woods with his Mingos.

The French captain, unperturbed by this threat, orders his men to begin pulling the structure down. Jamie and the others watch, ignored by the French, as a pair of younger officers begin to site and drive in stakes.

"*Voleurs de terres,*" says LaCroix when he sees one take a reading with a compass in hand.

Jamie explains to him and Killbuck that the men are laying out the shape of the new fort they will build, many times the size of the little strong house.

We'll go to Shingas now, says Killbuck. He'll want to know about our new neighbors.

"*BÉNIS-MOI, MON PÈ, CA' J'AI PÉCHÉ—*"

The Abbé studies her silhouette through the lattice. A woman, for certain, but not an *acadienne.* An atrocious accent, not really French—

"*Je pense qu'il m'aime, mais pou'quoi voudrait-il plus de chagrin?*"

Who needs no more sorrow? Who are you talking about? asks the Abbé.

"*Mon amou', qui d'autre?*"

Does your love have a name?

You don't need to know his name, she says, just tell me what I should do.

Why don't you begin again, the Abbé suggests, starting with how long it has been since your last Confession, and then enummerate your sins.

He hopes there aren't too many. Bâtard is due at the rear of the church at any moment—

"*Je pa' 'vec le bon Dieu tous les soirs,*" she says, "*mais il ne m'a pas donné un signe.*"

Signs from Heaven, he tells her, are most often reserved for saints and mystics. And the Good Lord answers our prayers with courage and grace, not with advice on romantic pursuits.

"*Le problème est que nous ne sommes pas la même couleur,*" she sighs.

Not the same color.

Only a few of the Mi'kmaq women speak French, and none sound like this. The Abbé is intrigued. Cursing, coveting, and carousing account for the bulk of holy offense here in Beauséjour, which is why he usually leaves the tallying of sins and assigning of penance to young Père Couture. But Cornwallis, the English governor, has just offered a reward for the Abbé's capture, dead or alive, and the people must be given a display of boldness and disdain. They may come to drag me from this church I have built under the eyes of God, he has announced from the pulpit, but I will not play the fugitive in my own land.

Fifty English pounds' reward is quite a compliment.

The English schooners that his Mi'kmaq emissaries commandeered off the shore from Halifax are in the hands of *la marine française* now, with their prisoners, unharmed, already ransomed and back where they belong. The mission was so well planned and the advantage of surprise so great that few shots were fired, and therefore Bâtard's warriors not honor bound to draw their scalping knives from their belts. The English should be mollified—they are the trespassers here, whatever the fine print in the unconscionable Treaty may say.

"*Ses enfants pourraient utiliser une mère*," says the young woman, and the Abbé begins to run down his mental list of widowers in the area.

With so many children, she says, and not one of them accepted as white.

It must be Desjardins.

It must be Desjardins, the miller, with his unruly troop of children, half of them bastards until the Abbé insisted on a Christian ceremony for him and little Chipchowech, who was also called *le Rouge-Gorge* and who died with ruined lungs over a year ago.

And if she is talking about Desjardins, this must be the *negresse* people have been gossiping about, the one who lives with the insolent Lieutenant and his *putain écosaisse* just across the road.

The people here do not confess only their own sins in the booth. In the early years of *la résistance* it was the perfect venue for hearsay, for gathering intelligence, even for directing intrigues. Anxious confessors would ask if it was an actual sin to trade with the English or to obey their laws, and the Abbé could deliver his lecture on the danger of consorting with heretics, then dig a little for commercial and military information. Broussard especially loved planning sorties for their crusade from the *cabinet*, made of thick, polished oak and impossible to eavesdrop upon as long as the next penitant is kneeling in the pews at a respectable distance.

The Mi'kmaqs *bautisés*, however, frown upon mixing the spiritual and the martial, and prefer that he leave the sanctuary of the church to come smoke pipes of tobacco with them before strategizing a raid.

It will be hard to give him up, *mon pè*, says the black woman. I am so alone here.

Le Loutre has seen the *negresse* at Mass, head covered, kneeling alone, hands clasped in prayer before her with a beautifully carved wooden rosary draped over her fingers. Desjardins is a somewhat less faithful worshiper, a shrewd trader whose mill supplies the flour for both the fort and the town, including that used to make the Communion wafers the Abbé must bless once a month. He now recalls several confessors hinting, in the course of their own litany of wrongdoing, at a suspected *connaissance charnelle* between the miller and the African wench. And though le Loutre does not encourage *mélange de race*, it is an inevitable aspect of this barely civilized corner of God's Kingdom, and unions of this sort must be either forbidden or consecrated.

"*Dis à ton homme que je viendrai le voir,*" he says, knowing that snow will settle atop the molten lakes of Hell before René Desjardins will be pushed into something against his will. But a visit could be useful—le Loutre will remind the miller of the discomforts of eternal damnation, of the joys of holy matrimony, and perhaps persuade him to lay aside an adequate supply of flour for the inevitable seige by English military forces. There is a dry space in the secret passage beneath the new church building—

Say three Hail Marys and an Act of Contrition, he commands the *negresse*, who has admitted to no sin and may even be unaware of committing one.

And turn away from lust.

The Abbé listens to her mutter the beginning of the prescribed prayers in her strange, truncated French, and then blesses her before sliding the shutter between them. He peeks through the curtain to see a half-dozen kneeling transgressors waiting to unburden themselves. He leans out and calls to Père Couture, up at the altar communing with his Savior, bidding the young priest to come man the *cabinet*. Étienne Bâtard will be here at any moment, tomahawk hung from his belt and crucifix from his neck, and only the Abbé knows where the rifles are buried.

THE CHAIN BROKEN

WHITE MEN CANNOT BE TOLD WHAT IS GOOD for them but must be lured with scraps like camp dogs who have lost their ability to hunt.

The Half King waits in the rain with his handful of warriors, waiting for Silver Heels to return. The French delegation—an ensign in a bright white uniform with thirty-five men, mostly Canadians, are camped for the night. If young Washington, who the Virginias are now calling a Lieutenant Colonel, is still at the Great Meadows with his pretend soldiers, it could happen soon.

Washington has sent word that the French are searching for the Half King in order to kill him. The Half King has sent word to Washington that the French army, from their new fort, which they call Duquesne, are searching for him and his colonials, hoping to attack them. Neither is true, exactly, but these are the scraps that must be left if the dogs are to be brought together to fight.

There is a warning cry, and Scaraoudy steps out of the rain. He has brought only a half dozen more, all of them Mingos, two of them only boys.

They squat under a bear robe to talk, away from the warriors.

Is Shingas coming with more?

No, says Scaraoudy. Shingas believes we should wait and watch until we know which side will win.

Shingas is a coward. The French are not so many, and most of them far to the north, while the English—the English are like pigeons. One lands in a tree and you look away, and then when you look back there are a thousand in the branches.

The French have more soldiers here.

Have you looked carefully at their uniforms? asks the Half King. They look like beggars. They have no farmers here, no men to make wagons and guns, things that the English have not far away.

You hate the French.

I hate the French and do not trust the English. But the English have fear of our Great Council, have fear of the power of the Haudenosaunee. They can be controlled.

Scaraoudy is silent at this.

We will deal with Shingas and the Lenape later, says the Half King. Shingas is a dog who growls at his master and thinks himself a wolf.

Where are the French now?

Not far from the path to the Great Meadow, camping at the base of a wall of rocks.

So they are not a war party.

That does not matter. It is a young ensign, probably with another paper meant to scare the English and make them go away. He has a few more than thirty men, Canadians, with him, and believes that in this rain he needs no sentries.

These boys of mine carry weapons, but none is a warrior.

Ho!

And how many men, asks Scaraoudy, will Washington bring?

We shall see, says the Half King. This young man seems eager to bloody the edge of his hatchet.

They wait beside the path with the others then, making tents of their blankets and robes. The men are painted for war, but there has not been time for the proper ceremony, time to fast and speak with one's guiding spirits for strength and courage.

But it is only a small party of Canadians.

And even if they attack and are repelled, blood will be spilled, blood that should have flowed when the French marched in and took the strong house that the Half King had planned for and helped to build. They are a flighty people, the whites, with a poor sense of honor.

Nothing is spoken and an hour passes, and then another hour, the rain lightening, and then Silver Heels is at his side.

He has come, says the messenger. He wishes to fight.

Washington has brought forty men, a sorry lot, but probably the best of his small force in the Great Meadow.

"We have many more coming," says the young Lieutenant Colonel. "They are bringing heavy artillery, munitions—"

"Those men have not left the Potomac," the Half King tells him.

Washington seems not to hear, as white men will when you know something that they do not.

"Is the French party close?" he asks.

"I believe so," the Half King tells him. "With good fortune we will find them."

If you do not pretend you have to search in the woods, where the white men know they have no skill, they will begin to make plans and give orders. They set out down the path, Washington's men and the dozen Mingo warriors, with Silver Heels leading the way.

The Lieutenant Colonel walks very casually, rain dripping from his hat. He keeps looking around, and finally asks where the rest of the Indians are.

They are ahead of us, the Half King lies, scouting to find the French.

The Half King is glad that Washington did not bring more soldiers, as white men walking in the woods, whether it is a bright day or a rainy night, sound like a herd of buffalo on the trot and are no smarter than those woolly creatures. These at least have been ordered not to talk, and have the sense to each stay in sight of the man who walks before him, muskets held with the barrels pointing down to keep them from being filled with rain.

When they reach the place he agreed upon with Silver Heels, they stop and pretend to have a conference.

Walk till you are out of sight, the Half King tells Silver Heels, wait as long as it would take you to reach the French, and then come back.

"Have we found them?" asks Washington when he catches up, watching Silver Heels step off the path and into the trees.

"I believe so," says the Half King. "But we should be ready in case they are also out searching, and should stumble upon us."

The rain has stopped and the white soldiers are happy for a moment of rest. Washington has them ready their muskets. Silver Heels returns in only a short while, nodding to Scaraoudy and the Half King.

"Come with us," says the Half King, taking Washington by the arm, "and remember the way that we go."

The Half King and Scaraoudy and Washington follow Silver Heels into the trees then, the Lieutenant Colonel trying to remember signs—a rotting tree trunk, one fallen tree leaning against a live one—as they go, the trees taking shape now as night gives way to morning.

They smell the campfires before they see them.

They stop and crouch low, whispering, when the French soldiers come into sight, half dressed, cooking their breakfast before a wall of stone twice as high as a man, that provides shelter for their stacked rifles.

"If you can bring your men around to stand upon those rocks," whispers the Half King, "we will surround them to see that none escape."

"With a dozen warriors?"

The Half King smiles. "We will make the cry of a hundred. White men, when they are in a woods they do not know, fear this more than anything else."

They return to the path and Washington tells his men of his plan, reminding them to shoot no Indians in their excitement. The Half King sends Silver Heels to lead them so they do not get lost.

They wait for a short while, then the Half King and Scaraoudy each take their small party of warriors, separately, to creep up on the enemy. It is not so far. The Half King is not worried about the fight—if it begins to go badly his men know how to retreat, where to regroup. And the Virginias, even if many are killed, will report that a war has begun.

When they are in place he hears Scaraoudy make the sound of a turkey, indicating that he is also ready. The Half King can see the Virginias taking their position on the ledge above the men sitting with their coffee and bacon.

He cups his hands around his mouth and gives the call of the crow. Immediately there is a musket volley from the ledge, the sound of it echoing off the rock face, gunsmoke filling the ravine, and then cries in the French tongue and in the tongue common to all wounded and dying men. He can hear Washington's voice, shouting orders, the men below crying *aux armes, aux armes!* and a few shots and then a second volley from above and the Canadians are running toward them, most of them barefoot, and the Half King and his warriors rise up with their hatchets in their hands, whooping and running forward, the Half King knocking the first between the eyes and quickly kneeling to take his hair, hearing Scaraoudy's band also whooping, and then he strikes another who is running by on the knee, smashing it, and the man goes down, the Half King finishing him with three swift strokes and is scalping this one when he sees that the runners have turned and are hurrying back toward the stone ledge, hands in the air and calling *Nous nous rendons! Nous nous rendons!* and he grabs one of these by the shirt, spinning him around and then chasing him into the woods a ways before letting him go. The French at their new fort must hear of this.

By the time he gets back to the ravine, the firing is over and Washington has brought his men down to surround the survivors, perhaps two dozen, some of them wounded. He sees Scaraoudy and his warriors approaching, carrying bloody scalps in their hands. Scaraoudy's son, who they call Swift Runner, is one of these, wild eyed and trembling with his first killing. The Half King steps over the bodies of men killed in the first volley, moving to where Washington faces a French ensign in only the top of his white uniform, the front of it red with blood now, who is being held up by two of his men.

"*Nous ne sommes pas un parti de guerre!*" he is saying. "*J'ai été envoyer pour vous donner un lettre d'avertissement!*"

Washington, who does not understand French, looks confused.

"He says he was only sent with a letter for you, a warning," says the Half King, stepping close to the ensign, as if to translate. The ensign pulls a bloody paper from his breast, begins to unfold it with shaking hands. The Half King sees that he has been shot twice, once in the shoulder and once in the chest. He puts a hand on the young officer's neck, looks into his eyes.

"*Tu n'es pas encore mort, mon père?*" he asks, almost tenderly, and then brings his hatchet down onto the man's skull, cleaving it in two. The men who support him jump away, as does Washington, surprised, and the ensign's body slumps to the earth.

The Half King kneels, striking the man's head again and again until it is open, then scoops hot brains from within it and rubs them between his fingers, as if washing his hands. The Canadians are also on their knees, begging the Virginias for mercy, pleading to be protected from the red savages.

The Half King, brain matter sticking to his hands, finds Washington's eyes and holds them. White men like to believe that they are peace-loving creatures, that they have to be forced to kill.

Then I will force them.

ST. CYR STROLLS FROM BASTION TO BASTION ALONG the *banquette* of what his men derisively call *Fort Malséjour.* Whether it is a fortress or a prison remains to be proven, sitting on a slight rise in the flat, contested territory, offering an unobstructed view over the surrounding marshes, south across the lethargic stream they call the Missaguash River to the burnt ruins of Beaubassin and the wooden palisades of Fort Lawrence a mile away, and seaward to the *Baie de Fundy.* With the news from the Ohio Valley this terrain has taken on a more sinister aspect, no longer two forgotten garrisons meant to do nothing more than keep an eye on the other but the defiant sentinels of a pair of belligerants. Each side not only sounds its trumpets and raises its flag every morning, but the easy passage of locals within the walls of both forts has ended, and most interchanges now occur out front by the Indian camp, with the *acadiens* denied entry.

As if there is anything here worth hiding.

Only the far inland side of the five-pointed star is completely vulnerable, the ground beside it wooded and sloping upward, and it is now St. Cyr's job to remedy this. He is no engineer, but common sense has led him to employ the score of local laborers to reduce the forest with axe and saw, the boles of the saplings to be sharpened to a point and used for *abatis.* From up here he can see another party of hired *acadiens* digging a trench around the palisade walls, the *deblais* piled in a berm against the wooden poles. Earth, if thick enough, is superior to stone as a buffer to cannon-shot.

The *acadiens* are stronger, more eager workers than the soldiers garrisoned here, and unlike his handful of *bombardiers* have no objection to digging in the soil. They are a hardy, good-natured people, mostly illiterate, but loyal only unto themselves. Their delegations have consistently vowed to accept English citizenship if allowed to practice their religion and will not lift axe or spade for the French garrison without pay, preferably in goods rather than the dubious paper money issued from Québec. And yet Abbé le Loutre has only to raise a finger after Mass to have several dozen, without recompense, out building dykes along the river, filling the reclaimed marshland with seaweed and soil in hopes of planting. Dykes the English will surely breach if the fighting should reach *Acadie*, though natural flooding will probably destroy them first. The Abbé, who has often stated he will gladly sacrifice a life to sword or tomahawk rather than risk losing a soul to the heresy of Protestantism, must be tolerated, St. Cyr has been informed, for without him the *acadiens* might consider the English only something to be endured, like a coastal storm or an early frost.

But no orders yet, apparently not on either side, so they watch and wait.

St. Cyr pauses at each embrasure, sighting down the barrel of whatever caliber gun is mounted there, saluted by the *sentinelles*. He looks out over the marsh and imagines an attack by land. An ineffective barrage from the far side of the river to precede the rows of red-coated infantry, marching to the beat of their drummers till within range—half of them scythed down by rifle and cannon till there is a disorganzed retreat, with the painted Mi'kmaq running out from cover to hack the survivors to pieces.

No, it will come from the bay. His two largest guns, *canons de vingt-quatre livres*, remain trained on the watery horizon, the best of his *bombardiers* assigned to them. St. Cyr pauses at the westernmost bastion, looks inward. Soldiers on the parade ground below are piling stone to build vaults over the vulnerable casements, which will serve for shelter and as powder magazines during bombardment. A good officer is always a pessimist, expecting the worst and doing what he can to prepare for when it comes.

And good officers, in this *poste oublié*, are in short supply.

Whether the dregs of the French administration and military have been deliberately sent here or the rawness of the country has had a corrupting effect, the Canadian service is regarded as little more than an opportunity for looting. Nothing reaches here from either the home country or Québec in the quantity or condition promised—one time out of three, even the gunpowder they are issued is too damp to be of use. Officers and government officials brag openly of their pecuniary schemes, and the foot soldiers are dishearteningly aware of it. The militia are in somewhat better hands, fighting for their own land and future, but the poor souls dragooned back in La Rochelle or Calais and packed off to this dreaded *glaciére* have only the lack of tropical disease to be thankful for.

The Lieutenant is saluted by Guérin, hopping up from the barrel of the cannon he was seated on, half asleep. For sixteen *livres* a month, paid irregularly in *papier-monnaie*, one does not expect miracles.

"*Rien de nouveau?*"

"*Rien ne bouge, mon lieutenant.*"

This side of the pentangle overlooks the little, newly built town, and St. Cyr can see smoke rising from the chimney of his house just across from le Loutre's *eglise* and imagines his woman inside with her faithful *bonne*, doing woman things. Though it has become apparent over the years that Jeannie will never be a lady, that is not what is wanted here. Turn her out with these robust *acadiennes* who work in the fields beside their men, who chop firewood and milk cows and carry bundles of seaweed on their backs, and she will not be out of place. There is little society here to show her off to, the *grandes balles* of Québec and Montreál only lovely rumors in Beauséjour, and the few times he has accompanied her to a *fête acadienne* she has sung along with the locals in their atrocious French and danced like a peasant.

À Rome fais comme les romains.

De Vergor, the commandant, has made a few sly inquiries about her, perhaps not meant as an insult, but galling nonetheless. If I didn't have her here, St. Cyr admits, I would go mad.

Or take up with a Mi'kmaq woman.

Abbé le Loutre has been stirring them up again, and there are reports that Chief Bâtard and his *acadien* cohort Joseph Broussard were red-handed in the killings around Halifax before the peace was shattered. Commandant de Vergor received several polite missives, delivered somewhat apologetically by a messenger from Fort Lawrence, from the English governor, Cornwallis, demanding information as to the perpetrators of such outrage. At the time a kind of *accord du gentlemen* existed between the two outposts, an attempt to keep their troops from foraging in the same woods on the same days, even some comparing of notes as to rates of pay for local labor and barter with the savages. A premonition of conflict does not preclude civilized behavior. Nonetheless, St. Cyr kept constant inventory of his artillery supplies, suspecting that illicit trade with the enemy might be among his commandant's perversions.

Where were you born? he asks the *bombardier.*

In Brittany, near Morlaix, says Guérin.

Ah—like so many of the people here.

The *bombardier* looks horrified. The *acadiens* have been here long enough to be a different people, a different race, even—

"*Mais je suis français!*" he objects.

"*Sans doute.*"

Though his artillerymen are barracked with the regular infantry, St. Cyr attempts to maintain their comportment and morale at a higher level. Once a week now there is seige drill, every gun in the fort except, as a precaution, those facing the English fired, reloaded, and fired again. Half charges are used to counter de Vergor's moanings about waste of powder, and the townspeople, fishermen, and Mi'kmaqs are advised not to be where the balls are likely to come to earth or sea.

Thus far, there have been no casualties.

St. Cyr walks along the curtain to the next bastion, exchanges salutes with the *sentinelle* there, then continues onto the parapet that holds the main gate. Pichon, the dissatisfied new commissary, has climbed up the rampart to wait for him.

Pichon held the same position at the *grande forteresse* at Louisbourg, and his transfer, or perhaps banishment, to this remote garrison with a fraction of the number of troops is the subject of much conjecture.

"*Puis-je être franc?*" he begins.

Pichon does not waste words.

Of course you may be frank, St. Cyr assures him. Honest communication between officers is vital to the health of the service—

"*Il écrasse à nouveau la crème!*"

Il always means "the commandant" when Pichon is speaking, unless he uses *ce prétendant* or the more apt *l'incompétent* to describe de Vergor. And as the *garde magasin*, Pichon is well placed to know who is skimming the cream and how much of it has gone missing.

"*Il continue de prétendre que nous avons cent-cinquante,*" he fulminates, waving his arms. It has been months, what with deaths and desertions, since they have mustered more than one hundred thirty soldiers, so the commandant is collecting pay and supplies for almost two dozen phantoms. Worse, no replacements have been sent for—

"*Et il m'interdit de corriger cette croyance!*"

St. Cyr suffered the same frustration on his arrival, the habit of stretching or abandoning the truth epidemic in *la Nouvelle France*, but without political influence here he quickly surrendered to the *comme il faut*. Pichon is either blind to his own powerlessness or so fueled by rancor he choses to ignore it.

Perhaps, St. Cyr suggests dryly, you should write a protest to the authorities.

"*À qui?*" the man cries, indignant. "*Au bon monsieur Bigot? Le plus grand de tous les escrocs!*"

Bigot, the Intendant in Québec, has become notoriously wealthy in the position, controlling trade, food supplies, and prices in the colony, his name always uttered with a shrug to explain why goods here cost four times what they do in France.

"*C'est la vie, mon ami,*" says the Lieutenant, smiling sadly and adding his own hunch of the shoulders.

"*Et si on nous attaque?*" demands the commissary. "*Avec ce bouffon comme notre chef?*"

It is St. Cyr's nightly terror, picturing the fat, frivolous Compte de Vergor stuttering panicked and contradictory orders while under fire. Of course, there are times when the roar of the cannon render an ill-advised command inaudible—

If we are attacked, he sighs to the outraged commissary, both of them gazing across the marsh to the English fort, keep your head down and stay away from the gunpowder.

THE PIG BELIEVES IT IS ONLY ANOTHER FROLIC. SHOUTing children tag and chase each other, big-eyed with excitement, their fathers drinking tin cups of a potent cider made from apples as they hone their blades and the women feed the fires and set kettles of water to boil. One of the Cormier daughters, just into her teens and an experienced swineherd, leaves a trail of table scraps to lure the first of the chosen, snorting and snuffling, straight up to big Pierre Landry with a sledgehammer in his iron grip. Landry waits for the sow to look up at him from a pile of ripe-smelling cabbage, then drops her with a single mighty downstroke to the cheers of all about.

Il n'y a pas de fête sans massacre, thinks Jenny, a phrase she learned from St. Cyr back on his island. And though a *boucherie* of three pigs requires a good deal of labor, this is unmistakably a celebration. A pair of *violineaux* are warming up their fiddles, a long, long oak table is being set with plates and cutlery, and a few of the women, all in identical *câline* bonnets and white linen aprons, are singing one of the songs she has heard when they come together to boil wool.

The Robicheaux brothers quickly pierce the hind hocks with thick metal hooks, then haul the still-twitching carcass up by the attached cords till it is hanging from a stout branch, front trotters dangling several inches off the ground. Madame Cormier helps her daughter drag a large wooden tub beneath, and then Landry slices the pig's throat open, carefully guiding the first bright rush of blood with a hand around its snout.

Jenny stands with several other women and girls by a trough filled with seawater, waiting for instruction, certain that she has been invited here more to be studied than to be helpful.

She is thrilled to have been asked.

It takes some time for the pig to empty out, the Robicheaux brothers lugging one blood-filled tub away to be replaced by another. The fiddlers begin to play, seeming to first find the tune and then each other, playing alternately in harmony or in counterpoint, as the *fréres* Robicheaux heave kettles of boiling water over the body to clean the muck off and soften the bristles and Landry uses a different knife to flay the animal, constantly tugging the loosened skin back to hang from the backbone till it looks like a bulky man shedding a winter coat. A fourth *acadien*, perhaps one of the many Doucets, saws the trotters and head off then as the others hold the body steady, Landry pulls the sow's anus out slightly to tie it off, then makes a cut from the pelvis to the ribs to allow the pink-and-purple entrails to slither out into a basin held by the Robicheaux, who quickly transfer the bloated coils into the saltwater trough.

The men then take turns with an axe to chop the pig into two halves, leaving them dangling to dry before further butchering, while the women show Jenny how to separate the intestines from the stomach, then strip the fat from them, tossing it into a bucket, before pinching the sharp-smelling contents from the casings, four women stepping apart to stretch out a length. Each long section, as well as the emptied stomach, is rinsed in another trough full of river water, then worried and rolled till it is turned inside out, a slippery-slimy process that sets the younger girls giggling, before a final rinsing.

Sheep, cows, chickens—they never owned a pig in Scotland. Anmals were killed within the byre, shielded from envy. Jenny concentrates on her fingers as she handles the glistening innards, clumsy at first, then gaining a sense of the process, feeling their eyes on her, quietly evaluating. She has taken over most of the chores at home that can be done outside, the work helping her to feel a bit less useless, and hopes her *voisines* have noticed. Women her age who have no children are very rare here, and women who sit before a looking glass all day *pour se faire belle* are not to be found.

The fiddlers change their tune, both men and women singing along with the melody—

Mademoiselle voulez-vous danser
La bastringue, la bastringue?
Mademoiselle voulez-vous danser?
La bastrigue va commencer—

—while sections of the gut are cut, tied shut at one end, then filled with either chopped heart and liver or meat, fat, cornmeal and blood, using a funnel made from a cow's horn. Most of these are tied off and hung on a rack to cure, but a number are thrown immediately onto a grill already heating over a small fire, while beside them strips of skin, the hair scraped off, are crackling loudly in a pot of rendered fat.

The third pig, a boar, is not fully dead when its throat is cut, twisting and writhing upside down till its body is nearly drained, making a strange wet clicking noise rather than a scream. Jenny has seen cattle butchered, but cowhide is not so like human skin as the pig's, nor its diet as varied, and the smell as the innards are squeezed flat is nearly overwhelming. Emptied intestines, milky white now, are being separated and rolled into coils when Madame Cormier gestures her over to where the enormous boiled head of the first sow rests on top of a tall stump, snout pointed toward the clouds and hairy ears flopping backward. The woman hands Jenny a very sharp knife and indicates a stack of wooden bowls.

"*Enlever toute la viande*," she instructs, then steps away to help her daughters stuff *boudin*.

A test.

But Jenny has survived months on a fever hulk, survived the middle passage across treacherous seas, has even stared down the elders of a Scottish kirk, and this is only a wee spot of butchery—

The cheeks are easy once skin and fat are cut away, lovely oblongs of glistening meat, then the large muscles under the eye sockets and the fistful of firm flesh at the base of the skull. She places the large cuts of meat and smaller scraps into one bowl, the snout, ears, and skin into another, the fat and jelly into a third. Jenny, who has never taken a good look at a pig's teeth before, is amazed by their variety and sharpness, wondering if these people have a use even for them.

"*Bon travail*," says Madame Cormier when she returns, bloody up to the elbows.

There's so much of it, says Jenny.

The woman watches her cut and twist and yank for a moment before coming to the point

"*Vous parlez anglais?*"

Jenny allows that she does speak English, though it is not her mother tongue.

"*Et vous savez que les anglais nous menace.*"

St. Cyr has explained how most of *Nouvelle-Écosse* was dishonorably ceded to the enemy in the Treaty of Utrecht, that the English stronghold in Halifax was only built a few years ago, and that the land Beauséjour occupies has always been contested.

"*C'est pourquoi nous avons un fort,*" says Jenny, careful with the knife, sharper than any she has ever held.

The Lieutenant has also explained that though the *acadiens* here have sworn neutrality and would prefer to be left alone, both the French and the English are expecting their support if there is a war—

"*Ètes-vous captif?*" asks Madame Cormier.

"*J'étais captif de l'anglais,*" Jenny answers, knowing that the story of her captivity and rescue is already legend among the people here, "*mais maintenant je suis libre.*"

"Free" sounds false in her mouth, though it is true after a fashion.

"*Vous ne manque pas votre pays?*"

She knows it would please the woman to tell her, "This is my country now," but it is not true. And she has not missed Scotland since the day she stepped off the French privateer.

I have no country, she tells Madame Cormier.

Unlike Amély, who was not invited today, who thinks of Martinique as her living home and of Africa as where her soul will rest once she's dead.

"*Je suis content,*" Amély said, clearly wounded by the snub, when Jenny offered to stay home with her.

I've seen enough animals slaughtered.

The *violineaux* are playing something very slow and sad now, similar to an air Jenny has heard played on the Highland pipes. There is only a picked-over skull with tiny white pig eyes left on top of the stump.

And what do you do with this? she asks.

"*Rien*," Madame Cormier tells her, picking up the bowl filled with the tongue and other face meat.

We leave that for the crows.

A DOZEN INDIANS SIT WATCHING FROM THE STOREhouse on the hill at Christopher Gist's plantation. Jamie is with Killbuck and LaCroix, and there are some Shawnee and four very surly Mingos, who keep to themselves, and a wandering Lenape known as Delaware George who is always smiling and who nobody trusts. Killbuck spots the advance scouts first, four warriors trotting out from the pack trail and across one of the meadows Gist has not yet planted on.

Ottawa, he says. They'll be with the French.

Shingas has left them to be his eyes, having told Washington he would not fight for him but would have scouts along the river to warn him, then told Jamie and the others to do no such thing.

One of the Ottawa, though painted and naked to the waist, is as light skinned as Jamie. When none of the men waiting by the storehouse run away, he and the other scouts approach.

"*Êtes-vous avec l'anglais?*" he calls in French.

We are with nobody, Jamie answers.

The man steps close, looks Jamie over. Wait here, he says. Our captain will want to talk to you.

The Mingos move away to watch from some distance. Delaware George keeps smiling.

The troops arrive in a loose formation, trudging across the meadow and up the hill, regulars first, then the Canadian militia, with different bands of Indians, some with as many as thirty warriors, shifting around them.

Those are people from the north and from the west, says Killbuck. Ottawa, Abenaki, Algonquian, Nipissing, Wyandot—

If their captain wants us, says LaCroix to Jamie, you talk with him.

Your French is as good as mine.

But you're a better liar.

The white soldiers keep formation well enough to make it easy for Jamie to count—six hundred men, including the dozens at the rear dealing with the wagons and the cannon.

How many Indians? he asks.

More than one hundred, says Killbuck. But some of them won't continue.

How do you know?

Because there is enough to loot here.

The light-skinned Ottawa returns as the main force falls out to rest and a few squads search the storehouse and outbuildings.

He wants one of you, says the Ottawa.

All look to Jamie, so he follows the warrior to where the regular troops have already begun setting up tents. The captain is a long-nosed man in his forties.

"*Vous avez vu l'anglais?*"

Yes, Jamie tells him. They were here, and then they left.

"*Quand?*"

Three days ago. They have been building a road for the Ohio Company, and thought they would stand and fight here, but then got word of how many you were.

He does not say that it was Delaware George, always welcome in any fort, who brought the word.

"*Et combien?*"

There are four hundred *Virginien* with Washington, and another hundred *troupes anglaises régulières* waiting at Great Meadows.

"*Y a-t-il un fort là-bas?*"

They've made something like a fort there, says Jamie, but I have not seen it.

"*Combien de sauvages sont avec lui?*"

There were some families he was feeding, but all the warriors have gone.

The captain cocks his head and frowns at this news. "*Pourquoi?*"

They left him because they think he's going to lose, says Jamie. Why else?

Who is your chief? asks the captain.

"*Je suis un Loup, mais nous ne suivons pas les chefs,*" Jamie tells him. We follow our own hearts.

If you follow us, you'll see the English defeated.

Perhaps. The last time you fought, the English took prisoners and beat the brains out of the ensign.

That was my brother, snaps the long-nosed Frenchman. "*Je suis capitaine Louis Coulon de Villiers.*"

Jamie tells him the rest of what he knows, that the Virginias are badly supplied, driving the last two dozen of their cattle before them, that many of the men are sick and that the redcoat regulars were left behind because they wouldn't wield an axe or a shovel without extra pay.

Captain de Villiers compliments him on his French and asks, suspicious, where he learned it.

I lived with the Shawnee in the south, Jamie lies, with the band of Chartier. We traded with the French all the time.

He is able to wander among their camp as it is made then, neither the French regulars or the *canadiens* or the various groups of northern and western Indians paying any special attention to him. Washington had been similarly lax, perhaps assuming that either trusting or controlling the movements of savages was not possible. His eavesdropping garnered a consensus among the white soldiers that they would be ambushed at some point, perhaps by the very Indians traveling at their side.

Killbuck, squatting with some of the Algonquians who are comparing the things they have looted from Gist's storehouse, waves him over.

I was right, he says. These men are turning back tomorrow.

What should we do?

LaCroix and I will walk along with the French. But Shingas wants to talk to you tonight. He's ahead on the trail.

JAMIE WAITS TILL IT IS DARK, THEN TAKES HIS RIFLE AND slips around the Canadian sentries and finds the trail heading east. Gist and a Lenape named Nemacolin established the path only a few years ago, and Washington and his men have made it wide enough for wagons all the way to the Great Meadows.

It is the first time he has been sent alone in the woods. It is a gesture of trust, he knows, and as he walks Jamie wonders how it would be taken if he were to join the French captain for the war that seems to be starting. He has heard that Chartier has been made an officer, as well as another *metis* named Langlade. He wonders if any of the military men he met when he was a courier in France have been sent here—

Shingas is waiting by the path at the top of Chestnut Ridge.

The soldiers Washington killed are still there, he says, nodding toward a glen off to the right. The Half King's warriors took their hair and their clothes and left them naked.

Perhaps the French will bury them.

That would be proper, says Shingas. So they are coming—

Six hundred white soldiers, more than one hundred Indians.

Shingas nods.

Queen Alliquippa has brought her people away to join Washington at the Great Meadows, he says, hoping the English will protect them.

Yes, says Jamie. And I have heard that Scaraoudy has burned his dwellings at Logstown and is coming this way with his people.

Lots of smoke in the air, says Shingas, and the deer run this way and that.

They sit by the trail, listening to the night. It is warm, and feels like it will rain tomorrow.

I talked to the French captain, says Jamie. His brother was the ensign that the Half King murdered here.

Shingas frowns at the word for "murder."

It was badly done, he says. And now there will be more killing.

Shingas takes Jamie's rifle in his hands, troubled, turning it as if seeing such a thing for the first time.

How do you make this?

A rifle—?

The wooden part, I understand. This we could carve from a walnut tree.

It is a Brown Bess pattern rifle, well-used, the metal of the barrel somewhat pitted, but the lockwork functions and it shoots true at fifty yards—

It is a thing made of many parts, say Jamie.

Explain to me.

Jamie touches the barrel—

This is made of iron—

The metal of the black pots.

Yes. The iron is made into a flat sheet, then cut—

How do you get the iron?

It is inside rocks that are dug from the ground—

All rocks?

No. You have to know which rocks carry the iron. If there is a red stain on a rock, it is likely to have iron in it. Men dig the rocks, then crush them—

How?

I believe with balls of iron, like the ones shot from a cannon, but I'm not sure—

You've never seen this done?

No. I've read about it—

Shingas understands what reading is, can write his name on a piece of paper, but distrusts the activity.

So even white people, he says, need to use things that they do not understand.

They understand the use of it, but not always the making, no—

So you have crushed the iron rock—

And then it is melted—

One can melt rock?

If the fire is hot enough, yes.

For this many trees must be cut.

For the fires, most times, coal is used, not wood—

Coal—

Yes, it is a—

The shiny black rock.

You have seen it—

Inside of other rocks, yes. Is there a place where all the rocks are coal?

Places with lots of it, yes. But most of it is under the ground.

So you must dig.

In parts of the great island where I am from there are mines, holes in the ground that become long caves—places like the ones where the Lenape find the clay to make tobacco pipes. But often the coal is very deep under the ground, and the hole to get to it goes down and down—the person digging the coal must carry a torch with him, and dig a tunnel—

Like a rabbit or a mole—

Yes, very much like that.

Shingas shakes his head at the notion.

A Lenape will not do this. The People Who Live Beneath must not be disturbed.

Jamie nods. The people where I come from who do it are very poor. And once they are put to this job they may not leave it. If the mine—one of the great holes with tunnels of coal—is sold from one owner to another, the men and women who dig there are sold as well.

We do not buy or sell people—

You sell prisoners. Or trade them—

Those are not Lenape.

You don't sell your own people, then—

No matter how poor they are.

That is a good thing, says Jamie. Once the coal is burning very hot, and the rock has melted, the part that is iron can be separated—

But it is all liquid—

When you cook a bear, the fat is lifted away.

Yes—

And when it cools it becomes much harder—

Yes—

The iron, before it has cooled completely, is stretched into a sheet. Iron can then be heated again to bend it—

I have seen this done with the iron they put on the hooves of horses.

Then you know that a sheet of metal can be rolled into a tube—

Like this, says Shingas, holding the barrel, that makes the ball fly straight.

Yes—

And that the softer black metal can be melted and shaped into balls—

Yes—

But what of the powder?

Jamie tries to think of what he knows and how to explain it.

The gunpowder, he says, is a mix of different things. Most of it is charcoal—if you burn wood until it is hot embers, then cover it in sand—

I know this thing. Like coal, but very light in the hand—

That charcoal is crushed into a fine powder, and then mixed with another powder, that of a yellow rock—

With a strong smell when it is wet—

That one, yes. And then there is another rock made into a powder, called saltpeter, which is harder to find. As far as I know, most of this comes from India, a land far across the Great Water—

So these powders, when mixed—

Become another thing, gunpowder.

That is magic.

A kind of magic, but one that many white people understand. The Lenape make sugar from the sap of trees—

Yes—

Which is not magic. Somehow they learned how to do this—

It was a knowing given to us, protests Shingas. By He Who Made All Things.

Jamie doesn't know if the words he needs exist in Lenape, and wishes Davie Falconer, who could always explain his medical learning, were here to help him.

There are other kinds of knowing, he says. When the Lenape come to a river they have never seen before, do they already know how the current moves?

No. They must try their canoes in the water—

Much of the white man's knowing is like that. Trying things, mixing things to see what will happen.

Because He Who Created All Things gave them less knowing than he gave the real people.

That must be it, says Jamie.

Shingas points to the lockworks.

The flint in the rifle makes a spark—

Yes. As when we make a fire with it—

And the gunpowder explodes—

When he says *pòkte,* Shingas makes a small explosion with his fingers.

Yes, but because it is confined in the iron tube, it pushes the ball, very fast—

As fast as an arrow from a bow.

Yes. Maybe faster.

Shingas frowns. When my grandfather was my age, he says, we had no such things. Everything we used we had made ourselves, or had been given the knowing of at the Beginning of Things. But this—

He shakes the musket—

—this we cannot make nor understand. And if we do not have it and our enemy does, we will be defeated and made slaves. But to get it we must trade with the white man—

Yes—

—who will not stay where he is told to.

No, says Jamie. White men are not made that way.

Shingas hands the rifle back to Jamie.

Stay with the French until they fight the Virginias, he says. Be my eyes. And if you fire this, you do not do it as a Lenape.

IT IS RAINING HARD THE NEXT DAY WHEN JAMIE FALLS IN beside Killbuck and LaCroix, who have attached themselves to the Abenakis who walk behind the *canadiens.*

These are the safest Indians for us to travel with, says Killbuck.

The others don't like Lenapes?

The others don't like anybody. Especially the Ottawa.

Under the trees to the sides of the path, their paint running down their faces and bodies, the Ottawa look no more fierce than the warriors from any of the other tribes, or than the *canadiens*, many of whom are dressed in buckskin.

The troop ahead of them has slowed now. They must be getting close—

The path becomes much wider then, raw stumps where Washington's road builders have cut the trees, planks laid across the swampy places. Jamie can see that the Abenaki are getting nervous, guessing that the enemy ahead could fill this road with men—

There is a rifle shot ahead of them.

There is a rifle shot ahead of them and then Captain de Villiers is shouting orders, the troop divided into three forces and Jamie and LaCroix and Killbuck stay with the Abenaki, who attach themselves to the Canadians, forming the left wing of a skirmish line as they hurry out onto a broad meadow and begin to advance toward the fort. Less than a fort, actually, a small circular palisade of logs standing on end with a few raised platforms for swivel guns and outside trenches with breastworks raised before them on two sides. The swivel guns fire, falling short, and then the Canadians in front of Jamie take a knee and fire a volley, still some six hundred yards from the enemy. There are wagon horses and cattle wandering loose around the stockade and a few of these are hit, the horses running away across the meadow, and the French force is up and marching again as the last of the English—red-coated regulars facing them—retreat into their trench. A second volley is ordered, most of the cattle brought to the ground now, as well as a few camp dogs, and then a shouted order to scatter into the dense woods just north of the stockade.

Jamie finds an elm with good shelter, the rain less driving beneath it, and watches the Abenakis and Canadians find their firing positions and begin a steady sniping at the regulars in the trench. The stockade couldn't have been built in a worse spot, not only within musket range from the woods but in a natural depression, water beginning to pool up in front of the breastworks and no doubt filling the trenches themselves.

It is a miserable business on both sides, hundreds of snipers firing steadily from behind boulders, trees, stumps, hillocks, while the Virginias, far too many of them to fit within the tiny circle of palisade, are easy targets whenever they expose themselves to shoot back. Jamie sees the men on his side of the battle making little tent shelters from their blankets, holding their muskets under these to load dry powder and ball, then hurrying back to their vantages to fire. Hours pass with only an occasional cry of triumph when someone in the trenches goes down and is carried back into the stockade. Cartridge boxes and dead dogs are floating in the small ponds that have formed in front of the breastworks, and the swivel guns have been silenced, their positions too exposed for the crews to man them.

And then it really starts to pour. Jamie tries to find the spot beneath the elm where the sheet of falling rain is the least dense, shivering while the sniping from the woods grows more intermittent and the enemy in the trenches, which must be nearly filled by now, can only crouch in the muddy water with their heads tucked in.

Killbuck strolls up to squat beside him, laughing.

Only white men, he says, would try to kill each other while they are drowning.

It is nearly dark when the young Lieutenant Colonel hears the cry.

"*Voulez-vous parler?*"

It must be a trick. The French have them surrounded, outmanned, outgunned, have a huge party of savages should they attempt to escape in the dark through the woods, and must know that reinforcement is hopelessly stalled back in Virginia.

"*Voulez-vous parler?*"

Again.

The firing from the woods has ceased. Washington, kneeling in the ditch, water nearly to his hips, calls back.

"Who is that?"

A pause, probably for translation, then, "*Je suis le capitaine de Villiers, commandant des troupes du roi très chrétien Louis.*"

The ensign killed by the Half King back in the glen was a de Villiers—it must be a common name among them. He sees the bulk of Van Braam shift at the other end of the breastworks, the Dutchman wading on all fours to reach him.

"Dis is der captain. He vish us to speak—"

"I understood that much. But I can't very well invite him in to get a look at our condition, can I?"

He's seen a half-dozen men at his side killed or wounded, his dear friend La Péyronie among them, and according to the one runner who managed to crawl from Captain Mackay's trench, the regulars suffered even heavier losses. Several score of men were too sick to fight even before the engagement began, and now the scoundrels left inside the palisade have broken into the rum, with Colonel Muse, after his precipitate withdrawal from the field at first contact, the most notable offender. If they begin to sing, not unlikely given the ungovernable, eightpence-a-day idlers he has been saddled with, the French will know for certain that they need not call for a truce.

"Den you go oudt to meet him?"

An image recurs to the young Lieutenant Colonel, as it has often in the last weeks, of the Half King with his fingers digging into the French ensign's shattered skull. *Coulon de Villiers, sieur de Jumonville,* their firebrand scribblers called him in eulogy. Murdered. Assassinated. As if he were truly on some diplomatic errand—

"Tell him I'll send somebody out."

Van Braam turns to bellow out across the meadow.

"*Nous enverrons quelqu'un pour négocier!*"

Washington wonders if the Dutchman's French is as thickly accented as his English. He is competent as a fencing instructor, proficient, even, but as a translator—

"*Nous viendrons vous rencontrer,*" calls the French captain. "*Dites à vos soldats de cesser le feu!*"

Washington calls cease-fire and hears it echoed around the stockade. Nothing but the drumming of the rain on the mud all around them.

"You'll have to go in my stead," he tells the Dutchman. "Hear what they have to offer and report it to me—"

"I'll go with him."

La Péyronie, shot in the right breast just above the lung, has not spoken or stirred for so long that Washington has thought him dead.

"You're wounded."

"I can walk, I believe, with assistance." He nods toward Van Braam. "We must be very clear."

La Péyronie, a Huguenot, obviously speaks better French than the Dutchman, and the half-breed Montour is still out with a patrol, perhaps within earshot and considering how far to run.

"Very well, if you think you're able. We'll dispense with the white flag."

"*Nous sortons!*" calls Van Braam, then he and Washington help the wounded man to his feet, La Péyronie clutching the Dutchman's shoulder for support as they step with some difficulty around the breastworks.

Washington watches as a pair of French officers in white, looking wet but otherwise unperturbed, step out from the woods facing him and begin to make their way across the soggy marsh ground. The taller man, a captain by his insignia, pauses once to dump rainwater from his hat. Washington turns, finds Captain Stobo halfway down the trench, motions for him to come.

Stobo, who has acquitted himself admirably for a man in his first clash of arms, stands and strolls over, bending to reassure some of the men on the way.

"Sir?"

"Terms are being discussed. I want you to step into the stockade and keep those bloody rascals quiet."

"I'm afraid they're well beyond obeying orders, sir. Even your presence—"

"Charge your pistols, Captain, and employ them as you must."

"Yes, sir."

His emissaries return rather quickly, the Dutchman half carrying the Huguenot, who he lays gently against the muddy bank of the flooded trench.

"He is saying dot as England und France haf no declaration of hostility, no honor is lost mit surrender. But no surrender, der captain say he don't maybe control his savages so goot."

"That is his threat?"

The Dutchman shrugs. "He say, *'Je suis vraiment désolé'*—I am truly sorry, but dis is facts."

Washington turns to La Péyronie, but his friend has passed into unconsciousness. He orders two of the men to carry him in to Dr. Craik in the stockade, then turns back to the matter at hand.

"Go back to them," he tells Van Braam, "and ask them to put their offer, in complete detail, of course, in writing."

"I do dis."

The Dutchman lumbers away. If nothing else, his men in the trenches will be afforded some moments of rest, even sleep, if such be possible when half immersed in cold water.

This is only the preamble, of course, the musicians tuning their instruments for the symphony to come. Forts will be taken and renamed, retaken and named again, the Indians will fight on whichever side bribes them with the most attractive bounty, but in the long run, here in America, it will be a contest of will. And unfortunately Virginians have so far shown little zeal for the struggle, pinching their purses shut, and the Pennsylvanians unmanned by Quakerism—only the traders and the rough folk of the frontier settlements seem to understand what is at stake. This—don't call it a defeat, for it is but a setback, a practical retreat, if you will—this can be presented to the burgesses in a manner not totally unflattering. A resistance was made, the road is half complete—

Van Braam reappears, stepping out of the growing dark with the papers—two copies written in the same harried hand—tucked inside his coat. Captain Mackay is called to witness, and Mercer, Steven, and Hogg, as well as Stobo back out from the stockade, Stobo holding a candle close as the Dutchman struggles to make out the words and relay them to Washington and his officers.

> *"Cabidulation granted to Monsieur de Villiers, captain und commander of infantry und troops of his most Christian Majesty, to dose English troops actually in der fort of Necessity vich is build on der lands of der French King's dominions, July der Third, at eight o'clock at night, seventeen fifty-four—"*

"The 'French King's dominions' indeed," huffs Mackay.

> *"As our indention vas never to trouble der peace und goot harmony reigning between der two friendly princes, but only to avenge der—der killing—dot has been done a certain of our officers, bearer of a summons—"*

"An absolute prevarication," says Washington. "But go on."

> *"—und as also to hinder der esdablishment on der lands of der dominions of der King, meine master: upon these considerations, ve are ready to grant prodection or favor, to all der English in der said fort, upon der conditions hereafter mentioned—"*

Van Braam turns the paper over.

> *"Colonel Vashington und his garrison may return peacefully to der own country, while the King's forces promise to restrain, as much as in our power, der savages vot are mit us. Der English are permiited to take mit dem all der belongings excepting der artillery und munition."*

"That will need to be amended," says Washington. "Without munitions, their Indians will follow and slaughter us. Continue—"

> *"Der English vill be granted der honors of war: leafing der fort mit drums beating und mit one of der cannon, to show by dis means ve treat dem as friends. Dey may leaf der property und return for it later mit vagons, leafing behind dem as many troop as dey vish, on condition that vord of honor is given not to vork on any establishment on dis side of der mountain for whole year."*

"All based on the conceit that their King Louis has the slightest claim to this land."

> *"Since der English haf in der possession an officer und two cadets as vell as other prisoner vot dey took ven dey kill der Sieur de Jumonville, dey now promise to send dem mit escort to Fort Duquesne, vich is on der Belle Rivière. To secure der safe performance uff dis article uff der treaty, they vill leaf*—und here there is blank space for two names—*both of them captains, vot shall be delivered to us as hostage until der arrival uff our French und Canadians herein before mentioned. Ve on our part declare dot ve shall provide escort back in safety for der two officers, vich is all happening in two months und a half."*

A silence then. Washington takes the candle, holding it close to his face so his officers may see him.

"Gentlemen?"

"Our ammunition is barely adequate to keep the savages at bay for a march back to Virginia," says Hogg. "We have no alternative."

The other officers agree, only Captain Mackay demurring.

"I'll sign it," he says. "But I'm not leaving any of my people behind."

"Very well. If they'll allow us our rifles and powder, we'll accept."

"I volunteer to act as hostage."

It is Captain Stobo, the Scotsman who had arrived for duty in Winchester with his own blacksmith, game hunters, servant-mechanics, and covered wagon to carry his personal effects.

"You understand," says Washington, "that the disposition of the French prisoners to be exchanged is not in my hands, but held by the House of Burgesses."

Stobo smiles. "I shall trust in your influence, then."

Washington nods, turns to Van Braam. "I'm afraid you'll have to be the other, Jacob. You speak the language, you can keep an eye out for Stobo and eavesdrop on your hosts. As an officer and a gentleman I'm sure you will be permitted some liberty of movement upon your honor."

Van Braam spreads his arms. He is covered in mire, and like half of the officers and all of the Virginia troops, wearing only civilian clothes.

"I am not looking like gentleman," he says. "But I am thinking, as ve are maybe der same size—"

"I believe I may have something appropriate."

In his trunk Washington has a dress uniform, which he was hoping to wear as he marched out of the fort under enemy eyes. Blue coat with scarlet facings, silver fringe, full-laced waistcoat—

"I buy dis from you, but I'm having no money—"

"I'll take it from your next pay—shall we say thirteen pounds?"

"I thank you."

The Dutchman, not so parsimonious as others of his race, already owes Washington at least that much.

"Go back to them and have the agreement amended. You captains will advise your men and decide what may be carried and what left behind or destroyed. Let them know we need to make an impressive show tomorrow."

The officers bid him a good night and retire to speak with their companies. There is, in fact, singing coming from the stockade behind him, something soft and plaintive, probably Irish, from the feel of it. Washington tries to think of the other great military men who have been forced to surrender, only to triumph on a later occasion. If nothing else, this incident may convince Mr. Pitt and the other worthies in the home country that regular English troops will need to be sent, and soon. There is a stubborness, a sense of independence bred into these American-born that is incompatible with proper warfare.

The rain seems to abate with the cease-fire. Jamie watches the several meetings between de Villiers and his second in command with the big Dutchman who was at Logstown, papers carried back and forth, and eventually the Dutchman and another colonial officer, both in splendid uniforms now, strolling to the French encampment. He sleeps then, as he has learned to do, sitting against the wet bark of the oak tree, until daybreak, a steamy mist rising over the meadow.

Within an hour the French and their Indians have mustered and formed two parallel lines outside the little stockade. Jamie joins Killbuck and LaCroix, standing with the Abenaki.

Watch the Ottawa, says Killbuck. The others will follow them.

A trio of drummers leads the English out, marching between the facing lines of their enemy, carrying both dead and wounded and a great deal of baggage. As they move off across the meadow de Villiers gives an order and a detachment of his regulars enters the stockade and raises *la bannière blanche de la France* on the flagpole.

The white men worship these colored cloths, Killbuck observes, and the man nailed to the wood.

The English have halted at the edge of the woods to bury their dead and pile the baggage they'll leave behind. De Villiers orders that the stockade be searched and then burned, the Indians breaking ranks with the white troops and hurrying in to see what is worth taking. Jamie sees a layer of gunpowder floating atop the puddles left in the trenches, obviously dumped last night at Washington's order, then watches a flock of crows, cautious, landing nearby and beginning to hop closer and closer to the dead animals that lie all around the stockade.

The Ottawa warriors move as a group toward the English, passing directly in front of de Villiers.

"*Essayez d'être gentil avec eux*," mutters the captain, not meeting their eyes.

The Ottawa are soon joined by the other groups of Indians, loosely circling the English troop to shout insults at them in their various tongues. The Virginia colonel has assigned two dozen of his men to stand guard, muskets ready and facing outward, as their fellows finish the burying, perhaps thirty of the shallow graves dug, and the stacking of goods into three large piles. Jamie approaches a nervous boy still in his teens, one of the colonials.

"Yer leavin' a guid deal ahind fer us," he says to the boy, who stares at him as if he is a talking dog. "What are these mounds, then?"

"I saw you," says the boy. "You were there at Gist's plantation."

"Aye, when yer lanky officer tried tae talk us intae throwin' in with yer troop."

"And you fought for them."

"Ah fought fer naebody." Jamie holds his musket out in front of him. "This has no been fired fer a week noo."

The boy looks back to where his comrades are piling baggage. "Some of it we'll carry," he says. "Some we'll burn, and some we'll leave under guard with the most badly wounded."

"Ah've a piece iv advice fer ye, laddie. If they ax fer volunteers tae stay, dinnae be ane of them who says yes."

The boy looks to the Ottawa, hooting and pressing closer to the English troop, some even poking the guards with their fingers and laughing.

"They're not supposed to bother us."

"They'll do whate'er they like, and ye want tae be weel awee frae here when they set tae it."

There is a shout, and men turn to see that the French flag has been removed and the stockade is in flames. Jamie has no idea how they've managed to get the wet wood to burn.

As if this is a signal, the Indians begin to rush in among the English and grab booty from the piles of baggage, laughing and giving shrill cries. Washington orders his men not to fire. The Ottawa have dragged a medicine chest to one side, opening it to examine and then drink whatever is liquid within its contents.

"They can't do that!"

"Steady, lad," says Jamie. "Keep yer calm and keep yer hair."

Captain de Villiers strides across the meadow then, drawing his sword and shouting remonstrances at the looters, but he is ignored.

"*Je m'excuse, Monsieur,*" he calls to the Virginia colonel, "*mais vous savez comment ils sont!*"

If the young colonel does, indeed, know how they are, he is not pleased with it.

"This is outrageous," he says. "And in direct violation of our agreement."

It is clear that the French captain understands no English, and that neither man has control of the situation. The piles of goods are spirited away, and quickly there appear Ottawa and Abenaki and Nipissing warriors wearing white man's clothing with an attendant loss of dignity, in Jamie's opinion, a scarlet-painted Wyandot under a silver-laced tricorn hat seeming a travesty, and fortunately the English have committed all their rum to the puddles back at the stockade.

Three warriors have wrested an enormous Grand Union regimental flag away and are dancing about with it. Orders are barked, and the redcoats and rough-dresssed colonials form ranks and begin to march away, leaving a dozen men standing guard and two dozen lying on blankets and litters on the ground behind them. De Villiers stands with these, hopelessly advising the rioting Indians to behave themselves.

"Hop it, laddie," says Jamie to the boy. "Unless ye'd care tae switch sides."

The boy hurries after the departing troop.

A wooden chest is thrown in the air to smash it open, the contents kicked and scattered about. Jamie picks up a book—a copy of Defoe's *Memoirs of a Cavalier*, which is inscribed by a 'Robert Stobo' inside the cover. Jamie quickly drops it back into the mud, not wanting to be seen to be reading by the others around him. He finds a good straight razor and a small looking glass with the initials R.S. scribed on the back of it and is content to settle for these till he thinks of Ange back in Kittanning. More booty will have to be gathered, perhaps some good cloth and something shiny, if there is to be peace at home.

He is squatting amid the strewn baggage, examining his face in the reflection of the looking glass, when one of the Abenakis pokes him with an officer's riding crop.

The warrior, staring at him, asks something in his own tongue, then, when there is no response, switches to French.

"*Qu'êtes vous?*"

Not who, but *what* are you.

Jamie has no ready answer.

CARRINGTON, HIS ADJUTANT, HOLDS THE LANTERN high. The man is nearly stone deaf, too many years with the artillery service, but a wizard at reading lips. Now he discretely studies the shadows cast on the ceiling beams as Sergeant Archibald, whose mother, somehow, was French, attempts to decipher the letter.

"Hit says 'ere that their commandant—"

"De Vergor—"

"That's 'im—hit says 'ee's *méprisé de tous*—everybody 'ates the bugger—"

"Universally despised," offers Captain Hussey.

"An ellygant manner of statin' it, Captain—spot on. Not only that, 'ee's 'avin a *liason avec* the wife of 'is *valet*."

Captain Hussey sighs in disapproval. "Ah—the French. Go on, Sergeant—and do keep your voice down a tad."

Archibald squints at the paper, raising it closer to the lantern. It seems strange to resort to such hugger-mugger in one's own quarters, but Hussey understands that fish keep longer than secrets in an action-starved garrison.

"'Ee goes on ter call 'im *un homme terne*—a dull man—*bègue*—which means 'e's a stutterer—of unpleasing countenance and doubtful character."

"Rather unflattering, that."

The letter was passed, surreptitiously, during a formal prisoner exchange, a trio of threadbare French deserters handed over for a young Englishwoman taken by savages on the outskirts of Dartmouth after witnessing the brutal murder of her husband and sons.

Commandant de Vergor, an overstuffed and addle-witted dandy, was in ill humor, no doubt thinking of the compensatory gifts he'd be expected to bestow upon the Indians for the deserters and the unlikelihood, given his dearth of uniformed personnel, of enjoying the luxury of hanging them.

"So he's telling us that Beauséjour is without leadership—"

"There's a Lieutenant, 'ee says, named St. Cyr, 'oos *compétent,* only 'is troops are of a poor quality and the guns at 'is disposal are—"

The sergeant mulls the text over for a moment, moving his lips and squinting—

"—*dérisoire*—I think it means pawtry—"

"Poultry?"

"*Paw*try. Not many—"

"Ah—"

"—when compared ter them as they got at their fortress at Louisbourg that this cove says 'ee wrote yer about before."

"Does he enumerate?"

The sergeant looks at him blankly. None of the Acadians, of course, can be trusted, and it is a wonder not only that among the dregs they've sent him here at Fort Lawrence he has a man who understands French, but that the man can actually *read* it, or any other language—

"Does he say how many *cannon*, Sergeant, or their caliber?"

Archibald scans down the page. The pretense of a peace between Britain and France had allowed for a certain amount of barter between the rival forts, the French commissary Pichon having even visited in person more than once, airing his discontent to Hussey rather forwardly and proposing, without a prompt, to try his hand at *espionnage.* Much more difficult now, with a declaration of hostilities, to pass information, and Pichon's extremely dodgy command of the English language has forced Hussey to enlist the good sergeant, who is as dense as a brick.

In two languages.

"'Ee's got a score of em, mostly twelve pounders," says Archibald finally. "Along with two big guns 'ee keeps trained on the sea."

Monsieur Pichon contends that his country's adventure in this benighted northern territory will be its financial ruin if not abandoned, and that it is his patriotic duty to hasten that outcome. The odd bit of silver or gold has also served to stir this patriotic ardor, the commissary explaining that the paper money issued from Quebec is near worthless here and will be scoffed at on his return to France.

"'Ee goes on ter warn about Abbé le Loutre—"

"What's *he* up to now?"

"The usual mischief, him with 'is red devils and that Acadian Broussard. 'Ee says ter expect another attack on Hallyfax soon."

The good *abbé* has foolishly entrusted Pichon to pen his missives to the authorities in Montreal, boasting of his intrigues and pleading for weapons and powder. Captain Hussey has relayed the salient bits of information to his superiors, cautiously withholding their source. The French have no monopoly on treason—

"Then 'ee goes on with quite a bit of military hadvice—"

"Do tell me."

The French commissary imagines himself something of a tactician, a fantasy Hussey has encouraged, if only to keep the source forthcoming—

"'Ee says when that i*névitable* day comes, Commandant de Vergor will attempt ter stop us from crossing the Missaguash, digging in behind the many walls—I think 'e means them dykes the *abbé* 'as 'ad 'em build—"

"No doubt—"

"—but if we do get across, though there's no cover, there's plenty of good spots ter dig trenches fer a seige—"

"A rather soggy endeavor, I daresay—"

"—which if we was ter lay it on 'eavy enough, them Acadians and Mickmacks is unreliable allies as will pose no threat—all yer got ter do is draw ’em out inter the open ter eraddycate em. But we got ter press on with ’aste before reinforcements can be sent from Louisbourg.”

Pichon has proferred similar plans for the taking of the Louisbourg fortress, weakened by smallpox and mismanagement, and has predicted the immediate surrender of the small garrison at their Fort Gaspereau if confronted by any sizable threat. He has given over census figures and supply estimates from Quebec, shipping schedules and troop orders, adding his scathing evaluations of the French officer class and of the Acadians as a race.

“‘*Une fois que vous avez triomphé*,’ ’ee says—once we’ve won—’ee says ’ow the Acadians should be no problem, them ’aving accepted English rule before and likely ter take that sensible route again. If not—*il ne devrait pas être difficile pour vous de les remplacer par des homologues anglais*—if not, hit shouldn’t be too ’ard ter replace em with—I dunno wot a hommylog is—”

“To replace them with English counterparts.”

The sergeant nods. “Makes sense ter me. And ’ee signs it ’ow ’ee always does—Tyrell.”

The wind moans through the wooden fort around them, candle flames and lantern flickering in his poorly chinked quarters. Captain Hussey will pass on the information to Halifax, hoping it may aid in provoking the order for assault—the only merit to this miserable posting is the hope of martial contest and advancement. The French are trespassing, all his maps reveal it clearly, they are trading with and harboring murderous savages and notorious highwaymen like Broussard—the situation cries out for a bold stroke.

“’Ooever ’ee is, Captain, do you *trust* this cove?”

Both the sergeant and Carrington are looking at him. He will have to impress upon them, once again, the need for absolute secrecy, citing the dire consequences should they let slip to anyone that there is a traitor, a man without morals or self-respect, in the enemy camp.

"Of course I don't trust him," says Captain Hussey. "But I be*lieve* him."

ANGE WEARS SOMETHING DIFFERENT FROM STOBO'S trunk every day. She has altered most of it, removed and repurposed lace, made brass buttons into pendants for her ears, tied his red sash around her body in various ways. Men get to carry the game they've killed into Kittanning, and their women are quick to step out and claim it. For some of the ceremonies women will wear things their men have bought from traders, just as the men will often wear white men's shirts they've traded for. Jamie has refused to wear anything he brought back from the Great Meadow.

I didn't defeat the man in battle or kill him, he tells Ange. I only took some things he'd left.

But she continues to tell the other women that he spared the Englishman's life and gave him to the French as a captive.

Most of the people in the village have made their own dwellings, some flimsy and ever on the verge of falling apart, many built to last. The *wikëwam* that Shingas and Cloud Woman share does not stand out among the others, while there are four men who have made small log cabins, dirt floored, but clearly modeled after white men's houses.

Tewea, who the English traders call Captain Jacobs, is building one of these. He has led his people—maybe fifty in all—down from the Juniata River after destroying their old village there.

White people too near, he says whenever people ask why.

Jamie helps to fell the trees, while Jacobs' son, who is called The Light, trims the branches off, making bundles of kindling for the other families who have come west. Every time four logs are ready Captain Jacobs and Jamie take turns with a drawknife to strip the bark off before they are piled to dry. Captain Jacobs, obviously considered a man of some substance here in Kittanning, was suspicious of Jamie at first, but when he joined him in the woods with a new axe that was part of the plunder from the rout of the Virginias, the chief only pointed to the next walnut he wanted down.

It does not seem like labor at all, though months were spent in Georgia Colony doing the same things for Jock Crozier. Examining the palms of his hands for new blisters, Jamie once again has the thought—I am neither a captive nor a slave.

Captain Jacobs is a large, thickset man, his face scarred by the pox, and from his tools and his knowledge of white man's carpentry it is clear that he has lived among or close to them for most of his life.

The things they trade to us, he says, stripped to the waist and glistening with sweat, are of little value to them. They did not make these things with their own hands—perhaps they have slaves who make them. If they give you a rifle for the bundle of skins that you bring them, you can be sure that bundle is worth twenty rifles. This is the way they grow wealthy and fill the world with their children.

Not all of them trade, observes Jamie.

Yes. And these are worth nothing. They cut all the trees to grow corn, their pigs dig in the earth, they kill all the does, so no new deer are born—

We kill deer as well.

Captain Jacobs seems to accept including Jamie within this "we" as he hacks away at the trunk of a tree.

But we are not so many, he says. They are like the pigeons that come in clouds, that break the branches of the trees with the weight of their number and leave the ground below white with their shit.

He carries a rage, Captain Jacobs, that he can barely keep a grip on, though nobody in the village seems to fear him. The blade of his axe is precise, wood chips flying with each stroke, but his attitude suggests murder more than harvest.

You've been cheated by them, says Jamie, chopping a stripped log in half.

Captain Jacobs unleashes a flurry of blows and the tree creaks, then leans, then crashes to the earth with much snapping of branches. He looks to Jamie, his face dark, panting from exertion.

I have moved to be away from them three times in my life, he says. This is the last.

THE FRENCH SENTRIES PAY LITTLE HEED TO CAPTAIN Stobo as he makes his daily promenade across the parapets. Contrecoeur, the commandant here at what they are calling Fort Duquesne, has given him the liberty of the structure and its surroundings, upon his honor. He and Van Braam have had no discussion of escape—too many savages about, eager for a reward or hungry for captives. The food is tolerable, perhaps a cut above what English soldiers might expect at so remote a garrison, and the rain has finally subsided.

Stobo finds himself counting steps, and smiles. The fort is a perfect square, eighty feet to a side, with bastions anchoring each corner and a dry ditch, some twelve feet across, dug all around the periphery. He has paced off the distance to both rivers as well, the Ohio lying to the west and the Monongahela to the south, both only a hearty stone's throw from the walls.

He pauses by the main gate, a drawbridge spanning it which is raised at night by a system of chains and levers, the main road leading away to the north, though most visitors and supplies arrive by water. A pair of log buildings for stores, a hospital and some barracks sit on either side of it just beyond the ditch. The road leads into the woods, now at least a musket shot away from his position, with a field of raw stumps lying between.

Stobo nods to one of the guards—"*bon après-midi, m'sieur*"—and continues walking toward the east bastion. There is a powder magazine buried beneath, almost invulnerable, unlike the wooden roofs of the buildings that ring the little parade ground.

A very presentable fortress.

Stobo has been able to study French with the *curé* assigned here and nearly every day has occasion to speak and barter with the Indians who wander in and out of the walls during daylight hours. He has even managed, with the help of the storekeeper, Garreau, to buy back from them several articles he recognizes from his own plundered trunk.

On the flat ground east of the fort are sixty small plank cabins for troops and junior officers, with a path, waggishly christened *l'Allée de la Vierge*, leading past them to an Indian village of thirty more huts and cabins. Judging from the traffic of French soldiers and junior officers on the path, few virgins remain within it. Corn fields hug the bank of the river for a half mile in each direction.

It was on a visit to the Indian village that he witnessed eight of the Virginia Regiment, including two good men from his own company, being held in a kind of corral by the savages. They were the men left to guard the wounded and baggage when Fort Necessity was abandoned, men protected by the Articles of Surrender. And when his protest was met with a Gallic shrug by Contrecoeur, the men doomed to be taken to Canada and sold or kept enslaved by the savages, he resolved to draw the map.

The river walls are palisades—round logs driven straight in the ground, nearly twelve feet high, with firing platforms running their length and loopholes cut for small arms below. The two inland walls are squared logs laid horizontally, with the space between them filled with stones and earth meant to resist artillery fire.

There are only eight cannon in all, half of them three pounders.

Van Braam, who feels more comfortable speaking French than he does English, sits with the officers at their interminable card games as Stobo strolls about the fort. The man's ability as an interpreter is questionable, with the French still emitting high-pitched indignation over Washington's admission, in the Articles of Surrender signed at Fort Necessity that miserable rainy night, that the young brother of de Villiers was *murdered*. The Dutchman certainly could not have spoken the word *assassinée* out loud, for as exhausted as Washington was, he would never have willingly admitted such a thing in an official document, true or not. And though they have been unsparingly cordial to him in his capacity as hostage, the French so overstate their "rights" in this country that they should have no need to further inflate their sense of moral superiority.

Turning to look within the walls, Contrecoeur's quarters sit at the right of the main gate as you enter, then the guard house, a barracks for some of the troops, a store, a tiny chapel, and a drafty building of rooms for the senior officers, including the one he and Van Braam currently share.

The Dutchman makes deep and rumbling noises throughout the night, perhaps a characteristic of his race.

There is a well in the center of the parade ground, and buildings within three of the four bastions—a kitchen housing a bake oven, a small prison, the blacksmith's shop, and a squalid little hovel for those cadets too young to touch razor to cheek.

The map required a good deal of planning and was several drafts in preparation, fitting so much information onto a single sheet of paper. And though he distrusts Van Braam's judgment rather than his loyalty, all was done in secret, the Dutchman still unaware of its existence, which will relieve him of the need for lying should

Stobo be found out. Yesterday he sent the first copy, hopefully to whoever is in command back at Wills Creek, by a Mingo named Moses the Song, who is known to be married to the sister of the sachem Tanaghrisson, the "great friend of the English" who left them a day before they forted up at Necessity. There is a rumor among the Indians that that worthy gentleman has either died of an illness or is about to be hanged by the English—with no speculation as to the reason why.

The Song, with those terrible distended earlobes flapping about, was selling him a pair of leather moccasins, very comfortable, in front of the storehouse when they fell to discussing the savage's next port of call.

"Moses go Venango, he go Logstown, he go Wills Creek—all the post, big trader. All the people know Moses."

Though brokenly conversant in both English and French, Stobo assumed the gentleman was not literate, but still folded the map with his observations penned on the back several times before sealing it with wax. And while the Song was such a smiling fellow, so amenable, that it was difficult to mistrust him, there was no sleep gotten last night, Stobo certain that at any moment he'd feel the point of a bayonet at his throat and hear Contrecoeur ordering him to the gallows.

Yet Moses is gone a full day, and Stobo is still at liberty.

Unless the burgesses in Virginia who hold the wretches from the Jumonville affair are either obdurate or incompetant, it should only be a matter of a month before he and Van Braam are exchanged. An officer lacking boldness might consider his duty done, and perhaps be content if the smuggled missive should merely go astray without condemning him.

Sporting try, so sorry it came to naught.

But Stobo has made a copy of the map and letter, and there is another man in camp, known as Delaware George, who arrived with a chief named Shingas this morning.

"*Il est un homme bon, ce Georges le Loup*," says Longueuil, the teenaged ensign who seems to have befriended Stobo. "*Pour un prix, il fera tout.*"

Contrecoeur has assured Stobo that as a man of property his credit will be respected, should any amenities become available for his purchase, but he suspects that the coins sewn into his regimental trousers will prove more useful in meeting Delaware George's "price" for his courier services. Moses the Song, happily, was mollified with only "hand this to the commandant at Wills Creek and he will treat you very well."

He spies the man, patching a canoe below the south wall, finally separate from Shingas, who strikes Stobo as too intelligent, too observant to be fully trustworthy.

"Ho there!" he calls. "Do you speak English?"

The Indian looks up to him, shading his eyes.

"English pretty good," he calls back.

"I come down, we parlay," says Stobo, wondering why he is suddenly uttering truncated phrases.

"You got silver, you got gold?"

"I most certainly have."

The savage, who wears a French infantryman's tricorn hat, grins broadly, missing some teeth, and beckons with a hand.

"You come down then, talk Delaware George."

THEY ARE NOT A MILE FROM THE FORT WHEN DELAware George shows Shingas the letter, which he has stuffed into his shot pouch.

He asked me to bring it to their chief at Wills Creek.

What is it? asks Shingas.

Writing on paper, all stuck together.

That's only beeswax, you can melt it again. Let me see.

George hands Shingas the paper, and he carefully breaks the seal and unfolds it.

Can you read their marks?

No, but look at this—it's a drawing of the fort.

Delaware George studies the map for a moment, breaks into a smile.

What a good drawing, he says. Like a bird is in the sky, looking down at the fort.

The writing probably tells how many men the French have, how many guns.

What do you think I should do with it?

We'll melt the wax again—

There was a mark on it—

But once that is gone no one will know what it was.

And then I take it to Wills Creek?

Shingas met Delaware George, a man who has never lived farther from a trading post than a toad can piss, on the far side of the river just before the fort came into view. If you want all men to know a thing, you tell George it is a secret.

Do you know the chief white man there?

No.

Then take it to Croghan at Aughwick. Tell him you have something from the Virginia captain held at the French fort, and you'll give it to him for three blankets.

George frowns, staring at the map.

For a drawing this good I want four blankets.

Shingas smiles. Ask for four. Croghan will offer you two, but don't give it to him till he gives you three.

It is worth four.

Tell him that after he sees the drawing.

Delaware George nods and takes the paper back, refolding it carefully, then pressing it between the palms of his hands, hoping to melt the wax a bit and seal it shut.

Croghan will give it to the English soldiers, says George, as if just realizing that the English and French are not brothers.

Yes.

Is that a good thing?

Shingas considers this as they walk along the bank of the great river.

Anything that puts white men *un*der our land instead of on top of it, he says, is a good thing.

WILDERNESS ROAD

"ME FEET IS TINGLIN', REG."

The 48th Foot are striking their tents on the hill behind the derisible clutch of palisaded logs that has been christened yet another Fort Cumberland. Sergeants are urging them to hurry, though the trek thus far has been slow and grueling, with countless pauses to allow the baggage train to catch up.

"We're still in camp, Bert. Save it fer the bloody mountains."

"Marchin' they only burn, then they go numb. But when they tingles, it's a premonition, like."

"Premonition of what?"

"Nothing good, I can tell ye that. Ye remember that day in Flanders?"

"Every time I try ter lift me right arm."

Cruikshank's right shoulder has been so compromised by the old wound that his friend must braid and powder his queu for him and coat it with tallow and flour on days when they are likely to face inspection. And firing a musket is agony—

"They tingled that morning when we left the monkery."

"Hit's called a monastery, Bert."

"Which we should of stayed in it, let them froggo dragoons run over somebody else."

"Hit's the unfamiliar environs got ye spooked. Strolling inter the unknown—"

"Oh, I *know* what's across that river, Bert. More bloody mountains, higher ones than we've already tramped over, jiggers tryin' ter make a nest in yer skin, and a bloody savage lying doggo be'ind every tree, bent on liftin' me 'air."

"The little ye've got left."

The drummers beat *Assembly*, and they hurry to form ranks. They'll be marching with Braddock's column today, moved up from old Dunbar's cadre along with the experienced men from the 44th. The idea is to have the best men, should they encounter their foe, in the van.

"P'raps I'll go find 'is Hexcellency the Gen'ral before 'ee climbs inter 'is coach," says Kirby, "and inquire if I could dispense with me topper till we're out of Indian country. The red devils see I'm nearly bald'eaded, they might spare me as not worth killing—"

"I wouldn't test the man, Bert. 'Ee's got a lot on 'is mind."

"What there is of it."

"Aww now, don't you join in on the poor old gent. 'Ee's doin' the best 'ee can."

The 48th had fought under Cholmondeley at Fontenoy and Culloden, but Cholmondeley abandoned them for the dragoons once they were shunted to Irish duty. Dunbar, their present Colonel, is held in low esteem, and as for General Braddock, well—

"'Ee's not a *war*rior, Reg. We've seen more combat in the Calf and Crown on a payday than 'ee's seen 'is 'ole career."

"Braddock's all right. His da' was a brigadier, at least, and I believe his granda' as well. 'Ee's got warfare in 'is blood—"

"And snuff all over 'is waistcoat—"

"Yer only miffed at the gen'ral cause 'ee sent yer doxy away."

"*And* 'er 'ole bleedin' tribe. They was sposed ter come with us, Bert, ter keep the bad Indians from foxin' us inter a hambush—"

They are silent as Sergeant Morse steps past them, glaring as usual.

The drummers, twenty of them for their section of the column, beat *March* then, and they head for the river, two abreast. Until they reached Fort Cumberland the column stretched at least four miles, but the general has been convinced to let Dunbar and the baggage lag—the heavy artillery in the wagons will only be needed if they have to beseige the French fort, and for that they should have time to regroup.

"We've still got a few of the better ones ter scout—"

"While them dozens that was sent away go over ter the French."

"More's the pity fer them, then. Yer 'aven't 'ad it squeezed properly fer a week now, Bert, that's why yer out of sorts. What was 'er name again?"

"I never could wrap me tongue around it. I just called 'er Bright Eyes."

"Sitting out there somewheres right now, she is, pining over the mem'ry of her lost love—"

"More likely she's out there eating the 'orse I give 'er in hexchange fer certain liberties."

Cruikshank cuts his eyes to Kirby. If the sergeant catches you turning your head on march, it's extra duty—

"Where'd ye get an 'orse? There's not enough of the jades ter pull our baggage up these 'ills, without ye go feedin' 'em ter the savages."

"Found 'im in the woods, where the rest went ter forage. Poor creature was starvin', 'ee was, all skin and bones. Done 'im a favor."

Cruikshank snorts.

"I've lost more than a stone since we left Winchester—don't do *me* any favors."

"Then the next day, she brings 'im back to me. 'Too skinny,' she says."

"Ye learnt their lingo?"

"She told me with *signs,* Bert. Our 'ole relationship was signs made with the 'ands."

"I bet I know one of them signs."

"Yer mind is a cesspool."

They reach the river and make a sharp right turn up along the bank. The ascent straight across from them, nearly a vertical wall of forest, was tried yesterday at the expense of three tumbrils full of axes and spades that went crashing into a ravine. Apparently a way has been found to go around the base of the mountain—

"Sounds like an ungrateful wench," says Cruikshank. "'Ere ye risk, what, fifty stripes? A hundrit? Not ter mention being put on 'alf rations, and the little doxy wants a fatter 'orse."

"Hit wasn't 'er, hit was 'er 'usband."

"She 'ad an *'usband?*"

"Not blessed by the vicar, no, but they 'ave their own harrangements. And this fella said 'ee wasn't about ter share 'is beloved, even fer only the odd poke now and then, wifout a fatter 'orse or a musket."

Cruikshank nearly misses a step. The drums help you stay in cadence, but this terrain along the bank is more path than road, tree roots grabbing for your ankles—

"Yer didn't give the 'eathen bastard a musket—"

"Course not, Reg, that's *trea*son."

There has been a drought, and the river is mercifully low. The men hold their muskets over their heads as they ford, the water only halfway up their gaiters and the current weak.

"So that was farewell ter Bright Eyes."

"I gave 'er a barrel of salt beef."

"Yer didn't—"

"One of them as was condemned and meant ter be left be'ind."

"And Mr. Bright Eyes haccepted this offering?"

"I told him hit was bait fer trapping—that's why hit smelt so ripe. Hit proved ter be sufficient fer one more night of bliss."

They march silently for a moment, Kirby looking troubled.

"Hit's a strange business," he says finally.

There had been at least fifty warriors camped just a quarter mile below the fort, shelters of sapling and bark thrown up for their women and children. The Virginians, as starved looking as the horses grudgingly sold to the expedition, advised it was best to steer clear of them. But that and the general's orders only added to their attraction. They seemed to be loosely under the control of a character called Scaraoudy, who speaks English and has a tomahawk tattooed on his chest and a bow on each cheek. He and his son are of the handful not dismissed by the general as "too bothersome," as is one called Montour who looks at least half white. Watching them dance at night soon lost its fascination, but once it became known that certain of the women might be amenable to commerce—

"Hit's just we're more familiar with transactions made in silver, Reg. If there'd been a knock shop set up by the fort I'd of volunteered ter be on the road crew, ter earn that extra sixpence per day—"

"Hit 'asn't been distributed."

Kirby is incredulous.

"Yer jokin'—"

"None of them poor buggers as 'volunteered' got a penny. 'Fer want of a market ter spend it in,' said 'is Hexcellency the Gen'ral. 'Hit will be reserved fer when we reach our winter quarters.'"

"Back in Virginia? That's months from now. And what about the poor buggers 'oo get topped by the froggos or the savages?"

"We 'aven't 'ad a single casualty yet, Bert."

"Me feet is *tingl*in'."

Cruikshank nods to the trail ahead on the far side of the river—a gap perhaps twelve feet across, full of stumps freshly cut, nearly as precipitous as the one tried the day before.

"Lookit this little 'ill we're coming ter—would ye like a pound of metal coins in yer knapsack ter 'aul up it?"

"Bright Eyes'd 'ave all the coins by now."

Cruikshank ponders this for a moment as they begin to climb, the drums beating steadly. They've been told that if there is a long roll it means the men ahead of them, already out of sight, have been attacked—

"Well I'm glad no mate of mine stooped ter clearing woods and pulling stumps. Hit's demeaning ter a proper sojer."

"Very true," says Kirby. "Mind you, we've done our share of scutwork—pulling ropes on those bloody wagons—"

"And wifout a penny's consideration fer our efforts."

"I've a mind ter write the King in protest."

"Ye can write, can ye?"

"After a fashion.'

"A man of letters, and still a private sojer. Imagine that."

They've had time at the fort at Wills Creek to have the camp-following women clean their uniforms, and as the sun hits them on the new-hewn path up the mountain they make a gaudy contrast to the solid green of the trees on either side—scarlet coats faced with yellow, leather and buckles polished, the tall mitres of the grenadiers ahead of them—and nobody but the squirrels, thick as gnats in these woods, to admire them. In the morning it always seems more like a parade than an invasion—

"I would've been a magistrate," says Kirby, wincing as he adjusts his chafing haversack, "but I didn't 'ave the Latin."

REGULATIONS STATE THAT OFFICERS OF RANK MUST travel in a carriage, but regulations must be adapted to circumstances and it is probably salubrious for the men—at least for the regulars—to view him riding amongst them.

General Braddock brushes snuff from his waistcoat, then waves mosquitos away from his face. The trouble with a healthy trencherman's paunch, normally the sign of good fortune, is that it provides a shelf to collect whatever does not properly reach the nose and mouth.

Gravies are the worst, spreading down and out to form outlines similar to those of Caribbean islands. He'll ride the bay till the first major stoppage and then switch to the dappled gelding he bought in Virginia, an animal reputed to be expert in running down foxes.

At least they are moving, and in the proper direction.

When he wrote to the governors in something more than a pique that he was prepared, unless they were able to muster more supply and personnel than their abysmal showing up to that point, to turn the entire column back to the docks and inform London that the colonials were in dereliction, if not open rebellion, there was some joy among his officer corps. Several months left stewing in this drear and desolate country has them longing for home, a state of mind to be avoided when engaged in foreign duty. The letters were meant as a hyperbolic threat to the governors, but surely a few of his younger men lost their wagers this morning when dismal Wills Creek was obscured by their dust, the column moving west instead of back east.

He has hopes that this campaign might serve to crown his pleasant but decidedly unspectacular military career with something written in the annals, and after the French have been harried back to the frigid north where they belong, perhaps a governship of one of these colonies, with its associated emoluments, will be forthcoming. Unlike in the army, a governor at sixty years is not remotely considered an old man. Albemarle, in fact, was until his recent passing the titular governor of Virginia despite never setting foot in it. A position worth a bob or two.

But of course they might desire him to actually *live* among these people.

In any case, another summer on Gibraltar, little to do in command but drink and perspire, both to excess, would have killed him. The Rock has served as a graveyard for many an officer's hopes, and he was not wrong to consider this commission a godsend.

The road—and it now deserves to be called that—is lined with the trunks of the trees that have been felled to make it, creating something like a wooden fence along the sides. Here it is a good twelve feet wide, with stumps pulled out in the center to let the wagons pass when they catch up. Without the thoroughfares built by General Wade in Scotland, the rebel hillskippers would remain inaccesible to this day—to rout your enemy, you first have to *reach* him.

Braddock's Road—the name has a pleasant weight to it.

Both Newcastle and Cumberland urged him, before his departure from London, to strive for moderation in expense. But that has proved impossible, the locals viewing the expedition not as an attempt to save their necks from the French and their hair from the savages, but as a sort of beached leviathan that everyone might take a bite of, charging criminal rates for their goods and services, in the rare cases when such are available in this hinterland. Even the governors, meant to be the King's agents here, have been of little help. Shirley, of course, has the taking of Fort Beauséjour and the rest of Acadia on his plate, and can't be expected to rob Peter to pay Paul, but Virginia's own Dinwiddie has been long on enthusiasm and short on delivery, his regiment and the other colonials, over half the General's force of two thousand, riddled with transported felons, runaway indentures, and frontier wastrels. He would say they are no worse than the refuse pressed at home in times of desperation, men untroubled by the concepts of discipline and loyalty, their valor precarious, but with no time for proper training there is no way to predict which way they'll jump when the first earnest shot is fired.

Sharpe of Maryland pleads the relative poverty of his constituents. But he at least has forwarded the remarkable map of Fort Duquesne, drawn by Captain Stobo who is being kept there as guarantee till the Virginia Assembly get around to returning the captives taken by young Washington during the Jumonville affair. That he was so easily able to smuggle it out points to a rather encouraging laxity on the part of his frog-eating hosts. The map will be of untold value if the French have not undertaken improvements or expansion, and one hopes that the valiant captain remains undetected until the column can free him.

Morris of Pennsylvania is full of apology in his letters, most likely sincere, but apologies won't move the General's men and equipment over fifty miles of wilderness mountains and rivers. Governor Shirley blames this intransigence on the preponderance of Quakers and Germans in that colony, and cites Maryland's Catholics as a further source of resistance. Not only is this disunion of the colonies with each other shocking, but each seems independently to have forgotten that the King's business is theirs as well.

A governor who cannot force his people to obey his edicts does not deserve the office.

The postal fellow from Philadelphia, Franklin, was well met, however, good for his word in sending nearly one hundred desperately needed wagons and some lovely parcels of comestibles for his officers, who, not being gentlemen of independent means, can't afford those things that make life tolerable on a long campaign.

Braddock passes a pair of the negro servants loaned as batmen to his younger officers, guiding horses laden with their employers' effects. They seem to be jolly fellows having a bit of a lark, perhaps mindful that they are not stooping in a sun-baked field of tobacco leaves as their less fortunate brethren do. The Virginians are wonderful hosts, ever ready to order their slaves to see after your comfort, their young ladies adept at leaving one rather puffed up with their attentions. And the country gentlemen there seem to have their own criteria of rank and privilege thoroughly worked out—Fairfax, Carter and Lee being the most desirable apellations—though only one of these, a mere stripling, was put forward to join the fight.

Mr. Washington, who has rejoined them after his battle with the flux, seems to be made of sterner stuff. Though a bit too proud for a youngster with only a dubious skirmish and an ignominious surrender under his belt, he at least has crossed this country before and dealt with the very savages whose loyalty is in the balance. He seems content enough to remain an aide without rank, and waits politely to be solicited before stating his opinion. Of those he has a plethora, most recently arguing, quite sensibly, that arriving at the forks *before* the French garrison of four hundred can be reinforced supersedes arriving with every man and piece of artillery in hand. And the man certainly *looks* a soldier—should they ever cast a statue of me, thinks Braddock, I'd pay to have them use Washington astride his steed for a model.

The General digs his bootheels into the bay's flanks, deciding to move to the head of the column before they reach St. Clair and his woodcutters. There is a lovely ripple effect, each pair of regulars he passes straightening a bit as they become aware of his presence—yes, much to be preferred to rattling over the mountains hidden in a carriage. Though the 44th and 48th have been brought back to full strength with drafts, the donating regiments naturally sending their worst men, they are still all British soldiers and will acquit themselves well when the time comes. There has been a good deal of fuss about the savages, but having met with them several times, he is thoroughly unimpressed. They seem petulant children, capable of murder should they catch you napping in the woods, but without the wit, discipline, or courage to face a well-timed volley, and it befuddles him as to why even Washington declares them key to the struggle in the Ohio Valley. The Delaware and Shawnee never even showed up to talk, and Scaraoudy has made light of their fighting prowess when compared to his own worthies, who were there in droves for over a month, drawing provisions and playing hell with discipline, their squaws, until he barred them from the camp, cunning jades who enticed the men—even a few of his officers—into debauchery and dereliction of duty. He is happy to see so few of the white camp followers with the column now, having had the nerve to demand more than the traditional sixpence a day for washing clothes—even the fairer sex here unashamed to take advantage of the remoteness of their surroundings.

His officers are a cut above the men they lead—though he can't bear Halkett of the 44th and the feeling is mutual, the man is at least a soldier. Dunbar wishes to be somewhere else, and Lord St. Clair, responsible for provisions and clearing the road, is a bit too much the hussar, a whirlwind of energy who leaves a good deal of devastation in his wake. No problem with any of them in a fight, but the getting there—it is a campaign designed by persons, not unskilled, in the case of the Duke of Cumberland, who have never glimpsed the terrain they have sentenced him to cross, using highly inaccurate maps as their guide. Then to discover that the success of the venture depends on a handful of Indian traders, with Croghan popular among the Indians but not, according to Washington, to be trusted, and Cresap and the rest of them no more than a parcel of *banditti*—it beggars the mind.

But if he can beat the logistics it will be cake.

Gist and Montour claim, from their Indian sources, that despite their access to a network of waterways the French fort remains undermanned and undersupplied—only four hundred in the garrison—and their rapport with the Ohio Valley Indians strained. When we reach the forks, thinks the General, they are most likely to burn the structures and flee, which would be something of a disappointment. Or, if their commander possesses a backbone, we just might have to break ground for a siege and justify the effort of dragging cannon, ball, and powder over these bloody mountains.

Braddock inhales loose snuff off his knuckles—this is a very mellow cherry—holds it in, half closing his eyes. Wonderful antidote to fatigue. Once the vexing details have been dealt with, a long march is quite a simple challenge, really, and requires a simple response.

Keep your flankers out and push on.

THE COMMANDANT IS STILL IN HIS NIGHTCLOTHES, bloated with sleep. The fisherman, Rostegui, lives at Cape Maringouin and has had to borrow a neighbor's horse, riding cautiously in the dark of night.

"*Avez-v-vous compté les n-n-n—*" says de Vergor, struggling with his words as he does whenever upset.

Did you count the ships? asks St. Cyr.

There were forty sloops and schooners, Rostegui tells them excitedly, and hundreds of soldiers on their decks, and two more ships with a cannon sticking out of every gunport.

When did they anchor?

Just at sunset, well out in the bay.

"*Ils attendent la m-m-marée,*" says the commandant.

The tide in the Bay of Fundy is extreme, perhaps only two hours in a day when ships of considerable draft can approach the shore.

"*Et comment pouvez-vous être certain que la f-f-lottille était anglaise?*"

The commandant has been assuring everyone that the fighting will remain down in the Ohio Valley, the English preparing to march upon Fort Duquesne—

I was born with eyes in my head, says Rostegui, and they were flying the English flag.

There won't be another daylight high tide till tomorrow afternoon, but there is so much to be done—

I request permission, sir, to lead a squad at daybreak to destroy the Pont à Buot over the Missaguash, says St. Cyr. No reason to make it easy for the enemy to bring their artillery near—

"*Il faut éviter la p-p-panique,*" says the commandant. A flotilla of the size this fellow claims to have seen must be on their way to attack the fortress at Louisbourg, anchoring in the bay only to avoid bad weather.

"*Mais Commandant—*"

"*Il n'y a pas p-plus de danger ici que dans les rues de P-Paris!*"

Nonetheless, de Vergor has the notary wakened to draft letters to Louisbourg, Québec, and Isle St. Jean pleading for reinforcement, and sends a runner into the village to wake the *acadiens* with an order to take up arms and muster outside the gates.

And then he returns to sleep.

"*Merci à vous, monsieur,*" says the Lieutenant to the exhausted fisherman when they are left alone. You have done a very great service. May I offer you my bed here at the fort?

St. Cyr has only lain in it this evening, still dressed, for a few hours after a triumphant session at cards. Just when my luck is turning, he thinks, *les putains d'anglais* have to appear—

There is time, if wisely used, to put up a resistance, perhaps even to hold out until help can arrive. Allowing space for crew and field equipment, he calculates that each English schooner might hold fifty soldiers, meaning an army of two thousand men will be deployed against their hundred-some *soldats non testés*, most of whom have never fired a shot in anger, and whatever *acadiens* and Mi'kmaqs choose to remain and fight.

If we can make their lives as miserable as our own, he says to Rostegui, perhaps they'll go away.

He wakes Vannes, who quit the card game owing him three hundred *livres*, to muster his infantrymen and appraise them of the situation, then exits through the *port d'embarquement* past the fuzz-faced sentry.

"*Alors,*" winks the *privée,* who can't yet be twenty, "*une visite à votre femme.*"

If only that were all.

Many of the officers and soldiers have found themselves a *copine*, most often a local widow or a Mi'kmaq woman, the beautiful young *acadiennes* being very protected, but his liaison with Jeannie is considered exotic and somehow more exciting. The commandant, having laid eyes on her only once or twice, is clearly jealous, and St. Cyr's card-playing *confréres* are quick with ribald comments whenever he tries to leave the table with time enough to enjoy her company. Nothing too insulting, but with the isolation and dearth of conversational topics, it has become a burden.

He walks quickly through the Mi'kmaq *campement*, only a trio of their rat-tailed dogs awake, sniffing his legs but not barking. If the elders have been informed of the news, they've decided it can wait till morning.

But there are already hastily dressed *acadiens* waiting in front of the church in Beauséjour, quickly surrounding him.

Is it true?

A fisherman saw them, he says.

What fisherman?

"*Il est de Cap Maringouin.*"

But those people are notorious liars!

Would a man hurry all that way in the dead of night, soliciting no payment, to tell us a lie?

The men consider this, unhappy to have been roused from their beds, most remembering the fate of their previous village. The Lieutenant wishes Broussard was here, a man they fear and trust—

Then what should we do?

Meet me at the fort at sunrise, bringing axes and shovels, he tells them. There is work to be done.

"*Ils sont venus?*" asks Abbé le Loutre, stepping out from his chapel just as the others disperse, dressed in a black robe and muddy boots, a musket at his side. The *abbé* has never mentioned

St. Cyr's avoidance of Mass or his *maîtresse* in the house across the street, treating him as a fellow military man.

"*Un bon groupe sont arrivés, peut-être deux mille.*"

The priest whistles at the figure, turns to look at his church.

A shame to have to burn another one down, he says, and hurries back inside.

Jeannie is still curled in bed, asleep. St. Cyr sits watching her for a while, pondering. Heroic resistance ending with surrender, he muses, is appreciated by one's superiors but never rewarded with advancement. There will be no glory unless they can hold out. And if not, Captain Hussey has proven to be a gentleman, and the English force is unlikely to be accompanied by Mohawks this far north.

So his hair is likely secure.

As he has been trained to do, St. Cyr pictures the field of battle from the enemy's perspective—with the disparity in numbers there will be no lining up in the field to exchange volleys, no opportunity for a cavalry charge to save the day. This will be decided by the artillery and the thickness of battlements.

And if Commandant de Vergor chooses to capitulate too rapidly, I may have to shoot him.

Jeannie stirs, turns and sees him, smiles dreamily.

Were the cards good to you?

"*Ils sont venus,*" he tells her. "*Une multitude d'anglais.*"

Jeannie sits up, eyes fully open, fingertips touching her throat.

"Aw, Christ," she says. "D'ye reckon they'll hang me?"

THE *ACADIENS* REPORT AT DAWN, ALMOST THREE HUNdred men, and though they follow St. Cyr's instruction, piling dirt and hauling squared logs to shore up the ramparts and the casements, it is with an anxious eye cocked toward the bay. Joseph Broussard is here with his four grown sons and his brother Alexandre, helping to egg the workers on, lending a hand with the timber. A dark-eyed man in his fifth decade of life with an energy that is contagious, Broussard is clearly the *chef de tous les hommes*. Moving from group to group, laughing and joking with his comrades, St. Cyr finds him a pleasing antidote to le Compte de Vergor, who paces back and forth on the same ten feet of the south wall, hands clasped behind his back, watching the sea. Though it is indeed an officer's duty to be seen by his troops at times of battle, this display does not so much strike confidence in the Lieutenant's heart as the hope that the commandant will make a convenient target for some enemy sniper.

"*Qu'en pensez-vous, mon lieutenant?*" calls Broussard from down on the parade ground.

St. Cyr indicates the fort with his hands.

These walls won't fall.

Too bad, says the warrior cheerfully. Then we're trapped inside of them.

The sails of the English *flotille* do not appear till the late afternoon, able to anchor four hundred yards out and send the men ashore in longboats, a dozen soldiers at a time from each of the two-score sloops. St. Cyr is at first relieved to see that most of their uniforms are the blue and green of colonial militia, mustering in formation on a flat spot ten feet above the rocky beach and then climbing, to the rattle of a quartet of drummers, the rest of the way to the high ground and Fort Lawrence, where they begin to put up their tents. There is no hurry, no confusion, the mass landing a pageant put on for the benefit of the soon-to-die. The Lieutenant catches a flash of red in his field glasses, refocusing them to follow a company of English regulars. These are artillerymen who wait, once ashore, to carefully unload four short field guns, six pounders, the new brass glistening in the late-day sun, and a squat, heavy mortar.

And now a sudden flurry in the *petite ville* of the Mi'kmaqs attached like a barnacle to the side of Fort Beauséjour, the women deftly stripping and rolling sheets of birchbark and bundling poles as the men collect their weapons and begin to paint themselves for battle. They won't dig or fell trees for another man, not even the Abbé, but seem always eager to fight.

If the odds are in their favor.

Seen through the glass, the invaders look tiny, swarming between the longboats on shore and the fort on the hill. They keep to land that is uncontestedly English till a trio of men in red officers' garb strolls out across the marsh and begins to pick their way toward the river. St. Cyr sends a pair of pickets out to meet them, and watches the exchange, shouted across the Missaguash, still rising with the tide, till both parties turn and head back to their respective forts.

The pickets, boots soaking and muddy, meet him at the *port d'embarquement*.

"*Que voulaient-ils?*"

They claimed they were searching for stray cattle.

A fitting occupation for a pair of English gentlemen.

I think they were looking over the ground their troops will have to cross to attack us, says one of the pickets.

"*Bien observé*."

The two young soldiers exchange a glance, then the bolder of them speaks.

What do you think our chances are?

There is a point at which a bold *façade* resembles lunacy more than fearlessness, and one's troops consider mutiny.

I think we're badly outnumbered, St. Cyr tells them.

Fort Beauséjour is a pentagonal star, its palisade walls backed with earth fifteen feet high, bastions at each of the corners, with a wide, six-foot-deep trench dug all around it—a charge from any direction would be slaughter for the attackers. No, the English will take their time, occupy the high, wooded ground to the north, raining shells down while they dig their own trenches, zigzagging across the marshland closer and closer until, if the French garrison has not already been bombed or starved out, they'll be near enough to pelt them with clods of earth.

Broussard, two pistols stuck in his belt now, intercepts the Lieutenant before he can climb back onto the wall.

"*D'accord*," he says, "*quel est le plan?*"

St. Cyr has always felt uncomfortable with the dirty war, never invited to conferences with Broussard or Abbé le Loutre or the Mi'kmaq chief to discuss what might next be done to discourage the English from further settlement. But here are the English with their colonials, dressed up like soldiers, ready to lay siege—

The English will wait till tomorrow to push across the river, he says. And as the easiest crossing will be at the Buot bridge—

"*Oui?*"

—you and your people might do us the favor of destroying it.

They both look to de Vergor above them, the commandant having some trouble in the breeze keeping his tobacco on the back of his hand long enough to snuff it into his nose.

Very discretely, of course, adds St. Cyr.

"*Avec plaisir, mon lieutenant*," says the outlaw, then hurries off to raise a party of arsonists.

IN THE MORNING OF THE SECOND DAY JENNY AND Amély climb into the bell tower of the church. The Lieutenant, with nothing better he can arrange for them, says they'll be safe here at least for today. Abbé le Loutre and Terèse Leger, his housekeeper, can be heard downstairs gathering all the gold, silver, and holy objects to be hidden. Amély has brought food and water enough for a few days, and from one of the bell tower openings they have a clear view of the English encampment.

With no Indians clustered outside the walls, Fort Lawrence has always been a tidier affair than Fort Beauséjour. At present there are two long, evenly spaced lines of white tents on the ground immediately below the wooden palisades, an orderly horde of uniformed men standing at attention in front of them. A trumpet is blown, drums are beaten, and suddenly the blocks of men swarm into frantic motion, the tents disappearing in minutes. Amély begins to mutter a prayer.

Jenny tries to reassure her. "*Ils ont encore à traverser le marais.*"

The marsh is difficult to cross even when not laden with pack and rifle, nearly a mile of it between the English fort and the little settlement of Beauséjour, and that without a tree to shelter behind. There is also the river, essentially a long, winding bog that rises and falls with the tide, bordered, on the *acadien* side, with several dykes that Abbé le Loutre has had the men build, the ground behind them raised and filled for planting. At the one dry crossing, Pont à Buot, the Lieutenant had the foresight to build a log blockhouse and dig several trenches, while the bridge itself has been destroyed in the night, only a few charred pillars sticking up from the murky water.

"*Et ils devront faire face aux canons du lieutenant,*" she adds.

Thinking to improve his mood when they first arrived, Jenny asked the Lieutenant to show her his guns, but they proved to be a sorry shadow of the armament he commanded in Martinique.

"*Petits canons pour tuer les mouches,*" he apologized after the very short tour. If only the guns could kill the flies, she thinks, a vast, biting, bloodsucking multitude of them bred in the marsh every year once the ground thaws. But if the English have nothing to hide behind—

They begin to march toward the river.

They begin to march toward the river, spread out in a column perhaps a half-dozen men across, and it is little comfort to Jenny how few of the uniforms are red. The men in the vanguard have only muskets, but those behind carry planks and large squared logs, carry the shining barrels of cannon that will be set up somewhere to fire at Beauséjour, town and fort. Back in Martinique Jenny spent an indolent day watching a narrow, slow-flowing river of ants move across a dirt road, many of them bearing twigs or cut pieces of palm leaf or bloated white eggs sacs in their jaws, no clue as to whether the procession was an attack, a retreat, or merely relocation from one home to another. She watched from the same spot all morning as they passed, went home for supper, and then returned to watch again with Amély, the glistening black column still moving at an ant's pace, stretching as far as one could see in both directions.

Until the shooting begins, this day has a similar feeling.

The English troops, carrying what they need to rebuild the bridge, pick their way across the expanse of wet ground, creeping forward while maintaining their formation. From the north opening of the bell tower Jenny and Amély can see French soldiers and rifle-bearing *acadiens* taking position in the blockhouse and trenches by the remains of the bridge, a long *abatis* of splintered trees laid in front of them.

Amély points. "*Il y a le lieutenant!*" she cries.

He is in the white uniform that hangs on him now, having lost so much girth here, supervising the placement of what Jenny recognizes as a quartet of swivel guns.

They see the *Abbé* and Madame Leger hurry away below them, carrying several bundles.

They eat chicken and boiled eggs with some of the dizzy-making cider the *acadiens* drink.

The enemy column—in those blue and green uniforms they might be Hessians or colonials—creeps closer to the river.

They hear axes cutting into trees from the direction of the French fort. On one side there is a gradual upslope, wooded, and since he arrived the Lieutenant has been pleading with Commandant de Vergor to order it leveled, leaving the enemy, should they be able to take position there, at least nothing to hide behind. But it is a convenient source of firewood, and de Vergor a man who goes about with his arms wrapped around himself, as if constantly freezing.

In the mid-afternoon a group of perhaps fifty near-naked Mi'kmaq warriors, armed and painted, trot over to the French soldiers in the trenches, squatting several yards behind them to watch. Despite their fearsome reputation for ambushes and raids at the edge of the deep forest, in the huge expanse of the marsh they appear vulnerable.

The English column comes to the river, then makes a sharp right turn to move along the south edge of it, not really a bank but only more soggy marshland. It must be somewhat firmer, though, as their field guns, six pounders by Jenny's reckoning, are now fitted onto wheeled carriages by the redcoats in the rear, then pulled along over the hummocks, each by a half-dozen soldiers in harness. The parade, now at right angle to her and Amély, looks to be nearly a quarter mile long.

Jenny sees gulls flashing white over the bay, sees somebody's cow, unfazed by men in uniform, grazing close to the entrenched Frenchmen. The rattle of the English drums seems a puny thing, an annoyance carried by the ocean-smelling breeze.

The fighting, when it comes, is far enough away that its sights precede its sounds. Jenny finds that she is holding her breath as she watches the enemy foot soldiers kneel and fire in volleys—first the smoke, then the crackling—while their brass cannon pound away at the blockhouse and swivel-gun emplacements. There are scattered wisps of smoke and random pops from behind the *abatis*, and the Indians and most of the *acadiens* quickly retire from the field, the uneven numbers and mode of combat not to their liking.

"*Zont trop nombreux*," says Amély, and indeed they are too many, the volume of their fire overwhelming the French even with their superior position and cover. The blockhouse is on fire. Jenny recognizes the Lieutenant's second in command, de Baralon, heading for the woods with a trio of soldiers and the two undamaged swivel guns in a cart, while St. Cyr himself leads his small detachment, carrying one wounded man, back along the river toward the village. The English do not pursue or even fire at them during this retreat, instead bringing up the timbers to start on a new bridge.

This will be a civilized battle, he told her this morning before returning to the fort, noting that neither Mi'kmaqs nor savage Highlanders would be in charge of the hostilities.

Gregoire Doucet is below, yanking on the bell ropes to set them pealing thunderously, Jenny and Amély covering their ears. Townspeople who have been watching, some from the roofs of their dwellings, begin to gather in front of the church, and Jenny and Amély scurry down the ladder and step out to join them. Lieutenant St. Cyr, his white uniform ruined with soot, calls out to the villagers.

"*Tout doit être brûlé!*" he shouts, while local men who left the skirmish early are already moving about with torches in hand, urging their neighbors to gather all valuables and flee. The village is in a direct line between Fort Beauséjour and the English and must not offer the enemy shelter nor sustenance. There is a panicked racket as stores of food are thrown open, squawking chickens chased down, children and cattle herded, some toward the fort and some across the marsh toward the sea and the fishing villages down the coast.

"*Vous devez détruire tout ce que vous ne pouvez pas porter!*"

St. Cyr takes Jenny's hand and pulls her into the house, Amély on their heels. There is not so much to save—some food, the Lieutenant's papers, a small bundle of clothing. Jenny, heart racing, recalls her sensations on the day of the Drummossie Moor, the sight of people climbing through the bracken with their life's possessions packed on their backs—

I suggest you take your chances in the countryside with the others, says St. Cyr. The fort will be crowded, bombardment will commence—

This is not her village being burned, not her country invaded. She belongs, if that word can be applied, to only two people in the world.

"*Je veux rester avec toi,*" says Jenny, throwing her arms around him. The Lieutenant smiles and squeezes her tightly, pleased.

We'll meet again when the siege has ended, he tells her. They'll send us into exile—maybe we'll see Paris together.

And is gone.

Smashing sounds from the street, the smell of wood burning. Amély picks up one end of the duffel they have thrown their goods into, looking at Jenny expectantly.

Tell me where we're going, she says, and Jenny is reminded that Amély is a slave. And she is the Lieutenant's woman, nothing, here, without him.

We follow the *maître*, she says.

Dozens of buildings are already in flames when they step outside. Joseph Broussard, the one they call Beausoleil, makes the Sign of the Cross with the burning oil lamp in his hand, then flings it into the open doorway of the church. There is fire reflected in his eyes when he turns to them—

Keep your distance, *mesdames*, he says. Churches burn like the devil.

A SIEGE, BY DEFINITION, IS A LEISURELY AFFAIR. CAPtain Hussey has relinquished his quarters to Colonel Monckton, commander of the expedition, and feels a mild sense of unease standing at attention across from his own desk. The Colonel, not only a military light but Member of Parliament for the family-controlled seat of Pontefract, spent a year here at Fort Lawrence immediately after its construction in '52, and is consequently well at home in the marshlands. He wears a very white, very expensive wig, even in the field, and has precalculated every aspect of the venture.

"We'll camp on their side of the river tonight," he declares, "at—what is it that they call that spot?"

"*Butte à Mirande,* sir," answers Hussey. "Roughly a mile downriver from their fort."

"Indeed. Tomorrow we'll finish the bridge and send out the engineers to determine the best vantage for our siege guns. Two dozen of the better colonials will do for an escort—don't want the Mi'kmaqs sneaking up to create a nuisance."

Even Hussey was given no hint of the invasion, a wise precaution considering the near impossibility of keeping a secret in this community, villagers of dubious loyalty free to wander in and out of both forts. He guessed that something might be in the works when much-needed supplies did not arrive from Boston with the first thaw, the high command wishing to keep news of the buildup of ships and men from reaching Acadia. If nothing else this invasion brings a welcome bounty of fresh food and new uniforms to his impoverished garrison.

"I assume there has been some improvement at Beauséjour since my tenure?"

"There has, sir, although I must say their commandant is a rather—a rather *fussy* gentleman. They've shored the walls up quite a bit, finished the casements and barracks—"

"The powder magazine?"

"Still rather vulnerable, if you ask me. One lucky mortar shot—"

Monckton raises his eyebrows. "You've been inside?"

"No—we're not quite that chummy. But the locals come and go freely enough, and one hears things. Actually, we've a man inside, an informant—"

He's held off revealing this to the Colonel, offering the information without its provenance. Mustn't seemed too chuffed with oneself—

"Well placed?"

"Their commissary. Extremely disgruntled—"

"It comes with the office—"

"He's been reporting to us almost weekly, whilst sowing discord amongst his colleagues—every claim he's made has borne out so far. I've kept his missives, though they're all scribbled in French—"

"Enlighten me."

Monckton is known as a cool head, having recently settled a near rebellion by the Germans living in Nova Scotia without a shot being fired and comported himself admirably in the fighting around Flanders during the War of the Succession. Hussey's dream, like any other captain with hopes for a career, is to serve under such an officer and impress him—

"Low morale, quite a number of desertions, chronically undersupplied—there's more than a spot of corruption involved in that—"

"Our greatest allies here," Monckton observes, "are the profligates in charge in Quebec."

"They've got a score of small guns to pester us with, a pair of twenty-four pounders they keep trained on the bay, and their artillery fellow is well regarded. However their other officers, including Monsieur le Compte de Vergor du Chambon, at least according to my source—"

"Yes?"

"They'd rather not *be* here."

"So a surrender with honor, and perhaps a year's hiatus from the burden of arms—?"

"I believe they'd be eager to hear your terms, sir."

"Once the requisite formalities have been observed, of course. How long, if it be available, for their reinforcement to arrive from the Louisbourg fortress?"

"Given that your appearance here has surprised even me, I'd say we have two weeks, sir. Though there's no accounting for the Acadians or the Indians—"

"Broussard and that bloody cleric still at it, then?"

"Yes, sir."

Colonel Monckton sits back, pondering. "The majority of them are no trouble—the Acadians—"

"Hard-working, rather friendly," Hussey agrees. "Though not especially keen on signing pledges of allegiance or altering their citizenship—"

Monckton nods, looking perturbed. "Our Lieutenant Governor, after whom this fort is named, is of the opinion that they are not to be trusted and should be packed off to somewhere far away."

"Leaving only the Mi'kmaq—"

"A tribe he desires to see eradicated."

"That will take more than a siege, sir. They are so extremely—i*tin*erant. You've noticed they've already pulled up stakes—"

"Waiting in the woods to fall upon us."

"It is a skulking manner of war, sir, but very effective, given the terrain."

The colonel stands, smiling. "We'll keep well in the open, then. Out of arrow shot."

"Le Loutre has gotten them all rifles by now. I'd wager their skill with a bow has greatly diminished."

"*Sic transit gloria Mi'kmaq*."

The captain has been informed that his own troops will serve only as hosts during the campaign, or perhaps as scouts, should that be required. Though feeling somewhat cramped now, billeted in his adjutant's tiny room, Hussey is looking forward to the meals, which promise to offer more variety than the venison and turnips he has been subsisting on.

"We are, as you know, hopelessly out of touch here," he says to the Colonel, cautious. "Might I know, sir—is that fellow from Hanover still King of England?"

There is a feeling, despite the arrival of two thousand Englishmen, of emptiness outside the walls of Fort Beauséjour. Where there was smoke and the yapping of camp dogs and little Mi'kmaq *coquins* chasing each other through a hodgepodge of pole-and-birchbark wigwams there is now only a field of stumps, and beyond that the heaps of charred wood and blackened stone chimneys where the *ville des acadiens* stood. Pichon tilts the spyglass beyond these till the invaders swim into view. They have built two bridges already, one to replace the Pont à Buot, where they have pitched their tents, and the other farther down the Missaguash, providing easier access from their ships to their own fort. Presently their colonials are engaged in laying planks end to end on the boggy marsh ground, no doubt to provide a road on which to move their larger guns into position. They seem to be heading it toward *la crête d'Aulac*, the rise just to the north of the battlement he is standing upon, where they will be able to pour fire into the French stronghold.

Just as he suggested in his last note to Captain Hussey.

His recommendation that an immediate surrender might be prudent has not been taken seriously, with Lieutenant St. Cyr holding on to some delusion that reinforcement might arrive in time from Louisbourg and Commandant de Vergor, ever practical, requiring a few more days to complete his looting of the post. Opening the fort to hundreds of village men, while perhaps comforting from a military perspective, has placed a devastating strain on the garrison's stores. Discounting the spirits, which le Compte de Vergor has appropriated as his private stock, there is food sufficient for less than a week. The cattle that have been driven inside have no feed and will need to be slaughtered very soon, and the local women and children who have fled to the hinterlands have done so with poultry and preserved food in hand. The overflow of men sprawl on the floors of the barracks at night, and in the daytime the parade ground is chockablock with uniformed soldiers resigned to their imminent capture and *acadiens* who are ready to bolt. Only St. Cyr seems determined to put up a *résistance*.

"*Il faut creuser!*" the Lieutenant cries out to the men, stripped to the waist, who are lugging baskets of earth dug from the middle of the *terrain de parade* and dumping them upon the earthworks that face the English out in the marsh, industriously digging their own trench just beyond cannon range. The workmen, mostly locals, exhibit a marked lack of enthusiasm. Though both St. Cyr and the commandant have assured them that help is already sailing their way, these are men who have had to burn their own homes, who have been promised by the English officials in Halifax that they are welcome to stay here if they will only sign a piece of paper and decline to carry arms for *leur patrie ancien*.

Several flying squadrons of geese, perhaps a hundred honking birds in all, wheel overhead in the darkening sky and then descend, group by group, to cover the marsh between the toiling Boston men and the walls of Fort Beauséjour. They waddle about, grazing with insouciance, somehow knowing that on this day they are safe.

There is a staccato rapping of drums as a mixed force is gathered below him, Lieutenant Vannes sufficiently recovered from last night's libations to lead a party—it looks like at least a hundred men—on some sort of foray. St. Cyr steps up to join Pichon on top of the bastion, surveying the situation with his own spyglass. Pichon coughs several times, finally capturing the Lieutenant's attention, and nods toward the men mustering below.

"*Où vont-ils?*"

They'll climb to the high ground outside, St. Cyr tells him, and attempt to hold it from the English.

Which is an impossibility given even twice their number—

"*Peut-être*—"

Those men will be killed, Pichon insists, for no effective purpose.

"*C'est la guerre,*" sighs the Lieutenant, adding his customary irritating shrug.

A sortie under a white flag to harvest some of those birds would yield far more benefit, but that is a calculation sadly beyond the powers of the military mind. The comedy must be played, *quoi qu'il arrive*. Pichon wishes he could pass on to the Lieutenant here Captain Hussey's assurance, just short of a promise, that upon surrender they will only be sent packing and forbidden, upon their honor, from further combat in the province. But though the majority of officers here share his dismal view of the entire conceit and end each dinner with a toast to the day they will be returned to true French soil, his familiarities with the English are bound to be misconstrued.

Let them resist, then, and doom us to bombardment.

As Vannes leads his party to the heights, a few dozen Mi'kmaq warriors, bedaubed with paint, suddenly emerge from the trees above them, beckoning. Uncanny the way they appear and disappear, unbidden, attuned to muses unknown to white men. Wolves must have similar instincts, knowing when to lay back, when to rush forward, their fangs bared—

St. Cyr steps away to stare intently at one of his cannon, as if the act could embue it with greater lethal effect. Pichon trains his spyglass on the geese. Every Christmas back in Sarlat his mother would roast one, stuffed with a *farce à l'oignon*, the meat drizzled with a hot apple puree and the rendered fat used to fry small potatoes. But here at Fort Beauséjour the Compte de Vergor, afflicted with the gout, is of the opinion that the rarer the flesh you consume the healthier, and Pichon has been compelled to choke down any number of undercooked local species at the officers' mess, with hedgehog, a gift from the Mi'kmaq chief Bâtard, only the least palatable.

Perhaps Monckton, the English commander, has brought a decent cook.

MEN STARE AT JENNY AS SHE MAKES HER WAY, HUNCHED in the rain under her hooded cape, to the commandant's quarters. There are a few other women who have come inside the walls, *acadiennes,* but she and Amély are the most speculated about among the soldiers, half begrudging and half admiring the Lieutenant for having two young women he is not married to at his disposal. The majority of the men left here mill about the parade ground and up on the battlements, idly muttering in small groups, ignoring St. Cyr's pleas for them to help strengthen the position. The uniformed soldiers believe digging and hauling to be beneath their station and the *acadiens* are nursing the resentment caused by the torching of their village. Both Abbé le Loutre and the Compte de Vergor have made speeches, attempting to raise their spirits, with the commandant promising that a fleet packed with experienced troops must certainly already be on its way from Louisbourg, but the mood remains sullen. A sentry holds the door to de Vergor's quarters open for her.

It seems the Indians have captured an English officer.

The commandant is there with her Lieutenant, as well as a pox-scarred sergeant, Hebert, Canadian born and aggressively proud of it. They stand facing a handsome English captain with hair the color of straw who sits in a chair in the middle of the room looking far too comfortable to be a captive.

"Terribly sorry I can't be of aid to you gentlemen, but I'm hopeless with foreign tongues—barely got past *veni, vidi, vici* in my Latin, to the great distress of my schoolmaster—ah—" he stands and offers a slight bow when he sees Jenny step in. "*Bonjour, Madame*—that much I do know."

He is nearly a foot taller than the Frenchmen and Canadian, his head nearly touching the rafters.

"I'd reckon they'd rather ye be seated," Jenny tells him, and he sits, smiling broadly.

"A Scotswoman!"

"Aye."

"And what circumstance, may I ask, has conveyed you to this remote outpost? I hope it wasn't those painted devils who ambushed me this morning—"

Jenny turns to St. Cyr. If he has asked her to translate it is because he doesn't trust the other men in the garrison who have a bit of English to keep the results of the interview to themselves.

"*Que voulez-vous que je lui demande?*"

The Lieutenant and de Vergor supply her with a number of questions, interrupting each other, St. Cyr openly contemptuous of his superior officer now that actual combat is upon them.

"I must say, your lot looks rather a jumble," the prisoner, whose name is Captain Hay, interjects. "We're here with the gaggle of raw colonials, but they can at least pre*tend* to be soldiers."

"They want tae ken hoo ye got yerself snatched by the Meemaws."

The English captain chuckles.

"Bit of a bollocks, that, if you'll excuse my French. I was leading a party on a recce in the woods above your position, when I was—how shall I say this?—indisposed by Nature—"

"Ye had tae drap yer drawers—"

"Quite. Something I ate on the ship, no doubt, and there are things one does not allow one's private soldiers to observe. I stepped away only a short distance, and thankfully had just completed my neccessaries when—they are *aw*fully silent of foot, aren't they? Stealthy brutes. I consider myself very fortunate to have been brought here instead of being made a meal of."

"They want tae ken the size of yer troop."

Captain Hay turns his head to grin at St. Cyr and the commandant.

"No problem there, it's rather an open secret given the terrain, what? We're a tad shy of two thousand foot soldiers, principally from Pennsylvania and Massachusetts—isn't it marvelous the place names they've come up with? So fanciful. And I might add that we've brought an impressive array of artillery—eighteen pounders, twenty-four pounders—beastly things, really—and of course a number of mortars to go up and over—" he describes a high arc with his finger and makes a whistling sound. "Indeed, despite your charming company, Madame, I'd much prefer to be out there with my cohorts than in here with you poor souls. I believe a request for surrender has already been tendered by our Colonel Monckton?"

Jenny relays the Englishman's words, and then de Vergor and the Lieutenant argue for a while, the commandant waving his arms, St. Cyr impassively maintaining that the fort, with his many improvements, is not such an easy nut to crack, and the *Canadien* sergeant walking a slow circle around Hay, glaring at him.

"If you'll indulge me," says the Englishman, making a little wave to get Jenny's attention, "as one Briton to another—have you any sense of what they intend to *do* with me?"

There is an edge to his politeness, Jenny feeling like the man would spit on her in any other circumstances.

"That depends," she tells him, "on them that captured ye."

"On the *sav*ages?"

"If ye're their captive, ye be*lang* tae them—right noo they've ainly loaned ye tae be questioned."

"Surely I won't be handed over to—"

"Mebbe the Meemews'll give ye tae the French here as a giftie, or mebbe the commandant will buy ye frae them—though we're very short on tobacca and *porcelaine*—which is the beads they like—and all the powder and guns is needed fer the fight."

Captain Hay is incredulous. "Please inform your commandant that as a *gentle*man—"

"The chief of the Meemews is named Bâtard, and he's a canny fella. I could stick in a word with him if ye'd like."

The steady drilling of rain is punctuated by the sound of rifle fire outside, a rapid crackling of a few volleys and then only random shots. The Englishman's grin returns.

"That will be our lads taking the heights," he says, and looks around as if assessing the sturdiness of the commandant's quarters. "I wouldn't expect the bombardment to commence until tomorrow, though."

Jenny translates this and there is another argument, this one ending with de Vergor bowing to the Englishman and speaking in soft, formal tones, while St. Cyr stalks out of the room, slamming the door behind him.

"The commandant says ye'll be left on parole within the fort, and he'll send a letter tae yer colonel promising ye'll be pervided all the comforts possible fer the duration of the engagement."

Hay, still seated, gives a slight bow to de Vergor. "Extremely kind of him. Then I take it the red men will be mollified?"

"Yer ransom has been paid."

"Very handsome indeed. Might I ask your name, good lady?"

She knows that the governor of Martinique received a document from the English, demanding the return of all the prisoners aboard the *Veteran*, with their names, ages, physical description, place of birth, and sentence listed. She knows also, from St. Cyr, that there are Scots exiled or even born just outside Paris, and that nobody here besides the Lieutenant and Amély are aware of her whole story.

"Ma name is Jeanne-Marie St. Cyr," she lies, "subject tae His Most Holy Majesty, the King of France."

AT LEAST THE RAIN HAS STOPPED, ONE LESS THING FALLing from the sky to worry about. St. Cyr and the messenger hug the base of the north wall, most of the men left inside lying upon the compressed-earth rampart, sheltered from the sight of the English cannoneers commanding the high ground. Lieutenant Vannes gave the defense of it up after the briefest of exchanges, explaining that resistance to a force of that size—he counted over five hundred of the enemy marching up the ridge—would only serve to sour their disposition when final terms were discussed. So the big guns are above them, pounding away at the walls, while on the other side the thirteen-inch mortars in the English trench, which is now within two hundred yards of Beauséjour, continue to shower them with explosive projectiles. There is a methodical, almost niggardly quality to the siege, as if expenditure of powder and ball has been calculated to the ounce, and the runners he sends to de Vergor, who is ensconced in the most secure of the casements, have divined the rhythm of it and do their scurrying accordingly. St. Cyr has pulled his own gunners off the battlements for the moment, too tempting a target, but has had them load their guns with grapeshot in case the English should lose their patience and attempt to overrun the fort. There are fewer *acadiens* in the garrison at each morning muster, but those leaving have had the decency not to abscond with any vital supplies.

The man who's just arrived, a *voyageur* named Brisbois bold enough to crawl through the marsh, then make a dash for the gate in broad daylight, has refused to deliver his news to any but the officer in command. St. Cyr kicks the casement door three times, hears the commissary's voice challenge him, and gives the ridiculous password. The door opens, Pichon looking annnoyed, de Vergor beyond him with his valet, packing things into a leather trunk.

"*Et maintenant?*" asks the commissary.

"*Nous avons des nouvelles,*" St. Cyr tells him. "*De Louisbourg.*"

Be quick about shutting that door, calls de Vergor as he waves them in impatiently.

"*Vous êtes Monsieur le commandant?*" asks the *voyageur,* suspicious. St. Cyr has ridden in their *pirogues*, has sat about a campfire with them—they are a race apart, dressing and arming themselves not unlike the savages, playing their squeeze-organs and singing through their noses, smoking whenever they can, *eau-de-vie* in their canteens, crucifixes hung from their necks—

"*Le Compte Louis du Pont du Chambon de Vergor,*" says the commandant, puffing up a little.

The *voyageur* glances at the others in the casement, hesitant—

"*Vous pouvez parler librement ici.*"

The *voyageur* nods, explains that he carries no written message for fear that it might be intercepted, but has memorized the words of *Monsieur le Gouverneur* Drucour, repeating them to himself for many miles and many days. These he proceeds to recite, as mortar shells explode on the parade and iron balls smash what is left of the north palisade into splinters.

The message is a disappointment, though not a surprise, to St. Cyr.

The *gouverneur* greatly regrets that his own fortress is at present facing a considerable threat from an English *flotille*, says the voyageur, concentrating with his eyes closed, and will be unable to send help at this time.

Pichon, the commissary, squawks that he told them as much two days ago. The commandant points an accusing finger toward the bearer of bad tidings.

"*M-m-mettre cet homme en isolation*," he orders.

And you gentlemen, he says, regarding St. Cyr, Pichon and his valet each in turn, must swear not to breathe a word to the garrison. "*Sans espoir, les hommes se comportent très m-mal.*"

Some men do not need to be without hope to behave badly, says St. Cyr, staring at his commandant, then briskly escorts the *voyageur* back out into the open, where a mortar shell explodes, disemboweling the last of the beeves.

The man, short and bandy-legged like most of his brethren, asks what he did to deserve being locked up.

"*Tu as bien fait, et je te remercie*," St. Cyr reassures him, patting him on the shoulder. He points to the east wall. The English have avoided the marsh beyond it, which nearly disappears with the high tide. "*Pouvez-vous échapper?*"

The *voyageur* grins, allowing that he is in fact a master of escape, and promises to speak to no one as he leaves. There is a woman waiting for him back in *Main-á-Dieu*—

St. Cyr leans on the side of the casement, listening intently after the man disappears over the wall. From the sound of the cannons on the ridge the officer there is letting his gunners practice, following the little *voyageur* with their fire until he is out of range.

THE ENGLISH HAVE CHOSEN TO HALT THEIR FIREWORKS at night. The uniformed soldiers are able to leave the casements and go back to their wooden barracks, half destroyed now, for a meal of salt cod and biscuit before their few hours of sleep. Jenny and Amély wait among the last of the *acadiens*, gathered on the angled berm of the wall, talking quietly among themselves. The *acadiens* have petitioned the commandant to allow them to fight in their own manner, meaning well away from Fort Beauséjour, but he has only repeated that aid is coming from Louisbourg, that soon, perhaps tomorrow, a French armada will appear and send the enemy running.

Everyone knows this is a lie.

De Vergor's *valet*, Babinot, long the object of ridicule because his wife is *impliqué* with the commandant, has taken his revenge by telling everyone in the garrison that Louisbourg has responded and no help has been offered.

"*C'est différent pour les soldats*," says Robicheaux, the baker, who has done very well for himself supplying the officers' mess here at the fort. Though the uniform makes them a target during the fighting, he explains, once a surrender is negotiated there are rules, a sense of honor among *les militaires*, that protect the soldier and his personal property. But the English, rightly or not, have long considered the *acadiens* to be their subjects, and may treat them as traitors condemned to the rope—

"*Personne ne va être pendu*," says the one they call Beausoleil.

Coming from Broussard, a reward offered for his capture and the man here most likely to be hanged, this is not reassuring.

The French have abandoned us, he says, and Jenny is struck again that these people think of themselves as French only when convenient or forced upon them, like children who have spurned a neglectful mother.

Well then—we'll abandon *them*!

There is hearty agreement with this sentiment. St. Cyr, not knowing what the English will make of her, has insisted she and Amély come down here, dressed for travel. Though their help with the wounded has been appreciated, Amély showing a real *aptitude* for healing, it will be safer for them to leave with the *acadiens*.

We're free men, says Broussard, moving his torch to look in the eye of every waiting civilian, and we intend to remain that way.

And then tells three of his sons to fetch ladders.

PICHON FINDS LIEUTENANT ST. CYR ON THE NORTHwest bastion, watching the *acadiens*—only eighty of them left now—go over the north wall.

You're not going to stop them?

Let them be a headache to the English, the Lieutenant tells him. They were doing us no good.

But we're here fighting for *them*—

The Lieutenant laughs. You know that isn't true.

Pichon peers toward the wall, gradually able to make out detail within the moving shapes.

Is that insufferable priest with them?

Abbé le Loutre departed from us last night, says the Lieutenant. Answering a higher call, no doubt—

Pichon has offered his services to the commandant as an emissary, hoping to remove himself from the daily barrage, but de Vergor has grown coy, wishing to be wooed with yet another request for capitulation before giving up the fort. Two men were killed and five injured today by mortar fragments, and there will be more casualties until the inevitable is accepted. A doctor will not waste his time on the terminally ill, he muses, a butcher knows he must get rid of meat when it begins to stink, but these military *coquettes*—

The Lieutenant's woman and her *negresse*, in hooded cloaks, climb the ladder on the north wall. Pichon looks to St. Cyr.

We must insist, he says to Pichon, his face registering no emotion, in the articles of surrender, that the *acadiens* are not punished.

Do you think the English will agree to that?

On paper, of course. But what is done once we've abandoned our position here—

The Lieutenant, a planter from one of the sugar islands and no more fit to wear the uniform than that imposter de Vergor, sighs and shrugs, then asks Pichon if he will miss Canada.

You know I will not. And neither will France, once we are able to cut it loose. The money wasted here, the honor lost—

Well, that's it, interrupts St. Cyr as the last of the locals disappears over the parapet. Now Madame Babinot is the only woman left in the fort.

Pichon scowls.

That cuckold of a *valet* should have poisoned de Vergor, he says.

That's the cook's job, corrects Lieutenant St. Cyr, the trace of a smile on his lips. "*Chacun à son propre métier.*"

DOZENS OF WHITE MEN ATTACK THE TREES WITH THEIR axes, others trimming what has fallen, before more white men, and some black, hook chains and goad their oxen, pulling huge logs to the sides or uprooting stumps in the center of the road. They work steadily, beaverlike in their perseverance.

Jamie squats with Shingas, Killbuck, and LaCroix, watching from deeper in the woods. Jamie has the saber in a sheath between his shoulder blades and the others carry tomahawks and muskets, but they are not painted for war.

A road like a great river, says Shingas, impressed.

The English are snakes, Jamie reminds him.

Shingas nods. When snakes fight, he says, one swallows the other. It is best to be friends with the snake with the bigger mouth.

Killbuck stands, steps toward the road. We'd better go meet them, he says, before they take us for savages and shoot us.

THE RED-COATED SOLDIERS SIT ON FRESH CUT STUMPS as they rest. A small canopy has been erected for their general, while his guests sit in the sun, also on stumps. The Virginian, Washington, stands nearby, difficult to tell what rank he holds from his uniform. Scaraoudy and Montour are there, as well as Silver Heels and some younger Mingos. Word has come that the Haudenosaunee council, meeting with whites in Albany, have sold all the lands west of the Susquehanna River, sold them from under the feet of the Lenape and the Shawnee and the Mingos living there, but Scaraoudy and Shingas have not spoken of it. Tanaghrisson the Half King, it is said, has died among the English, as if his spirit had been broken by their defeat in the Great Meadows.

Jamie can tell that Shingas is cowed by the multitude of redcoats he has seen, by the axemen and the teamsters with their wagons and the sailors along to rig pulleys for the steepest ascents and the horses and the herd of cattle that is driven along to feed the horde of invaders. Introduced as merely a local *sachem* by Scaraoudy, he has been presented with a single belt of wampum, white beads with a red tomahawk design at the center.

"I am well aware," says the general, this one named Braddock, "that these Frenchmen have invaded the territory immediately to the west of the Allegheny River—lands that your people have heretofore enjoyed the bounty of. Your father, King George, has sent me at the head of this great army to drive them away. If you—if you *people* would like to join our force, there will be gifts of muskets and powder and shot, and, of course, a great many things to be captured from the enemy."

In translating, Jamie is sure to emphasize, "Your father, King George." Croghan and the other English traders are always careful to call him only "your good friend." The general at least looks the Lenape in the eye, though his tone is that of a lecturer.

"I must remind you in this that we are many and strong, while the French are few and weak. You see the great road I am building, you can count how many soldiers follow the axes."

Jamie translates this, Shingas nodding, then responding, speaking slowly and clearly.

"Yer brother Shingas says he is impressed by the road ye've built through these lands, and asks the general what his father George intends tae dae with them should ye succeed in driving the French awee?"

The question seems to baffle the general, who is portly and sweating through his waistcoat.

"With the lands? They shall be *ours*, of course."

Jamie sees the tall Virginian standing beside General Braddock close his eyes in chagrin. Shingas, understanding what was said, bypasses Jamie to speak English.

"You say 'our land'?"

"It belongs to the Crown, of course. The land is ours by treaty with the Iroquois Confederation."

Scaraoudy, never one to lose his composure, stares at Shingas as if nothing out of the ordinary has been spoken.

Shingas stares back at him.

"Our cousins the *mengwe*," Shingas continues, still in English, "believe that any land they look on with their eyes is theirs to sell."

"British subjects shall populate this land once it is free of hostiles," says the general, fighting not to blink as sweat stings his eyes.

Jamie translates this to Killbuck.

Shingas turns to Jamie.

Perhaps I do not understand the words of the great General

Braddock, he says, controlling himself. My brother, the Beaver, would be better at this.

Tell me exactly what you wish to know, and I'll ask him.

Shingas states his question as carefully as he can, then looks into the general's eyes as Jamie translates it.

"Yer brother Shingas asks, will our people, and those of the Shawnee and those of the Mingo, if they join the war against the French, not *share* in the land and be able tae live on it and tae grow their crops and hunt as they have afore?"

It is hard to say whether the general is more annoyed at waiting for translations or by Jamie's Scots accent.

"No savage shall inerit the land," he says.

Jamie uses *awènhakeyok,* the word for a wild Indian. Shingas nods without taking his eyes from the general, then gives him a second chance, speaking carefully.

"Yer brother Shingas asks if he has truly heard the great General Braddock. Does he understand that the general will drive us intae the arms of his enemy, the children of King Louis?"

Braddock looks up to Washington. "Is he saying they're going over to the other side?"

"If we are not to live on this land," says Shingas in English, "why would we die for it?"

Washington raises a hand. "I think perhaps you misunderstand the general—"

"He understands me perfectly, Mister Washington," snaps Braddock. "He and his people merely decline to fight."

The general hauls himself to his feet, his very limited patience at an end.

"I'm certain that we can settle the French without any assistance from these people," he says to Washington. "Deal with the formalities, would you?"

He makes a perfunctory bow to the Lenape—

"Good day, sirs."

—then strides away.

The tall Virginian faces them, smiling unconvincingly.

"The general thanks the wise men of the Delaware, the Shawnee, and the Mingo for their generous offers of help in our efforts. However—"

THEY WALK WEST THROUGH THE FOREST, THE SOUND of axes biting into wood gradually fading. It is LaCroix who finally breaks the silence.

I've talked to the officer at Fort Duquesne, he says. The French will pay us three pounds for an English scalp.

And the English will pay us five pounds for that of a Frenchman, says Shingas. He looks to Jamie.

I have seen more of these redcoats on the great road than there are Lenape in the world. If we defeat these, are we then finished?

Did you see the *trees* that still surround their soldiers? asks Jamie.

Yes.

There are more than that many redcoats waiting over the Great Water.

Shingas stops walking for a moment, and it is as if he is trying to remember the trees, to count them in his mind. He resumes walking then, and does not speak again till they have reached the Allegheny River.

"BOSTON, OF COURSE, HAS THE PRETENSIONS OF A CITY, and their port is certainly well situated, Philadelphia is plagued by Quakers—I'm sure you people have a religious order something like them at home—who manage to be both sanctimonious and mercenary, and New York—well, I haven't actually *been* to New York—"

Captain Hay, though allowed his liberty within the little fort, has been able to do very little strolling about due to the incessant artillery assault laid on by his comrades in arms. Four days sequestered in this casement, considered the most secure by the French officers, have induced a kind of volubility not ordinary to his nature, especially when his audience understand so little of what he is prattling on about—

"—but I gather it is rather culturally impoverished, which one might say of the whole of the colonies, though I suppose that comes with the territory, so to speak. I had rather hoped to be posted somewhere in the Caribbean—"

St. Cyr, a good fellow from what he can gather, and another lieutenant named Vannes are there, awaiting the midday meal. When Pichon, the rather dyspeptic commissary, is present, they have a foursome for cards, but that worthy has gone off to the storeroom with the commandant, bickering over something in their impenetrable language—

"—balmy breezes, tropical fruits, pliant native doxies—you get the picture. Have you ever been? I know you froggos have got hold of some islands down there, at least for the moment—"

St. Cyr is listening, with little comprehension, to Hay, and half listening to the serenade of the cannon beyond the door. There is the deep, basso thump of the twenty-four pounders up on the ridge wearing away their north wall, and then the higher, snare-drum-and-cymbal play of the falling mortar shells, some of them duds, more of them blasting apart on or slightly after landing within the walls, sending jagged scraps of metal shrieking in all directions. These will occasionally hit the casement door, a sturdy barrier some six inches thick, with no more effect, at least as experienced from within, than someone hurling a fistful of gravel—

"—though of course the poor buggers involved in our last venture to Jamaica were *ter*ribly vexed with the fever—shiploads of them kicking off and tossed into the drink—so I expect it's a matter of what season you are there, and we military fellows aren't actually on holiday, are we? From a certain perspective it all seems a bit of a shambles, really, waste of effort and loss of lives and all that, but without a war we'd be out on our arses begging for employment, wouldn't we? Not to say our respective monarchs don't have their rationale, their divine rights and so forth—"

He is unable to stop himself, as if his words might provide some kind of barrier that even the heaviest cannonball cannot penetrate, as if talking is equal to breathing and if he stops the one—

"—and of course any posting is superior to duty in *Ireland*, unless you have a craving for potatoes without the roast beef they are meant to garnish. I suppose we're somewhat resented by the Acadian folk here and of course by those bloody Highlanders back home, but the *Irish*—a more obstreperous passel of bogtrotters you'll never encounter, convinced, somehow, that they are capable of governing themselves—"

There is a spot of brandy left, rather decent, and some *eau de vie* made from apples, an acquired taste he has not yet acquired. They've been eating off pewter, the commandant having packed the silver plate away "for safekeeping," and the cook is down to the inferior cuts of the beeves that have been slaughtered, bathing them, as the French are wont, in mysterious sauces. Better, though, than salted eel, with which he has been threatened on several occasions. Vannes is holding a small looking glass and trimming his moustache, while St. Cyr draws something absently on a scrap of parchment, palm trees perhaps—

"—when they've got our perfectly adequate Parliament only a stone's throw across the water to make their lives miserable—merely jesting, ha-ha—what would be your equivalent, Corsica, perhaps? Swarthy little fellows, almost Italian—"

The door is kicked three times in signal, and Vannes rises to open it. The commandant's surly *valet* stands there, the basket holding the cook's latest attempt at a decent meal in hand, just as a mortar round, a tin cylinder, lands and bounces between his legs, rolling toward the foot of the table they sit at.

"*C'est un explosif,*" St. Cyr has time to observe—

COLONEL MONCKTON AND CAPTAIN HUSSEY ARE PUZzling out the wording for the articles of surrender when the white flag appears. They have just come to Article 24, stating that any slaves held by members of the vanquished garrison will remain as their property, a *caveat* added due to Pichon's intelligence that one of the French officers has brought a negress with him all the way from Martinique.

"What's this, then?" says the Colonel, standing as a trio of Frenchmen step out through the western gate with the flag. "Tossing in the sponge so soon?"

"Perhaps they've run out of brandy," says Hussey.

The Colonel signals for his translator, an overeducated fellow also in charge of the regiment's marching band with a *connaissance* of the enemy's lingo far superior to that of Sergeant Archibald, and begins to climb out of the trench.

A sudden, welcome quiet as the order for cease fire is passed. It is the nicest sort of summer day up here, yellow butterflies dancing about, the sun sparkling off the distant bay as they meet upon the boggy marsh that lies between the fort and the closest trench, a dissipate French captain and two scrawny private soldiers facing Monckton, his regimental commanders Scott and Winslow, Captain Hussey, and the musical translator.

"The captain regrets to inform you," says the translator, "that the prisoner, Captain Hay, has just been killed, along with several French officers, in an explosion."

"Hay?"

Scott, embarrassed, leans toward Monckton.

"One of mine, sir. Captured by the savages while on reconnaissance."

The Frenchman continues—

"Given their strategic disadvantage and dwindling supply of victuals and ammunition," relays the translator, "Commandant de Vergor is ready to begin negotiations for the relinquishment of Fort Beauséjour."

"Then why isn't he bloody *present*?" asks Monckton.

The French captain seems discomfited when this is posed to him. His response is halting, as if fashioned of very thin tissue—

"He says Commandant de Vergor suffers an impediment of speech, leaving him ill-equipped for verbal arbitration."

Hussey stifles a laugh. There is more back and forth, establishing that the honor of France and *sa Majesté trés chretienne Louis* seem to have been satisfied.

"That's a comfort," says Colonel Monckton, "though *I* would have held out twice as long given the circumstances. Ask him how many combatants remain within."

The officer has an exact count.

"The garrison numbers one hundred and twenty-two men, eleven of them severely wounded."

"And the Acadians lodged there?"

"They seem to have all taken French leave, sir."

"Have the captain tell his verbally incontinent commander that terms will be delivered forthwith."

The parties exchange bows then, and head back to their respective positions. Captain Hussey is eager to visit the map in his headquarters and replace that tiny white-and-gold French flag with a tiny Union Jack, the first, he hopes, of many such readjustments in this north country.

"We'll have to rechristen the place once we occupy it, sir," he says. "Would Fort Monckton be presumptuous?"

"Bad form, naming things after oneself," mutters the Colonel. "I was rather thinking we should honor the King's youngest."

"Ah, Fort *Cum*berland," Hussey nods, worried he's come off a bit the bootlicker. "After the hero of Culloden."

PERHAPS THE MOST SURPRISING THING IS THAT IT hasn't happened before. Certainly the grenadiers are not familiar with Indians, one bare-chested savage appearing little different than the next to them, and with another white straggler or two slain and mutilated every few days along the road, the men are primed to shoot at anything in moccasins. Washington feels he might have helped avoid this, perhaps suggesting that their few native escorts paint a large cross upon their chests or something of the like, but he has been so thoroughly indisposed. The damnable flux has him hurrying into the trees several times a day with little warning, and though he takes the precaution of bringing a pair of the negro batman with him, armed to intercept skulkers, his capacity for coherent thought has been diminished.

They at least have the sense to carry the young man into camp on an improvised litter rather than slung over the shoulder like a hind, with Silver Heels and Fairfax, Queen Alliquippa's son, following with grim faces. With the axes ringing out from dusk to dawn and explosives used to remove boulders from their path and the flankers taking the odd shot at a wild turkey or phantom enemy, the little ripple of musket fire to the north seemed nothing special. But then the ashen Virginia ranger running in to report the tragedy, and now the body—

It is Scaraoudy's son, Swift Runner.

"We 'eard somefing of a ruckus be'ind us," says one of the grenadiers from the advance guard, "and come back ter find free of our lads, stripped and scalped, they was. Then we 'eard the whoopin' and hollering like they do, right near us from the woods, and these gents—" the grenadier nods to Silver Heels and Fairfax, "and a few uvver of our friendlies lights out after 'em. Hit seems like on their way back they run inter some of our colonial lads—"

"Put rifle down, hold hands up," says Silver Heels, who has a modicum of English. "Soldier shoot anyhow."

The boy's forehead is indented where the ball entered, and there is little left to the back of his head. General Braddock and Lord St. Clair ride up, the knot of onlookers moving aside to give them a clear view of the body, now laid on the ground.

"Finally got one, did we?" says the general.

"He's one of ours, sir," Washington tells him. "Scaraoudy's son."

"Bloody hell."

It has been a unique experience for Washington, no longer in the Virginia Regiment nor on the British Army roll, answering only to Braddock, the other officers not sure what to make of him. His observations and advice have not been ignored, however, and if he were not so weakened by the flux he might have fought harder to have them implemented. The general is an unimaginative fellow who goes strictly by the book, but the book was not written with this terrain or mode of warfare in mind.

"Three of our advance guard were ambushed, our Indians went in pursuit and were mistaken, on their return—"

"I'll want your help."

"General?"

"To break it to Scaraoudy. He seems to be their leader, if they have such a thing."

"He is scouting ahead, General. When he returns—"

"You'll tell him, then." The general is annoyed, waving mosquitos from his face. "We'll do a proper sendoff in the morning—drums, pipes, ten-gun salute. They like a bit of ceremony."

KIRBY AND CRUIKSHANK SIT ON TREE STUMPS, TAKING a moment before they rejoin their patrol.

"Ye'd think hit was the uniforms make all men look alike. But ye strip 'em nakit, get busy with yer knife—"

"Jenkins was a good mate."

"'Ee was that."

"What I say, they was rushed from be'ind, knocked on the 'ead before they 'ad time ter reflect upon it."

"I would 'ope so. There wasn't time enough fer any torture."

"We would 'ave 'eard the screams."

"Still, once ye've scragged yer enemy, what's the point of coming the butcher?"

"Ye'd say hit were a beastly thing ter do, but I can't fink of a *beast* would do the same. They might eat yer, but—"

"I'd like ter see 'em all dead."

"The Frenchies' savages—"

"The *lot* of em, no matter which side they pretend ter be on. Hit's like wooves. All of England used ter be crawlin' with slaverin' wooves, skulkin' about, carrying off yer infants in their jaws if ye so much as turned yer back, and hit weren't a fit place ter reside fer yuman beings like you an me, Bert. Hit weren't *civ*ilized. So the people got together and they e*rad*dycated 'em, is what they did. Ye won't find a single woof between Penzance and Newcastle. Wales and Scotland, I can't speak fer."

"There's one at the Tower."

"Waitin' ter be 'anged?"

"In the King's menagerie, with the lions and ellyphants and whatnot."

"Then we'll save one or two of the savages," says Cruikshank, "and ship 'em back ter the King."

THE NOISE ALONE IS IMPRESSIVE. A SCORE OF DRUMmers rattling away, half that many pipers, Braddock intoning with all of his officers flanking him in full dress uniform.

Courage.

Honor.

In the finest military tradition.

And then a squadron of grenadiers firing a volley into the sky over the freshly dug grave. The Virginias have been ordered to muster in the rear, empty-handed, penitent, and out of the bereaved father's sight. A dozen white men have fallen on the campaign, two from heatstroke, the others ambushed by marauders, but they were only teamsters or private soldiers, and were left buried beside the new road without ceremony. But the general has grudgingly accepted that Indian scouts are vital, and thus the Union and regimental flags hoisted over the assembly.

Scaraoudy himself is draped with every ornament he's been given by the white man over the years, gorgets and ribbons and medallions, and sports a beaver hat that might have been in fashion a century ago. Washington has done his best to frame the incident as the fault of the perfidious French, sending savage western Indians to hinder the march and commit their depredations, but the *sachem*'s reaction is unreadable, having uttered but one phrase since appraised of the misfortune.

"There is a hole in my heart."

THEY KEEP TO THE SPARSE WOODS, JENNY AND AMÉLY welcomed to attach themselves to Desjardins and his children, who in turn have joined Broussard and over three dozen *réfugiés* moving southwest from the besieged fort. The people carry bundles, small children, and babies in their arms, faces drawn, speaking little or not at all. Things could be worse, thinks Jenny, it could be winter with Aonach Beag to climb. We could be barefoot—

Broussard has sent out scouts to precede and to follow them, Desjardins' eldest son, Modeste, who is an avid woodsman, volunteering to walk in the lead. They stop briefly only when they have crossed a stream, waiting for stragglers, eating a bite of salt cod or parched corn. Jenny wishes she had moccasins like those worn by Broussard and his raiders, her store-bought shoes ill-adapted for travel through marsh and forest, her ankles already sore and swollen.

"*Pas d'anglais devant nous*," Modeste reports when they catch up to him at a little waterfall. He is already a head taller than his father, though still in his teens, and has the darkest skin of all the Desjardins children. Quiet and handsome, half the young girls in Beauséjour are in love with him, to the dismay of their parents.

"*Et nos frères rouges?*" asks Broussard.

Modeste says he has seen no sign of the Mi'kmaqs, though they may have been watching him.

"*Eh bien, nous continuerons.*"

The sky looks innocent of rain and they can hear the sea to their right as they move through the sap-smelling pines, Broussard warning them to move quietly, as the English may have boats out searching the coastline. Amély carries little Sophie, while Jenny lags to help Cyprien and Marguerite over the fallen trees. The *acadiens* have large families, so there are more children than adults, though not a one cries or asks where they are going. Landry carries his smallest on his shoulders, the little boy happily reaching to poke at pine cones hanging near his head. Eventually the trees give out and there is only marshland, the people keeping a wary eye on the bay as they walk two and three abreast along the rocky shore, feet remaining relatively dry at low tide. A few hundred yards out, a pair of dolphins swim parallel to them, curious, until they grow bored of the somber parade and disappear beneath the sparkling water.

When the Indians come, it is from behind. Chief Bâtard and Jules Theriault, a trader who lives most of the year with them, confer with Broussard for a moment, then Broussard waves Jenny over, looking grim.

The breath is already gone from her lungs when she arrives.

"*Je suis désolé*," says the Mi'kmaq chief, "*mais votre homme est tombé.*"

He's dead.

An unfortunate mortar shell, he explains, that led to the immediate surrender of the garrison. And though the *imbécile* Compte de Vergor was allowed to march his troop from the fort with drums rolling and flag held high, facing only a boat ride to Louisbourg and a promise to refrain from combat for half a year, St. Cyr's blasted remains have been left for the English to dispose of.

Nothing to be done about it now, adds Broussard, looking her in the eye. We can mourn later.

They move on then, the dozen Mi'kmaqs leading the way with Modeste, while the fate of the Lieutenant and Fort Beauséjour is whispered back through the exiled families. Jenny feels lightheaded, wishing she could go back, wishing she had been there, half believing the news to be untrue. But St. Cyr has explained to her, in his dry, superior manner, the effect on human flesh of an exploding mortar shell at close range. She hopes he was killed instantly.

Don't worry, says Amély, suddenly walking beside with an arm around her shoulder. You're not alone. I belong to you now.

Jenny finds herself weeping. "*Ce n'est pas vrai,*" she says. "*Je ne suis que la maîtresse, pas la femme.*"

Mistress or wife, Amély explains, I belong to you. That's how it works in Martinique.

"*Mais nous ne sommes pas en Martinique.*"

Amély shrugs.

One way or another, you own me now.

They have stopped, facing each other, the other travelers stepping silently around them.

Then I make you free, says Jenny.

Amély frowns, shaking her head. Be careful what you say—

I make you *free*.

Amély is crying as well now. "*Tu ne veux pas de moi?*"

You're not mine, Jenny tells her. You belong to yourself. You can go anywhere you wish.

They are standing at the very edge of the bay, nothing to see in a wide circle but flat water and flat land and a handful of passing *acadiens* with their heads held low. Amély shifts the squirming Sophie in her arms, pondering what has been said, then her face softens into a beautiful smile.

What good fortune, she says. Free to go anywhere the English won't arrest me or the *peaux-rouges* won't take my hair.

Then it's settled, says Jenny.

They begin to pick their way over the rocks again, side by side, slowly catching up with the rest of the party. Amély is humming a song to herself, something Jenny doesn't recognize.

"*Passe moi la petite fille*," says Jenny to her friend after a spell, reaching for little Sophie. She must be getting heavy.

SHINGAS HAS NOT SHOWN HIS FACE AT THE FORT. CAPtain Jacobs is here, and maybe a dozen more Lenape—LaCroix, Killbuck, Red Warrior, as well as Ange and a few of the other women. The progress of Braddock's army over the mountains, a great red flood that will scour the French from this country, has been reported on for weeks, and the officers here are rightfully anxious. They will need the support of as many tribes as they can muster to have even a prayer of resistance, and several hundred have gathered outside the walls to see what will be offered.

Jamie and LaCroix drift from group to group, LaCroix identifying the groups he can recognize by language or ornamentation—Shawnee, Mingo, Ottawa, Wyandot, Potawatomi, some Catholic Indians from the north—and Chartier is here, though he makes no sign of recognizing Jamie. None, apparently, are blood enemies of the others, though there is a wariness to their interaction—

We see each other at the trading posts, says LaCroix. But only the Shawnee are our brothers.

A pair of French officers step out from the front gate, a half-dozen drummers riffling behind them, and then soldiers carrying chests and bundles. The warriors and their women make a half circle around the officers, and Ange waves to Jamie, eyes agleam with excitement.

Even if you don't fight, like at the last battle, she said when she insisted on coming, there will be good things to carry home after it is over.

The taller one is Beaujeu, says LaCroix, and the younger is named Dumas.

Captain Jacobs and the other Lenape move to stand by Jamie and LaCroix to hear their translation. The drummers stop in unison, and Beaujeu steps forward to address them, declaiming in a voice that carries even to the men standing with the river at their backs.

"*Les Anglais se dirigent vers l'ouest,*" he begins, "*et prennent de plus en plus de vos terres.*"

He says the English are pushing westward, taking more and more of our land, Jamie translates. He says our good friend Louis wishes only to trade with us, to help us prosper. Are there settlements of French people among us? he asks. No. Only this Fort Duquesne, and the others like it to the north, where we can trade for the things we need and where we are always welcome to find shelter from our enemies.

Some muttering among the warriors, other translators catching up with Beaujeu's words.

"*Et maintenant,*" says Beaujeu, "*maintenant l'armée de notre ennemi Georges fait la guerre contre nous—*"

And now the army of our enemy George makes war on us, says Jamie to his tribesmen. His soldiers and their friends the *mengwe* kill French traders and threaten our villages. He asks us to join them in opposing the English. The French will give us muskets, powder, and shot, they will give us food to feed our families while we are away on the campaign—

Beaujeu spreads his arms dramatically. "*Parmi vous, quels grands chefs nous rejoindront sur le chemin de la guerre?*"

Suddenly you can hear the river flowing past.

Dumas and Beaujeu look stricken, certain that the call to arms would be immediately and enthuiastically answered.

A bit more muttering now among the different groups, and then Chartier steps forward, turning sideways so he is addressing both the French and the Indians.

"*Nous tiendrons un conseil ce soir et nous vous répondrons dans la matin.*"

He says we'll hold council tonight, then let them know in the morning.

Dumas and Beaujeu huddle together, as do several of the individual chiefs and their warriors. Finally Beaujeu turns back to them.

"*Nous attendrons votre décision.*"

And with that he gestures to the soldiers, who unceremoniously pick up the goods that were about to be offered and carry them back inside the fort, with the officers attempting to maintain their dignity as they follow, the drums barking a retreat.

What do you think? Jamie asks Captain Jacobs.

It depends on how the French wish us to fight, he says. I know I'm not stepping inside those walls.

A voice, strangely familiar, cries out from the river as a trio of canoes pull up to the bank, heads turning. Jamie moves to see, and the crowd parts to reveal a procession of Shawnee warriors climbing up to the fort, with Lachlan MacLeod, face painted half red, half black in the lead, loudly proclaiming in Shawnee the virtues of his chief—

Tremble in fear all ye who gather here, for Bone, great war chief of the Shawnee, approaches!

Bone, looking fierce and haughty, strolls behind the *seanachaidh*.

He who takes the scalp of white man and red man, he whose very name causes the hearts of his enemies to shrink with fear! Turn your eyes away, for he has come to wreak a terrible vengeance!

The men from the other tribes do not seem overly impressed. Lachlan slows as he approaches Jamie, taking a moment to recognize him.

"Jamie! Ye look a feckin' savage."

"And what aboot the company ye're keepin'?" The bard is still a wee sprite, but seven years with the Shawnee have strengthened him. Jamie, unlike his fellow warriors, does not carry a mirror, and often forgets what he used to look like.

Bone steps past him without a flicker of acknowledgement.

THE FRENCH HAVE THE GOOD SENSE TO FEED THE GATHered throng, and Jamie and Lachlan sit by each other, a bit removed from the others, as hot beef and a squash and corn stew is brought out in wooden trenchers.

"Pity they haven't hailed oot the cognac yet," says Lachlan.

"That will come after we've agreed tae fight."

Lachlan is as scrawny as ever, the strip of hair left unshaven on his head giving him the appearance of a plucked rooster.

"Every time Ah see a mon's tonsure hanging on a Shawnee's belt," says Jamie, "Ah expect it tae be yers."

"Ah've learnt the history of Bone's people back tae the day the Great Turtle formed the airth—they kill me, and they kill their past."

"Do they trust ye with a' that?"

"Their *seanachaidh* was an auld mon. He and the laddie he was training took the pox and deid." Lachlan shrugs. "They've naebody left but me."

"And yer great chief there—"

"Ah, Bone will play the zealot, but ye can understand why. They've been pushed frae pillar tae post, these Shawnee—they're spread a' over the country like a madwoman's shite—" He nods toward the French soldiers doling out food. "If this battle gaes well, Ah mean tae ask the froggies tae send me hame."

"Hame tae what?"

"I've nae idea—and there's days Ah wonder if it ever *twas*."

Two bonfires have been built some distance apart, their light bouncing red off the river's surface and revealing a sentry by the biggest cannon on the near bastion. The headmen and their warriors have crowded in between the fires, men taking turns standing to speak, followed by a babel of translation, words often passing through three languages before they are deciphered.

Shingas is here now, always seeming to know what has gone on before. He and Chartier speak first, each with an accurate appraisal of the size and might of the English force, though Shingas counts two more cannon. Both agree that the column will cross the Monongahela tomorrow and wonder if the French will put up only a show of battle, as the white people do, and then march away beating their drums.

Bone has taken the center of the circle now, his words sharp and staccato.

The English have many settlers, he says, and more come into our lands each day. If we let them win this war they will be stronger. If we can force them to leave, it will then be easy to kill the sons of Louis and rid our lands of the white people forever!

As this clatters through the various tongues, Jamie thinks of the Highland clan gatherings he's been to, always good for fisticuffs and perhaps a dirking, with each of the chiefs rising up to take their Erse for a walk even if only to remind their renters who the headman is. He wonders what old wounds and hatreds are stirred by this meeting.

Half Turtle of the Potawatomi stands—

My people can no longer survive without the things the white man brings, he admits, muskets, animal traps—

Rum and iron hatchets are not a fair trade for all that we have lost! cries young Pontiac of the Ottawa.

Some debate now, among and between the different groups, until Shingas rises again and steps to the center.

The esteemed chiefs Bone and Pontiac speak a great truth in this, he says. But the path of war is a difficult one—our women and children will suffer, many widows will be made. Instead, let the white man kill each other while we continue to trade with both. In time we can choose the side that will clearly win.

Bone is up beside him, suddenly staring at Jamie.

Shingas is a wise chief, he says without hiding his contempt. He has walked the middle of the path for many years. But I fear his eyes have been clouded—there is a white spy in his camp!

Some angry shouts, and Jamie is on his feet in an instant, knowing how badly this could end.

May I speak?

All who are here may speak, says Pontiac.

Jamie looks at Bone, choosing his Lenape words carefully but speaking with a vehemence—

This is not my land, he says. I was forced to come here by the English, who are snakes. I wish nothing more than to be across the Great Water—killing them.

He waits for this to be rendered into the various tongues, hearing a few cries of agreement when whatever their word for "kill" is uttered.

But if this is not to be—

He turns to look at the Shawnee, unblinking. If this is not to be, he says, I agree with the great warrior Bone. We should make war on the English now. What happens after they are defeated depends on the sons of Louis. I have started down the path of war beside the French once before. Their words bark louder than their muskets.

There is laughter from various sectors. Shingas holds up both hands to show the empty palms to the surrounding warriors.

I, Shingas, will wait and see how this war goes forward. If some of my warriors wish to fight now, I will not stand in their path. What is important is that red men do not kill red men.

The *mengwe* fight for the English, snaps Bone. And we will have to kill them.

But those are creatures without penises, says Shingas. I am speaking of human beings.

More laughter, and then, with no resolution, men begin to drift away from the fires.

"Just like the bluidy Hielanders," says Lachlan to Jamie when he is sure Bone has stepped away. "A'ways spoilin fer a fight, but nivver sure which side tae join."

Jamie finds LaCroix, and they walk north along the riverbank. He thinks of the redcoats, not far away now, thinks of their portly general with the snuff powder on his coat, thinks of lying in a ditch under the bodies of murdered Scotsmen, of rotting in chains, of climbing the gallows—

"*Nous allons nous battre!*" crows LaCroix when they reach the bark lean-to Ange has put up, one of scores, each now with its own little fire. She sits feeding pine branches to the flames, reflections flaring up in her eyes.

Ange nods toward the other campfires dotting the riverbank on both sides. "*Et les autres?*"

"*Peut-être, peut-être pas. On verra dans la matinée.*"

I'm fighting with the French, says Jamie as he sits. No matter what anyone else does.

Ange studies his face in the firelight, a look on it she has not seen before.

WASHINGTON HAS POMPEY FIX A CUSHION OVER THE saddle. The bloody flux has left him raw where he sits, and it should be most of a day's ride to the French fort. He's eager to see it—if Stobo's map is accurate, it must be quite impressive, sitting there at the forks, even ringed with the usual confusion of Indian hovels. With good fortune the enemy will mount at least a token resistance instead of burning it down and fleeing, and it will serve the King well in this part of the country.

He mounts the gray and gingerly eases into his seat. He attempted yesterday's trek without it, making a much better figure in front of the men, but finally it became so painful that he was forced to walk for the second half of the day. An officer's duty is to be visible, to be mobile, and for that horseback is a must. Your soldiers must—literally—look up to you. The regiments are forming ranks now, drums riffling, and the axemen have already gone forward with their escort. He knows that by noon the woods will become so widely spaced that the cutting will cease for the most part, and then they'll ease downslope to the Monongahela.

If there is to be an ambush, it will happen there. The way the river loops they will have to ford it twice, its depth no problem in this dry summer, but wading in water is an atrociously bad place to maneuver, absolutely no cover and impossible to take a knee to allow the second line to volley. They'll send scouts and flankers ahead, of course, but the enemy will have their own observers, and can move quickly without artillery—

Washington is wearing his silver gorget, even knowing these are enough prized by the savages to make him a special target. In a smaller engagement they would be careful not to aim at his mount, hoping to carry it away, but today, if there is in fact a reckoning, any confrontation will not be small.

A shame to lose such a fine animal, but one can't ride into battle on a yeoman's plug.

General Braddock, with young Shirley and another subaltern behind him, rides up along the line of colonials.

"You're getting some of your color back," he observes when he sees Washington. "Just in time for the festivities."

"We may only see their coattails."

"We'll make it plenty hot for em, I promise you that."

"I believe we shall."

"While you're riding," says the general as he trots by, eyes sparkling with anticipation, "give a thought to what we'll name their pile of timbers once it's ours. Something with a bit of *panache*."

And then he is gone to ride with the 44th.

The little enclosed trading post back at Wills Creek has been christened Fort Cumberland, not exactly an honor for the King's son. Pitt has his name on far too many places in the colony, and the river names—Ohio and Monongahela—lack specificity of location.

Fort *Brad*dock, then.

RED WARRIOR MIXES VARIOUS THINGS THAT HAVE BEEN dug out of the ground or stripped off bushes into the boiling water in a small iron pot on a little fire by the side of a secluded section of the river. Jamie and LaCroix duck themselves in the cold eddy while Killbuck sits on the bank rocking and chanting to the Great Spirit. Captain Jacobs has his own ritual, which requires him to be alone farther down the bank.

You have to put your head under the water, says LaCroix.

Why?

To make yourself pure.

Jamie finds a good spot and sits till the water flows over his head. Later today he will try to kill someone, and he might be killed himself. He makes his body loose and lets the little bit of current nudge him along the rocky bottom, trying to empty his mind and feel what it will be to be dead.

Not a bad feeling, now that the water has lost its sting.

They step ashore, naked, and squat by the fire as Red Warrior pours the black drink he's made into a wooden bowl. He begins to chant—simple words, really, if this is the day of my death let me face it with courage—and then Red Warrior and LaCroix drink from the bowl. LaCroix hands it to Jamie—

To make yourself pure.

Jamie throws the rest of what's in the bowl down his throat, the smell earthy and bitter. He only has time to turn his head away from the fire before he vomits the contents of his stomach onto the grass.

Well done, says Red Warrior.

"IS THIS THE SAME RIVER," ASKS REG AS THEY WADE across, "or another?"

"Either way we're bloody well knackered if the froggos be in them trees."

The soldiers carry their muskets at port arms, primed to fire, and search the far shore for any sign of movement.

"Can ye swim, Bert?"

"Not a stroke, as ye might remember from bloody Scotland. And I expect that wherever this river is likely to take us, there's a gentleman waiting wif a tommy'awk."

"Hit's so bloody 'ot, I'm of a mind ter give the water a try."

"Sergeant Morse would frown on that."

"That 'ee would. I can tell ye one thing—I've 'ad it up to me eyes with this walkin'."

"Ye should've joined the cavalry, Reg."

"Don't care fer 'orses, if ye'd know the truth of it. And the feeling is reciprycated."

"The surgeon gets ter ride in a wagon."

"Ye ever sawr off a man's leg, Bert?"

"'Aven't 'ad the pleasure."

"Hit's the butcher's trade, is all, but without a chop ter sit down ter eat at the end."

"Then I'm afraid ye've found yer calling, Reg. March in file, fire in volleys, and soak up lead."

Sergeant Morse is waiting on the far bank to help haul them up to dry ground.

"I might've known it was you two, flappin' yer gums."

"Private Cruikshank would prefer ter be carried the rest of the way, Sergeant."

"Is it much further?"

"Ye'll know we're there," says the sergeant, "when ye've a hatchet stuck between yer eyes. Move along."

The column stretches ahead of them, the trees here far apart with underbrush burned away some time ago. They can see Colonel Gage of the Virginias riding alongside his men, sitting tall in the saddle, only occasionally having to duck under the branches.

"Lookit this, Reg," says Private Kirby. "From 'ere on hit's a stroll in the park."

BY THE TIME THE FRENCH PUT OUT THE WEAPONS—muskets with rifled barrels, gleaming new hatchets, laid in rows atop traders' blankets—the day is sweltering. Soldiers knock the lids off powder barrels and the warriors begin to gather, only a few painted for war, still wary. Then the drums and pipes again, and the front gate is drawn up and Beaujeu and Dumas march out at the head of a few dozen French regulars and nearly a hundred Canadian militia, stripped to the waist. There is a murmur among the warriors.

If there is to be a battle, it will be fought Indian style.

The English have left their road and approach through your hunting grounds, says Beaujeu, just across the great river. Who will join us to fight them?

Jamie, LaCroix, Red Warrior, and Killbuck step forward at the same moment as Bone and his small band of Shawnee, as well as perhaps two dozen of the western tribesmen.

Beaujeu, sweat pouring down his face to smear the black bands painted across his cheeks, is clearly disappointed. Dumas, also stripped and painted with a white cross upon his chest, shouts out, raising a musket in his hand—

"*Y a-t-il d'autres hommes courageux parmi vous?*"

A long moment, Jamie feeling that the others are on the verge of coming over, and then Captain Jacobs steps forward and faces the throng of Indians—

I dreamed last night of a road through the forest, he says, as long as a great river. And I saw the trees, too many to count, that had been felled to make it. Each one of those trees was a white man in a red coat, a man we had cut down in our vengeance.

He grabs a rifle from the blanket next to him, raises it over his head—

I will pick up the hatchet for our friend Louis!

Pontiac steps forward then. I will join him!

More follow, a sudden rush for rifles and powder. Jamie guesses there are at least three hundred red men in the party now, whooping and vowing to take many scalps. The faces of the men he knows—LaCroix, Killbuck, Red Warrior—are transformed, and he raises his own musket and gives a cry in Erse as Dumas, crossing himself, steps past, muttering to himself—

"*Dieu nous pardonne!*"

THE WOODS HAVE BEEN BURNED OF UNDERBRUSH FOR hunting here, huge gaps between the trees allowing the ambush party to pass with a broad, uneven front, half-naked Beaujeu looking peculiar at the head of the uniformed French, the Canadians behind and the Indians in their tribal groupings loosely flanking them. Even in the intermittent shade of the trees it is hot, and Jamie's throat feels parched and raw. He hurries behind Red Warrior, who carefully studies his painted face, half red and half black, in his tiny looking glass as he moves along.

Jamie sees Bone and his cadre of Shawnee too near, and drifts through the ranks of the Canadians till he has joined the dozens of Ottawa who have come out. No sense in having to watch your back as well as the enemy before you.

They trot forward to flank the uniformed French, Beaujeu setting the headlong pace as if afraid a moment's pause will cost him his allies. The idea is that they will deploy along the banks of the Monongahela where Braddock's column is most likely to ford and catch them in the open.

Jamie wonders if Dougal felt the same sense of falling from a height, the same hollow stomach, at Prestonpans before the English appeared out of the rain and the desperate charge was unleashed. When Ange and the other women at the fort sang them away, their faces were not drawn with fear with but flushed with pride and excitement—

They start down the side of a shallow ravine, and not a hundred yards ahead come the English vanguard, Jamie recognizing George Croghan and Scaraoudy in front of the column of redcoats and Beaujeu is waving his hat as his regulars scramble into three rows, shoulder to shoulder, and the redcoats do the same—

"*Premier rang*," cries Beaujeu, "*visé!*"

The front line of French muskets roar as one and smoke fills the air, the volley answered immediately by the front line of kneeling redcoats, and Jamie sees Beaujeu fall. He joins the rush of Indians, both Chartier and Captain Jacobs running past him shouting, telling them all to get to the high ground and spread along the sides of the English column.

The redcoats hold their formation, exchanging volleys and tightening their lines as men fall, though they are retreating slightly, leaving their dead and wounded before them. Jamie chooses one side of a huge chestnut, a Canadian militiaman crouched at the other, looking down at the clustered redcoats not more than thirty feet away.

"The bluidy Campbells knelt behind a stane wall fer a' the battle," Dougal told him of Culloden, "and had their choice iv which iv us tae slaughter."

The redcoats are still facing the French regulars, who have taken shelter behind trees, and Jamie is able to step clear of the chestnut and take careful aim. An officer rides toward him, seemingly calm, calling to his men over the now steady rattle of gunfire—

"Steady now! Hold your positions! Hold fast!"

Jamie fires and through the smoke sees the officer slump forward, then slide to the ground, his horse so suddenly unmanned it wheels about and gallops back along the rapidly collapsing column.

A pattern to the killing emerges, Jamie and the men beside them loading their rifles with their backs against the thick tree trunks, just upslope from the enemy, then turning and popping out to take aim and fire into the mass of red, listening for the voice of whatever English officer is still able to shout orders, ready to duck back behind shelter when the grenadiers' muskets are raised for a volley. The volleys blow through the woods around them, clipping branches and stripping bark off trees, a low wall of smoke rolling behind, but they are neither frequent nor effective enough to defray the constant sniping from the French and Indians. Jamie empties his pouch of shot into the English advance guard and then is given another handful of balls by a Canadian militiaman scurrying from tree to tree. He can hear the battle roaring and crackling along the line stretching to the east, can see the rifle smoke of his fellows among the trees on the other side of the redcoats, can hear the cries of the wounded and merely panicked. It feels like more than an hour of this before the shrinking phalanx of redcoats begins to break apart, private soldiers running back to jam up against similarly besieged gaggles of men, redcoats and colonials mixed with weaponless axemen and teamsters whose horses have been killed, like flotsam thrown against the rocks by floodwaters, Jamie and the others working their way parallel from tree to tree, only bothering to aim carefully when the smoke has cleared enough to see a face.

There is a whoop and Captain Jacobs sprints across the narrow ravine, splitting the skull of a kneeling grenadier with his tomahawk and continuing his dash to the trees on Jamie's side. This feat is greeted with a chorus of yipping, howling, whooping, and Bone is the next to leap into the open and down a man with a blow from his carved war club, with the men beside the victim, though their bayonets are affixed, choosing to flee rather than retaliate.

It is a rout, and Jamie decides he will hunt only officers.

THE PANICKED ADVANCE GUARD STACKS UP AGAINST the main force, creating a denser target for the marauders to fire into. No room to turn the wagons around—

Washington, on his third horse, cuts off a militiaman running without a weapon.

"Arm yourself!"

"They're all around us!"

"And behind us as well! Find a weapon!"

There are plenty of those available by the bodies of the dead, though savages are rushing out from the cover of the trees now to snatch them up. The man ducks around Washington's horse, and if he still had his saber he'd have thrashed him with the flat of it, but men are forsaking their formations all along the line of march, some so addled they run straight into the clutches of their adversaries and now through the smoke he sees a pair of the brutes drag an officer—he can't tell which—off from his mount. Washington has lost his saber and his cushion and his beautiful gray horse and felt a ball slap through his coat more than once, but flight only emboldens the enemy. At Necessity there was at least the palisade at your back, nothing lethal to worry about from one direction, but in this swirl of butchery there is peril all about with no room to turn the wagons and open the way for an orderly retreat. The grenadiers under Gage and the Lord St. Clair's Virginians have fallen back upon them in disarray, probably having left their wounded to the depredations of the enemy, and what organized resistance remains is under the direction of bellowing sergeants. Colonel Halkett, riding up from the baggage train to assess the situation, has been killed, along with his son, and Lord St. Clair has been carried unconscious toward safety, if such a thing now exists in this wood, and the 48th seem to have lost all their officers but Gage himself. What is needed is a bayonet charge, in any direction, the savages and the French mongrels, most probably Canadians, who egg them on sure to break and run if their lives are threatened. Which at present, ensconced securely behind the surrounding trees, they are not.

A ball grazes the neck of his mount, but he is able to rein it back under control.

The men have certainly seen him about, but he is in direct command of none and in their present state of confusion they are unlikely to follow him. Braddock, who he last saw with his hat tied on his head with a very white handkerchief knotted under his chin, must be found and a counterattack ordered and quickly organized. Washington bends low over the horse's neck, steering it through the frantic muddle who blindly load and fire into the trees, as likely to be felled by his own men as by the enemy. The gunfire is constant and without order, while the animal screams of the savages further stir the chaos and the hanging smoke makes it nearly impossible to see the flanking trees, much less the villains who lurk behind them, and now the drums are beating *Retreat*, as if this unruly horde has not been attempting the very thing for a bloody hour.

It is only a wagon horse, a bony, saddleless creature quickly unhitched by a drayman and provided an improvised hackamore, and he has to struggle to keep it from bolting off into the trees. He feels dizzy, the flux having left him at half strength, but there is no rest on a battlefield. For an instant he sees one of the savages standing in the open, ramming a patch and ball down the barrel of his rifle and staring murderously straight at him. Washington slaps the wagon plug on the flanks as hard as he can and it plunges forward, skittering in between a pair of dead rangers lying on the ground, already scalped, as his hat is hit by a ball and spun sideways over one eye for a moment before he can secure it.

The interpreter.

That's why he recognized the man, the white renegade who spoke for Shingas at Logstown and stood watching when they marched out of Fort Necessity and who now has come within an inch of spilling his brain matter. But there is something settling, thinks Washington, about putting a face on this phantom enemy in defilade all about them. The interpreter will be an apt candidate for hanging once the tide has been turned.

Braddock is down.

Washington sees ahead to the men—it looks like Gage and the general's body servant, Bishop—carrying him back toward the baggage convoy loaded in a scarlet sash unrolled to serve as a hammock. The twelve pounders, which have been ineffectively raking the trees with case shot, have been silenced, the teams pulling the howitzers unhitched and pressed into flight. Quail before wolves, Washington thinks as dozens more hurry past him, abandoning hats and weapons, some of them shot down midstride. The survivors will make easy prey for the savages, all the way back to the river and perhaps beyond it.

By the time he reaches them, Gage and Bishop are lifting the general into a two-wheeled horsecart, easily turned around.

Washington dismounts and sees that Braddock's arm has been pierced through, the ball most likely passing into his lung, making it difficult for him to speak.

"Retreat," he gasps. "Get whoever is left back across the river."

Croghan arrives then, and the general stretches his good arm, trying to grab one of the Irishman's pistols.

"Let me end it here," he says. "Leave me and organize the retreat!"

Washington pushes Croghan back, kneels beside the general.

"We'll get you to the rear, sir. We'll regroup."

An Indian leaps out from the trees making an animal cry and then fires a ball that somehow manages to pass between without hitting any of them, before disappearing as quickly as he appeared.

He was wearing the red jacket of the 44th foot.

A HALF-DOZEN OTTAWA MEN ARE LAUGHING AS THEY run, taking turns trying to snatch the flapping reins of a white horse, its withers covered in gore, that does not want to be caught.

The bodies of redcoats and militia and axemen litter the main path and the sides of the ravine, with warriors, and now women who've come out from the fort, taking their scalps and stripping them of clothes and possessions. Jamie comes upon Ange yanking the only slightly bloodied white shirt off a dead grenadier.

Leave it, he tells her.

You defeated them.

They're my enemy. I don't want anything that belongs to them.

She looks at him, then at the shirt, which she holds out to examine.

That's stupid, she says.

Jamie walks away, stepping over and around the bodies. The English force, with perhaps half of their number slaughtered, is in flight, recrossing the river and still heading east, leaving their dead and all of their artillery behind. Their small herd of cattle has been captured, and scores of horses, and now abandoned drums are being tattooed by the victors in a dozen competing rhythms. Jamie sees Dumas, who waves him over to where a knot of French and Canadian officers gather around something spread out on the side of a tipped wagon.

"*Ceux-ci ont eté trouvé dans la voiture du général Braddock,*" he says, handing a much-folded scrap of paper to Jamie.

It is an elegantly drawn map of Fort Duquesne, with writing on the other side describing the garrison.

"*Vous avez un espion dans le fort.*"

"*Évidemment. Et ça ici?*" asks the fort's commander, Contrecoeur, pulling a document from a leather pouch.

Jamie reads for a moment as the Frenchmen watch his face.

"*Cette une lettre du Boucher,*" he tells them.

"*Boucher?*"

"The Duke iv bluidy Cumberland—the Butcher. *Le fils du roi Georges.*"

The French exclaim excitedly as Jamie reads on—

"*C'est son plan pour le conquête de l'Amérique du Nord.*"

And the very first step in the plan for that conquest was the taking of Fort Duquesne.

DOZENS OF BONFIRES BURN ALONG BOTH BANKS OF THE river, the night pierced by chanting and wild shouts of celebration and intermittent gunfire. Jamie and Lachlan walk through the various camps together, warriors singing and retelling their exploits from the battle. There is no feeling, Jamie realizes, quite like surviving a deadly fight unmarked and with none of your comrades killed. Some brandy has been passed out, with the French and even the Canadians back in their fort, the gate securely drawn up.

A scream of anguish cuts through the noise of carousing.

"Ah've never seen the entertainment in it," says Lachlan, nodding in the direction of the cry. "Just cut the puir bastart's head off and be finished with him."

Another scream—

"Would ye care tae hear ma ballad? The Shawnee tongue takes a meter very well—"

They come upon a pair of staked captives, one Mohawk and the other white, who have drawn a crowd. The captured Mohawk sings his death song as smoke rises around his face, excited warriors poking at him with burning sticks. Fires have been set on both sides, scorching his legs and torso—

Jamie, though still wearing his warpaint, is uneasy now that the liquor has flowed, feeling more threatened here than during the day's battle. The white man, a young English officer who has been beaten and cut with knives, catches Jamie's eye.

"You're a white man!"

The men who are torturing him, Shawnee, turn to examine Jamie and Lachlan.

"Help me! Please!"

"Ah cannae do a thing fer ye," says Jamie.

"You can kill me!"

"They would no appreciate that."

What is he saying to you?

It is Bone, holding a burning stick to the nipples of the Mohawk warrior.

"Please, I beg you—"

Jamie mutters to the English officer. "Ye'll need tae do what Ah say—"

What are you telling him?

Bone, stepping over and drawing his knife—

This man tells me he is a powerful sorcerer, says Jamie. He can put a spell on weapons, and he says he will give us this power if we spare his life.

The other Shawnee move closer, always interested in magic.

Let him prove it, says Bone.

Jamie sees Lachlan moving away, not sure how this will play out.

He says he can make your knife too dull to cut his throat.

The men around Bone laugh. Bone does not.

Do you believe this story?

No—but we can't lose much by testing it.

Bone smiles then, a terrible smile, and holds out his knife to Jamie.

You do it.

Jamie looks him hard in the eyes and takes the knife, muttering to the young officer, "Say a prayer, oot loud, and keek the mon in his eye."

The officer, who can't be much older than twenty, does as he is told.

"Our father, who art in Heaven, hallowed be Thy name. Thy kingdom come, Thy will be done—"

Jamie steps behind the young man, bringing the knife up. Bone and the other Shawnee step closer, rapt, wondering if this incantation will work. Lachlan steps back out of the light—

"—on earth as it is in Heaven. Give us this day—"

Jamie swipes hard with the knife, blood spraying hot to spatter the Indians, who hustle back, then laugh. Bone steps back up when the young officer's head droops down, blood still burbling from his throat.

He cheated us.

I told you I didn't believe that shit, says Jamie, offering the knife back to Bone.

Bone turns away without taking it. The Mohawk warrior's chant rises in pitch and volume, his legs now on fire—

IT IS CLEAR THAT THE CHILDREN HATE THE TRADE. Modeste, the eldest of the Desjardins brood, comes up missing at least once a week now, gone for longer and longer periods, off to hunt wild turkeys. His latest absence has been for four days, throwing his father into a black mood.

"*C'est son sang sauvage*," he will mutter, staring at the empty seat at their table. "*Ça lui chant*."

Of the other boys only Antoine is big enough to climb a ladder with a sack of grain on his back, and though his savage blood may not be singing to him, his daily labor is punctuated with moans and sighs. Desjardins has been working to fix the barrel hoist, but the previous *meunier* has let the mill fall to near ruin, with only the stones, a pair of quartz beauties imported from the Marne Valley, and a well-placed millstream making the old wreck worth the bother. Desjardins, with no family in Grand-Pré, listened to the farmers complain about the millers already here—Bourgeois a thief, Melandon an unreliable drunkard, Guidry dependable but situated on the far end of the peninsula—then took the chance that his trade would earn him a welcome. And the *habitants* have flocked to the establishment, if only to have a new *meunier* to gripe about.

Jenny spends much of her day in the attic loft, raking out the sacks of hot grind as they come up from below, shoveling whatever has dried sufficiently into the bolting hopper, emptying the cloth of bran and middlings once the finer flour has passed through. Desjardins sends his middlings to the navy cook in Louisbourg to make biscuit and throws whatever bran his horse doesn't eat into the river. Mercifully there is a window cut into the attic through which a breeze may enter, also providing Jenny with a clear view across the meadowland to the sea. She ducks to peer from it constantly, searching the horizon for English warships.

Which may come any day.

At times Jenny feels like she has been swallowed by a growling, belching monster, condemned to play a role in its internal functions, its digestion and elimination. Other days she feels as if she has become the slave—Amély cooks for them all and cares for the smallest of the children, like a wife, while Jenny and Antoine and occasionally Modeste do whatever Desjardins needs at the mill. Sacks of raw grain have to be hauled up to the bins, the grind, hot and damp, sacked again and brought up to the loft, bolted wheat flour stored to dry further and whiten, the three cats, vital to rid the mill of vermin, need water and a bit of petting, spiderwebs reappear as soon as they are brushed away, gears and belts need to be greased with lard, old sacks mended. Desjardins adjusts the millstones depending on the grade of flour or meal desired, keeps the water wheel, axles, and gears in operation, controls the flow from the hopper and collects his miller's toll, which here in Grand-Pré is understood to be one sixth of every run. There is soft bread on the table every night, Amély having become an excellent baker, and the rest is sold to Gaspard, one of the merchants who runs sloops through the English blockade to Louisbourg fortress.

It is hot in the mill, hard to breathe and dark, with the grain dust that hangs in the air more combustable than gunpowder. Desjardins insists the works be shut down a full two hours before allowing a candle inside. By the end of a day Jenny's clothes are stuck to her, and she continues to sneeze until it is time for bed.

"*Encore plus, Tante Jeanne,*" calls Antoine from the top of the ladder, hunching to flip the sack of grind onto the floor. Desjardins lets his sons grow their black hair long, like the *voyageurs* do, though they wear white men's clothes and have no tattoos. When the family—now with Jenny and Amély included—step into Sainte Solange each

Sunday there is a murmur, and a space is left unoccupied for them in the left rear of the church. There are other *acadiens* who have taken up with Indian women, but these are mostly traders who live somewhat separately from people of either race. Abbé le Loutre, having converted the girl who had become Desjardins' woman to his religion and baptized her in the Missaguash, saw no reason to deny her a consecrated marriage. Though exciting a bit of a scandal among his white parishioners, the act enhanced his status among the Mi'kmaq, inducing many more of them to follow the Cross and murder Protestants in its name.

Jenny tells Antoine to be careful on the ladder and lifts the sack from the bottom to dump its contents onto the drying floor. The whole structure shakes a little with the movement of the gears and the millstones, the grinding loud and steady as Desjardins feeds it grist, the mechanical racket almost blocking the roar of the millstream from out the window. Jenny bends again to look out, relieved to see only a pair of one-sail fishing shallops making their way into the Minas Basin.

The runner stone ceases to spin, and the building settles for a moment. At home you ground your own oats on a quern, unless you had a generous laird with a mill on his domain. But Grand-Pré yields more than any spot in the Highlands, fields and fields of golden wheat and barley, ample forage for the cattle, the sea right beside you to cast a net in. No wonder the English want to steal it.

She hears Amély calling below with *dîner* and turns to back down the ladder, with Charlemagne, the brindle cat, pouncing softly onto her shoulder to steal a ride.

They eat at a wooden table and bench Desjardins has built beside the stream, all the children but Modeste present and waiting for their *papa* to bless the food.

"*Bénissez-nous, Seigneur,*" he says, hands folded, head bowed. "*Et bénissez ce repas et ceux qui l'ont préparé.*"

There is plenty of white bread, butter, and *fayots au lard*, with a small crock of molasses to sweeten the beans. Desjardins has his glass of table wine, while the others drink milk. There is enough surplus flour from the miller's toll to trade for produce with farmers who don't raise wheat. Jenny has not seen a scrap of the Québec *papier-monnaie* since coming to Grand-Pré, even Gaspard and the other traders accepting only barter.

Amély is a competent if not a natural cook, still missing the spices of Martinique, but she clearly loves to see the children eating her food.

Don't be shy, she tells them, in the *patois* they barely understand, there's more where this comes from.

"*Quel est le discours en ville?*" asks Desjardins, who only goes to town on Sundays.

"*Elas, rien de nouveau,*" says Amély, waving flies from the stew pot.

Jenny knows from the look on her face that this must mean troubling news, something not to be discussed in front of the children.

"*Les anglais?*"

People say they're still on the *rivière Petitcodiac.*

Which is not so far from Grand Pré.

The *grand dérangement* began almost immediately after the fall of Beauséjour, those *acadiens* who had not run far or fast enough away from the fort, perhaps believing the articles of surrender would be honored, the first to be rounded up and deported. The English have since worked outward in a circle, burning homes, slaughtering cattle, surrounding farms and villages and herding the people first to Halifax and then shipping them to parts unknown to the south. There are rumors, but as so few of the *acadiens* are *hommes de plume* capable of writing a letter and nobody has returned in the flesh, they remain unverified. The people here in Grand-Pré, their faith in God somewhat shaken, look to Joseph Broussard and his Indian allies.

"*Broussard nous sauvera,*" they say, though he too has become something of a myth. "*Ils ne peuvent pas arrêter le Beausoleil.*"

But each time Captain Gaspard stops by in his sloop he tells of another community uprooted, another small port he must avoid. Broussard's raids are a thorn in the paw of the English lion, but he has barely slowed the rate of expulsion. There was a MacLeod in the western islands, Jenny remembers, notorious for selling his own people into servitude in the colonies. She wonders where they have settled, if they survived the voyage at all. She has been lucky here, these people clannish but warmhearted once they are used to you, regarding the Desjardins ménage as a curiosity rather than a threat.

Sophie, who is three and does not remember her natural mother, climbs onto Amély's lap to share her meal. She is the happiest of the children, too young to know they are refugees and delighted by all the cats they now own.

When there is no more grain left to grind, says Desjardins to Antoine, I'll teach you to bend iron.

It is the dilemma of the *meunier,* he has explained, the need for a second trade during the winter months. And the more skills a miller can master, the less he is at the mercy of millwrights and blacksmiths.

"*Oui, Papa,*" says Antoine, not raising his eyes from his plate. He is a brooder, never challenging his father openly like Modeste, but just as discontent with the future that has been planned for him.

There are dragonflies dancing above the eddies in the stream, golden plovers skipping across the mudflats that lead to the sea, an osprey hunting overhead. Lulled by the sun, Sophie puts her thumb in her mouth, her eyelids beginning to drop, and Amély croons her a *fais-dodo*—

Mama est en haut
Qui fait du gateau

Papa est en bas
Qui fait du chocolat

IN MARTINIQUE JENNY WOULD NAP IN A HAMMOCK AFter the midday meal, feeling spoiled and decadent, the most delicious sleep, free from *cauchemars,* she has ever experienced. In Martinique danger was far, far away, unlikely to sweep in from the sea as as it was for Pelée to suddenly vomit hot lava. Her few years there with St. Cyr seem a dream now, as if they never happened, and his absence from her life somehow just. Jenny has never lost the sense that she is cheating fate, that her wardens are just beyond the horizon, biding their time—

When they come, she says, gazing out to the sea, now empty but for a constantly shifting flock of gulls, where will we go?

Desjardins spreads his hands as if to indicate their position on the very edge of the earth.

"*Il n'y a plus de terre,*" he shrugs.

He takes Antoine back into the mill to help him lift the runner stone, which must be redressed for a load of corn, while the younger children head off to pick berries and Jenny helps Amély clear the table.

"*Qu'ont-ils dit en ville?*" asks Jenny.

Amély frowns, checks beneath the table to be sure little Sophie is asleep on her blanket.

Jules Theriault has just come back from raiding with Broussard, she says, shot in the foot so he needs a crutch to walk with. He saw Modeste.

"*Avec Broussard?*"

"'*Vec les Mi'kmaqs,*" says Amély, shooting a look to the mill building. He has joined his mother's people.

Desjardins has a respect for the Indians rare among the *acadiens* but believes they are doomed as a people, that their only hope is to become Christians, to learn the white man's way of life, to intermarry and dilute their savage blood—

When will you tell him?

"*Cette nuit. Pour protéger les enfants.*"

It will be hard on Antoine.

We'll lose him, too.

You think so?

"*Regard moi.*"

Amély stands to face Jenny with her arms slightly spread.

I have the blood of *le maître St. Cyr* in my veins, she declares, but will I ever be white?

The sun has moved so that the shadow of the mill building is upon them, Jenny feeling a slight chill.

And if I ever get babies with *mon cher Desjardins*, says Amély, they won't be either.

WITH THE REDCOATS DRIVEN BACK ON THEIR NEARLY finished road, Contrecoeur becomes profligate with French powder and shot, telling his red brothers that it is now time for them to purge all English-speaking settlers from their lands. Shingas and Jamie sit on the riverbank, a thin morning fog lying over the water like a blanket.

The plan said that they will attack the French at Niagara, at St. Frederic, at Louisbourg, Jamie tells him.

The English do not know how to fight, says Shingas. We have seen this.

Perhaps this is so, but only not in the woods. And perhaps we had good luck. The letter I read from Cumberland said thousands more will be sent.

Shingas nods, reflecting. I had another dream, he says. White people were running to the east—running from a great fire—

Soldiers—

The ones who come after the soldiers. White men and women and their children. The hungry ones.

They both ponder this.

Do you really think you can win your land back? Jamie asks the chief.

We will burn their houses and kill them wherever we find them, says Shingas. We will drive them back to the Great Water!

He seems more determined than confident

And you, my brother?

Jamie hesitates to answer, troubled by the tortures and drunkeness of the long night after the great victory.

Remember that you are no longer a white man, says Shingas. You are one of us, Lenape—

I will fight them, Jamie tells him. But only the redcoat soldiers.

Then you must stay with the French.

Jamie nods.

Do you really think you can win your land back? Shingas asks Jamie.

The chief asks this with no irony. Jamie's answer is defiant.

I do.

This is good, then. A man should not kill without reason.

THERE ARE SO MANY STATUES. IN THE KIRKS BACK home there might be a simple cross on the wall, nothing more, to distract you from the contemplation of your utter worthlessness. But these *acadiens catholiques*—three different bleeding Jesuses, a Saint Dominique gazing up to the heavens, the Stations of the Cross depicting the Savior's final tortures and execution carved in wood, and the woman the church is named for, Sainte Solange.

Jenny has come to like the Mass, though she understands only parts of it—the *curé* sing-songing in Latin, little Sophie curled on the pew beside her, asleep, Amély kneeling proudly beside Desjardins, the wooden rosary Jenny gave her so long ago laced between her praying fingers, Antoine and the other children arrayed beside them in descending order of height. Jenny does not pretend to be a Catholic, but comes each Sunday so they don't believe her to be a pagan. Though she doesn't take Communion, she does dip her fingers in the holy water and cross herself, an act, Amély assures her, that would leave any witch scarred as if by acid. There are enough rumors in Grand-Pré about Desjardins and his *ménage* without Jenny being suspected of practicing the dark arts.

But today is not a Sunday, and Jenny can't take her eyes off the headless woman.

Amély, unfamiliar with the story, repeated it to her excitedly after learning it on her first visit to the church. A pious young girl, desired by the son of the local warlord, resisting his advances and cruelly decapitated with a swordstroke. Then the miraculous part, Solange's severed head speaking Christ's name three times, before her body picks it up and carries it back into town, into her church, and up to place it on the altar before finally dropping completely dead.

The statue head, tears of blood running from sky-blue eyes and held gently in delicate plaster hands, is even with Jenny's at the end of the pew. Why hold it at waist level, she wonders, an unfamiliar vantage, instead of lifting it back onto the neck where one's view and balance would surely be better?

The church is filling up with men, only men, and Desjardins is not one of them.

Don't go, he told her this morning, having read the edict. If we let them separate us we are lost. But the village baker, Bertrand Aucoine, pled with her to come, saying that Père Landry could not be found and somebody with both languages would be needed. Abbé Chauvreulx and Abbé Lemaire have already been deported, and for months now the English have been barracked in and around the church, even raising a rectangular palisade around it and flying their Union flag from the steeple.

But the statues remain, so far unharmed.

Desjardins has asked Amély to marry him, and now that she is free and any children she might bear will be equally free, she has consented. Père Landry has agreed, eager to bring their union within the bounds of the Church, and the children seem happy with the idea of it. Jenny feels the tiniest bit of envy, feels sorry for herself, not quite a proper widow and so pointedly an outsider in this community. But of course she could be stumbling across the marshland with her head in her hands—

The men, several hundred of them crowded inside now, are uneasy. Their names checked from a list as they entered the stockade, quickly searched for weapons, though most of these have been surrendered voluntarily—why this summons? They are Neutrals, to a man willing to take the Oath sent from Halifax if only the clause demanding they take up arms against the French is removed. They have supplied firewood and foodstuffs to the camp here, this harvest being especially bountiful, as ordered. The men sit in the pews and stand around, muttering in low voices. A rise in their volume as a pair of the Massachusetts colonials, men who were at the siege of Fort Beauséjour, bring in a large table and place it in front of the altar.

And then militiamen with muskets held before them, stepping down the aisle, blocking the rear and front entrances, followed by Colonel Winslow in his bright blue coat bedecked with lace and braid, but wearing his own hair, marching down the aisle and turning a sharp about-face behind the desk.

"Does anyone here speak English?" asks the colonel as the men settle into a shocked silence. "*Parlay anglay?*"

Men turn to look at Jenny. Winslow gestures to her.

"Come up here, please."

Jenny, already feeling like a traitor, is followed by every eye as she comes up the aisle.

"You understand English?"

"Ah do."

The colonel gives her a penetrating look, then changes to a softer tone.

"Firstly, I'd like them to understand that I find what I'm about to say, what we're here to bring about, to be very disagreeable to my nature."

"*L'homme se sent trés mal à propos de ce qu'il va dire,*" she tells the men.

"However, it is not my business to animadvert, but to obey such orders as I receive."

But he's going to say it anyway.

Winslow pulls a sheet of paper from the breast of his coat, waves it over his head.

"This is a message—a decree issued by His Excellency, Charles Lawrence, Governor of Nova Scotia—"

"*C'est un décret du gouverneur anglais,*" Jenny tells them—

The colonel lowers the paper, frowning, and looks around at the anxious *acadiens.*

"The crux of the matter is that your land and tenements, your cattle and livestock of all kinds are forfeited to the Crown, along with all your other effects—your money and your household goods—and that you yourselves are to be removed from this Province."

They're taking everything, Jenny tells the men, and sending us away.

Angry muttering then, and shouts of defiance from a few of the men. But they are surrounded by armed militia, more of them outside, and there is no rescue to be had from Beausoleil and his raiders.

"I would remind the gentlemen that any of their friends not present, mistakenly believing they are exempt from the King's decree, shall be hunted by our troops as the partridge on the mount."

"*Tout homme qui court,*" says Jenny, thinking of Desjardins and Amély and the children, "*sera poursuivi par nos troupes comme une perdrix sur la monture.*"

"If we agree it to be absolutely necessary, a few of you will be allowed, with an escort, to go to your homes to ready your families and gather provision for the journey."

"And the rest of them?"

"Shall be held here as a guarantee of cooperation."

Jenny translates, and Gaudet, a man with eleven children, is the first to leave, flanked by a sergeant and two infantrymen with bayonets.

"May I ask how you've come to your knowledge of our language?" Winslow is staring at her again.

There is so much ocean between London and Martinique, she thinks, and perhaps even more between that island and this place. Certainly no judgment, for a crime you never committed, can follow so far.

"I was bairn in Paris," Jenny tells him, as casually as she can manage, "but ma da' was a Scotsman."

BOO

FO

THE VALLEY AFLAME

THEY KILL WITH ARROWS WHENEVER POSSIBLE. Arrows have the advantage of silence, affording no warning to a settler in the fields or returning through a path in the woods, and can be left in the bodies as a message to the white people. They carry their rifles in case any armed men are encountered, but this far east they are in the land stolen by the Quakers, the ones who do not fight.

"I have no rum, as we do not use it," says the bearded farmer at the door. "But I can offer thee tobacco."

"We will come in to smoke," Shingas tells him.

The farmer looks past him to his sons, who were stacking hay before the Indians arrived. Four of the Shawnee stand by the boys, pulling at their shirts and trousers as if curious to know what they are made of. Captain Jacobs is farther up the creek with most of the Lenape, the parties having split after they killed the two families this morning.

The farmer steps aside, not smiling, and tells his wife to fetch tobacco.

Red Warrior and Big Man have brought their own pipes, and the farmer provides several smaller ones, made of clay. The boys come in, pushed by the Shawnee, who do not sit at first but move about the cabin picking things up to examine them. The wife does not look as well fed as the Quaker women usually do, and has two small daughters peeking out from behind her dress.

"You have cattle in your barn."

"I do. But some of them belong to my neighbor, Mr. Berryhill."

Berryhill might be the man they killed on the road, riding an old horse in this direction. A stake was driven through his body so anybody using the road will see him.

"And horses."

"Yes—"

"And sheep."

"Sheep, and hogs. We have been blessed by our Creator."

The Pennsylvanias in their great city have twice promised to move the settlers from this land, which they have not even bothered to cheat away with a paper signed by the Haudenosaunee. But the Pennsylvanias are weak, and did not even raise a militia to follow the English general Braddock on his great road to death. The pity, so far east from Kittanning, is that these animals—cattle and horses and pigs and sheep—cannot be brought back there and will have to be herded into the barn to be burned. Perhaps one steer will be butchered and brought to the camp—he has explained to the warriors that the task is to kill as many settlers as possible and not to carry heavy things away.

Shingas points to the south.

"Who lives that way?"

The farmer, left standing as the Indians have all taken chairs or sit on top of the table, hesitates before he answers.

"The McClelland family," he says finally. "They are not of our faith, but are good people."

Shingas nods. He had never killed a man or a woman before this morning. He has cut the throats of hundreds of deer, has eviscerated elk while their bodies lie steaming in the snow, has split the skulls of hogs with a tomahawk, and this new killing felt no different to his hand. One of the Shawnee said that the power of the enemy slain would become his own, but who wants the power of a woman weeping on her knees? To be a killer of men, he thinks, one must take on the spirit of the marauding bear, its hide raw with vermin, blood in its tiny, stupid eyes, possessed by the need to murder. He hopes it will become easier.

"Art thou hungry?" says the farmer, hoping to lose only food.

"We will always eat," says Shingas.

When you pull on the bowstring there is a moment where either you must release the arrow or your arm will begin to shake—

One of the Shawnee drops a plate then, deliberately, and the wife makes a little cry when it smashes but does not stir from where she stands, a hand on the shoulder of each of her daughters. The farmer raises a hand as if to calm her.

"Do you know us?" Shingas asks him.

The farmer answers carefully. "You are Delaware people."

"We are your enemies."

"I consider no man my enemy," says the farmer.

"Then you are a fool."

One of the Shawnee, who missed the Braddock fight and is so young he has never been to war, has lost patience. He steps up to one of the sons, a boy about his same age, and begins to strike him with his tomahawk, only grazing his face with the first blow and then chopping down again and again on the boy's upraised arms. The warriors are up and upon the farmer immediately as the wife and daughters scream.

Don't kill the girls! Shingas shouts to them over the screaming. We'll take them as our own.

THERE ARE NO CHAINS ON THE *HANNAH*.

A sloop overcrowded with women and children, groups of twenty allowed the liberty of the deck for only an hour at a time, it is no wonder the pox has taken hold. Mrs. Bujold has lost three already and the two who are left, a boy and a tiny girl not yet on her feet, are unlikely to survive. There is no oakum to pick, no employment or diversion of any kind, and though they have been told that their husbands, brothers and sons are being held on the *Swan*, separated only by the muddle of other ships anchored in the Philadelphia harbor, none fully believes they will ever be reunited.

Jenny, the only woman on board without family, eavesdrops on the sailors and the guards sent from Grand-Pré and passes what information she can glean on to the anxious *acadiennes*.

Today it is the rumor they are being transferred.

Coffins have been brought on board each day for a week now, many of them tiny, with Père Landry rowed over to say his few words of Latin. He is not allowed to linger and answer questions. A council of important men in the city have kept them on this floating morgue since their arrival, but now Schoep, a night guard who sleeps in the city during the day and had been stationed with the Massachusetts volunteers in Grand Pré, says the governor has ordered them to the pesthouses on Province Island.

Jenny misses the willows.

The roads in Grand Pré are planted with willows, as are the edges of the fields, long rows of them that spread wide at the top, the trunks growing thicker every year. The English marched the men out from the church in groups of fifty, willows lining the road to the Gasperaux landing with the wives and mothers and children of the men standing beneath the willows, weeping, some on their knees, calling their farewells. Colonel Winslow allowed Jenny one trip to gather a warmer coat and the bundle of food Amély had left her, Desjardins having packed everything portable for their flight to find Broussard and Modeste, but after that she was kept close to help translate and was among the first brought aboard to sit on the cold ship waiting to sail. The food is more plentiful than that offered on the *Veteran*, but monotonous—the same portion of bread and salt pork every day—and the women complain that their teeth are coming loose. When it was the women's turn to come to the landing with their children they pushed carts down the same road, loaded with food and bedding and iron pots, most of which they were forced to abandon at the riverside, as the *Hannah* is only a sloop with limited space belowdecks. The night before they sailed the sky was alive with firelight, houses and barns from Piziquid to Port La Tour set ablaze by the English.

"And what of the stock," Jenny asked Schoep as he stood beside her on the rail, "the coos and sheep and horses?"

"What cannot be eaten or transported will be shot," he told her. "We are not sawages to burn dem alive."

He is not a bad-looking man, broad shouldered, with a shaven face and only a little trace of the Dutchman in his speech, though he does call her "Chenny." He is sitting on a tar barrel, as if waiting for her, when she is brought up for the final deck promenade of the day.

"Now dey are inquiring of you," he tells her.

"What aboot me?"

"Perhaps dere is some of der women here, suspect you haf been spying on dem, as you haf der English tongue. Tales haf been told."

"Ah was bairn in France—"

"Dere are some dot do not belief you."

"Ah'm already a prisoner."

"'Refugee' is what in der assembly dey are calling you. Der Neutral French is being considered refugees. Dere is some dot are saying you are needer French nor neutral."

"Ah'll be brought tae court?"

"I tink dey will not bosser mit dot."

Schoep has told her he's from the Pennsylvania Colony here, a recent widower, who volunteered to fight the French for Massachusetts because "der Dummkopf Quakers" hadn't the backbone to protect themselves.

"You will be left on der island tomorrow, der all of you."

"Ah've heert that—"

"Dem mit der pox separated from der healty—"

"The mothers winnae stand fer it."

"But if I was you, I would not linger while is going on dis inquiring."

The other women and their children shuffle about the deck in a rough circle as Jenny stands by Schoep, warmer on deck than in the hold.

"Ah've got a choice innit?"

Schoep smiles. He still has all his teeth, and says that out west where he's left his children with a sister he has a homestead. He nods toward a trio of full-sized coffins piled on the afterdeck.

"Dere is two waiting to be buried," he says, "and my enlistment is ending tomorrow."

"Two—"

"Mit one box empty. Der mate of der surgeon is particular friend of mine—"

"Yer askin' me to gae in the box?"

"It is never leaving my sight. You will be marked 'deceased' on der roll, and by middle of day in a wagon heading to der west."

She hadn't thought confinement would try her so, having survived it before. But the drowsy liberty of Martinique, the wary acceptance and bounty among the Acadians, has spoiled her for stale air and a ceiling too low to stand under. *Anything but this*, she has found herself brooding, *even the rope*.

"Ye say yer a planter—"

"I am—"

"Ye've a hoose near a burn."

"On a creek dot feeds into der Chuniata River."

"Does it flood?"

"Dis it has not done."

It is possible the women aboard will be reunited with their men in the pesthouses, and she'll be once again the odd one, rumored to be Desjardins' other doxy, and, just possibly, a spy for *les mauvais anglais*. The idea of being declared dead, her past erased, is tempting—

"Might I ask," he ventures, "if you are a Catolic?"

"Nae."

He nods. "Is no matter to me, but some of mine neighbors—"

"Ye have neighbors?"

"Dere is der Steinmetz farm a few miles downstream, and den der Mittleberger's a piece to der west. Enough in der area dot we got us a mill. Der man is a tief, like dem all, but he is knowing his trade."

Her father had a crofter picked out for her, a man near twenty years her senior named Duff who owned sheep and smelled of them. She thinks of how she was always amused at Amély's flights of romantic fascination, her slave girl dreams of a dark-skinned hero, a free man, who would buy her away—

"A body can no breathe in a box sae close," says Jenny.

"I haf drilled holes in der side and fill dem mit punk," says Schoep. "You can poke dem clear mit a finger when der time is coming."

"Ah—ye've been figurin' on this fer awheel."

"We can be married on der way or when we haf reached Kishacoquillas," says Schoep. "I leave dis op to you."

"With a crofter," her father used to say, "ye'll ne'er lack fer oots."

The boatswain sounds his piercing whistle, and Schoep hops down off the barrel to help escort the prisoners—the refugees—back into the hold. The aft compartment is filled with the pox-ridden, the fore with those waiting to be afflicted. The pesthouses will afford more room, hopefully, but there is no knowing who was kept in them before or what diseases they carried. And if the English are inquiring—

"Tell me," says Jenny as she starts for the hatch, "hae many bairns ye've got, and what are their names?"

HE IS PERHAPS FAR TOO ADVANCED IN YEARS FOR *LA guerre sauvage*. Scuttling through the frozen woods on foot, sleeping on pine boughs two nights out of three, constantly on the alert for enemy patrols. But a de Villiers serves where he is needed. There are other officers, mostly those recently come over from France, who refuse to soil themselves by association with the tribesmen, who sip their sherry and wait for the "real war" to begin. But in this new world the real contest is in the wilderness, with ambush and arson the principal tactics, and mercy—the English and their red brethren banished mercy when they murdered his half brother. De Villiers is Canadian born and proud of it, his family having paid too dearly for the land to give it up without mortal struggle.

At the moment, though, the drama lies in his upper jaw.

The teeth, *molaires* on the upper left side, were just beginning to assert themselves as his party left the fort. By the time of the raid they were in full revolt and now throb angrily with each quick step through the snow-choked forest. He has put one of the Loups, Killbuck, at the point, the long-legged, energetic fellow setting a pace on the already-beaten path that is quite literally blistering. De Villiers knew better than to wear the boots, but the Indians are in awe of a proper uniform, envious of buttons, silk, and braid, and moccasins most definitely spoil the effect. He has at least been able to leave his periwig back at the fort.

They are heading west to the frozen forks, bearing scalps and booty but no prisoners. It is an effort for him not to favor the more afflicted foot, but he knows from experience how tenuous an officer's control over these people can be, and any faltering, any sign of weakness must be avoided.

"Do not believe that they are children," his father counseled, before he and his brother Damonville were killed at Baie-des-Puants in an engagement with the Fox. "They have their religion, their allegiances, their jealousies and family attachments, just as we do. We are not the lodestar of their journey, but only, they hope, a passing phenomenon, like a season of inclement weather."

The key in the hot south had been to encourage and profit from their hatreds of each other, ancient, perhaps, making alliance with the Choctaw to eradicate the Natchez and Chickasaw. Superior weapons, perhaps even artillery to knock down a palisade of saplings—they are never too proud to borrow white man's tools of destruction. The mongrel band he has gathered here is even less predictable than his collection of regulars, Indians and African runaways was in Louisiana. While the Shawnee are adept travelers, fighting for land they believe they've lost, the northern Indians are out only for plunder—he knows he will lose them when they've won more than they can carry—and the Loups very new at it and alarmingly wild, like a young wolf set loose in a sheep paddock. De Villiers, who like his brothers was taken into the King's army at the age of eight, marvels at the looseness of their commitment to the campaign, with the Abenaki already asking when they can move on to Virginia, where there are negros to be stolen and sold to the *haute société* of Québec.

Though de Villiers has said nothing of it, one of the Shawnee has noticed his jaw swelling and given him the inner bark of some tree to slip between his teeth and gum, which is beginning to have a numbing effect. Not one of his charges was killed or even wounded on the raid, which will result in a joyous round of scalp-halloos when they reach the Indian dwellings that surround the fort. His adjutant, Duchambray, on the other hand, has gotten into some creeping vine that excites a terrible rash on the skin and loses no opportunity to bemoan his misfortune, much to the amusement of the savages.

Killbuck has stopped, and men from the various tribes surround him, all looking up into the branches of a tree.

A *raton laveur* who should be asleep for the winter has been discovered out on a branch barely thick enough to support its weight, ringed tail stiff with alarm, eyes wide on its masked countenance as below boasts are made and wagers placed. The warriors are in good spirits, and the likelihood of an English patrol venturing this close to Fort Duquesne almost nil. One of the young Shawnee is chosen, stepping away to find the ideal vantage point, then taking his tomahawk in hand and drawing it back to throw as he fixes on the stranded beast. He hurls the weapon, flying end over end till it thwacks the creature in the side, the blade not penetrating flesh but the impact enough to knock it sprawling from the branch and down to the swift dispatch that waits below.

The last of the settlers they killed, a man with some white in his beard, had been chased for sport across his stubbled field, over a fence and some ways into the woods till he fell with a half-dozen arrows in his back and legs, the warriors gathering around to point and claim authorship of each hit before finishing him with a blow from a hickory club. De Villiers prefers to survey the site to be attacked, discuss tactics, and then wait at some distance while the Indians go about their gory business. Though masters of stealth and silence, *la discipline* in the strict military sense is not a concept close to their hearts, and his instructions regarding the taking of captives or not are mostly ignored. There is always planning involved, a rationale, but providence—or its sinister cousin, doom—often controls the outcome.

Much laughter at the young Shawnee for only wounding the animal with his weapon, the tail awarded to him as an ornament. The raccoon, intent on its daily quest for sustenance, has had the misfortune to intersect with a war party that earlier lost its way in the woods and rather than attacking the intended settlement stumbled upon a section of girdled trees and made do with the farm they led to, a dozen Pennsylvania settlers brutally dispatched to *le bon Dieu*.

If there is a Celestial Plan involved in this, it is an indecipherable one. His Canadians, as well as most of the mission Indians in tow, ask to be blessed by the *curé* before a *sortie*, while the red pagans prepare themselves with fasting and incantation—is God there on the field of combat beside you, bloody-handed and taking sides, or does He watch from on high, pitying all of His creations?

The point of the raids, as described by Contrecoeur, is to spread terror, like a fire in a strong wind that drives all the forest creatures before it. Escaping these Indians employed as deadly avatars, the English settlers will flee back to the ocean, and then Frenchman and natives will enjoy the fruits of coexistence and trade, with white habitants, even if French-speaking, restricted to lands already cleared and cultivated.

But the wind is notoriously fickle.

They are moving again, Killbuck almost loping across the snow, and de Villiers finds himself struggling to keep up. The old wound in his thigh, suffered in the same battle where his father and brother were killed, has announced itself again, the arrowhead damaging enough on its entry but a bloody mess to extract. He falls behind, with only the brooding Scotsman for company.

A curious specimen this, unmistakably a Loup until closer inspection, speaking a Parisian-inflected French when interpreting and professing a deep hatred for the English. The man petitioned Contrecoeur to join the regulars at Fort Duquesne, to don the white uniform and swear fealty to *sa très sainte majesté Louis*, but was turned down, the commandant perhaps mistrusting the man's sanity or made cautious by the treachery of his fellow Scotsman Stobo. In any case he is the only man among them neither wearing nor bearing plunder from the raid, not even a single scalp on his belt to be redeemed with rum or gunpowder by the commandant, and he insisted on laying the bodies inside the cabin before it was torched rather than leaving them for the creatures of the night to feed upon. He moves with the grace of his red brethren but seems less than elated by the day's work.

"*Ça va, mon ami?*" asks de Villiers, in the tone he adopts with them all, more an elder brother and mentor than *officier supérieur.*

The Scotsman pulls a long face, eyes kept on the pathway, and asks when they will go to kill the redcoats in their fortresses.

Obviously a man of some education, but one who does not yet understand the dark heart of war. The Pennsylvanians on the frontier have begun to make strong houses, fortifying mills and cabins to provide a place of shelter and a storehouse for weapons, while organizing systems of warning that will make ambush somewhat more difficult. Their governor has placed a bounty on the heads of the Loup chiefs Shingas and Captain Jacobs. But these are *agriculteurs*, not warriors, the settlements isolated from each other, and nothing will truly protect them until the English mount a campaign on the scale of Braddock's march again.

It is they who will attack us, Louis Coulon de Villiers tells the Scotsman. And that will come soon enough.

AFTER IT ALL SHE HAS BECOME A CROFTER'S WIFE.

Her few dark hours in the coffin proved more comfortable than the long ride on the lazyboard of the boatlike Conestoga wagon filled with supplies for the farm, Schoep guiding the team from the back of the wheelhorse in front of her. What he describes as "roads" would not serve for footpaths in the Highlands, and twice they were almost swept away while crossing streams. They were married, she believes, at Harris Ferry, but without any German she is unaware of the details.

Schoep has two hundred acres on Kishacoquillas Creek, a third still in forest, with twenty acres of meadow that he irrigates with wooden pipes. He has a hired man named Enoch with one cheek always distended by chewing tobacco, he has two years time left from a redemptioner, young Peck, and a kitchen girl with a harelip named Hedda who seems to have been taken in by Schoep's wife before she died, and three little daughters, Frederika, Dagmar, and Katrin.

Jenny is there to work.

Loving with Schoep is quick and somewhat furtive, nightgowns rolled up, voices held in check so as not to wake the girls just beyond the wall, careful attention paid to her monthly bleeding.

"No more *kinder*," he says, "until dis trouble is settling down."

Six families were were murdered at Penn's Creek, on the west side of the Susquehanna, in October, women and children taken as captives, a Swiss man left with two tomahawks in his skull as a calling card. A week later settlers returning from Shamokin were ambushed, four of them shot dead, four more drowned.

"Dose people were careless," says Schoep.

In more peaceful days Schoep grew wheat, milling it at Old Town and sending it east for a good price. The land here is even more fertile than Acadia, and the people work even harder, families often separated by miles of wilderness. Schoep has built a stone house and barn, sheltering his stock, as the Germans do, through the worst of winter.

"Cold animal eat more den warm animal. We are saving der fodder dis way."

In November they thrash the rye, a pair of huge draft horses worked in a circle on the threshing floor of the barn, stamping over it again and again, then stooping to pull out the straw before running the remains through a Dutch mill to lose the dust and chaff before packing it into sacks.

In November, Great Cove and Kennalaways are attacked, two dozen plantations burned, and fifty of the settlers—who had been warned by the Pennsylvania government that they were on land still owned by the Delawares—killed or captured. At Tulpehocken the Kobel family, Mennonites, are slaughtered, even the children scalped. The Moravian town of Gnadenhutten is attacked, most of the Christian Indians in the mission house murdered, the survivors fleeing to nearby Bethlehem.

"We are forming militia," says Schoep. "Nobody is working in fields mitout protection."

So when he and Enoch and Peck clear new pasture or repair the worm fence or plow and harrow or reap the buckwheat before the first frost, they keep their rifles ever within arm's reach and watch the woods for movement.

In December, Hedda teaches Jenny to make clothing from the hemp and flax that has been put by, taking her through the retting, breaking, scutching, and hackling before setting her at the wheel, Jenny eventually able to understand most of the girl's nasal, heavily accented chatter.

A small fort is built by the trader George Croghan, situated where the creek meets the Susquehanna River. On Sundays the entire household travels down on horseback, the men drilling under Colonel Ward in the mornings and entertaining themselves with schnapps and hard cider in the afternoon. Schoep's sister Gertrudis is there, with her husband Boetticher and a slew of children. On the ride back the men are in no condition to repel savages.

Schoep buys a sow from a man named Gottfried who is abandoning his farm for the east, and it is carefully backed into its stall on the first day to ensure its future health.

"I am not believing in all of dese tings," says Schoep, "but what goot is taking a chance?"

It is clear that his first love is his farm—the grain fields, the peach and apple orchards, the clover, the black cattle and the sheep and swine and dunghill fowl, the walled garden next to the house—

"First year, mit der new-cleared ground, we are plowing tree times and den planting wheat, den oats or corn in der second year, den clover, and den we let it rest."

The idea is that if he never sires a son, the farm will grow and be divided among the girls, bait for industrious husbands.

In January, it is Lehi Township and the Irish Settlement, the farms around Smithfield, Neskopen, Shupp's Mill, Sherman's Creek, even Croghan's fortified trading post at Aughwick. The Quakers are finally outvoted in the Pennsylvania assembly, with paid militias formed and bounties offered for Indian scalps.

"Is turning our way now," says Schoep. "We stay here for harvest in Chuly."

A hollow is dug beneath the stacks of firewood and lined with stone—a place for the girls to hide and wait for attacking savages to leave. What will keep them from freezing while in there is not clear.

"Yer daft if ye think we're safe here," Jenny tells Schoep.

"We go east, we haf nussing," he tells her. "Already der farm is falling apart from when I go to Canada. Mit good harvest we go forward."

Though he mocks her gently for it, Jenny has the farmer show her how to load and fire a pistol, and carries it with her as she moves from task to task. One shot, she thinks whenever she finds the weight of it in her hand. If they come in number as they have in the other places, she can only hope she has the time and the nerve to use it on herself.

THERE IS NOBODY LEFT AT THE FARM TO KILL. THE FAMily gone perhaps a day before their arrival, some panic apparent in the disarray within the house, clothing left on the floor and a clotted bowl of oatmeal on the stovetop. The family Bible has been left as well, with the names of the children inscribed just inside the front cover—

Jonah
Nathaniel
Harriet
Ethan
Abigail
Ezekial
Priscilla
Hiram

Where they all slept is a mystery. Jamie leaves the book to the boisterous Shawnee, who like to smash and tear things, and moves on to the barn. Horseshit in the one stall but no horse and an impressive chest full of tools, someone here no doubt a skilled carpenter. He takes a pair of pliers, passes through the yard, the house itself already burning, and heads back to where they left de Villiers and most of the Lenape. On the way he finds a stone jug of hard cider, nearly full, half submerged in the little spring they passed quickly on the way in.

They have been moving steadily eastward, meeting little real resistance, and he prefers the days like this one when the terror has successfully fulfilled its purpose to the days when blood must be spilled. Nobody they've encountered has worn anything resembling a uniform, certainly not a red coat among them, and each morning Jamie has to remind himself which war he is waging. He tries to imagine the forest reclaiming the half-cleared land around the cabins they have burned, the game returning, the birds—the abandoned Shawnee and Lenape villages he's been through have fallen back to Nature within a year or two. They've raided along the Loyalsock where Shingas says he lived as a young boy when Madame Montour was a power there, and it is beautiful country, well worth fighting for. The Highlands had remained free in practice, if not by edict, until General Wade pierced it with his roads, but once the English have claimed an area on their maps, they are willing to sacrifice legions of their soldiers to fully own it.

He has not met with Shingas, marauding farther to the south, for months now, and has only the assurance of the French that the strategy is working throughout the colony, that the whites will be driven to the far side of the Susquehanna forever. It is a huge area, of course, and controlling it indefinitely will take a level of vigilance he's not certain the tribes are capable of or willing to maintain—

De Villiers sits on a stump with his hand on his jaw. He has grown increasingly morose the farther east they've come, despite the trail of destruction they've left behind. The rest of the war party, mostly Lenape, have not yet caught up.

"*Où sont les autres?*" asks Jamie.

Picking blueberries, says the Frenchman.

It has been a wonderful season for blueberries, raids often postponed or redirected so that the warriors can eat their fill, fingers stained purple and men calling out joyously when another patch is discovered. Jamie and Dougal picked sloe berries when they were small boys, Dougal daring him to eat them before the first frost. His mouth puckers at the memory. They sold them to Widow MacCrary, who made dye.

I brought you this, he says, offering de Villiers the jug of hard cider.

De Villiers pulls the cork, sniffs, makes a face.

"*C'est pas ma boisson,*" he says.

Jamie shows him the pliers.

It will help with this.

Ah, says the captain, this will rescue my sanity, if not my life.

De Villiers manfully begins to gulp the hard cider down.

You'll dispose of what's left, he orders, before our friends return.

No, you'll have to finish it.

"*Hélas*."

They sit in a very small clearing by a shallow creek with a towering white pine at the edge of it, the agreed meeting place for the raiders. They are in territory none of the men know, and landmarks must be identified and agreed upon if they are not to lose contact with each other. Weeks pass without encountering friends or allies, and though they leave markings on the trees boasting of their slaughter it is hard to imagine who will ever stumble upon them. The war could be over, the ink on a treaty powdered and dried by now, and it might be months before they learned of it—

Jamie looks around. Where are your own people? he asks. "*Les soldats français?*"

The captain has a handful of Frenchmen in the party. He sighs.

"*Tout le monde aime les bleuets*."

De Villiers pours the last of the cider down his throat, making a sour face, then stands and walks unsteadily to the immense white pine and back.

"*Je suis prêt*."

The rotting molar is on the upper left of the captain's jaw, and it takes some maneuvering to jacket it with a scrap of deerskin and get a proper grip with the pliers, de Villiers lying flat on the ground and Jamie above him with a knee on his chest. The extraction, though, is surprisingly quick, merely a hard upward jerk and it is out, roots and all, the captain making a sound like a lanced boar. Jamie folds the scrap of deerskin and has de Villiers push it up on the wound, hoping that Killbuck will know what to pack into the wound when he catches up. Within minutes the captain is sleeping.

Renault and Durocher are the first to wander into the clearing, both with the whites of their uniform jackets stained purple, Durocher with a loincloth and leggings on below the belt. They have picked up phrases of both Shawnee and Lenape and practice with bow and arrow whenever there is an opportunity, much to the amusement of their red brethren.

Is the captain drunk? asks Durocher, stepping around the prone de Villiers and looking shocked.

Jamie holds up the bloody molar, still pinched in the jaws of the pliers.

Only recovering.

I hope that improves his mood, says the *caporal*, Renault. Did you find the farm?

They've already fled, says Jamie.

"*Dommage*," says Durocher, who is an overgrown boy and writes love letters to a young woman that are impossible to post.

When Killbuck arrives he asks if he can have the molar. He has a necklace, left back in Kittanning, made from the teeth of bears, wolves, and elk.

But the tooth of a French captain, he says, is not so easy to find.

The girls make candles and sew and learn their words and letters. They are outwardly as stoic as their father, but many nights little Katrin cries out with nightmares and Jenny goes in to comfort her.

"Dreams aren't real," she whispers, trying not to wake the other two. "Not even the guid dreams."

"They put you on a fire and cook you and eat you," says Katrin.

"D'ye think yer father would alloo sich a thing?"

The little girl does not seem to be comforted.

Schoep's early peaches appear in May, his hogs gathering there to feast on the drops, snorting and hauling up onto their trotters whenever they hear a dull thud. Jenny helps to sow oats, takes charge of weeding the turnips in the truck garden. The girls feed the chickens and pull caterpillars off the new cabbage. McCord's Fort on the Conocheague is taken and burned by French and Indians, more than twenty settlers killed, and a party of men pursuing in hope of revenge are ambushed by marauders under Shingas and Captain Jacobs, each of them with a bounty on his head, to be paid in pieces of eight.

Schoep and Enoch and the indentured boy, Peck, spend a good deal of their time either plowing or applying the animal manure collected in the stables over the winter to where it is most needed. The girls sing for Schoep after supper, sing prettily in German, and while Jenny is putting them to bed he falls asleep in his chair by the fire, pipe growing cold in his lap.

Unlike the American farmers nearby. Schoep does not girdle his trees and plant crops beneath while waiting years for them to die. He and his workers cut them down and pull the stumps, grubbing out any roots that might snap a plow and saving the useful wood for building or burning. They are clearing a new section near the creek when Peck suddenly runs for his rifle and shoots at something across the water.

He is trembling when Schoep and Enoch join him, their own rifles in hand.

"I saw one," says the redemptioner. "He was near nekkid, with paint on his face. Just standing and watching us."

Schoep does not believe the boy, thinking it was a deer or perhaps only a turkey, but when they cross the stream to search they find one of Katrin's dolls, made by Hedda with yellow yarn for hair, pinned to a poplar tree by a horn-handled knife.

That night Schoep is still awake when Jenny comes back from singing the girls to sleep. They like it when she croons to them in Erse, accepting whatever wild story she tells them the words describe.

"I tink you go to der fort now," he says. "You and Hedda and der kinder. We men stay to harvest der wheat."

"If ye let the wheat just be fer a year, Ah've nae doot it'll grow again," says Jenny. "Besides, the miller's run tae Philadelphia."

"You go tomorrow," says Schoep, relighting his pipe. "Den I don't worry no more."

THERE IS A FORM TO REUNION AMONG THE LENAPE, which Jamie has observed many times between Shingas and Cloud Woman.

I am returned! Shingas would say, stepping into their *wikëwam*.

I am glad! Cloud Woman would reply, quickly shifting a pot over the fire to cook something for him. I thank the Great Spirit for keeping you safe.

And he would inquire as to the health of his children, of his brother the Beaver and his wife and children, and when satisfied with this sit to wait for the meal without another word being spoken. This whether the absence was for a day or for a month, Cloud Woman only learning the details of his journey when Beaver would come over to smoke and listen to the tale. Cloud Woman, unless there was game brought home to be dressed, would kneel patiently, listening and tending to the fire, knowing that sometime before they turned in for the night Shingas would present her with gifts, if there were any to be given, that she might display to remind the rest of the village what a good husband she had. Shingas has never been one for show—Captain Jacobs already has the horns of a dozen bucks upon his cabin roof—but never neglects his wife's feelings.

Ange has obviously never witnessed this form.

Jamie steps into the tentlike structure she has put up by the river—the Monongahela—in front of the walls of Fort Duquesne. She sits by the fire sewing beads onto a pair of her moccasins, looking up when she has finished a stitch.

So?

Very few men have been wounded, and only one killed so far

raiding the white settlers, but there is a war on and other wives sing songs of courage when their husbands leave to fight.

She looks to his belt, and finds no scalps hanging there.

She looks back to him, her eyes asking only what have you brought me?

Jamie steps out, then ducks back in carrying his plunder—a new Hanoverian *Jäger* rifle, a satchel full of lead balls and gunpowder, silver buttons from the vest of an English major, and two Hudson Bay blankets. He lays the blankets, with the buttons on top of them, on the ground next to Ange.

Captives?

I don't take captives, Jamie tells her once again.

There were plenty for the taking. LaCroix and Killbuck have brought three each back with them, hustling them along with slaps and kicks, LaCroix carrying the small boy when he couldn't keep up. They will be at the front gate of the fort by now, seeing what the French officers will give for them. The raids have been so successful that they trade only for women and children now, and there is a corral filled with unransomed captives in the middle of the Indian dwellings, growing more crowded each day. It serves as a kind of bank, Jamie figures, hostages a valuable commodity if one doesn't have to feed them for too long.

The white people capture few Indians, and those taken are quickly shot or hanged.

Jamie leaves Ange examining the buttons and goes to sit outside. By tomorrow she will be wearing them on her ears or around her neck or sewn to her dress, and will be happy to explain they were taken from an English general Jamie vanquished with only his knife. He sees other men from the returning de Villiers party hanging scalps to dry on the poles set up beside their lodgings—the French will have something of a ceremony in the morning, handing out bounties in cash or goods. A few traders have set up shop on the other side of the water, willing to sell rum and brandy to soldier or savage. Jamie has tried to explain to Ange the concept of a war, a finite thing with a beginning and an end, a victor and a vanquished, but she persists in regarding the present hostilities as a particularly abundant hunting opportunity, like a run of shad or a snowbound herd of elk.

She comes to sit beside him. The disappointment never lasts too long, and he is the only Lenape man who will have her as a wife.

But you killed some, she says.

Yes. Men with weapons.

It is not exactly true, some of the men only running to find their weapons, or at least that's what Jamie hopes they were doing. He supposes that Dougal did the other, the burning and the looting, on the Prince's march into the north of England, but killing crofters—

Some spirit must guide you in this, she says. To kill and take no proof of it—Buffalo Hair now has a cat, which will play with a vole, catching it again and again, eventually killing it, but will not eat it.

What does it eat?

Birds.

Jamie nods, then touches the cat tattooed on his chest.

I don't mean to dishonor you.

The women believe you possess a powerful medicine, says Ange, that allows you to understand any tongue that is spoken by man. They think you are too modest to shout your triumphs, too modest even to take the hair of the enemies you have killed.

And what do you think?

Ange lets her little twist of a smile creep onto her face then, the thing he likes about her the most.

I think you are a cloud that sits forever between two mountain peaks, she says. I think you are like me.

There is whooping and a series of scalp-halloos from the river then, and they turn to see the party of Shingas and Captain Jacobs arrive in six canoes, three of them carrying white captives bound hand and foot. Jamie rises to meet them.

I am glad to see you! calls Shingas when he sees Jamie. Captain Jacobs has gone before him carrying a pole with a dozen scalps hung upon it.

I am glad to see you as well.

How do you fare?

We have been successful, says Jamie. The white settlers run from us like water down a hill.

Ho!

Shingas looks weary, as if he has not slept for many nights.

Have you lost a warrior?

No, he says. The Great Spirit has cleared a path for us, He has guided our arrows to their marks. But I see that you are not pleased.

Ange says that there is a small bird who flies about the village, spying on everyone, who comes each morning to tell Shingas all their secrets. At first Jamie thought it was only her Lenape way of talking, till he found her one morning watching the *wikëwam* of Shingas and Cloud Woman, hoping to catch the bird at its work. Jamie knows he is only a man who sees everything without staring at it, a man who understands the behavior of other men as well as he does the habits of deer, bear, or possum.

I wish to fight the redcoats, says Jamie. But they are still in the north. These people of the colonies—

The Americas—

Are they calling themselves that? They have done nothing bad to me.

They walk together toward the fort, Shingas pondering this before he responds.

Their vision is poor, he says finally. They do not see that if they come back into our lands, again and again, we will only have to kill them, again and again.

I wasn't here before they came—

Neither was I. White people have always been upon the horizon, like a storm that is about to strike. But now I have learned to strike back.

Yes—

"I am called Shingas the Terrible," he says in English. "The whites wish to remove my head from my shoulders and place it on the point of a spear, to show all the settlers that the country is safe for them once more, as if killing one man will end what is wrong between us."

Red Warrior trots by them, pulling a half-dozen captives along by a rope. Jamie sees that the prisoners are looking at the walls of the fort, French flag raised above it, with hope in their eyes, a hope that will soon be dashed—

"The French cannae support mair hostages," Jamie says. "Will ye take them tae Kittanning?"

The village is overrun with them, says Shingas, somewhat ruefully. We have over a hundred already. They are of little use, and you have to feed them something—

You could let them go, says Jamie, and see if they can find their way to Philadelphia.

They would frighten all the game away, says Shingas, smiling. No, some we will sell or trade to other tribes, and the young ones will become Lenape, as you have.

He watches Jamie's face as they walk.

But only if their hearts are open.

THE GIRTY BOYS ARE TROUBLE. NOT SURPRISING, GIVEN their obvious dislike of their stepfather, Turner, and the unlikelihood of any quartet of adolescent boys remaining content while penned within a fifty-foot-square palisade, forbidden to venture out unless among their armed elders on a mission to gather wood or haul water. Their mother, Mary, has for some reason chosen Jenny as a confidant, seeking her out whenever she's managed to wheedle a few cups of rum from the militiamen.

"Girty was no fucking bargain, I can tell ye that," she confides in a voice that can likely be heard on the far side of the log wall that serves to protect them from savage marauders. "A good deal too fond of the drink, he was, and the one he'd choose to share a bottle with was this Delaware that lived in the holler, who white people called The Fish."

There is water in the trough today, hauled in bucket by bucket, and the handful of woman inside are washing clothes in it, dropping glowing, smoking rocks from an open fire in with a pair of tongs to keep it heated. Schoep was a bull about keeping the girls clean, always saying that "der oudside is telling you what is der inside," but here inside Fort Granville, playing in the piles of clay—

"This is back before the troubles started, the fix we're in now, and it wasn't so singular to see a white man drink with an Indian. A certain kind of white man." Mary has a baby in her arms, this one by John Turner, and she shifts it to the other hip from time to time.

"Turner, he was a neighbor, he and Girty would get into the stuff too, come home pie-eyed and singing, but Turner drawn the line at hobnobbin' with them red devils. Never liked 'em, never trusted 'em, which is the best policy in my book."

All the men over eighteen have been sworn into the militia now and supplied with an odd assortment of weapons, set out in groups of a dozen or more to scout the area for French and Indians, only rarely finding something edible to shoot. Schoep has come down the Juniata once with Enoch, hauling a canoe full of food for the fort and staying only to visit with the girls for an hour before heading back to the farm. Hedda does all the bread baking inside the fort and even has an admirer, a bucktoothed young man who spends a good deal of his day searching for a spot where he can clutch at her in privacy. There are none.

"Who knows what the row begun over," says Mary. "They're moody sonsabitches, your Delawares, like all Indians, and Girty was no better when he was in his cups, give me the back of his hand more than once and laid into the boys pretty hard when he could catch em. But row they did, nobody paying it no mind when their voices rose up, just a couple of souses making a racket. This was in the back room of—well, you wouldn't call it a tavern, really, just old Jeter's cabin where he sold whatever he cooked in his still. There was a scuffle heard, and then it got quiet, and it wasn't till Jeter wanted to sleep and asked the other fellas there to help him clear the back that they found The Fish passed out cold and Girty dead with a knife in his chest."

The boys dash by then, with Simon, the oldest and always the instigator, leading his brothers Thomas and James and the Schroeder boy in a clay ball throwing assault on his youngest brother George, with the rest of the children in the fort, including Schoep's girls, following with delight. Mrs. Turner—Mary—steps out to stand in front of the wet wash that is hanging on a rope line.

"You dirty this wash," she advises, "I'll tear your gizzards out!"

George wisely sprints for the other corner of the parade ground, pursued by his tormentors.

There is not much of a parade ground to parade on, a blockhouse occupying two of the stockade's corners and then the barracks, meant to house fifty men but now filled with more than a hundred each night, the overflow sleeping under the stars. Large mounds of clay, carted in with the idea of making a brick powder house some day, provide a small mountain range for the children to climb and push each other off of, accounting for the reddish stains Jenny is currently scrubbing at. The trader George Croghan, charged by the Pennsylvania Assembly to build several forts very quickly, must have felt that Granville's proximity to a spring and to the Juniata beyond it spared him of the effort of digging a well, meaning that water, carried into the fort in the half-dozen precious buckets, is rationed for drinking and available for the wash only once a week.

"Turner was one of them in the cabin that night," says Mary, returning to the trough. "The others wanted to hang The Fish, but no, he says, hanging's too good for an Indian. They thrown a bucket of cold water on him to wake him, then shown him what he done. 'Somebody kilt poor Girty,' he says, and then Turner brained him with that mallet they used to bung the kegs with. Brained him several whacks, John says, on account the red men got thick skulls."

"Sae ye married him," says Jenny, scrubbing.

Mary shakes her head, lifts a ball of sodden trousers from the hot water. "Within the month. I had them boys to care for, and a woman alone—"

There is a rifle shot from atop the wall then, and men come running. Jenny sees that the girls have huddled around Hedda, her hands white with flour, and moves to the wall to peek through a loophole.

There is a painted Indian standing on a stump in front of the fort, holding a wooden pole with a woman's white undergarment on it for a flag of truce. Jenny can see movement in the woods behind him, men there making little yipping sounds.

"You men come out, we fight fair, no hurt women!" calls the Indian.

"I don't believe we'll do that," answers Captain Ward. Jenny can see him above on the parapet, with Lieutenant Armstrong and John Turner, who is third in command. They are standing with their heads and shoulders exposed to fire, but seem unconcerned. On either side of them militiamen crouch with their rifles, ready if there is an attack.

"Mebbe only women inside the fort," says the Indian. "Maybe no man with bollocks between his legs."

"You'll have to come through or over these walls to find out," says Ward. He seems to Jenny like a real soldier, though not one born to the profession.

The Indian takes hold of his crotch with his free hand. "Mebbe we come back soon, mebbe somebody grow bollocks."

There is whooping from the treeline as he turns to stroll away, and then the Girty boys, on top of the northeast blockhouse, begin to throw balls of clay at him till their stepfather threatens to eviscerate them.

For the next several hours everybody not on the parapet with a weapon either stays inside the barracks or sits behind the piles of clay, the Indians sniping intermittently and calling insults in laughable French and worse English and presumably in their own tongue, though nobody in the fort understands it.

"That was Captain Jacobs," says Turner. "I know the rogue from up by the Kishacoquillas, when he was chummy with the trader there. I should have put a ball in his skull back then."

Only a few of the men in the fort are hurt by flying splinters, and the Indians either run out of ammunition or grow bored just before dusk, fading into the woods. By some miracle they fail to encounter the Boettichers and three other families who arrive with their wagons barely an hour later.

"I be taking der girls mit us," says their aunt Gertrudis, a large, long-faced woman who seems as stubborn as her brother but much more sensible. The girls, thrilled to see their many cousins and eager to leave the confinement of the fort, seem happy to leave. A conference is held with the travel party, who aim to go as far east as Harris's Ferry on the Susquehanna, and Colonel Ward and Lieutenant Armstrong, planning a route that they hope will help them avoid a meeting with the marauders. Hedda finds Jenny cranking wet clothes through a mangle, a task interrupted by the Indian attack.

"It's because I love him." The serving girl explains in her strange, nasal voice, that she and her young man are joining the wagons east, though there is nobody waiting for them there.

"Guid fortune tae ye then," says Jenny. Neither Gertrudis Boetticher nor her husband has offered a place for her in their new home, and she is supposed to be dead of shipboard fever back in Philadelphia. Though he's made no impression upon her heart, the pull of loyalty bids her to at least stay close to Schoep till the outrages have ended.

She hopes that Captain Jacobs and his party have not followed the Juniata south looking for farms to pillage.

"Yer not coming with us?"

"Nae," says Jenny, intent on the machine. "As lang as the girls are safe with their auntie, Ah've done ma part."

Hedda looks across the crowded parade ground. She was no help during the raid, hands shaking uncontrollably, crouched in a nest she'd made behind the flour barrels.

"If yer staying, then," she says, "I'd better show ye how to bake bread."

INDIANS DON'T SEEM TO CARE MUCH FOR PORK. THEY'LL gobble it straight out of the barrel if sharp set and there is absolutely nothing else, but Jamie has noticed after the raids that they mostly leave it to the French. They always prefer venison to beef, as he does now, and are suspicious of lamb. Killbuck carted off a plum pie from the last raid, sharing it with LaCroix, and now vows he'll capture a woman who knows how to make such a thing.

The French and Canadians are all in moccasins now, even Captain de Villiers who has a bad foot, and have been able to leave their snowshoes behind at the coming of spring. Jamie can tell the captain is concerned about his regulars, so much exposure to Lenape and Shawnee ways, to their casual attitude toward rank and status. They have learned to be stealthy and silent, have learned the stalker's patience, but it is clearly getting more difficult to control them once the prey is encountered, men trying to outdo their red brethren in daring and heartlessness. Currently they are tormenting the young ensign, Durocher, who has made the mistake of sharing a dismissive letter from the girl he left behind in Trois Rivières.

We will find you a better one at the next farm, jokes Coubertin. *Une grande paysanne* who is desperate for a man.

Can any woman be that desperate? asks *Caporal* Renault, looking the miserable ensign from head to toe. Perhaps a Quaker girl with no sense of smell—

She has crushed my heart, moans Durocher, who does not yet shave and has taken to yipping and whooping like the Indians to put the settlers in a panic before they are killed.

She has also crushed *tes bonbons, mon ami.* You need to forget this girl and find another who will restore your manhood, says Coubertin, snatching the letter away from the boy. And this I will use to wipe *mon cul* when I next am stricken with the flux.

Perhaps a *blind* Quaker girl with no sense of smell—

But there are no women at the next farm by the river. Only three men pulling stumps who see them and quickly grab rifles they've left behind a belly high pile of wood, shooting whenever anyone moves to get closer. They are far enough away from the little fort upriver not to worry about militia hearing them and coming to help, but eventually de Villiers tires of the stalemate and signals for Jamie to crawl over to him.

With that rifle, says the captain when Jamie has arrived, a few balls having whistled rather close to his head on the journey, you should be able to hit one easily.

Jamie sets up on his belly with the *Jäger* rifle braced atop a fallen log, sighting across the recently harvested field to the top of the woodpile. De Villiers then sends various of his Canadians dashing forward in small bursts, drawing the sheltered men up to shoot. On the fifth of these Jamie fires and sees the tallest of their adversaries fall back, struck square through the forehead. There is yipping and whooping from the crouching Indians and Durocher.

The remaining two grow more cautious, never appearing at the same spot to shoot, but shortly there is smoke drifting across the field, the distant farmhouse in flames. This proves too much for the stout crofter, who begins to run across the stubble toward his dwelling, a half-dozen warriors immediately popping up from where they've been watching to chase him down. He is a strong-looking man but no harrier, and makes it only halfway to his burning abode before he is overrun and tomahawked to the ground.

"*Tuez le dernier!*" shouts the captain, and all of the men are on their feet trotting toward the woodpile. The last defender, a skinny young man about the age of Durocher, suddenly stands, staring at them for a moment, then attempting to place the rifle barrel in his mouth and pull the trigger—but his arms prove too short and he is quickly clubbed to death and scalped.

It is a very well-run farm, Germans, in Jamie's estimation, with tidy stacks of wheat to set fire to and a barn full of well-fed livestock. He is relieved that no women or children have been found, Captain Jacobs' party having stumbled, by chance, upon the house while de Villier's men were engaged with the farmers. Jacobs, never a modest fellow, is wearing a girdle of raw scalps and bears important tidings—

The men at the fort would not come out to fight us, he says. But just this morning their officer left with most of the militia.

Why would he do that?

Captain Jacobs smiles, crinkling the tattoos on his cheeks.

He must be hunting for us.

"*Laissez tout ça!*" de Villiers shouts to the men who are laughing as they chase turkeys in front of the barn. We can come back for it later.

As they hurry back to the river Jamie notes that nobody has

taken the hair of the man he shot at the woodpile, though the French at Duquesne would redeem it in cash or trade, nor searched the body for loot.

His kill, his bounty. There is some honor left.

WHEN THEY COME BACK THERE ARE MORE OF THEM, and now Captain Ward has gone off with most of the militia, leaving less than two dozen men and the Girty boys to defend the fort. The firing seems to come from all sides this time, the horrible sounds the Indians make constant, and arrows are loosed high into the air, falling almost straight down onto their heads.

"They won't never bother with that," says a woodsman named Shockey who seems to have fought the savages before, "unless they know they can get in to pick them up later. Arras is nothing to waste."

Jenny, without the Schoep girls to mind, is expected to nurse the wounded, an impossibility given her total lack of experience and there not being a drop of water left within the walls.

"Yer fortunate it dinnae blind ye," she says to the young man as she wiggles wood splinters from beneath his eyes with a piece of brass wire doubled to make a tweezers. "Ah've nae remedy fer that."

Nor for little else, as badly wounded men, leaden balls penetrating various parts of their bodies, begin to be carried to her. If the men don't expose themselves to shoot, the raiders can come too close, hoping to fire the palisades, and snipers seem to be targeting the loopholes lower on the wall.

"I got one!" shouts one of the Girty boys, who so far seem to be enjoying the fight.

"Ye did not!" calls another.

"Did too! I'll show ye later if they don't take the body. Right through the mouth!"

Lieutenant Armstrong, who has been left in charge, comes down from the parapet to assure the women, only an angry *landfrau* left besides Jenny and the Girtys' mother Mary, and the handful of crying children that there is no great worry, as Ward has bequeathed them sufficient powder and ball for a siege and will surely return within a day or two. He does not mention the water situation.

"We'll just have to bear up," he says. "For there's no trusting them if we surrender."

French uniforms have been spotted in the trees, but again it is Captain Jacobs who seems to be leading the attack, strolling into the open from time to time to taunt them, seemingly immune to their volleys.

"*Dumme Männer,*" snarls the German woman when Armstrong is back on the wall. "Dey get us all killed."

The raid continues unabated for hours, no great fury to it but debilitating what with the heat and the lack of water and the feeling that there is nothing in the entire world surrounding them that is not hostile. Mary Turner has broken into the rum.

"They'll spare a young woman like yerself," she tells Jenny, red faced and unsteady on her feet, having passed her baby on to the *landfrau*. "They'll make a squaw of ye. Work their women like dogs, they do, and any young buck that takes a fancy—"

Jenny points a finger, bloody from probing the wound of a man with a ball in his hip, at the drunken woman.

"Ah'll accept ma fate withoot any prophecy, if ye dinnae mind," she says. "And if ye take any more drink ye'll fall on yer face."

Which happens shortly before night falls.

When it is dark, Indians creep up the ravine between the fort and the river and shoot flaming arrows into the logs of the palisade. It has been dry all month, and soon that whole wall is aflame, several men rushing to throw buckets of loose clay on what's burning as the raiders concentrate their firing—organized volleys now, with a Frenchman calling out orders—on the cracks and loopholes. Lieutenant Armstrong is wounded, his collarbone snapped in two, and another man hit in the jaw. The fire makes a strange glow, smoke and burning cinders drifting up into the black sky. Jenny presses a clean bit of cloth against the Lieutenant's wound, hoping to stem the bleeding. He glances over to Mary Turner, laid out on the ground at the corner of the blockhouse, immobile.

"Is she dead?"

"She's ainly sleeping through the ruckus."

"I wish that I could do as much."

Jenny ties a torn strip of linen around Armstrong's chest to hold the dressing in place, eases his arm onto the sling, and helps him to his feet The fire at the far wall is burning hot now, gaps growing wider between the charred upright logs, and the men inside have begun to pile whatever they can find—furniture, stove wood, a wagon bed—to make a barricade parallel to it. Once the burning wall is breeched, it will be their only protection. They work with red-rimmed eyes and deliberate motion, mouths so dry it is an effort for them to speak.

"That won't do," says Armstrong, and goes to join the men.

Jenny, feeling dizzy and exhausted, sits back on the ground to watch. The wounded men are in the little barracks building with the children, but every few minutes flaming arrows land on the roof of this structure, with the oldest Girty boy, Simon, now directed to stay up there with a bucket of clay from the mounds. If he lays on his belly he seems not to present a target to snipers in the surrounding trees, but whenever he has to crawl to put out another little flame he draws gunfire.

It is near midnight when they hear axes chopping on the other side of the burning wall and Lieutenant Armstrong leads a half-dozen men to it to counter the attempt. He is shot through the heart almost immediately, the other men leaving his body to run back behind the barricade.

The gunfire from outside ceases then, and a Frenchman's voice is heard, shouting something. Jenny walks to the barricade to hear better. Another voice then, translating, and this one sounds as if he's just stepped down from the Highlands.

"The colonel says we're a' gang tae sleep noo, as yer well surrounded. If ye'd care tae give the fort o'er, we'd be happy tae accept in the morn."

The wall keeps burning, oranges and reds dancing on Armstrong's body where it lies. The weary men look to John Turner, in command now.

"I don't know what else to do," he says.

THE MEN IN THE FORT WAVE A SHEET FOR A WHITE FLAG shortly after first light. The wall by the ditch is nearly burnt through—a good kick would knock a hole in it—but the man left in command opens the front gate for them to come in. Captain Jacobs knows him from before, a man named Turner, and clearly does not like him. De Villiers makes his usual plea for decorum before the looting and the snatching of prisoners begins, the Canadians grown as avaricious as the Lenape and Shawnee, with the French regulars ordered to commandeer any powder and shot left inside.

Besides John Turner there are eighteen men left, four of them badly wounded, a handful of near-grown boys, two women and some small children. Turner seems relieved when he counts heads among his conquerors, the combined parties numbering over one hundred fifty.

"We never stood a chance, did we?" he keeps saying, as if seeking exoneration for his decision to yield.

Jamie strolls around the little enclosure, casting an idle eye for something Ange might approve of. Two Shawnee are arguing over which has the right to scalp the dead lieutenant, Captain Jacobs having already taken his boots, while the prisoners are given useful articles to carry and ushered outside the walls, most of them begging for water. Jamie spies a tall barrel next to one of the blockhouses, gives it a push with his foot—it doesn't move as if it's empty. Lifting the cover off he discovers a youngish woman squeezed inside, and tips her out onto the ground.

"Whatever Ah say, ye dae it withoot complaint, and ye've a chance tae live through this," he tells her and she nods, staring at him as if he is a talking dog.

Jamie slips a noose around her neck and leads her out of the fort holding the cord, enduring a good deal of ribaldry from his comrades in arms.

"*Regarde le sauvage écossais*," laughs Coubertin, "*il s'est retrouvé une petite chouchou!*"

LaCroix is even more to the point.

You better enjoy that one before Ange gets ahold of her.

Jamie leads the woman to the stream and lets her drink. De Villiers has the English flag taken down and the pole reset several yards outside the fort with the French colors affixed to it, an act not wholly appreciated by the Indians in the party, and then charges Captain Jacobs with torching the structure. This destruction seems to be a special favorite of his, employing lamp oil, strategically placed hay bundles and even a bit of gunpowder to create a hasty but all-encompassing blaze, which de Villiers does not allow them to appreciate for long, the smoke bound to draw the fort's main force back and pitched battle very awkward with so many prisoners in tow.

Coubertin ceremoniously folds the letter he took from Durocher into a small leather pouch, allegedly fashioned from the cured skin of a Catawba warrior, and ties it to the flagpole before marching away.

Rejected love, he says, is a curse best left for one's enemies to discover.

They move as quickly as the prisoners can bear, heading west for

Kittanning, with the young women rarely letting her cord grow taut. Turner has been burdened with a heavy sack of rock salt, Captain Jacobs trotting beside to advise him, in adequate English, of the horrors he will suffer upon reaching the village.

"We put gun barrel in the fire," he says, "then push gun barrel up inside you."

Jamie drops back farther so the woman won't have to hear.

THERE ARE AS MANY PEOPLE IN THE VILLAGE AS THERE were in Grand-Pré. There are a lot of noises shouted back and forth, little near-naked children running up to point and poke at her, everybody smiling and laughing when a prisoner is struck by hurled chunks of pumpkin. There is a black woman among them, dressed like the other women, just watching from in front of her dwelling, and then several other women who seem very angry, congregating around John Turner and striking him with sticks. When he drops the sack he is carrying he is forced to lift it over his shoulder again, leaving him no defense from their blows.

"Bad bluid there," says the white savage who has claimed Jenny. "Ah dinnae ken what the story is."

And then there is a young woman, comely in her way, wearing strings of silver buttons hung from her ears, who accosts the man, shouting in their harsh language. She steps very close to Jenny, staring her in the face, and when Jenny refuses to blink pulls at her hair and slaps her hard in the face.

"Steady noo," croons the white Indian. "Ye mean naething tae her."

After they are paraded through the village, which is a hodgepodge of dwellings situated on both sides of a substantial river, Jenny and the other prisoners are pulled and driven to something like a corral, made with stakes and pricker bush, that holds another three dozen white captives and four negroes.

"Ye'll bide a weel in here," says the white Indian, "till Ah can think hoo tae dispose of ye."

There is a small reunion, a few of the new prisoners knowing some already there, and Mary Turner lights into her husband.

"Look where ye've got us!" she snarls at him. "Go in the fucking fort, ye say, we'll be safe there. It was a sorry day I ever laid eyes on ye!"

"Would ye be better off with Girty?" snaps Turner, backed up against a wall of briars.

"Girty," replies Mary, loud enough for her boys and the rest of the captives to hear, "would've died like a *man*."

But she is all woe and remorse an hour later when Captain Jacobs and three other Indians come to drag Turner out of the enclosure, making him kneel while his face is painted with black grease.

"Those are the ones they torture," says an old woman standing next to her. "He'll wish he had died before."

"My husband!" cries Mary Turner, clutching her baby in her arms. "They're taking my husband!"

His face painted, Turner is chased back into the village with kicks and blows. Some women come then with baskets of food, which they hand over the sides of the corral. It is mostly uncooked ears of maize, which the *landfrau* from Fort Granville makes sure is doled out evenly.

"*Alle* is staying maybe a liddle hungry," she says, "but nobody here is starving."

"Sometimes the French down at the Forks will buy women from them," the old woman tells Jenny. "But somebody said they're full up with captives. And nobody wants one old as me."

"Ye've survived this lang," Jenny says. "Ye'll come through."

She doesn't believe it, doesn't have any idea what will happen next and isn't eager to find out. Schoep's stories about Indian atrocities race through her mind, and she wonders if he was somehow overlooked by the raiding parties. There are so many people crowded into the corral that they have to take turns sitting on the ground in a special area. She and the old woman are told they can take a turn.

"What's that ye smell of?" asks the old woman when they are seated with another ten captives.

"Tis the cabbagey thing the Germans eat."

"Sauerkraut—"

"Aye. Ah tried tae hide in a barrel that was used fer it."

The woman nods. "They take some to live with them," she says. "Mostly the younguns and some of the women. They think it's an honor. So if you try to run and they catch you—"

She shakes her head dolefully.

"Sometimes they make us watch."

The raw maize has made Jenny's stomach hurt, and she wonders what's to be done if you're taken with a need—

"In the far corner there," says the old woman, as if reading her mind. "There's a ditch dug, and someone will hold up a blanket."

It is dark, the glow of fires and chanting voices rising from the river's edge when they come for Mary and the Girty boys. They are tied together in a coffle and led away, Indians with clubs and tomahawks held high in case anyone resists.

"They're relations of the man that was painted?" asks the old woman.

"Aye."

"Then they want them to witness what's done."

Turner's screaming cuts through the night, and does not abate for hours. There are two little German girls, their parents left dead back in Tulpehocken, who begin to cry hysterically. Jenny pushes through the other captives to find them, taking their hands.

"*Wir singen jetzt*," she says and begins to hum one of the tunes she learned from Schoep's daughters, getting their attention.

"*Sie kennen die Wörter,*" says the *landfrau*, finding them, and the girls begin to sing along, little voices shaky at first—

Der Mond ist aufgegangen
Die goldnen Sternlein prangen
Am Himmel hell und klar-

—then gaining power as Jenny and the *landfrau* join them, trying to drown out the screams and the shouts of the Indians—

Der Wald steht schwartz und schweiget,
Und aus de Weiesen steiget
Der weiße Nebel wunderbar-

—singing as many verses as they can remember. Then the old woman begins, with a voice much too strong and beautiful from a tiny stick of a person, singing a hymn that everybody in the enclosure seems to know—

When all Thy mercies, O my God,
My rising soul surveys,
Transported with the view, I'm lost
In wonder, love, and praise.

—most of them lifting their voices to join her—

Thy Providence my life sustained,
And all my wants redressed,
While in my silent womb I lay,
And hung upon the breast—

—till there is nothing in their ears but a song of praise—

To all my weak complaints and cries
Thy mercy lent an ear,
ere yet my feeble thoughts had learned
to form themselves in prayer!

TURNER'S BODY IS STILL TIED TO THE POST IN THE morning when they leave. It resembles a burnt tree stump, blackened and twisted. Ange, angry about the captive woman, went to watch just to spite him, but came back quickly.

He was only a weak man, she said, and this torture brings us no honor.

Charbonneau, the *voyageur* rowing up from Fort Duquesne agrees to guide them for a bundle of tobacco. Jamie and LaCroix do the rowing, following his canoe, with Ange sulking in their bow and the woman to be sold, unbound, sitting in the rear. The *voyageur* carries supplies and three sullen Canadians whose term of service ended nearly a year ago, as well as "a thousand requests from the garrison for *nos chefs dans le nord*," most of which are expected to be ignored.

The Allegheny current is strong, requiring a few short portages when it narrows and twists, but Charbonneau knows it well and entertains them at the fire on their first night out.

A river is a story, he says, drying his bare feet close to the flames. A story told by a very old man, who changes the details with every telling, though the plot remains the same and the story always ends up in the same place. As you row upon a river you've traveled before, you can think ahead—ah, here comes the part where—

He stuffs tobacco into his pipe.

—but of course that part of the tale may be told this time with more passion, or this time it is set in the winter months, which can change everything. I know hundreds of such stories, and the many versions of them.

He rolls up his sleeve to show them a tattoo, a bluish, meandering path that runs from his shoulder to his wrist.

"*C'est celui que les indiens du sud appellent le Mississippi,*" he explains. I learned this story when I was very young, and the Chickasaw people drew this on me from a map. That is why my Christian name is Amable Charbonneau, but other *voyageurs* call me La Charte.

He grows pensive then, picking up his squeezebox to play a mournful air that goes on and on.

You could play that on the pipes, says the captive woman in Erse, trying to catch Jamie's eye.

Jamie answers without looking at her, also in Erse.

But this will make you weep, he says, whereas the pipes will make you run.

What is that you're talking? asks Ange.

The language of my people.

It's an ugly language, she tells him, and you have ugly women there.

Jamie tries not to smile, Ange's moods as subtle as an open wound.

I don't care if you lay with her, she says, getting to her feet, as long as you get a good price for her. And soon.

Ange walks into the dark, her brother waiting till she is out of sight before he laughs.

Maybe you should sell her to me now, says LaCroix.

And you'll bring her back to Buffalo Hair?

He laughs again.

Not unless I desire to be castrated. Women are a problem, even if you hold their lives in your hand.

Jamie avoids the Scotswoman's eyes. She'd be well-looking with a good meal and a few nights' sleep, familiar to him somehow, though there must be a thousand like her in the Highlands. Or perhaps not—? He shudders to think what has become of it under the English heel.

The Canadians begin to sing the words to the air, feeling melancholy though they are headed home.

Though they have a home to go to.

IT IS NEARLY NOON THE NEXT DAY WHEN THEY REACH Venango where the Rivière aux Boeufs, which the English call French Creek, spills into the Allegheny. The town has been overwhelmed by the new-built Fort Machault and its outbuildings, which sit above the west bank of the river. There are nearly a dozen flat-bottomed *bateaux* pulled up before it, but little activity by the water.

We have enough women to cook and clean, says the commandant, who is not a happy man. And for the other, *nous avons les jeunes peaux rouges*.

And you've given them all the pox, Jamie wants to say to him, but holds his tongue.

And if I wished to enlist with my friend LaCroix? he says instead—

Enlist?

"*Comme un soldat régulier, pour combattre les anglais.*"

The commandant laughs at him.

If you want to fight the English, you'll have to go find them.

But if they come here—

If they come here, my friend, I have less than one hundred *canadiens dissolus* who do not wish to be here and a group of savages who will refuse to come within the walls. If the English come here with any serious force, I will be only too happy to surrender.

Then why are you here?

Continue up to Fort Le Boeuf, *mon ami,* and ask the commandant there this question. Perhaps he will have a more pleasing answer.

My boat is growing very heavy, says Charbonneau when they leave an hour later. Between the new requests they have given me to carry, and then the complaints, which weigh even more—

It is not a bad thing, paddling upstream. At least for now there is no danger for them on the Rivière aux Boeufs, and it is late summer, the sun warm on their skin. In Paris the Jesuits had explained their concept of the Limbo of the Infants, each holy man with his own interpretation. The most benevolent of these was that these tiny, unbaptized children lived in a Paradise complete but for the absence of the Lord—and that they would be united with Him on Judgment Day.

We are paddling in Limbo, thinks Jamie. Birds swoop down to snap up insects hovering over the water, ducks and their ducklings paddle in the shallows, dipping their heads for the slippery green that coats the rocks, a muskrat makes a V-shaped wake swimming parallel to them. This may be the natural paradise the old men get misty-eyed about around the fire when they speak about Before the White Man, the world of their grandfathers' fathers, leaving out the murder between tribes, which seems to have been constant, if not often devastating. Charbonneau feels it too, singing with the Canadians in the boat ahead, the discharged soldiers' spirits rising as they get closer to home. Even the Scotswoman in the stern, facing Jamie as he paddles, seems far too relaxed watching the scenery roll past for a captive whose fate is yet to be determined.

The river peters out at Fort Le Boeuf. The commandant there is no more welcoming.

We are here to guard supplies as they wait to go down the river, he says. We fight nothing but mosquitos.

And the woman?

Move on to Presqu'Île. All of the north trades there, at least a dozen tribes. One of them might want her, *comme une curiosité.*

THEY CAMP OUTSIDE THE FORT THAT NIGHT AMONG the Indians, who hang about for scraps. Ange speaks with some of them, but none have the language of her mother. Her people, the *Chats*, used to live by the water just to the north of here, before they were crushed by the Haudenosaunee and scattered to the winds. When she comes back to their fire her Long Knife is talking to the captive woman, and not in the proper tone of voice. She is glad that only her brother is here along with the white men, for none of the Lenape would approve. Captives must prove themselves before they are treated like humans, as he was forced to do.

Ange knows what he says when he speaks with the French officers. He wants them to take him back as a white man again, to wear their uniform and leave her behind, maybe even keep the white woman to lay with. The killing has done this to him. She has watched what the killing has done to other men in the village—some it has made stupid, or greedy, or crazed with blood. Some like Shingas it has driven to near silence. It has made her Jamie confused, made him believe the killing will be better if he wears the French uniform. Men are born to kill—animals to eat and take the hides from, other men, sometimes—but if they have to kill too many men the spirits of war grow bored and pay no attention. That is why her brother has come along. He knows he will never be fully Lenape, so he wonders if the French will take him as a warrior. He has left Buffalo Hair the papers and metal discs the French use to trade with, and told her to buy food from the ones at the forks if the winter becomes hard.

Buffalo Hair says he is a poor husband.

Ange has stopped brewing the plants that Cloud Woman showed her, the ones she used when all the men wanted to lay with her and she would let the ones she liked or who were especially generous. She has stopped drinking the brew some time ago, but still there is nothing in her belly but the few handfuls of corn she ate in the canoe this afternoon. Nothing lies across the path of creation but perhaps a bad spirit between her and Jamie, for children rarely come into the world unless they are welcomed.

And Lenape men, even ones who used to be white, will not turn their back on their children.

JAMIE THOUGHT IT WAS A CRUCIFIX HANGING AROUND her neck.

"Are ye Catholic?"

"Nae. Though ah've been tae their kirk a guid deal."

"If the French should ax ye aboot it, say ye are."

"Ah will."

"Hae did ye come tae this land?"

"Transported as a rebel, though Ah never raised ma hand."

Jamie nods. "And that hangin' aboot yer neck?"

She pulls the ring out then. He has to look at it closely to be sure, the woman tensing as if he'll snatch it from her. It can't be—

"Where did ye get this?"

She hesitates, maybe thinking up a story, then tells him the truth. "It was gien me. There've been times—but Ah thought twould be a sin tae sell it."

Jamie studies her face then. Eyes an unsettling light gray, almost clear, like fresh water held in a glass—

"Christ, Ah *ken* ye."

"Hoo's that, then?"

"Tis ma mother's ring."

She stares at him for a long moment. Jamie is made conscious of his shaved head, of the tattoos on his chest, for the first time in years—

"That's *you*, then. The gentleman on the horse."

"Aye."

The woman, who was little more than a girl then, looks him over from head to toe.

"Yer a different creatur noo."

"Ah am that," says Jamie. "Ah am that."

Then Ange comes back with a rabbit to be cooked.

You'd better not touch her, she says, throwing the rabbit down to be skinned and staring at the captive. She looks like she has a disease.

IN THE MORNING THEY BEGIN TO CARRY THE CANOES up the Venango Path.

This is a part of the story as well, says Charbonneau. But not an interesting one.

The land is very flat, mostly pine trees, and the Path well worn with wagon traffic. They pass a detachment of *canadien* militia, twenty men in all, marching in the opposite direction, and the recently discharged soldiers gleefully call of the horrors they will be facing in their new garrison, whatever it is, pointing to Jamie and LaCroix and saying they were French corporals from Bordeaux only six months ago.

The trees are full of blue jays and squirrels and by midday they are bathed in sweat.

"*Ne désespérez pas*," Charbonneau urges them, "*je peux sentir la grande eau*."

LaCroix claims he can smell it too, no near-Lenape about to be outdone by a *voyageur*, and within the hour the woods open up to a lake so large it seems an ocean.

If a river is a story, what is this? asks Jamie.

Charbonneau laughs. It's an open book, and one with blank pages.

He points straight out past the fort and over the water.

If we were able to row absolutely straight, the maps tell us there is a shore on the other side—maybe yes, maybe no, as I do not know a *voyageur* who has done this.

And if we paddle and paddle, says Jamie, always keeping the shore to our right, will we end up back in this same place?

If one believes in maps drawn by men who have never done such a thing.

The commandant of Fort de la Presqu'île has no use for Jamie or LaCroix.

All that we require in these *pays-d'en-haute,* he says, is a few officials in Québec who are not thieves or idiots. As for the woman, there is a priest here who might take her off your hands.

The men in the fort stare at Jamie and Ange and Jenny, for that is the woman's name, as they cross the parade ground, calling out offers to buy either or both of the women. They are mostly *canadiens,* though the commandant stated that a General Montcalm has arrived in la Nouvelle France with a squadron of professional soldiers from the mother country.

The real war is about to commence, the commandant declares.

There is a tiny cabin with a wooden cross nailed to its front wall and inside stands a young Jesuit speaking a lesson to a dozen Indian children sitting uncomfortably on wooden benches.

Notre Dieu, he says, is a forgiving God, but He sees all. Every sin shall be punished in the hereafter.

He studies the faces of the children, who seem more cowed than attentive.

And what are these sins?

The children, if they know the sins, are not eager to name them. The priest looks up as he sees a painted savage and a white woman standing by the door.

Ponder the nature of it as I speak with these people.

He moves past the children to them, walking with his hands folded in front of him.

"*Je suis le père Jérôme. Comment puis-je vous aider?*"

"*Elle est captive*," says Jamie, pointing to Jenny "*Écossaise*."

I have no money to buy captives.

"*Je peux travailler pour vous*," says Jenny. "*Ou pour quelqu'un d'autre, si vous voulez me vendre.*"

Both Jamie and Père Jérôme are surprised by this, the young woman's French correct but with a strange lilt to it.

"*Je peux cuisiner, coudre, nettoyer*—"

"*Et elle est catholique*," adds Jamie, as if her list of domestic skills is not enticement enough.

Jenny crosses herself as if she's done it a thousand times.

Père Jérôme nods, then studies Jamie's face, the tattoos on his bare chest—

And you, my son? What are you?

Jamie hesitates, no easy answer coming to mind.

I am between worlds.

The priest seems to accept this.

I can certainly use a housekeeper, he says, but have no money—

I'm not selling her.

Jenny looks to Jamie then. In Martinique people were exchanged as presents, willed to children, thrown into the bargain when land or sugar cane exchanged hands. She is being offered shelter—

"*Très bien*," says the young Jesuit. "*Votre nom mademoiselle?*"

"Jenny."

"*Nom de famille?*"

A sad smile plays at her lips.

I've several of those—I've been unfortunate with husbands—

"*Votre nom de jeune fille, alors?*"

Jenny Ferguson, she tells him. I was Jenny Ferguson, so many years ago.

The Indian children are staring at them, aware that some exchange is taking place. Jenny lifts the ring from around her neck and presses it into Jamie's hand.

"Ye'll have this back noo. Ye can't imagine the places it's been."

Jamie is struck by a feeling of loss when he walks out the door.

Ange is waiting on the parade ground, ignoring the stares of the militiamen, pleased to see that Jamie is alone, but still suspicious.

What did you get?

No money—

I knew it—

Only this—for you.

He hangs the gold ring around Ange's neck.

Ange examines the ring, turning it over in her fingers, tears forming in her eyes.

It's something white people give when they marry, says Jamie.

I know that.

LaCroix meets them by the canoes, having spoken with as many of the militiamen as would talk with him.

They say the real war is going to begin, he says, with real soldiers.

I was told the same, says Jamie.

They also say that de Villiers is heading north to join with this General Montcalm. They'll attack the British fort at Oswego, on the most eastern of the lakes.

Jamie nods.

It sounds like a real war.

THEY SAIL PART OF THE WAY ACROSS LAKE ERIE, CHARbonneau having traded the canoes for a larger *bateau*, and see no other craft till they reach the mouth of the Niagara and the little trading post there, now with a palisade around it and a few dozen homesick militia. They pause only to deliver news from the other forts and for Charbonneau to collect more requests and complaints and add three of his cousins, who have fortuitously just arrived from Montreál, to the crew. The discharged Canadians have become adept oarsmen by now, singing along with the *voyageurs* to maintain their rhythm—

Salut a mon pays
Apres un' longue absence
De mes anciens amis
O douce souvenance!

—until the river begins to tumble downhill, one series of rapids leading to the next, and their hearts rise up into their throats with terror. Charbonneau decides which of the chutes they will rush through, which they will pull the *bateau* ashore and carry it around, too busy shouting orders to entertain them with metaphor.

There are passages of swift running between the rocky sections, the power of an enormous lake funneled into the steep-sided river. After a harrowing dash in which they are twice nearly capsized, Jamie begins to feel a thickness in the air, which becomes a distant undertone, then something like a roar, a roar with no beginning and no end—

"*Qu'est-ce que c'est?*" asks LaCroix, having to shout now over the sound, though he is on the thwart just in front of Charbonneau.

All good stories have an exciting climax, says the *voyageur.* And we are coming to one of the best.

They row to the east bank of the river, where a half-dozen Indians, Seneca Haudenosaunee, are waiting. The men have a ring through their nose and a triangular pendant hung from that, which dangles before their lips—Jamie wonders how they can eat or drink without it getting in the way. Charbonneau pays them with French *livres* to help carry the *bateau* and the supplies, and they begin to climb, losing sight of the river for a while. Ange, carrying a pair of oars over each shoulder, has no problem keeping up. It seems like they have climbed three mountains by the time they rest at a point where they can look back at the falls.

The spill is in a horseshoe shape, water cascading down nearly two hundred feet into a vast pool that seems equally deep, a huge ball of mist and spray rising at the center, the thundering all the more impressive due to its relentlessness. Even the Seneca seem to be transfixed by the power of the spectacle, no doubt feeling in the presence of a Great Spirit. What Jamie feels is very *small*—it isn't his role in the current conflict that seems futile, but the war itself. Perhaps He Who Made All Things put this here, he thinks, as a reminder of our insignificance.

They remain quiet on the downhill portage, as if chastened.

IF A WAR MUST BE WAGED THE SUMMER MONTHS ARE the best. Food is plentiful and another body is not missed under the blanket as much when it is warm at night. Most of the men have been gone since the killing of the English near the forks, roving in several different parties to attack the white settlers, coming home for a few days with goods and captives they have taken. Cloud Woman worries that Kittanning is becoming the place where everybody leaves their prisoners, who must be fed and guarded if they are not to be welcomed as Lenape, replacing those killed in battle or dead from disease. Three brothers, one of them almost a man, were brought in from the fight at Fort Granville—one claimed by the Shawnee, the eldest by the Mingos, and the youngest, George his white name, taken in by Shingas to live with them. The mother and a baby have been sent back to the French at Fort Duquesne, since she was a quarrelsome woman and likely to be resentful after watching her husband burned alive.

George has grown his hair long and has begun to dress like the other boys his age here, fighting back enough during their games to earn some respect, but has a long path to walk before becoming a Lenape. He still sees himself at the center of all things, like most white people. But he is growing stronger and more observant, happy to gather berries or firewood, and has never tried to run away, even when not closely watched.

When Shingas is gone Cloud Woman weaves baskets by the fire, often staying up later than usual or even waking in the dark without worrying what time it might be and giving new life to the fire before taking her work in hand. There is always need for baskets, and they are a good thing to give to young women who have just been married or given birth. She has asked her youngest brother, Elk Dreaming, who is lame and unable to go raiding, to teach George to make arrows and use a bow, something he seems very eager to learn, so the boy is often at that *wikëwam* when the sun comes up.

A low mist hangs over the river and the paths through the village, the kind that will always burn off before noon. Cloud Woman brings some of the winter furs and blankets out, hanging them on the meat-drying rack to air. She sees no people awake and about yet, though the dogs are up and sniffing as usual. When they begin to yip and howl she knows it is bad.

The white men attack from two directions, hundreds of them shouting and firing their rifles and grabbing up burning sticks to try to light people's dwellings on fire. She runs back inside to wake George, telling him to pull his moccasins on, and then they join the women and children running off through the maize field and then into the river.

The invaders know what they want. Though there is gunfire and shouts and people running in every direction, they quickly gather around the enclosure where the new prisoners are kept and the house of Captain Jacobs, who arrived with his raiding party only a day ago. Cloud Woman and George and dozens of others swim to the shallows on the far side of the river, where no white men have come yet, and crouch in the mist there trying to see what is happening. She can hear the horse that was given to Shingas, its cries moving about the village as it runs from one terrifying scene to another, somehow never thinking to go to water, as a wild animal would.

The men left in the village are fighting back, as is Captain Jacobs, his cabin easy to see on the high ground where it dominates the village, an idea he must have been infected with when living near wealthy white people. Dozens of the whites have surrounded the cabin, most lying on the ground to shoot as Jacobs and probably his son are up in the space by the roof shooting down at them. Besides prisoners, most of what he brings back is gunpowder, sometimes whole barrels of it, and he has bragged that he will make peace with the white man only when they agree to teach him how to make such a thing.

More people swim across, saying that some of the white men are being killed too, so maybe they will go away. It is said that the English have offered a reward of seven hundred pieces of eight on the heads of both Captain Jacobs and her Shingas, and so perhaps the men around the cabin are greedy as well as wanting revenge. The cabin and several other buildings have been set on fire and the dogs, who bark but run away from trouble, are still howling.

Do you think they'll find us? asks George, who has been quick to learn as much Lenape as a very small boy might understand, and Cloud Woman cannot tell if he wishes to be found or to stay hidden. He may not know himself. Making him watch his father be tortured and killed was not a good thing, though George says that Turner was not their real father. They are cold crouching on the bank, wet from the river and the sun barely risen above the edge of the hills, but nobody leaves yet, waiting to see if the fighting will end or even turn toward them. Cloud Woman knows three good places to hide if it does. She sees Buffalo Hair, and is glad, because the English make the black ones into slaves, and she is glad that their Long Knife and his Ange and her brother LaCroix are away to the north, though they would fight hard if caught in the village. She has the knife she uses to skin deer in hand, but will run and hide before she is forced to use it. Even a wolf knows when to fight and when to lope away.

There is an explosion and much screaming. It is Captain Jacobs' cabin, one wall blown out and flames shooting higher than the roof now and one, two, three—his wife and his son and finally Jacobs himself leaping from the cock croft beneath the roof and shot by the white men waiting below. Some men from the dwellings on this side of the river begin to wade across, rifles in hand, calling to the runaways to go hide until it is safe. It won't ever be safe now, now that the whites know where they are and believe they can win their captives back here.

The fight goes on for another hour, gunfire rising and falling, and there are some bodies of white men and of Indians floating past on the current. Chikhikàn, who lives on this side, brings them blankets and leads them up the hill to a place where the view is better. They can see the white men forming into a group, and then retreating back into the woods, carrying whatever of their dead and wounded they have been able to find.

Women are weeping when they cross back to the other side. Nearly half of the dwellings have been burned, and there are dead people everywhere, those who were first only wounded finished with hatchets by the attackers. Captain Jacobs has been scalped and all his clothing stripped away. One wounded white man, one of the raiders, not a prisoner, is discovered and quickly killed with rocks. Cloud Woman finds that her own *wikëwam* is gone, probably targeted by the white men and pulled to pieces and scattered about.

They knew where people lived, says Buffalo Hair. Somebody who has been here drew them a map.

Cloud Woman sees the horse that her Shingas was given, body quivering as it stands, the rope it was tied with trailing on the ground. She speaks to it softly, stepping forward to take the rope, but it bolts away, sprinting across the field where beans and pumpkins were growing, trampled now by the invaders, and disappears into the trees.

Maybe it will come back when it grows hungry, she thinks, or maybe the wolves will get it.

"*Kwikhul,*" says George, claiming he will help her build another *wikëwam.*

This is a bad place now, she explains to him. We will bury the dead and find another to live in.

GOD IS AN ANGRY MAN. A MAN LIKE REVEREND CRAIGIE who ruled the kirk where they lived in the west, a bearded man with a permanent scowl and a sharp voice to admonish you with. But Père Jérôme's God must have another side, or how explain the priest's dedication to his own personal misery and his untiring efforts to convert the pagan Indians around Fort de la Presqu'île? Jenny finds it no great effort to maintain the fiction that she is a Catholic, attending Mass being a sort of entertainment in a place with very little else to offer, the sounds of the priest's Latin as mysterious and pleasing in its way as the strange sounds the Indian children make when they talk among themselves, words that seem to be pushed from their throats without engaging the lips. Her only misstep was the first time she knelt in Confession, knowing a bit of this ritual from Amély's descriptions of her own sessions—

"*Bénis-moi, mon père, car j'ai péché—*" she began, as was expected, but then could think of no sins to confess other than her lie about being of Père Jérôme's creed, which would give her away. He asked her to dig back in her memory, and the best she could do is admit to some guilt at not being more eager to be reunited with her latest husband, should he still be alive.

You have lost hope, my child.

Perhaps. Or perhaps I've only given up thinking there is anything one can do to control one's life.

Ah, but you're speaking of the *world,* Père Jérôme reminded her. That is only an illusion. It is our eternal *souls* we must care for.

Freed from the cabinet, she mutters the prayers he assigns to her, again relying on her memories of Amély. She imagines her friend with Desjardins and his children in the northern forest, hiding, running—

For the war has turned, and there has been little good news for the French since the victory of their General Montcalm at Fort William Henry, and even that marred by the slaughter of the surrendered English troops by his Indian cohorts. The French do not speak of this, of course, not in front of her, but Marie Claire, one of the Wyandot converts who hangs about the tiny church in the fort is full of news and gossip. The fortress at Louisbourg has been taken, as well as Fort Frontenac, cutting the French off from their forces in the Ohio Valley, and now there is a rumor that the hated William Johnson and his Iroquois are coming to attack Fort Niagara. Supplies and reinforcements do not arrive here at Presqu'île when promised, and then even the promises are given up.

When there is nothing more to do for Père Jérôme or his charges, Jenny likes to sit on the banks of the great lake, which is called Ontario, and look across the water. On a very clear day you can see a line of bumps on the horizon, the far shore, and there are always canoes and rafts and *bateaux* coming in and out, and some under sail when the weather is right, some boats much bigger than the one that brought her here. When Jenny thinks about her soul, which she is doing for the first time in her life, she likes to think of it as a thing at the side of a lake or an ocean, a thing not closed up in a walled palisade—

The soldiers in the garrison are rude, of course, ready with jokes about how Jenny "serves the good father," and even the Indian boys tease her, asking why she does not wear trousers when Père Jérôme is always in a robe. "*Le robe noire*" is what the Indians call him when he is out of earshot, and they regard him as something between an annoyance and their guide to salvation, believing his magic can be benevolent or turned to evil purposes depending on his mood.

A man to deal with cautiously.

Père Jérôme stared at her constantly for her first month in his service, putting her on alert for signs of an approach, but it turned out to be only another aspect of his self-abnegation.

If there is no temptation, he told her, apologizing when she finally asked that he not watch her so closely, there is no virtue in resistance.

It is the same with his meals, the priest insisting on only eating the simple fish, venison, and *sagamité* that makes up the local Indians' diet, while she is encouraged to fix something much more palatable for herself.

"*Ah, qu'est-ce que c'est?*" he will ask as she sits across from him—for he insists that she eat at the same time and table—and then nod as she explains the ingredients and method of preparation. Madame Rossignol, cook for the commandant here, is a great help in this, an Acadian refugee with a genius for making something new and interesting with what the fort has to offer.

And Jenny wishes never to face a bowl of boiled oatmeal again.

At night, after his first bout of prayer and meditation, Père Jérôme likes to sit by the fire and relate the histories of his idols, *les martyrs nord-américains*. The priest's eyes glow with firelight and sometimes with tears as he relates the stories, perhaps for Jenny's spiritual edification, but more likely because he loves them so.

The story of the Ox, Jean de Brebeuf, who came to minister to the Wyandot people in the days of Monsieur Samuel de Champlain, when *la Nouvelle France* was only in its infancy.

The story of Père Anthony Daniel, or of the missionaries Charles Garnier and Isaac Jogues, of their triumphs and their suffering.

Mostly of their suffering.

Jenny tends the fire as she listens, a skill the priest surprisingly lacks, considering his years spent among the Indians. He has two black robes and very few other clothes, eats only two small meals a day and engages in no activities that require cleaning up after. He does, however, often ask Jenny to accompany him when visiting the native huts, though she hasn't a word of any of their languages, explaining that her presence somehow reassures the people that they are not dealing with a sorcerer. Of the many obstacles set before the missionaries, says Père Jérôme, the most difficult to overcome was that when the influenza or the smallpox struck the villages, killing scores of people, many were convinced it had been brought as a curse by the black robes.

On the other hand, so many souls were redirected to Heaven by the quick action of the Jesuits in baptizing the poor savages in their dying moments—

God made the Wyandots, Jenny ventures—

As He made you and me, says Père Jérôme.

Then why did he put them in a place where there was no chance to learn His laws? I mean before the priests came—

I don't understand—

You say the people they baptized just before they died were saved—what about the ones who died before the missionaries came here?

If they had done no evil in their lives, they were cast into Purgatory.

Which is—?

Like Hell, but not eternal—

They burn?

Burn in a purifying fire, not a punishing fire.

But it hurts—

Of course. Fire is fire.

For how long?

Till the Day of Judgment.

That could be a long time.

Yes. But they suffer knowing there is an end to it, and then everlasting glory.

Maybe thousands of years—

It's why my work here is so important. To help these poor souls avoid such torment—

But some of them had no chance. They didn't reject salvation, they never knew of it.

Père Jérôme smiles patiently.

Mysterious are the ways of God's Providence.

To Jenny it seems more arbitrary than mysterious, but she has not pondered these things for long hours as Père Jérôme has. Most of his stories end with one of the Jesuits being brutally tortured and then murdered by the enemies of their converts.

And why, she asks, were the Wyandot fighting the Iroquois in the first place?

Over hunting rights, over land, because they had always been enemies and Satan was allowed free reign among them—

Like England and France.

Père Jérôme stares at Jenny for a moment.

Those are civilized nations, he says, and we French are fighting for the one true religion.

Ah—

On these nights Jenny can't sleep for questions. Infants who die unbaptized—are they sent to this Purgatory as well? And somehow burn without being consumed? And the ones baptized, who die and go to Heaven—do they grow into adults once there? And if not, who cares for them? Are mothers sentenced to give suck for Eternity? Or is there no need for food, the babies always smiling and joyous like in the paintings she's seen. If an Indian tortures and kills, but then finds the true religion and confesses his sins in the cabinet before he dies, is he then sent to Heaven to dwell beside the people whose brains he dashed out with a club? Kirk in Scotland was so much simpler—you were wicked and destined to burn after you died and had better not be caught enjoying yourself before that day came around.

She wonders if there had been priests like Père Jérôme, or even these murdered Jesuits, in Martinique when white people first arrived there. Because the ones she met there were much more interested in guiding you through this world than in preparing you for the next.

The blood of martyrs is the seed of the Church, Père Jérôme is fond of saying, and seems wistful that no situation requiring his life's sacrifice has yet arisen here at Fort de la Presqu'île.

Jenny sleeps, finally, and dreams of torture.

One morning a party of Shawnee raiders come through the fort, with three white men, captives, who they are using as beasts of burden. Jenny recognizes one of these from Fort Granville, a young man named Granger, who lived south on the Juniata. While the Shawnee are engaged in a trading palaver Jenny manages to speak with him.

"Can you help me?" he asks. "I've begged the French at every fort we've come to, but they pretend not to hear."

"It costs them dear tae redeem a captive," Jenny tells him. "And they've a' gan hard-hearted in this wilderness. But Ah'll ax ma priest if there's owt he can dae."

"They're the worst," says Granger. "Unless you're a Catholic, they've not a drop of pity. And these Shawnee—we see the farms after they've done their bloody work. They were at your farm just before Granville was taken."

"My farm?"

"You weren't told? They killed your Schoep and his two men."

She has assumed it all along, but the certainty hurts, Jenny thinking of the three little girls now orphaned—

Granger grows mute as they see one of the Shawnee approaching. The Indian speaks to Jenny in a harsh and guttural French—

"*Que veux-tu avec ce prisonnier?*"

"*Rien, je ne parle pas sa langue.*"

She finds Père Jérôme at lakeside, telling a group of his pupils of Jesus walking upon Galilee.

"I've just learnt that I'm a widda," she blurts to him. "*Mon mari est mort, tué par les indiens.*"

May his soul rest in peace, says the priest. You'll want to begin packing my things—I've been recalled to Québec.

Is something wrong?

Perhaps.

He looks eastward over the water, where the lake narrows some to drain into the *Rivière de Saint Laurent*. There are big cities there, Jenny knows, the soldiers in the garrison growing wistful when they speak of Québec or Montreál or even Trois Rivières.

We in the Society of Jesus are soldiers of the Lord, says Père Jérôme. And soldiers do not question their orders.

SHINGAS LISTENS WITH HIS BROTHERS TO THE MORAvian. Christian Friedrich Post is a small and humorless man wearing black clothes, but one who speaks from the heart.

We remember your kindness and friendship upon our arrival, says the Moravian, speaking of the long ago time when the Lenape lived far east of this place, Kuskuski, when they lived on the shores of the Great Water.

We remember how you fed us and taught us how to survive through the first hard winter. The path of friendship was open between us then, and we lived together without strife.

It is not exactly true, of course, the path often blocked by fallen trees and pits full of vipers, the friendship strained by the greed of white men and the whims of the Haudenosaunee. But there have been few periods of killing like the present—

The Governor, and your other Friends in Philadelphia, wish to open this pathway again.

The Moravian only speaks for the Pennsylvanias, and probably not for all of them, but his words must be heard. It is clear the French are losing their struggle with the English, their forts not supplied or kept strong with soldiers, their excuses more and more hollow as the months go by. Warriors cannot hunt for their families, and the French have little food to give, and now that the English have learned to fight and even begun to make their own raids, such as the one at Kittanning—

We wish you to bury the hatchet and raise not your hand against us, we wish you to return to your villages and live in peace as before—

The Moravian speaks Lenape well. Pisquetomen is clearly impressed with him, Pisquetomen who should have been named the headman of the Lenape, or even Beaver, both of them older than their brother Shingas. But Pisquetomen was too strong, and Beaver too wise, and the Pennsylvanias and the Haudenosaunee chose Shingas, thinking he could be more easily controlled. He hopes they know now that this is not possible.

We ask only that you pledge to step away from war and that you return all the white captives you have taken.

And our lands? asks Shingas.

The Pennsylvanias have torn to pieces the paper that was signed in Albany, says Pisquetomen. They no longer claim the lands west of the mountains.

Pisquetomen is respected among the Lenape and not so feared as Shingas among the English. He has never become Pisquetomen the Terrible. He has invited the Moravian to speak with them, the brave little man traveling west into the wilderness with no weapon in hand and only one white companion and his guide, Shamokin Daniel, who skulks in the darkness at the edge of the campfire.

Shingas knows that Daniel tried to betray the Moravian to the French when he spoke to the Indians gathered just across the river from their Fort Duquesne, the French officers present writing his words down and trying to kill him with their eyes.

The French are a broken reed, says Pisquetomen. When General Forbes and his troops come near they will have to abandon their great fort and flee up the river.

It would be better, thinks Shingas, if the Pennsylvanias had sent them this Moravian before the great army of redcoats began to march westward. Though their General Forbes is a sick man, perhaps dying, none believe he will be as foolish as Braddock. He has militia with him who know how to fight, who know enough to get behind a tree if they are being shot at.

Shamokin Daniel watches the talk with a sour look on his face. Last night he was drunk at the campfire, and began to curse the Moravian.

"Damn you," he said in English, "why do you not fight the French on the sea? You come here only to cheat the poor Indians and take their land."

It was impolite and spoken to the wrong person, but there is much truth to his words. The Lenape, in the days of his grandfather Tammany, once lived on the shore of the Great Water, but here they are, far to the west of the Mahoning. How has that happened?

If the path is made open again, says Shingas to the Moravian, will not the English wish to hang me? I have led so many raids, and now that they have killed Captain Jacobs—why would they not wish to complete their revenge?

They are strange people, the Moravians, as serious as the Catholic black robes but not so devious. They love to sing, and wish people to live together and share their wealth, more like Indians than white people.

That was a long time ago, says the Moravian. It is forgotten and wiped away.

Shingas has not forgotten the ones who were killed when they raided Kittanning, and he knows the whites have not forgotten those whose blood he and his warriors have spilled. But the English know that without the Lenape and the Shawnee and the Mingo, the French cannot stand before them. The French are here in Kuskuski, men sent to help build cabins for the winter, and surely have sent a runner to Fort Duquesne telling that the Moravian has arrived and is speaking for peace. But Shingas is not afraid of the French.

There lie many dead bodies between us, he says, uncovered on the ground, which fill our eyes with tears and our hearts with grief so that we can neither see nor speak together till they are put away.

Bodies soon become only bones, says the Moravian, and in time even those are scattered.

I know that the men who join the Pennsylvanias are promised land if they will fight, says Shingas. And I have heard from their great trader himself that they wish to own all that is under our feet.

The Moravian frowns at the mention of Croghan. Beaver has been speaking with the trader in secret, using Delaware George to carry words back and forth.

I would not trust the words of Irish papists, says the Moravian. They speak only with their mouths and not with their hearts.

Not all the Pennsylvanias are like your people, Shingas reminds him. And then there are the Virginias, who thirst for land as a drunkard thirsts for rum. They wish to kill us all and divide our lands among themselves—

This is not so—

You know this is true, but perhaps the Governor has stopped your mouth so that you cannot say it.

If the French had not come into this land, says the Moravian, perhaps believing his own words, we would never have come here. Someone has placed foolish notions in your head.

The Indians who have become Moravians live in the east and wear white people's clothing and sing many times a day. They have become like the white man's cattle, unable to protect themselves. Shingas knows that the Moravian here dreams of a world where all share and live together and there are no wars.

But life is not a dream.

Your nation has always encouraged their poor people to settle on our land, says Shingas. Where one of those people would settle, like pigeons, many would follow, and we were pressured by you and the Haudenosaunee to sell our lands, till we had jumped over the Allegheny hills and settled on the waters of the Ohio. Here we thought ourselves happy! We had plenty of game and a rich and large country that He Who Created All Things had made for Indians and not for white people. And yet your own king gave this land, by signing a paper, to a parcel of covetous white men from Virginia, who came and offered to build forts in our land, no doubt to make themselves masters and we their slaves. And then you sent your General Braddock into the heart of our country, and he spoke with his own lips to me that he intended the white people to take it from us. He was defeated, but now another great redcoat general is on the march, coming toward us, and you speak of opening the path of friendship!

The Moravian listens patiently. They are not ones to anger easily, and do not drink liquor, at least not before other men's eyes—

Brother, says Shingas, you understand from my words why our heart is much afflicted. But there remains a spark of love in it toward our brethren the English. We can drive the French away when we please, but we can never drive you away because you are such a numerous people, as numerous as mosquitos and nits in the woods, and this makes us fear your army and suspect that you covet our lands on the Ohio.

The Moravian weighs his response before speaking.

What would warm your heart toward us, he asks, and put your suspicions to rest?

Send not an army, Shingas tells him, but only five wise white men and their families to live among us. We will care for all their needs, but one should teach us to make gunpowder, another teach us the smelting of lead from ore, another the weaving of cloth blankets, another the making and mending of rifles, and the last the producing of iron. Then we would not need even a trading post of whites within our land.

But then we would never meet—

And therefore never shed each other's blood. Do this, and we will force the French to leave and will never raise the hatchet against the Pennsylvanias again.

The Moravian nods gravely.

I will carry these words, exactly as you have spoken them, to the Governor.

THE BROTHERS GATHER WITH THE OTHER IMPORTANT men, Lenape and Shawnee and Mingo, by the river. Beaver, who is trusted by all and can repeat a council's proceedings speaker by speaker, word by word, tells them of the Moravian's offer.

He speaks only for the Pennsylvanias, adds Shingas. Each of their other colonies is like a tribe, with their own headman and their own desires.

Their army is already marching toward the forks, says the headman of the Mingo.

And they will chase the French away, says Pisquetomen. And once they are inside the fort there they will find a reason not to leave it. But the fact remains that the French are weak in number and do not possess the will of the English. The fact remains that our children are hungry. The fact remains that the militia of the colonies have learned to fight, that their rangers are as dangerous as the Haudenosaunee or the Cherokee and they can come in the night to our villages and slaughter our people. I do not see the future clearly, but I do see that if we continue to support the French, we will be destroyed.

And this about returning all the captives, says the headman of the Mingo. Some we can give, but others we have taken into our families—

The English believe that if you are born white, you are doomed to stay that way forever, says Beaver. It is part of their religion.

The men look to Shingas.

What do you believe?

He thinks before he speaks. There are Lenape, he knows, who live in the east and have learned to lie, who eat and drink with the white politicians and wish to be thought of as powerful leaders, if only by those who see very little. Shingas was made a leader, it is not something he sought—

I believe that no matter what path we take, I will have a rope around my neck, he says. I am Shingas the Terrible.

IT IS NEARLY DARK WHEN THE FRENCH OFFICER FROM Fort Duquesne arrives and asks that they meet him by his fire. He does not mention the Moravian, who Pisquetomen has removed to a safe place, a place that is not comfortable for the Moravian or his protectors, but far enough from the village that they may slap the mosquitos that surround them without fear of being betrayed.

The French officer has brought a wide belt of wampum, which he holds out to them.

As you must know, the English are coming with a great army to destroy both you and me. I therefore desire, my children, that you hasten with all your young men to the forks to help us drive them away forever.

The headman of the Shawnee present, who the English call Captain Peter, takes the belt in his hands.

I have just heard something better from our brethren the English, he says, and will not go with you. But perhaps others of the men here will consent to fight.

He hands it to the headman of the Mingo, who immediately drops it on the ground.

You have boasted often of your fighting—now let us see it. We are tired of losing our young men in your service with barely a crust of bread to show for it.

The warriors then begin to treat the string of wampum as a snake, flipping it at each other with sticks and jumping away that it might not touch them.

The French officer looks to Shingas for help.

Surely you will come to our aid.

If I fight at your side, he says, others of my people will suffer. You and the English began this war—now see if you can finish it yourselves.

THERE IS NO GREETING WHEN THEY ENTER FORT SAINT Jean. Though two of the bastions are made of stone, the soldiers inside are gathered to repair one of the wooden ones, which has rotted in the fetid swamp air. Lieutenant Coustenoble, badly shaven and in a uniform that needs replacing, supervises the work as Jamie and LaCroix introduce themselves.

"*Ils ne m'envoient rien pour nourrir mes hommes,*" grumbles the officer without looking at them, "*il ne reste que peu de poudre sèche, nos uniformes sont en lambeaux.*"

Several of his men are holding long poles, attempting to keep the bastion from collapsing as other men fit new timber beneath it in support—

We ask only for powder and flints to fight the English—

"*Louisbourg se rend, Frontenac tombe, Duquesne est abandonné, et maintenant une armée se dirige vers le Québec*—"

"*Québec? Vraiment?*"

The Lieutenant finally looks at them, seeing a pair of dirty but unpainted *métis.*

Where have you been?

On the frontier, says LaCroix.

Coustenoble shakes his head.

The English have more of everything—men, guns, ships—and now the fucking Indians have deserted us.

But here we are!

He scowls at them.

The Shawnees and the Loups—they have told the English they will fight no more. Even *Shingas le Terrible* has laid down his hatchet.

They scramble backward as there is a loud crack and the superstructure of the bastion falls, soldiers scattering to avoid being crushed. Dust hangs in the air.

"*Merde,*" says the French lieutenant.

THE PLAINS OF ABRAHAM

UNLESS ONE IS BORN A PRINCE IT TAKES A GREAT battle to make a general.

Or to destroy him.

Major General Wolfe—they've elevated him to that rank, but only for the duration of the present campaign as a sop to certain older, politically well-connected, and, if he must be frank, rather incompetent officers—is rowed from his headquarters tent on the Île d'Orleans to the Pointe de Lévis under the eyes of the French entrenchments that line the cliffs on the other side of the river. Well out of rifle range, though receiving a ball in the brainpan at this point might be considered a kindness. The voyage from Louisbourg up the St. Lawrence nearly killed him, the usual nausea with a touch of scurvy as seasoning, and now the damnable gravel again, his bladder in agony and urination a function involving ground glass passing through his member to produce a spray of blood-tinged piss.

And the soldiers are calling him General Pikestaff.

Though Île d'Orleans does not offer a vantage of any great altitude, a decent look at their objective can be had over the masts of his anchored fleet—Quebec, sitting like a crown on the vertiginous headland, its Upper City all gleaming alabaster and gold, the Lower Town, partially hidden behind Cap-aux-Diamants, a hodgepodge of warehouses and poorish cottages. Sounds carry across the water—bugle calls, voices shouting in French, the occasional rattle of drums or rifle practice, all cutting through the constant hissing roar from the Montmorenci falls just downstream. It is a beautiful location, a city worth defending. And if Monsieur General Montcalm is able to prevail over his jealous and militarily suspect governor, Vandreuil, it will prove a hard nut to crack.

The rowers ship oars, and they glide onto the rocky beach. Monckton's American rangers, usually the worst soldiers in the universe, took the heights here just a day ago, though considering the Canadian and savage rabble that faced them this is no great accomplishment, with the brigadier then bringing his entire force, some two thousand men including the bloody company of Highlanders, over to occupy it. Major General Wolfe seized this occasion to have his manifesto posted to the local *hoi polloi*—

> The King of Great Britain does not wage war against the Industrious Peasant, the sacred order of Religion, or defenceless women or children. The people may remain unmolested—but, if by a vain obstinacy and misguided valour they presume to appear in arms, they must expect the most Fatal Consequences; their habitations destroyed, their sacred temples exposed to an exasperated soldiery, their harvest utterly ruined—and thus the miserable Canadians must in the winter have the mortification of seeing the very families for whom they have been exerting but a fruitless and indiscrete bravery perish by the most dismal Want and Famine.

—translated into French by some sort of Huguenot subaltern and sincerely meant to curb the usual looting and sexual depredations attendant with an army of rum fiends and street sweepings, if they will only refrain from making a nuisance of themselves.

Monckton is there to meet him. Chosen by himself, like Brigadier Murray, with no expectations besides loyalty, obedience, and a modicum of sense, Monckton surprised him yesterday by reacting to a rumor of a French counterassault by spreading his command out on this beach to be picked away at by marksmen and cannoneers lodged on anything the French could find to float past them.

"We're ready for you, sir," says Brigadier Monckton with a smart salute. He brings some reputation from the taking of Fort Beauséjour, though consensus has it that the French commandant there was criminally inept, if not openly treasonous. Major General Wolfe was assured, upon accepting this commission, that he would be able to pick his own subordinates, and was able to pass up a goodly number of fossils who would have been head-shaking and tut-tutting his every decision, when decisiveness is half of the battle, not only in defeating the enemy but in maintaining the fear and respect of your own troops.

"Any new opposition?"

"Only some ambuscades, at the edges of our camp. We've had a few men scalped and mutilated."

"By Canadians or savages?"

"It doesn't seem to matter, sir. And my own rangers will miss no opportunity to—"

"Cowardly rascals who dare not show themselves," snarls Wolfe. "From now on, no sentries within rifle shot of the woods."

"We'll have to fell some trees, then—"

"I expect you shall. Shall we take a look?"

The climb is disagreeably steep, the Major General imagining the casualties had the French bothered to place some professional soldiers at the top, and it requires some effort for him to hide his exhaustion. Having pledged his fragile carcass to this endeavor, his dearest hope is that it will not fail him before the Union Flag flies over Quebec. When he arrived back in Halifax there was a letter waiting for him with news that his father had finally given up the ghost. The old man died a Colonel, and surely would have gone higher were it not for so many years of "peace" occasioned by the Treaty of Utrecht during his prime years, and was blessed with a splendid constitution, weakened only by his months spent on fever ships during the follies off Cartagena and Santiago. Not so his eldest son. Slender, pale, with a set of internal organs designed for torment, there is nothing like the ruddy-faced, fleshy picture of health as exemplified by Brigadier Robert Monckton to put Wolfe in an ill humor.

"By my reckoning there are several spots where our guns will be able to reach the Lower Town," says the brigadier.

"Which will do us little good beyond the satisfaction of rendering hellish the lives of the civilian population."

"That, as well as our ability to cut off their supply lines—"

"If we're fated to starve them out, I shall die of either the flux or of boredom in the meantime. We'll have to either draw them out of their fortress or march in and overrun them."

The first seems unlikely—Montcalm no fool, as demonstrated by his success in the attacks on Oswego and Fort William Henry, as well as his defense of Fort Carillon. The second option is truly daunting, with the French dug in on high ground with adequate weaponry and sufficient troops—though four out of five are only Canadian militia—to make any incursion a bloody one.

The French guns on their floating batteries are providing the inconvenience of a constant and rather sloppily scattered bombardment, the sort of thing which no longer causes the Major General to so much as quicken his stride. An officer must seem impervious to flying balls and bits of metal and therefore unconcerned, and if he be mounted his steed must possess the identical *sangfroid*. Townshend, the unsufferable third brigadier who was foisted upon him by Mr. Pitt, was only last night at mess relating the tale of Brigadier General Prideaux, decapitated when he stepped in front of one of his own mortars at Niagara.

"Not the last fellow to lose his head after a rapid promotion," added

Townshend, rather pointedly. The man considers himself a wag and something of a sketch artist, and should be gracing a table at a Fleet Street coffeehouse rather than impersonating a field commander.

The soldiers at the top are busy digging trenches shored up by fascines of new-cut saplings and building boxlike gabions of stone. They appear appropriately miserable, scuttling about with heads ducked and shoulders hunched as the enemy cannonade throws up earth and rock about them, only occasionally dismembering a thoroughly unlucky comrade.

"Those works will serve more for the men than the artillery," Monckton admits. "We're of course waiting for you to choose the optimal venue."

Captain Stobo is brought to him. The Virginia colonial left as an honor hostage at the Fort Necessity fiasco who then smuggled a map of Fort Duquesne out under some long French noses was transported to Quebec and condemned to be executed for illicit correspondence with the enemy, saw that sentence suspended, and then made a daring escape with a few other English prisoners, a woman and two children, that included the commandeering of both a shallop and a schooner in the service of the French and an odyssey up the St. Lawrence all the way to Louisbourg, missing the fleet's departure by only a day.

He is a Scotsman but seems rather intelligent and resourceful.

Wolfe extends his spyglass and sights it on the foremost of the French big guns. Their crews are fussing about the bores of the cannon, a more serious barrage no doubt about to commence.

"Tell me what I'm looking at."

Stobo stands behind the Major General, looking over his shoulder.

"If you've got artillery near the water's edge, that would be the Batterie Royale to the left and the Batterie Dauphine several blocks to the right of it, with wharves and wharehouses separating them. Raising the glass a little you'll see the Bas-Ville—the Lower Town—a good number of warehouses, dwellings of the tradesmen and their laborers, with the old Place Royale and Notre Dame des Victoires smack in the middle of it. As you can see, they've had time to wall up any doorways or windows facing us, add a palisade around the batteries—"

"It won't serve them any advantage."

"I expect not. Moving upstream—that's to the left—"

Wolfe scowls but pans his glass left—

"—you'll see the Sillery Landing, then the sheer cliffs—that's Cap-aux-Diamants, some hundred meters high—"

"You've measured it?"

"A habit I picked up at Fort Duquesne. That's a well-fortified redoubt at the top, and then moving further in the same direction you see Anse-au-Foulons at the base and more precipice—scalable, I suppose, but easily guarded—that if climbed would bring you out onto the Plains of Abraham, to the southwest of the city, with a good deal of open ground to cover before you reach the wall."

"Tell me about the wall," says the Major General, moving his glass to study the Upper City.

"They appear to have extended it a good deal since I left, good solid stone, six meters in height where complete, with plenty of firing embrasures. That wall curves around the back of the Haute-Ville all the way from the top of Cap-aux-Diamants to the bank of the St. Charles River. It's obstructed from your view, but they were building an entrenchment from the Intendant's Palace back to the Hôpital Général along that river—most likely out of our firing range from here—and then more wall on the north side of the river to Beaufort."

"They're all along the crest on that side of the city."

"It's the most likely spot for a landing—the promontory goes up in something like terraces, very convenient if you're carrying heavy cannon. That area is where Montcalm is billeting the majority of his forces—"

"Not inside the walls?"

"There are a few barracks mixed in with the religious edifices, and the gun crews—he's got at least a hundred cannon on that wall—they'll be kept on alert within. But I believe Montcalm is principally concerned with preventing us from coming ashore. A retreat into the Upper Town can be effected rather quickly—I saw them drilling for it."

"You met Montcalm?"

Stobo shakes his head. "Never had the pleasure. But the governor, Vandreuil, who has quite a bit of say in military strategy, interviewed me and presided rather testily at my court-martial."

"Your impression?"

Stobo allows himself a smile. "Vain, pretentious, jealous of his power—extremely *French*, in other words—and not pleased to share the stage with the good general."

Wolfe pushes the spyglass shut, and sees that even more junior officers have arrayed themselves expectantly around Monckton.

"Not here," he snaps and begins to stride away.

The thing about command is that wherever you go, others will follow, perhaps blindly. He uses his *aides de camp*, Smith and Bell, to keep the junior officers away when he wishes to be private, which, truth be known, is most of the time. People find their level, one hopes, and he can think of a dozen officers he's met along the way who have settled comfortably into a rank and never budged from it, their attitude and behavior informing all that "I have arrived, do not expect more from me." Certainly the army would never function if its officers were all strivers like himself, ambition impelling one toward bold maneuvers and ill-advised frontal assaults—but one does appreciate a spot of audacity in a commander. The Major General has never been a gambler, despite the pressure from his fellows to display his dash and fearlessness at the card table, but at some point in this campaign he knows he will have to risk all or be replaced for his irresolution.

If only the chink in the armor, the vulnerable heel of Achilles can be discovered, a way in without losing half his command in the process—

He puts his glass on the French across the river every few minutes, the gaggle of following officers waiting eagerly, and then moves on without comment. They know to keep any suggestions they might have to themselves unless asked.

And he does not ask.

Hangman Hawley was a walking oath, never content to keep his own counsel when he could roar his views to all and sundry like a Cheapside tavern keeper. Mordaunt was ever the gentleman, but a paragon of vacillation, while Ligonier's pet Jeffrey Amherst, phlegmatic but thorough, has the envied talent of finding himself in the most fortuitous place at the proper time. As for his own qualities, the Major General has not met a more energetic or prepared officer than himself in all his service, and has so far enjoyed that combination of pluck and luck that marks a sterling career.

But it will only be judged by the outcome of this venture just begun.

After an hour's stroll and much employment of the spyglass, Wolfe finds the right spot to place the guns, called Pointe-au-Pères, about a mile west of Monckton's headquarters.

"This will do, gentlemen. I trust we'll be making it a good deal warmer for them by tomorrow morning."

Admiral Saunders, in command of the fleet below, has warned Wolfe his ships must be out to sea by early October or risk being iced in and destroyed. It leaves him adequate time to mount an offensive, and he knows that Pitt and the others back home are keeping accounts—a timely victory always less an offense to the treasury than a protracted seige. When he thinks of it all, the ships and their seamen, the tons of artillery, the thousands of troops, all of it under the purview of one frail man, it can seem the very apogee of hubris.

But there is nobody he can think of better fit for the undertaking than Major General James Wolfe.

THERE ARE DEER WHERE HE'S NOT SEEN THEM FOR years. Mature bucks, thick necked from holding up huge racks of antler, does by the dozen, twin-spotted fawns hidden in the tall grass, flighty as ever but so numerous that it's a rare passage through the woods where one does not encounter several, white flagtails erect as they bound away. Their coats are reddish-brown at this time of year, many of the does pregnant, and Eustache can hear them from his cabin at night, feeding on fallen chestnuts and the leaves of the new growth. It is like the Anishinaabe stories his wife remembers from the old men, of how the Creator of All Things made the world and desired it to be.

But the Indians, the Canadian *coureurs de bois,* the French and English soldiers are all too thoroughly engaged in their butchery of each other to hunt.

Eustache watches the three travelers, *métis* by the look of them, walking up the path to his cabin. He is stretching a raccoon skin out on a frame, his rifle primed and within easy reach.

They stop, respectfully, several paces away, and he can see that one of the men, darker skinned, has a bundle of green skins on his back.

"*Bonjour, Monsieur,*" says the lighter skinned man. "*Êtes-vous Eustache?*"

"*Oui, le même.*"

"*Nous avons des peaux à échanger.*"

Eustache nods toward the flat spot where goods are laid out—or were, when there was a regular trade.

"*Voyons les*—"

The woman, who looks not unlike his own Marie-Madeleine twenty years ago, but with a kind of burning resentment in her eyes, lifts the hides off the darker man's back and rolls them out in display. Killed within a day or so, barely treated.

These will be a lot of work, Eustache tells them, without moving to look closer.

We understand that.

And the market—

The market is crying out for deerskin, gloves to be made, vellum, breeches even, but as for finding a merchant ship heading back to France—

—well, there's no way to get them to the market, with the English all about our ears.

They've been here?

The lighter man, intent.

They've been close enough.

Marie-Madeleine is boiling a stew inside, fragrant with juniper berries, and if these were people he was ever likely to meet again he'd invite them to eat. They can't be starving, and must have left a good deal of meat behind for the scavengers.

We only want some powder and shot, says the darker man.

From their tattoos he's guessing Lenape, but there are so many different tribes up here now, hoping for scalps or booty, it is hard to say. They are at least not fucking Mohawks. Marie-Madeleine will be stirring the pot with a stick in one hand and a hatchet in the other, listening to the parley.

Eustache nods, puts the raccoon down and lifts a small wooden barrel of black powder.

You can have what's left in this. The fucking militia came through and found my shot when they searched the cabin.

They just took it?

He shrugs.

There's a war on. Nobody in a uniform thinks they have to pay.

The lighter man takes the powder.

Where were they headed?

"Au Québec, comme le monde entier."

That's where they're coming together?

The final stand. If Québec falls—well, I hope you can speak some English.

The men kneel and carefully transfer the powder from the barrel into their leather pouches. The woman, who is as beautiful as Marie-Madeleine was, wears a gold ring on her finger like a white woman. He shudders to think who was slaughtered to obtain it.

"*Y a-t-il un grand fort au Québec?*" she asks him.

The whole city is a fort, he tells her. And once you go inside it you won't be able to leave. Like the trap I caught this raccoon with.

There are more panthers now, he and Marie-Madeleine hear them coughing and screaming at night, with plenty to feed on. In different times they would be trapped as well, for their hides and to keep them from killing the fawns and yearlings. There is a balance to these things, and a trader must always be aware of how the scale is tipping—

The woman nudges the green skins with her foot.

If we carried these to Québec, they'd give us a lot more.

Eustache laughs.

In Québec, he tells her, they're only buying scalps.

SOMETHING IN THE AIR HERE IS TRYING TO SMOTHER him. Colonel de Bougainville breathed perfectly on the ocean passage, equally well coming down the Saint Laurent, and yet at the first sight of the jewel upon the heights that is Québec he felt a thickening in his chest, and by the time he had climbed to the Haute-Ville and the Governor's Palace he was red faced and wheezing. There is no science to suggest it, but perhaps the bearing of disappointing news—

If one's house is on fire, they had told him in Paris, one does not worry about the barn.

And so his return to the now-besieged city with barely a fraction of the troops and supplies Général Montcalm had thought vital to retaining possession of the great north territory, his return to the miasma of envy and distrust that lies between the governor and the general, to the moral cesspool where a prominent citizen much in debt to the avaricious M. Bigot through indiscretions at the gaming tables has been granted the commission to provide for the uprooted *acadiens*, then allowed to redirect the government monies given him for their care to settle his obligation to the Intendant, while dozens of the poor souls have starved or frozen to death over the last hard winter.

De Bougainville puts his mouth over the ceramic jar and breathes in, slowly and deeply. There are various substances recommended by the friendly *sauvages* that have been boiled within it, principally the oils of peppermint and wintergreen. The action induces a pleasant sensation in his throat and chest, and he wonders if soaking a rag in the concoction might allow him to enjoy it outside the tent. If other officers may indulge in snuff—

The tribes, which remain friendly only in proportion to the gifts and promises they receive, have proven to be a necessary evil in this vile campaign, as indispensable in the thick woods as cavalry horses on an open plain. They are probably no more cruel or capricious than the minions of the Great Khan, though certainly more difficult to lead, deciding from day to day—no, from moment to moment—to follow their own leaders or not, and certainly without loyalty to something as abstract to them as the French crown. The spirit of independence thus permeating the air seems contagious, the Canadian militia and even many of the regular soldiers brought from home intoxicated by it, discipline and order become a nightmare to maintain.

Perhaps that's what's been compromising his lungs here.

Montcalm has given him the five grenadier companies, Duprat's volunteers, three light companies of regulars, and a few militia, plus the men he has posted at likely disembarking places along the shore. It is a game with Monsieur Wolfe's troops as he moves them up and down the river, each large redeployment needing to be countered, movement upon the land slower or equal to that on the English barges depending on tide and current. Two great beasts huffing and feinting at each other, one of greater size but the other with a secure and elevated den to retreat to, each tiring of the display, each consuming massive amounts to sustain themselves each day, the countryside stripped. De Bougainville, a student of human nature as well as mathematics and the sciences, cannot imagine the English grandees in London being any less niggardly than his own superiors in France. Wolfe will be forced to make a move, a massive commitment, and soon.

Nothing like a full-on battle to clear the air.

IT WAS TRULY WONDERFUL BEFORE THE BOMBS STARTED falling. St. Cyr's friends who had been there and even some who had not used to go on about Paris, but Jenny can't imagine it can be grander than Québec's Haute-Ville was in the spring when the English armada and the troops it brought up the Saint-Laurent were only rumors. The buildings of the religious orders—Jesuits, Recollects, Ursuline and Augustinian nuns, the bishopric and the Cathedral, the Seminary with its lovely gardens—seemed palaces to her even before she viewed the governor's mansion within Fort Saint Louis and the sumptuous *résidence* of the Indendant, where dwells the very Monsieur Bigot who everyone at Fort Beauséjour had a story about. And private houses with carriages waiting in front of them, restaurants and coffee shops and bakers and tailors, all embraced within the curtain of masonry wall that is still being put up even as the shells burst and the fires are never quite extinguished. London has the wonderful bridge and some impressive buildings where you are brought to be condemned, but it was smoky and dirty, full of people who looked as poor as Highland crofters and not half as hale. Fort-Royal and Saint Pierre on Martinique are colorful miniatures, fashioned more with thatch and bamboo than with stone, likely to blow away in a high wind. Philadelphia she passed through in a wooden coffin. But this, even if she has had to find poorer lodging in the crooked streets of the Bas-Ville, is a *city*.

Upon arrival Père Jérôme passed her off onto the canonesses of St. Augustine, who have decided she is a somewhat reformed prostitiute.

You're doing very well, says Soeur Béatrice whenever they pass in the corridor at the Hôpital Général, where all the healing has moved now that both the Hôtel-Dieu and the Ursulines' Chapel are under fire.

Our Father rejoices in a lost lamb reclaimed, says Soeur Jonquille when they make beds together, and the *Mère Supérieure* will pat her back and whisper, "*Tu es pardonnée, mon enfant*," at least once a day.

The source for this idea must be Soeur Hortense, one of the youngest of the nuns, who was raised in Martinique. She must have heard of Jenny and St. Cyr there, and the story has grown legs. Despite their pity and condescension, living with the sisters is pleasant, and despite the cannonade from Pointe de Lévis across the river and now from the Montmorenci heights as well, day and night, she feels strangely—*safe*.

The good Lord protect us, the *Mère Supérieure* will mutter, crossing herself each time one of the explosions shakes the ground beneath their feet or looses a dusting of plaster onto their wimpled heads.

The good Lord, thinks Jenny, St. Cyr's words coming to her with a smile, with the aid of a well-managed battery of twenty-five pounders.

IT IS HOT WORK FOR THE CREWS, SERVING THE PORT guns now, Briggs somehow able to see all the cannon on the middle gun deck at once without ever moving his head, listening to their ministrations, perhaps, and then waiting for the slightest upward roll of the hull before shouting fire!, the deck above expected to be ready to follow immediately. There is no time to stick one's head out the gunport to assess the effect of the cannonade—their fellows on the top deck will cheer when something that will inconvenience the French has been hit—and any gunner not already deaf as a post will soon be rendered so. The bores are elevated to their maximum, unusual in a ship-to-ship battle but appropriate if bombarding a redoubt dug in up on a promontory. When the muzzles become dangerously hot, Briggs will send a runner up to the captain and they will come around to give the starboard twenty-five some glory.

The French are firing back, of course, but a ship of the line might as well be a scrap of flotsam in this great river, whereas every burst from the *HMS Centurion* is bound to hit something above, and they can hear their huge land-based guns on the other side of the Montmorenci River contributing to the assault. There was a strange hiatus at four bells, afternoon watch, the men allowed to sit, dripping with sweat, waiting for the order to resume that came nearly an hour later. It has been explained that they had run out of projectiles and a new supply was being ferried out on one of the landing rafts. They've been going at it since early this morning, two transports, the *Russell* and the *Three Sisters* loaded with infantrymen having been grounded in the shallows, waiting for the tide to drop enough to send them into the beach on longboats. The channel has proven much shallower than predicted, their ship having to stay out a good thousand yards from the shore, which will certainly diminish the effectiveness of their labors. Why after so many weeks of observation and pointless maneuver have not the great minds in charge of this venture foreseen these obstacles? Perhaps not worth pondering, with the cannon such insatiable monsters that thought itself must be postponed for quieter moments—

Briggs is a markedly unemotional fellow, his air of distance perhaps a function of his inability to hear anything not explosive, but every now and then as they are swabbing, loading, ramming, running the guns back into place, there will escape from his lips something like a shout of joy.

"Feed the beast, lads!" he will roar. "'Ee's always keen fer more!"

"IT'S ABOUT BLOODY TIME, BERT, IS ALL I'VE GOT TER SAY."

They have been rowed back and forth providing target practice for the French artillery for at least three hours now, from one grounded transport to another, while the enemy militia on the steep hill above them duck under a constant but rather loosely scattered barrage and their anemic, slender reed of a commander, Major General Wolfe, decides whether to go through with the planned mass assault or call it a day.

"Hit's the *tide*, Reg. When the tide is too 'igh there's not sufficient beach fer us ter muster up on before we climb to the top and make short work of them froggos."

"If they call this one off I've a mind ter jump out and swim ashore—"

"Never keep yer powder dry that way, Reg."

"Little do they care. We'll be wading in with our muskets 'eld over our 'eads and the water up ter our chinstraps, you mind me. Military genius, that's what's lacking 'ere."

"The French've got all the natural hadvantages on us, primarily the 'igh ground. Just think if you was up there on the 'ill, Reg, lookin' down at 'undreds of redcoats waiting ter come ashore—"

"Fer eight bloody hours—"

"What would yer sentiments be regarding the impending hexchange of 'ostilities?"

Cruikshank thinks for a moment. Scores of them are squashed together in the boats like tinned sardines, the day humid with a grumbling threat of storm, having sweated through their unseasonably heavy uniforms and forbidden, by sergeant's orders, to remove their mitred hats even to wipe their brows.

"*Eager,*" he says finally. "I'd feel eager ter get the bloody circus started, is what, after all the nonsense that's come before. Maybe the frogs aint weak-kneed from the flux and attacked by fecking black flies day and night and afraid ter step inter the bushes to do a man's business at the risk of 'is scalp being lifted, but I'll wager ye they'd like ter get it over one way or the other."

There is a signal from the grounded *Russell* and suddenly the cox has his navvies pulling for the shore.

"What's this?"

"From what I sees, there don't appear ter be much more beach than an hour ago."

"Second thoughts, is it?"

"I'll tell ye true, Bert, if we don't get ter shoot some Frenchies terday, I'd settle fer that lot of Royal bloody Americans in the next boat."

"Now, now—"

"Ye know our fellow cut theirs up pretty badly—"

There had been a duel last night, sabers, their Captain Octerlony engaged with a presumptuous German named Wetterstrom of the colonial regiment. Blood had been drawn almost simultaneously and the seconds able to rush in to declare honor satisfied before either combatant was rendered unfit for today's duty. The two groups have been pitching their tents alongside each other since the move to Pointe Lévis, and the heat, flies, bad food and interminable waiting—which under Major General Wolfe entails hours of drilling and makework projects—have helped the usual ribbing between units escalate into a dullish mutual hatred.

"And they called us *scare*crows, Bert, too bloody stupid ter lay down or take a tree if we're hambushed—"

"They 'aven't 'ad the bennyfit of our many years of hexperience, is all. We'll see 'ow they fare when we stroll up this little slope ahead. Not a blade o' grass ter 'ide behind."

For they are indeed coming to shore, closer, closer—the bottom of the boat scraping onto a shoal well short of it—

"All out!" shouts Sergeant Miles. "'Old yer muskets 'igh, lads!"

"I told ye so, Bert."

"We're already soaking wet, Reg. It'll be a relief."

"I'll be relieved when I'm back in Brixton tossing an ale down my throat—"

They wade in on their toes, muskets and powder boxes held as high as possible, the water level moving up to their next-to-last button before it begins to drop, while taking less harrying gunfire than they were in the longboat.

"They're coming out of that redoubt, Bert—"

"Out the *back* end of it, if my eyes don't trick me. Must 'ave 'eard you and me is in the vanguard, Reg."

"If they're going ter run, they 'ad better keep going—"

Some of the Royal Americans from another boat reach the shore first, waving their hats and, in a few cases, their posteriors at the grenadiers.

"Cheeky bastards."

"I don't fancy follerin' in their wake."

The footing on the rocky beach is firm enough that they are able to muster quickly into formation, each new boatload swelling their number. The taunting from the Royal Americans continues and the drummers from each contingent are rattling away now, stirring the blood, and banners are raised and neither Private Cruikshank nor Private Kirby is certain they actually hear an order to charge but suddenly they have fixed their bayonets to their muskets and are trotting, no, running as fast as their equipment will allow toward the rocky cliff ahead and the enemy who wait at the top of it, cheering as the heavens crack and it begins to rain, rushing pell-mell into the fray they've been told will end this war—

THE LAND ITSELF IS THE ENEMY, THINKS WOLFE FOR THE hundredth time today, for the thousandth time since they sailed under the guns of Quebec. He is in command of a great number of very good troops, while Monsieur Montcalm can count on a great deal fewer and of dubious quality, but the Frenchman has the land and today even the bloody *tide* to protect him. It is apparent to the Major General, as he wields his glass on board the *Russell*, that the French positions on the slopes above the redoubt are a good deal closer and more numerous than he had thought. Yes, Monckton is landing his people from Pointe Lévis now and Townshend, if his incompetence does not exceed his impertinence, should be bringing his across the Montmorenci below the falls to reinforce, but the advance party of grenadiers and Royal Americans have taken the cheese and are now caught in the trap, having bolted up to overrun the abandoned redoubt like a rabble of amateurs. Hidden in smoke on the heights above, the entrenched French militia fire round after round down upon them, the *Centurion* and the big guns across the Montmorenci silent now, useless to return fire without hitting their own men. What had seemed a bold if decidedly risky plan, the concerted attack of a weak point with three coordinated forces, is now revealed to have been folly even in concept.

Oh, the grenadiers and Royal Americans, if any survive, will feel his wrath, but the blame is not theirs. The pressure to act, to appear decisive, and too much consideration given to his restless subordinates have brought him to this. The prudent course, given the immutable power of the geography, would be to starve them out, to wait for Amherst to take Montreal and Trois Rivières, to choke off French shipping in the St. Lawrence, to continue to reduce the farms and townships up and down the river to ashes. But that would require much more time and much greater expenditure—Mr. Pitt has ordered a victory won with the blood of Englishmen, not with the gold in the King's Treasury.

Hervey Smythe is beside him, a question perched on his furrowed brow.

"Send somebody to turn that idiot Townshend around before the river's too high to cross back over, and have them prepare to row me in," says the Major General. "If we must retreat, it shall be with order."

THE BLOODY HIGHLANDERS WON'T MOVE. THEY HAVE hurried back along the beach to the ford, the water rising and current gaining force, and yet here stands Brigadier Townshend in the rain, rapping his walking stick against the side of his boot while Fraser is hustled over to him.

"What seems to be the problem, Colonel?"

The erstwhile Master of Lovat salutes him. There is some resemblance to Hogarth's wonderful portrait of the Auld Fox, but the son's face bears none of the cunning, none of the joyful wickedness. Intelligent enough, perhaps, and stubborn as any "North Briton" is wont to be—

"Sir, Ah cannae leave ma people ahind."

"Those who have been killed or wounded will—"

"Them who've been left on the *boot*, sir. The one as was run aground this morn."

"Ah."

The *Russell* and the *Three Sisters*, having both been battered a good deal by enemy artillery, will not float for another hour or more, and must certainly be put to the torch before they are abandoned.

Townshend sighs, turns to his runner. "Carruthers, hop down

to the beach, would you, and ask Major General Wolfe if he would please order that the men on both of the catboats be ferried back to safety. There's a good lad."

The boy sprints away and Townshend looks back to the Highlander, who he knows to be capable of weaning the Scotch from his discourse in other circumstances.

"May we proceed?"

"When Ah keek them oot of the water—"

Townshend was Cumberland's *aide de camp* when he issued the orders at Culloden Moor—no prisoners. The story is that this particular Fraser—Simon, son of the notorious beheaded Lord—arrived too late at the battle to be inconvenienced by the Duke's edict. And as the geography of the Highlands rendered complete extermination untenable—

Wolfe himself was one of the authors of the current experiment, allowing these hillskippers to once again carry a weapon, wear their tartans, gargle their excuse for a language, and torture the air with their execrable pipes if willing to fight for the King—on foreign soil, of course—with the addendum that it "would be no great mischief" if most were destroyed in the process. They have proved willing, even eager soldiers, no slackers at Louisbourg when the lead was flying. But once a rebel—

"I applaud your concern for your countrymen, Colonel, but you do understand that the tide is rising, and that if we're to be able to ford the river—"

"We'll stay ahind and wait fer them, if need be."

"You'll do nothing of the sort.. An order has been passed, and your people in the boats will be accommodated. You will join the rest of us in our march back to camp."

Fraser considers this order a mite too long.

"May I remind you at this moment, Colonel Fraser, how fortunate you are that I am not Major General Wolfe?"

And then there is the smile, the Auld Fox's smile just as Hogarth had drawn it, making Townshend wish he had his own pen and ink handy.

"Extremely fortunate, sir," says the grinning Scotsman, "and may Ah say that it's yer maist admirable quality."

YOU'RE NOT ONE OF THEM, SAYS THE YOUNG *COUREUR de bois* with a shoulder that has been smashed by a ball, staring up at her. Jenny has not spoken, and assumes he means she's not a nun.

And you're not one of *them*, she replies, wiping some of the paint near the wound off with a wet bit of cloth. Canadian men will go out with Indians, dressed in their fashion, bare-chested with painted bodies and faces. The word has filtered back that the English general Wolfe has declared such combatants to be eligible for scalping by his troops, but the custom has not been abandoned.

I grew up with the Abenaki, he says, attempting to smile. He lies on a pallet on the floor with two dozen French and militia waiting to be brought in to the surgeon. In another wing lie the English and Americans wounded and captured after their disastrous rush today, fortunate only in that they were dragged aside before the Langlade's Ottawas could knock them on the head.

That's no excuse, says Jenny, able to see that the young man's shoulder is not blue from paint but from the mortification. Can you lift that arm?

I'd rather not. What are you?

At the moment I'm your nurse.

You're not French.

Neither are you.

You're not Canadian, either.

That's true.

After a while you stop thinking about it, says the *coureur de bois*.

You skin a man's head as easily as you skin a deer. The English have got the habit now, and the American rangers—

Are you a Catholic?

Yes.

And what do your priests say?

This time he manages a real smile, gritting his teeth.

They tell us that to protect our land and our people from the evil of Protestantism, anything is permitted.

The Bas-Ville has been evacuated for days, the warehouses burned, the Place Royale and Notre Dame des Anges only shells now, and even the Cathedral in the Haute-Ville has collapsed. Before the English arrived General Montcalm encouraged those with no stomach for a siege and somewhere else to go to leave Québec, and many did. But now every gate to the city has been barricaded except the Palace Gate that sits across from where the pontoon bridge over the St. Charles River was, and that is impossible to leave through without a *laissez-passer.* When citizens protested, Montcalm threatened them with the Indians, which has caused a good deal of tension between the Canadian militia, who are itching to go tend to their harvests, and the French regulars, who are stuck here and relieved that the English have finally grown the testicles required to attack them.

Jenny hands the young man a scrap of deer hide.

Bite on this if it hurts you too much.

Soeur Béatrice passes carrying a full bucket of bloody water from the surgery.

You are an inspiration to us all, she beams and waddles past Jenny.

The captured soldiers do not seem inspired when she enters their waiting place.

"Is there any of ye kens this fella?" she asks as she stands over a redcoat who has died, bleeding out on the straw beneath him.

"'Ee was in my company," says a man with a shattered kneecap. "Grenadiers."

"Ye ken his name?"

The man ponders for a moment with no result.

"Replacement, 'ee was, joined us at 'Allyfax. The sergeant only called 'im 'ye bloody eedjit' and things iv that sort."

"Well, he's deid noo."

"Yer a Scotswoman."

"Of a sort, aye," says Jenny, cautiously moving down the row of casualties, tasked with putting them in some kind of order of desperation.

"But ye've joined a French convent."

"It's calt a vocation," she says. "Yer taken by the Holy Spirit."

"But yer not wearin' the whatchercallit—the 'abit."

"Mine was covered with bluid," she lies. "Which is wont tae upset the sufferers."

They have given her small squares of cloth with numbers written on them, and she pins them to their clothes, a young, deathly pale militiaman holding his hand over his throat receiving Number One.

"Do I get oner them?" asks the grenadier.

"Ye'll be ane of the last tae be seen. There's plenty worse aff here, as ye can witness."

The grenadier looks around at his gory comrades.

"We lost our 'eads, is all. Sawr them Frenchies up on the 'ill, calling down ter us, gasconading about 'ow we was too timid ter come and get them, and—well—the lads didn't wait fer an order ter charge. We took the 'ill, too, right smart we did, and then every Jacques and Pierre on the 'igher ground around us starts shooting as fast as 'e can pack 'is powder down. We didn't turn our backs, I'll say that much fer discipline, but we was drove down that 'ill with 'alf our number gone ter glory. A fatal hexcess of enthusyasm is all it was."

"Ye'll no have tae fight anymair," says Jenny, pinning a number in the twenties on his lapel.

"And what use am I, then?"

"Ye've been a sojer fer a lang weel?"

"Before the first 'air sprouted on me chin."

"Ye'll have stories tae tell."

"Aye, in the poor'ouse."

He watches as Jenny spreads more hay on the floor. With the constant bombardment and patrols from both sides lurking about at night, there are always more wounded.

"Yer bound ter be defeated, ye know," says the grenadier, softly. "Sooner or later."

There has been much grumbling among the *habitants* about Governor Vandreuil and General Montcalm waiting, only waiting for the English attack, while the enemy seem to be on all sides of them, shifting hundreds of men on boats from one point to another every day. The news that has managed to be smuggled through enemy lines is not encouraging—forts Carillon, Saint-Frédéric, and Niagara have all been taken by the English, and no new troops have left France as reinforcement. People are limited to two ounces of bread a day, when available, while Bigot still entertains lavishly in his palace. Jenny has never met a king, and never hopes to, but imagines them as spoiled and overgrown children, playing with toy boats and lead soldiers on a map of the world, while here over the water the Hôpital Général has to use the stables to accommodate all the dead and the dying caught in their game.

"And I hope ye see that day if it cooms," Jenny tells him.

The grenadier listens for a moment, the thudding and explosions crushing what's left of the Haute-Ville before them. The Augustinians are a contemplative order, and three times a days the sisters kneel with eyes closed and palms pressed together, the concussions of the artillery shells rattling the pews in the little chapel connected to the hospital. Jenny's jaw aches from grinding her teeth whenever she is conscious, and she is not sure if she dreams of explosions or they are just outside the supply room they are using for a bedchamber.

"We're safe 'ere?" he asks.

"Aye, fer noo. Yer guns cannae reach sae far."

He nods, then glances down at his bloodied leg.

"D'ye think they'll cut it off?"

"Ah'm no a surgeon," she says. "But Ah ken that aince yer on the table, they dinnae care what colors ye wear. It's a' just arms an legs."

The grenadier considers this, and then he is weeping.

An exploding shell hits closer than usual, and plaster dust sifts down upon them.

"Ma best mate was kilt today," says the redcoat. "Shot through the 'ead. 'Is name was Reggie."

"Ah'm sorry tae hear it," says Jenny, and realizes that she, surprisingly, is telling the truth.

The redcoat shrugs his shoulders, wipes his eyes on his sleeve. "Hit's what we're made fer."

MASONRY AND DUST FLY IN THE AIR ABOVE THEIR heads as a cannonball smashes through what's still standing of a tall cathedral building, the stone already blackened by fire. Jamie, Ange, and LaCroix run with their heads bent low, following a dozen Mi'kmac warriors led by a Canadian in buckskins. They hurry around a corner, and before trotting away he indicates that they are to sit in the little courtyard in front of a barracks miraculously undamaged by the endless barrage. The Indians look at the buildings around them, some with actual holes through their walls and none with a roof intact, and mutter unhappily. The courtyard is littered with debris, and French regulars in dirty uniforms and provincial militia wearing rags enter and exit the barracks without a glance at them.

Our father was here once, says LaCroix, looking around. He said there were buildings cased in gold.

An explosive shell lands, perhaps a block away, and Jamie feels his body lifted off the paving stones.

Do you think they'll feed us? asks Ange.

There might not be much left to eat, Jamie tells her. Ange has been complaining of hunger since they left Fort Saint Jean, eating as much as him and LaCroix combined whenever something is available. He wonders if it is her way of protesting the decision to stay north.

Another small group of warriors is led to them, Shawnee by their scalp locks. From his gait Jamie recognizes Bone and is relieved to see Lachlan still breathing, though not versifying beneath the hammering of the English artillery. He grins when he sees Jamie—

"And haven't they hanged ye yet?"

"Tis the Shawnee Prophet himsel'."

"If Ah could keek the future, Ah doot Ah'd have come here."

Jamie stands, and the men embrace. Bone nods coolly to Jamie, then sits with his warriors to wait.

"Ye've come far," says Jamie.

"We were forty miles short of Philadelphia when it a' went tae shite."

Jamie sits again. "They've telt me that Shingas has made peace with the English."

"Aye, and maist of the Shawnee as well." Lachlan nods to Bone. "Present company exceptit."

He looks Jamie over. LaCroix traded his looking glass in at Trois Rivières for a sack of corn and some stomach powders for Ange, and there is not an unbroken window in Québec for Jamie to find his reflection in.

"There's a price on yer heid, Jamie."

"I trust it's considerable."

"Twa hunnert pounds fer the Dellyware renegade knane as Long Knife."

A French officer approaches the sitting warriors.

"*Bon après-midi, mes amis*—"

Lachlan cocks his head. "And where have Ah seen this froggo afore?"

I thank you for coming to join us, says the officer, bowing slightly. Which of the great chiefs are here?

A moment of silence, then Lachlan answers him in Erse—

The great chiefs died at Culloden.

The officer stares at him for a moment, stunned, then laughs, answering in Erse as well.

They did, God bless their souls.

"Ye were with the Perthshire men in the second line—"

It is clearly not a pleasant memory for the gentleman. "I fought that day with MacDonald of Glengarry's, on the left. He fell beside me."

He bows again. "Chevalier Guillaume de Johnstone—*a votre service*."

There are three quick crashes, iron balls smashing into a nearby building, and then Bone's harsh voice croaks a challenge.

De Johnstone looks to Lachlan.

"He'd like tae noo why he's been led tae be trapped within these walls."

"Ah. Tell him we're gathering as many of you people as we can to fight under Monsieur Chartier, the *métis* gentleman from the lakes."

Bone snorts when he hears Chartier's name, mutters something, and rises to lead his men away.

"Not pleased, is he?"

"He says to let him know when there are some white men to kill."

THERE HAS BEEN A HIATUS IN DRAWING THE MAJOR General. At the beginning of the campaign his scarecrow body and pallid skin, his red hair worn unpowdered, his lack of chin, his strange gait, and his insufferable condescension invited—no, de*mand*ed a satirist's brush—the man is a walking caricature, for God's sake. But for the week after the failed landing when Townshend and the other senior officers attempted to divine meaning from the surgeon's hangdog countenance as he emerged from Wolfe's cabin—was their commander dead, dying, delirious, only vaguely aware of his own identity and mission?—further lampooning would have been in poor taste. He is back, though, if not the picture of health, at least ambulatory and capable of human discourse.

Not that any of *that* will be encouraged.

Wolfe himself is easy by now, Townshend feeling he could render him with his eyes shut—the ferret face, pipestem legs, exaggerated (only slighty, mind you) queue of reddish hair sticking out behind his head—but the others will take some effort, and he will eventually be required to gaze into a looking glass for an honest assessment of his own less remarkable countenance. Tis but a tiny curve to the lips—there, now—to capture the Major General's most common expression. How would one characterize it—pique? Irritation? A frank disenchantment with his own inadequacies?

Ah—dis*dain*.

It is difficult to recall a person or situation the Major General was ever heard to approve of, his low opinion of creatures other than himself varying only in degree of aversion. He solicits no advice, and then chides you for lack of initiative, he is quick to criticize with either a haughty barb or dismissive glance, ill-tempered with even his closest aides, energetic to the point of frenzy, and at the moment just returned from death's parlor to agree, of all things, on an assault plan not of his own devising. Whether it is the fiasco of his previous attack, more than four hundred casualties suffered before disengagement was effected, or the impregnable quality of the enemy's situation that has led him to this concession is hard to say—however, once accepted, he has immediately banished his subordinates from any involvement in the details of the operation. Townshend has taken to interrogating his junior officers as to what rumors are circulating in the camp, as Wolfe is wont to occasionally blurt some hint of his intent to the stray lieutenant fortunate enough to be present when he has an idea.

The drawings have been an excellent diversion, a manner of flushing thoughts and emotions Townshend can otherwise express only in his letters home to his wife—but it was admittedly not prudent to share them in the officers' mess. That the moronic Captain Benchley would believe the Major General would be equally amused by his satiric portraiture and show him one of the more scathing of the drawings passed around—a panel from his homage to Hogarth entitled "*A Prig's Progress*"—could not have been foreseen, and Townshend's relation with his superior officer has quickly fallen from an attitude of glacial forbearance to one of undisguised loathing. Fair enough. But there is a battle to fight, a war to be won, and as a brigade commander some clue of what is being cooked up for a do-or-die offensive would be appreciated.

Here's Monckton to a T—the multiple chins, the phlegmatic corpus, the air of genial fellowship—he is an annoyingly decent chap—following the leader with his arms stretched out for balance.

Since the Major General's miraculous recovery, companies have been sent out daily to punish the civilian inhabitants of the region, Wolfe furious that the *habitants* have not taken his posted manifestos to heart, instead hiding their hard-won foodstuffs from foraging troops, failing to inform upon their countrymen or somehow dissuade the various bands of savages attached to the French command from their atrocities.

Or perhaps he just needs to punish somebody.

Murray is not a challenge—the narrow, envious phiz of the Scot, the hawk's beak, the willingness to be led, if grudgingly, into the next folly, a trait notably exhibited in his defense of Sir John Mordaunt after the abortive raid on Rochefort.

Another of Wolfe's brilliant conceptions.

It is a sickening mode of combat, this scorched-earth bullying, and Townshend will be jubilant when he is released from it. In Belgium, yes, there were civilians forced to flee, some even killed when caught in a crossfire or lingering too long in a town marked for bombardment. But this entire affair—the wholesale murder on the Pennsylvania frontier, the constant ambush by Indians or Canadians dressed as Indians, their own American rangers swaggering about with scalps hanging from their belts, the forced exodus of the Acadian farmers—if this is to be modern warfare, he will seek to change profession.

Now the self-portrait—unfair to temper the acid in the pen when you've applied it to others. Not the fittest officer of the King's infantry, nor the most prepossessing, but a gentleman, a viscount-in-waiting, and, despite a shorter battlefield *resumé,* a creditable tactician. But here blindfolded, as are his fellow brigadiers.

The year has run out on them, and it is truly "now or never." Admiral Saunders is rightfully adamant that his ships must leave soon or be crushed in winter ice, over a third of the men are too sick for combat with more falling ill each day—whatever Townshend's misgivings about the Major General, he does not envy the fellow. He saw Wolfe only this morning, pale as a ghost, feverish eyes fixed on something just ahead, passing by him without a word or a glimmer of recognition.

His few utterances regarding tomorrow's apocalypse, wherever he has chosen the initial landing to occur, have made one thing very clear—Wolfe doubts the gamble will succeed but is prepared, perhaps even looking forward to dying in the attempt to pull it off.

One of his better pieces, in all objectivity, as he blows upon it to dry the ink. The determined beanpole of a Major General striding forward with three desperate, blindfolded brigadiers stumbling after—*The Deaf Leading the Blind.*

Wolfe is resigned to his doom. All that is left to discover, thinks Townshend, is how many of us he'll take with him.

IF YOU CLIMB ONTO THE PARAPET YOU CAN SEE THE flashes from the English batteries across the river, can remind yourself that it is not natural for incendiary bombs to fall out of the sky day and night, that there is somebody out there with fixed intention to kill you. Jamie has gone up twice, needing that reassurance, as it has been difficult in the last few days to pinpoint exactly what he is meant to be doing here. Fighting, killing, has become a state of being, as constant and unquestioned as the weather. On calm days one is either seeking or fleeing from the enemy. On stormy days actual blood is being shed. There have been a few instances of strategy, if not reflection, where a plan to kill is considered, but more often it has been a kind of wandering with intent to kill, if one targeted farm or village is too well protected for attack the one a half mile down the river serves just as well.

I am a warrior, he was able to tell himself at the beginning, and my people have been forced to raise the hatchet. And then, for what he is sure were very practical reasons, most of the great men in his tribe have settled with the English and stepped away from the path of war.

Yet he fights on.

They walk along the base of the wall, exhausted French soldiers barely noticing them, their way lit by fires in the Haute-Ville that nobody has bothered to put out. Jamie follows after Ange and LaCroix, trying to convince them to stay for the final battle.

We have come all this way, he says.

And it will be a long journey home, says LaCroix. We don't want to be caught by the first snow.

Neither do the English. They'll have to attack soon, within days, or leave in their ships.

They'll be back the next year, then.

Not if they suffer a great defeat.

LaCroix seems not so much frightened as disoriented, as if the world he understands has ceased to exist.

I've heard that the English have cannibal women fighting for them, he says.

Cannibals—?

Warriors who wear skirts and eat the men they kill.

People are afraid. They make up stories.

I also am afraid, says LaCroix. The French soldiers—if they survive to surrender they'll be put on a ship and sent back to their country. What will the English do to me?

We gave our word—

LaCroix turns to face him, firelight glittering in his eyes. They treat me like a dog. I am their dirty half-breed son! Why should I die for them?

Ange, who has grown heavier and more sullen every day here, stands behind her brother.

Maybe that's what you wish, she says to Jamie. To be put on a boat to France. You probably have a woman there.

Jamie holds his arms out.

And what French woman would have me? Look at me—

I *am* looking, says Ange.

Jamie realizes too late that what he's said is an insult. He looks like a Lenape warrior. He looks like Ange and LaCroix. He touches the cat and turtle tattoos on his chest.

These spirits are at war within me, he says. And right now the one that is stronger tells me I must stay and fight. They killed my brother, took my land, they rule over my people—

Ange nods, understanding.

You love the dead more than you love me.

"*Bonne chance, mon frére,*" says LaCroix, taking Jamie's arm for a moment, then he and Ange climb over the parapet and are gone into the night.

THE COURTYARD IS LIT BY TORCHES, WARRIORS OF various tribes sitting and sleeping on the dirty blankets they've spread out on the ground. Lachlan sits with Bone and the small party of Shawnee left, while he can see the Ottawa Pontiac and two dozen of his people gathered around Chartier. They'll all leave at dawn for another ambush—

"Ah thought ye'd gan o'er the wall," calls Lachlan.

Jamie shakes his head, sits.

"We're the last of a breed, Jamie MacGillivray. A breed of feckin' madmen."

"LaCroix left because he heert there were cannibals. Indians—they're like bluidy children."

"Mair like bluidy Hielanders. And here we sit, as a'ways, oot-numbered and with our backs tae the wall."

When the killing began there was the ceremony attached to it, a deep respect for death. You fasted, you purged, you painted yourself and let the spirit of murder—there is no other word for it—enter your body and guide your actions. But there has been so much, so often, so randomly, no time to prepare oneself for it and the other warriors soon drunk with killing and drunk with rum whenever found in the aftermath—it has been a long and violent nightmare, and Jamie fears waking up to take stock of it.

"Cannibals wearing dresses," he grumbles.

"He means Fraser's regiment."

Jamie stares at the *seanachaidh*.

"Have ye no heert?" says Lachlan. "The young laird has raised a group of the lads tae fight fer the English crown. They went ashore at Louisbourg."

The words make no sense. Jamie feels nauseous.

"And noo ye'll tell me they're *can*nibals as well," snorts Jamie, unbelieving. "Bluidy fecking children."

MILITARY CAREERS, LIKE GOOD STORIES, REQUIRE A satisfying conclusion. Yes, a good number of formerly vital commanders linger on at half pay, haunting their manors, gilding memories over port at their clubs, some even on the rolls of Parliament, but their stories are understood to be over. This tale has run on much too long and his body cannot support it any longer. The morning will witness an act of desperation—accepted, he hopes, as valor—which will close the book on him, one way or the other.

The Major General has only just shared the assault plan with his brigadiers, two of them cowards and the other a villain, and silently endured their objections. The naval fellows have been no more encouraging, but have at least confirmed that the tides are propitious for the first landing. Between boldness and folly lies Fortune—and to that he shall surrender himself. He has not informed the brigadiers that he will be just behind those first volunteers, that if the sliver of opportunity proves to have been an illusion, he will pay for it with his life.

Not a glorious *finale*, perhaps, but at least a bloody end to it.

MONSIEUR LE COMPTE LOUIS DU CHAMBON DE VERGOR does not cherish sleeping in tents. Nor does he enjoy dwelling in this raw country, and hopes the responsible people in the home government will soon come to their senses, cut their losses, and allow him to return to a more civilized life. He does not welcome the mockery—oh, never to his face of course, but ever since the court-martial over Beauséjour he has been aware of the murmurings—from both proper officers and their Canadian imitators. He does not relish receiving orders from Montcalm's puppy, Monsieur de Bougainville, that leave him camped at the edge of an unscalable precipice, allegedly to guard against an infiltration by the English, a physical impossibility lest they sprout wings. It smacks of punishment, which he does not deserve.

Should the enemy redcoats suddenly achieve flight, the road leading to the Plains of Abraham and the walled city beyond it is a mere pathway, and could easily be held by three dozen indifferent soldiers—these he has kept in the tents, allowing the other two thirds of his command, Canadian militia more adept with rake and hoe than musket and spontoon, to return to Lorette and see to their harvests, as well as that on his own property.

The excellent M. Bigot, after his most recent *soirée*, led the captain into his munificently supplied wine cellar, there pointing out which vintages were to be repatriated once the inevitable has occurred and they are allowed to quit this field of dubious battle, and which bottles condemned to grow dusty and acidic upon Canadian soil.

"To our imminent return," the Intendant toasted, and de Vergor was able to sample something divine from the Aquitaine.

"*Vive le roi, et au diable le Canada!*" he answered.

The captain pulls his sleepmask over his eyes, the hour for feigned vigilance having passed. There is, however, the matter of the infernal artillery barrage to be accounted for, which though directed at the ruins of the Haute-Ville a tad more than a mile up the river is nonetheless inconducive to rest. De Vergor presses the devices he has been given, a combination of beeswax and sawdust, into his ears till the fit is snug, loudly instructs his aide to be sure the sentry is changed once during the night, and gets as comfortable as can be hoped on the pallet that has been provided him. Disturbing reveries lately, in which he is much pointed at, guilty of an unnamed offense, leading to his premature arousal in a state of anxious confusion.

Perhaps tonight will be better, despite the heat. Perhaps, he thinks, I shall wake to find we are on the dock mustering in companies, about to board a ship bound for *la belle France*—

THE OARLOCKS HAVE BEEN OILED AND STUFFED WITH rags, longboats gliding with the current over the black water without a splash. Tonight is different, the countless days of rowing and drifting, rowing and drifting up and down the river, shadowed by equal numbers of marching Frenchmen on the cliffs, are over. This is no feint—they are the cat's paw, and if this incursion proves to be folly, they will be sacrificed.

The boatmen have shipped oars and are out before the hull bottom can scrape rock, holding the craft steady. The volunteers have been drilled for this disembarkment, a kilt proving so much more convenient for stepping over the gunwale than trousers, each man out and firmly planted before his musket is handed down. A quick crouching on the tiny strip of bank, not a word spoken, then Captain Delaune signals to climb. Weapons slung over the back, both hands free to grasp and pull at the slick rock face and bits of vegetation, "better quiet than quick," as he's been reminded a hundred times.

It is nearly straight up, but there is a way.

He is not surprised that the 78th Foot has supplied half the volunteers for this mission—though Major General Wolfe had ample occasion to observe them coming ashore through the cannon-shot at Louisbourg and witnessed their charge and taking of the Lighthouse Battery, swords besting artillery pieces, they are, barring the American rangers, still considered the most expendable of his minions here. If they are not to be treasured, they can at least be respected—

He struggles a half-dozen men behind the point man, Donald MacDonald, chosen for linguistic skill rather than mountaineering. Colonel Fraser himself would be here on the cliff but for a wound—his father the Auld Fox must be shaking with laughter wherever he dwells, assuming he has been reunited with his head. Above are the French, whose timely arrival and support might have changed the outcome of the rebellion. And perhaps today's events will lead, some day, to the restoration of the Fraser lands.

Perhaps not.

"There's nae mair kings of Scotland," Simon Fraser has told the regiment. "We fight noo fer the honor of our race."

They fight, thinks Dougal MacGillivray as the boot of the man above him finds leverage upon his shoulder, because military service is preferable to starvation.

They are nearing the top when an unsteady voice calls out.

"*Qui vive?*"

"*C'est un troupe de secours,*" hisses MacDonald, rapidly if not with perfect inflection. "*Fait votre rapport à votre officier de service—nous allons prendre le relais ici.*"

Jamie should be here, he thinks, helping to deceive the frogeaters.

There is a pause as the sentry considers this order, then a bit of a scuffle, and Dougal reaches the top just in time to see, in the waning moonlight, a frightened Canadian with a pistol held to his temple and a dirk at his throat.

"*Pas un son,*" Delaune whispers to him, waiting for the second dozen of the party to gain the summit, then signaling them to hurry forward toward the ghostly white tents that lay ahead.

There is a musket flash and a shot, then more, scarcely a dozen before they have overrun the encampment, more than half of the tents unoccupied. It is as if the French, snugly boarded up for months, have left one door unlatched.

Most of the guardians have managed to run away, but there is one blubbering fellow who sits on the ground in his white nightshirt, a ball in his ankle, yellow plugs of wax in his ears, indicated by two of his sullen troopers to be in command of the post.

"*Ne me f-f-faites pas mal, s'il vous plaît,*" he begs. "*Le Québec est à v-vous!*"

THERE IS A LIGHT RAIN FALLING AS THEY GATHER IN front of the shell of some formerly grand edifice, the Sillery battery firing down the river, just enough light to recognize faces. Chartier, wearing the tunic of a militia captain, walks among them, surveying his group of perhaps three dozen warriors and half as many Canadian irregulars. He stops before Jamie and Lachlan, smiling as he recognizes them.

"*Bonjour mes petits*," he says to them. "*Bienvenue a Québec—le bijou du nouvelle monde.*"

Following Chartier like a shadow is a huge warrior, the skin of his near-naked body etched with as many scars as tattoos. He is tearing at a strip of dried meat with his teeth, looking at nothing in particular.

"Fergal MacGregor," says Lachlan, "is that *you?*"

"*Attention*," warns Chartier, tapping his temple, "*il est fou.*"

Jamie speaks to the giant in Erse.

Fergal? How are you?

No understanding lights the man's eyes.

Do you remember us?

He keeps chewing.

Not a chatterbox, but he kills English like the devil, says Chartier, running a finger across his throat.

It is then that the Chevalier de Johnstone clatters into the courtyard on a white horse, looking stricken—

"*Ils ont grimpé les falaises! Les Anglais sont dans les plaines d'Abraham! Nous formerons des rangs à la porte Saint-Louis!*"

They run then, weapons in hand, joining a company of provincials and then more French regulars, who are given a quick blessing *en masse* by a priest and then formed by shouting officers into vaguely coherent units and marched through the Saint Louis gate and over the line of small buttes to look upon the

Plains of Abraham, a mile-wide expanse of flat ground and cornfields that has somehow, at the far end, filled with red-coated English soldiers—

And then the pipes, screaming.

Jamie does not recognize the air, if he ever knew it. He looks to Lachlan as a painted Wyandot warrior beside them makes the Sign of the Cross and mutters—

"*Ce sont les cannibales!*"

"Did Ah tell ye?" says Lachlan.

"Ah'll no raise ma hand agin them," says Jamie.

"Then ye've plenty mair tae choose frae."

There are thousands of them, in fact, already formed in their firing lines, just waiting, banners aloft, drummers riffling.

And the pipes, and men in tartan kilts.

They can't all be Campbells.

The enemy lines waver, then begin, in an orderly fashion, to lie on the ground as the cannon from the long western wall come into play, projectiles whistling overhead and plowing up turf as they strike among the blanket of redcoats. Jamie looks around—he sees Bone and his Shawnee men trotting toward the trees that line the serpentine St. Charles, at the English left flank.

"Yer chief is gang tae snipe at them," he says to Lachlan.

"Ah'll stand here," says the *seanachaidh*, an expression of grim resolve on his face. "Tis a finer vantage fer the story."

It is too late to retire behind the walls—the English will have their cannon upon the field soon—and a desperate charge is perhaps the only hope. Too late, Dougal told him of Culloden Moor, we already understood that it was too late, but ran nonetheless and threw ourselves on their bayonets—

Most of the Indians around them are gone, gone to harry the redcoats from cover, or perhaps just gone home with their tales of battle to tell, when Général Montcalm rides to the fore on a dark horse. He is a smallish man, dressed in splendid green and gold, waving a saber over his head.

"*Êtes vous préparés, mes enfants?*" he cries, and there is a cheer along their lines, regulars in the center, mongrel battalions to the left and right.

"Prepared fer slaughter," mutters Lachlan. "As ever."

"*Ligne—avancez!*" comes the cry, repeated up and down their still forming lines.

They begin to move down the gentle slope of the buttes, Jamie and Lachlan drifting toward the center so as not to be opposite the Highlanders. There is smoke drifting across the field now, some houses by the St. Charles having been fired, and there is a constant crackling of gunfire on the periphery. When the redcoats are ordered to stand up it is like a wave, row after row of them rising from the shelter of the ground, and the artillery from the walled city ceases along with the light rain. The sun is fighting its way through the clouds.

The English have two field pieces up already, firing cannister shot at them, a man falling here and there, and Jamie sees that, but for the very center, he is part of an advancing and disorganized flood, patches of cornstalk and brush funneling regiments upon one another, the newest militia recruits bewildered but carried along with the flow, and he feels swept as he did in the Porteous riot, no option but to ride it to the end.

The redcoats stand with inhuman discipline, muskets loaded but still shouldered, their officers pacing in front of them with backs to the enemy, hold steady, hold fire, they'll come to us—and the gap between the forces closes quickly. At what Jamie guesses is more than a hundred yards, too far, men around him begin to kneel and fire, the militia then flopping to the ground to reload or reassess their commitment, the regulars marching forward and fixing bayonets. The redcoats, as they did at first under Braddock near the forks, quickly close ranks, stepping over the dead, the wounded crawling or carried back through the lines. But here there are not woods and skirmishers hard upon them, here there is only a mob of the enemy walking straight into their killing range.

Jamie tries to picture, as he has before many an attack, his brother Dougal cut still breathing from the gallows and eviscerated before the morbid throng, fury the best engine to drive one through a fight. But instead he sees him at Culloden Moor, dashing into the maelstrom of lead and steel—

"Like bluidy sheep in a pen!" cries Lachlan as they are pushed into the horde of white-jacketed soldiers, stacked into four, five, maybe even six dense rows, and when there is a gap to see them Jamie can count the buttons on the redcoat grenadiers' tunics. But there is no charge, no screaming and waving of claymoors, only a scattered *Vive le Roi!* as they stride ever forward, and then the steady voice of an English officer—

"Make ready—"

Jamie nudges Lachlan so they are sheltered behind a phalanx of Guyenne regiment infantry—

"Present—"

—fighting the urge to throw himself down and dig for cover, as any sane Lenape warrior would have done long before—

"Fire!"

The mighty slap of the front line volley clears the field of men in front of them and Jamie dives for the ground, looking up to see Lachlan torn apart by the firing of the second. He fires his rifle into the smoke, rolls onto his back, deftly moving his hands through the motions of reloading. There is nothing to hide behind. The English volleys roll, deafening, one after the other, barely a second between one and the next, and Jamie can see, through the smoke, the French and Canadians retreat, backing up at first, and then those not fallen turning to run toward the buttes and the ruined city beyond them.

He points his rifle into the rolling wall of smoke, fingers the trigger—then lets the ball remain unspent. What point killing a man you can't even see? he thinks before the next volley sweeps over his head like a giant scythe and the air is made sharp with the reek of sulphur. Someone is bellowing, and Jamie turns to peer through the haze and there is Fergal, blood gushing from his body at the several places he's been shot, a hatchet in one hand and a sword in the other, wheeling and lunging like a wounded bear at the group of redcoats who step forward to surround him, jabbing with their bayonets whenever there is an opening. The MacGregor's eyes are crazed, blood spurts from his mouth with each scream, and even when brought to his knees by a sergeant's halberd he continues flailing, as if all Jamie's years of stifled wrath have been made flesh, raging and sputtering, spewing out a final curse in Erse before a passing grenadier captain takes careful aim with his pistol and blows the back of his head off.

Jamie tosses his rifle well away and sits up, a sudden peace filling his body. The Catholic Wyandot he saw before kneels several feet to the left, struggling to breathe with both lungs shot through, brokenly muttering his death song. The first of the English front line reach him, a burly corporal grabbing the Wyandot's scalp lock and twisting his head sideways.

"Should we just lift the bugger's 'air or take the 'ole noggin' fer a keepsake?"

"Let him die in peace, ye bluidy savages," calls Jamie.

Several of the men turn their attention to Jamie then, stepping over to stand above him.

"Wot's this, then?"

"Hit made a noise like a yuman being."

"Hit don't *look* like one."

"Bloody bushwhacking Canadian is wot it is, painted up like a red Indian—"

"We've got some tricks fer *you*, mate. Serve ye up in pieces, we will—"

Jamie wishes the last thing he is to see in this world was not red uniforms and gunsmoke. He should have been killed before this, though, at Culloden, but arrived too late—

A major looms over him, bending to stare at his face, then rap him on the head with the flat of his sword.

"You there," he says. "What's your name?"

Long Knife, says Jamie in Lenape.

"You're not French—"

"Ah'm Lenape. What you English call Delaweer."

"What you are," says the major, pricking Jamie's chest with the point of his sword now, "is a renegade and a traitor, and I shall see that you are hanged for it. You two—bring him along!"

The major strolls away. Two of the grenadiers yank Jamie to his feet, dragging him along after the third line as it crosses the Plains of Abraham, pausing only to skewer any enemy left breathing.

"That'll teach ye to keep yer gob shut," grumbles the corporal.

The warrior's death song ends as he is pinioned to the ground with bayonets.

THEY HAVE CARRIED THE MAJOR GENERAL FAR ENOUGH back to be safe from further harm, but the gore soaking his shirt indicates there is little to be done.

"Don't bother with that," he says when a surgeon is sent for. "It's all over with me."

A colonel runs up, breathless, cheeks glowing, his smile fading only when he notes the general's body draped over Lieutenant Brown's lap.

"Is he dead?" asks the colonel, a Yorkshireman.

Brown holds a finger to his lips.

"What of the battle?" Wolfe is able to ask, his frail chest fighting for air.

"They run, sir."

"*Who* run?"

"The enemy, sir. They give way all along our line."

A wisp of a smile on the pale man's face. "One of you lads hurry to Colonel Burton, have him march Webb's to the river and cut off the bridge."

This order implemented, he turns his face from the sky. "Now, God be praised, I can rest."

The redcoats are halfway across the river when the sisters sweep her away to one of their cells. Their eyes are averted as they help peel off her dress, blood-spattered now from the new wave of casualties, and hurry her into the habit. The clothing is starched and heavy, and by the time the wimple has been adjusted on her head Jenny feels that she has become a different person.

"*Tu es Soeur Solange—ici depuis trois ans,*" they tell her.

The redcoats stomp into the hospital, looking for armed men, shooing the sisters and the wounded away from the windows.

"We're taking over 'ere," states a sergeant with a nose like a radish who shies away from the nuns as they pass near. "So noner yer bloody tricks."

I don't understand what you're saying, Jenny replies in French as she tightens a bandage around a moaning Canadian's head. We only wish to serve the wounded.

The sergeant scowls, angrily gesturing for her to step back with the other sisters.

It matters little which king rules over you, comforts Soeur Jonquille, taking her arm, if your heart is pure.

I am Sister Solange, Jenny thinks, shrinking herself into the crisp habit and dropping her eyes modestly to the floor. Carrying my head in my hands—

"THAT'S THE ONE!"

An English lieutenant and a colonial soldier in green stand over him. The lieutenant kicks his foot.

"What's your name?"

Again Jamie gives his name in Lenape.

"He speaks English—and French," says the colonial. "I saw him when they held me at Kittanning."

"Ah'm calt Lang Knife. Of the Turtle Clan."

"You are a renegade," says the lieutenant.

"There was a bounty on his head—him and Shingas and Captain Jacobs—"

"We'll leave his feet dangling soon enough," says the lieutenant. "A traitor to his nation and to his race."

Fuck the English, says Jamie in Erse.

They leave then and the man chained beside him, a deserter shot through the groin this morning, begins to weep.

Jamie is glad for the man who escaped Kittanning, probably during the Armstrong raid. Keeping captives, keeping slaves, is not good for people. Even back in the Highlands when he was full of dreams, having a half-dozen gillies to do his bidding was never appealing.

He wishes the parting with Ange had been better.

They both knew it was likely the last they would see of each other, but she only turned away, angry and hurt. No matter the strangeness of their coming together, her fierce ambitions—when they held close together at night he never felt alone in the world. But you can't belong only to one person, you have to stand on one side of the tree or the other—

Ange, with all her sharp edges, has been a gift, a gift he has not valued enough, not knowing these last years have been nothing but a hiatus, a brief stroll about before the rope is tightened again around his neck.

He should be rotting beneath Drummossie Moor.

THEY ARE KEEPING THE SPECIAL PRISONERS—THE RENegades, the deserters—in what was a wine cellar, cool, narrow, with a vaulted brick ceiling. He winds his way from man to man, holding a torch low to see their faces. Some of them are wounded, as yet untreated, all of them in chains. The Indian has an iron collar around his neck, bolted by a short bit of chain to the wall. He kneels to look closer, the man staring past him soullessly.

"Is that you, then?"

The Indian's eyes float to him, focus—

"Dougal?"

"Aye."

Jamie gives a laugh that is almost a sob. "I thought they'd topped ye back in London."

"They scragged a few mair, and then lost the stomach fer it."

Dougal sits on the dirty straw beside his brother.

"Ah heert there was a Scotsman captured as also spake the French tongue, and Ah thought no wee it could be ma Jamie—but just look at ye—"

"Look at *me*!? A MacGillivray fighting fer the bluidy English—"

"Och—life moves on, Jamie—with or withoot us—"

"The clan—"

"Is a clan in name ainly! Ah went back tae Scotland when they tossed me frae their prison. Everywhere ye turned, they were upon us, like the Black Death—"

"And noo ye do their dirty work fer them."

"We're paid enow tae feed our families, we're allooed tae carry arms, tae feel like men again—"

"Is that what it takes?"

"Perhaps."

Jamie points to the turtle tattoo on his chest.

"These people—they dinnae have a king. Their chiefs dinnae live in a stane hoose aboon the rest. But their loyalty tae each other—"

"Dae the red men no fight other red men?"

"Aye, but nae mon is forced tae raise the hatchet. If somebody wants tae leave, fer his family, fer whatever reason—"

"Then they'll suffer fer that, won't they?"

Jamie has no answer for this. Dougal watches the shadows the torchlight makes on the ceiling.

"We've been telt that when this is o'er, we can stay here in Canada if we choose tae," he says. "A thousand miles frae bluidy King George, a new land—"

"The land is as auld as Scotland," says Jamie. "And ye'll have tae tear it awee frae them that's on it."

Dougal gets to his feet. The guard at the door has only been provided a half crown's worth of patience, and he is making rumbling noises in his throat.

"Ye'll a' be taen tae Halifax in the morn, fer the trial and hangings. Ah'll dae what Ah can fer ye."

"Ah'm glad ye dodged the rope, Dougal. It daes ma heart guid tae keek yer face."

Dougal nods, steps away over the feet of the condemned.

AS BOTH COMMANDING GENERALS, WOLFE AND MONTcalm, have been killed in the fighting, and Monckton seriously wounded, it falls to Brigadier Townshend to negotiate terms of surrender with the governor. Bougainville is still behind them, of course, with a considerable force that could complicate the issue, but Monsieur Vandreuil and his closest counselor, Intendant Bigot, seem impatient to be on the promised boat back to their homeland. The transportation of the other French nationals, thinks Townshend, shall be a headache he will gladly pass on to the navy, while the Canadians will be his own to deal with as he will.

The hagiography of the late lamented Major General Wolfe will begin as soon as the glorious news of victory reaches London, despite the fact that in his opinion the man acquitted himself no better or worse than Braddock, whose name shall ever be married to the word "defeat." Thus are the fortunes of war. The willowy hero will certainly receive better treatment than in the satirical scribblings of his mordant brigadier—he'll merit oils on a large canvas and a hanging in the royal palace. Gainsborough, perhaps? Or his rival Joshua Reynolds? Wolfe will be lying dressed in simple scarlet, limpid as if just pulled down from the Cross, with various notables encircling him, few, if any, who actually attended his death. Townshend will be absent, he is certain, protecting the flank and the river in the far and hazy background, from whence will come running the crier of victory, waving his hat. Perhaps a crouching, mostly naked Mohawk gentleman, respectfully pondering the sacred moment, and some ambitious colonel who was a hundred miles distant during the battle but has paid the painter's tavern bill.

And unless Jeffrey Amherst can contrive to get himself killed during the relatively simple taking of Montreal, it shall be James Wolfe who is known as the conqueror of the north. Count on him to take all the glory and none of the responsibility.

While Governor Vandreuil attempts to craft terms of surrender sufficiently flattering to his honor, the first group of opponents will be ferried away to their fate this morning. It is difficult to imagine any state of misery, drunkenness, or mental deficiency that would induce one to row or swim across the swift currents of the St. Lawrence to defect to the French, of all people, and yet there are a dozen such turncoats who've had the misfortune to have survived yesterday's bloody harvest and be taken prisoner. They'll be marched down the banks of the St. Charles and around to the dock that was taken below Beauport, thence to Halifax and the end of the rope. War is an expensive hobby, as Mr. Pitt is wont to remind them in his letters, and it will be Townshend's task to convince the *habitants* that it offers them no profit in compensation. They are touchy about their religion, dependent on remaining armed to protect themselves from the western tribes, and likely to resist any edict forcing them to learn a new, if superior, language. But he is certain they will not begrudge him stretching the necks of a passel of traitors—

THERE ARE PERHAPS TWO HUNDRED FRENCH REGULars near the head of the column, disarmed and lightly guarded, chatting among themselves as they cut over the headland to the Beauport cliffs. Then a squadron of musket bearing grenadiers, followed by the manacled prisoners, with a dozen Highlanders bringing up the rear. Jamie watches a seahawk out over the St. Lawrence as he walks, leg irons mercifully left off till they are on the boat. The seahawk barely shifts its wings, riding the air currents, watching for something to swoop down upon.

The angle of the sun makes a glare on the water, and he wonders if a raptor's eye can somehow see through that to the fish that might swim below. If a wolf can smell a bitch in heat a mile away, and geese find the same pond after each wintering to the south—

A canoe is moving parallel to them.

Far down and well out from the bank, it is only one of dozens of small craft—longboats, supply rafts, tiny sloops—moving about between the Île d'Orleans and the mainland, two tiny persons steering it with their paddles as the current takes them upstream, where Jamie has never been before. One of them might be a woman—

Jamie looks to his left. Some flat ground where yesterday there were tents, then a solid wall of trees running up the side of the heights. He looks down to his right again—the canoe is still there, keeping pace.

He has stood upon the platform, felt the rough hemp at his throat, and found it an experience he'd rather not repeat. But a ball in the back of the head—

He bolts out of line, leaping over the precipice, falling, rolling, scrambling to his feet then careening farther, struck on the face by branches as musket fire erupts behind him and he hears his brother's voice, shouting in Erse—

Aim high, he's one of ours!

He falls again and tumbles to the bank, more shouts now as men are braving the cliff face in pursuit of him. He is up on his knees as the canoe slices the water in front of him, slowing.

Your friends are terrible shots, LaCroix observes as Jamie steps into the river, lead balls pocking the surface here and there.

Ange reaches to grasp him under the shoulder as he rolls into the belly of the canoe, his face and body battered, his wrists bleeding around the iron cuffs—

Stay down there, she says, till we've passed the big ships.

They paddle then, with no appearance of concern, moving quickly with the current and hugging the bank to provide a poor angle for anyone still firing at them from above.

The seahawk is drifting along overhead, as if supervising the escape.

And Ange, he realizes as he watches her rhythmically reach and pull with the oar, gracefully leaning into each stroke, is carrying his child.

Where will we go? he asks her.

To the west. Where the white people can't find us.

They hear bagpipes playing then, Fraser's Highlanders on the march somewhere behind them. A frown creases Ange's forehead.

What is that terrible noise?

Spirits, says Jamie MacGillivray, in Lenape. Spirits of the dead.

The seahawk stays with them as they pass, barely noticed, through a forest of English warships, the river ahead waiting to tell its tale.